KT-420-627

David Baldacci is the author of international bestsellers *Absolute Power*, *Total Control*, *The Winner*, *The Simple Truth*, *Wish You Well*, *Last Man Standing*, *The Christmas Train*, *Split Second*, *Hour Game* and *The Camel Club*. He lives in his native state of Virginia.

For more information visit his official website at www.david-baldacci.com

PRAISE FOR DAVID BALDACCI AND HIS NOVELS

LAST MAN STANDING

'Baldacci grabs you by the balls and squeezes
steadily until you don't know whether to scream
out in pain or pass out with pleasure'
Punch

'Baldacci's most accomplished thriller.
The action . . . is nonstop and expertly drawn'
Publishers Weekly

WISH YOU WELL

'Reveals his talent as a storyteller of the
highest merit'
Punch

'Abounds with affection for the state
he makes his home'
USA Today

'Succeeds as a departure for Baldacci . . .
a tender . . . inspirational story . . .
some wonderfully lyric prose'
Denver Post

ABSOLUTE POWER

'A brilliant thriller'
Guardian

'Accomplished and amazing – one of the hottest
reads around'
Daily Mail

'Baldacci's prose is fluent and racy . . .
This book is sure to make a killing'
The Times

'First rate . . . Baldacci cuts everyone's grass –
Grisham's, Ludlum's, even Patricia Cornwell's –
and more than gets away with it'
People

THE WINNER

'Yet another winner . . . The excitement builds
. . . The plot's many planted bombs explode
unpredictably'
New York Times

THE SIMPLE TRUTH

'A plot strong enough to make the bath go cold
around you'
Independent on Sunday

SAVING FAITH

'An adrenaline-pumping plot that could, once
again, make you late for work'
Heat

TOTAL CONTROL

'Wonderfully tricky. His genius is to keep readers
guessing, and reading while he's tossing out twists
like so much confetti . . . David Baldacci is a
superb storyteller, and even better writer . . . he
compels you to read, and read, and read.
You won't argue'
Literary Review Service

DAVID BALDACCI

last man standing
&
saving faith

PAN BOOKS

Last Man Standing first published 2001 by Warner Books USA.
First published in Great Britain 2002 by Simon and Schuster UK.
First published in paperback 2003 by Pan Books.
Saving Faith first published 1999 by Warner Books USA.
First published in Great Britain 1999 by Simon and Schuster UK.
First published in paperback 2003 by Pan Books.

This omnibus first published 2006 by Pan Books
an imprint of Pan Macmillan Ltd
Pan Macmillan, 20 New Wharf Road, London N1 9RR
Basingstoke and Oxford
Associated companies throughout the world
www.panmacmillan.com

ISBN-13: 978-0-330-44663-1
ISBN-10: 0-330-44663-0

Copyright © Columbus Rose Ltd 2001, 1999

The right of David Baldacci to be identified as the
author of this work has been asserted by him in accordance
with the Copyright, Designs and Patents Act 1988.

This book is a work of fiction. Names, characters, places, organizations,
and incidents are either products of the author's imagination or used fictitiously.
Any resemblance to actual events, places, organizations, or persons,
living or dead, is entirely coincidental.

All rights reserved. No part of this publication may be
reproduced, stored in or introduced into a retrieval system, or
transmitted, in any form, or by any means (electronic, mechanical,
photocopying, recording or otherwise) without the prior written
permission of the publisher. Any person who does any unauthorized
act in relation to this publication may be liable to criminal
prosecution and civil claims for damages.

3 5 7 9 8 6 4 2

A CIP catalogue record for this book is available from
the British Library.

Printed and bound in Great Britain by
Mackays of Chatham plc, Chatham, Kent

This book is sold subject to the condition that it shall not,
by way of trade or otherwise, be lent, re-sold, hired out,
or otherwise circulated without the publisher's prior consent
in any form of binding or cover other than that in which
it is published and without a similar condition including this
condition being imposed on the subsequent purchaser.

last man standing

To all the wonderful teachers and other volunteers across the country who have helped make the All America Roads project a reality.

———————————

This book is also dedicated to the memory of

Yossi Chaim Paley
(April 14, 1988–March 10, 2001)

The bravest young man I ever met.

"A wrongly accused man is always vilified
by the ignorant masses.
Such a man should fire at will,
he is bound to hit something."
—ANONYMOUS

"Speed, surprise and violence of action."
—HOSTAGE RESCUE MOTTO

1

1

Web London held a semiautomatic SR75 rifle custom built for him by a legendary gunsmith. The SR didn't stop at merely wounding flesh and bone; it disintegrated them. Web would never leave home without this high chieftain of muscle guns, for he was a man steeped in violence. He was always prepared to kill, to do so efficiently and without error. Lord, if he ever took a life by mistake he might as well have eaten the bullet himself, for all the misery it would cause him. Web just had that complex way of earning his daily bread. He couldn't say he loved his job, but he did excel at it.

Despite having a gun welded to his hand virtually every waking moment of his life, Web was not one to coddle his weapons. While he never called a pistol his friend or gave it a slick name, weapons were still an important part of Web's life, though like wild animals guns were not things easily tamed. Even trained lawmen missed their targets and everything else eight out of ten times. To Web, not only was that unacceptable, it was also suicidal. He had many peculiar qualities, but a death wish was not one of them. Web had plenty of people looking to kill him as it was, and once they had nearly gotten their man.

About five years prior he had come within a liter or two of spilled blood of checking out on the floor of a school gymnasium strewn with other men already dead or dying. After he had triumphed over his wounds and stunned the doctors tending him, Web started carrying the SR instead of the submachine gun his comrades-in-arms toted. It resembled an M16, chambered a big .308 bullet, and was an excellent choice if intimidation was your goal. The SR made everyone want to be your friend.

Through the smoked-out window of the Suburban, Web eyed each fluid knot of people along the corners and suspicious clumps of humanity lurking in darkened alleys. As they moved farther into hostile territory, Web's gaze returned to the street, where he knew every vehicle could be a gun cruiser in disguise. He was looking for any drifting eye, nod of head or fingers slyly tapping on cell phones in an attempt to do serious harm to old Web.

The Suburban turned the corner and stopped. Web glanced at the six other men huddled with him. He knew they were contemplating the same things he was: Get out fast and clean, move to cover positions, maintain fields of fire. Fear did not really enter into the equation; nerves, however, were another matter. High-octane adrenaline was not his friend; in fact, it could very easily get him killed.

Web took a deep, calming breath. He needed his pulse rate to be between sixty and seventy. At eighty-five beats your gun would tremble against your torso; at ninety ticks you couldn't work the trigger, as blood occlusion in veins and constricted nerves in shoulders and arms combined to guarantee that you would fail to perform at an acceptable level. At over one hundred pops a minute you lost your fine motor skills entirely and wouldn't be able to hit an elephant with a damn cannon at three feet; you might as well slap a sign on your forehead that read KILL ME QUICK, because that undoubtedly would be your fate.

Web pushed out the juice, drew in the peace and for him there was calm to be distilled from brewing chaos.

The Suburban started moving, turned one more corner and stopped. For the last time, Web knew. Radio squelch was broken when Teddy Riner spoke into his bone microphone or "mic." Riner said, "Charlie to TOC, request compromise authority and permission to move to yellow."

Through Web's mic he heard TOC's, or Tactical Operations Center's, terse response, "Copy, Charlie One, stand by." In Web's Crayola world, "yellow" was the last position of concealment and cover. Green was the crisis site, the moment of truth: the breach. Navigating the hallowed piece of earth that stretched between the relative safety and comfort of yellow and the moment of truth green could be quite eventful. "Compromise authority"—Web said the words to himself. It was just a way of asking for the okay to gun down people if necessary and making it sound like you were merely getting permission from your boss to cut a few bucks off the price of a used car. Radio squelch was broken again as TOC said, "TOC to all units: You have compromise authority and permission to move to yellow."

Thank you so very much, TOC. Web edged closer to the cargo doors of the Suburban. He was point and Roger McCallam had the rear. Tim Davies was the breecher and Riner was the team leader. Big Cal Plummer and the other two assaulters, Lou Patterson and Danny Garcia, stood ready with MP-5 machine guns and flash bangs and .45-caliber pistols, and their calm demeanors. As soon as the doors opened, they would fan out into a rolling mass looking for threats from all directions. They would move toes first, then heels, knees bent to absorb recoil in case they had to fire. Web's face mask shrunk his field of vision to a modest viewing area: his miniature Broadway for the coming real-life mayhem, no expensive ticket or fancy suit required. Hand signals would suffice from now on. When bullets were flying at you, you tended to get a bit of cotton mouth anyway. Web never talked much at work.

He watched as Danny Garcia crossed himself, just like he did every time. And Web said what he always said when Garcia crossed himself before the Chevy doors popped open. "God's too smart to come 'round here, Danny boy. We're on our own." Web always said this in a jesting way, but he was not joking.

Five seconds later the cargo doors burst open and the team piled out too far away from ground zero. Normally they liked to drive right up to their final destination and go knock-knock-boom with their two-by-four explosive, yet the logistics here were a little tricky. Abandoned cars, tossed refrigerators and other bulky objects conveniently blocked the road to the target.

Radio squelch broke again as snipers from X-Ray Team called in. There were men in the alley up ahead, X-Ray reported, but not part of the group Web was hunting. At least the snipers didn't think so.

As one, Web and his Charlie Team rose and hurtled down the alley. The seven members of their Hotel Team counterparts had been dropped off by another Suburban on the far side of the block to attack the target from the left rear side. The grand plan had Charlie and Hotel meeting somewhere in the middle of this combat zone masquerading as a neighborhood.

Web and company were heading east now, an approaching storm right on their butts. Lightning, thunder, wind and horizontal rain tended to screw up ground communications, tactical positioning and men's nerves, usually at the critical time when all of them needed to operate perfectly. With all their technological wizardry, the only available response to Mother Nature's temper and the poor ground logistics was simply to run faster. They chugged down the alley, a narrow strip of potholed, trash-littered asphalt. There were buildings close on either side of them, the brick veneer blistered by decades of gun battles. Some had been between good and bad, but most involved young men taking out their brethren over drug turf, women or just because. Here, a gun made you a man, though you might really only be a child, running outside after watching your Saturday morning cartoons, convinced that if you blew a large hole in someone, he might actually get back up and keep playing with you.

They came upon the group the snipers had identified: clusters of blacks, Latinos and Asians wheeling and dealing drugs. Apparently, potent highs and the promise of an uncomplicated cash-and-carry business cut through all troublesome issues of race, creed, color or political affiliation. To Web most of these folks looked a single snort, needle nick or popped pill from the grave. He marveled that this pathetic assemblage of veteran paint hackers even had the energy or clarity of thought to consummate the simple transaction of cash for little bags of brain inferno barely disguised as feel-good potion, and only then the first time you drove the poison into your body.

In the face of Charlie's intimidating wall of guns and Kevlar, all but one of the druggies dropped to their knees and begged not to be killed or indicted. Web focused on the one young man who remained standing. His head was swathed in a red do-rag symboliz-

ing some gang allegiance. The kid had a toothpick waist and barbell shoulders; ratty gym shorts hung down past his butt crack and
a tank shirt rode lopsided across his muscular torso. He also had an
attitude several miles long riding on his features, the kind that
said, *I'm smarter, tougher and will outlive you.* Web had to admit,
though, the guy carried the rag-look well.

It took all of thirty seconds to determine that all but Bandanna
Boy were looped out of their minds and that none of the druggies
were carrying guns—or cell phones that could be used to call up
the target and warn them. Bandanna Boy did have a knife, yet
knives had no chance against Kevlar and submachine guns. The
team let him keep it. But as Charlie Team moved on, Cal Plummer
ran with them backward, his MP-5 trained on the young back-
alley entrepreneur, just in case.

Bandanna Boy did call after Web, something about admiring
Web's rifle and wanting to buy it. He'd give him a sweet deal, he
yelled after Web, and then said he'd shoot Web and everyone else
dead with it. HA-HA! Web glanced to the rooftops, where he knew
members of Whiskey Team and X-Ray were in their forward firing
positions with rounds seated and lethal beads drawn on the brain
stems of this gaggle of losers. The snipers were Web's best friends.
He understood exactly how they approached their work, because
for years he had been one of them.

For months at a time Web had lain in steamy swamps with
pissed-off water moccasins crawling over him. Or else been
wedged into wind-gusted clefts of frigid mountains with the custom-built rifle stock's leather cheek pad next to his own as he
sighted through his scope and provided cover and intelligence for
the assault teams. As a sniper he had developed many important
skills, such as learning how to very quietly pee into a jug. Other lessons included packing his food in precise clusters so he could
carbo-load by touch in pitch-darkness, and arranging his bullets
for optimal reloading, working off a strict military model that had
proved its worth time and time again. Not that he could easily
transfer any of these unique talents to the private sector, but Web
didn't see that happening anyway.

The life of a sniper lurched from one numbing extreme to another. Your job was to achieve the best firing position with the least amount of personal exposure and oftentimes those twin goals were simply incompatible. You just did the best you could. Hours, days, weeks, even months of nothing except tedium that tended to erode morale and core skills would be sliced wide open by moments of gut-wrenching fury that usually came at you in a rush of gunfire and mass confusion. And your decision to shoot meant someone would die, and you were never clear whether your own death would be included in the equation or not.

Web could always conjure up these images in a flash, so vivid were they in his memory. A quintuplet of match-grade hollow points would be lined up in a spring-loaded magazine waiting to rip into an adversary at twice the speed of sound once Web's finger pulled the jeweled trigger, which would break ever so sweetly at precisely two-point-five pounds of pressure. As soon as someone stepped into his kill zone, Web would fire and a human being would suddenly become a corpse crumbling to the earth. Yet the most important shots Web handled as a sniper were the ones he *hadn't* taken. It was just that kind of a gig. It was not for the faint-hearted, the stupid or even those of average intelligence.

Web said a silent thank-you to the snipers overhead and raced on down the alley.

They next came upon a child, maybe all of nine, sitting shirtless on a hunk of concrete, and not an adult in sight. The approaching storm had knocked at least twenty degrees off the thermometer and the mercury was still falling. And still the boy had no shirt on. Had he ever had a shirt on? Web wondered. He had seen many examples of impoverished children. While Web didn't consider himself a cynic, he was a realist. He felt sorry for these kids, but there wasn't much he could do to help them. And yet threats could come from anywhere these days, so his gaze automatically went from the boy's head to his feet, looking for weapons. Fortunately, he saw none; Web had no desire to fire upon a child.

The boy looked directly at him. Under the illuminated arc of the one flickering alley lamp that somehow had not been shot out, the child's features were outlined vividly. Web noted the too-lean body and the muscles in shoulders and arms already hard and clustering around the protrusion of ribs, as a tree grows bark cords over a wound. A knife slash ran across the boy's forehead. A puckered, blistered hole on the child's left cheek was the unmistakable tag of a bullet, Web knew.

"Damn to hell," said the child in a weary voice, and then he laughed or, more accurately, cackled. The boy's words and that laugh rang like cymbals in Web's head, and he had no idea why; his skin was actually tingling. He had seen hopeless kids like this before, they were everywhere around here, and yet something was going on in Web's head that he couldn't quite figure. Maybe he'd been doing this too long, and wasn't it a hell of a time to start thinking that?

Web's finger hovered near his rifle's trigger, and he moved farther in front with graceful strides even as he tried to rid himself of the boy's image. Though very lean himself and lacking showy muscles, Web had enormous leverage in his long arms, and strong fingers, and there was deceptive power in his naturally broad shoulders. And he was by far the fastest man on the team and also possessed great endurance. Web could run six-mile relays all day. He would take speed, quickness and stamina over bulging muscles any day. Bullets tore through muscle as easily as they did fat. Yet the lead couldn't hurt you if it couldn't hit you.

Most people would describe Web London, with his broad shoulders and standing six-foot-two, as a big man. Usually, though, people focused on the condition of the left side of his face, or what remained of it. Web had to grudgingly admit that it was amazing, the reconstruction they could do these days with destroyed flesh and bone. In just the right light, meaning hardly any at all, one almost wouldn't notice the old crater, the new rise of cheek and the delicate grafting of transplanted bone and skin. Truly remarkable, all had said. All except Web, that is.

At the end of the alley they stopped once more, all crouching low. At Web's elbow was Teddy Riner. Through his wireless Motorola bone mic, Riner communicated with TOC, telling them that Charlie was at yellow and asking permission to move to green—the "crisis site" of the target, which here was simply a fancy term for the front door. Web held the SR75 with one hand and felt for his custom-built .45-caliber pistol in the low-slung tactical holster riding on his right leg. He had an identical pistol hanging on the ceramic trauma plate that covered his chest, and he touched that one too in his pre-attack ritual of sorts.

Web closed his eyes and envisioned how the next minute would play out. They would race to the door. Davies would be front and center laying his charge. Assaulters would hold their flash bang grenades loosely in their weak hand. Subgun safeties would be off, and steady fingers would stay off triggers until it was time to kill. Davies would remove the mechanical safeties on the control box and check the detonator cord attached to the breaching charge, looking for problems and hoping to find none. Riner would communicate to TOC the immortal words, "Charlie at green." TOC would answer, as it always did, with, "Stand by, I have control." That line always rankled Web, because who the hell really had control doing what they did?

During his entire career Web had never heard TOC reach the end of the countdown. After the count of two, the snipers would engage targets and fire, and a bevy of .308s firing simultaneously was a tad noisy. Then the breach charge would blow before TOC said "one" and that high-decibel hurricane would drown out even your own thoughts. In fact, if you ever heard TOC finish the countdown you were in deep trouble, because that meant the breach charge had failed to go off. And that was truly a lousy way to start the workday.

When the explosive blew the door, Web and his team would invade the target and throw their flash bangs. The device was aptly named, since the "flash" would blind anyone watching, and the "bang" would rupture the unprotected eardrum. If they ran into any more locked doors, these would yield quickly either to the impolite knock-knock of Davies's shotgun or to a slap charge that looked like a strip of tire rubber but carried a C4 explosive kicker that virtually no door could withstand. They'd follow their rote patterns, keying on hands and weapons, shooting with precision, thinking in chess maneuvers. Communication would be via touch commands. Hit the hot spots, locate any hostages, and take them out fast and alive. What you never really thought about was dying.

That took too much time and energy away from the details of the mission, and away from the bedrock instincts and disciplines honed from doing this sort of thing over and over until it became a part of what made you, *you*.

According to reliable sources, the building they were going to hit contained the entire financial guts of a major drug operation head-quartered in the capital city. Included in the potential haul tonight were accountants and bean counters, valuable witnesses for the government if Web and his men could get them out alive. That way the Feds could go after top guys criminally and civilly from a number of fronts. Even drug lords feared an IRS full frontal assault, because seldom did kingpins pay taxes to Uncle Sam. That was why Web's team had been called up. They specialized in killing folks who needed it, but they also were damn good at keeping people alive. At least until these folks put their hands on the Bible, testified and sent some greater evil away for a very long time.

When TOC came back on, the countdown would begin: "Five, four, three, two . . ."

Web opened his eyes, collected himself. He was ready. Pulse at sixty-four; Web just knew. *Okay, boys, pay dirt's dead ahead. Let's go take it*. TOC came through his headset once more and gave the okay to move to the front door.

And that's precisely when Web London froze. His team burst out from the cover heading for green, the crisis site, and Web didn't. It was as though his arms and legs were no longer part of his body, the sensation of when you've fallen asleep with a limb under your body and wake up to find all the circulation has vacated that extremity. It didn't seem to be fear or runaway nerves; Web had been doing this too long. And yet he could only watch as Charlie Team raced on. The courtyard had been identified as the last major danger zone prior to the crisis site, and the team picked up its pace even more, looking everywhere for the slightest hint of coming resistance. Not a single one of the men seemed to notice that Web was not with them. With sweat pouring off him, every muscle straining against whatever was holding him down, Web managed slowly to rise and take a few faltering steps forward. His feet and arms seemingly encased in lead, his body on fire and his head bursting, he staggered onward a bit more, reached the courtyard, and then he dropped flat on his face as his team pulled away from him.

He glanced up in time to see Charlie Team running hard, the target in their sights, seemingly just begging them to come take a piece of it. The team was five seconds from impact. Those next few seconds would change Web London's life forever.

2

Teddy Riner went down first. Of the two seconds it took him to fall, the man had been dead for one of them. On the other side Cal Plummer fell to the ground like he'd been pole-axed by a giant. As Web watched helplessly, up and down the compact lines heavy ordnance impacted with Kevlar and then flesh, and then there was nothing else. It didn't seem right for good men to die so quietly.

Before the guns started firing, Web had fallen on his rifle and it was wedged under him. He could barely breathe; his Kevlar and weapons seemed crushed against his diaphragm. There was stuff on his mask. He couldn't know, but it was part of Teddy Riner, throw-off from the monster round that had blown a hole the size of a man's palm through his body armor and sent part of Riner flying back to where Web lay, dead last of Charlie Team and, ironically enough, the only one still living.

Web still felt paralyzed, none of his limbs responding to pleas from his brain to move. Had he suffered a stroke at age thirty-seven? Then suddenly the sounds of gunfire seemed to clear his head, the feeling finally returned to his arms and legs and he managed to rip off his mask and roll on his back. He exhaled a gush of foul air and screamed in relief. Now Web was staring straight up at the sky. He saw spears of lightning, though he couldn't hear even the belly rumbles of the thunder over the gunfire.

He had a powerful if insane urge to lift up his hand into the maelstrom above him, perhaps to confirm the presence of the bullets racing past, as though he were a youngster told not to touch a hot stove and who would then, of course, think of nothing else. Instead he reached down to his belt, undid the latch on a side pouch and pulled out his thermal imager. On the blackest night the TI would pick up an entire world invisible to the unaided eye, zeroing in on the core heat signature that burned in just about everything.

Though he was unable to see them even with the TI, Web could easily sense the vapor trails thrown off by the net of bullets zipping across above him. Web also observed that the dense gunfire was coming from two separate directions: the tenement building dead ahead and a dilapidated structure to the immediate right. He looked through his TI at the latter building and saw nothing but jagged glass. And then Web observed something that made his body tense even more. The muzzle flashes were erupting at the same time at each of the shattered windows. They moved across the apertures, stopped for a few seconds, and then moved back across, as the gun barrels he could not see yet knew were there completed their controlled firing arc.

As the gunfire began anew, Web rolled over on his belly and stared at the original target building through his imager. Here too there was a line of windows in the lower level of the target. And the same muzzle flashes were occurring with the exact same synchronized arc of movement. Web could now make out the long barrels of the machine guns. Through the TI the silhouettes of the guns were brick-red, the metal molten hot from the amount of ammo they were spraying. No human outline, though, came up on his thermal, and if any man had been in the vicinity, Web's imager would have nailed him. He was for sure looking at some kind of remote-controlled firing post. He now knew that his team had been set up, ambushed, without the enemy putting a single man at risk.

The slugs ricocheted off the brick walls behind and to the right of him, and Web felt bits of shrapnel hitting all around, like hardened raindrops. At least a dozen times the deflections had skimmed his Kevlar, but most of their speed and lethality had already been depleted. He kept his unarmored legs and arms tight to the asphalt. However, not even his Kevlar could withstand a

direct hit, for the machine guns were almost certainly doling out
.50-caliber ordnance, with each round as long as a butter knife
and probably armor-piercing too. Web could gauge all this from
the supersonic cracking sound made by the guns and the signature muzzle flash. And the vapor trail of a .50-caliber was also
something pretty damn unforgettable. In fact you *felt* the snap
before you even heard the round. It raised every hair on your
body, as lightning did right before its fatal blow.

Web screamed out the names of his teammates one by one. No
answer. No movement. No moans, no body twitches to show that
life was still out there somewhere. And still Web yelled out their
names again and again, like some insane roll call. Everywhere
around him garbage cans exploded, glass burst, walls of brick were
being eroded as if bludgeoning rivers were carving canyons. This
was Normandy Beach, or more aptly Pickett's Charge, and Web
had just lost his entire army. Alley vermin fled the slaughter. That
courtyard was as clean of such rodents as it ever had been. No city
inspector had ever done as good a job as rhythmic .50-caliber ordnance did that night.

Web didn't want to die, but every time he looked at what was left
of his team, a part of him wanted to join them. The family fought
and died together. It held some appeal for Web. He actually felt his
legs tense for such a leap to eternity, yet something stronger took
hold and he stayed hunkered down. To die was to lose. To give up
was to let everyone perish in vain.

Where the hell were X-Ray and Whiskey? Why weren't they fast-
roping to the rescue? The snipers on the buildings overlooking the
courtyard couldn't come down without getting ripped apart,
though, yet there were other snipers on the roofs of the buildings
along the alley Charlie had come through. They could rope down.
But would TOC give them the green light? Maybe not, if TOC
didn't know what was going on, and how could they? Web didn't
even know what the hell was going on, and he was right in the
middle of it. Yet he couldn't exactly hang around waiting for TOC
to make up their mind until a stray round made it a clean sweep of
Web's team.

He felt a thin layer of panic settle over him despite years of training designed specifically to banish that weakness from his psyche. Action, he needed to be doing something. His bone mic lost, Web snared his portable Motorola from its shoulder Velcro patch. He pushed the button, yelled into it. "HR fourteen to TOC, HR fourteen to TOC." No response. He changed to the backup frequency and then to a general purpose one. Still nothing. He looked at the radio and his spirits sank. The front was smashed from where he had fallen on it. Web slithered forward until he reached Cal Plummer's body. When he tried to grab Plummer's two-way radio, something hit Web's hand and he pulled it back. A ricochet only; a direct hit would've taken his hand off. Web counted five fingers still there, and the intense pain made him want to fight, to live. If for no other reason than to destroy whoever had done this, although Web's bag of tricks was almost empty. And for the first time in his career Web wondered if the opposition he now faced was actually better than he was.

Web knew that if he stopped thinking he still might leap up, firing at nothing that could be killed. So he focused on the tactical scenario. He was in a carefully confined death zone, automatic firing arcs on two sides, forming a ninety-degree angle of destruction and providing no human agent that could be stopped. Okay, that was the field situation. Now what the hell was he supposed to do about it? What chapter was that in the manual? The one that read, "You're screwed"? God, the sounds were deafening. He couldn't even hear his heart pounding. His breath came in short gasps. Where the hell were Whiskey and X-Ray? And Hotel? They couldn't run any faster? And yet what really could they do? They were trained to gun down human targets at both long and close range. He screamed out, "There's nothing for you to shoot!"

Chin tucked hard to his chest, Web started in surprise as he saw the little boy, the shirtless one from the chunk of concrete. Hands over his ears, the kid was crouched at the edge of the corner, along the alleyway Web and company had come from. If he moved out into the courtyard, Web knew the boy's body would be going into a morgue bag—probably two morgue bags, because the .50 rounds could actually cut the kid's skinny body in half.

The boy took a step forward, nearing the end of the brick wall and almost at the courtyard. Maybe he was intending to come help. Maybe he was waiting for the gunfire to stop so he could strip the bodies of any valuables, snagging their weapons for later resale on the streets. Maybe he was just flat-out curious. Web didn't know or really care.

The guns stopped firing, and just like that there was quiet. The boy took another step forward. Web screamed at him. He froze, obviously not expecting the dead to yell at the living. Web inched up his hand, called to him to keep back, but the gunfire started again and drowned out the end of his warning. Web slithered on his belly under the hail of fire, shouting at the boy with every twist and thrust of his pelvis. "Stay back! Get back!"

The kid didn't flinch. Web kept his gaze on him, which was difficult when you were double-timing on your gut, afraid that if you raised your head another centimeter you would no longer have a head. The boy finally did what Web thought he would do: He started to fall back. Web crawled faster. The kid turned to run and Web yelled at him to stop. Shockingly, he did.

Web was almost to the edge of the alley. He was going to try and time this just right, for there was now a new element of danger for the child. During the last pause in the firing Web had heard synchronized footsteps and shouts in the distance. They were coming. Web thought it must be everybody: Hotel and the snipers, and the reserve unit that TOC always kept back for emergencies. Well, if this didn't qualify as an emergency, nothing ever would. Yes, they were hustling to the rescue, or so they thought. What they were really doing though was running blind with no reliable intelligence.

The problem was the kid heard them coming too. Web could tell the boy knew exactly what and who they were, like a scout sniffing the earth and deducing from that the location of great buffalo herds. The boy was feeling trapped, and for good reason. Web knew that for the alley kid to be seen around people like Web was a death sentence here. The powers that be would just assume he was a traitor and deposit his body in the woods as his reward.

The child twitched, looked behind him even as Web picked up his pace. Web lost half his equipment whipping along the rough asphalt like that, a two-hundred-pound serpent on speed. Web could feel the blood coming from a dozen scratches on his legs, hands and face. His left hand stung like a couple thousand wasps were partying there. The body armor was so damn heavy now, his body ached with each thrust of his arms and legs. Web could have dropped his rifle, but he still had use for it. No, he would never let go of the damn SR75.

Web knew what the kid was going to do. Retreat cut off, he was going to go for it, race across the courtyard and then disappear into one of the buildings on the far side. The boy could hear the bullets as well as Web could. Yet he could not *see* the lines of fire. He could not dodge them. And yet Web knew the boy was about to try.

The child jumped out of the blocks, and Web leapt off his belly at the last possible second so that the two met right at the fringe of safety in a collision Web would win ten times out of ten. The child kicked at Web; his knotty fists struck him about the face and chest as Web's long arms wrapped around him. Web went back farther into the alley, carrying the kid. Kevlar was not easy on the hands, and the boy finally stopped punching and looked at Web. "I ain't do nothing. Let me go!"

"You run out there, you die!" Web yelled over the gunfire. He held up his bloody hand. "I'm wearing body armor and I can't survive out there. Those bullets will cut you in half."

The boy calmed as he studied Web's injury. Web carried the kid farther away from the courtyard and the guns. Now they could at least talk without shouting. From some odd impulse, Web touched the bullet wound on the boy's cheek. "You've been lucky before," Web said. The boy snarled and jerked away from him, breaking free of Web's grip. He was up, ferretlike, before Web could blink and had turned to run back down the alley. "If you go at them in the dark," Web said, "your luck runs out. They'll blow you away."

The kid stopped and turned back. For the first time his eyes truly seemed to focus on Web. Then he peered beyond to the courtyard. "They dead?" he asked.

In answer Web slipped the big rifle from his shoulder. The boy took a step back at the sight of the intimidating weapon.

"Damn, mister, whatcha gonna do with that?"

"Stay here and keep down," Web said. He turned back to the

courtyard. Sirens were everywhere now. The cavalry was coming, too late, as the cavalry always did. The smartest thing to do would be nothing. Yet that just wasn't going to cut it. Web had a job to finish. He ripped a piece of paper from the notebook he carried on his belt and scribbled a quick note. He then pulled off the cap he wore under his helmet "Here," he said to the kid. "Walk, don't run, back down the alley. Hold up this cap and give this note to the men coming this way." The boy took the items, his long fingers curled around the cloth of the cap and the folded paper. Web pulled his flare gun from its pouch and loaded in a flare. "When I fire, you go. Walk!" Web said again. "Don't run."

The boy looked down at the note. Web had no idea if he could even read. Around here you didn't assume that children received the fundamentals of education that other kids took for granted. "What's your name?" Web asked. The boy needed to be calm now. Nervous people made mistakes. And Web knew the charging men would cremate anyone who came rushing at them.

"Kevin," the boy answered. As he said his own name, he suddenly looked like the frightened little kid that he was, and Web felt even guiltier about what he was asking the boy to do.

"Okay, Kevin, I'm Web. You do what I say and you'll be okay. You can trust me," he said, and then felt guiltier still. Web pointed the flare gun to the sky, looked at Kevin, nodded reassuringly and then fired. The flare would be their first warning. The note carried by Kevin would be their second. The boy moved off, walking, but walking fast. "Don't run," Web yelled. He turned back to the courtyard and slid his thermal imager onto the rifle's Picatinny rail and locked it into place.

The red-colored flare bloodied the sky and in his mind Web saw the assaulters and snipers stop and consider this development. That would give the boy time to reach them. Kevin would not die, not tonight anyway. When the next pause in the wave of fire came, Web burst out from the alley, rolled and brought the rifle up as he assumed a prone firing position and flipped down the rifle's bipod, pressing the weapon's butt flush against his shoulder. The three windows dead ahead were his first targets. He could see the muzzle flashes with his own eyes easily enough, but the thermal allowed him to draw a bead on the heated outlines of the machine guns. That's what he wanted to hit. The SR75 roared and one machine gun nest after another exploded. Web rammed in another twenty-round mag, aimed the rifle and pulled the trigger, and four more machine guns were finally silenced. The last gun nest was still firing when Web crawled forward and lobbed a concussion grenade into its throat. And then there was silence until Web emptied both of his .45s at the now-silent window openings, ejected cartridges tumbling out of the weapons like parachutists from a plane's belly. When the last shot was fired, Web doubled over, sucking in precious air. He was so hot he thought he might spontaneously combust. Then the clouds opened and the rain came down hard. He looked over and saw an armor-coated assaulter cautiously edge into the courtyard. Web tried to wave to him, but his arm wouldn't follow through; it just hung limply by his side.

Web surveyed the shattered bodies of his team, his friends spread over the slick pavement. Then he sank to his knees. He was alive and he didn't really want to be. The last thing Web London remembered from that night was watching drops of his sweat fall into the blood-tinted pools of rain.

3

Randall Cove was a very big man endowed with great physical strength and also remarkable street instincts that he had further honed over many years of working them. He was an FBI undercover agent and had been one for nearly seventeen years. He had infiltrated Latino drug gangs in LA, Hispanic crews on the Tex-Mex border and heavyweight Europeans in south Florida. Most of his missions had been startling and, at times, nail-biting successes. He was currently armed with a .40 semiautomatic chambering hollow points that would collapse to small pancakes when they entered a body, wreaking internal havoc and probably death. He also had a sheathed knife with a serrated edge that he could use to slash vital arteries in a blur. He always prided himself on being professional and reliable in his work. Right now some ignorant people would condemn him as a vicious criminal who should be locked up for life or, better yet, executed for his terrible sins. Cove knew he was in serious trouble and he also realized he was the only one who could get himself out of it.

Cove crouched low in the car and watched as the group of men climbed in their vehicles and headed out. As soon as they passed, Cove rose, waited a bit and then followed them. He pulled his ski cap tighter over his newly shorn head, the dreadlocks all gone, and about time too, he had decided. The cars stopped up ahead and Cove did too. When he saw the group of men emerge from the vehicles, Cove pulled a camera from his backpack and clicked away. He put away the Nikon, pulled out a pair of night binoculars and adjusted the distance magnifier. Cove nodded to himself as he tallied the men one by one.

He inhaled and let go of one last deep breath and took a fast-forward reel on his life thus far as the group disappeared into a building. In college Cove had been a bigger, faster version of Walter Payton; a consensus All-American from Oklahoma, every NFL team was throwing bales of cash and other perks at him. They were, that is, until a ruptured ACL in both knees during a freakish spill at the scouting combine had reduced him from a supernatural guaranteed number-one pick to a man with merely normal abilities who no longer excited NFL coaches. Millions of potential dollars had disappeared instantly and the only way of life he had ever known had vanished along with them. He had moped for a couple of years, looking for excuses and pity, and his life had spiraled downward until it had nowhere else to go, and then he had found her. His wife had been a divine intervention, he had always believed, saving his miserable, self-pitying carcass from oblivion. With her help, he had straightened himself out and fulfilled a secret dream of his to be a real-life G-man.

He had bounced here and there in the Bureau. It was a time when opportunities for black men were still severely limited. Cove had found himself pushed toward drug undercover work, because his superiors had bluntly informed him that most of the "bad dudes" were people of his color. You can walk the walk and talk the talk and you look the part too, they had said. And he couldn't argue with that, really. The work was dangerous enough to never be boring. Randall Cove had never easily tolerated being bored. And he put away more crooks in a month than most agents put away in their entire careers, and these were big fish, the planners, the true moneymakers, not the nickel-and-dime streetwalkers one bad snort from a pauper's grave. He and his wife had had two beautiful children and he was thinking seriously of calling it a career when the bottom had dropped out of his world and he no longer had a wife or kids.

He snapped back as the men came out, climbed in the cars, drove off and Cove once more followed. Cove had lost something else that he could never get back. Six men had died because he had

messed up badly, been snookered like the most green agent there
was. His pride was hurt and his anger was molten. And the seventh member of the shattered team deeply intrigued Cove. The
man had survived when he should have been dead too and apparently nobody knew why, though it was early in the game yet. Cove
wanted to look the man in the eye and say, *How come you're still
breathing?* He didn't have Web London's file and he didn't see himself getting it anytime soon. Yeah, Cove was FBI, but yeah, everyone was no doubt thinking he had turned traitor. Undercover
agents were supposed to live right next to the edge, weren't they?
They were supposedly all head cases, right? What a thankless job
he'd been doing all these years, but that was okay because he had
done it for himself, nobody else.

The cars pulled into the long drive and Cove stopped, took
some more pictures and then turned around. That was apparently it for tonight. He headed back to the only place he could be
safe right now, and it wasn't home. As he rounded a curve and
sped up, a pair of headlights seemed to appear out of nowhere
and settled in behind him. That wasn't good, not on a road like
this. Attention from his fellow man was not something Cove ever
sought or encouraged. He turned; so did the car. Okay, this was
serious. He sped up again. So did the tail. Cove reached down to
his belt holster, pulled out his pistol and made sure the safety
was off.

He glanced in the rearview mirror to see if he could tell how
many folks he was dealing with. It was too dark for that, no streetlights out this way. The first bullet blew out his right rear tire, the
second bullet his left rear. As he fought to keep control of the car, a
truck pulled out from a side road and hit him broadside. If his window had been up, Cove's head would have gone right through it.
The truck had a snowplow on its front end, though it was not wintertime. The truck accelerated and Cove's car was pushed in front
of it. He felt his car about to roll and then the truck pushed his
sedan over a guardrail that had been placed there principally to
protect vehicles from plummeting down the steep slope that the
curve of road was built around. The car's side smashed into the dirt
and then rolled, both doors popping open as the sedan continued

its cartwheeling, finally landing in a heap at the rocky bottom of the slope and bursting into flames.

The car that had tailed Cove stopped and one man got out, ran to the twisted guardrail and looked down. He saw the fire, witnessed the explosion as fuel vapor met flames and then ran back to his car. The two vehicles kicked up gravel leaving the scene.

As they did, Randall Cove slowly rose from the spot where he'd been thrown when the driver's door had been ripped open by the first impact with the ground. He had lost his gun and it felt like a couple of ribs were cracked, but he was alive. He looked down at what was left of his car and then back up at where the men who had tried to kill him had raced off. Cove stood on shaky legs and started slowly making his way back up.

Web clutched his wounded hand even as his head seemed primed to explode. It was like he had taken three quick slugs of straight tequila and was about to reflux them. The hospital room was empty. There was an armed man outside, to make sure nothing happened to Web—nothing *else* anyway.

Web had been lying here all day and into the night thinking about what had happened, and he was no closer to any answers than when they first brought him here. Web's commander had already been in, along with several members of Hotel and some of the snipers from Whiskey and X-Ray. They had said little, all of them reeling in their personal agony, their disbelief that something like this could have happened to them. And in their eyes Web could sense their suspicions, the issue of what had happened to him out there.

"I'm sorry, Debbie," Web said to the image of Teddy Riner's widow. He said the same to Cynde Plummer, Cal's wife and also now a widow. He went down the list: six women in all, all friends of his. Their men were his partners, his comrades; Web felt as bereaved as any of the ladies.

He let go of his injured hand and touched the metal side of the bed with it. What a sorry wound to bring back with him. He hadn't taken one round directly. "Not one damn shot did I get off in time," he said to the wall. "Not one! Do you realize how un-

believable that is?" he called out to the IV stand, before falling
silent again.

"We're going to get them, Web."

The voice startled Web, for he had heard no one enter the room.
But of course a voice came with a body. Web inched up on his bed
until he saw the outline of the man there. Percy Bates sat down
in a chair next to Web. The man studied the linoleum floor as
though it were a map that would guide him to a place that held
all the answers.

It was said that Percy Bates had not changed a jot in twenty-five
years. The man hadn't gained or lost a pound on his trim five-ten
frame. His hair was charcoal-black without a creep of white and was
combed the same way as when he first walked into the FBI fresh
from the Academy. It was as though he had been flash-frozen, and
this was remarkable in a line of work that tended to age people
well ahead of their time. He had become a legend of sorts at the
Bureau. He had wreaked havoc on drug operations at the Tex-Mex
border and then gone on to raise hell on the West Coast in the LA
Field Office. He had risen through the ranks quickly and was currently one of the top people at the Washington Field Office, or
"WFO," as it was called. He had experience in all the major Bureau
divisions and the man knew how all the pieces fit together.

Bates, who went by Perce, was usually soft-spoken. Yet the man
could crumple a subordinate with a look that made one feel un-
worthy to be occupying a square foot of space. He could either be
your best ally or your worst enemy. Maybe that's how a man
turned out after growing up with a name like Percy.

Web had been on the end of some of the classic Bates tirades
before, when he had been under the man's direct command in
his previous professional life at the Bureau. A good deal of the
abuse had been deserved, as Web had made mistakes as he
learned to be a good agent. Yet Bates did play favorites from time
to time and, like everyone else, sometimes went searching for
scapegoats to pin blame upon when things went to hell. Thus,
Web did not accept the man's statements right now at face value.
Nor did he accept the subdued tone as a token of peace and good-
will. Yet the night Web had lost half his face in the fury of combat, Bates had been one of the first people by his bedside, and

Web had never forgotten that. No, Percy Bates was not a simple equation, not that any of them were. He and Bates would never be drinking buddies, yet Web had never believed one had to do shooters with a guy to respect him.

"I know you've given us the prelims, but we'll need your full statement as soon as you're able," said Bates. "But don't rush it. Take your time, get your strength back."

The message was clear. What had happened had crushed them all. There would be no outbursts from Bates. At least not right now.

"More scratches than anything," Web mumbled in response.

"They said a gunshot wound to your hand. Cuts and bruises all over your body. The docs said it looked like somebody had taken a baseball bat to you."

"Nothing," Web replied, and then felt exhausted by saying the word.

"You still need to rest. And then we'll get your statement." Bates rose. "And if you're up to it, and I know it'll be hard, it would help if you could go back down there and run us through exactly what happened."

And how I managed to survive? Web nodded. "I'll be ready sooner than later."

"Don't rush it," Bates said again. "This one ain't gonna be easy. But we'll get it done." He patted Web on the shoulder and turned to the door.

Web stirred, trying to sit up. "Perce?" In the darkness the whites of Bates's eyes were really the only things visible of him. To Web they were like a pair of dice hanging, showing deuces somehow. "They're all dead, aren't they?"

"All of them," Bates confirmed. "You're the only one left, Web."

"I did all I could."

The door opened and then closed, and Web was alone.

Outside in the hallway, Bates conferred with a group of men dressed exactly as he was: nondescript blue suit, button-down shirt, muted tie, rubber-soled black shoes and big pistols in small clip holsters.

"This will be a media nightmare, you know that," said one of them. "It already is, in fact."

Bates stuck a piece of gum in his mouth, substitute for the Winstons he had given up for the fifth time now and counting. "The needs of suck-wad journalists are not high on my priority list," he said.

"You have to keep them informed, Perce. If you don't, they'll assume the worst and start making it up. There's already been stuff on the Internet you wouldn't believe, that this massacre is tied to either the apocalyptic return of Jesus or something to do with a Chinese trade conspiracy. I mean, where do they get this crap? It's driving the media relations people nuts."

"I can't believe anybody would have the guts to do this to *us*," said another man, who had grown gray and plump in the service of his country. Bates knew this particular agent had not seen anything other than the top of his government desk in more than a decade but liked to act as though he had. "Not the Colombians, the Chinese or even the Russians could have the guts to attack *us* like that."

Bates glanced at the man. "It's 'us' against 'them.' Remember? We try to cram it down their throats all the time. You think they don't want to return the favor?"

"But my God, Perce, think about it. They just slaughtered a squad of our men. On our home turf," the old fellow blustered indignantly.

Perce looked at him and saw an elephant without tusks, just about ready to drop and die and become dinner for the jungle carnivores. "I didn't realize we had laid claim to that part of D.C.," said Bates. He had last slept the day before yesterday and was now really starting to feel it. "In fact, I was under the impression that that was *their* home turf and we were the visiting team."

"You know what I mean. What could have prompted this sort of attack?"

"Shit, I don't know, maybe because we try so damn hard to pull the plug on their billion-dollars-a-day drug pipeline and it's starting to really piss them off, you idiot!" As he said this, Bates backed the man into a corner and then decided the guy was far too harmless to be worth a suspension.

"How's he doing?" asked another man, with blond hair and a nose red from the flu.

Bates leaned against the wall, chewed his gum and then shrugged. "I think it's messed more with his mind than anything else. But that's to be expected."

"One lucky guy is all I can say," commented Red Nose. "How he survived it is anyone's guess."

It took barely a second for Bates to get in this man's face. He was obviously taking no prisoners tonight. "You call it luck to watch six of your team get ripped right in front of you? Is that what the hell you're saying, you dumb son of a bitch?"

"Geez, I didn't mean it like that, Perce. You know I didn't." Red Nose coughed a good one, as though to let Bates know he was sick and in no shape to fight.

Bates moved away from Red Nose, thoroughly disgusted with them all. "Right now I don't know anything. No, I take that back. I know that Web single-handedly took out eight machine gun nests and saved another squad and some ghetto kid in the process. That I do know."

"The preliminary report says Web froze." This came from another man who had joined their ranks, yet he was one who clearly stood above them all. Two stone-faced gents were in lockstep behind the intruder. "And actually, Perce, what we know is only what Web has told us," said the man. Though this person was obviously Percy Bates's superior in official rank, it was equally apparent that Bates wanted to bite his head off yet didn't dare.

The man continued. "London's got a hell of a lot of explaining to do. And we're going into this investigation with our eyes *wide* open, a lot more wide open than last night. Last night was a disgrace. Last night will never, ever happen again. Not on my watch." He stared hard at Bates and then said with sarcasm driven home with a sledgehammer, "Give London my best." With that, Buck Winters, head of the FBI's Washington Field Office, stalked off, followed by his two robotic escorts.

Bates gazed with loathing at the man's back. Buck Winters had been one of the principal frontline supervisors at Waco and had, in Bates's opinion, contributed to the eventual carnage with his ineptness. Then, in the funny way of big organizations, Winters had received promotion after promotion for his incompetence until he had reached the top of WFO. Maybe the Bureau was just unwilling to admit it had messed up and believed that promoting from the ranks of the leadership of the Waco fiasco was a strong message to the world that the Bureau considered itself blameless. Eventually, many heads had rolled because of the flameout of David Koresh in Texas, but Buck Winters's head was still firmly attached to his shoulders. For Percy Bates, Buck Winters represented much that was wrong with the FBI.

Bates leaned against the wall, crossed his arms and chewed his Wrigley's so hard his teeth hurt. He was certain that old Buck would be running off to confer with the FBI director, the attorney general, probably even the President. Well, let him, so long as they all kept out of Percy Bates's way.

The group of men slithered away singly and in pairs until just Bates and the uniformed guard remained. Finally Bates moved off too, hands in his pockets, gaze fixed on nothing. On the way out he spit his gum into the trash can. "Assholes and idiots," he said. "Assholes and idiots."

4

Web, dressed in a set of blue surgery scrubs, carried a bag with his personal belongings and stared at the sunlit sky that filled the window of his hospital room. The layers of gauze around his wounded hand were irritating; he felt like he was wearing a boxing glove.

He was about to open the door to leave when it opened all by itself. At least that's what Web thought until the man appeared there.

"What are you doing here, Romano?" said Web in surprise.

The man didn't acknowledge Web right away. He was just under six feet tall, about one-eighty, very powerful-looking in a wiry way. He had dark wavy hair and wore an old leather jacket, a Yankees baseball cap and jeans. His FBI shield was pinned to his belt; the grip of a pistol poked out from its clip holster.

Romano looked Web up and down until his gaze came to rest on the man's bandaged hand. He pointed at it. "Is that it? Is that your damn *wound*?"

Web looked at his hand and then back at Romano. "Would it make you happier if the hole was in my head?"

Paul Romano was an assaulter assigned to Hotel Team. He was one very intimidating guy among many such folks and you always knew where you stood with the man, which was usually nowhere good. He and Web had never been close—principally, Web thought, because Web had been shot up more than he had, and Romano strongly resented the perception that Web was more heroic or tougher.

"I'm only going to ask you this once, Web, and I want it straight, man. You bullshit me and I'll pop you myself."

Web looked down at the guy and stepped a bit closer so that his height advantage was even more evident. He knew this ticked off Romano too. "Gee, Paulie, did you bring me some candy and flowers too?"

"Just give it to me straight, Web." He paused and then asked, "Did you wimp out?"

"Yeah, Paulie, those guns somehow shot themselves all up."

"I know about that. I meant before that. When Charlie Team went down. You weren't with them. Why?"

Web felt his face growing warm and he hated himself for it. Romano usually couldn't get to him. Yet the truth was, Web didn't know what to tell the man.

"Something happened, Paulie, in my head. I don't know exactly what. But I didn't have anything to do with the ambush, in case you suddenly lost your mind and were thinking that."

Romano shook his head. "I wasn't thinking you turned traitor, Web, just that you turned chickenshit."

"If that's all you came to tell me, then you can go on and get the hell out now."

Romano looked him up and down again and Web felt like less and less of a man with each pronounced glare. Without a word, Romano turned and left. Web would have preferred the man had exited on the heel of another insult rather than silence.

Web waited another few minutes and then opened the door.

"What are you doing up?" asked the surprised guard.

"Docs discharged me, didn't they tell you?"

"Nobody told me anything like that."

Web held up his bandaged hand. "Government isn't paying for another night on account of a scratched hand. And damn if I'm paying the difference on my paycheck." Web didn't know the guard, but he seemed like the type to be sympathetic to such a commonsense plea. Web didn't wait to get an answer but just walked off. He knew the guard had no grounds to stop him. All he would do was communicate this development to his superiors, which he was assuredly doing right now.

Web ducked out a side exit, found a phone, called a buddy and an hour later he was inside his split-level thirty-year-old rancher in a quiet Woodbridge, Virginia, suburb. He changed into jeans, loafers and a navy blue sweatshirt, ripped off the gauze and replaced it with a single Band-Aid of blazing symbolism. He wanted no pity from anyone, not with six of his closest friends right now lying in the morgue.

He checked his messages. There weren't any of importance, yet he knew that would change. He unlocked a firebox, pulled out his spare nine-millimeter and thrust it into his belt holster. Although he had not technically shot anyone, this was still an SRB—or Shooting Review Board—matter now, since Web had most definitely fired his weapons. They had confiscated his guns, which was akin to taking his hands. Next, they had advised him of his rights and he had given them a statement. It was all standard, by-the-books practice and yet it still made him feel like a criminal. Well, he wasn't about to walk around without hardware. He was paranoid by nature, and the massacre of his team had made him a walking schizoid, capable of seeing real threats in babies and bunnies.

He went out to the garage, cranked up his 1978 coal-black Ford Mach One and headed out.

Web had two vehicles: the Mach, and an ancient and iron-gutted Suburban that had carried him and his Charlie Team to many Redskin football games, to the beaches in Virginia and Maryland, to beer-drinking outings and on assorted other manly campaigns up and down the East Coast. Each guy had had his own assigned seat in the Suburban, based on seniority and ability, which was the way everything was divvied up where Web worked. What outstanding times they had had in the big machine. Now Web wondered how much cash he could get for the Suburban, because he didn't see himself driving the beast anymore.

He jumped on Interstate 95, headed north and fought through the obstacle course that was the Springfield Interchange, which apparently had been designed by a highway engineer strung out on cocaine. Now that it was undergoing a major overhaul scheduled to last at least ten years, the driver navigating it each day had the option of laughing or crying as years of his life slipped by while the traffic's progress was measured in inches. Web sailed over the Fourteenth Street Bridge, cleared the Northwest quadrant where all the major monuments and tourist dollars were kept and was quickly in a not-so-nice part of town.

Web was an FBI special agent, but he did not see himself as such. First and foremost he was a Hostage Rescue Team (HRT) operator, the Bureau's elite crisis response group. He didn't dress in suits. He didn't spend much time with fellow agents outside HRT. He didn't arrive on the crime scene after all the bullets had stopped flying. He was usually there from the get-go, running, dodging, firing, wounding and occasionally killing. There were only fifty HRT operators, because the selection process was so grueling. The average time at HRT was five years. Web had bucked that trend and was going on his eighth year of duty. It seemed that HRT was being called upon a lot more often these days and to hot spots all over the world, with HRT's unwritten policy of being wheels up in four hours from Andrews Air Force Base. Well, the curtain had fallen on his part of that show. Web was teamless now.

It had never occurred to Web that he would be the sole survivor of anything. It just didn't seem in his nature. They all had joked about it, even had morbid betting pools on who would die one moonless night. Web had almost always been first on the list, because he always seemed to be first in the line of fire. Now it was torturing Web, though, not knowing what had gotten between him and the seventh coffin. And the only thing worse than the guilt was the shame.

He pulled the Mach to the curb and got out at the barricade. He showed his ID to the men posted there, who were all stunned to see him. Web ducked down the alley before the army of reporters could glom on to him. They had been reporting live here since the massacre from their tall-mast satellite broadcast trucks. Web had caught some of the news from the hospital. They were feeding the public the same facts over and over, using their little charts and pictures, and sporting their little dour expressions, and saying things like, "That's all we know right now. But stay with us, I'm certain we'll have more later, even if we have to make the shit up. Back to you, Sue." Web jogged down the alley.

Last night's storm had long since blown itself into the Atlantic. The air pushing behind it was cooler than the city had had in a while. Built on a swamp, Washington, D.C., handled heat and humidity better than cold and snow. When the snow fell, the only street likely to be cleared was the one in your dreams.

He ran into Bates halfway down the alley.

"What in the hell are you doing here?" Bates said.

"You said you wanted my take on things, so I'm here to give it to you." Bates glanced at Web's hand. "Let's get going, Perce. Every minute counts."

From the exact spot where the Chevy had dropped them off, Web retraced the steps of his squad. With every stride Web took toward the target, he could feel both his anger and his fear swell. The bodies were gone; the blood was not. Even the hard rain apparently was incapable of clearing it all away. In his mind, Web blitzed through every move he had made, every emotion he had felt.

The ruined machine gun nests were being dismantled and examined by a team of people who consistently pulled legal convictions out of microscopic scraps. Others walked the square courtyard kneeling, stooping, tagging things, probing and basically looking for answers from objects that did not appear willing to give any. Watching them, Web was not confident. It was highly unlikely that crystal-clear tented arches and plain whorls were just waiting around on the guns to be plucked by the fingerprint techs. Whoever had planned this intricate ambush wouldn't be that careless. He stepped between the bloodstains like he was tiptoeing around a graveyard, and wasn't he really?

"Windows were painted black so the guns couldn't be spotted until they started firing. No light reflections off barrels, no nothing," said Bates.

"Nice to know we were done in by professionals," replied Web bitterly.

"You did a number on the fifties." Bates pointed to one of the ruined weapons.

"An SR75 will do that for you."

"They're mini-guns, military design. Six-barrel Gatling style,

tripod-mounted with the pods bolted to the floor so the firing position wouldn't deviate. There were feeder box and conveyor belt
attachments and four thousand linked rounds per gun. Firing
rates were set at four hundred a minute, though its maximum
setting is eight thousand."

"Four hundred was plenty. And there were eight guns. That's
thirty-two hundred slugs flying at you every sixty seconds. I know
because all except one ricochet missed me by a few inches."

"With that low firing rate those guns could shoot a long time."

"They did."

"Power drive was electric, and they were chambering armor-
piercing rounds."

Web just shook his head. "Did you find what tripped them?"

Bates led him over to a brick wall on the side farthest from the
alley Web had come down. It was part of the building perpendicu-
larly placed to the targeted abandoned tenement house and the
source of one-half of the firing arc that had wiped out Charlie, save
Web. What was invisible in the dark was only a bit more apparent
in the daylight.

Web knelt down and looked at what he recognized as a laser device. A small hole had been punched in the brick and the laser point
and power pack inserted into it. The hole was deeper than the power
pack so that once inside the hole, it was pretty much invisible. The
snipers wouldn't have been able to ID it from where they had their
posts set up, even if they had been looking for such a thing, and their
intelligence had given them no indication of it, as far as Web knew.
The path of the laser was knee height and the invisible light stream
no doubt had run across the courtyard when activated.

"Beam breaks, firing starts and doesn't stop except for a few seconds' pause after each cycle until the ammo's gone." He looked
around in bewilderment. "What if a dog or cat or somebody just
strolling by here tripped the laser before we got there?"

From Bates's expression, it was clear he had already considered
this possibility. "I'm thinking people were discreetly warned to
stay away. Animals are another issue. So I'm thinking the laser was
armed via remote."

Web rose. "So they waited until we were just about there before activating the laser. That means the person would have to be reasonably close by."

"Well, he hears you guys coming, or he gets intelligence to that effect. He waits until you've maybe turned the corner and he hits the remote and runs."

"We didn't see a damn soul in the courtyard, and my thermal didn't pick up a ninety-eight-point-six temp anywhere."

"They could've been in the building—hell, any one of these buildings. They point the device out one of the windows, hit the button and they're long gone."

"And the snipers and Hotel saw nothing?"

Bates shook his head. "Hotel's story is they saw zip until the kid brought them your note."

At the mention of Hotel, Web thought of Paul Romano and his spirits sank even more. Romano was probably at Quantico right now telling everyone that Web had turned coward and let his team die and was trying to blame it on a mental lapse. "Whiskey? X-Ray? They had to see something," Web said, referring to the snipers on the rooftops.

"They saw some things, but I'm not prepared to discuss it quite yet."

Web's instincts told him to let that one alone. What would the snipers say? That they saw Web freeze, let his team charge on without him and then drop to the ground while his comrades-in-arms got obliterated? "How about the DEA? They were with Hotel, and there was a crew of them in reserve too."

Bates and Web looked at each other and Bates shook his head.

The FBI and DEA weren't the best of friends. The DEA, Web had always thought, was like a little brother kicking at his older sibling's shins until big brother hit back, and then the little punk ran off and tattled.

"Well, I guess we have to accept that until something makes us not," commented Web.

"Guess so. Were any of you wearing night-vision equipment?"

Web immediately understood the logic of the question. NV goggles would have picked up on the laser, transforming it into a long, unmistakable band of light.

"No. I pulled my thermal after the shooting started, but assaulters don't wear NVs. You get any source of ambient light while you're wearing them, then you are basically blind if you have to take them off and start shooting. And the snipers probably wouldn't have been using them during the assault; they screw up depth perception too much."

Bates nodded toward the gutted buildings where the guns had been set up. "The techs examined the guns. Each had a signal link box. They're thinking that there was a delay of a few seconds between when Charlie Team tripped the laser and when the guns were activated in order to make sure the team was squarely in the kill zone. The courtyard and firing lanes were large enough to allow for that.

Web suddenly felt dizzy and put his hand against the wall. It was as though he were reexperiencing the paralysis he had suffered during the doomed attack.

"You should've given yourself some more time to recover," said Bates as he slid an arm under Web's to help support him.

"I've had paper cuts worse than this."

"I'm not talking about your hand."

"My head's fine too, thanks for your concern," Web snapped, and then relaxed. "Right now I just want to do, not think."

For the next half hour Web pointed out the locations and descriptions of all the persons they had passed that night, and everything else he could recall from the time Charlie left the final staging area to the moment the last bullet was fired in the courtyard.

"You think any one of them could have been working with the target?" said Bates, referring to the people Web and company had passed in the alley.

"Down here anything's possible," replied Web. "There was obviously a leak. And it could have come anywhere along the line."

"There's a lot of possibilities there," Bates said. "Let's go over some."

Web shrugged. "This wasn't a triple-eight-beep scenario," he said, a reference to the three number eights that appeared on his pager representing a command for all HRT operators to haul butt to Quantico. "Last night was selected as the target date in ad-

vance, so everybody met at HRT to get our gear and team config-
urations ready and then we moved out in the Suburbans. We did
the prelim staging at Buzzard Point and then drove to the last
staging area. We had a U.S. attorney available in case we needed
some additional warrants issued. The snipers were already in
place. They went in early posing as HVAC rehab workers doing a
job on roof units on two of the buildings along the strike path.
Assaulters did our down-and-dirty with the local police just like
always. After we left the last point of concealment, Teddy Riner
requested and received compromise authority because of the unfriendly logistics. We wanted to be able to shoot on the fly if we
had to. We knew that hitting the place from the front and exposing ourselves to fire in the courtyard was risky, but we also
thought they wouldn't expect it. Plus the way the building was
situated and configured, there weren't a lot of options. We got the
green light to move to crisis site and then we were going to execute on TOC's countdown. We had one primary exterior breach
point. The assault plan was to split once we were inside and hit
from two points while Hotel and DEA blew in from the rear, with
a unit in reserve and the snipers as backup firepower and cover.
Hard and fast, just like always."

The two men sat on a pair of trash cans. Bates tossed his pack of
gum in the trash, pulled out his cigarettes and offered one to Web,
who declined.

"The local police knew the target, didn't they?" Bates asked.

Web nodded. "The approximate physical location. So they can
keep a presence, help quadrant off the area and keep people on the
outside of the perimeter out of the way, look for associates of the
target tipping them off, that sort of thing."

"How much advance time you figure the locals had in case there
was a leak from there?"

"Hour."

"Well, nobody set up that death trap in an hour."

"Who was the undercover on this one?"

"Goes without saying that you take this name to the grave with
you." Bates paused, presumably for emphasis, and then said,
"His name is Randall Cove. A real vet. Working the target from

deep inside. I mean deep, like down-in-the-sewer deep. African-American, built like a truck and could do the street stuff with the best of them. He's done a million of these gigs."

"So what's his story?"

"I haven't asked him."

"Why not?"

"I can't find him." Bates paused and then added, "Do you know for certain if Cove was aware when the hit was happening?"

Web was surprised by this question. "Your end would know that better than mine. I can tell you for a fact that we were not briefed that the undercover or any snitches would be at the target. If they were supposed to be there, they'd tell us in the pre-op. That way we'd know who they were, what they looked like and we'd cuff 'em and get 'em out just like everybody else, so the real target wouldn't get a heads-up and kill them."

"How much did you know about the target?"

"Druggies' financial ops, with bean counters present. Heavy security. They wanted the money guys as potential witnesses that we were to treat as hostages. Bag 'em fast and get them out before anyone figured out what we were doing and popped them so they couldn't rat. Our strike plan was approved, ops orders written; we got blueprints of the target and built a copy of it at Quantico. Practiced our butts off until we knew every inch. Got our rules of engagement, nothing out of the ordinary, suited up and climbed in the Suburban. End of story."

"You guys do your own surveillance, snipers on glass," Bates said, referring to snipers observing the target through binoculars and spotting scopes. "Anything pop on that?"

"Nothing special or else we would've been told in our briefing. Except for the possible witness angle, to me it was just a glorified dope house raid. Hell, we cut our teeth on those."

"If it was just a dope house, they wouldn't have needed you guys to crack it, Web. WFO could've used its SWAT team."

"Well, we were told the logistics were really tricky, and they were. And we knew the targets were supposed to be real nasty and were packing some ordnance SWAT didn't think they could handle. And then you had the issue of the potential witnesses. That was enough to make it our gig. But none of us were expecting eight remote-controlled mini-guns."

"Obviously it was all bullshit. Fed to us like mother's milk. Except for the guns, the place was empty. Ambush all the way. There were no bean counters, no records, no nothing."

Web rubbed his hand against the bullet gouges on the brick. Many were so deep Web could see the concrete block underneath—armor-piercing, for sure. The only good thing was death for his team would have been instantaneous. "The snipers had to see something." He was hoping they had seen whatever had made Web freeze. Yet how could they?

"I haven't finished talking to them," was all Bates would offer on that point, and again Web chose not to press it.

"Where's the kid?" Web hesitated, trying to remember. "Kevin."

Bates also hesitated for a second. "Disappeared."

Web stiffened. "How? He's a kid."

"I'm not saying he did it on his own."

"We know who he is?"

"Kevin Westbrook. Age ten. Got some family around, but most are guests of the state. Has an older brother, street name of Big F, the F standing for what you think it does. Head street ganger as big as a tree, and smart as a Harvard MBA. Deals in meth, Jamaican sinsemilla, the really cool stuff, though we've never been able to build a case against him. This area is sort of his turf."

Web stretched the fingers of his injured hand. The Band-Aid wasn't doing the trick right now, and he felt guilty for even thinking about it. "That's a pretty big coincidence that the little brother of the guy who runs this area was sitting out in the alley when we came by." Even as he talked about the boy, Web could feel a change come over his body, as though his very soul were sliding out and moving on. He actually thought he might pass out. Web was starting to wonder if he needed a doctor or an exorcist.

"Well, he does live around here. And from what we found out, his home life isn't all that great. He probably avoided it if he could."

"This big brother missing too?" Web asked as his balance began to return.

"Not that he actually lives at a normal address. When you're in the kind of business he is, you keep moving. We don't have any direct evidence tying him to even a misdemeanor, but we're looking for him real hard right now." He stared at Web. "You sure you're okay?"

Web waved off this comment. "How exactly did you lose the kid?"

"That's not real clear right now. We'll know more after we finish going through the neighborhood. Somebody had to see those weapons coming in and that machine gun nest being put up. Even around here that qualifies as a little unusual."

"You really think anybody here's going to talk to you?"

"We have to try, Web. We only need one pair of eyes."

The men fell silent for a while. Bates finally looked up, his expression uncomfortable.

"Web, what really happened?"

"Say what you really mean. How come it wasn't a perfect seven-for-seven?"

"I *am* saying it."

Web gazed across the courtyard at the exact spot where he had hit the asphalt. "I came out of the alley late. It was like I couldn't move. I thought I'd had a stroke. Then I went down right before the shooting started. I don't know why." Web's mind suddenly went blank and then came back, like he was a television and there had been a lightning strike nearby. "It was over in a second, Perce. A second was all it took. The worst timing in the history of the world." He looked at Bates to gauge his reaction to this. The narrowed eyes of the man told Web all he needed to know.

"Hell, don't feel bad. I don't believe it either," said Web. Bates remained silent, and Web decided to get to the other reason he had come here. "Where's the flag?" he asked. Bates looked surprised. "The HRT flag. I have to bring it back to Quantico."

On every mission HRT undertook, the senior member was given the HRT flag to carry with him in his gear. When the mission was completed, the flag was to be returned to the HRT commander by the senior member of the team. Well, now that happened to be Web.

"Follow me," said Bates.

An FBI van was parked at the curb. Bates popped open one of

the back doors, reached in and pulled out a flag folded military style. He handed it to Web.

Web held the flag in both hands, staring down at the colors for a moment, every detail of the slaughter once more working through his head.

"It's got a few holes in it," Bates observed.

"Don't we all," said Web.

5

The following day Web headed down to Quantico to the HRT facility. He drove along Marine Corps Route 4 past the campus-style FBI Academy that was home to both FBI and DEA grunts. Web had spent thirteen very intense and stressful weeks of his life at the Academy learning how to be an FBI agent. In return Web was paid peanuts and lived in a dorm room with a shared bath and he even had to bring his own towels! And Web had loved it and had devoted every waking moment to becoming the best FBI agent he could because he felt he had been born for the job.

Web had walked out of the Academy as a newly minted and sworn agent of the FBI with his Smith & Wesson .357 wheel gun, which required a staggering nine pounds of pull to fire. Rarely did one shoot oneself in the foot with the weapon. Recruits now carried .40 Glock semiautomatics with fourteen-round magazines with a much easier trigger pull, but Web still had fond memories of his Smith & Wesson with the three-inch bull barrel. Fancier didn't necessarily mean better. He had spent the next six years learning how to be an FBI agent in the field. He had sweated through the infamous FBI paperwork mountain, ferreted out leads, drummed up informants, answered criminal complaints, kept his butt on wiretaps, undertaken all-night surveillances, built up cases and arrested people who badly needed to be. Web had gotten to the point where he could concoct a battle plan in five minutes while he was driving a Bureau car—or Bucar, as it was always called—a hundred and ten miles an hour down the highway steering with his knees and shoving shells into his shotgun. He had learned how to interrogate suspects, establishing baselines and then asking them tough questions designed to knock them for a loop, to later gauge when they were lying. He had also learned how to testify without being cracked by slick defense lawyers whose only goal was to not discover the truth and instead to bury it.

His superiors, including Percy Bates (when Web had been transferred to the Washington Field Office after several years in the Midwest), had filled his personnel file with commendation after commendation, impressed with his dedication, his physical and mental skills and his ability to think on his feet. He had worked outside the rules at certain points, yet most of the really good agents did, he thought, because some of the Bureau rules were just plain stupid. That was also something Percy Bates had taught him.

Web parked, got out of the car and headed into HRT's building, which would never be termed beautiful by anyone who could actually see. He was welcomed with open arms, and tough, hardened men, who had seen more death and danger than the average citizen could possibly imagine, broke down with him in private rooms. HRT was not a place where anyone rushed to show his vulnerabilities and emotions. No man wanted to be firing guns and risking his life next to the shy, sensitive type. You left your warm fuzzy aura at the door and just brought your alpha male kick-ass side to work. Everything here was based on seniority and ability; those two attributes usually, though not always, paralleled each other.

Web returned the flag to his commander. Web's chief, a lean, muscular man with salt-and-pepper hair and a former HRT operator who could still outwork most of his men, accepted the flag with dignity and a handshake that dissolved into an embrace in the privacy of the man's office. Well, thought Web, at least they didn't hate his guts.

The HRT's admin building had been built to hold fifty personnel, yet now a hundred people called it their home away from home. There was a two-holer for all those folks, so the pee lines were long even for elite crime-busting Feds. There were small offices behind the reception area for the commander, who was at the rank of an

ASAC, or assistant special agent-in-charge, and his down-the-line chain of command that consisted of one supervisor for assaulters, and one for snipers. The HRT operators had honeycomb cubicle areas across the hallway from each other, split between snipers and assaulters. There was only one classroom in the building, which also doubled as a conference and briefing room in the space-challenged complex. There was a line of coffee mugs on a shelf on the rear wall of the room. Whenever the choppers landed here, the force of the blades would make the mugs vibrate. Somehow that sound had always been very soothing to Web. Team members coming home safe, he supposed.

He stopped by to see Ann Lyle, who worked in the office. Ann was sixty, much older than the other women who worked in administration, and could be truly termed the matriarch and unofficial mother hen of the hardcore lads who called HRT home. The unwritten rule was that you did not curse around Ann or use any other sort of uncouth language or gestures. Both rookie and veteran operators who ran afoul of this policy quickly found themselves the target of retribution ranging from glue in their helmets to taking a particularly hard shot during a training drill, the kind that left you wondering if one of your lungs had fallen out. Ann had been with HRT almost since its inception after working at the WFO for many years and had become a widow during that time. Childless, she let her entire life revolve around her work, and she listened to the young, single agents and their problems and doled out sensible advice. She also served as HRT's unofficial marriage counselor and had on more than one occasion prevented a divorce. She had come to Web's hospital room every day while he was waiting to get his face back, far more often than his own mother had bothered to. Ann regularly brought home-baked goodies to the office. And she was known as the primary information source for all things having to do with the Bureau and HRT. She was also a whiz at navigating the Bureau's requisition morass, and if HRT needed something, no matter how big or small, Ann Lyle made sure they got it.

He found Ann in her office, closed the door and sat across from her. Ann's hair had been white for several years now, and her body had lost its shape, but her eyes were still youthful-looking and her smile was truly beautiful.

Ann rose from her desk and gave Web a much-needed hug. Her cheeks were wet from tears. She had been especially close to the members of Charlie Team, who took great pains to show her their affection for all she did for them.

"You don't look good, Web."

"I've had better days."

"I wouldn't wish this on anybody, not even my worst enemy," she said, "but you're the last person in the world this should have happened to, Web. Right now, all I want to do is scream and never stop."

"I appreciate that, Ann," said Web. "I still don't know what happened, really. I've never frozen like that before."

"Web, honey, you've spent the last eight years of your life getting shot at. Don't you think that adds up? You're only human."

"That's just it, Ann, I'm supposed to be more than that. That's why I'm at HRT."

"What you need is a good long rest. When's the last time you took a vacation? Do you even remember?"

"What I need is some information and I need you to help me get it."

Ann accepted this change in subject without comment. "I'll do what I can, you know that."

"An undercover named Randall Cove. He's MIA."

"That name sounds familiar. I think I knew a Cove when I worked at WFO. You say he's gone missing?"

"He was the inside guy on the HRT hit. Guess he was either in on it or else got his cover blown. I need whatever you can find on him. Addresses, aliases, known contacts, the works."

"If he was working in D.C., his home won't be around there," said Ann. "There's an unofficial twenty-five-mile rule for UCs. You don't want to run into one of your neighbors while you're working your shift. For big-time assignments they might even bring the agent in from another part of the country."

"Understood. But twenty-five miles out still leaves a lot of possibilities. Maybe we can get a record of phone logs, communications with WFO, that sort of thing. I don't know how you manage it, but I really need whatever you can get."

"UCs mostly use disposable phone cards with low amounts on them to call in with. Buy them at convenience stores, use them up, chuck them and buy another. No record of anything that way."

Web's hopes dimmed. "So there's no way to trace?" He had never had to track down an undercover agent before.

Ann smiled her beautiful smile. "Oh, Web, there's always a way. You just let me dig around a little."

He looked at his hands. "I'm feeling kind of like a guy at the Alamo that the Mexicans somehow missed."

Ann nodded in understanding. "There's some fresh coffee in the kitchen and a chocolate walnut cake I brought in. Go help yourself, Web, you've always been too skinny." Her next words made Web look up into that wonderfully reassuring face. "And I'm watching your back here, honey, don't think that I'm not. I know what's what, Web. I hear everything, uptown or down. And nobody, and I mean nobody, is going to pull anything on you while I'm sitting here."

As he walked out, Web wondered if Ann Lyle would ever consider adopting him.

Web found an empty computer terminal and logged on to HRT's database. It had occurred to him, as he was sure it had to others, that his team's annihilation might have been a simple case of revenge. He spent considerable time going through past cases where HRT had been called up. Memories came flooding back to him of chest-thudding victories and heart-wrenching failures. The problem was that if you added up all the people who had been affected by an HRT mission and factored in family and friends, along with fringe crazies chasing any cause they could get their demented hands around, the numbers ran into the thousands. Web would have to leave that to somebody else to run down. He was certain the Bureau computers were crunching that data right now.

Web passed down the main hallway and lingered in front of the photo displays of past HRT operations. Here there were visual images of many stunning successes. The credo of hostage rescue was, "Speed, surprise and violence of action," and HRT put big-time action to those words. Web looked at a photo of a terrorist on the most-wanted list who had been plucked from international waters ("grabs," they called them) like an unsuspecting crab taken from a sand hole and whisked away to stand trial with a lifelong prison term to follow. There were photos of a joint international task force operation on a drug farm in a Latin American country. And finally there was a picture of a very tense hostage situation in a high-rise government building in Chicago. The result was all hostages were saved, with three of the five hostage-takers dead. Unfortunately, it didn't always work that way.

He walked outside the admin building and observed the lone tree there. It was a species of the state tree of Kansas, planted there in memory of the HRT operator who had been killed in a training accident and who had hailed from there. Each time Web had passed that tree he had said a silent prayer that it would be the only one they would ever have to plant. So much for answered prayers. Soon they'd have a damn forest here.

Web really needed to be doing something, anything that would make him not feel like a total failure. He went to the equipment cage, snagged a .308 snipe rifle and some ammo and headed back out. He needed to calm down and, ironically, firing guns did that for him, as it required a precision and focus that would block out all other thoughts, however troubling.

He passed the HRT's original headquarters building, which was narrow and tall and looked like a glorified grain silo instead of home for an elite law enforcement unit. Then he stood and looked out at the sheered-off hillside where one of the shooting ranges was situated. There was a new thousand-yard rifle range, and work crews were in the process of leveling an adjacent forest in order to add to the HRT's ever-growing complex, which also included a new indoor shooting range facility. Behind the outdoor shooting range, the trees were leafy green. It had always seemed an odd juxtaposition to Web: nature's beautiful colors serving as a backdrop to where he had stood for so many years learning better ways to kill. Yet he was the good guy, and that made it all right. At least that's what the bill of goods that came with the badge had very strongly implied.

He set up his targets. Web was going to play a game of sniper's poker. The cards were slightly fanned out across the target holder such that only the tiniest portion of each card, other than the front card, was visible. The goal was to build a winning hand. The trick was you could only count a card that you hit cleanly. If your round even nicked another card, you couldn't claim the card you were shooting at. And you only got five shots. The margin of error was impossibly tiny. It was just the sort of nerve-wracking task to relax a person, if that person happened to be an HRT grunt.

Web set himself up a hundred yards away from the targets. Lying flat on the ground, he placed a small beanbag under the .308's stock to support his upper body weight as he settled in. He aligned his body with the recoil path to minimize muzzle jump; his hips were flat against the ground, his knees spread shoulder-width and ankles flat to the ground to shrink his target profile in case someone was aiming at him. Web dialed the proper settings on the scope's calibration wheel and figured in wind too. The humidity was high, so he added an extra half-minute click. As a sniper, every shot he had ever fired during a mission had been recorded in his log. It was a very valuable record of environmental effects on bullets fired and also might explain why a sniper had missed a target, which was the only time anybody gave a damn. When you hit your target you were just doing your job, you didn't get a key to the city. There was no detail too small when it concerned killing at long range. A hint of a shadow across your objective lens could easily make the less-than-vigilant shooter wipe out a hostage rather than the person holding him.

Web lightly squeezed the pebbled pistol grip. He pulled the stock to his shoulder, pressed his cheek to the stock, set the proper eye relief and gripped the butt pad with his weak hand to steady the .308's bipod. He sucked in a breath, eased it out. No muscle could come between Web and his sniping. Muscle was erratic; he needed bone on bone because bone didn't flinch. Web had always used the ambush technique when sniping. This entailed the shooter waiting until the target entered a predetermined kill zone. The sniper

would plant his crosshairs just ahead of the target and then count
the mil-dots in the reticle to calculate distance to target, angle of
incidence and speed. You also had to judge elevation, wind and humidity and then you waited to kill, like the proverbial spider in the
web. You always shot into the skull for a very simple reason. Targets shot in the head never fired back.

Bone on bone. Pulse at sixty-four. Web let out one last breath;
his finger slid to the trigger and he fired five shots with the precise
motion of a man who had done this very thing well over fifty thousand times. He repeated the process four more times, three times
at a hundred yards, and the last hand of poker was played out at
two hundred yards, which was the outer reaches of distance for
sniper's poker.

When he checked the targets Web had to smile. He had a royal
flush in spades on two hands, aces with king high on two others
and a full house on the hand at two hundred yards; and not one
mark on any other card. And not one round thrown either, which in
Bureau parlance meant not a shot missed. This allowed him to feel
good about himself for about ten seconds and then the depression
came roaring back.

He returned the weapon to the equipment cage and continued
his stroll. Over at the adjacent Marine Corps facility was the Yellow Brick Road, which was a hellish seven-and-one-half-mile obstacle course with fifteen-foot rope drops, bear pits with barbed
wire just waiting for a slip and fall and also sheer rock cliffs. During his HRT qualification days, Web had run that course so many
times he had memorized every single disgusting inch of it. Team
events had involved fifteen-mile runs, loaded with upward of
fifty pounds of gear and precious objects carried, such as bricks
that must not touch the ground lest your team lose. There were
also swims through icy, filthy water, and fifty-foot long ladders
pointed straight to God. That had been followed by a trek up
"heartbreak hotel," a mere four-story jaunt, and the optional
(yeah!) leap off the gunwale of an old ship into the James River.
Since Web's joining HRT, heartbreak hotel had been tamed somewhat, with guide wires, railings and nets. It was undoubtedly
safer but, in his opinion, a lot less fun. Still, those with a fear of

heights most definitely need not apply. Rappelling from choppers into thick forest really separated the men from the boys, where if you missed your brake point a hundred-foot oak got to know your insides far too well.

And along the way to graduation each recruit had to navigate the hothouse, which was a three-story concrete tower with steel shutters over the windows, welded shut. The interior configuration, with its mesh floors, allowed a fire at the bottom to shoot smoke all the way to the top in seconds. The luckless recruit got thrown into the third floor and had to use his sense of touch, guts and instincts to find his way to the bottom and out to safety. Your reward for surviving that was a bucket of water in the eyes to clear out the smoke there, and the chance to do it again a few minutes later with a hundred-and-fifty-pound dummy on your back.

Crammed in between all that was tens of thousands of rounds fired, classroom drills that would have perplexed and confounded Einstein, fitness grinders that would have left many an Olympian heaving from exhaustion, plus enough paralyzing split-second decision-making scenarios to make a man give up booze and women, crawl in a padded room and start talking to himself. And every step of the way were the real HRT operators grading your sorry butt on every mistake and every triumph, and you just hoped you ended up with far more of the latter, but you never really could tell, because the HRTs never talked to you. To them you were scum, busting-your-ass scum, but still scum. And you knew they wouldn't even acknowledge your presence until and if you graduated. Hell, they probably wouldn't even attend your funeral if the tryout managed to kill you.

Web had somehow survived it all, and upon graduation from the New Operators Training School, or NOTS, as it was known, he had been "drafted" as a sniper and spent two more months at the Scout Sniper School of the Marine Corps, where he had learned from the very best the skills of field craft, observation, camouflage and killing with rifle and scope. After that Web had spent over seven years as first a sniper and later an assaulter either being bored to death at long standoffs, often in miserable conditions, or else shooting or being shot at all over the world by some of its most deranged inhabitants. In return he got all the guns and ammo he wanted and a pay scale equivalent to what a sixteen-year-old could earn programming computers during his lunch hour. All in all it had been really cool.

Web walked by the hangar facility, which housed the team's big Bell 412 helicopters, and the much smaller MD530s, which they all referred to as the Little Birds, because they were fast and agile and could carry four men on the inside and four more on the skids at a speed of 120 knots. Web had ridden the Little Birds into some hellish situations and the 530s had always brought him back out, a couple of times dangling upside down from a rope hooked to the chopper's swing arm, yet Web had never been picky about exactly how he survived a mission.

The motor pool was behind a chain-link fence. Web stopped and zipped up his jacket against a chilly wind. The sky was quickly becoming overcast as a storm system swept into the area, something it routinely did this time of day at this time of year. He went inside the fence and sat atop the team's sole armored personnel carrier, a hand-me-down gift from the Army. His gaze swept across the row of parked Suburbans. The vehicles had been reconfigured with ladder packages such that they could drive right up to a building and extend the ladder and go knock-knock-surprise! on the fifth floor of some criminal's lair. There were mount-out trucks that carried their gear, Jet Skis, food service trucks and a rigid-hull boat with inflatable gunnels that had been designed by Navy SEALs. The thing had twin Chrysler V-8s whose effect Web could only equate to being inside a building while it was being demolished via wrecking ball. He had ridden in it on numerous occasions—or more aptly had survived it.

They had it all here, from equipment for jungle assaults to arctic expeditions. They trained for every contingency, put everything they had into the work. And yet they could still be beaten by coincidence, by the blundering luck of inferior opponents or by the skillful planning and insider knowledge of a traitor.

It started to rain, so Web ducked inside the training facility, which was a large warehouse-style building with long corridors to simulate hallways in hotels and moveable, rubber-coated walls. It

was very much like a Hollywood studio back lot. If they were lucky
enough to get the blueprints of a target, HRT would reconstruct it
on-site here and train within exact parameters. The last set they
had built here was for the operation where Charlie had ceased to be.
As Web studied this configuration, it hadn't occurred to him that he
would never see the insides of the actual target for real. They had
never even gotten to the front door. He hoped they would tear out
the guts of this place soon, get it ready for the next operation. The
result couldn't be any worse, could it?

The rubber-coated walls here absorbed the slugs, for HRT often
practiced with live fire. Stairways were made of wood that would
not allow ricochets; however, the team had discovered, fortunately
without serious injury, that the nails in the wood could catch a bullet and send it on to unintended places. He passed by the aircraft
fuselage mockup that had been constructed so they could practice
on skyjacking scenarios. It hung from the rafters and could be
raised or lowered for training purposes.

How many imaginary terrorists had he shot down in here? The
training had paid off, for he had done it for real when an American
airliner had been stormed in Rome. The terrorists had ordered the
plane flown to Turkey and then on to Manila. Web and crew had
gone wheels up at Andrews Air Force base within two hours of
learning of the skyjacking. They had followed the hijacked plane's
movements from their airborne perch in an USAF C141. On the
ground at Manila where the jetliner was being refueled, the terrorists had tossed out two dead hostages, both Americans, one of
them a four-year-old girl. A political statement, they proudly an-
nounced. It was the last one they would ever make.

The hijacked plane's takeoff had been delayed first by weather
and then by mechanical failure. At around midnight local time,
Web and his Charlie Team had boarded the plane disguised as mechanics. Three minutes after they got on the plane, there were five
dead terrorists and no more slain hostages. Web had shot one of
them with his .45 directly through the diet Coke can the guy had
been holding up to his mouth. To this day he still couldn't drink
the stuff. Yet he never regretted pulling the trigger. The image of an
innocent little girl's body on the tarmac—American, Iranian,

Japanese, it didn't matter to Web—was all the motivation he would ever need to keep pulling the trigger at rank evil. These guys could claim all the geopolitical oppression in the world, call upon all the grand and omniscient deities in their religious warehouses, make every half-assed justification they wanted to, so they could detonate their bombs and fire their weapons, and none of it meant a damn thing to Web when they started killing innocent people, and in particular kids. And he would fight them for as long as they wanted to perform their perverted little dance of sin and mayhem across the globe, for wherever they could go, so could he.

Web moved through small rubber-walled rooms where posters of bad guys pointing guns at him hung on support poles. He instinctively drew a bead with his finger and blew them away. With an armed person you always keyed on hands, not the eyes, because no one in history had ever been killed by a pair of eyes. As he lowered his "gun," Web had to smile. It was all so easy when no one was actually firing at you. In other rooms were the heads and upper torsos of dummies on poles, their "skin" and bulk replicating that of a real human. Web threw side kicks to their heads followed by a series of paralyzing kidney punches and then moved on.

From inside one room he heard some movement and looked in. The man there had on a tank shirt and cammie pants and was wiping the sweat from his muscular neck, shoulders and arms. Long ropes dangled from the ceiling. This was one of the rooms where the men practiced their fast-roping skills. Web watched as the man went up and down three times with graceful, fluid motions, cords of muscles in his arms and shoulders tensing and then relaxing.

When the man finished, Web stepped inside and said, "Hey, Ken, don't you ever take a day off?"

Ken McCarthy looked over at Web and his gaze was not exactly what Web would have called friendly. McCarthy was one of the snipers who had been overhead along the alley the night Charlie Team had disappeared under the wave of .50s. McCarthy was black, thirty-four years of age, a Texan by birth as well as an Army brat who had seen the world on Uncle Sam's dime. He was a former SEAL yet did not exude the flagrant cockiness that most SEALs tended to. Only five-ten, he could bench-press a truck and held advanced multidegree black belts in three different martial arts. He was the most skilled water operator HRT had, and he could also place a bullet between a person's eyes at a thousand yards in the dead of night while straddling a tree limb. A three-year veteran of HRT, he was quiet, kept mostly to himself and lacked the ghoulish sense of humor that most operators had. Web had taught him things McCarthy hadn't known or was having trouble picking up, and in return McCarthy had shared some of his remarkable skills with Web. To Web's knowledge McCarthy had never had a problem with him, yet the man's look right now possibly heralded an end to that streak. Maybe Romano had turned everyone against him.

"What're you doing here, Web? Figured you'd still be in the hospital nursing your injuries."

Web took another step toward the man. He didn't like McCarthy's tone or words, yet he could understand where they were coming from. Web could also understand where Romano was coming from too; it was just that sort of a place. You were expected to do your job, perfectly. Perfection was all they asked for here. Web hadn't come close. Sure he had knocked out the guns, after the fact. That counted for zip with these men.

"I take it you saw it all."

McCarthy slipped off a pair of workout gloves and rubbed his thick, heavily callused fingers. "Would've fast-roped down to the alley, but TOC told us to sit tight."

"There was nothing you could do, Ken."

McCarthy was still looking at his feet. "Finally got the go-ahead. Took too long. Hooked up with Hotel. Took damn way too long," he said again. "We kept stopping, trying to raise you guys on the mic. TOC didn't know what the hell was going on. Our chain of command sort of broke down. Guess you knew that."

"We were prepared for everything except what went down."

McCarthy sat on the rubber mat floor and drew his knees up. He glanced up at Web. "Heard you were a little late coming out of the alley and that you kind of fell down or something."

Or something. He sat down next to McCarthy. "The guns were triggered by a laser, but the laser was probably activated by a remote so the fifties wouldn't kick on prematurely and hit the wrong target. Somebody had to be around there to do that." Web let that last statement hang as his gaze remained on McCarthy.

"I've already talked to WFO."

"I'm sure."

"It's an ongoing AFO, Web," he said. An AFO was an investigation of an assault on a federal officer, actually lots of them in this case.

"I know all that too, Ken. Look, I'm not sure what happened to me. I didn't plan it that way. I did all I could." Web drew a long breath. "And if I could take it all back right now, I would. And I've got to live with that every day of my life, Ken. I hope you can understand that."

McCarthy lifted his head and his hostile look faded.

"There was nothing to shoot, Web. There wasn't a damn thing for the snipers to blow away; all that training and no party to show it off at. We had three guys on the buildings overlooking the courtyard and not one of them could get even a decent bead on the mini-guns. Hell, they were afraid to fire because they thought one of their ricochets might nail you."

"How about the kid? Did you see the kid?"

"The little black kid? Yeah, when he came down the alley, with your cap and the note."

"We passed him going in too."

"You guys must have blocked our view. And the light in that alley really reflected weird up where we were."

"Okay, how about the other guys? The dudes doing the drugs?"

"We had a sniper on them the whole time. They never left where they were until the firing started, then they took off running. Jeffries said they seemed as surprised as anybody. When TOC gave us the green light, we took off."

"What happened then?"

"Hooked up with Hotel, like I said. We saw the flare, stopped, fanned out. Then the kid came to us. We got the note, your warning. Everett and Palmer went forward as scouts. Too damn late." McCarthy paused here, and Web saw a single tear slide down the man's youthful, handsome features; normal features like what Web had once possessed.

"I never heard gunfire like that in my life, Web. I've never felt helpless like that in my whole life."

"You did your job, Ken, and that's all you can do." Web paused and then said, "They can't seem to find the kid. Know anything about that?"

McCarthy shook his head. "Couple guys from Hotel took charge of him. Romano and Cortez, I think."

Romano again. Shit, that meant Web had to go talk to the man. "What'd you do?"

"I went into the courtyard with some of the others. We saw you, but you were out of it." He looked down again. "And we saw the rest of Charlie." He glanced at Web. "A couple of the snipers told me how you went back out there, Web. They saw what you did and still can't believe you did it. Said you must have the luck of the Irish somewhere in your back pocket to have gone back out there. I don't think I could have."

"Yes you would, Ken. And you would've done it better than me." McCarthy seemed startled at this praise.

"After you came back out of the courtyard, did you see the kid?"

McCarthy thought about this. "I remember him sitting on a trash can. By that time, everybody was showing up."

"Did you see any suits take custody of the kid?"

McCarthy thought again. "No, I sort of recall Romano talking to somebody, but that's all."

"Did you recognize any of them?"

"You know we don't interface with the regulars that much."

"How about DEA?"

"That's all I can tell you, Web."

"You been talking to Romano?"

"A little."

"Don't believe everything you hear, Ken. It's not healthy."

"Including from you?" McCarthy asked pointedly.

"Including from me."

As Web drove away from Quantico, he realized he had a lot of ground to cover. This was officially not his investigation, yet in some ways it was more his than anyone else's. But he had to take care of something else first, something even more important than finding out who had set up his team. And finding out what had happened to a little boy with a bullet hole on his cheek and no shirt to his name.

6

Six funerals. Web attended six funerals over three days. By the fourth one, he couldn't muster a single tear. He walked into the church or the funeral home and listened to people he mostly didn't know talk about fallen men he knew better than he understood himself in some ways. It was as though all of his nerves had been boiled away, along with part of his soul. In a way he felt incapable of reacting as he was supposed to. He was terrified he would start laughing when he should be mourning.

At the services half the caskets were open, the rest not. Some of the dead men had fared better with the size and placement of the wounds that had killed them and thus had open caskets. However, staring at pale, collapsed faces and rigid, shrunken bodies in metal boxes, inhaling flower fragrance and hearing the sobs of all those around him made Web wish he could just lie down in a box too and be put away in the ground to hide forever. The funeral of a hero; there were far worse ways to be remembered.

He had wrapped his hand back up in the layers of gauze because he felt guilty walking among the bereaved without a trace of a wound. It was a pathetic thing to be concerned with, he knew, yet he felt like a walking slap in the face to the survivors. All they really knew was that Web London had somehow gotten off with barely a scratch. Had he run? Had he left his comrades to die? He could see those questions in some of the people's faces. Was that always the fate of the sole survivor?

The funeral processions had passed between endless lines of

men and women in uniform and hundreds of others dressed in the neat suits and sensible shoes of the FBI. Motorcycles led the way, citizens lined the streets and flags everywhere flew at half mast. The President and most of his Cabinet came, along with many other VIPs. For a few days, the entire world talked of nothing else except the slaughter of six good men in an alley. Not much was said about the seventh man, and for that Web was mostly grateful. Still, he wondered how long that moratorium could possibly last for him.

The city of Washington was deeply stricken. And it was not entirely over the fate of the slain men, for the broader implications were troubling. Had criminals really become so brazen? Was society coming apart at the seams? Were the police not keeping pace? Was American law enforcement's crown jewel, the FBI, losing its luster? The Middle Eastern and Chinese news services were having a particularly delicious time reporting yet another example of Western mayhem that would one day bring arrogant America to its soft knees. Cheers were no doubt racing up and down the streets of Baghdad, Teheran, Pyongyang and Beijing at the thought of the old USA falling apart one miserable media-fueled crisis at a time. The pundits on American soil were spouting so many absurd scenarios that Web no longer even opened a newspaper or turned on a TV or radio. If anyone had asked him, though, he would have said that the whole world, and not just the United States, had been screwed up for a long time.

There had been some relief from this crossfire, though its catalyst was another appalling tragedy. A Japanese commercial jetliner had crashed off the Pacific Coast, so the newsmongers had chased after that story and left the alley and its dead behind for now. A single news truck was still there, but scraps of three hundred bodies floating in the ocean was a far bigger draw than a days-old story about a team of dead FBI agents. And for that Web was also grateful. *Leave us alone to grieve in peace.*

He had been debriefed "uptown" at the Hoover Building and at the WFO on three different occasions, by several teams of investigators. They had their pads and pencils, their recorders and some of the younger agents even had laptops. They had asked Web many more questions than he had answers for. However, when he told each group that he didn't know why he had frozen and then fallen, the pencils had stopped scribbling on paper, fingers had stopped clacking on keyboards.

"When you say you froze, did you see something? Hear something to make you do that?" The man spoke in a monotone, which, to Web, was one imperceptible inflection short of incredulity or, worse, outright disbelief.

"I don't really know."

"You really don't know? You're not sure if you froze?"

"I'm not sure. I mean, I did. I couldn't move. It was like I was paralyzed."

"But you moved after your team was killed?"

"Yes," Web conceded.

"What had changed to allow you to do that?"

"I don't know."

"And when you got to the courtyard, you fell?"

"That's right."

"Right before the guns opened fire," said another investigator.

Web could barely hear his own answer. "Yes."

The silence that followed these meager responses came close to dissolving Web's already bludgeoned insides.

During each debriefing, Web had kept his hands on top of the table, his gaze steady on each questioner's face, his posture in a slight forward lean. These men were all professional, seasoned inquisitors. Web knew that if he looked away, sat back, rubbed his head the wrong way or, worse yet, crossed his arms, they would instantly conclude he was a lying sack of shit. Web wasn't being untruthful, but he wasn't telling all of the truth either. Yet if Web started talking about how the vision of a little boy had had a weird effect on him, perhaps inexplicably caused him to freeze, thus saving his life—or about then feeling weighed down as though encased in concrete and then seconds later being able to freely move—he would be finished at the Bureau. The higher-ups tended to frown on field agents making insane comments. Yet he had one thing going for him. Those machine gun nests didn't disintegrate by themselves. And his rifle rounds were embedded in all of them. And the snipers had seen everything, and he had warned Hotel Team and saved the boy on top of it. Web made sure he said that. He made sure all of them knew that. *You can kick me while I'm down, friends, just not too hard. I'm a damn hero after all.*

"I'll be all right," Web had told them. "I just need a little time. I'll be all right." And for one awful moment Web thought that might be the first actual lie he had told all day.

They would call him back in as needed, they told him. For now, they just wanted him to do nothing. He was to take plenty of time to get himself together. The Bureau had offered the assistance of a counselor, a mental health professional, in fact they had insisted on it, and Web said he would go, although there was still a stigma at the Bureau for those seeking such help. When things looked okay, Web was told, he would be assigned to another assaulter or sniper team, if he so desired, until Charlie could be rebuilt. If not, he could take another position within the Bureau. There was even talk of allowing him to burn an "office of preference" transfer that would allow him to proceed directly to "Go" in the form of an office he would retire from. That sort of treatment was usually reserved for senior-level agents and symbolized that the Bureau was really unsure of what to do with him. Officially, Web was in the middle of an administrative inquiry that might well blossom into a full investigation, depending on how things shook out. Well, no one had given Web his Miranda rights, which was both good and bad. Good because Web getting his Miranda warning would mean he was under arrest, bad in that anything he said during the inquiry could be used against him in civil or criminal proceedings. The only thing he had done wrong, apparently, was having survived. And yet that was a source of guilt far stronger than anything the Bureau could charge him with.

No, really, whatever he wanted, Web was told, he could have. They were all his friends. He had their full support.

Web asked how the investigation was going and didn't get an answer in return. So much for their full support, Web thought.

"Get better," another man had told him. "That's *all* you need to focus on."

As he was leaving from his last debriefing, he got one final question. "How's the hand?" the man asked. Web didn't know the guy,
and although the question seemed innocent enough, there was
something in the fellow's eyes that made Web want to deck him.
Instead, Web said it was just fine, thanked them all and left.

On the way out from the last session he had passed the FBI's
Wall of Honor, where hung plaques for each of the FBI personnel
killed in the line of duty. There would be a major addition coming
to the wall, the largest single one in the history of the Bureau, in
fact. Web had sometimes wondered if he would ever end up on
there, with his professional life compacted into a chunk of wood
and brass hanging on a wall. He left Hoover and drove home, besieged by many more questions than he wanted to confront.

FBI also officially stood for Fidelity, Bravery and Integrity, and
right now Web didn't feel he possessed any of these qualities.

7

Francis Westbrook was a giant of a man, with the height and girth of a NFL starting left tackle. Regardless of the weather or season, his clothes of choice were silk tropical short-sleeved shirts, matching slacks and suede loafers with no socks. His head was bald, his large ears were covered with diamond studs and his enormous fingers were festooned with gold rings. He wasn't a dandy of any sort, but there simply weren't that many things he could spend his drug earnings on without the law or, even worse, the IRS sniffing around. And he also liked to look good. Right now Westbrook was riding in the backseat of a large Mercedes sedan with black-tinted windows. To the left of him was his first lieutenant, Antoine Peebles. Driving was a tall, well-built young man named Toona, and in the passenger seat was his chief of security, Clyde Macy, the only white guy in Westbrook's entire crew, and it was easy to see that the man carried that distinction with great pride. Peebles had a neatly trimmed beard and Afro, was short and heavyset, but he wore his Armani and his designer shades well. He looked more like a Hollywood exec than a high-level drug entrepreneur. Macy looked like a breathing skeleton, preferred his clothes black and professional-looking and with his shaved head could easily have been mistaken for a neo-Nazi.

This represented the inner circle of Westbrook's small empire and the leader of that empire held a nine-millimeter pistol in his right hand and seemed to be looking for someone to use it on. "You want to tell me one more time how you lost Kevin?" He looked at

Peebles and clutched the pistol even tighter. Its safety was in the grip and Westbrook had just released it. Peebles seemed to recognize this and yet didn't hesitate in responding. "If you let us keep somebody on him twenty-four and seven, then we'd never lose him. He goes out sometimes at night. He went out that night and didn't come back."

Westbrook slapped his enormous thigh. "He was in that alley. The Feds had him and now they don't. He's mixed up with this shit somehow and it happened in my damn backyard." He smacked the gun against the door and roared, "I want Kevin back!"

Peebles looked at him nervously, while Macy showed no reaction.

Westbrook put a hand on the driver's shoulder. "Toona, you get some of the boys together and you gonna hit every part of this damn town, you hear me? I know you already done it once, but you do it again. I want that boy back nice and safe, you hear me? Nice and safe and don't come back till you done it. Damn it, you hear me, Toona?"

Toona glanced in the rearview mirror. "I hear you, I hear you."

"Set up," said Peebles. "All around. To put the blame on you."

"You think I ain't know that? You think 'cause you went to college that you smart and I'm stupid? I know the Feds coming after my ass on this. I know the word on the street. Somebody's trying to get all the crews together, almost like a damn union, but they know I ain't joining shit and it's messing up their plan." Westbrook's eyes were red. He hadn't slept much in the last forty-eight hours. That was just his life; surviving the night was usually the big project of the day. And all he could think about was a little boy out there somewhere. He was getting close to the edge; he could feel it. He had known this day might come, and still, he was not prepared for it.

"Whoever got Kevin, they gonna let me know it. They want something. They want me to jump my crew in, that's what they want."

"And you'll give it to them?"

"Anything I got they can have. So long as I get Kevin back." He paused and looked out the window, at the corners and alleys and cheap bars they were passing, where his drug tentacles slithered.

He did a brisk business in the suburbs too, where the real money was. "Yeah, that's right. I get Kevin back and then I kill every one of the mothers. I do it myself." He pointed the pistol at an imaginary foe. "Start with the knees and work my way up."

Peebles looked warily at Macy, who still showed no sign of any reaction; it was as though he were made of stone. "Well, nobody's contacted us so far," said Peebles.

"They will. They didn't take Kevin 'cause they want to shoot hoops with him. They want me. Well, I'm right here, they just got to come to the party. I'm ready to party, bring it the fuck on." Westbrook spoke more calmly. "Word is one of them dudes didn't eat it in that courtyard. That right?"

Peebles nodded. "Web London."

"They say machine guns, fifty-caliber shit. How's a dude slip that?" Peebles shrugged his shoulders and Westbrook looked at Macy. "What you hear on that, Mace?"

"Nobody's saying for sure right now, but what I hear is the man didn't go in that courtyard. He got scared, freaked or something."

"Freaked or something," said Westbrook. "Okay, you get some shit on this man and you let me see it. Man walk away from something like that, man got something to tell me. Like maybe where Kevin is." He looked at his men. "Whoever shot them Feds up got Kevin. You can count on that."

"Well, like I said, we could've had him on round-the-clock," commented Peebles.

"What the hell kind of life is that?" said Westbrook. "He ain't got to live that way, not because of me. But the Feds come after my ass, then I'll just point them boys in another direction. But we got to know which way that is. With six damn Feds dead, they ain't gonna be looking to cut no deals. They'll want some serious ass to fry and it ain't gonna be mine."

"Whoever took Kevin, there's no guarantee they'll let him go," said Peebles. "I know you don't want to hear this, but we have no way of knowing if Kevin's even alive."

Westbrook lay back against the seat. "Oh, he's alive, all right. Ain't nothing wrong with Kevin. Not right now anyway."

"How can you be sure?"

"I just know and that's all you need to know. You just get me something on this Fed mother."

"Web London."

"Web London. And if he ain't got what I need, then he'll wish he died with his crew. Hit it, Toona. We got bizness."

The car sped on into the night.

8

It took Web a couple of days to make an appointment with a psychiatrist whom the Bureau used on an independent contractor basis. The FBI had trained people on staff, but Web had opted for someone on the outside. He wasn't sure why, yet spilling his guts to anyone on the inside right now didn't seem like a good idea. Rightly or not, tell the Feds' shrink, you're telling the Feds, was Web's thinking, to hell with patient confidentiality.

The Bureau was still pretty much in the Dark Ages when it came to the mental health of their people, and that probably was as much the fault of the individual agents as the organization. Until several years ago, if you worked at the FBI and were feeling stressed or were having problems with alcohol or substance abuse, you pretty much kept it to yourself and dealt with it in your own way. The old school agents would have given no more thought to seeking counseling than they would about leaving home without their gun. If an agent was seeking professional help, no one knew about it, and certainly no one talked about it. You were, in a sense, tainted goods if you did, and the indoctrination process of being a member of the Bureau seemed to instill both a stoicism and stubborn independence that were difficult to overcome.

Then the powers that be had finally decided that the stress of working for the FBI, reflected in rising rates of alcohol and drug abuse and the high incidence of divorce, needed to be addressed. An Employee Assistance Program, or EAP, was instituted. Each FBI di-

vision was assigned an EAP coordinator and counselor. If the in-
house counselor couldn't handle the situation, he or she would refer
the patient to an approved outside source, as Web had opted to have
done. The EAP wasn't widely known at the Bureau and Web had
never gotten any written materials on its existence. It was just sort
of whispered ear to ear. The old stigma, despite the Bureau's efforts,
was still there.

The psychiatric offices were in a high-rise building in Fairfax
County near Tyson's Corner. Web had seen Dr. O'Bannon, one of
the psychiatrists who worked here, before. The first time was years
ago when HRT had been called up to rescue some students at a private school in Richmond, Virginia. A bunch of paramilitary types
belonging to a group calling themselves the Free Society, who apparently were seeking to create an Aryan culture by means of their
own version of ethnic cleansing, had burst into the school and immediately killed two teachers. The standoff had lasted almost
twenty-four hours. HRT had finally gone in when it appeared im-
minent that the men were going to start killing again. Things were
going perfectly until something had alerted the Frees right before
HRT was ready to pounce. The resulting shootout had left five of
the Frees dead and two HRT personnel injured, Web critically so.
The only other hostage to die was a ten-year-old boy named David
Canfield.

Web had been almost close enough to the child to pull him to
safety when things went to hell. The dead boy's face had intruded
into his dreams so often that Web had voluntarily sought counseling. At that time there was no EAP, so after he had recovered from
his injuries Web had discreetly gotten O'Bannon's name from another agent whom O'Bannon was seeing. It had been one of the
hardest things Web had ever done, because, in effect, he was admitting that he couldn't handle his problems. He never talked
about it with other HRT members and he would have cut out his
tongue before he would reveal that he was seeing a shrink. His colleagues would have only seen that as a weakness, and at HRT there
was no room for that.

The operators at HRT had had a previous encounter with mental health counseling, and it had not gone well: After Waco, the

Bureau had brought in some counselors who had met directly with the stricken men as a group instead of individually. The result would have been comical if it hadn't been so pathetically sad. That was the last time the Bureau had tried that sort of thing with HRT.

The most recent time Web had seen O'Bannon was right after Web's mother had died. After quite a few sessions with O'Bannon, Web concluded that things were never going to be right on that score and he had lied and told O'Bannon that he was just fine. He didn't blame O'Bannon, for no doc could make that mess right, he knew. It would have taken a miracle.

O'Bannon was short and heavyset and often wore a black turtleneck that made his multiple chins even more pronounced. Web remembered that O'Bannon's handshake was limp, his manner pleasant enough, and yet Web had felt like running for the door the first time the two had met. Instead, he had followed O'Bannon back to his office and plunged into some dangerous waters.

"We'll be able to help you, Web. It'll just take time. I'm sorry we have to meet under such difficult circumstances, but people don't come to me because things are wonderful; it's my lot in life, I suppose."

Web said that was good and yet his spirits sank. O'Bannon clearly had no magic that would make Web's world normal again.

They had sat in O'Bannon's office. There was no couch but rather a small love seat not nearly long enough to lie down upon. O'Bannon had explained it as, "The greatest of all misperceptions in our field. Not every psychiatrist has a couch."

O'Bannon's office was sterile, with white walls, industrial furnishings and very few items of a personal nature. It all made Web feel about as comfortable as sitting on death row waiting to do a last dance with Mr. Sparky. They made small talk, presumably to ease Web into opening up. There was a pad and pen next to O'Bannon, but he never picked them up.

"I'll do that later," O'Bannon had said when Web asked him about his lack of note-taking. "For now, let's just talk." He had a darting gaze that had been unsettling to Web, though the psychiatrist's voice was soft and relatively soothing. After an hour the session was up, and Web could see nothing much that had been accomplished. He knew more about O'Bannon than the man knew about Web. He had not gotten around to any of the issues disturbing him.

"These things take time, Web," O'Bannon had said as he led Web out. "It'll come, don't you worry. It just takes time. Rome wasn't built in a day."

Web wanted to ask him exactly how long it would take to build Rome in this case, but he said nothing except good-bye. At first Web had believed that he would never go back to see the short, pudgy man with the blank office. And yet he had. And O'Bannon had worked through the issues with him session after session, getting him to deal with things. But Web had never forgotten the little boy who had been gunned down in cold blood with Web mere feet away and unable to save him. That would have been unhealthy, to ever forget something like that.

O'Bannon had told Web that he and others at his psychiatric practice had catered to the needs of Bureau personnel for many years and had helped agents and administrative staff through lots of crises. Web had been surprised at that because he assumed he was one of the few who had ever sought professional counseling. O'Bannon had looked at him in a very knowing way and said, "Just because people don't talk about it doesn't mean they don't want to address their issues or don't want to get better. I can, of course, reveal no names, but trust me, you are definitely not alone in coming to me from the FBI. Agents who hide their heads in the sand are just ticking bombs waiting to explode."

Now Web wondered if he was a ticking bomb. He went inside and over to the elevators, each step heavier than the previous one.

With his mind clearly elsewhere, Web nearly collided with a woman coming from the other direction. He apologized and pushed the elevator button. The car came and they both got on. Web punched the button for his floor and stepped back. As they headed up, Web glanced over at the woman. She was average height, slender and very attractive. He put her age at late thirties. She wore a gray pantsuit, the collar of a white blouse topping it. Her hair was a wavy black and cut short, and she had on small clip earrings. She carried a briefcase. Her long fingers curled around

"No big deal. My mistake. Thanks for the coffee." He rose.

"Mr. London, would you like me to tell him you were here?"

"It's Web. And no, I don't think I'll be back on Wednesday."

Claire stood too. "Is there something I can do to help you?"

He held up his cup. "You already made the java." Web took a breath. It was time to get out of here. "What are you doing for the next hour?" he asked instead, and then was stunned to hear his own words.

"Just paperwork," she said quickly, her gaze downcast, her face slightly red as though he had just asked her out to the prom and instead of saying no to his advance she was deciding, for some unknown reason, to encourage it.

"How would you like to talk to me instead?"

"Professionally? That's not possible. You're Dr. O'Bannon's patient."

"How about human to human?" Web had absolutely no idea where any of these words were coming from.

She hesitated for a moment and then told him to wait. She went into an office and then came back out a few minutes later. "I tried reaching Dr. O'Bannon at the university, but they couldn't track him down. Without talking to him, I really can't counsel you. You have to understand, it's a touchy thing ethically, Web. I'm not into poaching patients."

Web abruptly sat down. "Wouldn't it ever be justified?"

She mulled this over for a few moments. "I suppose if your regular doctor wasn't available and you were in crisis, it would be."

"He's not available and I'm in an honest-to-God crisis." Web was being absolutely truthful, for it was like he was back in that courtyard, unable to move, unable to do a damn thing to help, useless. If she still refused him, Web wasn't sure he could even manage to get up and leave.

Instead she led him down the hallway to her office and closed the door behind them. Web looked around. There could not have been a greater difference between Claire Daniels's digs and those of O'Bannon. The walls were a muted gray instead of stark white, and cozy with femininely floral curtains instead of industrial shades. There were pictures hung everywhere, mostly of people, presumably family. The degrees on the wall evidenced Claire Daniels's impressive academic accomplishments: degrees from Brown and

Columbia Universities and her medical sheepskin from Stanford. On one table was a glass container that had a label reading, "Therapy in a Jar." There were unlit candles on tables and cactus lamps in two corners. On shelves and on the floor were dozens of stuffed animals. There was a leather chair against one wall. And by God, Claire Daniels had a couch!

"You want me to sit there?" He pointed to it, trying desperately to keep his nerves in check. He suddenly wished he wasn't armed, because he was starting to feel a little out of control.

"Actually, if you don't mind, I prefer the couch."

He collapsed in the chair and then watched as she switched her flats for slippers that were lying next to the couch. The momentary sight of her bare feet had prompted an unexpected reaction from Web. There was nothing sexual about it; it made Web think of the bloodied skin in the courtyard, the remains of Charlie Team. Claire sat down on the couch, pulled a pad and pen off the side table and uncapped the pen. Web took a series of small breaths to arrest his nerves.

"O'Bannon doesn't take notes during the session," he commented.

"I know," she said with a wry smile. "I don't think my memory is as good as his. Sorry."

"I didn't even ask if you're on the Bureau's approved list of outside contractors. I know O'Bannon is."

"I am too. And this session will have to be revealed to your supervisor. Bureau policy."

"But not the content of the session."

"No, of course not. Just that we met. The same *basic* rules of confidentiality apply here as they would in a normal psychiatrist and patient relationship."

"Basic rules?"

"There are modifications, Web, because of the unique job you have."

"O'Bannon explained that to me when I was seeing him, but I guess I was never really clear on it."

"Well, I'm under an obligation to inform your supervisor if during a session anything is revealed that poses a threat to yourself or others."

"I guess that's fair."

"You think so? Well, from my point of view, it gives me a great deal of discretion, because where one hears something benign, another hears genuine threats. So I'm not so sure that policy is very fair to you. But just so you know, I have never had occasion to use that discretion and I've been working with people from the FBI, DEA and other law enforcement agencies for a long time."

"What else has to be revealed?"

"The other major one is drug use or specific therapies."

"Right. The Bureau is a stickler for that, I know," said Web. "Even over-the-counter stuff you have to report that you're taking. It can actually get to be quite a pain in the ass." He looked around. "Your place is a lot more comfortable. O'Bannon's office reminds me of an operating room."

"Everybody approaches their work differently." She stopped and stared at his waist.

Web glanced down and saw that his windbreaker had fallen open there, and the grip of his pistol was visible. He zipped up the jacket, as Claire looked down at her pad.

"Sorry, Web, it's not like it's the first time I've seen an agent with a gun. Though I suppose when you don't see them every day—"

"They can be scary as hell," he finished her thought.

He eyed the array of furry toys.

"What's with all the stuffed animals?"

"I have a lot of children as patients," she said, adding, "unfortunately. The animals make them feel more at ease. To tell the truth, they make me feel more at ease too."

"It's hard to believe kids would need a psychiatrist."

"Most of them have eating disorders, bulimia, anorexia. Usually centered on issues of control between them and their parents. So you have to treat the child *and* the parent. It's not an easy world for children."

"It's not all that great for adults either."

She gave him a look that Web interpreted as a quick appraisal. "You've been through a lot in your life."

"More than some, less than others. You're not going to make me take an inkblot test, are you?" He said this as a joke, but he was actually serious.

"Psychologists perform Rorschach, MMPI, MMCI and neuro-testing, I'm just a humble psychiatrist."

"I had to take the MMPI when I joined Hostage Rescue."

"The Minnesota Multiphasic Personality Inventory, I'm familiar with it."

"It's designed to ferret out the crazies."

"In a manner of speaking, yes. Did it?"

"Some of the guys failed it. Me, I figured out what the test was for, and just lied my way through it."

Claire Daniels's eyebrows lifted slightly and her gaze once more went to where his gun was. "That's comforting."

"I guess I'm not real clear on the difference. Between psychologists and psychiatrists, that is."

"A psychiatrist has to take the MCATs, then do four years of medical school. After that you have to serve three years of residency in psychiatry at a hospital. I also did a fourth-year residency in forensic psychiatry. I've been in private practice ever since. As medical doctors, psychiatrists can also prescribe medication, whereas psychologists generally can't."

Web clasped and unclasped his hands nervously.

Claire, who was studying him closely, said, "Why don't I tell you how I go about my work? Then, if you're comfortable with that, we can continue. Fair enough?" Web nodded in agreement and she settled back into the cushions. "As a psychiatrist, I rely on understanding patterns of normal human behavior, so that I can recognize when certain behavior falls outside the norm. An obvious example is one you're no doubt familiar with: serial killers. In the vast majority of cases such people have suffered consistent, terrible abuse as children. They, in turn, exhibit clear patterns of rage when young, like torturing small animals and birds as they single-mindedly transfer the pain and cruelty foisted upon them onto living things less powerful than themselves. They move on to larger animals and other targets as they grow older, stronger and bolder, and eventually progress to human beings when they reach adulthood. It's actually a fairly predictable evolution of events.

"You also have to listen with a third ear of sorts. I take what someone tells me at face value, but I'm also looking for cues underlying those statements. Humans are always layering their statements with other messages. A psychiatrist wears many hats, often at the same time. The key is to listen, I mean really listen to what you're being told, in words, body language, that sort of thing."

"Okay, how would you like to start with me?"

"I usually have a patient fill out a background questionnaire, but I think I'll skip that with you. Human to human," she added with a very warm smile.

Web finally felt the heat in his belly start to ease.

"But let's talk a little about your background, all the typical information. Then we can move on from there."

Web let out a deep breath. "I'll be thirty-eight next March. I did the college route and then somehow got into the University of Virginia law school and actually managed to graduate. After that I worked in the commonwealth attorney's office for about six months in Alexandria until I realized that life wasn't for me. I decided to apply to the Bureau along with a buddy of mine. It was really on a whim, to see if we could do it. I made the cut, he didn't. I survived the Academy and I've been with the FBI for a lucky thirteen years. I started out as a special agent, cutting my teeth on this and that in a string of field offices across the country. A little over eight years ago, I applied to HRT. That stands for Hostage Rescue Team. It's part of CIRG, Critical Incident Response Group, now, though that's a fairly recent development. They kill your ass in the selection process and ninety percent of the applicants don't make the cut. They sleep-deprive you first, break you physically and then force you to make snap decisions of life and death. They make you work and sacrifice as a team but still compete against one another, because there aren't many slots available. It was a real walk in the park. I saw former Navy SEALs, Special Forces guys, Deltas even, break down, cry, pass out, hallucinate, threaten suicide, mass murders, anything to make their tormentors stop. By a miracle, I somehow got through and then spent another five months at the New Operators Training School, or NOTS. In case you couldn't tell, the Bureau is big on acronyms. We're based at Quantico. I'm an assaulter right now." Claire looked confused. "HRT has Blue and Gold Units, with four teams in each. They mirror each other, so we can handle two crises in two different places simultaneously. Half the teams are made up of assaulters or the main attack force, the other half are snipers. Snipers train at the Marine Corps Scout Sniper School. We switch off periodically, cross-train. I started out as a sniper. They used to really get the short end of the stick, though after HRT was reorganized in 1995 it's gotten a lot better. Still, you lie in the mud and rain and snow for weeks, spying on the target, learning the weaknesses of your opponents that will help you kill them later. Or maybe even save their lives, because watching them, you may spot something that will tell you that they won't shoot back in certain situations. You wait to take your shots of opportunity, never knowing if the shot you take will trigger some damn firestorm."

"You sound like you've experienced something like that."

"One of my very first assignments was Waco."

"I see."

"Right now I'm assigned to Charlie Team in the Blue Unit." *Was*, Web mentally corrected himself. There was no more Charlie Team.

"So you're not an FBI agent per se?"

"No, we all are. You have to have at least three years at the Bureau and a superior performance rating to even apply to HRT. We carry the same shields, the same credentials. But we HRT guys keep to ourselves. Separate facilities, no other duties outside HRT. We train together. Core skills, knots, CQB."

"What are those things?"

"Knots covers combat and firearm training. CQB stands for close-quarters battle training. Firearms and CQB are the most perishable skills, so you're constantly working them."

"Sounds very military."

"It is. And we are very military. We're split into active duty and training. If you're on duty and a mission comes up, you go. Any downtime for active duty operators is spent on special projects and special skills like rope climbing, chopper rappelling, SEAL training, first aid. And also field craft, what we call snooping and pooping in the woods. The days go quickly, believe me."

"I'm sure," said Claire.

Web studied his shoes and they sat there quietly for a while. "Fifty alpha males together is sometimes not a good thing." He smiled. "We're always trying to one-up each other. You know those Taser guns that shoot out electrified darts and paralyze people?"

"Yes, I've seen them."

"Well, we had a contest one time to see who could recover the fastest after getting hit by one of those."

"Good God," exclaimed Claire.

"I know, crazy." He added, "I didn't win. I went down like I'd been hit by an NFL lineman. But that's sort of the mentality. Ultracompetitive." He became more serious. "But we're good at our jobs. And our jobs aren't easy. What nobody else wants to do, we do. Our official motto is, 'To save lives.' And we mostly succeed. We try to think of every contingency, but there's not a lot of room for error. And whether we succeed or not could come down to a chain on a door you weren't expecting when you're doing a dynamic entry, or turning left instead of right, or not firing instead of firing your weapon. And these days if the target gets a little nick while he's trying to blow our heads off, everybody starts screaming and suing and FBI agents start falling like flies. Maybe if I'd checked out after Waco, my life would really be different."

"Why didn't you?"

"Because I have a lot of special skills that I can use to protect honest citizens. To protect the interests of this country from people who would do it and them harm."

"Sounds very patriotic. Some cynics might take you to task over that philosophy, though."

Web stared at her for several seconds before answering. "How many TV pundits have ever had a sawed-off shotgun stuffed up their noses while some deranged lowlife freaked on meth has his finger on the trigger deciding whether to end their lives? Or waited out in the middle of nowhere USA, while some pseudo-Jesus psycho, who finds it in his holy book somewhere that it's all right to screw his disciples' kids, messes with the psyche of the whole country and then ends his fifteen minutes of fame in a fireball that takes every abused child with him? If the cynics have a problem with my motivation or methods, then they can get out there and do it. They'd last all of two seconds. They expect perfection from the good guys in a world where that just is never going to happen. And the bad guys could've ripped the heads off a thousand babies, and you're still going to get their lawyers screaming holy hell if you give them a hangnail while you're trying to arrest them. Now, the higher-ups at the Bureau do make mistakes when issuing orders and some of them shouldn't be holding the jobs they have because they're incompetent. I wasn't at Ruby Ridge, but that was a disaster from minute one and the Feds were more to blame than anybody else for innocent people dying. But it's ultimately guys like me, following those orders, who get their nuts cut off because they had the *audacity* to risk their lives to do what they believe is the right thing and get paid jack-shit for the privilege. That's my world, Dr. Daniels. Welcome the hell to it."

Web took a deep breath, started trembling and looked over at Claire, who looked as stunned as he felt. "Sorry," he finally said, "I'm kind of a *patriotic* jerk when it comes to all of that."

When Claire spoke, she sounded contrite. "I think I should apologize. I'm sure you find your job thankless at times."

"I'm kind of finding it that way right now."

"Tell me about your family," she said after a few more moments of awkward silence.

Web sat back and put his hands behind his head, as he once more took several small breaths. *Sixty-four beats a minute, Web, that's all you need, man. Sixty-four smacks a minute. How hard can it be?* He leaned forward. "Sure. No problem. I'm an only child. I was born in Georgia. We moved to Virginia when I was around six."

"So who is the *we* here? Your mother and father?"

Web shook his head. "No, just me and my mother."

"And your father?"

"He didn't come. The state wanted to keep him awhile longer."

"Was he employed with the government?"

"You could say that. He was in prison."

"What happened to him?"

"Don't know."

"Weren't you curious?"

"If I had been, I would have satisfied that curiosity."

"All right. And so you came to Virginia. What then?"

"My mother remarried."

"And your relationship with your stepfather?"

"Fine."

Claire said nothing, apparently waiting for him to continue. When he didn't, she said, "Tell me about your relationship with your mother."

"She's been dead nine months now, so we don't have a relationship."

"What was her cause of death?" She added, "If you don't mind my asking."

"The Big B."

Claire looked confused. "You mean the Big C? Cancer?"

"No, I mean the Big B, booze."

"You said you joined the FBI on a whim. Do you think it could have been more than that?"

Web shot her a quick glance. "You mean, did I become a cop because my real father was a crook?"

Claire smiled. "You're good at this."

"I don't know why I'm still alive, Claire," Web said quietly. "By all rights I should be dead along with my team. It's driving me crazy. I didn't want to be the sole survivor."

Claire's smile quickly faded. "That sounds important. Let's talk about that."

Web's hands ground against each other. Then he stood and looked out the window. "This is all confidential, right?"

"Yes," Claire said. "Absolutely."

He sat back down. "I went into the alley. I'm hauling butt with my team, we're almost at the breach point and then . . . and then—" He stopped.

"And then I, shit, I froze. I couldn't move. I don't know what the hell happened. My team went out into that courtyard and I couldn't. Then I finally get going and it feels like I weigh a thousand pounds, like my feet were in concrete blocks. And I dropped, because I couldn't keep myself up. I just went down. And then—" He stopped, a hand went to his face, not the damaged side, and he pushed hard there, as though keeping things that wanted to come out from doing so. "And then the guns started. And I lived. I lived, and none of my team did."

The pen sat idle in Claire's hand as she looked at him.

"It's okay, Web, you need to get this out."

"That's it! What in the hell can I add to that? I freaked out. I'm a damn coward!"

She spoke very calmly and precisely. "Web, I understand that this is extremely difficult to discuss, but I'd like you to go over the exact events leading up to you 'freezing,' as you referred to it. As accurately as you can remember. That might be very important."

Web went through the details with her, starting from the moment the Chevy doors popped open to the point where he couldn't do his job, where he had watched his friends die. When he had finished he felt totally numb, as though he had given away his soul as well as his pitiful story.

"It must have felt paralyzing," she said. "I'm wondering whether you felt any earlier symptoms before it hit you so completely. Something like a drastic pulse change, rapid breathing, a feeling of dread, cold sweats, dry mouth?"

Web thought about this for a bit as he again went over in his mind every step he had taken. He started to shake his head in answering no, but then he said, "There was a kid in the alley." He wasn't about to reveal to Claire Daniels the importance that Kevin Westbrook was taking in the investigation; however, there was something that he could tell her. "When we passed him he said something. Something really odd. I remembered his voice sounded like an old man's in some ways. You could tell from his appearance that life had not been exactly kind to him."

"You don't remember what he said?"

Web shook his head. "I'm drawing a blank on that, but it was something weird."

"But *what* he said made you feel something, something beyond the usual pity or sympathy?"

"Look, Dr. Daniels—"

"Please, call me Claire."

"Okay, Claire, I'm not looking to make myself out to be a saint. With my job I go into some real hellholes. I try not to think about all the other things, like the kids."

"It sounds as though if you thought that way you wouldn't be able to do your work."

Web shot a glance at her. "Is that what you think might have happened to me? I see the kid and it snapped something in my brain?"

"It's possible, Web. Shell shock, post-traumatic stress syndrome that induces physical paralysis along with a whole host of other physical debilitations. It happens more often than people think. The stress of combat is unique."

"But nothing had happened yet. Not one shot fired."

"You've been doing this for many years, Web; it can all accumulate inside you and the *effect* of that accumulation can manifest itself at the most inopportune moments and in the most unfortunate ways. You aren't the first person to go into battle of sorts and have that kind of reaction."

"Well, it's the first time it's happened to me," Web said with an edge to his voice. "And my team had been through just as much as me, and none of them locked up."

"Even though this was the first time it's happened to you, Web, you have to understand that we're all different. You can't compare yourself to anyone else. It's not fair to you."

He pointed a finger at her. "Let me tell you what's fair. What's fair is me maybe making a difference that night. Maybe I could have done something, seen something that would have warned my guys, and maybe they'd still be living and I wouldn't be sitting here talking to you about why they're not."

"I understand that you're angry and that life is often not fair. You've doubtless seen hundreds of examples of that. The point is how best for you to deal with what happened."

"How exactly do you deal with something like this? It doesn't get any worse than this."

"I know it may seem hopeless, but it would be worse if you can't work through your issues and move on with your life."

"Life? Oh, yeah, that's right, I guess I have something of a life left. You want to switch with me? I'll give you a real deal."

"Do you want to go back to HRT?" she asked flatly.

"Yes," he said immediately.

"You're sure?"

"I'm absolutely sure."

"Then that's a goal that we both can work toward."

Web ran a hand up his thigh and stopped at the bulge of his pistol. "Do you really think that's possible? I mean, at HRT if you can't cut it mentally or physically, well, then you're gone." Gone, he thought, from really the only place he had ever fit in.

"We can try, Web, that's all we can do. But I'm pretty good at my job too. And I promise that I'll do all I can to help you. I just need your cooperation."

He looked squarely at her. "Okay, you've got it."

"Is there anything particularly troubling in your life right now? Any especially stressful issues out of the usual?"

"Not really."

"You mentioned that your mother had died recently."

"Yes."

"Tell me about your relationship with her."

"I would've done anything for her."

"So I take that as you were very close to her?" Web hesitated for so long that Claire finally said, "Web, right now the absolute truth is important."

"She had her problems. Her drinking, for one. And she hated what I do for a living."

Claire's gaze drifted again to where Web's gun rested under his jacket. "Not so unusual for a mother. What you do is very dangerous." She glanced at his face and then quickly looked down. Web, though, had noted it.

"It can be," he said evenly, and turned the damaged side away from her; it was a movement he had grown so adept at he usually didn't notice he was even doing it.

"I'm curious about something. What did you inherit from her? Did she leave you anything that means something to you?"

"She left me the house. I mean, she didn't leave it to me, she didn't have a will. Under the law it went to me."

"Do you plan to live there?"

"Never!"

Claire jumped at his tone.

He said quickly but in a calmer tone, "I mean, I've got my own house. I don't need hers."

"I see." Claire made a note and then seemed to consciously shift gears. "By the way, have you ever been married?"

Web shook his head. "Well, at least not in the conventional way."

"What do you mean?"

"The other guys on my team all had families. I felt like I had a bunch of wives and kids through them."

"So you were very close to your colleagues?"

"In our line of work, you tended to hang together. The better you knew each other, the better you worked together, and down the road that could save your life. Plus, they were just great guys. I liked being with them." As soon as he finished saying this, the fire in his belly returned. Web jumped up and headed to the door.

"Where are you going?" an astonished Claire called after him. "We've just started. We have a lot more to talk about."

Web paused at the door. "I've talked enough for now."

He closed the door behind him, and Claire made no move to follow. She put her pad and pen down and stared after him.

9

At Arlington National Cemetery, Percy Bates walked from the visitors' center up the paved road that led to the Custis-Lee House. After Robert E. Lee had chosen his native state of Virginia and leadership of the Confederate forces over a similar offer from the Stars and Stripes at the outset of the Civil War, the federal government had responded to this rebuff by confiscating Lee's home. Anecdotal history stated that the Lincoln Administration had offered the property back to the Confederate general during the war. All he had to do was come and pay the back taxes. In person. Lee, of course, had not taken Lincoln up on the offer and his estate had been turned into what was now the country's most prestigious national cemetery. That bit of history had always made the Michigan-born Bates smile, although the mansion was now a memorial of sorts to Lee and was popularly known as Arlington House.

Bates reached the front of Arlington House and looked out over what many considered the finest view in all of Washington and perhaps the country. From here, the entire capital city lay at your feet. Bates wondered if old Bobby Lee ever thought this as he got up each morning and looked out.

The cemetery covered over six hundred acres of grounds and was dominated by simple, uniform white headstones. There were also some very elaborate memorials to the dead, erected by survivors or other grateful parties; however, the sea of white headstones, which at the right angle created the illusion of snow-covered ground even in summer, was what most people remembered from their visit here. Arlington National was the final resting place for American soldiers killed while fighting for their country, five-star generals, an assassinated President, seven Supreme Court justices, explorers, famed minorities and many others who qualified to be interred at this national shrine. There were well over 200,000 dead buried here and that number increased at the rate of eighteen bodies every weekday.

Bates had come here numerous times. On several occasions he had attended funerals of friends and colleagues. Other times he had come as a tour guide of sorts when his family had company in town. A favorite thing to do was watch the changing of the guard by members of the U.S. Third Infantry, who maintained around-the-clock vigil over the Tombs of the Unknowns. Bates checked his watch. He would be just in time if he hurried.

As he arrived at the tombs area, Bates could see that the crowd was already gathering, mostly out-of-towners with their cameras and kids. The guard on duty was performing his excruciatingly precise routine of marching twenty-one steps, pausing for twenty-one seconds, switching his rifle to his other shoulder and then marching back along the same narrow path.

Bates had often wondered if the rifle the guards carried was even loaded. However, Bates believed that if anyone ever tried to pillage or defile one of the tombs, he would be met with a swift and painful response. If there was sacred ground for the military in this country, this was it. Arlington Cemetery ranked right up there with Pearl Harbor.

As the changing of the guard started and the crowd grew and moved in for their photo opportunities, Bates glanced across to his left and then started working his way through the rows of tourists and down the steps. The changing of the guard was an elaborate ceremony and would take some time to fully complete. The spectacle drew just about everyone in the cemetery, but not Percy Bates.

He walked around the large Memorial Amphitheater that was situated adjacent to the tombs area. Bates continued strolling, crossed over Memorial Drive and walked around the *Challenger*

Space Shuttle Memorial. Then he turned back and entered the amphitheater. He walked down to the stage area with its large columns, pediments and balustrades; moved over to a wall there and pulled out a map of the cemetery, held it up and studied it.

The man was hidden from Bates's or anyone else's view. He had a pistol in a belt holster and one hand rested on its grip even as he drew nearer to where Bates was standing. He had shadowed Bates around most of the cemetery, making certain that the FBI agent was alone. He moved closer.

"Didn't think you were going to show until you gave me the high sign back there," said Bates. The map completely hid his face from whoever might be watching.

"Had to make sure conditions were right," said Randall Cove. He remained in hiding behind a section of wall.

"I made sure I wasn't followed."

"Whatever any of us can do, somebody out there can do better."

"Can't exactly argue with that. How come you always like to meet in a cemetery?"

"I like the peace and quiet. I rarely get it anywhere else." Cove paused and then said, "I got set up."

"I figured as much. But I've got six men dead and the seventh one is a question mark right now. Did your cover get blown from the inside? Instead of killing you, did they feed you bad stuff to set up HRT? I need details here, Randy."

"I was in that damn building myself. Went in as a potential player with those folks and wanted to check out their operation. I saw desks, files, computers, geeks running around spouting numbers, cash, product, the whole nine yards. With my own eyes I saw it. I don't call up you guys on something like that unless I've seen it for myself. I'm no rookie."

"I know that. But that building had zip in it when we got there. Other than eight trashed machine guns."

"Right. Trashed. Talk to me about London. You trust him?"

"As much as I trust anybody."

"What's his story? Why is he still kicking?"

"I don't think he knows. He says he froze."

"Damn good timing on that."

"He shot those guns up. Saved a little kid in the process."

"That's a real special little kid. Kevin Westbrook."

"So I know."

"Look, we went into this thing hunting the elder Westbrook 'cause the higher-ups thought it was about time to bring him down so they could toot their own horn. But the more I got into it, the more I realized he's small fish, Perce. He makes a good living but not a great one. He doesn't shoot up neighborhoods, keeps a low profile."

"But if not him, who?"

"There're about eight main street sellers in this town and Westbrook is just one of them. Collectively they sell a ton of the shit. Now, you multiply that action by every major metropolitan area from here to New York and south to Atlanta, and you got yourself a real heavyweight."

"What, are you saying one group controls all that flow? That's impossible."

"No, what I'm saying is that I think one group is controlling the flow of Oxycontin from rural areas to metropolitan areas up and down the East Coast."

"Oxycontin, the prescription drug?"

"Right. They're calling it hillbilly heroin, because the illegal trafficking started in rural areas. But now it's moving to the cities. See, that's where the real money is. The hicks in the mountains don't have the kind of cash the city folks do. It's synthetic morphine, for chronic pain or for the terminally ill. Abusers crush it, snort it, smoke it or inject it, and they get popped like something close to heroin."

"Yeah, except it's time-released, so you do a whole pill like that, bypassing the time release, you could kill yourself."

"A hundred deaths and counting so far. It's not as potent as heroin, but it's got double the kick of morphine and it's a legal drug, and that makes some people believe it's safe even if abused. You even got old people selling one pill on the street to cover the cost of the rest of their prescription because their insurance doesn't. Or else you get docs to write up bogus prescriptions or you burglarize pharmacies or homes of patients using it."

"It's bad," agreed Bates.

"That's why the Bureau and DEA ran their joint task force. And it's not just Oxy, you got the older stuff like Percocet and Percodan too. Now you can get 'Perks' on the street for ten to fifteen bucks a pop. But they don't pack the wallop of Oxy. You'd have to take sixteen tablets of Percocet to get the same high as one eighty-milligram Oxy pill."

During this discussion Bates had looked around casually several times, to see if anyone was observing him, yet there was no one. Cove had picked a good place to meet, actually, Bates concluded, since no one could see him, and the way Bates was facing the wall and holding the map up, he appeared simply to be a tourist in need of directions.

Bates said, "Well, the government watches dispensation of controlled narcotics, of course, and you get a doc and a pharmacy dispensing tens of thousands of the same pills, it raises red flags, but you also don't have to worry about getting it over the border."

"Right."

"How come I didn't know this Oxy angle, Randy?"

"'Cause I just figured that part of it out. I didn't know I was dealing with an Oxy pipeline when I first stumbled into this. I just thought it was your run-of-the-mill coke and heroin. But then I started seeing and hearing stuff. Most of the drug seems to be coming in from little pockets up and down Appalachia. For the longest time it just used to be little mom-and-pop operations, mostly by people hooked on the drugs themselves. But I'm sensing a single force out there that's putting all this together and shipping it to the big cities. See, that's the next step. This could be the mother of all gravy trains and somebody's figured it out, at least around here. Bringing it up to the standards of a real drug operation but with profit margins triple what the cartels or anybody else is doing and with a lot lower risk. That's the people we want. That's actually who I thought was operating out of the building HRT hit. I thought we could crack this thing wide open if we got to the bean counters. And it'd make sense to hide your money clearinghouse in a big city."

"Because in the rural areas that sort of thing would stick out," Bates completed his thought.

"You got it. And they have plenty of incentive. Say you work up to moving a million pills a week with a street value of a hundred mil; well, you get my point."

"But whoever's driving the product, they'd have no incentive to waste an HRT unit. That'll bring them grief they just don't need. Why would they do that?"

"All I can tell you is the operation I saw in that building was *not* Westbrook's. It was huge. Lots of activity, way more than his business could generate. If I thought it was just Westbrook, I would have said no-go on the HRT hit. We would've gotten a little fish, but the big one would've just floated away. With that said, I think Westbrook is distributing the product in D.C. and so are the other crews. But hard proof of that I don't have. The guy's real smart and he's seen it all."

"Yeah, but you got to someone in his crew. That's valuable."

"Right, but snitch today, dead tomorrow in my line of work."

"So somebody really put on a damned Broadway production for us by loading up that warehouse to make it look like a big-time drug operation. Any thoughts on that?"

"Nope. After I passed along the intel to you guys and the hit was set, whoever snookered me didn't need old Randall Cove anymore. I'm figuring I'm lucky to be alive, Perce. In fact, I'm wondering why I am alive."

"So is Web London. I guess after a massacre there's always a lot of that going around."

"No, I mean somebody tried to waste me after the HRT hit. Cost me my Bucar and a couple of cracked ribs."

"Jesus, why didn't you let us know? You have to come in, Randy. Get fully debriefed, so we can figure this out."

Bates looked around once more. This was taking too long. He would have to move on soon. He could only look at the cemetery map for so long without arousing suspicion. But he didn't want to leave without Randall Cove.

"No way in hell am I doing that, Perce," replied Cove in a tone that made Bates lower his map. "I'm not doing that because this shit hits way too close to the bone."

"Meaning exactly what?" said Bates with an edge to his voice.

"Meaning that this shit stinks from the *inside* and I'm not putting my life in somebody's hands unless I know they're going to play fair with me."

"This is the FBI, Randy, not the KGB."

"Maybe to you it is. You've always been an insider, Perce. Me, I'm about as outside as somebody can get. I come in now, without knowing what happened, then all of a sudden they might not ever find me again. I know a lot of folks uptown think I was behind what happened to HRT."

"That's crazy."

"Crazy as six dudes getting wiped? How'd they manage that without inside info?"

"That crap happens in our line of work."

"Okay, you telling me you haven't noticed stuff falling down everywhere? Blown assignments, two undercover agents getting killed in the last year, Bureau strike teams showing up to do their thing and finding nobody home to play, major drug busts going down the tubes because folks got tipped off. I think there's some big, stinking rat right in the Bureau selling a lot of folks down the river, including me!"

"Don't go conspiracy theorist on me, Randy."

Cove's voice grew calmer. "I wanted to let you know I wasn't in on it. You got my word because that's all I got to give right now. I hope to have more later."

"So you're on to something?" said Bates quickly. "Look, Randy, I believe you, okay, but I've got people I've got to answer to. I understand your concerns, a lot of bad things have been happening, and we're trying to find the source, but you've got to understand my concerns too." He paused. "Damn it, come on, I'll give you every assurance that if you come in now, I will watch over you like it's my father on his deathbed, okay? I hope you feel that you can trust me, after all we've been through together. I've gone to bat for you before." There was no answer from Cove. "Look, Randy, tell me what you need to come in and I'll see what I can do." There was still no answer. Bates swore under his breath and darted behind the wall. Across the space he saw the door leading out from the other side. He went to it, but it was locked. He ran back around the amphitheater and out into the open. The guard ceremony was breaking up and large crowds had spilled out onto paved walkways and cemetery ground. As Bates looked everywhere, he knew he had already lost him. Despite his large physical size, Cove had spent many years learning how to blend in with any surroundings. For all Bates knew, he was dressed as a groundskeeper or possibly a tourist. Bates threw his map in the trash and trudged off.

10

The neighborhood Web was driving in was identical to most others in the area. Modest postwar homes with boxy shapes, gravel driveways and metal awnings. The front yards were tiny, but there were big back spaces where detached garages lurked and grills sat in protected areas and split-trunk apple trees gave comforting shade. This was the land of working-class families who still took pride in their homes and never took it for granted that their children would go to college. Today men fussed with old cars in the coolness of their garages, women gathered on front porch stoops to drink coffee, smoke cigarettes and exchange gossip under a sun that was very hot for this time of year and skies that were finally clear of the last storm. Kids in shorts and tennis shoes raced up and down the street on scooters that actually required one to use his legs to make it go.

As he pulled up in front of Paul Romano's house, Web could see Paulie, as everyone called him, laboring under the hood of a vintage Corvette Stingray that was his absolute pride and joy, his wife and kids rating a little farther down on the love and gush meter. Originally from Brooklyn, Paul Romano was a "get your fingers dirty" kind of guy and fit in a neighborhood like this, with its mechanics, power linemen, truck drivers and the like. The only difference was Romano could kill you in a hundred different ways if he wanted to and damn if there was anything you could do about it. Paul Romano was one of the ones who talked to his guns, gave them names like you would a pet. His MP-5 was Freddy, as in Freddy from *Nightmare on Elm Street*, and his twin .45s were Cuff and Link, named after the turtles in the

movie *Rocky*. Yes, as hard as it was to believe, Paul Romano from
Brooklyn was a big Sly Stallone fan—although he was forever complaining that that "damn Rambo character was one wimpy ass."

Romano looked up in surprise as Web walked over and peered
into the guts of the Nassau-blue 'Vette with a white convertible
soft top. Web knew the car was a model year 1966, which was the
first production year of the famous 427-cubic-inch block engine
that carried 450 horses inside, because Romano had told him and
all the other HRT guys this about a thousand times. "Four-speed
manual close ratio. Top speed of about one sixty-five. Blow anything off the street," he had said until Web was sick of hearing it.
"Police cruisers, morphed street shit-cans, hell, half the damn
stock cars racing at the smaller tracks."

Web had often wondered what it would have felt like to be a kid
pulling wrenches and tearing apart cars in the driveway with your
old man. Learning stuff about carburetors, sports, women, all the
things that made life worth living. *Like, hey, Pop, you know how she's
next to you and you're wondering, should I slip my arm around her, and
maybe take a chance placing my hand there? Yeah, there, Pop, help me out,
you were young once, weren't you? Don't tell me you never thought about
stuff like that, because I'm standing here, aren't I? And when should I go in
for the kiss? What signs should I be looking for? Pop, you won't believe this,
but I can't figure these crazy women out. Does it get easier when they get
older?* And the old man would wink, smile knowingly, take a swig
of beer, a long drag on a Marlboro and sit down, wipe off his greasy
hands on a rag and say, *Okay, listen up, Junior, this is how you work it.
Let me lay it out for you here, and you better write this down 'cause this is
the gospel, son.* Staring into the Corvette's chest cavity, Web wondered what that exchange would feel like.

Romano eyed Web and didn't mention the 450 HP Big Block that
could blow away morphed street shit-cans. All he said was, "Beer's
in the cooler. Buck a can. And *don't* make yourself comfortable."

Web reached inside the small Coleman at his feet and popped
open a Budweiser without, however, leaving a dollar bill in payment. "You know, Paulie, Bud's not all there is. Got some wicked
South American brews you should try."

"Right, on my salary?"

"We make the same money."

"I got a wife and kids, you got shit."

Romano gave the socket wrench a few more pulls and then stepped past Web and fired up the engine. It sounded powerful enough to burst through the thin metal keeping it all together.

"Purring like a kitten," said Web as he sipped his beer.

"Hell, like a tiger."

"Can we talk? Got some questions."

"You and everybody else. Sure, come on. Got all the time in the world. What the hell am I supposed to do on my day off, enjoy myself? So what do you need? Some ballet tights? I'll check with my wife."

"You know I'd appreciate you not ragging my ass to everybody at Quantico."

"And I'd appreciate you not ordering me around. And while we're at it, get the hell off my property. I got standards on people I hang with."

"Let's just talk, Paulie. You owe me that."

Romano pointed the wrench at him. "I owe you nothing, London."

"After eight years doing this crap, I think we *both* owe each other more than we'll ever be able to cover."

The two men stared at each other until Romano finally put down the wrench, wiped off his hands, turned the tiger off and headed toward the backyard. Web took this as an invitation to follow. Yet, part of Web was thinking that maybe Romano simply was going to the garage to get a bigger wrench to hit him with.

In the backyard the grass was cut short, the trees pruned, a fat rosebush billowed out from one side of the garage. The temperature must have been near eighty in the sun, and it felt good after all the rain. They pulled up a couple of lawn chairs and settled down. Web watched as Romano's wife, Angie, hung clothes on the line to dry. She was from Mississippi originally. The Romanos had two kids, both boys. Angie was petite and still curvy with big blond hair, bewitching green eyes and a "let me eat you up, darlin'" look. She was always flirting, always touching your arm or grazing your leg with her foot, saying that you were cute, but it was all innocent stuff. It drove Romano nuts sometimes, yet Web could tell he really loved that other guys were attracted to his wife. That was just part of what made Romano tick. And yet when Angie Romano got pissed off, you had better look out. Web had seen that side of her too at some HRT get-togethers; the little woman could be a hellcat on speed—she had made intensely confident guys who shot big guns for a living dive for cover when she was on the warpath.

Paul Romano was a Hotel Team assaulter now, but he and Web had come to HRT in the same class and been paired as snipers for about three years. Romano had been with the Deltas before joining the FBI. Though Romano was built like Web, lacking big muscles, the muscle he did have was like cable. You couldn't break it, and the guy's motor never quit. No matter what you threw at him, he never stopped. Once, during a night raid on a drug boss's Caribbean stronghold, the assault boat had dropped Romano off too far from shore, and the guy, carrying sixty pounds of gear, had plunged into fifteen feet of water. Instead of drowning like everybody else would have, he hit the bottom, stood, somehow got his bearings, held his breath for a mere four minutes, walked to shore and participated in the attack. Because there had been a snafu in communications and the target wasn't exactly where he was supposed to be, Romano had actually ended up nailing the drug lord himself after killing two of his bodyguards. And the only thing Romano had bitched about afterward was getting his hair wet and losing the pistol named Cuff.

Romano had tattoos over most of his body, dragons, knives and snakes, and a cute little ANGIE in a heart on his left biceps. Web had run into Romano on the very first day of the HRT selection class for that year, when most of the applicants had stood naked and scared, awaiting the terror they all knew was ahead of them. Web had been checking out all the other guys, looking for scars on knees or shoulders that evidenced physical weakness or expressions on faces that demonstrated mental paralysis. This was both free enterprise and Darwinism at their full, feverish pitch, and Web had been looking for anything to get an edge over the competition. Web knew that only half of them would survive the first cut that would take place in two weeks, and only one in ten of those would get an offer to come back and really kill himself.

Romano had come from the FBI's New York City SWAT team, where he had the reputation of being extremely intimidating among a group of intimidating folks. He hadn't looked scared standing in a room with seventy stripped males that first day of HRT qualifying. To Web, he had looked like a guy who loved pain, who was just itching for HRT to start clobbering his butt with it. And the guy could dole out the hurt too. Back then Web hadn't known himself if he would make the cut for the HRT slots, yet he had known from day one that Paul Romano would. The two had always been supercompetitive and the guy regularly made Web mad, but Web had to admire the man's ability and courage.

"You wanted to talk, talk," said Romano.

"Kevin Westbrook. The kid from the alley."

Romano nodded at his beer. "Okay."

"He's missing."

"The hell you say!"

"You know Bates? Percy Bates?"

"No. Should I?"

"He's heading up WFO's investigation. Ken McCarthy said you and Mickey Cortez were with Kevin. What can you tell me?"

"Not much."

"What'd the kid say?"

"Nothing."

"So who'd you pass him off to?"

"Couple of suits."

"Get their names?"

Shake of the head.

"Hey, Paulie, you know the difference between talking to you and talking to a wall?"

"What?"

"Not a damn thing."

"What do you want me to say, Web? I saw the kid, I watched the kid and then the kid was gone."

"Are you telling me he didn't say one thing to you?"

"He was pretty tight-lipped. He told us his name and gave us his address. We noted that down. Mickey tried to talk to him some more but got nothing. Hell, Cortez doesn't even talk to his own kids. See, we weren't all that sure what the boy's role in all this was. I mean, we're hauling ass to the courtyard, see your flare and stop. Then this kid comes out of the dark with your cap and a note. I wasn't sure if

he was on our side or not. I didn't want to screw up legally by asking him stuff I shouldn't."

"Okay, that was actually smart of you. But you passed him off to
the suits without a word? How the hell does that compute?"

"They flashed their creds, said they were there for the kid and
that was that. It's not like we had the authority to say no. HRT
doesn't do investigations, Web, we just bang 'em and hang 'em.
The suits do the snooping. And I had other things on my mind. You
know me and Teddy Riner were in Delta together."

"I know, Paulie, I know. So about what time was that, when the
suits showed up?"

Romano thought about this. "We weren't there that long. It was
still dark. Say, two-thirty or so."

"Pretty efficient for WFO to get its act in order and send guys for
the kid that quickly."

"So what'd you want me to say to them? Hey, guys, you can't
have the kid, you're way too efficient, and the FBI just doesn't
work that way? Boy, that'd do wonders for my career. I could kiss
my GS fourteen salad days good-bye with that one."

"The suits, can you give me a description?"

Romano thought this over. "I already told the agents."

"A bunch of other suits. So tell me. It won't kill you. Trust me."

"Right. If I was that stupid you wouldn't have to stop at the
bridge because you could sell me Brooklyn too."

"Come on, Paulie, assaulter to assaulter. Hotel Team to what's
left of Charlie."

Romano thought about this for a bit and then cleared his throat.
"One of them was a white guy. A little shorter than me, thin but
wiry. Satisfied?"

"No. Hair?"

"Short and blond—he's a Fed, what else is it going to be? You
think J. Edgar walked around with a ponytail?"

"Some folks claim he did. That and a dress. Young, old, in between?"

"Thirties. Had on your standard-issue Fed suit, maybe a little
nicer than that, actually. A lot nicer than anything you have in your
closet, London."

"Eyes?"

"He had on shades."

"At two-thirty in the morning?"

"Well, they might have been tinted prescription glasses. I wasn't exactly gonna interrogate the guy on his choice of eyewear."

"You remember all that and you can't remember the guy's name?"

"He flashed his creds and I zoned out. I'm in the middle of a crime scene with people running everywhere and six of our guys with their heads blown off. He came for the kid and he took the kid. He walked the walk and talked the talk. Hell, he probably outranked my ass."

"What about his partner?"

"What?"

"His partner, the other suit, you said there were two of them."

"Right." Romano didn't look so certain now. He rubbed at his eyes and sipped his beer. "Well, see, that guy didn't actually come over. The one suit pointed at him, said it was his partner and that was that. That other guy was talking to some cops, so he never actually came over."

Web looked at him skeptically. "Paulie, that means you don't know for sure if the guy you talked to was even with that other guy. He could've been working all alone and just been blowing smoke up your butt. Did you tell the *real* honest-to-God FBI all this?"

"Look, Web, you were an honest-to-God Fibbie. You're used to investigating this kind of crap. I was a Delta. I only joined the FBI so I could jump to SWAT and then onto HRT. It's been a long time and I've forgotten how to play detective. I just bang 'em and hang 'em. Just bang 'em and hang 'em, man."

"Well, you might just have hung a little boy."

Romano stared at him angrily for a few seconds and then slouched down and looked off. Web figured Romano was thinking about his own two sons. Web wanted the guy to feel guilty, so this blunder would never happen again. "That kid's probably in some landfill right now. He has a brother. Some badass named Big F."

"Don't they all," growled Romano.

"Kid hasn't had much of a life. You saw the bullet hole on his cheek. At all of ten years old."

Romano took a slug of beer and wiped his mouth. "Yeah, well, six of our guys are dead and they shouldn't be and I'm still wondering why it wasn't seven." He shot Web a nasty look as he said this.

"If it makes you feel any better, I'm getting some professional help now trying to figure that out." This was a huge admission for Web to make, particularly to Romano, and he immediately regretted it.

"Oh, yeah, that makes me feel so good I'm gonna run through the streets yelling 'Web's seeing a shrink, the world is safe.'"

"Give me a break here, Paulie, you think I wanted to freeze out there? Do you think I wanted to see my team get shot up? *Do* you?"

"I guess you're the only one who can answer that," Romano fired back.

"Look, I know this all looks bad, but why are you giving me such a hard time?"

"You want to know why? You really want to know why?"

"Yeah."

"Okay, I did talk to that kid, or let me put it better. The kid talked to me. You wanta know what that kid said?"

"I'm sitting here, Paulie."

"He said you were so scared you were bawling like a baby. He said you begged him to please don't tell anybody. You were the biggest piece of chickenshit he'd ever seen. He said you even tried to give him your gun because you were scared to use it."

Talk about your ungrateful kid. "And you believed that crap?"

Romano took a swig of his beer. "Well, not the part about the gun. You ain't giving that damn SR75 to nobody."

"Thanks a lot, Romano."

"But the kid must have seen something to make him say stuff like that. I mean, why would he lie about everything?"

"Oh, I don't know, Paulie, maybe because I'm a cop and he's just not big into law enforcement types. Why don't you go ask some of the snipers about it? They can tell you if I was crying or shooting. Or maybe you wouldn't believe them either."

Romano ignored this. "I guess people turn chickenshit all the time, course I wouldn't really know about that."

"You know, you're a real bastard."

Romano put down his beer and half rose out of his chair. "You want to find out how much of a bastard I really am?"

The two looked to be working up to blows when Angie came over and said hello to Web and gave him a comforting hug along with some soothing words.

"Paulie," she said, "maybe Web would like to stay for dinner. I'm making pork chops."

"Maybe I don't want Web to stay for damn pork chops, okay?" growled Romano.

Angie bent down and grabbed Romano's shirt, jerking him up. "Excuse us for a sec, Web," she said.

Web watched as Angie dragged her husband over to the side of the garage and gave him what Web could only describe as a dressing down of intimidating proportion. She tapped her bare foot and waggled her hand in his face and did a very fine impersonation of a drill sergeant taking a serious bite out of an enlisted man's ass. And Paul Romano, who could kill just about anything that lived, just stood there, head down, and quietly took it from his "little woman." Angie finally led him back over to Web.

"Go ahead, Paulie, ask him."

"Angie," said Web, "don't make him—"

"Shut up, Web," snapped Angie, and Web shut up. Angie smacked the still-silent Romano on the back of the head. "Either ask him or else you'll be sleeping in the garage with that stupid car of yours."

"Do you want to stay for dinner, Web?" asked Romano as he stared at his lawn, arms folded across his chest.

"A pork chop dinner," prompted Angie, "and why don't you try saying it like you actually mean it, Paulie?"

"Would you like to stay for a pork chop dinner, Web?" asked Romano in the meekest little voice Web had ever heard, and damn if he didn't even look Web in the eye when he said it. That Angie was a miracle worker. With all Romano's suffering, how could Web say no, although the truth was, he was really tempted to decline the invitation just to tick the guy off.

"Sure, Paulie, I'll stay, thanks for thinking of me."

As Angie went in to start dinner, the men worked on their beers and stared at the sky.

"If it makes you feel any better, Angie scares the crap out of me too, Paulie."

Romano looked over and for the first time, at least in Web's recent memory, he actually smiled.

Web looked down at his beer. "I guess you told uptown what the kid said."

"Nope."

Web glanced up, surprised. Romano just stared straight ahead.

"Why not?"

"Because it wasn't true."

"I appreciate that."

"I know when kids are lying their asses off, my own boys do it enough. I guess I was just pulling your chain. Guess that's gotten to be a habit."

"But I really can't believe the kid said all that, Paulie. I saved his butt. Hell, he got lucky twice. It's only thanks to me he didn't have another bullet hole in his head.

Romano looked at him, puzzled. "That kid didn't have a bullet wound."

"Sure he did, on his left cheek. And he had a knife slash on his forehead too, long as my pinky."

Romano shook his head. "Look, Web, I was with the kid and maybe I wasn't paying all that much attention to him, but I wouldn't have missed something like that. I know what a bullet wound looks like because I got one of my own. And I sure as hell have popped enough guys to know what they look like."

Web sat up very straight. "What was his skin color?"

"What the hell are you talking about, what was his skin color? He was black!"

"Damn it, I know that, Paulie! I mean light-skinned? Dark?"

"Light-skinned. Smooth as a baby's ass, and not a mark on him. From my lips to the Pope, I swear."

Web smacked the arm of the chair. "Damn!" Kevin Westbrook, at least the one Web had run into, had chocolate brown skin.

After dinner with the Romanos, Web visited Mickey Cortez and got the same story. He'd heard no other statements from the kid. No ID on the suit who had taken him away, but corroboration on the time. And no bullet wound on the boy's cheek.

So who had made the kid-switch? And why?

11

Fred Watkins climbed out of his car after another long day for the U.S. attorney. It took him an hour and a half to drive into Washington each day from his northern Virginia suburb and about the same coming home. Ninety minutes to drive barely ten miles—he shook his head at the thought of it. His work wasn't over either. Despite having risen at four A.M. and having labored ten hours already today, he had at least another three hours awaiting him in the small study he used as an office in his house. A little dinner and some brief quality time with his wife and teenage kids and he would burn the midnight oil. Watkins specialized in high-profile racketeering cases at the Department of Justice in Washington after a long stint as a humble commonwealth's attorney in Richmond prosecuting whatever miscreants came his way. He enjoyed the work and felt he was doing a real service for his country. He was reasonably well compensated for doing so, and though the hours were sometimes long, his life had turned out all right, he believed. His oldest would be going off to college in the fall, and in another two years so would his youngest child. He and his wife had plans for traveling then, seeing parts of the world they had only viewed in travel magazines. Watkins also had visions of taking an early retirement and teaching as an adjunct professor of law at the University of Virginia, where he had received his degree. He and his wife were thinking of maybe even moving to Charlottesville someday permanently and escaping forever the traffic dungeon that northern Virginia had become.

He rubbed his neck and breathed in the fresh air of a nice, cool evening. A good plan overall; at least he and his wife had a plan. Some of his colleagues patently refused to think beyond tomorrow, much less years from now. But Watkins had always been a practical, commonsensical man. That's how he had always approached his law practice and that's how he dealt with life.

He closed the car door and headed up the sidewalk to his house. On the way he waved to a neighbor pulling out of her driveway. Another neighbor was grilling next door, and the smell of cooking meat filled his nostrils. He might just fire up the barbecue tonight too.

Like most people in the Washington area, Watkins had read about the ambush of the Hostage Rescue Team unit with great interest and sinking despair. He had worked with some of those folks on a case once and had nothing but good things to say about their bravery and professionalism. Those guys were the best, at least in his book, and they did a job that virtually no one else would be willing to do. Watkins had thought he had had it tough until he saw what those fellows went through. He felt especially sorry for their families and was even thinking about inquiring if a fund had been established to help them. If there wasn't such a fund, Watkins was thinking about starting one. Just another item to add to the old to-do list, but that's just how life worked, he guessed.

He never saw it until it rose from the bushes and charged right at him. Watkins yelled out and then ducked. The bird missed him by inches; it was the same damn blue jay. The thing seemed to lie in wait for him most nights, as though trying its best to scare him into a premature coronary. "Not this time," said Watkins to the fleeing creature. "Not ever. I'll get you before you get me." He chuckled and walked up to the front porch. As he opened the front door, his cell phone rang. *Now what?* he thought. Few people had this number. His wife, but she wouldn't be calling him because she had no doubt seen him pull in the driveway. It had to be the office. And if it was the office, that meant something had happened that would probably take up the remainder of his evening and perhaps even require him to turn around and drive back into town.

He pulled out his phone, saw that caller ID was unavailable and thought about not answering it. But that just wasn't how Fred

Watkins did things. It might be important, yet maybe it was just a wrong number. No, no barbecuing tonight, he thought as he punched the talk button, ready to confront whatever it was.

They found what remained of Fred Watkins in the neighbor's bushes across the street where the blast that disintegrated his house had delivered him. The instant he'd hit the talk button a tiny spark from his phone ignited the gas that had filled his house, gas that Watkins had little chance of detecting when he opened the door because of the smells of grilling meat next door. Somehow his briefcase had survived, still clamped in a hand that was now virtually all bone. The precious papers were intact and ready for another attorney to take over from the deceased lawyer. The bodies of his wife and children were found in the wreckage. Autopsies would show that all of them had already died from asphyxiation. It took four hours to extinguish the fire, and two other homes were engulfed before the conflagration was put out. Thankfully no other people were seriously injured. Only the Watkins family had ceased to exist. The question of how he and his wife would spend their retirement years after a lifetime of hard work was laid to rest with them. They had no problem finding Watkins's phone, because it had melted to his hand.

At about the time Fred Watkins's life was ending, ninety miles south in Richmond, Judge Louis Leadbetter was climbing into the back of a government car under the watchful eye of a United States marshal. Leadbetter was a federal trial judge, a position he had held for two years after being elevated from being chief judge of the Richmond Circuit Court. Because of his relative youth—he was only forty-six—and his exceptional legal ability, many folks in powerful places had their eye on Leadbetter as eventually a candidate for the Fourth Circuit Court of Appeals, and perhaps even one day taking his seat on the Supreme Court of the United States. As a judge in the legal trenches Leadbetter had overseen many trials of varying complexity, emotion and potential volcanic eruption. Several men that he had sentenced to prison had threatened his life. Once he had almost fallen prey to a letter bomb sent by a white

supremacist organization that hadn't cared for Leadbetter's stead-
fast belief that all persons, regardless of creed, color or ethnicity,
were equal under the eyes of God and the law. These circumstances
dictated that Leadbetter receive additional security, and there had
been a recent development that had further increased concerns for
his safety.

There had been a daring prison escape by a man who had sworn
revenge on Leadbetter. The prison where the man had been held
was very far away and the threats were from several years ago, yet
the authorities were wisely taking no chances with the good judge.
For his part Leadbetter simply wanted to live his life as he always
had and the beefed-up security was not particularly appealing to
him. However, having barely escaped death once, he was practical
enough to realize that the concern was probably legitimate. And he
didn't want to die violently at the hands of some piece of filth who
should be rotting away in prison; Judge Leadbetter wouldn't want
to give the man the satisfaction.

"Any news on Free?" he asked the U.S. marshal.

That the man who had escaped from prison was named Free
had always rankled Leadbetter. Ernest B. Free. The middle initial
and surname weren't his real ones, of course. He had had his
name legally changed when he had joined a paramilitary neo-
conservative group whose members all had taken that name as
symbolism of the perceived threats to their liberty. In fact, the
group called themselves the Free Society, ironic since they were
violent and intolerant of anyone who didn't look like them or
who disagreed with their hate-filled beliefs. They were the type
of organization that America could certainly do without and yet
they were also an example of the vastly unpopular types of
groups that the First Amendment to the United States Constitution was constructed to afford protection to. But not when such
groups killed. No, not when they killed. No bit of paper, no matter how cherished, could protect you from the consequences of
that.

Free and other members of his group had broken into a school,
shot two teachers to death and taken numerous children and
teachers hostage. Local authorities had surrounded the school, and

a SWAT team had been called up, but Free and his men were heavily armed with automatic weapons and body armor. Thus, federal lawmen specializing in hostage rescue had been called up from Quantico. At first things looked like they would end peacefully, but shooting had erupted from inside the school and eventually the Hostage Rescue Team had gone in. A horrific gun battle had ensued. Leadbetter could still vividly recall the heartbreaking sight of a young boy lying dead on the pavement, along with two teachers. A wounded Ernest B. Free had finally given up when his accomplices had been gunned down.

There had been some question as to whether Free would be tried in federal or state courts. While it was believed that the school was targeted because it was a cutting-edge magnet school for integration and enhancement of race relations, and Free's racist views were well known, it still would have been hard to prove, Leadbetter recognized. To start with, the three people killed—the two teachers and the young boy—were white, and thus prosecuting Free under a federal hate crime statute looked relatively weak. And while technically Free could have been charged with assaults on federal officers, it seemed the best shot was to make things simple and try him in state court and seek the death penalty for the multiple murders. The result was not one any of them had intended.

"No, Judge," replied the marshal, snapping Leadbetter out of his reminiscing. The marshal had been looking out for Leadbetter for a while now and they had quickly established a good rapport. "If you ask me, that man's plan is to head to Mexico and then on to South America. Hook up with some Nazis, people of his own kind."

"Well, I hope they get him and put him right back where he belongs," said Leadbetter.

"Oh, they probably will. Feds are on it and they sure got the resources."

"I wanted that bastard to get the death penalty. That's what he deserved." It was one of the few regrets that Leadbetter had as a circuit court judge. But Free's defense counsel had, of course, raised the issue of insanity and even tiptoed along the fringe of alleging a claim of brainwashing by the "cult," as he had described the organization Free belonged to. The attorney was just doing his job, and in the minds of the prosecution, it apparently had raised just enough doubt about the odds of a solid conviction that they had struck a deal with Free's counsel before the jury had come back in. Instead of a potential death penalty, Free had gotten twenty to life with the possibility, however slight, that he might someday be paroled. Leadbetter hadn't agreed with the deal, yet he really had no choice but to sign off on it. The media had taken an informal poll of the jury later. Free had the real last laugh then. All jury members would have voted for conviction and all would have recommended the death penalty. The press had had a field day with that one. Everyone had ended up with egg on his face. Free had been transferred, for a variety of reasons, to a maximum security prison in the Midwest. That was the place he had escaped from.

Leadbetter looked over at his briefcase. Folded neatly inside was a copy of his beloved *New York Times*. Leadbetter had been born and attended school in New York City before heading south and settling in Richmond. The transplanted Yankee loved his new home, but each evening when he got home, exactly one hour was spent reading the *Times*. It had been his habit for all his years on the bench and his copy was specially delivered to the courthouse before he left each day. It was one of the few acts of relaxation the man was able to enjoy anymore.

As the marshal drove out of the court's garage, his phone rang and the answered it. "What's that? Yes, sir, Judge. Yes, sir, I'll tell him." He put the phone down and said, "That was Judge Mackey. He said to tell you to look at the last inside page of the front section of the *Times* if you want to see something really amazing."

"Did he say what it was?"

"No, sir, just that you were to look and then to call him right back."

Leadbetter glanced at the paper, his curiosity running high. Mackey was a good friend and his intellectual interests ran similar to Leadbetter's. If Mackey thought something fascinating, probably so would he. They were stopped at a light now. That was good because Leadbetter couldn't read in a moving car without getting violently ill. He pulled the paper out, but it was too dark to see in the car. He reached over and turned on the reading light switch and opened the paper.

The annoyed marshal looked back and said, "Judge, I told you not to be turning that light on. It makes you a durn sitting duck—"

The tinkle of glass stopped the marshal cold, that and the sight of Judge Louis Leadbetter toppling facedown onto his precious *New York Times*, its pages now soiled with his blood.

12

Kevin Westbrook's mother, Web learned, was probably dead, though no one could tell him for sure. She had disappeared years before. A meth and crack addict, she had most likely ended her life with the prick of a dirty needle or snort of impure powder. The identity of Kevin's father was unknown. Apparently these were not unusual gaps in personal history in the world where Kevin Westbrook dwelled. Web drove down to a section of Anacostia even the cops avoided, to a crummy, falling-down duplex amid others just like it where Kevin reportedly lived with a hodgepodge of second cousins, great-aunts, distant, kind of, sort of uncles or step brother-in-laws. Web wasn't really clear on the boy's living situation and, apparently, neither was anyone else. It was the new and improved American nuclear family. The area looked like a reactor had been hemorrhaging nearby for a few decades. Apparently, no flowers or trees could grow here; the grass in the small yards was a sickly yellow; even the dogs and cats in the street looked ready to keel over. Every person, place and thing looked totally used up.

Inside, the duplex was a dump. From outdoors the stench of rotting garbage was overpowering, and indoors there were offensive odors heightened even more by the close quarters. This lethal combination hit Web so hard when he walked through the doorway, he thought he might end up kissing the floor. Lord, he'd take tear gas over this homemade toxin any day.

The people who sat across from him didn't look unduly worried

that Kevin was not among them. Maybe the child routinely disappeared after a shootout of staggering proportions. A sulky young
man sat on the couch. "We already talked to the cops," he said,
more spitting the words at Web than saying them.

"Just following up," said Web, who didn't want to think about
what Bates would do to him if he found out Web was nosing
around on his own. Well, he owed it to Riner and the other guys, to
hell with official Bureau policy. Still, the butterflies were numerous
and reproducing freely in his belly.

"Shut your mouth, Jerome," said the grandma-type who sat
next to Jerome. She had silver hair, big glasses, an enormous
bosom and a no-bullshit attitude. She had not given Web her name
and he had not pushed it; it was in the FBI file no doubt, but he
had tracked it down from other sources. She was as large as a small
car and looked like she could take Jerome, no problem. Hell, it
looked like she could take *Web*, no problem. She had asked to see
Web's badge and credentials twice before unchaining the door. "I
don't like letting people I don't know into my house," she explained. "Police or otherwise. This area ain't been safe for as long
as I can remember. And that's from *both* sides of the table." She
said this with raised eyebrows and a knowing look that penetrated
right to Web's federal law enforcement soul.

I really don't want to be here, Web wanted to tell her, *particularly
since I'm holding my breath so I won't puke.* When Web sat down
he could see between the wide cracks in the floorboards all the
way down to the hard clay the house was built on. This place
must be toasty warm in the winter, he thought. It was about
sixty-five outside right now and it felt like thirty inside. There
was no comforting sound of a furnace going and no smells of
good food simmering in Grandma's nice kitchen. In one corner of
the room was a pile of diet Pepsi cans. Somebody was watching
her weight. Yet next to that was a mound of McDonald's trash.
Probably Jerome's, thought Web. He looked like a Big Mac and
fries kind of guy. "I can understand that," said Web. "Have you
lived here long?"

Jerome simply snorted while Granny looked down at her clasped
hands. She said, "Three months. Other place we were in, we'd
been there a long time. Had it fixed up nice."

"But then they decided we made too much money to be living in such a nice place, and they kicked us out," added Jerome angrily. "Just kicked us out."

"Nobody said life was fair, Jerome," she told him. She looked around the filthy place and drew in a heavy breath that seemed to drain all of Web's hope away. "We gonna fix this place up too. It'll be fine." She didn't sound too sure, Web noted.

"Have the police made any progress on Kevin's disappearance?"

"Why don't you go ask them?" asked Grandma. "Because they ain't telling us nothing 'bout poor Kevin."

"*They* lost his ass," said Jerome as he slid farther down into the mound of sagging, heavily stained cushions that passed for a couch. Web couldn't even tell if there was a frame left. The ceiling was split open in three different spots that Web could see and it sagged down so far you almost didn't need stairs to get to the second floor, you could just reach and pull yourself up. The walls had black mold growing over them, and there was probably lead paint in there as well. And no doubt asbestos clung around the pipes. There was rodent excrement everywhere, and Web would have bet a thousand bucks that termites had eaten most of the wood in the place, which was probably why it had that little lean to the left he had observed as he had come up the front sidewalk. The building inspectors must have just written off this whole area, or else they were drinking coffee somewhere and laughing their butts off.

"Do you have a picture of Kevin?"

"Course we do, gave one to the police," said Grandma.

"Got another?"

"Hey, we ain't got to keep giving you stuff," snarled Jerome.

Web leaned forward and let the grip of his pistol show very prominently. "Yes, Jerome, you do. And if you don't lose the attitude, I'll just haul your ass downtown and we can go over your record for any outstanding warrants that'll put your little butt away for a while, unless you want to try and bullshit me and claim you've never been arrested, slick."

Jerome looked away and muttered, "Shit."

"Shut up, Jerome," said Grandma. "You just shut your damn mouth."

There you go, Granny, Web thought.

She pulled out a little wallet and lifted out a photo. She handed it across to Web, and when she did, her fingers started to tremble a little and her voice caught in her throat, but then she straightened everything out. "That's my last picture of Kevin. Please don't lose it."

"I'll take good care of it. You'll get it back."

Web glanced down at the photo. It was Kevin. At least the Kevin Web had saved in the alley. So the kid Cortez and Romano had babysat was somebody else who had lied and said he was Kevin Westbrook. That took some planning, but it also would have to have been on the fly. And yet for what purpose?

"You said you gave the police a photo of Kevin?"

Grandma nodded. "He's a good boy. He goes to school, you know, most every day he does. A special school because he's a real special little boy," she added proudly.

Down here, Web knew, going to school was an accomplishment to tout, perhaps second only to surviving the night.

"I'm sure he is a good boy." He looked over at wild-eyed, felony-in-waiting Jerome. *You were a good boy too once, weren't you, Jerome?* "Were they uniformed police?"

Jerome stood. "What, you think that we're stupid? They was FBI, man, just like you."

"Sit down, Jerome," said Web.

"Sit down, Jerome," said Grandma, and Jerome sat.

Web thought rapidly. So if the Bureau had a photo of Kevin, then they had to know that they'd had the wrong boy, however briefly, in custody. Or did they? Romano had been clueless about there being two boys. He had just described him as a black kid. What if that was the entire official report? If the fake Kevin Westbrook had disappeared before Bates and the others got on the scene, then all they'd know was a black kid around ten years old named Kevin Westbrook who lived at such-and-such address near the alley was missing. They'd come here and talk to the family, get a picture, like they had done, and go about their investigation. It's not like they'd for sure go ask Romano and Cortez for a positive ID, especially if they had no reason to suspect a switch. And Ken McCarthy had said the snipers hadn't gotten a look at the real

Kevin when Charlie Team had passed him on the way in. Perhaps only Web knew about the deception.

Web looked around, and for the sake of the grandmother, or whatever her relation to Kevin was, he tried hard not to show his disgust. "Did Kevin actually live here?" Bates had said Kevin's home life was miserable and that he probably avoided it when he could, which would explain why he'd been out alone in the middle of the night instead of here in bed. The physical surroundings truly were awful, but probably no worse than many of the other homes down here. Poverty and crime were everywhere and the marks they left were in no way pretty. Yet Granny seemed solid as a rock. A good person, and it seemed like she genuinely cared for Kevin. Why would he avoid her?

Granny and Jerome exchanged a glance. "Most of the time," said Granny.

"Where would he live other times?"

Neither of them said a word. He watched as Granny looked at her very substantial lap and Jerome closed his eyes and swayed his head, apparently to some bitchin' music in his head.

"I understand Kevin has a brother. Does Kevin live with him *sometimes*?"

Jerome's eyes popped open and Granny stopped looking at her lap. In fact, from the expressions on their faces it was as though Web were pointing a gun at them and had just told the pair to kiss their respective butts good-bye.

"Don't know him, never seen him," said Grandma quickly as she sat there rocking back and forth like something suddenly was hurting her. She didn't look like she could take anybody right now. She looked like an old woman scared out of her wits.

When Web looked over at Jerome he jumped up and was gone before Web could even rise. Web heard the front door open and then slam shut and then came the sound of feet running away.

Web looked back at Granny.

"Jerome don't know him neither," said Grandma.

13

The morning came for the official memorial service, and Web rose early, showered, shaved and dressed in his nicest suit. The time to formally honor and mourn all of his friends had come, and all Web wanted to do was run like hell.

Web had not spoken with Bates about what he'd learned from Romano and Cortez, nor about his visit to Kevin's home. Web wasn't exactly sure why he hadn't, only that he wasn't feeling in a real trusting mood, and because Bates would no doubt chew him out for interfering in the investigation. To Web, Bates had identified the kid as Kevin Westbrook, which meant either the boy had told him that was his name or Bates had gotten it from Romano and Cortez if the boy had disappeared before Bates had arrived on the scene. Web would have to confirm which it was. If Bates had seen the other kid, then when he had taken Kevin's photo from the grandmother, he'd have known there were two different kids involved.

So Web had given a kid with a bullet wound on his cheek a note to take to his HRT guys. That kid had told Web his name was Kevin. The note had been delivered, but apparently not by the same kid Web had given the note to. That meant that between him giving the kid calling himself Kevin the note and the note being delivered, the boy had been switched with another kid. That could only have taken place in the alley between where Web was and the charging HRT unit. That wasn't a whole bunch of space, yet it had been enough to pull the switch, which meant other people had been lurking somewhere in that alley, waiting for this to happen, maybe waiting for a lot to happen.

Was Kevin's coming down that alley planned? Was he working for his brother, Big F? Was he supposed to check for survivors, and had he not expected to find any? And when he did find Web alive, had that thrown a monkey wrench in somebody's plan? And what the hell could that plan have been? And why pull one kid out and put another one in? And why did the fake Kevin lie and say Web was a coward? And who was the suit who had taken the replacement kid? Bates had been pretty tight-lipped about losing the kid. Was the suit Romano had talked to even an FBI agent? If not, how could one imposter have walked right in with creds and bravado impressive enough to fool Romano and Cortez and waltz off with *another* imposter? It was bewildering, and Web was so full of doubt that turning to Bates for answers and information sharing was not real high on his list of action items.

He parked the Mach One as close to the church as he could. There were many cars already there, and the parking spaces relatively few. The church was a somber-faced stone monolith built in the latter part of the nineteenth century when the architectural commandment had been, "Thou house of worship shalt have more turrets, balustrades, Ionic columns, broken pediments, arches, gables, doors, windows and cool masonry curlicues than thy neighbor."

It was at this holy temple that Presidents, Supreme Court justices, members of Congress, ambassadors and other, lesser dignitaries of varying degrees did their praying, singing and, very occasionally, confessing. Political leaders were often photographed or filmed going up or down its broad steps, Bible in hand and God-fearing looks on their features. Despite the separation of church and state in America, Web had always believed that voters liked to see a little piety in their elected officials. No HRT members had attended this church, yet the politicos had to have a grand stage to say their words of consolation. And the little backwoods house of religion near Quantico, where some of the members of Charlie Team had actually done their worshiping, apparently didn't cut it.

The sky was clear, the sun warming and the slight breeze refreshing. It was too fine an afternoon for such a depressing thing as a memorial service, it seemed to Web. Yet he went up the church steps, each click of his polished shoes on the stone simulating the ding of a wheel gun's cylinder being turned, one chamber, one bullet, one potentially spent life at a time. Such violent analogies were Web's lot in life, he supposed. Where others saw hope, he only witnessed the raw sores of a festering, degenerating humanity. God, with that attitude, it was no wonder he was never invited to parties.

Secret Service agents were everywhere, with their shoulder holsters, poker expressions and curly ear cords. Web had to go through a metal detector before entering the church. He showed his gun and his FBI creds, which told the Secret Service the only way Web and his gun would be parted was if he was dead.

As soon as he opened the door, Web almost bumped into the rear of the mass of people that had somehow squeezed itself into the space. He took the rather uncouth tactic of flashing his FBI shield, and the seas parted and he was allowed to move through. Over in one corner a camera crew had set up and was broadcasting the entire spectacle. What idiot had authorized that? Web wondered. And exactly whose idea was it to invite the whole frigging world to what should have been a private ceremony? This was how the survivors were to remember their dead, at a circus?

With the help of some fellow agents Web managed to wedge himself into one of the pews and then looked around. The families were in the front two rows, which had been roped off. Web bowed his head in prayer, saying one for each of the men, lingering the longest on Teddy Riner, who had been a mentor to Web, a crackerjack agent, a wonderful father, a good man all around. Web dropped a couple of tears as he realized how much he had really lost in those few seconds of hell. Yet when he looked up front to where the families sat, he knew he had not lost as much as those folks had.

The truth was beginning to set in with the younger kids, for Web could hear their wails at Daddy being gone forever. And the sobbing and screaming continued through all the tired speeches, from the get-tough-on-crime bullcrap from the politicians to the preachers who had never met any of the men they were eulogizing.

They fought the good fight, Web wanted to stand up and quietly say.

They died protecting all of us. Never forget them, for they were all unforgettable in their own way. End of eulogy. Amen. Let's hit the bars.

The memorial service finally was over, and the congregation heaved a collective sigh of relief. On his way out, Web spoke with Debbie Riner and offered some words of comfort to Cynde Plummer and Carol Garcia and exchanged hugs and snatches of more words with some of the others. He squatted down and talked to the little kids, held small trembling bodies in his arms and Web just didn't want to let go. This simple physical giving threatened to make Web start bawling. Tears had never come easily to him, and yet he had shed more of them in the last week or so than he had in his entire life. But the kids were just killing him.

Someone tapped him on the shoulder. As he rose and turned, Web thought he would be comforting one more bereaved person. However, the woman staring back at him did not appear to need or want his sympathy.

Julie Patterson was the widow of Lou Patterson. She had four kids and had been expecting a fifth but had miscarried it three hours after learning she had become a widow and single mother. A look at her glassy eyes told Web that the woman was heavily drugged with what he hoped were doctor-ordered prescriptions. And Web could smell the liquor. Pills and booze was not a good combo to serve oneself on a day like today. Of all the wives, Julie had been least close to Web, because Lou Patterson loved Web like a brother and Web had easily sensed that Julie was jealous of that relationship.

"You really think you should be here, Web?" said Julie. She tottered in her black heels, her eyes not entirely able to focus on him. Her words were slurry, her tongue moving on to form others before they had completed the last. She was puffy, her skin pale yet blotched red in spots. She had not carried the baby long enough for her belly to swell, and this lost opportunity seemed to have deepened the woman's hurt. She should be home in bed and Web wondered why she wasn't. "Julie, let's go outside and you can get some air. Come on, let me help you."

"Get the hell away from me!" Julie shouted in a voice loud enough to make those within twenty feet of them stop and stare.

The TV crew saw this exchange too, and both the cameraman and reporter apparently simultaneously saw potential gold. The camera swung in Web's direction and the reporter headed over.

"Julie, let's go outside," Web said again quietly. He put his hand lightly on her shoulder.

"I'm not going anywhere with you, you bastard!" She ripped Web's hand off and he grunted in pain, cupping his wounded hand near his body. Her fingernails had bitten right into the hole there, ripping out the stitches; it started to bleed.

"Wasamatter, your little hand hurting, you gutless sonovabitch? You with the Frankenstein face! How'd your mother stand looking at you? You freak, you!"

Cynde and Debbie tried to talk to her, console her, but Julie pushed them away and got close to Web again. "You froze up before the shooting started, only you don't know why? And then you fell down? You 'spect us to buy that bullshit!" Her liquor breath was so intense Web had to close his eyes for a moment, and that only magnified his sense of faltering balance.

"You coward. You let them die! How much did you get? How much did Lou's blood get you, you asshole?"

"Ms. Patterson." This came from Percy Bates, who had swept up next to them. "Julie," he said very calmly, "let's get you to your car before the traffic gets really bad. I've got your kids right over here."

Julie's lips trembled at the mention of her children. "How many are there?" Bates looked confused. "How many kids?" Julie asked again. One hand slid to her empty belly and stayed there, and wet spots from tears marked the front of her black dress. Julie focused once more on Web, her lips curling back in a snarl. "I was supposed to have five of them. I had five kids and a husband. Now I got four kids and no Lou. My Lou's gone. And my baby's gone, damn you! Damn you!" Her voice edged upward again, her hand was making crazy circles on her belly, as though she were rubbing a magic lamp, perhaps making a wish for the baby and husband to come back. The camera was eating up all of this. The reporter was scribbling furiously.

"I'm sorry, Julie. I did all I could," said Web.

Julie stopped rubbing her belly and spit in his face. "That's for

Lou." She spit again. "That's for my baby. Go to hell. You go to hell, Web London." She slapped his face, hitting him right on his ruined cheek, and she almost fell over with the effort. "And that's for me, you bastard! You . . . you freak!"

Julie's energy was spent and Bates had to grab the woman before she collapsed to the floor. They got her outside and the nervous crowd started to drift away into small pockets of discussion; many of them cast angry backward glances at Web.

Web did not move. He had not even wiped away Julie's spit. His face was red from where she had hit him. He had just been proclaimed a freakish monster and a coward and a traitor. Julie Patterson might as well have cut off his head and took that with her too. Web would've beaten to death any man who had said those things to him. But coming from a bereaved widow and mother, her insults had to be accepted; he felt like taking his own life instead. None of what she said was true, yet how could Web deny her any of it?

"Sir, it's Web, right? Web London?" said the reporter at his shoulder. "Look, I know this is probably a really awkward time, but the news sometimes can't wait. Would you be willing to talk to us?" Web didn't answer. "Come on," said the reporter. "It'll only take a minute. Just a few questions."

"No," said Web, and started to leave. He wasn't sure until right then that he actually could even walk.

"Look, we're going to talk to the lady too. And you don't want the public to have only her side of things. I'm giving you a shot to tell your story here. Fair is fair."

Web turned back and grabbed the man by the arm. "There are no 'sides.' And you let that woman alone. She's had enough for the rest of her life. You let her alone. Stay away from her! You understand me?"

"Just doing my job." The man carefully edged Web's hand off his arm. He looked at the cameraman. *Excellent*, was the unspoken thought that seemed to travel between the two men.

Web walked out the door and quickly left behind the church of the famous and well heeled. He climbed in the Mach, fired it up and headed off. He stripped off his tie, checked his wallet to make sure he had some cash, stopped at a liquor store in the District and bought two bottles of cheap Chianti and a six-pack of Negra Modelo.

He drove home, locked all the doors and pulled the shades on all the windows. He went into the bathroom, turned on the light and looked at himself in the mirror. The skin on the right side of his face was slightly tanned, relatively smooth, a few odd whiskers in spots he had missed with his razor. A nice side of skin, not bad at all. "Side of skin." That was how he had to analyze it now. The days were long gone when anyone could remark on his handsome face. Julie Patterson had had no trouble commenting on his mug, though. *But Frankenstein? That was a new one, Julie.* Given time to think about it, he wasn't feeling quite so understanding towards the woman right now. *You would've lost Lou a long time ago if Frankenstein hadn't done what he'd done that cost him half his damn face. Did you forget that? I haven't, Julie. I see it every day.*

He turned slightly to fully reveal the left side of his face. No whiskers sprouted there. And the skin never really did tan. The doctors had said that this might happen. And there didn't seem to be enough of it, the skin was stretched so tight. Sometimes, when he wanted to laugh or smile really wide, he couldn't because that side of his face just wouldn't cooperate, as though it were telling him to kiss off, buddy, look what you did to me! And the damage had reached to the edge of his eye such that the socket was pulled more to the temple than normal. Before the operations, it had given him quite an unbalanced appearance. Now the look was better, but the two sides of his face would forever be misaligned.

Under the transplanted skin were lumps of plastic and metal that had replaced destroyed bone. The titanium in his face set off the airport detectors just about every damn time. *Don't worry, guys, it's just the AK-47 I've got stashed up my butt.*

Web had endured numerous operations to bring his face back to this point. The docs had done a good job, though he would always be considered disfigured. At last the surgeons had told him they had reached the end of their professional skills and even their medical miracles, and they'd wished him well. It had been a more difficult adjustment than he had thought, and to this day he couldn't say he was actually through it. It wasn't the sort of thing you ever really got over, he supposed, since it stared back at you in the mirror every day.

He cocked his head a little more, inched down his shirt collar and the old bullet wound on the base of his neck was fully revealed. It had come in above his armor line, and how it missed all vital arteries and his spine was nothing short of miraculous. The wound resembled a cigar burn, a big-ass cigar burn on his skin, he had joked when lying in the hospital bed with one side of his face missing and two large holes in him. And all the guys had laughed with him, though he had sensed the nervousness amid all the chuckling. They were reasonably sure he was going to make it, and so was he. Yet none of them knew what physical and emotional nightmare lay under those bandages. The plastic surgeons had offered to cover up the bullet wounds. But Web had said no. He had had enough with doctors stealing skin from places on his body and gluing it to others. This was as good as old Web was going to get.

He touched his chest where the other "cigar burn" was in full, blooming glory. It had entered his body and exited at the back of his shoulder, somehow skirting his Kevlar on both ends, and still had enough kick left to erase the head of a guy behind him who was about to cleave Web's skull with a machete. And who said he wasn't lucky? Web smiled at himself in the mirror. "Lucky is as lucky does," he said to his reflection.

HRT had always held Web in the highest possible regard for the heroism he had shown that night. It had been the school hostage situation in Richmond, Virginia, executed by the Free Society. Web had recently switched from sniper to assaulter and was still feeling his way a bit, eager to show his mettle in the front lines. The explosion had occurred from a homemade concoction thrown by one of the Frees. It would have hit Lou Patterson if Web hadn't leapt and knocked him out of the way. The fireball caught Web dead on the left side of his face, knocking him down and melting his shield against his skin. He had ripped the shield off along with a good part of his face and kept fighting, the adrenaline that always came with battle the only thing blocking out the horrible pain.

The Frees had opened fire and Web had taken a bullet through his torso, and the second round had tagged his neck. Many innocent men would have died but for what Web had done *after* receiving these injuries. Instead of weakening him, the shots seemed to have energized him, for how he had fought, how he had killed men trying to kill him and his team! He had dragged injured comrades to safety, including the late Louis Patterson, who had taken a round through the arm a minute after Web had saved him from the flames. The acts Web performed that night had far surpassed what he had done in that courtyard; for he had been so badly wounded at the time, no mere hand scratch that time, no simple Band-Aid that day. To both veteran and new operators at HRT, Web was a legend. And at the highly competitive alpha male agency, there was no better way to elevate oneself on the pecking order than bravery and skill shown in the heat of battle. And all it had cost him were a few vanity points and most of the blood in his body.

Web didn't even remember the pain. But when the last bullet had been fired and the last man had fallen, he too had slumped to the ground. He had touched the open wound on his face and felt the blood pouring out of him from the two wounds, and Web knew it was finally his time to die. He had gone into shock in the ambulance and by the time the doctors at the Medical College of Virginia got to him he was almost flat-line. How he had come back that night was anyone's guess, Web certainly didn't have an answer. Never a religious man, he had started to wonder about things like God.

The recovery had been the most painful thing Web had ever done. Though he was a hero, it was no guarantee that Web would be able to rejoin HRT. If he couldn't carry his full weight, they wouldn't want him, hero or not—it was just the way things were. And Web would never have wanted the terms to be anything else. How many weights lifted, how many miles run, walls climbed, choppers rappelled from, rounds fired? Fortunately, the wounds to his face had not affected his eyesight or aim. Without perfection there, you were gone from HRT. The psychological battering of his recovery, however, had been even worse than the physical cramming. Could he fire when called up? Would he freeze in a crisis and place his team in jeopardy? Well, no, he never had, at least not until that damn courtyard came along. He had come back, all the way back. It had taken almost a year, but no one could say he didn't de-

serve to return on his own, with no corners cut. Now what would
people say? Would he make it back this time? The trouble wasn't
physical this time; it was all in his head and thus was a hundred
times more terrifying.

Web made a fist and put it right through the mirror, cracking the
drywall behind it. "I didn't let them die, Julie," he said to the shattered glass. He looked at his hand. It wasn't even bleeding. His luck
was holding, wasn't it?

He opened the smashed medicine cabinet and took out the bottle of mismatched pills. He had collected them over time from a variety of sources, some official, some unofficial. He used them to
help him sleep occasionally. He was careful, though, because he'd
almost become addicted to the painkillers while they were rebuilding his face.

Web flicked off the light and Frankenstein was gone. Hell, everybody knew monsters were more comfortable in the dark.

He went downstairs and carefully laid out all his bottles of booze
and sat in the middle of them, like a general with his aides going
over a battle plan. Yet he didn't open a single bottle. The phone
rang every few minutes, but Web never answered it. There were
knocks on the door; he let them go. Web sat there and stared at a
wall until it grew quite late. He rummaged through the mismatched pills and took out a capsule, looked at it and then put it
back. He leaned back against a chair and closed his eyes. At four
A.M. he fell asleep on the floor of the basement. Web still had not
bothered to wash his face.

14

Seven in the morning. Web knew this because the mantel clock was chiming when he lifted himself groggily off the basement floor. He rubbed at his back and neck; as he sat up, his foot hit one of the bottles of wine and it fell over and cracked slightly and Chianti leaked across the floor. Web threw the bottle away, grabbed some paper towels and cleaned up the spill. The wine stained his hands red, and for a dazed moment his sluggish mind told him he'd been shot in his sleep.

The noise outside the rear lower window made him race up the stairs and grab his pistol. Web went to the front door with the intent of circling around back and getting the drop on whoever was out there. Maybe it was just a stray dog or squirrel, but Web didn't think so. Human feet trying their best to keep quiet just had a certain sound to them if you knew how to listen, and Web knew how to.

When he opened the door, the surge of people toward him almost caused Web to pull his gun and fire. The reporters were waving microphones and pens and sheets of paper and calling out questions so fast, they cumulatively appeared to be speaking Mandarin. They were screaming for him to look this way or that way so they could take his picture, film his video, as though he were some celebrity or, perhaps more apt, an animal in the zoo. Web looked past them to the street, where the media ships with their tall electronic masts now were docked outside his modest rancher. The two FBI agents assigned to watch over his house seemed to be attempting to hold back the masses but were clearly losing the battle.

"What the hell do you people want?" Web cried out.

One woman wearing a beige linen suit, her blond hair sculpted, pushed forward and planted her high-heeled feet on the brick stoop bare inches from Web. Her heavy perfume made Web's empty stomach turn queasy. She said, "Is it true you're claiming that you fell down right before the rest of your squad was killed but can't explain why? And *that's* why you survived?" The hike of her eyebrows signaled exactly what the woman thought of that preposterous story.

"I—"

Another reporter, a man, shoved his microphone near Web's mouth. "There have been reports that you didn't actually fire your weapon, that the gunfire stopped on its own somehow and that you were actually never in any danger. How do you respond to that?"

The questions kept coming as the bodies pressed closer. "Is it true that when you were at the Washington Field Office you were put on probation for a shooting infraction that resulted in the wounding of a suspect?"

Web said, "What the hell does that—"

Another woman elbowed him from the side. "I have it on good authority that the boy you 'allegedly' saved was actually an accomplice to this whole thing."

Web stared at her. "An accomplice to what? To who?"

The woman gave him a penetrating look. "I was hoping you could answer that."

Web slammed the door, raced to the kitchen, grabbed the keys for the Suburban and headed back out. He pushed through the crowd and looked at his fellow agents for help. They came forward, yanked and pulled on a few people, yet to Web it seemed their hearts clearly were not in it, and they refused to meet his gaze. *So that's how it's going to be*, Web thought.

The crowd suddenly surged closer, sealing off the path to his truck.

"Get out of my way," Web yelled. He looked around. The entire neighborhood was out watching this. Men, women and children who were his friends or at least his acquaintances were staring at this spectacle with wide eyes, open mouths.

"Are you going to respond to Mrs. Patterson's charges?"

Web stopped and looked at this questioner. It was the same reporter from the memorial service.

"Are you?" the man said grimly.

"I didn't know Julie Patterson had the authority to bring charges," said Web.

"She made it abundantly clear that you either acted with cowardice or were somehow involved. Paid off."

"She didn't know what she was saying. She's just lost her husband and unborn child."

"So you're saying the charges are false?" the man persisted and pushed the microphone closer. Somebody jostled him from behind and his arm jerked forward and the microphone hit Web in the mouth, drawing blood. Before he knew it, Web's fist had shot out and the man was lying on the ground holding his nose. He didn't appear to be all that upset. In fact, he was screaming to his camera unit, "Did you get that? Did you get that?"

They all pressed forward more, and Web, being in the middle of this circle, was pushed around by the sheer weight of the crowd. Cameras were snapping in his face, blinding him. Fat video machines were feeding away, dozens of voices were jabbering at once. As the knot of people and machines jostled him around, Web's feet got tangled in a cable and he went down. The crowd moved in, but he pushed his way back up. This was far past being out of control. Web felt a bony fist hit him in the back. When he turned, he recognized the attacker as a man who lived down the street and who had never cared much for Web as a neighbor or human being. Before Web could defend himself, the man ran off. As Web looked around, it was clear that the crowd was not filled just with reporters ravenous for a Pulitzer. This was a mob.

"Get the hell away from me," Web screamed. He yelled at the two agents, "Are you guys going to help or not?"

"Somebody call the cops," said the perfumed blonde, pointing at Web. "He just assaulted that poor man, we all saw it." She bent down to help up her fellow reporter while a slew of cell phones appeared from out of pockets.

Web looked around at a level of chaos he had never before experienced, and he had seen more than most. But he had had enough of this. Web pulled his pistol. The FBI agents saw this and were suddenly interested once more. Web pointed the pistol straight up and fired four shots into the air. On all sides of him the mob now was in full retreat. Some dropped to the ground, crying out, pleading for him not to shoot them, that they were just doing their job, miserable though it might be. The perfumed blonde let her dear reporter friend drop back to the muddy earth and turned and ran for her life. Her heels sank in the soft grass and she ran right out of them. Her fleshy bottom made a nice target if Web had been so inclined. The reporter with the bloody nose was crawling on his belly shouting, "Are you getting this? Damn it, Seymour, are you getting this?" Neighbors swooped up their kids and fled to their homes. Web put his pistol away and walked to his Suburban. When the federal agents moved toward him, all he said was, "Don't even think about it." He climbed in the truck and started it up. He rolled down the window. "Thanks for the assist," he told the two men, and then drove off.

15

"A re you out of your mind?" Buck Winters stared over at Web, who stood by the door of the small conference room at the Washington Field Office. Percy Bates was next to Web. "Pulling and firing your gun, in front of a bunch of reporters, no less, and them taping the whole damned thing. Have you lost your mind?" he said again.

"Maybe!" Web shot back. "I want to know who leaked information to Julie Patterson. I thought the Charlie Team inquiry was supposed to be confidential. How the hell did she know what I said to the investigators?"

Winters looked at Bates in disgust. "Bates, you were this guy's mentor. How the hell did you foul it up so bad?" He looked back at Web. "There are a bunch of different guys looking into this thing. Don't act like a virgin and be surprised when something slips, particularly to a wife who wants to know what the hell happened to her husband. You lost your head, Web, and you screwed up, and it's not like it's the first time."

"Look, I walk out my door and get mobbed, and my own guys not lifting a hand to help me. People were punching me, screaming accusations in my face. I did what anybody would've done."

"Show him what he's done, Bates." Bates quietly went over to a TV sitting in the corner. He picked up the remote and punched some buttons. "Compliments of the media department," Winters added. The tape started to run and Web was looking at the inside of the church during the memorial service. Specifically, he was watching Julie Patterson rubbing her childless belly, screaming at him, spitting in his face, slapping him with all her strength. And him just standing there silently taking it. His statement about having done all he could was mysteriously absent, or at least couldn't be heard. On the tape all he said to Julie was, "I'm sorry." It made Web look like he had pulled the trigger on Lou Patterson himself.

"And that's not the best part," said Winters, who rose and snatched the remote from Bates. He hit the device and Web watched as the scene outside his house ran across the TV. It had been craftily edited such that the atmosphere of the mob scene was gone, the edges of the camera shots crisp and narrow. The individual reporters were depicted as being tough—pushy, even—but polite, professional in every way. The one fellow Web had slugged looked particularly heroic, not even bothering to hide his bloodied nose but going on about his business of introducing the madness the viewer was about to see. And then there was Web looking like a rabid animal. He was screaming, cursing and then he raised his gun. The film speed made him almost appear to pull the gun in slow motion so that it seemed deliberate, controlled and not a man fighting for his life. There were some chilling cinematographic moments too of neighbors running with their children, escaping from this mad fiend. And then there was Web standing alone. Cold, hard, as he put the gun away and walked calmly from the chaos *he* had caused.

Web had never seen anything so slick outside a Hollywood movie. He looked sadistic, evil, the man with the Frankenstein face. The camera had gotten several close-ups of the damaged skin, yet with no mention of how he had come by such injuries.

Web shook his head and looked at Winters and said, "Damn it, that's not how it happened. I'm not Charlie Manson."

Winters bristled. "Who cares if it's the truth or not! Perception is everything. Now that's running on every TV station in town. And it's hit the national pipe too. Congratulations, you're a breaking news story. The director flew back from a high-level meeting in Denver when he was briefed on this. Your ass is in the fire, London, in the fire."

Web slumped in a chair and said nothing. Bates sat across from him and tapped a pen against the table.

Winters stood in front of him, his hands clasped behind his back. To Web, it seemed the guy was really enjoying this.

"Now, you know that the Bureau's SOP in responding to something like this is to do nothing. We've followed the ostrich-head-in-the-sand before. Sometimes it works and sometimes it doesn't, but the higher-ups like the passive tactic. The less said, the better."

"Bully for them. I'm not asking the Bureau to do jack-shit on my behalf, Buck."

Bates picked up the conversation. "No, Web, we're not taking this lying down. Not this time." Bates ticked the points off on his fingers. "First, the media relations guys are putting together a highlight film of our own. The world right now thinks you're some sort of psycho. They're going to find out you're one of the most decorated agents we have. We're issuing press releases detailing all of that. Second, although he wants to strangle you right now, Buck here is holding a televised press conference at noon tomorrow to clearly state what an outstanding agent you are, and we're going to run our highlight film in all its glory. And we're going to release some details of what happened in that alley that will damn sure demonstrate that you didn't turn and run but managed single-handedly to take out enough firepower to wipe out an Army battalion."

Web said, "You can't do that while the investigation is still going on. You could blow some leads."

"We're willing to take the risk."

Web looked over at Winters. "I don't give a damn what these people say about me! I know what I did. And what I don't want is to do anything to jeopardize finding who wiped out my team!"

Winters placed his face a couple of inches from Web's. "If I had my way, your ass would already be gone. But to some in the Bureau you're kind of a hero, and the decision has been made that we're going to bat for you. Believe me, I argued against it, because from a PR point of view it doesn't really help the Bureau, it's just to make you look good." He glanced at Bates. "But your friend here won that battle."

Web looked in surprise at Bates.

Winters continued, "But not the war. And I'm not looking to

make you some damn martyr." Winters glanced at Web's damaged face. "A disfigured martyr. Now Perce is going to take you through the Bureau's little dog-and-pony show that we're doing to clean up your mess. I'm not going to stay for that, because it would make me nauseous. But listen up, London, and you listen really good. You're hanging by a thread right now, and I'd love nothing better than to cut that string. I'll be watching you so close I'll be able to count every one of your breaths. And when you screw up, and you will, then the hammer comes down and you are gone for good, and I'll smoke me the biggest damn cigar I can find. Is that clear?"

"Yeah, a lot clearer than your orders at Waco were."

Winters straightened up and the two men stared intently at each other.

Web said, "I always wondered, Buck, how come you were the only one in the chain of command—excuse me, the chain of *chaos*—that didn't get his career path cut off for that mess. You know, while I was sitting out there on sniper duty a couple of times I actually thought you were working for the Branch Davidians because of all the dumb-shit decisions you made."

Bates said sharply, "Web, shut your damn mouth." He looked anxiously at Winters. "I've got it from here, Buck."

Winters stared at Web for several more seconds and then headed to the door, but he looked back. "If I had my way, there wouldn't be an HRT, and I'm going to have my way yet. And guess who'll be the first son of a bitch to go? How's that for chain of command!"

Winters shut the door and Web let out a big breath he wasn't even aware he'd been holding. And then Bates got right in his face. "I put my neck out for you, called in every chit I've ever earned at the Bureau and you almost screwed it up, taking on Winters like that. Are you really that big a damn idiot?"

"I guess I must be," Web answered defiantly. "But I didn't ask for any of this. The press can strip me clean, but nothing, nothing is going to mess up the investigation."

"You're going to give me a coronary, you really are." Bates finally calmed down. "Okay, here are your marching orders. You're going to lay low for a while. Don't go home. We'll get you a car from the motor pool. Head out somewhere and stay there awhile. The Bureau will foot the bills. We'll communicate via your secure cell phone. Check in regularly. As bad as you looked on the tube right now, you'll look just as good when we tell our side. And if I find you anywhere near Buck Winters during the next thirty years, I will personally shoot you myself. Now get out of here!" Bates went to the door, but Web remained sitting.

"Perce, why are you doing all this? You're taking a big risk standing up for me."

Bates studied the floor for a few moments. "This is gonna sound sappy, and maybe it should, but anyway it's the truth. I'm doing this because the Web London I know has risked his life for this agency more times than I can remember. Because I've watched you lying in a hospital room for three months not sure if you were going to make it. You could've retired then with full pay, gone out on top. Gone fishing or whatever the hell it is retired FBI do. But you came back and got in the line of fire again. I don't know many guys that have ever done that." He drew a long breath. "And because I know what you did in that alley even if the rest of the world doesn't. But they're going to damn sure know it, Web. There aren't many heroes left anymore. But you're one of them. That's all I'm going to say about it. And don't you ever, ever ask me again."

The man walked out and left Web to contemplate another side of Percy Bates.

It was almost midnight and Web was on the move. He was climbing over fences and sneaking through neighbors' yards. The goal tonight was a simple if absurd one. He had to break into his *own* home through a rear window because the media were still moored out front waiting to board him. And then sink him. Two uniformed Bureau security officers were there too, backed up by a Virginia state police cruiser, its blue waggle lights slicing through the darkness. Web hoped there would be no more mobs, no more riots. So long as no one spotted him climbing in his own bathroom window, that is. Then all bets were off.

Web quietly packed a duffel in the dark, threw in some extra rounds of ammo, some other pieces of equipment that he thought might come in handy, then crawled back out. He cleared the fence and slipped back into his neighbor's yard and then stopped. He opened the duffel, pulled out a battery-operated ambient light monocular that made the dark look as clear as day, albeit with a greenish tint, and looked through it. He surveyed the army camped outside his house and focused the magnifier for a better look. All those people whose sole purpose in life right now was to get any possible dirt and damn the truth made Web decide that paybacks, however small, should be taken when the opportunity arose. And right now he could use a generous fix. Web pulled out a flare gun, loaded in a cartridge, aimed the weapon to the sky at a spot right over the top of this fine group of people and fired. The flare sailed upward, exploded and lit the heavens a brilliant yellow. Web watched through his monocular as the pack of fine, exemplary people looked up with fearful eyes and then ran screaming for their lives. It truly was the little things that made life so sweet: long walks, rain showers, puppies, scaring the crap out of a bunch of sanctimonious reporters.

He jogged back to the Crown Vic that Bates had arranged for him and drove off. Web stayed that night at a dump motel off Route One in south Alexandria where he could pay in cash, no one bothered him and the only room service was the McDonald's bag you brought with you or the soda and snack machine chained to a graffiti-stained support column outside his room. He watched TV and ate his cheeseburger and fries. The he pulled out from his duffel his bottle of pills and swallowed two of them. He fell into a deep sleep and for once nightmares didn't rouse him from it.

16

Early on a Saturday morning, Scott Wingo navigated his wheelchair up the ramp and unlocked the door to a four-story nineteenth-century brick building that housed his law office. Divorced, with grown children, Wingo had a thriving criminal defense practice in Richmond, the city of his birth, where he had remained his whole life. Saturdays were a time for him to go into the office and not be bothered by pealing phones, clacking keyboards, harassed associates and demanding clients. Those pleasantries were left for during the week. He went inside, made a pot of coffee, spiked it with his favorite Gentleman Jim bourbon and rolled his way to his office. Scott Wingo and Associates, Counselors at Law, had been a Richmond institution for almost thirty years. During that time Wingo had gone from being a sole practitioner working out of an office the size of a closet, basically defending anyone with enough cash to pay him, to head of a firm with six associates, a full-time PI and a support staff of eight. As the sole shareholder of the firm Wingo pulled down seven figures in a good year, and even mid-six money in bad times. His clients had also grown more substantial. For years he had resisted taking on the drug people, but the cash flow was undeniable and Wingo had wearied of seeing far inferior attorneys drawing down those dollars. He comforted himself with the knowledge that anyone, regardless of what heinous thing he had done, deserved a competent—even inspired—defense.

Wingo had considerable skills as a courtroom lawyer, and his presence before a jury had not been diminished one iota by his confinement two years ago to a wheelchair because of ongoing diabetes and kidney and liver ailments. In some ways, he felt his ability to reach out to a jury had been enhanced by his physical predicament. And many a member of the state bar envied Wingo's string of victories. He was also loathed by those who felt he was simply a means for rich criminals to avoid the rightful consequences of their terrible misdeeds. Wingo naturally didn't see it that way, but he had long ago stopped trying to win that argument because it was one of the very few issues he had ever come upon that didn't seem worth arguing about.

He lived in a substantial home in Windsor Farms, a very affluent and coveted area of Richmond; drove a specially configured Jag sedan to accommodate his disability; took luxurious trips overseas when he wanted to; was good to his children and generous and on good terms with his ex-wife, who still lived in their old home. But mostly he worked. At age fifty-nine Wingo had outlived many predictions of his premature death. Those had come either because of his various medical conditions or because of threats from disgruntled clients or folks on the other side of a crime who felt justice had not been served largely through Wingo doing what he did best, which was finding reasonable doubt in twelve peers of the defendant. Yet he knew that his time was running out. He could feel it in his tired organs, in his poor circulation, his general fatigue. He figured he would work until he died; it wouldn't be such a bad way to go.

He took a sip of coffee and Gentleman Jim and picked up the phone. He liked to work the phones, even on the weekends, particularly in calling back people he didn't want to talk with. Rarely would they be in on Saturday morning and he'd leave a polite message telling them he was sorry to have missed them. He did ten of these and felt like he was being very productive. His mouth was growing very dry, probably from all the talking, and he took another shot of the whiskey coffee. He turned to a brief he was working on that would, if granted, suppress evidence in a burglary ring matter he was involved in. Most people didn't realize that trials were often won before anyone stepped foot inside a courtroom. In this case if the motion were granted there would be no trial because the prosecution would have no case.

After several hours of work and more phone calls, he took off his glasses and rubbed his eyes. The damn diabetes was wreaking havoc with just about every part of him and he had found out last week that he had glaucoma. Maybe the Lord was getting him back for the work he was doing here on earth.

He thought he heard a door open somewhere and figured one of his overpaid associates might have wandered in to actually perform some weekend labor. The young folks these days, they just didn't have the same work ethic of Wingo's generation, even though they made outrageous sums. When had he *not* worked a weekend for the first fifteen years of his practice? The kids today grumbled about working past six. Damn if his eyes weren't killing him. He finished the cup of coffee, but his thirst returned just as bad. He popped open a desk drawer and drank from the bottle of water he kept there. Now his head was throbbing. And his back was aching. He put a finger on his wrist and counted. Well, hell, his pulse was out of whack too; yet that happened just about every day. He had already taken his insulin and wouldn't need another shot for a while; still, he wondered about speeding up the schedule. Maybe his blood sugar had plummeted somehow. He was always adjusting his insulin, because he could never get the damn right dosage. His doctor had told him to stop drinking, but that was just not going to happen, Wingo knew. For him, bourbon was a necessity, not a luxury.

He was sure he heard the door that time. "Hello," he called out. "Is that you, Missy?" Missy, he thought, Missy was his damn dog that had died ten years ago. Where the hell had that come from? He tried to focus on the brief, but his vision was now so badly blurred and his body was doing such funny things that Wingo finally started to get scared. Hell, maybe he was having a coronary, though he felt no pain in his chest, no dull throb in his left shoulder and arm.

He looked at the clock but couldn't make out the time. Okay, he needed to do something here. "Hello," he called out again. "I need some help here." He thought he heard approaching footsteps, but then no one ever came. *Okay, damn it,* he thought. "Sons of bitches," he yelled. He picked up the phone and managed to guide his hand to the nine and then twice on the one. He waited, but no one came on the line. That was our tax dollars at work. You dial 911 and get jack. "I need some help here," he called into the phone. And then he noted there was no dial tone. He hung up and lifted the receiver again. No dial tone. Well, shit. He slammed the phone down and missed the cradle and the receiver fell to the floor. He pulled at his shirt collar because it was getting hard to breathe. He'd been meaning to get one of those cell phones but never had gotten around to it. "Is anybody out there, damn it?" Now he could hear the footsteps. His breathing was becoming impossible, like something was wedged down his gullet. Sweat was pouring off him. He looked up at the doorway. Through his clouded vision he could see the door opening. The person came in.

"Mother?" Damn if it wasn't his mother, and she would be dead twenty years this November. "Mother, I need some help, I'm not feeling too good."

There was no one there, of course. Wingo was just hallucinating.

Wingo slid to the floor now, because he couldn't keep himself up in the chair any longer. He crawled along the floor to her, gasping and wheezing as he did so. "Mother," he said hoarsely to the vision he was experiencing. "You got to help your boy, he ain't doing too good." He got to her and then she just disappeared on him, just like that, right when he needed her. Wingo put his head on the floor and slowly closed his eyes.

"Anybody out there? I need help," he said one last time.

17

Francis Westbrook was feeling seriously hampered. His usual haunts, his normal places of conducting business were not available to him. The Feds, he knew, were looking for him, and whoever had set him up was no doubt trying to get the jump on him too. Westbrook couldn't assume anything else. In his line of work extreme paranoia was really the only thing keeping him alive. Thus he was hanging out, at least for the next hour, in the back of a meat warehouse in Southeast D.C. Ten minutes' drive from where he was sitting and freezing his ass off was the Capitol and other great national buildings. Westbrook had lived his whole life in Washington and had never been to a single monument. These grand edifices to a great nation meant absolutely nothing to him. He didn't consider himself an American, a Washingtonian or a citizen of anything. He was just another brother looking to get by. His goal when he was ten was to live to fifteen. Then his objective was to make it to twenty before he was killed. Then twenty-five. When he hit thirty a couple of years ago he had given himself a party worthy of a person achieving octogenarian status, because in his world, he had. Everything was relative, maybe more so in the eyes of Francis Westbrook than other people.

What was occupying most of his thinking now was how he had screwed up with Kevin. His desire to let the boy have a somewhat normal life had led him to be careless about Kevin's safety. He had once had Kevin with him all the time, but then a crew dispute had erupted into a full-fledged battle and Kevin had been shot in the face and almost died. Francis hadn't even been able to take him to the hospital because he probably would've been arrested. After that, he let Kevin live with some quasi-family, an old lady and her grandson. He kept close watch on Kevin and visited him as often as he could; however, he let the boy have his freedom because every child needed that.

And the fact was Kevin was not going to grow up like Francis. He was going to have a real life, away from guns and drugs and the quick drive to the medical examiner's office with a tag on your toe. Being around Francis too much, being witness to such a life, any young man might be tempted to stick his toes in the water. And once you did, you were caught for life, because that sweet-looking pond was pure quicksand and filled with water moccasins all claiming to be your friend until you weren't looking and one of them sunk his fangs in your neck. That was not going to happen to Kevin, Francis had pledged when Kevin had been born, and yet maybe it already had. It would be truly ironic if Kevin did not outlive him.

While Westbrook headed up one of the more lucrative drug operations in the D.C. metro area, he had never been arrested for anything, not even a misdemeanor, though he was going on his twenty-third year in the "bizness," having started very young and never looked back, because there was nothing to look back to. He was proud of that clean record, despite his felonious ways. It was not all luck; in fact, most of it was due to his carefully crafted survival plans, the way he gave information when it was needed to the right people, who in return then let him carry on his thing peacefully. That was key, don't rock the boat, don't be causing trouble on the street, don't be shooting nobody or nothing if you can help it. Don't give the Feds a hard time, because they got the manpower and money to make your life hell and who needed that shit. His life was complicated enough as it was. And yet without Kevin his life was nothing.

He looked over at Macy and Peebles, his twin shadows. He trusted them as much as he trusted anyone, which was not all that much. He always carried a gun and had needed it on more than one occasion to save his life. You only had to learn that lesson once. He glanced toward the door where big Toona had just come in.

140   DAVID BALDACCI

"Toona, you got me some news, ain't you? Some good news 'bout Kevin."

"Nothing yet, boss."

"Then get your sorry ass back out there till you do."

A sour-looking Toona immediately left and Westbrook looked at Peebles.

"Talk to me, Twan."

Antoine "Twan" Peebles looked chagrined and carefully adjusted his expensive reading glasses. The man's eyesight was excellent, Westbrook knew, he just thought wearing spectacles helped him to look the part of an executive, trying to be something he never would be, legitimate. Westbrook had made his peace with that issue a long time ago. Really the choice had been made for him the moment he had been born in the backseat of a Cadillac up on cinder blocks, his mother snorting coke even as Francis had slipped out between her legs into the arms of her man of the moment, who had promptly set the child aside, cut the cord with a dirty knife and forced the new mother to perform oral sex on him. His mother had told him about this later, in graphic detail, as though it were the funniest story she had ever heard.

"It's not good news," said Peebles. "Our main distributor said until the heat died down on you, he wasn't sure he could provide us with any more product. And our inventory levels are pretty low as it is."

"Damn, now ain't *that* a shock," said Westbrook. He sat back. Westbrook had to put on a strong front before Peebles and Macy and his people, yet the fact was he had a real problem. Like any reseller of sorts, Westbrook had obligations to folks down the line. And if they couldn't get what they needed from him, they would get it from somebody else. His survival time would not be long. And once you disappointed folks, they almost never did business with you again. "Okay, I'll deal with that later. This Web London dude, what you got?"

Peebles opened a file he had pulled from a leather briefcase and adjusted his reading glasses once more. Using his monogrammed handkerchief, Peebles had carefully wiped off the seat he was sitting on and had made it clear that holding a meeting inside a meat warehouse was far beneath his dignity. Peebles liked rolls of cash in his pockets and nice clothes and nice restaurants and the nice ladies doing whatever he wanted for him or to him. He didn't carry a gun, and for all Westbrook knew, Peebles didn't even know how to shoot one. He had come up at a time when drug operations had been far less violent and run in a more orderly way, with accountants and computers and business files, and taking dirty money and making it clean, and having stock portfolios and even vacation homes that one traveled to in one's private jet.

Ten years older than Peebles, Westbrook had come up purely on the streets. He had run crack for pennies a bag, slept in rat holes, gone hungry more often than not, dodged bullets and fired them into others when he had to. Peebles was good at what he did; he made sure that Westbrook's operation ran smoothly and that product came in when it was supposed to and went out to the people that it was intended for. And he also ensured that accounts receivable—Westbrook had belly laughed when Peebles had first used that term with him—that accounts receivable were promptly paid. Money was efficiently laundered, excess cash flow prudently invested, innovations in the industry kept abreast of, the latest technology utilized, all under the watchful eyes of Antoine Peebles. And still Westbrook couldn't bring himself to respect the man.

When personnel issues arose, though, which basically meant that somebody was trying screw them, Antoine Peebles quickly stepped aside. He had no stomach for that part of the business. That's when Westbrook took over and handled things. And that's where Clyde Macy really earned all the dollars that he was paid.

Westbrook looked over at his little white boy. He had thought it a joke when Macy had come to him for work. "You on the wrong side of town, boy," he had told Macy. "Whitey-town's up Northwest way. You go get your ass to where it belongs." He had figured that would be the end of that until Macy had popped two gents trying to mess with Westbrook and, as Macy had explained at the time, he'd done it on a *pro bono* basis, just to prove his value. And the little skinhead had never failed his boss. Who would have thought it, big black Francis Westbrook being an equal opportunity employer?

"Web London," said Peebles, who stopped and coughed and then blew his nose, "has been with the FBI for over thirteen years and with Hostage Rescue for about eight. He's highly thought of. Got lots of commendations and things like that in his file. He was badly injured and almost died during one mission. Militiamen thing."

"Militiamen," said Westbrook. "Right, that's white people with guns think the government's fucked *them* over. They ought come see us black folk, see how good they really got it."

Peebles continued, "There's an investigation currently going on into the shooting in the courtyard."

"Twan, tell me something I don't know, 'cause I'm freezing my ass off and I see you are too."

"London's going to a psychiatrist. Not one at the Bureau, an outside firm."

"We know who?"

"It's a group at Tyson's Corner. Not sure yet of the psychiatrist seeing him."

"Well, let's get that nailed down. He'll talk to the shrink about things he ain't talk to anybody else about. And then maybe we have a talk with the shrink."

"Right," said Peebles as he made a note.

"And Twan, can you tell me what the hell they were going after that night? Don't you think that might be important shit?"

Peebles bristled at this. "I was just about to get to that." He rustled through some more papers while Macy meticulously cleaned his pistol, wiping away from the barrel dust motes that apparently only he could see.

Peebles found what he was looking for and glanced up at his boss. "You're really not going to like this."

"There's a lot of shit I really don't like. Tell me."

"Word is that they were going after you. That building was supposed to house our entire financial operations. Bean counters, computers, files, the whole deal." Peebles shook his head and looked offended, as though his personal honor had been impugned. "Like we'd be stupid enough to have that centralized. They sent HRT in because they wanted to bring the money guys out alive, to testify against you."

Westbrook was so stunned by this that he didn't even take Peebles to task for saying "our" financial operations. They were Westbrook's, clear and simple. "And why the hell they think that? We ain't never even used that building. I ain't never even been in the damn place." A thought suddenly seized Westbrook, but he decided to keep it to himself. When you wanted to deal, you needed to bring something to the party, and maybe he had something, something to do with that building. When Westbrook was just starting out on the streets, he had actually known that place real well. It was part of government-funded tenement housing built in the 1950s and designed to give poor families the subsidies they needed to get back on their feet. What it ended up being twenty years or so later was one of the worst drug areas in the city, with killings nightly. White kids in the suburbs watched TV at night while Westbrook had watched homicides in his own backyard. But there was something about that building and others like it that maybe the Feds didn't know. Yeah, that one went in his "deal-making" file. He started feeling a little better, but just a little.

Peebles perched his glasses on the end of his nose as he eyed Westbrook. "Well, I'm assuming the Bureau had some undercover working this thing and that agent must have told them otherwise."

"Who's the damn agent?" asked Westbrook.

"That we don't know."

"Well, that's shit I *got* to know. People going around lying about me, I want to know who it is." Something very cold had suddenly seized in Westbrook's chest even as he tried to put on a strong front. Now he was not feeling so good. If a Bureau agent had targeted what he thought was Westbrook's operations center, then this meant the FBI had turned its attention to him. Why the hell had they done that? He wasn't that big an operation and he sure wasn't the only game in town. A bunch of crews did things a lot worse than he did. Now, nobody walked over him and nobody touched his turf, but he had played it low and cool for years, causing nobody trouble.

Peebles said, "Well, whoever tipped the Bureau off knew what strings to pull. They don't call up HRT unless they got something very serious to go on. They hit that building because it was supposed to be filled with evidence to be used against you. At least that's what our sources say."

"And what'd they find there, except the guns?"

"Nothing, place was empty."

"So the undercover was full of shit?"

"Or else *his* sources were."

"Or else they set him up, to set me up," said Westbrook. "See, Twan, the cops ain't going to care what's *not* there. They still gonna think my ass was behind it 'cause it's on my turf. So whoever did this was taking no risk. They stacked the deck against me right from the go. Ain't no way I could win that. Am I right, Twan, or you see it different?"

Westbrook studied Peebles closely. The man's body language had very subtly shifted. Westbrook, who had made the noticing of such things an instinct, an instinct that had saved his life numerous times, definitely picked up on it. And he knew its source. Despite his college education and his skill at managing the business, Peebles was just not as quick as Westbrook was at sizing up a situation and coming to the right conclusion. His street instincts paled in comparison to his boss's. And there was a simple reason for that: Westbrook had spent years surviving on those instincts and all the while honing them to an even sharper precision. Peebles had never had to do that.

"You're probably right."

"Yeah, probably," said Westbrook. He stared grimly at Peebles until the man finally looked down at his papers.

"So the thing is, as I *probably* see it, is we know jack-shit about London, only that he's seeing a shrink 'cause he froze up. He could be in on it and just faking everybody out and saying it's all in his head."

"I'm certain he is in on it," commented Peebles.

Westbrook sat back and smiled. "No, he ain't in on it, Twan, I was just seeing if you could finally show me some street mind. You ain't there yet, bro. Not by a long shot."

Peebles looked up in surprise. "But you said—"

"Yeah, yeah, I know what I said, Twan, I can hear myself talk, okay?" He hunched forward. "I been seeing the TV and newspapers, catching up on this dude Web London, Twan. Like you say, man's a damn hero, got his ass shot up and all."

"I've been following it too," said Peebles. "And I didn't see any-thing that convinced me London's not in on the setup. In fact, the widow of one of his own men thinks he was in on it. And did you see what happened outside his house? The guy pulled his gun and fired on a bunch of reporters. He's crazy."

"No, he fired in the air. Man like that, if he had wanted to kill any-body, they'd be dead. That man, he knows guns, that's easy to see."

Peebles wasn't backing down. "I think the reason he didn't go out in that courtyard was because he *knew* the guns were there. He went down right before the guns started shooting. He *had* to know."

"Is that right, Twan? He had to know?"

Peebles nodded. "You wanted my informed opinion, that's it."

"Well, let me inform your damn opinion some more. You ever been shot at?"

Peebles looked over at Macy and then back at Westbrook. "No. Thankfully."

"Yeah, that's a hell of a lot to be thankful for. Well, see, I have. You too, right, Mace?"

Macy nodded and put his pistol away as he followed this dis-cussion.

"See, folks don't like to get shot at, Twan. It just ain't natural to like something like getting your head blown off. Now, if London was in on it he coulda done lots of shit to stay away from that hit. He coulda shot himself in the foot during training, ate some bad food and put himself in the hospital, run into a wall and broke his arm, all sorts of shit so his ass not even been anywhere near that place. But he was, he hauling butt with all the rest of his crew. Then he can't haul no more and his team gets shot up. Now, a man on the take, what's he gonna do if he is stupid enough to go on the gig? He gonna sit back, maybe fire a few rounds in there and then go see the shrink saying his mind's messed up. But what a guilty man ain't gonna do is go out in that courtyard and mess with those machine guns. He gonna stay nice and safe and collect his money for setting everybody up. Now, this man, he went out there and did something even I ain't got the balls to do." He paused. "And he done something else just as crazy."

"What's that?"

Westbrook shook his head and decided it was really fortunate for

Peebles that he was so good at the business end because he was surely lacking everywhere else. "Unless the whole world's lying their asses off, that man saved Kevin. Ain't no way a guilty man gonna bother with that shit."

Peebles sat back, looking thoroughly whipped. "But if you are right and he's not involved, then he won't know where Kevin is."

"That's right. He ain't. In fact, I ain't know nothing, do I, except shit that don't matter?" He said the last with a hard stare right at Peebles. "And I ain't no closer to getting Kevin back than I was a week ago, am I? You happy about that, Twan? 'Cause I ain't."

"So what do we do?" asked Peebles.

"We keep a line on London and find out what shrink he's seeing. And we wait. Them folks took Kevin didn't do it for nothing. They'll come to us, and then we see what happens. But let me tell you this: I find out somebody sold me and Kevin out, baby, they could run to the South Pole and I'd find 'em and feed 'em to the polar bears limb by limb, and folks think I'm shitting, they better hope they never find out."

Despite the severe chill in the room, a bead of sweat crept down Peebles's brow as Westbrook adjourned the meeting.

18

The air here was not fresh, the smells noxious at times, yet at least it was warm. They fed him all the food he wanted and it was good. And he had books to read, though the light was fairly poor, but they had apologized for that. And they had even given him sketchpads and some charcoal pencils when he had asked for them. That had made his imprisonment easier. When things were going badly in his life, he could always turn to his drawings for a measure of solace. And yet despite everyone's kindness, every time someone came to the room he was convinced that it would be the moment of his death, because why else would they have brought him here but to kill him?

Kevin Westbrook looked around at a room that was far bigger than the one he had at home, yet it seemed close all around him, as though it were shrinking or he was growing larger. He had no idea how long he had been here. Without the rise and fall of the sun, telling time was not possible, he had found. He never thought about calling out anymore. He had tried that once and the man had come and told Kevin not to do that. He said it very politely and in a nonthreatening way, as though Kevin had merely walked across a prized flower bed. Yet Kevin could sense that this man would kill him if he yelled out again. It was always the soft-talking ones who were the most dangerous.

The clanking sound was always there, that and the hissing and the sound of running water nearby. Collectively it would probably cover any noises he could make, but it was very irritating, and interrupted his sleep. They apologized for that too. They were much more polite than captors probably should be, thought Kevin.

He had looked for ways to escape, yet there was only one door to the room, and it was locked. So he read his books and drew his pictures. He ate and he drank and he waited for the time when somebody would come and kill him.

While he was sketching another drawing decipherable only to him, Kevin flinched when he heard the footsteps. As he listened to the door being unlocked, he wondered if that time had come.

The man was the same one who had told him not to yell. Kevin had seen him before but didn't know his name.

He wanted to know if Kevin was comfortable, if he needed anything else.

"Nope. You treating me real good. But my grandma be worried about me. Maybe I ought be getting on home now."

"Not right now," was all the man said. He perched on the large table in the middle of the room and eyed the small bed in the corner. "You sleeping well?"

"Okay."

Then the man wanted to know, one more time, exactly what happened between Kevin and the man in the alley, the one that had grabbed Kevin, given him the note, sent him on his way.

"I didn't tell him nothing, because I ain't had nothing to tell him." Kevin's tone was more defiant than he would have liked, but the man had asked him these questions before and he had told him the same answers and he was growing weary of it.

"Think," said the man calmly. "He's a trained investigator, he may have picked up on something you said, though it didn't seem important when you said it. You're a smart boy, you'll be able to remember."

Kevin held the piece of charcoal pencil in his hand, squeezing it until his joints cracked. "I went down the alley like you told me to. I done what you told me to, and that's all. And you say he ain't gonna be moving or nothing. All messed up and stuff. Well, that ain't happen. He scared the crap out of me. See, you were wrong about that."

The man put out a hand and Kevin flinched, but the man merely rubbed him gently on the shoulder. "We didn't tell you to go near that courtyard, did we? We said to just sit tight and we'd come get you. See, we had everything timed out perfectly." The man laughed. "You really made us jump through some hoops, son."

Kevin felt the hand tighten on his shoulder and despite the man's laughing he could tell the fellow was upset so he decided to change the subject. "Why you have that other boy with you?"

"Just something for him to do, just like you did. He made some nice money, just like you did. In fact, you weren't supposed to see him, but we had to change things, see, because you weren't where you were supposed to be. Cut it pretty darn tight." The hand tightened some more.

"So you already let him go?"

"Go ahead with your story, Kevin, that boy's no concern of yours. Tell me why you did what you did."

How did Kevin explain this? He had had no idea what would happen when he had done what they told him to. Then the guns started firing and he was scared, terrified, but it had been a terror rife with curiosity. It had been a curious dread, actually, to see what he had wrought; as though, say, you'd dropped a rock from a bridge onto a highway with no purpose other than to scare some motorists, only to see your handiwork result in a fifty-car pile-up and numerous deaths. And so when he should have run like hell, Kevin had gone farther down the alley to see what he had done. And the guns, instead of making him flee, had somehow drawn him closer, like both the horror and allure of a dead body. "And then that man yelled at me," he now told his captor. Lord, how that had scared him. Rising up from all those bodies, that voice telling him to get back, stay back, warning him!

Kevin looked at the man after describing all this. He had done what they had told him for one of the oldest reasons in the world, money, enough to help his grandma and Jerome get into a nicer place. Money enough to allow Kevin to believe he was helping out, taking care of others, rather than always being taken care of. His grandma and Jerome had warned him about accepting offers of fast money from people who trolled his neighborhood looking for folks to do things they shouldn't. Many of Kevin's friends had been so taken in, now dead, crippled, imprisoned or disillusioned for life. And now he had been added to that miserable pile, at all of ten years old.

"And then you heard the others coming from down the alley," prompted the man smoothly.

Kevin nodded as he thought back to that moment. He had been so scared. Guns in front of him, men with more guns cutting off his only avenue of escape. Except across that courtyard. At least he had thought so. That man had stopped him from doing that; had saved his life. Didn't even know him and he had helped him. That was a new experience for Kevin. "What was the man's name again?" he asked.

"Web London," the man said. "He's the guy you talked to. He's the one I'm really interested in."

"I told him I ain't done nothing," Kevin said again, hoping that the same answer once more would make this man leave and let him get back to his drawing. "He told me if I went out there I'd get killed too. He showed me his hand, where he been shot. I started to run the other way and he say if I do that, they kill me too. That's when he give me the hat and the note. He shot that flare off and told me to go on. And that's what I did."

"Good thing we had another boy lined up to take your place. You'd been through a lot."

Somehow Kevin didn't think it was such a good thing for the other kid.

"And London actually went back into the courtyard?"

Kevin nodded. "I looked back once. He had that big-ass gun. He went back in there and I heard that gun go off. I was walking fast." Yes, he had walked fast. Walked fast until some men had appeared out of a doorway and snatched him clean. Kevin had caught a glimpse of the other boy, roughly his age and size, yet who was a stranger to Kevin. He looked just as scared as Kevin. One of the men had quickly read the note, asked Kevin what had happened. And then the other boy had been given the cap and note and sent off to deliver it in Kevin's stead.

"Why you bring that other boy?" Kevin asked again, but the

man didn't answer. "How come you sent him with the note and not me?"

The man ignored the question. "Did London seem at all out of it to you? Like he wasn't thinking clearly?"

"He tell me what to do. He thinking pretty good from where I be standing."

The man took a deep breath and shook his head, obviously pondering this. Then he smiled at Kevin. "You'll never realize how extraordinary that is, Kevin. Web London must be truly special to have done that."

"You ain't tell me all what was gonna happen."

The man continued to smile. "That's because you didn't need to know, Kevin."

"Where's the other boy? Why you bring him?" he asked again.

"You think of every contingency, then most times things turn out okay."

"Is that other boy dead?"

The man rose. "Let us know if you need anything else. We'll try and take care of you."

Kevin decided to toss out a threat of his own. "My brother be looking for me." He hadn't said this before, but he had been thinking it, every minute he had. Everybody knew Kevin's brother. Just about everybody he knew feared his brother. Kevin prayed that this man feared him too. Kevin's spirits sank when he could clearly tell from the man's face that he didn't. Maybe this man wasn't afraid of anything.

"You just rest up, Kevin." The man looked at some of his drawings. "You know, you've got a lot of talent. Who knows, maybe you could've ended up *not* like your brother." The man closed and locked the door behind him.

Kevin tried to stop them, but the tears just came in a rush down his cheeks, dripped onto his blanket. He rubbed them away, but more took their place. Kevin sank into a corner and wept so hard he kept losing his breath. Then he pulled a blanket over his head and sat there in the darkness.

19

Web drove the Crown Vic down the street his mother used to live on. It was a neighborhood on its last legs, its potential never realized and its vitality long since exhausted. Yet the location, thirty years ago considered rural, was now smack in the middle of prime suburbia, what with the continued sprawl of the metropolitan area, where commuters rose from their beds at four to get to the office by eight. In five years' time, a developer would probably buy up all the dilapidated properties, bulldoze them under and new homes costing too much would arise from the dust of old ones sacrificed for too little.

Web got out of the Crown Vic and looked around. Charlotte London had been one of the older people living here, and her house, despite Web's efforts, was about as run-down as the rest. The chain-link fence was a few rusting strands from collapse. The house's metal awnings sagged with water and carried grime that could no longer be cleaned away. The lone maple in front was dead, with brown leaves on it from the year before scraping a sad tune in the breeze. The grass had not been cut for a while because Web had not been around to push the mower. He had fought a valiant effort over the years to keep it as it had once been but had finally given up because his mother had taken little interest in maintaining her home and yard. Now that she was dead, Web figured he would be selling the place at some point; he just didn't want to deal with it right now, maybe never.

Web went inside and looked around. Right after her death he

had come here. The place had been a mess, exactly as his mother had left it. He had spent an entire day cleaning the house and ended up carrying ten thirty-gallon bags of trash to the curb. Then Web had kept the electricity, water and sewer going after his mother's death. It wasn't that he ever envisioned himself living here, but something just wouldn't let him go. Now he surveyed the rooms, clean except for dust and the occasional cobweb. He settled down, checked his watch and flipped on the TV just as a soap opera was interrupted for a special news event. This was the promised FBI news conference. Web scooted forward and adjusted the picture and sound.

Web gaped as Percy Bates appeared at the podium. Where the hell was Buck Winters? Web thought. He listened as Bates ran through Web's distinguished career at the FBI and some feel-good film was shown of Web accepting various awards, medals and citations from the Bureau heads and one from the President himself. Bates spoke of the horror in the courtyard and Web's bravery and grit in doing what he had done when confronted with such an overwhelming foe.

One shot was of Web in the hospital with half his face bandaged. This made Web reach up and touch the old wound. He felt proud and cheap at the same time. He suddenly wished Bates had not done this. This "promo" wasn't going to change anyone's mind. It just made him seem defensive. The journalists would crucify him, probably accuse the Bureau of covering their ass by shielding one of their own. And maybe, in a way, they were. He let out a low moan. He didn't think it could get any worse, yet it just had. He turned off the TV, sat there and closed his eyes. In his mind he felt a hand on his shoulder, but there was no one there. This seemed to always happen to him when he came here; his mother's presence was everywhere.

Charlotte London had kept until her death the shoulder-length hair that had over the years turned from glorious, sexy blond to elegant, luxurious silver. Her skin had been unwrinkled because she was allergic to the sun and had covered herself from it all her life. And her neck had been long and smooth with tight muscles set at the base. Web wondered how many men had been seduced by that delicate but overpowering curve. When he was a teenager Web had had dreams about his young, sexy mother that to this day he still felt shame for.

Despite the drinking and less-than-healthy eating habits, his mother had not gained an ounce in forty years and the weight had remained pretty much in its original locations. When she really put herself together, she had been a knockout at age fifty-nine. It was too bad that her liver had given out. The rest of her could have kept going for a while longer.

As beautiful as she had been, it was her intellect that attracted most people. Yet the conversations between mother and son had been downright bizarre. His mother did not watch TV. "They call it an idiot box for good reason," she had often said. "I'd rather read Camus. Or Goethe. Or Jean Genet. Genet makes me laugh and cry at the same time, and I don't really know why, for there is arguably nothing humorous about Genet. His subject matter was vile. Depraved. So much suffering. Mostly autobiographical."

"Right. Sure, Genet, Goethe," Web had told her several years before. "G-men, like me, sort of." His mother had never gotten the joke.

"But they can be wonderfully compelling—erotic, even," she had said.

"What can?" he had asked.

"Vileness and depravity."

Web had taken a deep breath. He had wanted to tell her that he'd seen some vileness and depravity in his time that would have made old Jean Genet barf up his lunch. He had wanted to un-equivocally inform his mother that these evils were nothing to joke about, because one day somebody filled to the brim with vileness and depravity might appear on her doorstep and violently end her life. Instead he had remained silent. His mother had often had that effect on him.

Charlotte London had been a child prodigy, astounding folks with her broad-ranging intellect. She had entered college at age fourteen and earned a degree in American literature from Amherst, graduating near the top of her class. She had spoken four foreign languages fluently. After college Charlotte had traveled the world alone for almost a year, Web knew, because he had seen the photos and read her journals. And that was back in the days when young women didn't do that sort of thing. She had even written a book chronicling her adventures, and the book was still selling to this day. Its title was *London Times*; London had been her maiden name, and she had changed it back after her second husband had died. She had had Web's surname legally changed from Sullivan after she had divorced her first husband. Web had never carried his stepfather's name. His mother would not allow it. It was just how she was. And to this day he never knew why he had been given such an odd name as Web with only the one *b*. He had gone up and down his maternal family tree and the answer wasn't there. His mother had steadfastly refused even to tell Web who had named him.

When he had been little, his mother had shared with Web much of what she had seen and done on her teenage travels, and he had thought hers the most wonderful stories he had ever heard. And he had wanted to go on trips with her just like that and write in his journal and take photos of his beautiful, adventurous mother against the backdrop of pristine water in Italy or on a snowcapped mountain in Switzerland or at an outdoor café in Paris. The beautiful mother and the dashing son taking the world by storm had dominated his boyhood thoughts. But then she had married Web's stepfather and those dreams went away.

Web opened his eyes and rose. He went to the basement first. Thick dust covered every surface, and Web found nothing remotely close to what he was looking for. He went back upstairs and into the rear of the house where the kitchen was. He opened the back door and looked outside at the small garage that housed, among other things, his mother's ancient Plymouth Duster. Web could hear the cries of children at play nearby. He closed his eyes and rested his face against the mesh as those sounds sank in. In his mind Web could almost see the football being thrown, the coltish legs hustling after it, a very young Web thinking that if he didn't catch that ball, his life would end. He sniffed the air, the smell of wood smoke mingling with the sweet aroma of freshly cut fall grass. There was nothing better, it seemed, and yet it was only a scent, never lasting for very long. And then you were pretty much right back in the shit of life. The shit, he had discovered, was never temporary.

In his vision, the young Web ran harder and harder. It was growing dark and he knew his mother would be calling him in soon. Not to eat, but to run over to the neighbors to bum cigarettes for his stepfather. Or to hustle down to the neighborhood Foodway with a couple dollars and a sad tale for Old Man Stein, who ran the place with a bigger heart than he should have. Always hustling down to the Foodway was young Web. Always singing the sad Irish song, his mother coaching him on the lyrics. Where had she learned it, the sad song? Web had asked her. As with the origin of his given name, she had never answered him.

Web could vividly remember Mr. Stein squatting down with his big glasses, old cardigan and neat white apron and graciously accepting the crumpled dollar bills from "Webbie" London, as he liked to call Web. Then he would help Web pick out food for supper and maybe even breakfast. These groceries, of course, always cost far more than two dollars, and yet Stein had never said a word about the cost. Yet he had not been so reserved about other things.

"You tell your mother not to drink so much," he had called after Web as he had run off home carrying two bulging bags of groceries. "And you tell that devil of a husband of hers that God will strike him down for what he has done, if a man's hand does not do so sooner. And if only God would allow me that honor. I pray for it every night, Webbie. You tell her that. And *him* too!" Old Man Stein was in love with Web's mother, as were just about all the men in the neighborhood, married or not. In fact, the only man who didn't seem to be in love with Charlotte London was the man she was married to.

He went upstairs and stared at the attic pull-down stairs in the middle of the hallway. This was where he should have started his search, of course, but he did not want to go up there. He finally grabbed the rope pull, hauled down the stairs and climbed up. He clicked on the light, his gaze darting to every darkened corner as soon as he did so. Web took another deep breath and told himself that simpering cowards rarely accomplished anything with their lives, that he was a big, brave HRT assaulter with a loaded nine-millimeter in his holster. He moved into the attic and spent an hour compulsively going through more elements of his history than he really cared to.

The school yearbooks were here with the awkward pictures of boys and girls trying to look older than they were, when only a few short years would pass before they would desperately be trying to do the opposite. He also spent time deciphering the yearbook scribbles from classmates outlining lavish plans for their futures, which had not come true for any of them that Web knew of, including himself. His old varsity jacket and his football helmet were there in a box. There was a time when he could remember where every scratch on the helmet came from. Now he couldn't even remember the jersey number he had worn. There were old and useless schoolbooks, journals that had nothing in them but stupid pictures drawn by bored hands. *His* bored hands.

In one corner was a clothes rack with garments from the last four decades gathering dust, mold and moth holes. There were also old records warped in the heat and cold. There were boxes of baseball and football trading cards that might now be worth a tidy fortune if Web hadn't used them as targets for dart games and BB shooting. There were pieces of a bicycle Web vaguely remembered owning, along with a half dozen burned-out flashlights. There was also a clay figurine his mother had sculpted, and quite well; but it had been bashed around so much by his stepfather that the figure was now not only blind but also lacking ears and a nose.

It was all a sad memorial to a quite ordinary family that actually had been anything but ordinary in certain ways.

Web was thinking of giving up when he found it.

The box was under a collection of his mother's college books, the works of long-dead philosophers and writers and thinkers. Web quickly looked through the box's contents. It was enough to start with. He would be one poor investigator if he couldn't follow it up to something. He was surprised he had never noticed it before while growing up in this house. But he had never been looking for it back then.

He jerked around and stared at the farthest corner from him. It was dark, shadowy and he could almost swear something had moved there. His hand eased to his gun. He hated this attic. Hated it! And yet he didn't really know why. It was just a damn attic.

He carried the box to his car and on the way back to his motel Web used his cell phone to call Percy Bates. "Nice job, Perce. What a difference a day makes. But what happened to old Bucky?"

"Winters backed out at the last minute."

"Right. In case I go crashing down. And so he left you to do it for him."

"I actually volunteered when he waffled on it."

"You're a good guy, Perce, but you'll never rise higher in the Bureau if you keep doing the right thing."

"Like I give a crap about that."

"Any breaks?"

"We traced the guns. Stolen from a military facility in Virginia. Two years ago. Big help. But we'll chase it down every path until it dies on us."

"Any sign of Kevin Westbrook?"

"None. And no other witnesses have come forward. Apparently everyone down that way was struck deaf and dumb."

"I guess you've talked to the people Kevin lived with. Anything come out of that?"

"Not much. They haven't seen him. Like I said, he avoided that place anyway."

Web chose his next words carefully. "So nobody to love the kid? No old lady or grandmother lying around?"

"There is an old woman. And we think she's Kevin's mother's stepmother or something like that. She wasn't real clear on the relation either. You'd think it'd be pretty simple to say one way or another, but talk about your extended families. Dads in prisons, moms gone, brothers dead, sisters hookers, you got babies dropped off everywhere with anybody who looks halfway respectable, and that's usually the older folks. She seemed genuinely worried about the boy, but she's scared too. They're all scared down there."

"Perce, did you ever actually see Kevin before he went missing?"

"Why?"

"I'm trying to put together a time line between when I last saw him and when he disappeared."

"A time line. Damn, wish I'd thought of that," Bates said sarcastically.

"Come on, Perce, I'm not trying to step on anybody's toes, but I saved that boy's life and I'd kind of like him to keep it."

"Web, you know the likelihood of the kid turning up alive is pretty damn slim. Whoever took him wasn't planning a surprise party at Chuck E. Cheese's for the boy. We've searched every place we can think of. Got APBs out in all the surrounding states, and even on the Canadian and Mexican borders. It's not like they'd hang around the city with the kid."

"But if he was working for his brother, he might be safe. I mean, I understand this Big F is one mean bastard, but popping your little brother? Come on."

"I've seen worse and so have you."

"But did you see Kevin?"

"No, no, I didn't personally see the kid. He was gone before I got there. There, you satisfied?"

"I spoke with the HRT guys who were babysitting him. They said they turned him over to a couple of FBI suits." Web had decided not to mention Romano's statement that actually only *one* man had been definitively involved, because he wanted to hear Bates's take on it.

"You'll be no doubt stunned that I talked to them too and found out the same thing."

"They couldn't tell me the names of the agents. Any luck there?"

"It's a little early in the game."

Web now gave up any pretense of congeniality. "No, it's really not, Perce. I spent a lot of years doing what you do. I know how these cases go down. If you can't tell me by now who the suits were, that means they weren't FBI. That means a couple of impostors got inside an FBI crime scene, *your* crime scene, and made off with a key witness. Maybe I can help."

"That's your theory. And I don't want or need your help."

"Are you telling me I'm wrong?"

"What I'm going to tell you is to keep the hell out of my investigation. And I mean what I say."

"It was my damn team!"

"I understand that, but if I find out you're doing anything, asking one question, following up one lead on your own, then your ass is mine. I hope I'm making myself clear."

"I'll call you when I crack the case."

Web clicked off and quietly berated himself for blowing his last asset at the Bureau. He had been as subtle as a dump truck, but Bates just seemed to bring out the bulldog in folks. And to think he had originally called merely to thank the guy for the press conference!

20

Claire stretched her arms and stifled a yawn. She had been up too early and had worked too late the night before; such had become her life's routine. Married at nineteen to her high-school sweetheart, she had been a mother at twenty and divorced at twenty-two. The sacrifices she had made over the next ten years while she pursued her medical and psychiatric degrees were too numerous for her to recall. Yet she had no regrets about her daughter, now a freshman in college. Maggie Daniels was healthy, bright and well adjusted. Her father had wanted no part in his daughter's upbringing and he would be given no role in her adulthood either. Actually, that was up to Maggie, Claire knew, but she had never asked much about her dad and had taken single parenting in stride. Claire had never really gotten back into the social circles and she had finally come to the conclusion that her career would be her life.

She opened her file and studied the notes she had made there. Web London was a fascinating subject for any student of human psychology. From the little Claire had gathered before his very abrupt departure from her office, the man was a walking billboard of personal problems. From the obvious issues in his childhood to his disfigurement as an adult to the sort of dangerous work that he did and seemed to derive so much from, a person could devote her professional life to such a patient. The knock on her door interrupted her thoughts.

"Yes?"

The door opened and one of Claire's colleagues stood there. "You might want to come and see this."

"What is it, Wayne? I'm kind of busy."

"FBI press conference. Web London. I saw him leaving here the other day. You counseled him, right?"

She frowned at his question and didn't answer it. But she got up and followed him out to the reception area, where there was a little TV set up. Several other of the psychiatrists and psychologists who had offices here, including Ed O'Bannon, were already assembled and watching the screen. It was lunchtime and none of them appeared to have patients. Several of them held parts of their meals in their hands.

For the next ten minutes or so, Claire Daniels got a much more in-depth look at the life and career of Web London. She found herself putting her hand up to her mouth when she saw Web in the hospital, most of his face and torso bandaged. The man had been through a lot, more than someone should have to go through. And Claire was feeling an incredibly strong urge to help him, despite how dramatically he had ended their session. When the press conference was over and people started to filter back to their offices, Claire stopped O'Bannon.

"Ed, you remember I told you about seeing Web London when you weren't available?"

"Sure, Claire. I appreciate you doing that, actually." He lowered his voice. "Unlike some of the others around here, I know I can trust you not to pilfer my patients."

"Well, I appreciate that, Ed. But the truth is I've taken a particular interest in Web. And he and I really hit it off at our session." She added very firmly: "And I want to take over his counseling."

O'Bannon looked stunned and shook his head. "No, Claire. I've seen London before, and he's a bit of a tough nut. He and I never really finished exploring it, but he seems to have serious mother-son issues."

"I understand all that, but I really want to work on his case."

"And I appreciate that, but he's my patient and there is something to be said for continuity of treatment, starting with keeping the same doctor."

Claire took a deep breath and said, "Can we let Web decide?"

"Excuse me?"

"Can you call him and let Web decide on which of us he'd prefer?"

O'Bannon looked very annoyed. "I hardly think that's necessary."

"We really seemed to click, Ed, and I think that perhaps another pair of eyes on his case might be beneficial."

"I'm not liking what you're insinuating, Claire. My credentials are impeccable. In case you didn't know, I served in Vietnam, where I dealt with combat syndrome cases, shell shock, prisoners of war who'd been brainwashed, and I was very successful."

"Web is not in the military."

"HRT is about as military as you can get for a civilian agency. I know the breed and I speak their language. I think my experience is uniquely suited to his case."

"I'm not implying anything to the contrary. But Web did tell me that he wasn't completely comfortable with you. And I know you would agree that the best interests of the patient are paramount."

"I don't need you to lecture me on professional ethics." He paused for a moment. "But he said that—that he wasn't completely comfortable with me?"

"Yes, but I think that's more a reflection on the fact that you're right, he is a tough nut. For all I know, he may not like me once we get going in treatment." She touched O'Bannon on the shoulder. "So you'll call him? Today?"

O'Bannon grudgingly said, "I'll call him."

Web was driving when his phone rang. He checked the readout on the screen. It was a number in Virginia he didn't recognize.

"Hello?" he answered cautiously.

"Web?"

The voice seemed very familiar, but nothing clicked.

"It's Dr. O'Bannon."

Web blinked. "How did you get this number?"

"You gave it to me. During our most recent session."

"Look, I've been thinking that—"

"Web, I talked to Claire Daniels."

Web felt his face growing warm. "Did she tell you we talked?"

"She did. But she didn't tell me what you had talked about, of course. I understand that you were in a bit of crisis and Claire tried to get hold of me before talking to you. That's really why I'm calling."

"I'm not exactly following this."

"Well, Claire said that you two really seemed to hit it off. She seemed to think that maybe you would be more comfortable with her. Since you're my patient, you and I need to consent to such an arrangement."

"Look, Dr. O'Bannon—"

"Web, I want you to know that we were successful in the past in dealing with your issues and I think we can be again. Claire probably was just embellishing somewhat on your uncertainty about me. But just so you know, Claire does not have the experience I do. I've been seeing FBI agents for longer than she has. I don't like to say this, but between you and me, Claire would be out of her league with you." He paused, apparently awaiting Web's answer. "So, we're good, you'll continue to see me?"

"I'll go with Claire."

"Web, come on!"

"I want Claire."

O'Bannon was silent for a bit. "Are you sure?" he finally said curtly.

"I'm sure."

"Then I'll have Claire get in contact with you. I hope you two click," he added brusquely.

The line went dead and Web continued driving. Two minutes passed and the phone rang again. It was Claire Daniels.

"I guess you feel like quite the pursued man," she said in a disarming tone.

"It's nice to be popular."

"I like to finish what I start, Web, even if it means upsetting a colleague."

"Claire, I appreciate everything, and I know I told O'Bannon it was okay, but—"

"Please, Web, I think I can help you. At least I'd like to try."

He thought about this for a bit as he stared over at the cardboard box. What treasures did it hold? "Can I reach you at this number?"

"I'll be here until five."

"After that?"

He pulled into a gas station and wrote down Claire's cell and home phone. He said he'd call her back later and clicked off. Web punched the numbers into his phone's memory, pulled back onto the road and tried to think all this through. What he didn't like was that she was trying really hard, maybe too hard.

Web drove back to the motel room. He checked his messages at home. A few people who had seen the press conference had called to wish him well. And an equal number of voices he didn't recognize were basically telling him that they wanted to punch him in his cowardly, messed-up face. Once Web thought he heard Julie Patterson's voice and kids bawling in the background, but he couldn't be sure. He wouldn't exactly be at the top of the woman's phone list.

He sat on the floor with his back to the wall and suddenly felt so sorry for Julie he started to shake. Sure, things were going rough for him right now, but that would blow over. She had the rest of her life to work through, with the weight of a lost husband and child forever around her neck and four young kids to raise on her own. She was a survivor, like Web. And survivors hurt the most of all, for they had to pick up the pieces somehow and go right on living.

He dialed the number and a child answered. It was the oldest, Lou, Jr., all of eleven years old and the man of the house now.

"Louie, is your mom in? It's Web."

There was a long pause. "Did you get our dad killed, Web?"

"No, I didn't, Louie. You know better than that. But we're going to find out who did it. Go get your mom, son," he added firmly.

Web heard the boy plunk down the phone and walk off. While he waited, Web felt himself start trembling once more, for he had absolutely no idea what he would say to the woman. His nervousness grew as he heard footsteps approaching the phone and then it was picked up, but the person said nothing.

"Julie?" he finally said.

"What do you want, Web?" Her voice was tired. Ironically, the weary tone was more painful to Web than her angry screams at the church.

"I wanted to see if there was anything I could do to help."

"There's nothing you or anybody else can do."

"You should have somebody with you. It's not good to be alone right now."

"My sister and mother came down from Newark."

Web took a breath. Well, that was good. Julie at least sounded calm, rational. "We're going to find who did this, Julie. If it takes the rest of my life. I just want you to know that. Lou and the others meant everything to me."

"You do what you need to do, but that won't bring them back, Web."

"Did you see the press conference on TV today?"

"No. And please don't call again." She hung up.

Web sat there while he absorbed this. It wasn't that he had actually expected her to say she was sorry about trashing him the other day. That was far too much to expect. What bothered Web was that he felt dismissed by her. *Please don't call again?* Maybe the other wives felt the same way. Neither Debbie nor Cynde nor any of the others had contacted him to see how he was doing. Then again, he reminded himself, their loss was much greater than his. They had lost their husbands. He had just lost his friends. He supposed there was an enormous difference. It was just in his case there didn't seem to be.

He ran across the street to a 7-Eleven and bought a cup of coffee. It had started to drizzle and the temperature had dropped. What had started as a beautiful warm day now was gray and wet, so common for this area, and so reinforcing for his suicidal spirits.

Web returned to his room, sat on the floor and opened the cardboard box. The documents were musty, some mildewed, the few photos yellowed and torn. And yet he was enthralled by it all, for he had never seen these things before. Partly it was because he had never known his mother had kept these items from her first marriage. And he had also never searched the house for them before either. Why not, he wasn't sure. Perhaps his relationship with his stepfather had smothered all interest Web had in dads.

He arranged the photos fanlike on the floor and then examined them. His father, Harry Sullivan, had been a handsome man. Very tall and broad-shouldered, he had wavy dark hair worn in a greased pompadour and possessed a confident look as he stared out from the photo. He looked like a 1940s-era film star, young and commanding, with a mischievous gleam in his blue eyes. Web could see how Harry Sullivan could be attractive to a young woman who was naive perhaps despite her intelligence and her world travels. Web wondered what his father would look like now, after years in prison, after decades of what he assumed was a fast life to nowhere.

In another photo, Sullivan had his arm around Charlotte's tiny waist. The man's arm was so long it curled around her torso and his fingers were placed just under her breasts, maybe even touching them. They looked very happy. Indeed, Charlotte London in her pleated skirt and flip hairstyle looked more beautiful, more enchanting and more excited to be alive than Web had ever seen her. Yet that was part of youth, he supposed. They hadn't experienced the hard times yet. Web touched his cheek. No, the hard times weren't great, and they didn't necessarily always make you stronger. Looking at her so full of life, Web had a hard time believing that the woman was actually dead.

As the rain started to pour harder outside, Web sat in his motel room and sipped his coffee and looked at some of the other items. He fingered the Sullivans' marriage certificate. Web was surprised his mom had kept that. Then again, it *was* her first marriage, however awry it might have gone. His father's signature was surprisingly small for such a big, confident-looking man. And the letters were badly formed, as though old Harry were embarrassed by the exercise of signing his name, unsure of how to make out the letters. An uneducated man, Web concluded.

He laid down the certificate and picked up another slip of paper. A letter. At the top was the heading of a correctional facility in Georgia. The date of the letter was a year after mother and son had fled the convict that the husband and father had become. The letter was typewritten, but Harry Sullivan's signature appeared at the bottom. And this signature was written bolder, the letters larger and more exactly formed, as though the man had been really working at it. But then, he had had a lot of "free" time in prison.

The contents of the letter were brief. It took the form of an apology to Charlotte and Web. When he got out, he would be a changed man, he claimed. He would do right by them. Well, actually, the letter said that Harry Sullivan would *try* hard to fulfill all these promises. Web had to concede that it was perhaps brutal honesty on Sullivan's part, not an easy thing for a man rotting slowly in prison. Web had conducted enough interrogations to know that steel bars and big locks and no future as a free person tended to make people lie shamelessly if they thought it would help their cause. He wondered if the divorce papers had reached his father soon after he had sent the letter. What did that do to a man in prison? His freedom taken and then his wife and son gone too? It certainly didn't leave a person with much. Web had never faulted his mother for doing what she did, and he didn't fault her now. Yet these little snippets of his family history made him feel a little sorry for Harry Sullivan, wherever he might be, dead or alive.

Web put the letter aside and spent the next couple of hours going through the other contents. Most were items completely useless to him in tracking down his father, yet Web spent time over them all, if just to get a better feel for the man. His hand closed around two objects that promised a lead. One was an expired driver's license that had his father's photo on it, and the other, more importantly, was his Social Security card. These opened up all sorts of possibilities. Web also had another angle to work.

He swallowed his pride, called Percy Bates and apologized to an almost embarrassing degree. Then he told him Harry Sullivan's name, Social Security number and a guesstimate of the dates of Sullivan's incarceration in the Georgia prison. Web had thought about calling Ann Lyle with this request but he didn't want to go to that well too often. Ann had enough to do, and HRT really needed her full attention right now. Besides, she hadn't gotten back to Web yet on Cove, and he didn't want her to feel pressured.

"Who is this guy?" Bates wanted to know.

When Web had applied to join the Bureau, he had had to put down his real father's name, and the investigators had wanted further particulars. He had asked his mother back then to supply more information on the man, but she had absolutely refused to discuss it. Web had told the investigators he didn't know the whereabouts of his father and had no information to help them track him down. As far as he knew, that had been the end of it. He had passed the background check and was off and running in his FBI career. His last contact with his father had been at age six, and the Bureau couldn't exactly hold it against Web that his father was a con.

"Just some guy I need to find," Web told Bates. Web knew that the Bureau was very thorough in its background checks and could very well have information about Web's father. Web had just never felt inclined to check the file over the years. And yet Bates might know that Harry Sullivan was Web's father. If so, he was lying very well.

"Any connection to the investigation?"

"No, like you said, that's off-limits, but I'd really appreciate the favor."

Bates said he'd see what he could do and then hung up.

Web packed the box away and slid it into a corner. He pulled out his cell phone and dialed his voice mail again. He had been obsessive about it since the courtyard and not really sure why. When he heard the voice, he was glad he was so diligent. Debbie Riner wanted to know if Web could come to dinner tonight. He immediately called her back and said he would. She had seen the piece on TV. "I never had any doubts, Web," she said. He let out a long breath. Life seemed a lot better right now.

He brought up the number he wanted on the phone screen. It was after five, so Claire Daniels wouldn't be at her office. His finger hesitated over the button. And then he called her. She was in her car heading home, she told him. "I can see you first thing in the morning. Nine A.M.,"she said.

"So, you've got all my problems solved?"

"I'm efficient, but I'm not that quick." He found himself smiling at this remark. "I appreciate you letting me counsel you. I know change is hard."

"Change I can handle, Claire. It's the going crazy part that's bothering me. I'll see you at nine."

21

The dinner with Debbie Riner and her children did not go nearly as well as Web had hoped. Carol Garcia was there too, with one of her kids. They sat around the dining room table, made small talk and mostly avoided matters having to do with the total destruction of their lives. When the Garcias made the sign of the cross on their chests, Web thought about what he told Danny Garcia before every mission. Web had been right, for God had not been with them that night. Yet all Web said was, "Would you pass the potatoes, please?"

HRT operators didn't really encourage support groups among their wives. In some cases it was because they didn't want their spouses to gossip among themselves about their husbands. Operators showed many sides of themselves at training and during missions, and not all good ones. An inadvertent slip by one of them to his wife could spread like wildfire among the women if they seriously networked. In other cases it was to discourage the wives from collectively worrying themselves to death, swapping incorrect information, speculation and outright falsehoods generated by fear of where their husbands were, how long they would be gone, whether they were dead.

The kids poked at their food, slouched in their seats and clearly did not want to be there. They treated Web, who had been their bosom friend, playing and joking and watching them grow up, like they had no idea who he even was. Everyone, even Debbie Riner's seven-year-old daughter, who had loved Web from almost the day she was born, looked relieved when he said his good-byes.

"Keep in touch," Debbie said, pecking him on the cheek. Carol merely waved to him from a safe distance, while she clutched her glassy-eyed son to her wide hips.

"You bet, sure thing," Web said. "Take care. Thanks for dinner. You need anything, just let me know." He drove off in the Vic, knowing he would most likely never see them again. Time to move on, that was clearly the message of the dinner.

At nine sharp the next morning Web stepped into Claire Daniels's world. Ironically, the first person he saw was Dr. O'Bannon.

"Web, good to see you. Would you like some coffee?"

"I know where it is. I'll get it, thanks."

"You know, Web, I was in Vietnam. Never under fire, I was a psychiatrist back then too. But I saw a lot of guys who were. Things happen in combat, things you never think will. But you know what, you'll probably be stronger for it. And I worked with POWs who'd been tortured by the damn Viet Cong. It's terrible what they were put through, classic physical and mental manipulation, ostracizing troublemakers, robbing them of every scrap of moral and physical support. Controlling their lives down to the position of their sleep, turning each individual against the other in the name of the group, as it was defined by their captors. Now, of course it's not ethical for one psychiatrist to poach patients off the other, although, frankly, I was a little surprised about what happened with Claire. But I think Claire would agree that the paramount issue here is your best interest, Web. So if you ever change your mind about working with Claire, I'm here for you." He slapped Web on the back, gave what Web assumed was intended to be an encouraging look and walked off.

Claire came out of her office a few moments later, saw him and they made their coffees together. They watched as a uniformed repairman with a box of tools came out of the closet housing the office's electrical and phone lines and left.

"Problems?" asked Web.

"I don't know, I just came in," answered Claire.

As they were making their coffees Web checked the woman out. Claire was wearing a blouse and knee-length skirt that showed off nice tanned calves and ankles, but her hair, though short, was in a bit of disarray. She seemed to note Web's observation and swiped at the errant strands.

"I've been fast-walking around the building in the mornings to get a little exercise. Wind and humidity aren't really good for hair." She took a sip of her coffee and added some more sugar. "You ready?"

"As ready as I'll ever be."

Once in her office Claire perused two files for a bit while Web stared over at a pair of sneakers in the corner. Probably what she fast-walked in. He looked over at her nervously.

"First of all, Web, I want to thank you for having enough confidence in me to let me take over your treatment."

"I'm not really sure why I did," he said candidly.

"Well, whatever the reason, I'm going to work hard to make sure your decision was a good one. Dr. O'Bannon wasn't very happy about it, but the primary concern is you." She held up a small file. "This is the file Dr. O'Bannon gave me when I took over your case."

Web attempted a weak smile. "I would've thought it would have been thicker."

"Actually, I was thinking the same thing," was Claire's surprising reply. "It shows the notes from a number of standard sessions; he prescribed various medications, antidepressants, again nothing out of the ordinary."

"So? Is that good or bad?"

"Good, if it helped you, and I'm assuming it did, since you returned to a productive life."

"But?"

"But maybe your case deserves a little more digging. I have to tell you that I am surprised that he didn't hypnotize you. He's very skilled at that, and that is usually part of his course of treatment. In fact, O'Bannon teaches a course at GW, where every third or fourth year he hypnotizes a student and does things like making them block out a letter from the alphabet so they'll look at the word 'cat' on the blackboard and pronounce it 'at.' Or make them believe a gnat is flying around their ear, things like that. We do that as part of a routine to demonstrate visual- and auditory-induced hallucinations."

"I remember we talked about it the first time I saw him years ago. I didn't want to do it, so we didn't," he said flatly.

"I see." She held up a much thicker folder. "Your official Bureau file, or at least part of it," she said in response to his inquisitive look.

"So I gathered. I thought they kept that confidential."

"You signed a release when you agreed to counseling. The file is routinely given to the therapist for help in treatment minus any top-secret or other sensitive information, of course. Dr. O'Bannon transferred the file to me when you became my patient. I've been going over it thoroughly."

"Good for you." Web cracked his knuckles and looked at her expectantly.

"You didn't mention in our initial interview that your stepfather, Raymond Stockton, died from a fall in the house when you were fifteen."

"Didn't I? Huh, I thought I did. But you didn't take notes, so you have no way of checking, do you?"

"Trust me, Web, I would've remembered that. You also told me you got along with your stepfather, didn't you?" She looked down at the papers.

Web felt his heart rate accelerate and his ears burn. Her interrogation technique was classic. She had baselined him and had just now jerked his chain using a five-hundred-pound gorilla for added leverage. "We had some differences, who doesn't?"

"There are page after page of assault claims in here. Some filed by neighbors, some by you. All against Raymond Stockton. Is that what you refer to as 'some differences'?" He flushed angrily and she quickly added, "I'm not being sarcastic, I just want to try and understand your relationship with the man."

"There's nothing to understand because we didn't have a relationship."

Claire consulted her notes again, flipping back and forth, and Web watched every movement with growing anxiety.

"Is the house that your mother left you the same one where Stockton died?" Web didn't say anything. "Web? Is it the same—"

"I heard you!" he snapped. "Yeah, it's the same one, so what?"

"I was just asking. So, do you think you're going to sell it?"

"Why do you care? Do you do real estate on the side?"

"I'm just getting a sense that you seem to have issues about the house."

"It wasn't a real nice place to have a childhood."

"I understand that completely, but often to get better and move on you must confront your fears head-on."

"There's nothing in that house I need to confront."

"Why don't we talk about it some more?"

"Look, Claire, this is getting pretty far afield, isn't it? I came to you because my team got blown away and it's messed me up. Let's stick to that! Forget the past. Forget the house and let's just forget fathers. They've got nothing to do with me or who I am."

"On the contrary, they have a great deal to do with who you are. Without understanding your past I can't help with your present or your future. It's that simple."

"Why don't you give me some damn pills and we'll call it a day, okay? That way the Bureau's satisfied that I did my little mind massage and you did your job."

Claire shook her head. "I don't work that way, Web. I want to help you. I think I can help you. But you have to work with me. I can't compromise on that."

"I thought you said I had combat syndrome or something. What does that have to do with my stepfather?"

"We merely talked about that being one possibility for what happened to you in that alley. I didn't say that it was the only possibility. We need to thoroughly explore all angles if we're to really address your issues."

"Issues—you make it sound so simple. Like I'm moping about having acne."

"We can use another term if you prefer, but it really won't affect how we approach the problems."

Web covered his face with his hands and then spoke through this shield. "What the hell exactly do you want from me?"

"Honesty, to the extent you can give it. And I think you can, if you really try. You have to trust me, Web."

Web removed his hands. "Okay, here's the truth. Stockton was a creep. Pills and a boozer. He never got past the sixties, apparently. He held some low-level office job where he got to wear a suit to work and fancied himself another Dylan Thomas on his off-hours."

"So what you're telling me is he was some sort of frustrated dreamer, perhaps even a phony?"

"He wanted to be more of an intellectual and more talented than my mother, and he wasn't, not by miles. His poetry was for shit; he never got anything published. The only thing he had in common with old Dylan was the fact that he drank too much. I guess he thought the bottle would inspire him."

"So he beat your mother?" She tapped the file.

"Is that what it says in the file?"

"Actually, what it doesn't say in the file is even more interesting. Your mother never filed charges against Stockton."

"Well, I guess we have to believe the record, then."

"Did he beat your mother?" she asked again, and once more Web didn't answer. "Or did he just beat you?" Web slowly lifted his gaze to her, yet still said nothing. "So just you? And your mother let this occur?"

"Charlotte wasn't around a lot. She'd made a mistake in marrying this guy. She knew it, so she avoided it."

"I see. I guess divorce wasn't an option."

"She'd done that once. I don't think she felt like bothering with it again. It was easier just to drive off into the night."

"And she left you with a man who she knew abused you? And how did that make you feel?"

Web said nothing.

"Did you ever talk to her about it? To let her know how it made you feel?"

"Wouldn't have done any good. To her, the guy never existed."

"Meaning she repressed the memory?"

"Meaning whatever the hell you want it to mean. We never talked about it."

"Were you home when your stepfather died?"

"Maybe, I don't really remember. I've sort of repressed it too."

"The file just said your stepfather fell. How did he fall?"

"From the top of the attic stairs. He kept his secret stash of mind goodies up in the attic. He was wigged out, missed a step, cracked his head on the edge of the opening going down and broke his neck when he hit the floor. The police investigated and it was ruled an accidental death."

"Was your mother home when it happened, or had she gone out on one of her *drives*?"

"What, are you pretending you're an FBI agent now?"

"Just trying to understand the situation."

"Charlotte was home. She was the one who called the ambulance. But like I said, he was already dead."

"Have you always called your mother by her first name?"

"Seems appropriate."

"I imagine you had to feel relief at Stockton's death."

"Let's put it this way, I didn't cry at the funeral."

Claire leaned forward and spoke in a very low voice. "Web, this next question is going to be very difficult, and if you don't want to answer it now, fine. But in instances of parental abuse, I have to address it."

Web held up both hands. "He never touched my private parts, and he never made me touch his private parts, okay? Nothing like that. They asked back then and I told the truth back then. The guy wasn't a molester. He was just a cruel, sadistic asshole who made up for a lifetime of insecurities and disappointments by beating the shit out of a boy. If he had messed with me like that, I would've found a way to kill him myself." Web realized what he had just said and hastily added, "But the guy saved everybody the trouble by taking his tumble."

Claire sat back and put aside the file. This small measure relieved Web's anxiety somewhat and he sat up. She said, "You obviously remember your time with your stepfather and loathed it for good reason. Have you thought more about any memories with your natural father?"

"Fathers are fathers."

"Meaning what, you lump your real father and Raymond Stock-ton together?"

"Saves the trouble of thinking about it too much, doesn't it?"

"The easy way out usually solves nothing."

"I wouldn't know where to begin, Claire, I really wouldn't."

"All right, let's go back to the courtyard for a bit. I know it'll be painful, but let's go through it again."

Web did so and it was painful.

"All right, the first group of people you met, you don't remember that having any sort of effect on you?"

"Nothing other than wondering if one of them would try to kill us or tip somebody off, but I knew the snipers had them covered. So other than the potential of instant death, everything was cool."

If she was put off by his sarcasm, the woman didn't show it. That actually impressed Web.

"All right, in your mind's eye, picture the little boy. Do you re-member any better exactly what he said?"

"Is that really important?"

"At this stage we really don't know what's important and what's not."

Web sighed heavily and said, "Okay. I saw the kid. He looked at us. He said . . ." Web stopped here because he could see Kevin clearly in his mind. The bullet hole in his cheek, the slash across his forehead, he was a little wreck of a kid who had obviously al-ready lived a long, crappy life. "He said . . . he said, 'Damn to hell,' that's what he said." He looked at her excitedly. "That's it. Oh, and then he laughed. I mean, this really weird laugh, like a cackle, really."

"At which part did you feel affected?"

Web thought about this. "I'd have to say when he first spoke. I mean, it was like this fog pushed into my brain." Web added, "'Damn to hell,' that's exactly what he said. It's happening again, I can feel my fingers tingling. This is nuts."

Claire wrote some notes down and then looked at him. "That's pretty unusual for a young boy to use that phraseology, especially from the inner city. Certainly 'damn' and 'hell' would be used, but 'damn to hell'? I mean, it sounds sort of archaic, like from another era. Maybe Puritanical, fire and brimstone. What do you think about that?"

"To me it sounds like from the Civil War or around that time, actually," said Web.

"It's all very strange."

"Trust me, Claire, the whole night was strange."

"Did you feel anything else?"

Web thought hard. "We were waiting for final orders to hit the target. Then we got them." He shook his head. "As soon as I heard the orders in my earpiece, I froze. It was immediate. You remember I was telling you about the Taser guns we messed around with at HRT?" She nodded. "Well, it was like I'd been hit with one of those electrified darts. I couldn't move."

"Could someone have actually shot you with a Taser gun in the alley? Could that be why you froze?"

"Impossible. No one was that close, and the dart wouldn't have penetrated my Kevlar. And last but not least, the thing would've still been sticking in me, right?"

"Right." Claire made more notes and said, "Now, you stated before that even though you froze, you were able to actually get up and move into the courtyard."

"It was the hardest thing I've ever done in my life, Claire. It was like I weighed two thousand pounds, nothing on me was working right. And it finally won and I just fell and stayed there. And then the guns started up."

"When did you start to recover?"

Web thought about this. "It felt like years where I couldn't move. But it wasn't all that long. Right when the guns started firing, I felt everything start to come back. I could move my arms and legs, and they were burning like hell, like when your arm or leg falls asleep and the circulation starts going again? That's what my limbs felt like. And it wasn't like I needed them at that point, I pretty much had nowhere to go."

"So it just came back on its own? You don't remember doing something that might have paralyzed you? Maybe a back problem suffered in training? Have you ever had any nerve damage? That could immobilize you too."

"Nothing like that. If you're not in top-notch condition, you don't go on an operation."

"So you heard the guns firing and the feeling started to come back to your body?"

"Yes."

"Anything else?"

"The kid, I'd seen a million just like him. And yet he seemed different. I couldn't get him out of my head. It wasn't just that he'd been shot, I've seen kids like that too. I don't know. While the guns were firing I saw him again. He was crouched down next to the alley. Another step and he'd have been cut in half. I screamed for him to get back. I belly-crawled over to him. I could tell he was scared to death. He heard Hotel Team coming from one end, me from the other, these damn guns firing. And I could tell he was going to run for it, across the courtyard, and that'd be it. I just couldn't let that happen, Claire. So many people had already died that night. He jumped and I jumped and I caught him, got him calmed down because he was yelling that he hadn't done anything, and of course when a kid says that you know he's hiding something.

"Like I said, I got him calmed down. He asked if my team was dead and I told him yes. I gave him the note and my cap and shot the flare. I knew that was the only way Hotel wouldn't kill him coming at them in the dark. I just didn't want him to die, Claire."

"It must have been an awful night for you, but, Web, you should feel good about saving him."

"Should I? What did I save him for? To go back to the streets? See, this is a special little kid. He's got a brother named Big F who runs one of the local drug ops. He's bad news."

"So maybe all this could involve some of this Big F person's enemies?"

"Maybe." He paused and decided whether to reveal this or not. "Somebody switched kids. In the alley."

"Switched kids? What do you mean?"

"I mean the Kevin Westbrook that I saved in that alley was not the boy that delivered the note to Hotel Team. And the little boy that disappeared from the crime scene was not the Kevin Westbrook I saved."

"Why would somebody do that?"

"That's the sixty-four-thousand-dollar question, and it's driving me nuts. What I do know is I saved Kevin Westbrook's butt in that courtyard and the kid he was switched for told Hotel Team that I was this big coward. Why would he do that?"

"Sounds like he was almost trying to intentionally discredit you."

"A kid I didn't even know?" Web shook his head. "Somebody *was* trying to make me look bad, that's for sure, and must have told the kid just what to say. And then they waltzed right in and waltzed out with the fake kid. He's probably dead. Hell, Kevin's probably dead."

"Sounds like somebody put a lot of planning into this," said Claire.

"And I'd love to know why."

"We can only try, Web. I can help you with some of it, but the investigation part is way out of my bailiwick."

"It actually may be out of my league too. I haven't really been doing much detecting over the last eight years." He played with a ring on his finger. "O'Bannon gave me a little pep talk on combat syndrome when I came into the office this morning."

Claire hiked her eyebrows. "Oh, did he? His Vietnam angle?" She seemed to be trying hard not to smile.

"I didn't think it was the first time he'd used that line. But is that what you think it is—I mean, despite this other stuff with the kid?"

"I can't tell you that, Web, not yet."

"See, I know soldiers get that way. Folks shooting at them and they freak. Everybody can understand that."

She eyed him closely. "But?"

He started talking very quickly. "But most soldiers get a little boot camp and then they're thrown into the firestorm. They know *nothing* about killing somebody. They know nothing about what it's like to be in the line of fire for real. Me, I've trained most of my adult life to do this job. I've had stuff coming at me that you wouldn't believe, Claire. From machine gun fire to frigging mortar rounds that if they hit me there'd be nothing left of me. I've managed to kill men with most of the blood in my body pooling on the floor. And never once, not one damn time, did I ever lose it like I did that night. And there hadn't even been one damn shot fired at that point. Tell me, how the hell is that possible?"

"Web, I know that you're looking for answers. We have to keep plugging. But I can tell you that when we're dealing with the mind, anything is possible."

He stared at her, shaking his head and wondering where the hell he could get off whatever road he was on. "Well, Doc, that's not a whole lot of help, is it? How much is the Bureau paying you to tell me nothing?" He abruptly got up and left.

Once again Claire didn't try and stop him, not that she could have. She had had patients walk out on her before, although never during their first two sessions. Claire settled back in her chair and started going over notes and then picked up a recorder and started dictating.

Unknown to Claire, hidden in the smoke detector attached to the ceiling was a sophisticated listening device that ran off the building's electrical current and also had a battery backup. Every psychiatrist and psychologist who worked here had a similar listening device secretly housed in his office. The phone closet in the office housed additional electronic taps, one of which had broken down, prompting the "repairman's" visit that morning.

These prying ears had swept up enormous amounts of intelligence on every patient who had come through the doors. Over the last year over one hundred FBI agents from all divisions, including undercover, Public Corruption, WFO, uptown and HRT, and over twenty spouses of those personnel, had come here expecting the utmost confidentiality as they revealed their secrets and problems. They had received anything but that.

As soon as Web stormed out of the office, Ed O'Bannon slipped out as well, rode the elevator down to the garage, climbed in his brand-new Audi coupe and drove off. He picked up his cell phone and punched in a number. It took a few rings, but the phone was finally answered.

"Is this a good time?" he asked anxiously.

The party on the other end answered that it was as good as any if the conversation was short and to the point.

"London came here today."

"So I heard," said the voice. "My guy was there to repair a glitch. So how's it going with old Web?"

O'Bannon swallowed nervously. "He's seeing another psychiatrist." He quickly added, "I tried my best to stop it, but no go."

O'Bannon had to hold the phone away from his ear, so loud and angry was the response from the other person.

"Listen, it's not what I intended," said O'Bannon. "I couldn't believe he would actually see another psychiatrist. It came out of the blue. . . . What? Her name is Claire Daniels. She used to work for me. She's been here for years, very competent. Under other circumstances there wouldn't be a problem. I couldn't make too much of a stink without them getting suspicious."

The other person made a suggestion that caused O'Bannon to tremble. He pulled the car off the road. "No, killing her would only arouse suspicion. I know London. Too well, maybe. He's smart. If anything happens to Claire, he'll latch on to that and never let it go. That's just how he is. Trust me, I've worked with the man a long time. Remember, that's why you hired me."

"But that's not the only reason why," said the other person. "And we pay you well, Ed. Real well. And I don't like it one bit that he's seeing this Daniels chick."

"I've got it under control. If I know London, he'll come a few times and then blow the rest of it off. But if anything else comes of it, we'll know it. I'll keep on top of it."

"You better," said the other. "And the second you no longer have it under control is the time we step in." The line went dead and O'Bannon, looking very distraught, pulled back on the road and drove off.

22

Web had spent considerable time in the Vic cruising the streets near where the slaughter had taken place. He was on unpaid leave and not part of the official investigation. Thus he could request no backup, should he need it, nor did he have a clear idea of what he was looking for. The darkness of the streets was broken by the uniform glare of traffic lights. There were cameras at many of these intersections ostensibly to photograph drivers who ran red lights. However, Web thought they actually might be serving the dual purpose of surveillance devices in these high crime areas. He had to appreciate the ingenuity of the local criminals, though, because many of the cameras had been knocked out of their viewing lanes. Some pointed to the sky, others to the earth, a few at buildings, still others had been smashed. Well, so much for Big Brother.

Web kept checking messages at home. No more wives had called. Cynde and Debbie had probably worked the grapevine, informed the others that they had done the dirty work of getting him clear of all their lives. Web could almost hear the ladies' collective sigh.

Web had finally made another appointment to see Claire. She did not mention his parting insult and second abrupt exit from her office. She merely noted the time and said that she would see him then. The woman must have a really thick skin, he thought.

There were several other people in the waiting room when Web got there. None of them made eye contact and Web attempted none. He supposed that's the way it was in a shrink's waiting room. Who wanted strangers to see you attending to your insanity?

Claire came out and got him with a reassuring smile and handed him a fresh cup of coffee, the cream and sugar already in it, just like he liked it. They settled in her office.

Web slid a hand through his hair. "Look, Claire, I'm sorry about last time. I'm not usually that big a jerk. I know you're just trying to help and I know none of this is easy to figure out."

"Don't apologize for doing exactly what you should be doing, Web, which is getting all these thoughts and feelings out in the open so that you can deal with them."

He gave her a weak smile and said, "So where to today, Doc? Mars or Venus?"

"To start off with let's explore post-traumatic stress disorder and really see if it applies to your case."

Web inwardly smiled. Now, this he could handle. "Like shell shock?"

"That term is very often misused, and I want to get a little more precise. Now, clinically speaking, you have probably suffered traumatic stress with the events that transpired in that courtyard."

"I'd probably agree with that."

"Well, let's test that conclusion. If that is the diagnosis, then there are several proven methods of coping with it, including stress management techniques, proper nutrition and sleep patterns, relaxation drills, cognitive reframing and prescription anxiolytic medications."

"Damn, sounds simple," he said sarcastically.

She looked at him in what Web thought was a strange way.

"Sometimes it is simple." She looked down at her papers. "All right, have you noticed any changes in yourself physically? Chills, dizziness, chest pain, elevated blood pressure, difficulty breathing, fatigue, nausea, anything like that?"

"The first time I went back to the courtyard and went over what happened, I felt a little dizzy."

"Anything since then?"

"No."

"All right, have you been excessively excitable since then?"

Web didn't have to think long. "No, not really."

"Any type of substance abuse to help you cope?"

"Nothing! I've been drinking less, actually."

"Flashbacks of the event?"

Web shook his head.

"Do you feel numb, wanting to avoid life, people?"

"No, I want to find out what happened. I want to be proactive."

"Are you more angry, irritable or hostile than normal with people?" She looked at him and smiled. "Present company excluded."

Web returned the smile briefly. "Not really, Claire. I think I've been relatively calm, actually."

"Persistent depression, panic attacks, heightened anxiety or phobia formations?"

"Nothing like that."

"Okay, do you have repetitive memories of the event that intrude suddenly on your thoughts? Traumatic dreams or nightmares, in other words?"

Web spoke slowly as he picked his way through this mental minefield. "The night in the hospital, after it happened, I had some bad dreams. They had me drugged up, but I remember I kept apologizing over and over to all the guys' wives."

"Perfectly natural under the circumstances. Anything since then along those lines?"

Web shook his head. "I've been really busy with the investigation," he said by way of defense. "But I think about it all the time. I mean, what happened in that courtyard, it crushed me. Like a pile driver. I've never experienced anything like it."

"But in your line of work you have experienced death before?"

"Yes, but never to any of my team."

"Do you find you've blocked part of what happened out of your mind, something we refer to as memory dysfunction or amnesiac syndrome?"

"No, I pretty much remember every damn detail," Web replied wearily.

While Claire looked down at her notes, Web blurted out, "I didn't want them to die, Claire. I'm sorry that they did. I would do anything to have them back."

She looked up at him and put aside her notes. "Web, listen to me very carefully. Just because you don't have the symptoms of post-traumatic stress disorder does not mean you don't care what happened to your friends. It doesn't mean you're not suffering. You have to understand that. What I see in you is a man who is suffering all the normal symptoms of having gone through an ordeal that would have left most people unable to function, at least for quite a long time."

"But not me."

"You have unique skills, years of training and a psychological makeup that aided you considerably in being selected for HRT in the first place. I've learned a lot more about HRT since you came to me. I know that the physical pounding and stress they put you through is extraordinary, but the ordeal they put you through mentally is even more daunting. Because of *both* your physical and psychological makeup, you can deal with more than just about anyone, Web. You survived that courtyard, obviously not just with your life but also with your mind intact."

"So I don't have post-traumatic stress disorder?"

"No, I don't think that you do."

He looked down at his hands. "Does this mean we're done?"

"No. Just because you're not traumatized over what happened in that courtyard doesn't mean you don't have some issues that need working through. Perhaps some issues that have been with you since long before you joined HRT."

He sat back, instantly suspicious; he couldn't seem to help himself. "Like what?"

"That's what we're here to talk about. You mentioned that you felt a part of your colleagues' families. I'm wondering if you ever wanted a family of your own."

Web thought about this for a while before answering. "I always thought I'd have a big family, you know, lots of sons to play ball with and lots of daughters to spoil, let them wrap old dad around their pretty little fingers, and me smiling all the way."

Claire picked up her pad and pen. "And why didn't you?"

"Years got away from me."

"Is that all?"

"Isn't that enough?"

She looked at his face, both the good and the bad. Web turned away just like he had last time.

"Do you always do that?"

"Do what?"

"Turn the injured side of your face away when someone looks at it."

"I don't know, I don't really think about it."

"It seems to me, Web, that you think very carefully about everything you do."

"Maybe you'd be surprised."

"We haven't talked about personal relationships. Are you dating anyone?"

"My job doesn't leave a lot of time for that."

"Yet the other men on your team were all married."

"Maybe they were just better at it than me," he said curtly.

"Tell me, when did you receive the injuries to your face?"

"Do we really have to go there?"

"It seems as though you're uncomfortable with this. We can go on to something else."

"No, what the hell, I'm not uncomfortable about it." He stood, took off his jacket, and while Claire watched in growing amazement, Web undid the top button on his shirt to reveal the bullet wound on his neck. "I got the *injuries* to my face right before I got this *injury.*" He pointed to the wound on the base of his neck. "Some white supremacists called the Free Society took over a school in Richmond. While my face was on fire, one of them got me with a .357 Magnum round. Nice clean wound, went right through me. Another millimeter to the left, I'm either dead or a quad. Now, I got another one, but I won't show you the hole. It's right here." He touched the wound near his armpit. "That bullet was what we in the business call a Chunneler round. You know, like the tunnel under the English Channel and those monster drills that dug it? It is damn wicked ordnance, Claire, steel-jacketed. It spirals into you at about Mach Three. And if anything gets in its way, it's pulverized. It went right through me and then killed the guy behind me who was looking to pop my head open with a machete. If it had been a dum-dum round instead of steel-jacketed, the bullet would still be in me and I'd be dead from a machete sticking in my skull." He smiled. "I mean, can you believe the timing on that one?"

Claire looked down, remaining silent.

"Hey, Doc, don't look away, you haven't seen the best yet." She glanced up as he cupped his chin with his hand and angled the damaged side of his face so it was fully on display for her. "Now, this beauty came from a flame gusher that almost took out my good buddy Lou Patterson—you know, the late husband of the woman who dissed me to the whole world? I'm sure you saw that on TV, right? Damn shield melted right to my face. They tell me a doctor and a nurse fainted when they saw me at the hospital in Richmond. The whole side was a raw, open wound. Somebody said I looked like I had already decomposed. Five operations, Claire, and the pain, well, let me tell you the pain just doesn't come any better. They had to strap me down more than a few times. And when I saw what was left of my face, all I wanted to do was put a gun in my mouth and chew on a round, and in fact I almost did. And after finally getting past all of that and checking out of the hospital, it was really fun to see how the women ran screaming when they saw old Web coming their way. My little black book just went right down the old toilet. So, no, I really don't date that often, and marriage just seemed to take a backseat to important things like taking out the garbage and cutting the grass." He sat back down and buttoned his shirt. "Anything else you want to know?" he asked amiably.

"I actually saw the Bureau press conference where they revealed a lot about how you received your injuries. What you did was incredibly heroic. Yet it seems like your view of yourself is someone who is unattractive and unacceptable to women." Then she added, "And I'm also wondering if you think you would have made a good father."

Damn the woman, she just didn't quit. "I'd like to think so," he said evenly, trying very, very hard to keep his temper in check.

"No, I'm asking you if you *do* think so."

"What the hell kind of question is that?" he said angrily.

"Do you think if you had children, you would have ever abused them?"

Web came halfway out of his chair. "Claire, I'm about two seconds from walking out of here! And not coming back."

She stared him down. "Remember, when we first started therapy, I said you had to trust me. Now, therapy is not easy, Web, particularly if you have issues you don't want to address. All I'm trying to do is help, but you need to deal straight with me. If you want to waste time with histrionics, that's your call. I'd prefer to be more productive."

Psychiatrist and lawman stared at each other for a very long moment. Web finally was the one to blink and he sat back down. He had just achieved a much better appreciation for Romano's plight with Angie. "I wouldn't have beaten my kids. Why would I, after what Stockton did to me?"

"What you say seems perfectly logical. However, the reality is that most parents who abuse their children were also abused as children. It's not as easy as learning from our parents' mistakes because our emotional psyche doesn't work that efficiently. And children aren't equipped to think that way. They are powerless to resist the abuse and thus they repress the hatred and anger and feelings of helplessness often over many years. It doesn't just go away by itself, this boiling pot of confusion, feelings of betrayal or the low self-esteem that accompanies the abused child—Daddy or Mommy can't love me because they hit me and it must be my fault, because Daddy and Mommy can do no wrong. Abused children grow up and have children, and sometimes they work through their problems and become outstanding parents. Other times, the anger and hatred that has lain dormant for so long comes out and is directed at their own children, just as it was done to them."

"I would never raise my hand to a child, Claire. I know what I do for a living might make me seem that way, but I'm not like that."

"I believe you, Web. I really do. But more to the point, do *you* believe you?"

His face flushed again. "You are really throwing me here, lady."

"Let me phrase it more directly, then. Do you think it just possible that your decision not to marry and have children may have come from the fact that you were abused and you feared you may abuse your own children? It's not unheard of, Web; it's really not. Some might claim it's the ultimate sacrifice, in fact."

"Or the ultimate running away from your problems."

"Some might claim that too."

"What do you think?"

"It could very well be you're both. But if that is the reason you've held back from marriage and a family, we can work through it, Web. And while I can understand how the injuries to your face might make it difficult for *some* women to be attracted to you, don't think all women are like that, because they're not."

He shook his head and then stopped, glanced up at her, held her gaze. "When I was sitting out in the middle of Montana during yet another standoff with yet another group pissed off at the government, I'd spend my morning watch drawing beads on the guys with my sniper rifle as they passed by the window. I spent several hours every day just waiting for the moment when I'd have to kill one of them. That sort of thing just wears you down, Claire, the waiting-to-kill part. So when I was off watch, sitting under the stars in the evenings out there in the middle of nowhere Montana, I used to write letters home."

"To whom?"

Web looked a little embarrassed and took a few moments to get going, for he had never revealed this before to anyone. "I pretended I had kids." He shook his head and couldn't even look at her now. "I even made up names like Web Junior, Lacey. My youngest was Brooke, with red hair and teeth missing. And I'd write them all letters. I actually sent them to my house, so they'd be waiting there when I got home. In the middle of waiting to kill a bunch of losers in Montana who were so outgunned it wasn't even funny, I'm writing to Brooke Louise and telling her Daddy will be home soon. I actually started believing I had a family back home. It's really the only thing that got me through, because I finally did have to pull that trigger and the population of Montana dropped by a couple." He stopped and wiped his mouth, swallowed what seemed to Web like a mountain of belly bile and stared at the carpet. "When I got home, there were all those letters waiting for me. But I didn't even read them. I already knew what they said. The house was empty. No Brooke Louise."

He finally looked up. "That's pretty crazy, isn't it?" he said. "Writing letters to kids you don't even have?"

Without trying to, Web could see that he had finally gotten to Claire Daniels.

When Web left Claire's office and saw the two people conversing in low voices in the waiting area, he blanked for a second, because the context was wrong. O'Bannon was standing there, and that fit, for the man worked here, after all. The woman he was there with, though, she shouldn't be here. When she glanced over and saw Web standing there, Debbie Riner actually gasped.

O'Bannon saw Web too and came over to him, his hand extended.

"Web, I didn't know you were going to be in today. I guess there was no way I would know, Claire and I don't exactly share calendars, bit of an ethical nightmare if we did."

Web didn't take the doctor's hand; he kept staring at Debbie, who seemed frozen, like she had just been caught in a tryst with O'Bannon.

O'Bannon looked between them. "Do you two know each other?" Then he smacked his forehead and answered his own question. "HRT."

Web moved over to Debbie, who was pulling a tissue out of her purse.

"Deb? You're seeing O'Bannon?"

"Web," O'Bannon said, "that's really confidential."

Web waved the little man off. "Yeah, I know, top secret."

"I never liked this common waiting area—it's not good for patient privacy, but there's no other configuration possible," O'Bannon said, though the two were clearly not listening to his complaint. Finally, he said, "See you, Debbie." To Web he said, "Take it easy, Web. I'm sure Claire's doing wonders for you." He looked at Web inquiringly.

She is, Doc, Web wanted to say. *The woman's doing such wonders for me, she's driving me nuts.*

Web held the door for Debbie and they walked to the elevators. She wouldn't look at him and Web felt himself growing red in the face, with anger, embarrassment, he wasn't quite sure what.

He finally said, "I'm seeing a shrink to help me through what happened. I guess you are too."

She blew her nose and finally looked at him. "I've been seeing Dr. O'Bannon for well over a year, Web."

Again he stared blankly at her, and didn't even hear the elevator doors open.

"Are you going down?" Debbie wanted to know.

They got out on the street and were about to go off in different directions when Web swallowed his confusion and said, "You got time for a cup of coffee, Deb?" He was absolutely certain that she wouldn't have any time at all for the likes of him.

"There's a Starbucks around the corner. I know the lay of the land quite well around here."

They sat with their Grande cups in a lonely corner while shiny machines whirred, slurped and sputtered for their thirsty customers.

"Over a year, you say? You've been seeing a shrink all that time?"

Debbie stirred sprinkles of cinnamon deep into her cup. "Some people are in therapy their whole lives, Web."

"Yeah, other people. Not people like you."

She looked at him in a way she never had before. "Let me tell you about people like me, Web. When Teddy and me were first married he was regular military. I knew what I was in store for, assignments overseas where no one spoke your language, or else in swampy backwater USA where you had to drive a hundred miles to go to the movies. But I loved Teddy and I went, eyes wide open. Then he went Delta. And the kids started coming, and while we mostly stayed in one place, Teddy never was in that place. Half the time I didn't know where he was. Dead or alive. I'd read about it in the newspaper or see it on CNN like everybody else. But we got through that. Then he joins HRT, and I thought it might actually be better. My God, nobody told me HRT was even crazier than Delta, Web, or that my husband would be gone more than he ever was before. I could take it when I was twenty with no kids. I'm not twenty anymore, Web. And I've got three kids that I raised pretty much on my own, on Teddy's paycheck, which, after all those years of serving his damn country, was about what a cashier at Kmart earns. I was there every day for my children and all my youngest wants to know is, why did Daddy have to go away? Why can't Daddy come home? And I have absolutely no answer to give her."

"He died fighting the good fight, Deb. He died for his country."

Her fist came down so hard on the table, the slurping customers all turned and stared. "That's a bunch of bullshit and you know it." With a monumental effort, she gathered herself.

To Web, the woman seemed like an erupting volcano desperately trying to recall its lava.

She said, "He made his choice. He wanted to be with his buddies and his guns and his adventures." Her voice grew calmer, sadder. "He loved you guys. He loved *you*, Web. God, you have no idea how much he did. Far more than he cared about me, or even his own kids, because he didn't know them half as well as he knew you. You guys fought together, you saved each other's lives, each day you walked in harm's way and were good enough and trained hard enough to make it through. As a team. The greatest damn team there ever was. He talked to you about things he never would with me. He had this whole other life I could never be a part of. And it was more exciting, more of a rush than anything else he had." She spread her arms wide. "How can a mere wife and family compete with all that? Teddy would only tell me things here and there about what he was doing, just little tidbits to keep peace in the family." She shook her head. "There were so many days I hated all of you for taking him away from us." She put a tissue to her eyes to catch the tears.

Web wanted to put his hand out and touch her, but he didn't know if that would be welcome. He felt guilty of grand and awful crimes, and he never realized he'd even been indicted.

"Did Teddy go to therapy too?" he asked quietly.

Debbie wiped her eyes clear and took a sip of her coffee. "No. He said if anyone at HRT found out he was seeing a shrink they'd throw him off the team, that there was no room for guys with weaknesses on HRT. And, besides, he said, he had no reason to go to a shrink. There wasn't anything wrong with *him*, even if I had some crazy problem. He didn't want me to go, but I put my foot down for once in my life. I had to, Web, I had to talk to somebody. And I'm not the only HRT wife who's seeing a psychiatrist. There are others, like Angie Romano."

Angie Romano! Web wondered if she came to talk about Paulie. Maybe he beat her. No, more likely *she* beat Paulie. "I'm sorry you weren't happy, Deb. You deserve to be." At his house Web had a hundred pictures of himself and his Charlie buddies doing fun things together. And not one wife appeared in any of those photos because they had never been invited to come. Web had judged others without walking in their shoes. It was not a mistake he cared ever to repeat, for the exposure of one's ignorance could be so devastating and complete.

She looked at him, reached out and touched his hand, even attempted a smile. "So, now that I've unloaded on you like a ton of bricks, how's your therapy going?"

Web shrugged. "It's going. I'm not sure where. I know it doesn't come close to what you lost, but it suddenly occurred to me that those guys were all I had in my life. And they're gone and I'm still here and I'm not sure why. I don't think I'll ever be sure why."

"I'm sorry what Julie Patterson did to you. She's totally screwed up. She was never that stable to begin with. She resented you guys, I think, most of all."

"Julie could do it to me again and I'd take it again," he said flatly.

"You should get out now, Web. You've paid your dues. You've damn well served your country. You've given enough. They can't ask for any more of you."

"I figure after about thirty years of psychobabble, I'll be as good as new."

"It does work, Web. O'Bannon's even hypnotized me; got me to think about things I never thought I could. I guess they were hidden really deep inside." Debbie gripped his hand more tightly. "I know the dinner at my house was awful. We didn't know what to say to you. We wanted to make you feel comfortable, but I know we didn't. I'm surprised you didn't run out screaming before dessert."

"It wasn't your job to make me feel comfortable."

"You've been so good with everybody's kids over the years. I want you to know how much we all appreciated that. And there's not one of us who isn't glad you survived. We all know how you've risked your life over the years to keep our husbands alive." She reached across and touched the damaged side of his face, sliding her soft fingers up and down the rough, jerry-rigged surface and Web did not pull away.

"We all know the price you've paid, Web."

"Right now it seems worth it."

23

Toona popped back into the driver's seat and closed and locked the door. He stretched out a long arm and handed the envelope back to Francis, who was sitting in the rear section of seats in the jet-black Lincoln Navigator. Macy sat in the middle section, a pair of sunglasses on, though the vehicle's glass was tinted. He wore an ear radio and a holstered gun. Peebles was not with them.

Francis looked at the envelope but didn't take it. "Where'd you get this, Toona? Don't be handing me shit you ain't know where it comes from. I taught you better'n that."

"It's clean. They already checked it out, boss. Don't know where it come from, but it ain't no letter bomb or nuthin'."

Francis snatched the letter away and told Toona to drive on. As soon as his hand touched the object in the envelope, Francis knew what the letter was. He opened it and took out the ring. It was small and gold and wouldn't have even fit over his pinky, but it had fit Kevin's middle finger just fine when Francis had bought it for him. On the inside of the ring was engraved the names Kevin and Francis. Actually, it read, FRANCIS AND KEVIN. FOR LIFE.

Francis felt his hands begin to shake and he quickly glanced up and saw Toona staring at him the rearview mirror. "Drive the damn car, Toona, or you're gonna find your sorry ass in a Dumpster with my whole pistol mag in your damn head."

The Navigator pulled away from the curb and sped up.

Francis looked down at the envelope and carefully slipped the letter out. It was all block print, something you might see in some mystery show. Whoever had Kevin was asking—no, telling Francis to do something if he wanted to see the boy alive again. What they were telling him to do was odd. Francis would have expected a demand for money or for him to give up all or part of his territory and he would have done it, gotten Kevin back and then tracked down his abductors and killed all of them, probably with his bare hands. But there was no such demands, and thus Francis was confused and suddenly more afraid for Kevin than he already had been, because he had no clue as to what these people were up to. He had seen first-hand the motivations that made people do everything from taking someone's money to taking someone's life. He thought he'd seen it all. And from the contents of the letter these people were obviously aware of something that Francis was too, something special about the location of the building where all the Feds had gotten shot up.

"Where'd this letter come from, Toona?"

Toona's gaze in the rearview mirror caught his. "Twan said it was at the downtown place. Somebody slipped it under the door."

The downtown place was a condo that was one of the few places that Francis used more than a couple times. It was held in the name of a corporation whose sole purpose was to allow Francis the drug lord to actually own something legally without the police knocking his door down. He had fixed it up nicely, with original artwork of some ghetto brothers he admired and who were trying to do almost the impossible and live life straight. That's right, Francis Westbrook was a patron of the arts of sorts. And the condo was also filled with custom-made furniture that was big enough and sturdy enough to allow him to lounge on it without breaking it. The address of the condo had been one of his most jealously guarded secrets and it was the one place where he could actually relax. Now someone had discovered the location, had violated the place, and Francis knew he could never go back there.

He folded up the letter and put it away in his pocket, but he held the tiny ring in his big hand and looked at it. Then he slipped the photo out of his shirt pocket and looked at it. It had been taken on Kevin's ninth birthday. Francis had the boy on his shoulders. They had gone to a Redskins game and had on matching jerseys. Francis was so big that most people at the stadium thought he was a Redskin. That's right, big and black, must be good for nothing except playing ball for outrageous bucks. He remembered, though, that Kevin had thought that very cool. Better than your old man being a drug dealer, he supposed.

And what did his son really think of him, the man he believed was his big brother yet who was really his daddy? What did he think when he got caught in a cross-fire intended to kill Francis? Francis remembered holding Kevin with one arm, shielding him from more harm, while his other hand held a gun and he was firing at the sons of bitches who had turned a birthday party into a kill zone. Couldn't even take him to the damn hospital, had to give him to Jerome. And Kevin screaming that he wanted his brother and Francis not being able to do anything about that, because the cops were all over D.C. General after the shootout. They were just waiting for men with bullets in them to show up, and on would go the cuffs. The cops had been looking for a long time for some excuse to put his butt away. And Francis would've left on a nice lengthy visit to some super-max prison for the benign act of dropping his wounded son off so doctors could save his life.

He felt tears welling up in his eyes and he tried hard to push them away. He could only recall crying twice in his life. When Kevin was born, and when Kevin had been shot and almost killed. His plan had always been to make enough money to last him two lifetimes, his and Kevin's. Because when Francis retired from the "bizness" and left for his little island somewhere, his son was coming with him, away from the drugs and the guns and the premature deaths happening all around them. Maybe he would even summon the courage to tell Kevin the truth: that he was his father. He wasn't really sure why he had created this lie about being his big brother. Was he afraid of fatherhood? Or were lies just an essential part of Francis Westbrook's life?

His cell phone rang, just like the letter said it would. They must be watching him. He slowly held it up to his ear.

"Kevin?"

Toona turned his head around when he heard the name. Macy sat impassively.

"You all right, little man? They treating you okay?" Francis said into the phone. He nodded at the answer he heard. They spoke for about a minute and then the line went dead. Francis put down the phone.

"Mace?" he said.

Macy instantly turned and looked at him.

"Mace, we got to get to this Web London dude. Things have changed."

"You talking killing or information exchange? You want him to come to us, or us go to him? Be better if he found us, if you're talking info. You want him dead, though, I'll go to him and it's done."

Macy was always logical like that. He read your mind, thought for himself, reviewed the possibilities and took the pressure off his boss from having to do all the analysis, making all the tough decisions. Francis knew that Toona would never be like that, and even Peebles was limited in that capacity. Damn ironic that a little white boy with a vicious streak would become his number one kind of guy, his soul mate of sorts as much as black and white could be.

"Info, for now. So he comes to us. How long you reckon?"

"He's been seen nosing around in that Bucar of his probably looking for clues. I'd say it wouldn't take all that long. He comes our way, we got a nice carrot to dangle in front of him."

"Let's do it. Oh, and Mace, nice call on that other thing." Francis glanced at Toona.

"Just doing my job," replied Macy.

Kevin looked up at the man as he put the phone away.

"You did real good, Kevin."

"I want to see my brother."

"One step at a time. You just talked to him. See, we're not bad people. Hell, we're into family stuff, see." He laughed in a way that made Kevin think he wasn't into family at all. He rubbed his finger where his ring had been.

"Why you let me talk to him?"

"Well, it's important that he knows you're okay."

"So he do what you tell him to do."

"Damn, you really are one smart kid. You want a job?" He laughed again, turned and left, locking the door behind him.

"What I want," Kevin called after him, "is out of here."

24

Web had not read a paper in several days. He finally bought a copy of the *Washington Post* and went through it over coffee at a table near the large fountain at the Reston Town Center. He had been making slow circles of the Washington metropolitan area and racking up some serious motel bills for the Bureau. Web occasionally looked up and smiled at the kids climbing up on the ledge and throwing pennies into the fountains while their mothers held on to their shirttails so they wouldn't go plunging into the water.

He had gone through Sports, Metro, Style, working his way backward to the front section. On page A6 his nonchalant attitude disappeared. He reread the article three times and looked closely at the accompanying photos. When he sat back and digested it all, he found himself coming to conclusions that didn't seem possible, so far-fetched were they. He touched the damaged side of his face and then pressed a finger against the spot of each bullet hole. After all this time was he going to have to confront it again?

He punched his speed dial. Bates wasn't in. Web had him paged. The guy called back a few minutes later. Web told him about the article.

"Louis Leadbetter. He was the judge down in Richmond who tried the Free Society case. Gunned down. Watkins was the prosecuting attorney in the case. He goes in his house and it implodes. All on the same day. And then you got Charlie Team. We were the team that responded to the Richmond Field Office's request. I killed two of the Freebies myself before I got my face toasted and two holes in me. And then you have Ernest B. Free himself. Busted out of prison, what, three months ago? One of the guards was paid off, got him out in a transfer van and ended up with his throat slit for his trouble."

Bates's reply was surprising. "We know all that, Web. We've had our computers crunching that stuff, and then those two deaths, murders, happened. And there's something else."

"What?"

"You better come on down."

When Web arrived at the WFO, he was escorted to the strategic operations room that had all the bells and whistles one would expect at the deep-pocketed crime-busting federal behemoth, including the standard-issue copper-coated walls, sophisticated interior security system, white noise at all vulnerable portals, retinal and palm scanners, stacks of high-powered computers, video equipment and, most important, fresh coffee in high quantities and a mound of hot Krispy Kreme doughnuts.

Web poured himself a cup and said hello to some of the folks scurrying around the large room. He looked at computer-generated diagrams of the courtyard and its environs that had been tacked to large boards and mounted on the walls. There were pins at various places on the diagrams that represented, Web knew, significant points of evidence or clues. The bustle of feet, the nonstop clack of computer keys, the ringing of phones, the rustle of paper and the ballooning body-heat index told Web that something was up. He had been part of these war room operations before.

"Oklahoma City set the standard way too high," said Bates with an ironic smile as Web sat down across from him. "Now everybody expects us to examine a few hunks of metal, check a few video-tapes, run a few plates, hit some computer keys and bingo, we have our man hours later." He dropped his legal pad on the table. "But it almost never works that way. Like everything else, you need some breaks. Well, we just got a bunch telegraphed to us. Somebody definitely wants us to know he's out there."

"I'll take a lead however it comes in, Perce. Whoever it is can't control how it's followed up."

"You know I really hated it when you left WFO to go climb ropes and shoot big guns. If you'd stuck with me, you might have made a decent FBI agent one day."

"You make your bed, you lie and die in it. You said there was something else?"

Bates nodded and slid a news clipping over to Web, who looked down at it.

"Scott Wingo . . . that name rings a bell."

"Yeah, he defended our friend Ernest B. Free. I wasn't at the trial, of course. I was still recuperating. But the guys who were there talked about Wingo."

"Slick and smart. He cut his guy a sweetheart deal. And now he's dead."

"Murdered?"

"Atropine was applied to his telephone receiver. You pick up the phone, you naturally press it against your skin, near your nostrils and such. Atropine is absorbed through the membranes much faster than via the bloodstream. Causes your pulse to go into over-drive, breathing constricted, can make you hallucinatory, all within an hour or so. If you have bad kidneys or other circulatory problems so the body can't quickly rid itself of the stuff, that would speed up the poison's effect. Wingo was diabetic, had heart problems and was confined to a wheelchair, so atropine was the perfect choice. He went in alone on Saturdays, so nobody would be around to help when he started feeling the atropine hit him. And on weekends he was known to return a lot of calls, or so the folks in Richmond tell us."

"So whoever killed him knew both his medical history and his work routine?"

Bates nodded. "Leadbetter got shot when he turned on the light to read an article another judge supposedly told him about. The marshal who took the call said it was a Judge Mackey. Of course, it wasn't."

"The phone again."

"That's not all. Watkins's neighbor was pulling out of his drive-way at the time Watkins was walking up to his house. He told police that he saw Watkins reach into his pocket and pull out his phone. The guy couldn't hear the phone ringing, but he said it looked like Watkins was answering a call. Gas in the house, he hits the talk button. Boom."

Web said, "Wait a minute. A cell phone isn't like a light switch. It doesn't have the right type and amount of electrical spark to ignite gas."

"We examined the phone, or what was left of it. The forensic folks actually had to scrape it off Watkins's hand. Someone had planted a solenoid inside the phone that would cause the exact type of spark necessary to ignite that gas."

"So somebody had to snatch his phone, probably while he was asleep or away from it for any length of time, plant the solenoid and then they had to be watching him when it happened to get the timing that exact."

"Yep. We checked the logs for Watkins's and the marshal's phones. Both calls were made with disposable calling cards you buy with cash and then discard. No record."

"Like undercover agents use. I take it yours hasn't surfaced yet?"

"Forget our undercover."

"No, I'll just come back to him later. So what's the latest on Free?"

"Nothing. It's like the guy's gone to another planet."

"Is the organization still active?"

"Unfortunately, yes. You probably remember they disavowed being part of the hit on the school in Richmond and Ernie wouldn't rat on his soul mates, said he'd planned the job himself without their knowledge, so there went that case. The other gunmen were dead, two of them thanks to you. We couldn't crack any of the other members and get them to testify, so the Free Society was never even charged with anything. They laid low for a while because of all the negative publicity, but word is they're coming back with fresh blood."

"Where are they now?"

"Southern Virginia, near Danville. You better believe we've got that place covered. We figured old Ernie would head there after his escape. But so far, nothing."

"After all this, can't we get a search warrant for their headquarters?"

"What, we go to the magistrate and say we've got three murders, six if you count Watkins's family, and we think this Free Society might be behind them, but we've got absolutely no evidence linking them to the hit on HRT or anybody else? Wouldn't the ACLU just love to hit that one out of the park?" Bates paused. "It all makes sense though. Prosecutor, judge, perfect motive for revenge."

"But why the defense lawyer? He saved Ernie from lethal injection. Why take him out?"

"That's true, but you're not talking about rational people, Web. For all we know, they're pissed because their fellow madman served one day in prison. Or maybe Ernie had a falling out with the guy and when he got out he decided to take them all out."

"Well, at least that should end the killings. There's nobody left."

Bates reached in a file and pulled out another slip of paper and a photograph. "Not quite. You remember there were two teachers gunned down at the school too."

Web took a deep breath as the painful memories came flooding back. "And the boy, David Canfield."

"Right. Well, one of the slain teachers was married. And guess what? Her husband was killed three days ago in western Maryland while driving home late one night from work."

"Homicide?"

"Not sure. It was a car crash. Police are still investigating. Looks like a hit and run."

"Telephone involved?"

"There was one in the car. After we contacted them, the police said they would check the phone logs to see if he received a call right before the crash."

"How about the other teacher's family?"

"The husband and kids moved to Oregon. We've contacted them and they're under twenty-four-hour surveillance right now. And we're not stopping there. You remember David Canfield's parents? Bill and Gwen?"

Web nodded. "I was in the hospital at MCV for a while. Billy Canfield came to visit me a couple of times. He's a good guy. He took the loss of his son really hard, who wouldn't? I never met his wife, and I haven't seen Billy since."

"They moved. Live up in Fauquier County now, run a horse farm."

"Anything strange happen to them?"

"We contacted them as soon as we made the connection. They said nothing out of the ordinary had occurred. They knew about Free's escape. And to quote Bill Canfield, he said he doesn't want our help and he hoped the bastard came after him because he'd just love to blow his head off with a shotgun."

"Billy Canfield is no shrinking violet. I could tell that when he came to the hospital to see me; rough, tough and opinionated. Some of my team who testified at the trial told me he was a pretty loud presence there too. Came close to contempt citations a couple of times."

"He ran his own trucking firm and then sold it after his kid died."

"If the Frees are behind the killings in Richmond, Fauquier County is a lot closer than Oregon. The Canfields really could be in danger."

"I know. I've been thinking of taking a ride out there and trying to talk some sense into him."

"I'll go with you."

"You sure about that? I know that what happened at that school in Richmond is something you'd be better off not revisiting."

Web shook his head. "That's not something you ever put behind you, Perce, I don't care how much time goes by. The two teachers died before we got there. I couldn't do anything about that, but David Canfield was killed on my watch."

"You did more than anybody could have, including almost getting killed. And you got a permanent badge from it right there on your face. You have nothing to feel guilty about."

"Then you really don't know me."

Bates studied Web closely. "Okay, but let's not forget about you, Web. If wiping out Charlie Team was the Frees' goal, they haven't accomplished it yet. You're the last man standing."

Barely, thought Web. "Don't worry, I look both ways before crossing the street."

"I'm serious, Web. If they tried once, they'll try again. These people are fanatics."

"Yeah, I know. Remember, I got the 'permanent badge.'"

"And another thing. At the trial Wingo filed that countersuit against HRT and the Bureau for wrongful death."

"That was bullshit all the way."

"Right. But it allowed them to make some discovery on HRT. The Free Society probably learned some things about your methods, procedures and such. It could have helped them in setting up the ambush."

Web hadn't considered this yet. It actually made a lot of sense.

"I promise if I get any weird-ass phone calls, you'll be the first to know. And I'll check my receiver for atropine. Now tell me about this undercover. Maybe the Frees are involved, but they had to have some inside help. Now, I know he's black and it's hard for me to believe the Frees would work with a man of color, but we can't afford to discount anything right now. You told me Cove was a loner. What else do you know about him?" Web hadn't heard back from Ann Lyle on his inquiries into Cove, so he had decided to go right to the source.

"Oh, lots of stuff. It's right in that file over there, marked 'FBI Undercover Agents, All You Ever Wanted to Know.'"

"Perce, this guy could be the key."

"He's not! Take my word for it."

"All I'm saying is I worked these kind of cases. And contrary to what you think, I didn't forget how to be an FBI agent when I joined HRT. I had a great teacher, and don't let that swell your head. And another pair of eyes is another pair of eyes. Isn't that what you always beat into me?"

"That's not how it works, Web, sorry. Rules are rules."

"I seem to remember you telling me differently way back when."

"Times change, people change."

Web sat back and pondered whether he should play his trump card. "Okay, what would you say if I told you something you don't know but that could be important?"

"I'd say why the hell didn't you tell me before?"

"I just figured it out."

"Yeah, right."

"Do you want to hear it or not?"

"And what's in it for you?"

"I give you info on the case, you do the same for me."

"How about I make you tell me for nothing?"

"Come on, for old times' sake."

Bates tapped the file in front of him. "How do I know it's really something I can use?"

"If it's not, then you owe me nothing. I'll trust your judgment."

Bates eyed him for a few more moments. "Go."

Web told him about the switch with Kevin Westbrook. As he went on, Bates's face grew more florid and Web could tell the man's pulse was nowhere near sixty-four and had probably left double digits far behind.

"When *exactly* did you figure this out? And I want it to the minute."

"When I was having a beer with Romano and I mentioned that the Kevin Westbrook I saw had a hole in his cheek from a bullet wound. The kid he had, he said, didn't. Cortez corroborated that. And don't go after those guys. I told them I'd fill you in ASAP."

"Sure you did. Who would switch the kids and why?"

"Not even a good guess. But I'm telling you the kid I saved in the alley and the kid Romano turned over to the 'alleged' FBI agent were two different boys." He tapped the table. "So what's your judgment? Worth it or not?"

In answer Bates opened a file, although he recited the facts from memory. "Randall Cove. Age forty-four. Been with the Bureau his whole career. He was an All-American tailback from Oklahoma but blew out his knees before the NFL draft. Here's a recent photo." Bates slid it across and Web looked at the face. The guy had a short beard, dreadlocks and eyes that could only be described as piercing. The vitals said he was a big man, about six-three, two-forty. He looked powerful enough to take on a grizzly and maybe win. Web hunched forward and while he pretended to study the picture in greater depth he was actually reading as much as he could from the file Bates had open. His years as an FBI agent had left him with many tricks to help his short-term memory retention until he could write things down. And he had also become very proficient at reading upside down.

Bates said, "He could take care of himself, knew the street better than most kingpins. And cool under pressure."

"Yeah, Princeton white-breads named William and Jeffrey just never seem to fit in with Drug Town, USA, I wonder why," said

Web. "You mentioned before that he didn't have a wife or kids. So he never married?"

"No, his wife's dead."

"And they didn't have kids?"

"He did."

"What happened to them?"

Bates shifted uncomfortably in his seat. "It happened a while back."

"I'm all attention."

Bates let out a long breath and didn't seem like he was going to start talking.

"I lost my whole team, Perce, I'd kind of appreciate full disclosure here."

Bates sat forward and clasped his hands in front of him. "He was working an assignment in California. Heavy cover because it involved the Russian mob, and those guys will fire a missile up your ass for coughing around them. They make the Mafia look like preschoolers." Bates stopped there.

"And?"

"And his cover got blown. They traced his family."

"And killed them?"

"Slaughtered would be more like it." Bates cleared his throat. "I saw the photos."

"Where was Cove?"

"They had intentionally diverted him away so they'd have a free hand."

"And they didn't go after him too?"

"They tried, later. They waited until he buried his family, nice guys that they were. And Cove was waiting for them when they came."

"And he killed *them*?"

Bates started blinking rapidly and Web noted a sudden tic over the man's left eye.

"Slaughtered. I saw those photos too."

"And the Bureau just let this guy keep working? What, they don't believe in early retirement for agents with butchered families?"

Bates spread his hands in resignation. "The Bureau tried, but he wouldn't go. He wanted to work. And to tell you the truth, after what happened to his family, the guy worked longer and harder than any UC we ever had. They transferred him to WFO to get him out of California. Let me tell you, he got into places we were never able to get into before. We got convictions on serious large-scale operators all across the board because of Randall Cove."

"Sounds like a hero."

Bates finally smoothed out his tic. "He's unorthodox, goes his own way a lot, and the higher-ups can only take so much of that, even from the undercover dudes, slaughtered family or not. But none of it really stuck to Cove. I can't say it hasn't hurt his career, I mean, it's not like the Bureau has a place for a guy like this outside of undercover, and I'm sure he knew that too. But he plays the Bureau games. Always covered his back. You take the dirt with the good and the guy always delivered. Until now."

"And the trace on his family by the Russians—would that have been in any way the Bureau's screw-up?"

Bates shrugged. "Cove didn't seem to think so. He's been plugging away ever since."

"You know what they say about revenge, Perce, it's the only dish best eaten really cold."

Bates shrugged again. "Possibly."

Web was just starting to get worked up. "You know, it just gives me the warm fuzzies that a guy like that was able to stay in the Bureau and maybe lead my team down the primrose path to Armageddon to avenge his wife and kids. Don't you guys have some kind of quality control over this shit?"

"Earth to Web, undercover agents are a different breed. They live a lie all the time and sometimes they get in too deep and get turned or just go nuts all on their own. That's why the Bureau switches people in and out, changes assignments and lets them recharge their batteries."

"And they did all that with Cove? Switched him out, let him recharge his dreadlocks? Gave him crisis counseling after he buried his family?" Bates was silent on this. "Or was he so good at his job that they just let him keep rocking along until he finally erupted all over *my* team?"

"I'm not going to discuss that with you. I *can't* discuss that with you."

"What if I told you that was unacceptable bullshit?"

"What if I told you, you were getting way too close to the line?"
The men glared at one another until the fires died down.

"And his snitches? Were they all-pro too?" asked Web.

"Cove always played it close. He had access to them only, not anybody else. That's not exactly Bureau procedure, but like I said, you couldn't argue with the guy's results. Those were his rules."

"So we know any more about this target? You said it was the financial guts of some drug op. Whose?"

"Well, there's some difference of opinion about that."

"Oh, swell, Perce. I love a puzzle at both ends."

"This stuff is not an exact science, Web. The area where your mission went down is controlled pretty much by one crew, Big F's—I told you that."

"So it was his operation we were hitting in that building."

"Cove didn't think so."

"He didn't know for sure"

"What, you think the bad guys carry union cards or ID reading, 'I'm a member of X crew'?"

"So what was Cove's opinion?"

"That the money operation was that of a much bigger player. Maybe the ring supplying a drug called Oxycontin to the D.C. area. You heard of it?"

Web nodded. "DEA guys talk about it all the time down at Quantico. You don't have to drug-lab the stuff or worry about sneaking it past customs. All you have to do is get your hands on it, which you can a dozen different ways, and then start printing money."

"A criminal's Nirvana," added Bates dryly. "It's one of the most potent and frequently prescribed painkillers on the market right now. It blocks pain signals from the nerves to the brain and gives you a feeling of euphoria. Normally, it works on a twelve-hour time release, but if you crush it or smoke it you get a brain rush that some say is almost equal to heroin. It also can throw the abuser into respiratory arrest, which it has frequently."

"Nice little side effect. Are you telling me you have no idea who his inside guy might have been?"

Bates tapped the file in front of him. "We have some ideas. Now, this is totally unofficial."

"At this point, I'll take rumors and lies."

"For Cove to get in as deep as he was, we figure the snitch has to be in the inner circle, pretty tight. He was working the Westbrook angle when he stumbled into the Oxy piece. But I have to presume that whomever he was using to infiltrate Westbrook's operation is the person who helped him get on to this new development. Antoine Peebles is Westbrook's COO, for want of a better term. He runs a damn tight ship and it's largely because of him that we haven't been able to lay a finger on Westbrook. Here's Westbrook, and the other one is Peebles." He slid across two photos.

Web looked at them. Westbrook was a monster, far bigger even than Cove. He looked like he'd been through a war, his eyes, even staring out from the paper two-dimensionally, had the keenness that you always saw in survivors. Peebles was an altogether different picture.

"Westbrook is a warhorse. Peebles looks like he should be graduating from Stanford."

"Right. He's young and we figure Peebles is the new breed of drug entrepreneurs, not as violent, more businesslike and ambitious as hell. Word on the street is that someone's looking to band all the local distributors together, to make them more efficient, enhanced bargaining power up the line, economies of scale, a real business approach to it."

"Sounds like old Antoine may want to be CEO instead of just COO."

"Maybe. Now, Westbrook came up through the streets. He's seen and done it all, but we've heard that he may be looking for an exit from the drug business."

"Well, Peebles may have a different agenda if he's the one behind the organization of the local crews. But giving away valuable stuff to Cove doesn't exactly figure with being the heir apparent. If you bust the operation, what does Peebles have left to run?"

"That's a problem," conceded Bates.

"Who else is in the picture?"

"Westbrook's main muscle. Clyde Macy."

Bates handed him the photo of Macy, who, to put it kindly, looked like he should be taking up space on death row somewhere. Macy was so white he looked anemic; a skinhead with the sort of calm yet merciless eyes that Web associated with the worst serial killers of his experience.

"If Jesus saw this guy coming at him, he'd scream for a cop."

"Apparently Westbrook only works with the best," commented Bates.

"How did Macy fit in with all the brothers? He looks like a white supremacist."

"Nope. Apparently just doesn't like hair. We don't know much about him before he came to D.C. Though we could never prove it, he was believed to be a foot soldier for a couple kingpins who got sent to federal Shangri-La in Joliet. After that he came to D.C. and joined Westbrook. He has a well-deserved rep on the street for loyalty and extreme violence. A real crazy-ass, but professional in his own way."

"Just as any good criminal should be."

"His first big act of malice was putting a meat cleaver in his grandma's head because, he claimed, she was shortchanging him at dinnertime."

"How come he's walking around free after a murder rap like that?"

"He was only eleven, so he did time at a juvie detention center. Since then, the only crime the guy's committed is three speeding tickets."

"Nice guy. Mind if I keep these photos?"

"Help yourself. But if you run into Macy in a dark alley or a well-lit street, my advice to you would be to run."

"I'm HRT, Perce. I eat guys like him for breakfast."

"Right. Keep telling yourself that."

"If Cove's really as good as you say, then he didn't just walk into an ambush. Something else is going on."

"Maybe, but everybody makes mistakes."

"Did you confirm that Cove didn't know when we were coming?"

"I did. Cove was not told the date of the hit."

"How come he didn't know?"

"They didn't want any leaks, and he wasn't going to be there anyway, so he didn't qualify as a need-to-know."

"That's great, you didn't trust your own undercover. That doesn't mean he couldn't have gotten the information from another source. Like WFO?"

"Or like HRT?" Bates shot back.

"And the potential witnesses being there, was that intel from Cove?" Bates nodded. "You know, Perce, it would have been nice to know all this up front."

"Need-to-know, Web. And you didn't need to know that to do your job."

"How the hell can you say that when you don't have a damn clue how I do my job?"

"You're getting close to that line again, my friend. Don't push it!"

"Does anybody give a damn that six men were killed in the process?"

"In the grand scheme of things, Web, no. Only people like you and me care."

"So, anything else I *don't* need to know?"

From his large stack of documents Bates pulled out a very thick expandable file, slid out one of the manila folders and opened it. "Why didn't you tell me Harry Sullivan was your old man?"

Web immediately rose and poured himself another cup of coffee. He didn't really need the extra caffeine, but it gave him time to think of a response or a lie. When he sat back down Bates was still looking over the file. When he glanced at Web, it was clear Bates wanted an answer to that question before he would give up the material.

"I never really thought of him as my father. We parted company when I was barely six. To me, he's just a guy." After a moment, he asked, "When did you find out he was my father?"

Bates ran his finger down one of the pages. "Not until I pulled your entire background-check file. Frankly, looking at this arrest and conviction record, I'm surprised he had time to get your mother pregnant. Lotta stuff in here," he added enticingly.

Web wanted to snatch the file out of Bates's hands and run from the room. However, he just sat there, staring at the upside-down pages, waiting. The bustle of the room had receded for him now. It was just him, Bates and, on those pages, his father.

"So why are you suddenly so interested in, as you say, 'just a guy'?" asked Bates.

"I guess you get to a certain age, things like that start to matter."

Bates put the folder back and slid the entire file across to Web. "Happy reading."

25

The first thing Web noticed when he got back to the motel was that there was a fresh oil patch in the parking space he had been using. Nothing unusual, really, for another guest could have used that spot, though it was directly in front of Web's unit. Before he unlocked the door, he checked out the doorknob while pretending to fumble for his room key. Unfortunately, even Web could not tell if the lock had been picked or not. It hadn't been forced, but somebody who knew what he was doing could pop the simple lock in the time it took to sneeze and leave not a trace.

Web opened the door, his other hand on the butt of his gun. It took him about ten seconds to discover that no one was in the tiny room. Nothing was out of place, and even the box he had taken from his mother's attic was there, each piece of paper exactly where he had left it. However, Web had five different types of tiny booby traps set up throughout his room and three of them had been tripped. Over the years, Web had developed this system whenever he was on the road. Well, whoever had searched his room was good but not perfect. That was comforting, like knowing the four-hundred-pound brute you were about to rumble with had a glass chin and occasionally wet his bed.

Ironic, that while he'd been meeting with Bates, someone had searched his room. Web had never been naive about life, because he had seen the worst of it, as both a child and an adult. Yet the one thing he had always thought he could count on was the Bureau and all the people who gave it life beyond the technical forms and guns. For the first time in his career, that faith had been shaken.

He packed his few belongings and was on the road within five minutes. He went to a restaurant near Old Town Alexandria, parked where he could see his car through the restaurant's window, ate his lunch and made his way through Harry Sullivan's life.

Bates had not been joking. Web's old man had been a guest of some of the finest correctional facilities the country had to offer, most of them in the South, where Web knew they grew some exceptionally fine human cages. His father's offenses were myriad yet had a common theme: They were typically low-level financial crimes, business scams, embezzlement and fraud. From some of the old court transcripts and arrest records in the file, Web could see his old man's main weapon had been a smooth tongue and more chutzpah than any one human being should be toting around.

There were various photos of his father in the file, from the front, right and left sides, with the little line of prisoner identification numbers running underneath. Web had seen many mug shots of arrested people, and they all looked remarkably the same: stricken, terrified, ready to slice wrist or blow out temple. Yet in all his mug shots Harry Sullivan was smiling. The bastard was grinning, like he had put one over on the cops, even though he was the one busted. But his father had not aged well. He was no longer the handsome man he had been in the photos in the attic box. The last series of shots showed a very old man, though he was still smiling, albeit with fewer teeth. Web had no reason to care about him, yet it was difficult for him to witness the man's decline in all its impersonal Kodak glory.

As Web read some of the trial testimony of his father, he couldn't help but laugh in places. One slick operator emerged from the lines of dialogue as the cagey con battled with prosecutors determined to put him away.

"Mr. Sullivan," asked one D.A., "is it not true that on the night in question you were—"

"Begging your pardon, lad, but what night would that be again? Me memory's not what it was."

Web could almost see the lawyer rolling his eyes as he answered, "The twenty-sixth of June, sir."

"Ah, that's right. Go on, now, lad, you're doing fine. I'm sure ye mum's proud of yer."

In the transcript the court reporter had typed parenthetically, "Laughter in courtroom."

"Mr. Sullivan, I am *not* your lad," replied the lawyer.

"Well, forgive me, son, for I'm not quite experienced in such matters, and I surely meant nothing by it. Truth is, I don't know what to be calling you. Though in the ride over from the jail to this fine courthouse I heard others call you names I wouldn't be saying to me dearest enemy in the world. Words that woulda made me poor God-fearing mum roll over in her good Catholic grave. Attacking your honesty and integrity, and what man can be standing for mucha that?"

"I could care less what criminals say about me, sir."

"Begging your pardon, son, but the worst of it be coming from the guards."

"Laughter again," the stenographer had typed. Huge thunders of laughter, Web concluded, judging from the regiment of exclamation points tacked on the end.

"Can we continue, Mr. Sullivan?" said the lawyer.

"Ah, now, you be calling me Harry. It's been me name since me Irish arse came into this world."

"Mr. Sullivan!" This came from the judge, Web read, and in those two words he seemed to sense a long laugh, though Web was probably wrong. But the judge's last name *was* O'Malley, and perhaps he and Harry Sullivan shared a hatred of the English, if nothing else.

"I certainly won't be calling you Harry," said the lawyer, and Web could almost see the righteous indignation on the man's features for having to carry on such a conversation with a common criminal and getting the worst of it.

"Well, now, lad, I know it's your job to put me old, withered self into a cold, dark cell where men treat other men with no dignity atall. And all over a wee misunderstanding that might amount to nothing more than bad judgment, or perhaps a pint or two more than I should have had. But even so, you call me Harry, for though you've got to see this terrible deed through, there's no reason we can't be friends."

As Web finished the file on that particular chapter in his father's life, he had to note, with some satisfaction, that the jury had acquitted Harry Sullivan on all counts.

The last crime his father had been sent to prison for had gotten him twenty years, by far his longest sentence. So far he had punched fourteen years of the time in a prison in South Carolina that Web knew to be a sweat-hole one short step from hell, and he had six more years to go unless he got paroled or, more likely, died behind bars.

Web took the final bite of his pastrami and the last swallow of his Dominion Ale. There was one more file to check. It did not take long to read and left Web stunned and even more confused.

The Bureau was good; they left no stone unturned. When they checked somebody's background out, damn it, man, you were checked out. If you were applying to work at the Bureau in any capacity, they talked to everybody you had any contact with in your entire life. Your first-grade schoolteacher, your paper route manager, even the pretty girl you had taken to the prom and subsequently slept with. And they had no doubt also spoken with her father, to whom you had to explain your miserable conduct afterward when the secret got out, even though it was his innocent little girl who had ripped off your pants and brought the extra-lubricated condoms. Your Boy Scout troop leader, your in-laws, the bank manager who had turned down your first car loan, the woman who cut your hair—nothing, absolutely nothing was sacred when the FBI was on the case. And damn if they hadn't managed to track down old Harry Sullivan.

He had been newly ensconced in his little South Carolina retirement cell, and he had given the background-checking agents his two cents on Web London, his son. "My son." It was a phrase Harry Sullivan had used thirty-four times during the meeting because Web took the time to count them.

Harry Sullivan gave "my son" the best damn recommendation anyone could give another person, though he had only known "my son" for the first six years of his life. But according to Harry Sullivan, a proper Irishman could tell if "my son" had what it took from nearly the day the diapers came off. And his son had what it took to be the finest FBI agent there ever was or ever would be and they could quote him on that. And if they wanted him to come up to Washington to tell the powers-that-be that very thing, he gladly would, though it would be with leg and arm shackles he'd be trooping in, yet his heart would still be bursting with pride. There was nothing on earth that was too good for "my son."

Web continued reading and his head dropped lower and lower as he did so, and then finally it almost hit the table with Harry Sullivan's last written statement: "And would the good agents, the fine agents," he'd begun, mind telling "my son" that his father has thought about him every day over all these years, never once letting him out of his heart, and though it was not likely that they would ever hook up again, that Harry Sullivan wanted "my son" to know that he loved him and wanted the best for him? And to not think too badly of the old man for how things had turned out? Would the good agents mind telling "my son" that, for he'd be much in their debt if they did. And he would be proud to buy them each a pint or two if the opportunity ever arose, though the prospects did not look at all promising for that, given his current living arrangements, though one just never knew.

Well, they never had told Web anything. Web had never seen this report until right this minute. Damn the Bureau! Was there never any room to bend the rules? Did everything have to be lockstep, their way or the highway? And yet Web could have discovered this information years before if he had really wanted to. He just hadn't wanted to.

The next thought that hit Web made his features turn grim. If the Bureau had sent Claire Daniels Web's file, was she already privy to some or all of this information regarding Harry Sullivan? If so, why hadn't she bothered to tell him that?

Web packed the file up, paid his bill and walked back to the Vic. He drove to one of the Bureau's motor pools, switched vehicles and drove a late-model Grand Marquis out another gate not visible from the street he had come in on. The Bureau wasn't exactly rolling in available Bucars, but the Grand had come in for a ten-thousand-miler, and Web had persuaded the supervisor that he deserved a nicer set of wheels than the twenty-year vet uptown at HQ the car was assigned to. If anyone had a problem with that, Web had added, go talk to Buck Winters, he's my best friend.

26

Bates was still in the strategic ops room when the man entered. Bates looked up and did his best to keep the dismay off his face.

Buck Winters sat down across from him. The crease on his suit was Bureau letter-perfect, the shine on his wing tips equally regulation. The insertion of his pocket handkerchief looked like it had been done with a ruler. The man was tall, broad-shouldered, with confident, intelligent features, a walking poster boy for the FBI. Maybe that's how he had risen so far.

"I saw London leaving the building earlier."

"Just checking in per his orders."

"Oh, I'm sure he is." Winters laid his palms flat on the table and seemed to study every feature on Bates's face. "Why the hell do you care so much about that guy?"

"He's a good agent. And like you said, I was sort of his mentor."

"That's not something I'd lay claim to, frankly."

"He's almost gotten himself killed for this place a lot more than you or me."

"He's a hothead. All those HRT guys are. They're not part of us. They go their own way and thumb their noses at the rest of us, like they're somehow better. What they really are is a bunch of alphas with big guns just itching to use them."

"We're all on the same team, Buck. They're a specialized unit that takes care of stuff nobody else can. Yeah, sure, they're cocky, who wouldn't be? But we're all FBI agents; we're all working toward the same goal."

Winters shook his head. "You really believe that?"

"Yeah, I really do. If I didn't, I wouldn't be here."

"They've also been the cause of some of the Bureau's worst moments."

Bates dropped his file. "That's where you're dead wrong. The Bureau throws them into the fire on a moment's notice and when something pops, usually because of knuckleheaded orders from the top that any guy on the front lines expected to execute said orders could tell you in a heartbeat won't work, they take all the heat. I'm actually surprised they haven't ask to be split off from *us*."

"You've never played the games you need to, to move up here, Perce. You're at the glass ceiling or, in your case, the steel ceiling. There's no getting through it."

"Well, I like right where I am."

"Piece of advice: When you stop rising here, you eventually start falling."

"Thanks for the career advice," Bates said curtly.

"I've been getting your memos on the investigation. Frankly, they're pretty sparse."

"So are the results of the investigation."

"Cove, what's the status? You were sort of vague on that."

"Not much to report."

"I trust you're working under the assumption that any Bureau undercover who hasn't shown after all this time is either dead, or if he isn't dead, he's been turned and the way we should be looking for him is through an APB."

"Cove hasn't turned."

"So you've talked to him? Funny, I didn't see that in any of your reports."

"I'm still feeling my way. But I did receive information from Cove."

"And what did our illustrious undercover say about this mess?"

"That he thinks he was set up."

"Gee, that's stunning," said Winters sarcastically.

"That he doesn't want to come in because he thinks the rat is somewhere in the Bureau." Bates stared hard at Winters when he said this, though he wasn't really sure why. It wasn't like Winters would be leaking secrets, would he? "He knows all about the leaks happening and the blown missions. He thinks what happened to HRT was another one of those."

"Interesting theory, but I'm assuming he has no proof of that."

That question struck Bates as odd. "None that he cared to share with me," he answered. "I've got it under control, Buck. I know how busy you are, and I don't want to clutter your legendary vision with small details. You have my word that if anything big is going down, you'll know beforehand. That way you can do the media circus. You're really good at that."

Winters could hardly have missed the sarcasm yet apparently chose to ignore it. "If I remember correctly, you and Cove were really tight at one time. California, right?"

"We worked together."

"About the time his family got hit."

"That's right."

"A disaster for the Bureau."

"Actually, I always thought it was a disaster for the Cove family."

"What's got me puzzled is how all this went down. As I understand it, Cove had discovered a drug crew's financial operations in that building."

"And HRT was called up to hit it," said Bates. "There were potential witnesses in there. HRT specializes in getting those kind of folks out alive."

"Boy, they really did a bang-up job of that. They couldn't keep themselves alive."

"They were set up."

"Agreed. But how? If not Cove, how?"

Bates thought back to his meeting with Randall Cove at the cemetery. Cove believed there was a leak inside the Bureau that accounted for all the things going wrong. Bates studied Winters for a moment. "Well, in order to accomplish something like that I would suppose that somebody would have to have inside information of the highest order."

Winters sat back. "Of the highest order. From inside the Bureau, you're saying?"

"Inside is inside."

"That's a very serious allegation, Bates."

"I'm not alleging anything. I'm just pointing out one possibility."

"It would be a hell of a lot easier to turn one undercover agent."

"You don't know Randall Cove."

"And maybe you know him too well. So well, you can't see the forest for the trees."

Winters rose. "No surprises, Bates. Nothing substantial goes down unless I know about it ahead of time. Clear?"

As Winters left, Bates muttered under his breath, "Waco clear, Buck."

Web was in his car when Ann Lyle called.

"Sorry it took me so long, but I wanted to get something solid for you."

"That's okay. I just got some stuff on Cove from the Bureau; understandably it was like pulling teeth."

"Well, I got you some*one*."

"Who? Cove?"

"I'm good, but I'm not that good, Web. I've drummed up a D.C. police sergeant who was a regular contact of Cove's when he worked the WFO beat years ago."

"A local cop as a contact for an FBI undercover? How's that?"

"It's not unusual for UCs to use a cop they trust to act as a go-between, Web. Cove had one of those during his first stint here, and the guy's willing to talk to you."

He pulled the car over, grabbed pen and paper and wrote down the name Sonny Venables, who was still a uniform in D.C.'s First District. Ann also gave him the man's number.

"Ann, anybody else got hold of the Venables angle?"

"Not that Sonny said, and I think he would've mentioned it. He was Cove's informal contact on his first tour through D.C., and that was a long time ago. Some folks might not make the connection. Though Sonny Venables tends to stand out," she added.

"You sound like you know him."

"Web, honey, when you've been around as long as I have, you tend to know everybody. I worked a lot with the D.C. cops."

"And Venable's willing to talk to me? Why?"

"The only thing he said was he had heard of you. And I threw my two cents in, for what it was worth."

"But we still don't know his take on things?"

"I guess that's up to you to find out." Ann clicked off.

Web called the number. Venables wasn't in, and Web left his name and cell number. Venables called him back twenty minutes later and the two arranged to meet later that afternoon. Web also asked him another question and Venables said he would see what he could do. If the guy could give Web a handle on Cove, then Web might be able to follow it up. However, something was bothering Web about Bates, namely that he had never told Web that Cove had worked at WFO before his stint in California. Not that it really mattered. He had given Web a look at the guy's file, and Web would have picked it up on his own, he supposed. He just hadn't had enough time to go through the man's entire history. But why not tell Web?

Venables had asked Web to meet him in the early afternoon at a bar around the area of his beat, nothing unusual about that. Web knew that that way you could quench your thirst and maybe over-hear some info that might help you crack a case later. Cops were nothing if not efficient with their time.

Sonny Venables was white, mid-forties and a veteran of almost twenty years on the force, he told Web as they were buying their beers. He was over six feet tall and beefy, the kind of body mass one got from pumping lots of weights; the man looked like he could military-press a semi. He wore a baseball cap that read ALL FISHER-MEN GO TO HEAVEN and wore a leather jacket with the NASCAR logo on the back. His neck was almost as thick as his very wide head. His voice had a twangy commonsense southern charm to it, and Web noted the circular outline of a can of tobacco chew in the back pocket of his jeans as they walked to a booth in the bar. They found a quiet corner and settled down with their beers.

Venables worked the night shift, he told Web. He liked it, more excitement. "Be hanging it up soon, though, right at twenty years. Go off and fish, drink beer and watch fast cars go around a little track the rest of my time, like most good cops do." He smiled at his own words and took a long pull of his Red Dog beer. From the jukebox Eric Clapton was going on and on about Layla. Web looked around. Two guys were playing pool in the back room, a stack of twenty-dollar bills and a couple of Bud Lights siting on the edge of the table. They occasionally glanced over at the booth, but if they recognized either Venables or Web, they made no sign of it.

Venables eyed Web over the rim of his beer mug. The man's face held enough wrinkles to be considered experienced and craggy. A man who had seen a lot in life, mostly bad, Web judged, just like him.

"Always wondered about you HRT guys."

"What's to wonder? We're just cops with a few more toys at our disposal."

Venables laughed. "Hey, give yourself some credit. I got a few FBI buddies who tried out for HRT and came back with their tails between their legs. Said they'd rather deliver a damn baby with just a stick between their teeth for the pain than go through that again."

"From the picture I saw of Randall Cove, he looked like he could've cut it at HRT."

Venables studied the head on his beer for a bit. "You're probably wondering what Randy Cove had in common with the likes of a redneck-looking gent like myself?"

"It crossed my mind."

"We grew up together in a backwater of Mississippi so small it never really did have a name. We played sports together all the way through because there wasn't much else to do around there. And our little backwater was state football champs two years in a row. We also played together at Oklahoma." Venables shook his head. "Randy was the greatest running back I ever saw, and the Sooners have turned out more than their share of those. I was fullback. First string, three years running, just like him. Blocked for Randy on every play. Threw my body in there like a damn runaway train and loved every minute of it, though I'm really starting to feel the effects of it now. See, you just needed to get Cove a little bit of daylight and that boy was gone. I'd look up from a pile of bodies and he'd already be in the end zone, usually with a couple of guys hanging on him. We were national champs our senior year and he was the reason. Oklahoma didn't believe in the forward pass back then. We just handed the damn ball off to Randy Cove and let him do his thing."

"Sounds like a friendship that would endure."

"It did. I never had the talent to play pro ball, but Randy sure as hell did. Everybody, and I mean everybody, wanted him." Venables stopped there and ran his fingers along the top of the table. Web decided to just wait the man out.

"I was with him at the combine when he blew out his knees. We both knew it, as soon as it happened. It wasn't like it is today. Just go in and clean it up and then you're back on the field the next year pretty much good as new. His career was over. Just like that. And football, man, football was all he had. We sat on that damn field and cried together for nearly an hour. I never even did that at my own mama's funeral. But I loved Randy. He was a good man."

"Was?"

Venables played with the pepper shaker and then sat back, tilted his cap farther up on his head and Web saw a lock of curly gray hair spring out.

"I take it you know what happened to his family," said Venables.

"I heard about some of it. Why don't you tell me what you know."

"What's to tell? Bureau screwed up and it cost Randy his wife and kids."

"You saw him back then?"

Venables looked like he wanted to throw his beer in Web's face. "I was a damn pallbearer at the funerals. You ever carry a four-year-old's casket?" Web shook his head. "Well, let me tell you, that's something you don't ever forget."

"Is that what Cove told you, that it was the Bureau's fault?"

"Didn't really have to tell me. I was a cop. I know how those things shake down. Ended up in D.C. because my wife's from here. Randy started out with the Feds here too. I guess you know that. Used me as a go-between because he knew he could trust me, and that's a rare thing in his line of work."

"It seems to be a rare thing in a lot of lines of work."

The two men shared a knowing look that seemed to come at a good time, perhaps strengthening a fledgling bond.

"Then Randy got transferred out to California and that's where his family got hit."

"I understand he took out his revenge."

Venables laid a cold gaze on Web, a look that clearly said the man had far more secrets than he would ever care to part with. "Wouldn't you have?"

"I guess maybe I would. Cove must really be something. The Russians are no lightweights."

"Try growing up the wrong color in shit-poor Mississippi." Venables leaned forward, putting his elbows on the table. "I heard about you. From the papers, some from Ann Lyle." He stopped and seemed to be checking Web out. Then Web realized Venables was staring at the messed-up side of Web's face.

"In almost twenty years on the force, I've pulled my gun maybe a dozen times, and fired it on six occasions. Four times I missed what I was shooting at, and twice I didn't. I've never been hurt on the job, not even a hangnail, and that's something to brag about in this town, especially these days. Now I'm in the First District, which isn't lily white and rich Northwest, but it's not exactly the Sixth and Seventh Districts in Anacostia, where your team got shot up. And I have great respect for guys on the thin blue line who've taken it and gotten back up. You seem like a damn walking ad for that."

"I never asked to be."

"Point is I respect you or else I wouldn't be sitting talking to you. But the thing is you'll never get me to believe that Randy has done anything wrong. I know undercover work screws with your mind and Randy's got no reason to feel good about the Bureau, but what happened to your team is not something he'd ever be a party to, I want you to understand that."

"And I want you to understand that while you seem sincere as hell and I wouldn't mind sharing another beer with you some other time, I can't accept a statement like that at face value."

Venables nodded in understanding. "Well, you'd be a real dumbshit, I guess, if you did."

"He could've walked away. I checked on that. Bureau offered him a new life, full pension. Why do you think he didn't take it?"

"And, what, spend the next forty years mowing his grass in a cookie-cutter suburb in the Midwest? That's not Randy. What else was he going to do except keep on plugging? It may sound funny, but he took pride in his work. He thought he was doing good."

"So do I. That's why I'm here. I'm going to find out the truth. If Cove was part of it, I may take out my revenge just like he did. I can't promise you I won't, friend of his or not. But if he had nothing to do with it, I'll be his best buddy. And believe me, Sonny, most folks would rather have me as a friend than an enemy."

Venables sat back and seemed to be considering this. Then he apparently made up his mind and hunched forward, eyed the pool players chalking their cues, smoking their cigs and sipping their beers, and started talking in a very low voice. "I have no idea where Randy is. Haven't heard from him since before this all went down. Way before, in fact."

"So he never talked to you about what he was working on?"

"You got to understand, I was his contact on his first gig through D.C. Now, I've seen him on his latest tour through here, but not for business, so to speak. I knew he was working on something pretty big, but he never told me what."

"So you two weren't that close anymore?"

"As close as you can be to somebody like Randy. After what happened to his family, well, I don't think he could really be close to anybody again. Not even to old Sonny Venables from Mississippi and all those damn blocks I threw for him."

"He ever mention another contact he might have been using on the force?"

"No, if he was using anybody, it would've been me."

"When's the last time you saw him?"

"Little over two months ago."

"How'd he seem?"

"Tight-lipped, mind somewhere else. Not looking too good, actually."

"He hasn't been back to his place in a while. The Bureau checked that out."

"I never knew where that was; we always met on neutral ground because of his work. We'd just talk about old times, really. Just somebody to talk to is what he wanted, I think. If he needed me to pass something on, I did."

"How'd he get in touch with you when he wanted to meet?"

"He'd never call me at home. Called at the precinct. Used a different name every time. And each time we met he'd tell me the new name he'd be using next when he called, so I'd know it was him."

"And he hasn't called?" Web eyed him closely. Venables appeared to be dealing straight with him, but one never really could be sure.

"No. Not one word. I started to worry something happened to him. In his occupation, that's a legitimate concern."

Web sat back. "So I guess you can't really help me track him down."

Venables finished his beer. "Let's take a walk."

They went outside and strolled down a street that was pretty empty. The workday wasn't over yet and most folks were probably still in their offices, counting the minutes until they could bolt, Web figured.

"On his first tour through WFO there was a place that Randy would use as a drop spot if he wanted to leave me a message. He told me he'd also use it to change clothes, as a safe house of sorts."

"The Bureau know about it?"

"No. Even back then I don't think he trusted the higher-ups at the Bureau all that much. That's why he used me, I guess."

"Probably a smart move. Have you been there lately?"

Venables shook his head. "Guess I'm a little afraid of what I might find, not really sure why. Don't even know if Randy uses it anymore. It could have been demolished, for all I know."

"Care to give me that address?"

"You smoke, don't you?"

"No, I don't."

"You do now." Venables pulled a pack of Winstons out of his coat pocket and handed it to Web, who took it. "Better light up, in case anybody's watching." Venables handed him a book of matches.

Web lit up and tried not to gag and then slipped the pack into his pocket. "I appreciate the help. But if Cove was involved . . ." He let his voice trail off.

"If Randy did something like that, I don't think he'd want to go on living."

As Sonny Venables walked off, Web went back to his car, ripped open the Winstons and clutched the rolled-up piece of paper inside. He looked at the address written on it. Also inside the pack of cigarettes were three small photos folded over. Web had asked Venables about any light-skinned black kids about Kevin Westbrook's age who had been reported missing in the city in the last month, and this obviously was what he had found. Web looked at the three photos; they were all slightly different versions of Kevin, he decided. All hopes of a decent life, their expressions told him, had already been torn from them. He drove off.

Twenty minutes later Web stared out the car window, his spirits hovering near an all-time low. Venable's offhand remark had proved to be right on target. Where once stood Randall Cove's old safe house there was an open construction pit; a tall crane rose in the middle of this hole, and a group of construction workers were just now walking off the job after what looked to Web to be a hard day's work. Judging from the degree of work already performed there, Web had to assume that Cove had not been using his old digs in the recent past. It was a total dead end. Web crumpled up the piece of paper with the address written on it and threw it on the floorboard. But he still had one more angle to take on Randall Cove.

He called Romano from the car. "You up for a little snooping around?"

He picked up Romano and they headed south toward Fredericksburg.

Romano looked around the car's interior. "What a piece-of-shit car."

"It's a Grand Marquis, the director is probably driven around in one of these."

"Still a piece of shit."

"I'll try to do better for you next time." He glanced at Romano and wondered what Angie told her shrink about him. With Romano as a significant other, she probably had a lot to talk about to a mental health professional.

"How're things at HRT?"

"Same old, same old. We haven't been called up for anything. Just training. I'm getting bored with that, man."

"Hang in there, Paulie, you'll be getting to fire your guns pretty soon."

"Maybe I should go join the French Foreign Legion or something like that."

"You just won't admit when you have it good."

"The guys been talking about you some, Web."

He should have been expecting this change in the conversation, but it still surprised Web. "So, what's the word?"

"Pretty even split for and against."

"Gee, I thought I was more popular than that."

"It's not that. Nobody thinks you're a coward, Web. You've done too much crazy stuff over the years. Almost as crazy as me."

"But . . ."

"But some of the guys think if you freeze once, you'll freeze again. What happened to you wouldn't have made a difference in what happened to Charlie Team, but next time it might."

Web stared straight ahead. "I guess I can't argue with that logic. Maybe *I* should go join the French. You armed?"

"Do politicians lie?"

Randall Cove lived on the outskirts of Fredericksburg, Virginia, roughly fifty miles south from Washington, D.C., and Cove's work arena, which roughly doubled Ann Lyle's twenty-five-mile rule of thumb on the minimum distance undercover agents should keep between their abode and their beat. Cove's home address was one of the pieces of information Web had surreptitiously read from Bates's file.

Just missing the brunt of rush-hour traffic, forty minutes later they pulled down the quiet suburban street where Randall Cove lived. It was a line of carbon-copy townhouses, many with rental signs out front. There were no moms or kids outside, though the weather was pleasant, and there were very few cars parked on the street. The community actually looked abandoned, and Web knew it would be until the commuters started arriving from D.C. and northern Virginia. This place had bedroom community written all over it, no doubt with mostly single people or childless couples living here until their salaries or expanded family demands prompted them to move. He could understand why Cove would pick such a place to live. No curious neighbors, people keeping to themselves and no one around during the day when he was probably at home. Most undercover agents in the drug arena did their hunting at night, he knew.

There was a government-plated Bucar parked in front of the house. "Fed babysitter," commented Romano. Web nodded and pondered how best to handle it. He drove up to the Bucar and he and Romano got out.

The agent rolled down his window, glanced at Web's and Romano's FBI identifications and then at Web.

"You're famous now, don't even need to show your creds," said the agent, whom Web didn't know. He was a young guy, full of vigor and promise, and Web figured he was probably hating life right now, watching a house no one expected Randall Cove to ever come near again. He got out of the car and extended his hand to the pair.

"Chris Miller, out of the Richmond Field Office." He flashed his own credentials, which he pulled from his right breast pocket so that he could shake with his strong hand, which was how the FBI trained you to do it. If the Bureau did nothing else, it enforced upon its agents a stark commonality of how they performed the smallest details. Without looking, Web knew that Miller had an extra layer of lining in his jacket so the gun he carried there wouldn't wear a hole in it. He also knew that when he had pulled in behind Miller and approached the car, Miller's gaze had been on the rearview mirror and then locked on Web's eyes, for eyes always told a person's intent.

The men shook hands and Web glanced at the quiet and dark townhouse. "You guys pulling round-the-clocks here?"

"Eight, eight and eight," said Miller wearily. He checked his watch. "And I've got three more hours on my shift."

Web leaned against the sedan. "So I take it not very exciting."

"Not unless you count a cat fight I watched about two hours ago." He paused, eyed Web closely and then blurted out, "You know, I've been thinking about trying out for HRT."

"Well, we can always use a few good men." *Six of them, in fact,* Web thought, *to rebuild Charlie Team.*

"I hear the tryouts are hellacious."

Romano almost snorted. "Take everything you've heard and raise it by a factor of ten, and then you're getting close to the truth."

From his skeptical look Miller obviously didn't buy that, Web could tell. Yet he was young and overconfident in his abilities, as the young always were.

"Were you at Waco?" Miller asked. Web and Romano nodded. "You get any shots off?"

"I've actually tried to banish it from my subconscious," said Web. *Wouldn't Claire Daniels be proud?*

"I could see that," said Miller in a doubtful manner that made Web feel sure the young agent actually did not get the point.

"How long you been with the Bureau?" asked Romano.

"Almost two years."

"Well, when you get the big three under your belt you can try out for HRT. Give me a buzz sometime. If you're serious about HRT, I can show you around." Romano handed him his card.

As Miller tucked the card away in his pocket, Romano and Web exchanged amused glances.

"Man, that would be great," said Miller. "I hear you guys have some awesome firepower."

The initial draw for many, Web knew, was the guns. Several men he knew had joined the Bureau solely for the opportunity to carry and fire fancy weapons. "That we do. And we'll show you exactly why it's always best if you *don't* have to use them."

"Right." Miller looked disappointed, but he would get over it, Web knew. There was an awkward silence, and then Miller asked, "Uh, can I help you guys with anything?"

"We just drove out here because I wanted to see the place. You know anything about the guy?"

"Not all that much. I know he's involved in what happened to you guys. Makes you wonder how somebody can turn like that, on their own kind, I mean."

"Yeah, it sure does." Web looked around the row of townhouses. They backed up to woods. "Hope you got somebody covering the rear."

Miller grinned. "*Something,* anyway. K-9s in the backyard. It's fenced in. Somebody tries to go in that way, they got a surprise. Cheaper than posting two agents out here, I guess."

"I guess." Web checked his watch. "Getting close to dinnertime. You eaten?"

Miller shook his head. "I brought some crackers and stuff along. And a bottle of water. Went through that. And like I said, I got three more hours before my relief shows up. Worst part is having no place to use the john."

"Tell me about it. Worked a bunch of surveillance details in the Midwest. Covered thousand-acre farms that were suspected drug distribution facilities and some trailer parks looking for good old boys that thought decent work included robbing banks and shooting people with sawed-off shotguns. Had to either hold it, pee in a bottle or just stand out in the fields and let it go."

"Yeah," said Romano. "And when I was a Delta we used to squat together in rows in whatever piece-of-shit place we were in and take our dumps. You get to know guys real well when you're crapping next to them. I had to shoot a guy once right when I was taking a shit. Man, let me tell you that was awkward."

Miller didn't look like any of those avenues of relief held sway with him. He was dressed very sharply, Web noted, and no doubt peeing in a bottle or taking the chance of exposing himself wasn't part of the young agent's image.

"There's a Denny's up the road. You want to take a dinner, we'll stay put until you get back."

Miller looked uncertain about abandoning his post.

"Offers like that don't come along every day, Chris." Web partially opened his jacket so Miller could see he was armed. "And yeah, I got some shots off at Waco. Go have yourself a good meal."

"You sure it'll be okay?"

Romano answered in his most intimidating voice. "If anybody comes along who shouldn't, they'll wish they got the dog over us."

At that, Agent Miller quickly got in his car and drove off.

Web waited until he was out of sight before he went to his trunk, pulled out a small device along with a flashlight, looked around and then walked with Romano up to the front door of Cove's house.

"Damn, that dude would last all of two minutes at HRT," said Romano.

"You never know, Paulie. You made it, didn't you?"

"You really gonna pop this place?"

"Yeah, I'm really gonna. You have a problem with that, go sit in the car."

"There's not much in life I have a problem with."

The pick gun made fast work of the simple front door lock and Web and Romano were inside in a few seconds. Web closed the door and turned on his flashlight. He saw the alarm panel next to the front door, but it was not armed. Presumably only Cove would have known the pass code. They walked down the short hallway and entered the living room. Web hit all corners with the light. Both men's hands were on their pistol grips. The place was very sparsely furnished. Cove probably didn't spend much time in here anyway, Web assumed. They did a quick search of the main floor and found nothing of interest, which didn't surprise Web. Cove was a veteran, and vets didn't exactly leave detailed records of what they were doing lying around for folks to find.

The basement was unfinished. There were a few boxes down there. Romano and Web quickly went through them. The only item Web lingered over was a framed photograph of Cove, his wife and their children. Web shone the light at an angle so it wouldn't reflect off the glass. Cove was in a suit, no dreadlocks in sight, his features handsome and confident. His smile was contagious. From simply looking at the photo, Web felt the corners of his mouth curl. One big arm was around his wife and the other enveloped both his children. His wife was remarkably beautiful, with shoulder-length hair, a big smile of her own and eyes that could have reduced any man to the quivers. The boy and girl favored their mother. They would have grown up into beautiful people, no doubt, at the same time their mother and father grew old together. That was how life was supposed to work out anyway, and rarely did, at least for people who did what Cove and Web did for a living. The photograph captured the other side of

Randall Cove, focusing on the man as husband and father. Web envisioned the former All-American tailback tossing a football to his son in the backyard; maybe the boy had inherited his old man's athletic skills. Perhaps he could've had the professional career that had been denied his father. In a Hollywood movie that might happen, but it rarely did in the unfairness of real life.

"Nice family," commented Romano.

"Not anymore." Web didn't bother to explain.

He put the photo back in the box and they headed upstairs. As his light glanced off the rear sliding door, something flung itself against the glass. In unison Web and Romano pulled their guns until they heard the barking and realized it was the K-9 doing its job.

Well, at least a dog would never rat on you; maybe that was the real reason they were man's best friends, thought Web. They kept your secrets to the grave.

They hustled to the upstairs level, wanting to be done long before Miller got back. Web didn't like conning a fellow agent, but he definitely didn't want to be caught conducting an unauthorized search of a major suspect's home. Bates would throw away the key on that one and Web probably couldn't blame him. There were two rooms up here connected by a bathroom. The front room that overlooked the street was Cove's bedroom. The bed was made and the closet held few clothes. Web lifted a shirt out and held it up to himself. Web could have almost fit his leg into one of the arms of the shirt. Web wouldn't have wanted to play defense against the man; one might as well try and tackle a van.

The room that was on the rear side of the house was empty. It was set up as a bedroom but apparently had never been used as one. The inside of the small closet had no hanger scratches on the walls, and the carpet held no imprints of furniture having been there. Web and Romano were about to leave when Web noticed something. He looked at the windows in this back room and then went through the connecting bath and into the front bedroom and looked at the windows there. They had miniblinds for privacy; logical, since this room overlooked the street. Web went back through the bathroom and into the other room. There were shades on these windows too but not miniblinds, noted Web; these were old-fashioned roll-up shades. The back bedroom overlooked dense woods, so privacy wasn't really an issue. Web looked out the window and saw where the sun was falling. The back room faced to the north, so it would get no afternoon light that required shades to block. And since the room wasn't being used, why have shades at all? And if one did elect some sort of window treatment, why not the same throughout the house? At least with miniblinds one could allow some light in and still have a reasonable degree of privacy. With shades it was all or nothing, and with little light back here as it was and no overhead light built in, this room would stay in perpetual darkness. It didn't make a lot of sense, but perhaps Cove had inherited this arrangement from a previous owner and had no interest in changing it.

"What's got your antenna up?" asked Romano.

"The man's choice in shades."

"You going feminine on me?"

Web ignored Romano and stepped to the window. The shades were fully pulled up. Web took the rope and jerked. The shade did its thing and came down, nothing out of the ordinary there. He stepped to the other window and did the same thing. The rope was stuck, and the shade did not come down. For an instant Web was about to just call it quits and leave. But then he shone his light up at the trip mechanism on the shade and saw that it had been bent such that the rope pull wouldn't work anymore. He bent the trip back into place and pulled on the rope. Down came the shade, and Romano gaped as the envelope that had been secreted in the rolled-up shade literally dropped into his hands.

Romano stared at him. "Damn, you are good at this."

"Let's go, Paulie." Web pulled the shade back up and they jogged down the stairs. Romano checked to make sure the coast was clear and then they slipped out. Web pulled the front door closed behind him.

Web and Romano got in their car and Web turned on the overhead light and settled down to review what they had found.

He opened the envelope and pulled out the yellowed news clipping. It was from the *Los Angeles Times*, and it was reporting on the deaths of an undercover agent's family at the hands of the Russian mafia. The official speaking on behalf of the Bureau gave a sting-

ing attack on the criminals and vowed that they would be brought
to justice. The official was identified as someone very close to the
investigation. He was actually the case supervisor of the undercover agent, whom they refused to identify even though the names
of the slain family members had been made public. Web could only
shake his head at the name of the Bureau official.

Percy Bates.

Miller drove up a few minutes later, got out and walked over to
the car. He patted his belly. "Thanks for the assist, guys."

"No problem," said Romano. "We been there, done that."

"Anything come up while I was gone?"

"Nope, all clear."

"Hey, I'm off duty in about two hours. You guys interested in
having a beer?"

"We—" Web glanced past Miller because the failing sunlight
had just glanced off some reflective object in the distance.

"Web, look out," Romano cried out, because he obviously had
seen the same thing.

Web reached across to Miller, grabbed his tie and tried to pull him
down. The shot hit Miller dead center of the back and came through
his chest, zipped right in front of Web and shattered the glass on the
passenger side. Romano was already out of the car and behind one
of the wheels. He poked the gun over the hood but didn't fire.

"Web, get the hell out of there."

For a split second Web held on to Miller's tie even as the young
agent slid down the side of the car. The last thing Web saw was the
dead man's eyes staring at him and then Miller hit the ground.

"Web, get your ass out of that car or I'll shoot you myself."

Wed ducked down as another shot shattered the rear side window of the Bucar. Web slid out and took up position behind the
rear wheel. At the Academy you were taught that squatting behind
car wheels was the place to be because there were few weapons
that could penetrate all that metal.

"You see anything?" asked Romano.

"Just that first reflection. Off a scope. A damn good thousand
yards away, in the woods, between those two sections of townhouses. Miller's dead."

"No shit. I'm figuring something like a .308 chambering steel-jackets with a Litton ten-powerscope."

"Great, the same stuff we use," replied Web. "Just keep your damn head down."

"Oh, thanks for telling me, Web. I was just about to jump up screaming for my mommy."

"We can't fire back; our pistols don't have that range."

"Why don't you tell me something I don't know? You got any goodies in your trunk?"

"I would if it were my car."

Another shot hit the sedan and both men ducked. Yet another shot came and the left front wheel blew. Another and steam rose from the radiator.

"Don't you think somebody might try calling the cops?" complained Romano. "What, you got snipers in the suburbs every day?"

"My phone's in the car."

"Well, don't try and get it. Whoever's out there knows what he's doing."

They waited another five minutes and no more shots hit; then they could finally hear sirens in the distance. Web edged his head up over the side and looked through the car's windows. He didn't see any more reflections from the woods.

The police finally showed and Web and Romano held up their creds and motioned for the cops to get down. After another few minutes Web crawled over to the squad car and explained the situation. No more shots came and then apparently all the county cops showed up, along with a half dozen state troopers. The woods were combed without finding anyone, although a dirt road leading out to the main one on the other side of the subdivision Cove lived in had fresh tire tracks. And they also found a number of spent rifle shells. Romano had been right: steel-jacketed .308s.

Chris Miller was officially pronounced dead and the ambulance came and took him away. Web noted the wedding band on his finger before they zipped the body bag shut. Well, Mrs. Miller was going to get the dreaded visit from the Bureau tonight. He shook his head and looked over at Romano.

"I'm really getting sick of this life."

27

Web and Romano had given their statements about three times each. And Bates had come down and had taken a bite out of Web's butt for conducting an unauthorized investigation.

"I told you they'd be gunning for you, Web. But you stubborn son of a bitch, you just won't listen," ranted Bates.

"Hey, take it easy," said Romano.

"Do I know you?" said Bates, as he got right in Romano's face.

"Paul Romano, Hotel Team assaulter." He put out his hand.

Bates ignored the gesture and turned back to Web. "Do you realize that Buck Winters is looking for any excuse to squash you?" He glanced at Romano. "To officially cremate all of HRT? And you're playing right into his hands."

"All I'm trying to do is find out what happened to my guys," rejoined Web. "And you'd be doing the same thing if you were me."

"Don't you throw that bullshit in my face." Bates stopped cold because Web was holding up the newspaper clipping.

"I found this in the house."

Bates slowly reached out and took the clipping.

"You want to talk about it?" asked Web.

Bates led them away from the crime scene and over to a quiet slice of ground. He glanced at Romano and then at Web.

"He's okay," said Web. "Cleared for all sorts of top-secret stuff."

"Even did joint VIP protection on Arafat once," said Romano. "Now, you talk about a target, lots of people after that man."

"You didn't mention you were working with Cove when his family was killed," said Web.

"I don't owe you my life story," snapped Bates.

"Maybe you just owe me an explanation."

Bates folded the clipping up and put it in his pocket. "It was really nobody's fault. Cove didn't mess up and we didn't either. It was a fluke and the Russians got lucky. I wish I could take it back, but nobody can. Randy Cove is a hell of an agent."

"So Cove has no reason to be seeking payback?"

"No. I've talked to him. He almost got popped not that long after Charlie Team. He said he saw that building filled to the brim with everything that was supposed to be there."

"So his story is he got set up to feed us bad intel. Out went the files and in came the guns?" said Web.

"Something like that. It was a short time fuse. Cove said he was in the building shortly before you guys hit it. He thought he'd infiltrated a big-time drug op."

"Perce, I'm not looking to tell you how to do your job, but the smart thing may be to bring him in. With his cover blown, he sounds like he needs protection."

"Cove can take care of himself. And he can do more on the outside. In fact, he might be getting close to a big-time drug supplier."

"That I don't care about. All I want are the guys who set us up."

"That's just it, Web, they might be one and the same."

"Well, that doesn't make a lot of sense. Why would a drug supplier want to have the Bureau coming after them loaded for bear?"

"There could be any number of reasons. Paybacks, to keep distributors in line. Even to set up a rival to take the heat and reduce the competition."

"You let me have a crack at those guys," said Romano, "and I'll reduce something, like their life span."

"So I take it he's not reporting in regularly," said Web.

"How'd you know that?" said Bates.

"If he's really that good, he'll know that everybody thinks he's in on it. So he lies low, doesn't trust anybody and goes about his own investigation, trying to get to the truth before somebody gets him."

"That's a pretty good deduction."

Web said, "Actually, I'm just speaking from experience."

"Speaking of experience, I finally got a call back from Bill Can-field. I've got an appointment to meet him tomorrow at his farm. Care to join me?"

"I said I would. You want to come too, Paulie?"

Bates stared at him. "Are you the same Paul Romano that was with Delta Force and then New York SWAT?"

"There's only one Paul Romano," said Romano without a trace of conceit.

"Arafat, huh?"

"Hey, when you want to send the very best . . ."

"Good, consider yourself temporarily reassigned. I'll talk to your commander."

Romano looked stunned. "Reassigned doing what?"

"Doing what I tell you to do. See you two tomorrow."

Web dropped off Romano at home.

Before he got out, Romano said, "Hey, Web, you think this new gig pays more? Angie's been talking about getting a new washer-dryer and maybe finishing the basement."

"If I were you, I wouldn't mention anything like that to Angie. You'll be lucky if it doesn't pay less."

Romano shook his head as he got out. "Story of my life."

Web pulled away and drove aimlessly. He felt miserable about Chris Miller and didn't envy the people who would have to tell his wife. He hoped Miller didn't have any kids, but he looked like the kind who would. Damn, there was just too much misery in the world. Finally he decided he needed another dose of old-fashioned police work.

Web took the outer loop of the Capital Beltway around to Interstate 395, headed north and steered the Mercury Bates had gotten for him across the dilapidated Fourteenth Street Bridge that an airplane tak-ing off from National Airport in a snowstorm had actually fallen on years ago. He pointed the car toward an area of town where few law-abiding citizens, other than those who were lost or those who carried a gun and a badge, ever dared venture, especially at this hour.

The scene was a familiar one to Web. It was the same route his squad had followed their last night on earth. Web knew the car and its government plates just screamed "Fed Man," but he really didn't care. For an hour he cruised up and down every dead-end street, every alley, every hole in the wall that looked promising. Several times he passed patrol cars that were nosing around looking for trouble, which here was akin to being a cat in an aviary: What you wanted was damn near everywhere.

He was just about to give it up when his gaze caught on the flash of red under a streetlight. He slowed the car, grabbed his trusty binoculars from the bag and got a better look. It was probably nothing, for many wore the do-rag here and many of them were red. Red for blood; even people down here had a sense of purpose and also humor about their work. A few seconds later Web's pulse kicked to a higher gear. The gent was even wearing the same clothes. A tank shirt over barbell shoulders and shorts below the butt crack. It was his good old neighborhood purveyor of fine crack cocaine and other illegal drugs from the alley where Charlie Team had run its last lap.

Web cut the car's engine, let the car drift to a stop and quietly got out. He thought about taking his shotgun but then decided his pistol would be enough. It was hard to pounce holding a shotgun. He gripped his pistol and slowly made his way down the street, keeping to the shadows. There was a streetlight under which he had to pass on his way to the kid. Just when he stepped into its pool of light, there came a scream from somewhere. The kid looked up, saw him. Web swore under his breath and took off running.

"Still want to deal on my rifle?" Web called out to him as he hustled forward.

The kid bolted down the alley. Web knew he shouldn't do it, not even armed, and he stopped. Going down that alley without any backup, he might as well phone in his casket order. It was still a tough decision because Web wanted Bandanna Boy in the worst sort of way. In Web's connect-the-dots manner of thinking, maybe Bandanna was the one who hit the remote that had activated the laser that had tripped the machine guns that had sent Web's dearest friends into oblivion. He finally made up his mind.

Another night, my friend. And next time I won't stop until my hands are around your damn neck.

Web turned to go back to his car. That's when he saw them coming. They seemed in no hurry. There were maybe a dozen of them. Along with their elongated shadows against the brick he saw the array of weapons they were carrying. Cut off from his car, Web ducked down the alley and started running hard. He heard the group behind him do the same.

"Shit," he said to himself. Could anybody say setup?

The light from the street lamp was quickly left behind and Web could only rely on the presence of some dregs of ambient light from the sky and the sounds of running feet ahead and behind him. Unfortunately, in this high-walled labyrinth the echoes were not reliable guides. Web made lefts and rights until he was hopelessly lost. He turned one last corner and stopped. He imagined half the group had probably headed around to block his escape, though for all he knew he was running in circles. He thought he could still hear them coming, but he couldn't tell from where. He ducked down another alley and stopped. Listened. Quiet. Quiet he didn't like. Quiet meant stealth. He looked left, right and then up. Up. Up sounded good. He climbed a nearby fire escape and then froze. The footsteps were close. He soon saw why. Two of them came around the corner. They were tall, lean, with shaved heads and dressed in leather and baggy low-riding prison shuffle jeans and big jailhouse shoes with thick heels they were no doubt just itching to grind into Web's face.

They halted and looked around. They were directly underneath him. Just like Web had done, they looked left and then right. He figured it would only be a matter of seconds before—as he had done—they looked up. So he swung down and each foot collided with one head and both men slammed into the brick wall. Web landed a little awkwardly, his ankle twisting under him. Since each husky fellow was groaning and attempting to get up, he landed the butt of his pistol against the backs of their necks, and they went down for a long winter's nap. He grabbed their guns, threw them all into a Dumpster standing nearby and then sprinted off.

He could still hear running feet and also an occasional gunshot.

Web didn't know if it was his pursuers or simply your run-of-the-mill gangbanger dispute that happened around here every night. He rounded another corner and was hit low and hard. The impact knocked him off his feet, and he lost his weapon as he sprawled on the asphalt. He rolled and came up, fists cocked.

Bandanna Boy was standing there, a knife almost as big as he was in hand. He was grinning the same shit-eating grin that he'd had in the alley on the night that Charlie Team had disappeared.

Web noted he held the weapon with some skill. The kid probably had fought a hundred knife fights. He was shorter than Web, yet more muscular, probably quicker. This was to be a classic test of youth against experience. "Well, come on and eat some experience, young man," muttered Web as he prepared to defend himself.

The kid lunged at Web, whipping the knife blade around so fast Web could hardly follow. Yet he didn't really have to, because Web executed a loop kick that clipped Bandanna's legs out from under him and he went down hard. The kid was up quickly, but only in time to take one of Web's size twelves to the head. With the kid stunned, Web was all over him. He locked down the arm holding the knife and proceeded to break Bandanna's grip on both the knife and his forearm. With his security of the blade gone and a jagged shaft of his forearm staring him in the face, the kid fled, his cries of pain sweeping the alley with him, and his shit-eating attitude lying next to the knife on the bloody ground. Web shook his own fuzzy head clear and started to stumble over to retrieve his gun. He never made it.

Web could only watch silently as the group of men appeared from all corners, blocking the path to his weapon. They carried sawed-off shotguns and pistols. Web could sense they were all so very happy to see him here, outnumbered as he was ten to one. Web figured he had nothing to lose by taking an aggressive posture. He held out his FBI shield. "I could bust every one of you on weapons charges. But I tell you what, I'm feeling generous and not up to all the paperwork, so you just pack up and go about your business, and we'll forget about it. For now. But don't be pulling this shit again."

Their response was to move forward. Web's response to that was to move back until he felt the wall behind him, and further retreat and ultimate escape would have to be confined to his imagination. Then two of the crew directly in front of him were tossed to the side so violently it was like gravity had been suspended from underneath them. In this gap Web found himself staring up at the largest man he had ever seen outside a professional football game. The giant was six-foot-six or -seven and if he carried less than four hundred pounds on his frame, Web didn't know how. He realized that this new antagonist must be the legendary Big F.

The man was dressed in a short-sleeved burgundy-colored silk shirt that was so large Web could have used it for a blanket. Beige linen pants covered long legs that actually looked short, so thick and massive were they. He had on no socks, his bare feet were in suede loafers and his shirt was open to the navel, even though it was only about fifty degrees with a sneaky little breeze that quickly got under one's skin. His skull had a shadow of fuzz covering it. His facial features matched his great size, with a heavy blob of nose and conical ears, each pierced with about a dozen diamond studs that gleamed impressively even in the poor light.

He wasted no time and strode right up to Web. When Big F reached out to grab a fistful of him, Web delivered a vicious blow to the man's gut that would have dropped a heavyweight boxer. All he got from Big F was a grunt. Then he lifted Web off the ground, reared back like he was preparing to hurl a shotput and threw the two-hundred-pound Web a good ten feet down the alley. The rest of the gang hooted, cursed and otherwise had themselves a little federal agent ass-kicking party, high-fiving, exchanging growls and knuckle-banging each other with animalistic glee.

Web had not even gotten to his feet before the man was on him again. This time he hooked Web by his belt, lifted him up and sent him sailing into a line of garbage cans. Web came up fast, gagging for air and nauseous with the pounding he was taking. Before Big F could get to him, Web shot forward, lowered his shoulder and laid his very solid frame directly into the man's gut. Web might as well have slammed himself into a pickup truck, for all the good it did. He dropped to the asphalt without having budged Big F one damned inch. His shoulder felt dislocated. Web got to his feet, feigned being seriously hurt and then exploded with a leaping kick that caught Big F flush on the side of the head. Splotches of blood appeared at the corner of Big F's ear, and Web noted with satisfaction that he had relieved the man of some of his diamond studs, leaving jagged bits of earlobe in their bloody wake.

Yet Big F was still standing, like one of the brick buildings surrounding them. Web had knocked hundred-pound body bags right off their supports with that kick. How could this be? Well, he had no time really to think about how it could be because Big F, moving faster than a man his size should ever have been able to, delivered a forearm the size of a six-by-six to the side of Web's head that came one dizzying star from knocking him out. A few seconds later, Big F was half carrying and half dragging Web down the alley, his shoes and jacket lost somewhere along the way. His pants were ripped and his legs and arms were bleeding from being dragged over the pavement.

Apparently just for fun, since Web was putting up no further resistance, Big F tossed him headfirst against a Dumpster. This did knock out Web, and he stayed that way until he felt himself being thrown onto something soft. He opened his eyes; it was the interior of the Mercury. He flinched when he saw Big F slam the door and walk away. The guy hadn't said one word, and Web had never been more humbled in his life. No wonder Granny and Jerome had acted the way they had. Hell, Jerome was probably still running.

Web sat up slowly and felt around for broken bones. When he opened his right hand a paper fluttered out of it. Web saw the numbers and words scribbled on it, looked over in amazement at where Big F had been but was no longer. He put the slip of paper in his pocket, pulled out his keys, revved up the Mercury and burned rubber off the rear wheels getting the hell out of there, leaving behind his jacket, his shoes, his pistol and a big chunk of his confidence.

28

It was early in the morning and Web was soaking in the tub in another crummy motel. Every part of him ached. The long scrapes on his arms and legs burned like there was a branding iron pressed to them. He had a knot on his forehead from where his noggin had met Dumpster and a gash along the good side of his face that probably still had some grains of asphalt inside. Boy, he was aging really well. He should try out for male modeling when he left the Bureau.

The phone rang and Web swung his hand out and snagged it. It was Bates.

"I'll pick you and your buddy up in an hour at Romano's house." Web groaned.

"What's wrong?" asked Bates.

"Late night. Got a bitch of a hangover."

"Oh, I'm so sorry, Web. One hour. Be there or find another planet to live on." Bates hung up.

Exactly one hour later Bates picked up Web and Romano and they headed to Virginia horse country.

Bates looked at Web's fresh injuries. "What the hell happened to you?" asked Bates. "You better not have trashed another car, because after the Mercury you're riding a bicycle." Bates glanced over at Web's car parked at the curb.

"I slipped getting out of the bathtub."

"You did all that getting out of the tub?" Bates clearly did not believe this.

"You know what they say, Perce, most accidents happen at home."

Bates stared at him for a long moment before deciding not to pursue it. He had a lot of other items on his to-do list.

After an hour's drive they got off the highway and drove for miles along twisting roads and hairpin curves bracketed by thick woods. They missed a turn somewhere because they ended up on a dirt road barely wide enough for their car. Web looked over at a sagging metal gate and the sign next to it that read, EAST WINDS FARM NO HUNTING, FISHING OR TRESPASSING. VIOLATORS PROSECUTED TO THE FULLEST EXTENT OF THE LAW.

East Winds, they knew, was the name of the Canfield farm. They must have come in on the rear side, Web concluded. He smiled as he read the sign. Well, damn, these people meant business; he was shaking with fear. He glanced at Romano, who was looking at the sign and smiling too because he was probably thinking the same thing. The fencing here was low, rail board on post. The place was in the middle of nowhere. "Somebody who knew what they were doing could hop that fence in a second, go to the main house, kill the Canfields and everyone else there, have a drink, watch some TV and no one would probably know until the spring thaw," opined Romano knowledgeably.

"Yeah, and since murder isn't one of the offenses listed on the sign," added Web, "I guess he'd be free from prosecution."

"Keep that crap to yourself," growled Bates. However, Web could tell the guy was worried. This place was vulnerable.

They finally found the correct turn and reached the front entrance to East Winds. The gates reminded Web of the ones in front of the White House. And yet with all the exposed property, the big gates were a joke from a security perspective. Above the entrance was an arch of metal scrollwork with the name of the farm written large. And to top it all off, the gates were open! There was a call box, however, and Bates hit the button. They waited and someone finally came on.

"Special Agent Bates with the FBI."

"Come on up," said the voice. "Follow the main road and take the first right up to the main house."

As Bates pulled forward, Web pointed out, "No closed-circuit TV. We could be Charlie Manson and company, for all they know."

They headed straight. The rolling green land stretched as far as they could see, much of it enclosed by horizontal rail fencing. Large rolls of hay lay in the fields. Off to one side was a small pond. The main road was asphalt and ran straight for a while and then curved right around a swath of towering oak and hickory, with scrub pines wedged between. Through the trees to the right they caught glimpses of an enormous structure.

They finally came to a large two-story stone house with high Palladian windows and broad sliding doors below and topped with a large tin-sheathed cupola patinaed by the elements, with a weather vane of a horse and rider mounted on top. To Web it looked like a color Martha Stewart might try to copyright and then sell to the masses as something far more chic than simple weather rot.

They turned right, away from the carriage house, and passed down a long paved drive. Some of the largest maple trees Web had ever seen were situated in rows on each side of the drive, forming a natural roof of limbs and leaves.

Web looked up ahead and his eyes widened. It was the largest house he had ever seen and it was constructed all from stone, with an enormous front portico supported by six massive columns.

"Damn," said Romano, "that looks to be about the size of the Hoover Building."

Bates parked the car in front and started to get out. "It's a house, Romano, and put your tongue back in your mouth and try not to embarrass the Bureau."

The massive door opened and a man stood there.

Billy Canfield had not aged well, thought Web.

He was still tall and trim, but the broad shoulders and deep chest—which Web remembered from the man's visits to Web in the hospital—had fallen in. His hair was now thinner and almost fully gray and the face had grown even craggier. As Canfield walked out to see them, Web noted the limp in the man's gait and he saw where one knee turned inward more than normal. Canfield, he figured, would be in his early sixties now. Fifteen years ago he had married for the second time, to Gwen, a woman much younger than he was. He had grown children from his first marriage, and he and Gwen had also had their own boy, the ten-year-old who had been killed by members of the Free Society at the school in Richmond. Web still

saw David Canfield's face often in his dreams. The guilt had not lessened over the years; if anything, it had grown more intense.

Canfield eyed each of them fiercely from under thick tufts of
eyebrows. Bates put out his strong hand and held up his credentials with the other, just like the Bureau taught you, observed Web.

"I'm Agent Bates with the FBI's Washington Field Office, Mr.
Canfield. Thanks for letting us come out."

Canfield ignored Bates and instead looked over at Web. "I know
you, don't I?"

"Web London, Mr. Canfield. I'm with Hostage Rescue. I was down
in Richmond that day," he added diplomatically. "You visited me in
the hospital. That meant a lot to me. I want you to know that."

Canfield nodded slowly and then put out his hand to Web, who
shook it. "Well I appreciate what y'all tried to do then. You did all
you could, risked your life and all for my boy." He stopped and
looked over at Bates. "But I told you on the phone that nothing's
happened out here and if that son of a bitch comes my way he'll
end up dead and not the other way round."

"I understand that, Mr. Canfield."

"Billy."

"Thank you, Billy, but you have to understand that three people
with a connection to what happened at that school in Richmond,
and possibly a fourth person, have already been killed. If the Free
Society is behind it, and I have to tell you that as yet we have no direct proof that they are, but if they are, you could be a target. That's
why we're here."

Canfield looked at his watch. "And what, you want to put me
under lock and key? I got a damn horse farm to run, and let me tell
you it don't run on autopilot."

"I understand that, but there are unobtrusive steps we can
take—"

"Y'all want to keep talking, you got to come on with me. I got
things to do."

Bates exchanged glances with Web and Romano and then
shrugged. They followed Canfield over to a jet-black Land Rover
and climbed in.

Canfield didn't wait for seat belts to be put on. He hit the gas and they sped off. Web was in the front seat next to him. As they drove along, he surveyed the farm.

"Last I heard, you owned a trucking company in Richmond. How'd you end up on a horse farm in Fauquier County?"

Canfield slipped a cigarette out of his shirt pocket and lit up, cracked the window and blew smoke out. "Gwen doesn't let me smoke in the house. Take my shots when I can," he explained. "Now, that's a damn good question, Web, from trucking to horses. I ask myself that sometimes and sometimes I wish I was back in trucking. I was born and bred in Richmond and like it there. That city creeps into your bones for better or worse, and I've seen both sides of that coin.

"But Gwen's always loved horses; she grew up on a farm in Kentucky. I guess it gets in your blood too. All it's done for me is make my blood *pressure* go through the roof. Anyway, we decided to make a go of it. Jury's still out on how we're doing. Sunk every damn dime I have into this place, so at least we have the incentive to make it work."

"What exactly do you do on a horse farm?" asked Romano as he leaned forward. "See, the only horses I've seen are the ones that pull the carriages around Central Park. I grew up in the Big Apple."

"Sorry to hear that, Yank," said Canfield. He looked around at Romano. "Didn't catch your name."

"Romano, Paul Romano. Friends call me Paulie."

"Well, we're not friends, so I'll just call you Paul. Now, the main thing you do on a horse farm is bleed money, Paul. Bleed it like it's ice in a damn hailstorm. You pay out your ass for a property like this and all the people to help run it. You get you some horses and they eat you out of house and home. You pay outrageous stud fees so some son-of-a-bitching horny stallion with a few track victories to its name will impregnate your mares. And then nature delivers you some foals that proceed to chip away at what little money you got left. As the foals grow into yearlings, you spend enough on the little sons of bitches to send a dozen kids to Harvard. And then you hope and pray that maybe one of 'em shows some promise and you can sell it to some poor sucker and maybe get a five percent return on your money for working your ass off sixteen hours a day. And if you don't, then the bank that you've sold your life to comes and takes every single thing you've ever owned in your whole life and you die dirt poor without a roof over your head, a stitch of clothes on your back or a single person you could call a friend." He looked back at Romano. "That's about it, *Paul*. You got any other questions?"

"Nope, that about covers it," said Romano as he sat back.

They reached a compound consisting of barns, stables and other buildings, and Canfield drove underneath a pediment wooden arch that Canfield said was based upon the one at George Washington's Mount Vernon; only that it cost more.

"This is the equestrian center. Horse stalls, big hay barn, manager's office, trainers work center, wash stalls, riding rings and the like. God's Little Acre if ever there were one," said Canfield, and he laughed as he climbed out of the Rover. The FBI agents followed him.

Canfield called out to a man who was talking to a number of what looked to Web to be farmhands. "Hey, Nemo, come on over here for a sec."

The man walked over. He was about Web's height, yet burly, with the powerful physique of someone who worked with his body for a living. He had short, wiry black hair, slightly graying at the temples, and strong, handsome features. His clothes were clearly ranch: loose-fitting jeans and a faded denim shirt. Pointed-toe boots were on his feet. They weren't fancy, no alligator or kangaroo skin and no silver toe clips. They were dusty and creased from hard use and worn away where Web figured stirrups met the leather. Muddy canvas gloves stuck out from his back pocket. He took off his sweat-stained Stetson as he walked over and wiped his brow with a rag.

"Nemo Strait here is my farm manager. Nemo, this is a bunch of folks from the FBI. They've come here to tell me I'm in danger because they let the asshole that killed my son break out of jail and he might be gunning for me."

Strait gave them all a terrifically unfriendly stare.

Web put out his hand. "I'm Agent Web London."

Strait shook his hand, and Web felt the extra force the man gave to the grip. Nemo Strait was a very strong gent and obviously wanted to let Web know it. Web caught the man checking out his damaged mug. For most it evoked sympathy, which Web loathed. Nemo, though, came away just looking a little surlier, as though he had suffered far greater wounds on a good day. Web instantly liked the man.

Canfield pointed at Web. "Now, this fellow here actually tried to save my boy, which is more than I can say for some others involved in the process."

"Well, in my opinion the government's not good for much 'cept messing up folks' lives," said Nemo, looking at Web. His voice was pure country, with little dips in between each syllable, mimicking the bobbing of his prodigious Adam's apple. For some reason, Web envisioned big Nemo performing country and western karaoke and being just a stitch at it.

Web looked over at Bates, who said, "What we're trying to do here is help you, Billy. If somebody tries something with you, we want to be here to stop it."

Canfield surveyed his property and then stared at Bates. "I got ten men full-time on my farm and every one of them is pretty good with a gun."

Bates shook his head. "We waltzed right in here and you didn't even know who we were. You came out the front door unarmed and alone. If we were looking to kill you, you'd already be dead."

Canfield smiled. "What if I told you I had some of my boys watching you from the time you stepped on the property? And that they were pointing something at you that wasn't their fingers?"

Web and Romano glanced around without seeming to do so. Web had a sixth sense about people aiming guns his way and he was wondering why it hadn't kicked in.

"Then I'd tell you your *boys* probably would end up shooting some innocent people," said Bates.

"Well, hell, that's what I got insurance for, I guess," Canfield shot back.

"I checked the records, Billy. During the trial you received death threats from Ernest Free among others. The Bureau put you under protection then."

Canfield's features grew very grim. "That's right, every time I turned around there was some suit with a gun staring at me and reminding me that my little boy was dead and buried. So, no offense, but I've had enough of you folks to last the rest of my life. That's about as clear as I can make it."

Bates squared his shoulders and got closer to Canfield. "The Bureau is offering you protection again. And until Ernest Free is caught and we're sure that you're not in danger, I'm kind of insisting on it," added Bates.

Canfield folded his arms across his chest. "Well, then we got us a problem, because this is the United States of America and a person has the right to choose who comes on his property and who doesn't and I'm asking you to get the hell off my land right now." Strait moved closer to his boss and Web saw some of the other farmhands also draw nearer. He also noted that Romano's hand had eased to his pistol grip.

One big fellow made the truly enormous mistake of putting his hand on Romano's shoulder. In an instant the man was facedown on the ground, Romano's knee against the base of his spine, one .45 in the guy's ear, and another .45, which Romano had pulled from the second holster he wore on the back of his waistband, pointed at Canfield's other men.

"Okay," said Romano, "any of you other buckaroos want to bring it on?"

Web quickly stepped forward before Romano killed them all. "Look, Billy, I shot two of the Frees, and if I had gotten the chance I would have blown Ernest away too. But the bastard got lucky and took a round through his shoulder instead, and I walked out with half a face and missing most of my blood. Now, I really believe that we all want the same thing here; we're just differing a bit on how to get there. What if Romano and I came to stay with you on the farm? No suits, just jeans and boots. We'll even help with the work. But in exchange you have to cooperate with us. You'll have to listen to us when we tell you there might be a problem, and if we tell you to get your butt down, you get down. It looks like the Frees have already taken out several people and they did it in ways that were pretty damn ingenious. So while I'm sure your men are really good at what they do, it might not be enough if these people really want to take you out. I can see that you're not the sort of guy who likes other people to tell you what to do, but I also don't believe you want to give the Frees the satisfaction of killing you. You and your wife have already been through that hell with your son. I don't believe you want her to have to grieve again over you."

Canfield looked at Web a long moment. And for that entire time Web wasn't sure if the man was going to jump him or maybe order his men to open fire. Finally, Canfield looked down and kicked the dirt. "Let's go on back to the house and talk about this." He motioned for Strait and his men to go back to work. Romano helped the man up and even dusted him off.

"Nothing personal, slick, I would've done that to anybody who touched me. Get the message?"

The man grabbed his hat and hustled off. From the look of fear in the man's eyes, Web didn't think he'd be "touching" Romano ever again.

Canfield and the agents climbed in the Rover. As they were driving back, Canfield looked over at Web.

"Okay, I'm not disputing that what you say makes a lot of sense, but I'm not looking forward to revisiting that part of my life. And I'm kind of hating it that these assholes are pulling me back into that shit hole."

"I understand that, but—" Web was interrupted by the ringing of a cell phone. He checked his phone, but it wasn't his. Bates and Romano did the same thing. Canfield pulled a phone out of a storage panel in the Rover and looked at it. It wasn't ringing. He glanced at the floorboard and reached down and picked up the phone that was lying there.

"Somebody must have left their phone in here, although it's not Gwen's and I don't know who the hell else drives this truck. Probably somebody wanting to sell me something." He was about to punch the talk button when Web grabbed the phone out of his hand, hit the window button on his door and threw the phone out.

Canfield looked at him. "What in the hell do you think you're doing?"

They watched as the phone flew through the air and then hit the ground in the middle of an empty dirt field. Nothing happened. Canfield pulled the Rover to a stop. "You get your ass out there and go get that damn phone—"

The explosion was powerful enough to rock the Land Rover and send a cloud of black smoke and flames a hundred feet in the air.

All the men stared at this fiery spectacle for several seconds. Finally a shaken Canfield looked over at Web. "When do you boys wanta start?"

29

Web drove down the street to his mother's home. He still didn't know what the hell to do with it. To sell it would require him to fix it up and he would have to do that himself, since his bank account wouldn't allow the convenience of hiring professionals to do it. And yet he had no desire to tighten one hinge or replace one shingle on the place.

Web was here because it had occurred to him that if he was going to be staying out at the farm for a while he would need some clothes. He didn't want to go back to his own home right now. The reporters were probably still staking it out. However, he kept some clothes at his mom's house too. He also wanted to return the box containing much of Harry Sullivan's life to the attic. Being constantly on the move now, Web didn't want to chance losing it. He also wasn't sure what to do about his father. Should he call the main prison? Was that the place to get reacquainted with his old man? Yet chances were, at his age, Harry Sullivan was going to die in prison. This might be Web's only shot. It was funny how almost being blown to bits by a bomb in a phone made you reorder your priorities.

His musings about his father stopped when his phone rang. It was Claire, and she sounded nervous yet determined.

"I've been giving our sessions a lot of thought, Web. I think we need to change tactics somewhat. I'm curious about a few things and I think they can be better addressed in a different sort of way."

"Well, that's incredibly vague, Claire. What exactly are you talking about?"

"From our discussions so far, Web, it seems to me that many of your issues stem from your relationship with your mother and stepfather. During our last session you told me that you had grown up in your mother's house and that you had recently inherited it from her."

"So?"

"And you also mentioned that you would never consider living there. Also that your stepfather died there."

"Again, so what?"

"I think there might be something else there. You remember I said I listen for cues from my patients? Well, I'm getting a big one from you here."

"What does an old house have to do with my *issues*?"

"It's not the house, Web, it's what might have happened in the house."

He persisted. "What might have happened in the house other than my stepfather kicking the bucket that has anything to do with me?"

"Only you know that."

"And I'm telling you that's all I know. And I really don't see how my freezing in an alley has anything to do with my growing up in that house. That was a long time ago."

"You'd be amazed, Web, at how long the mind can keep something under wraps until it erupts one day. Your encounter with the little boy in the alley could have triggered something from your past."

"Well, I'm telling you I don't know what that is."

"If I'm right, you do know, Web, only your conscious mind doesn't realize it."

He rolled his eyes. "What kind of psychobabble crap is that?"

In response Claire said, "Web, I'd like to hypnotize you."

He was stunned. "No."

"It really could help us get somewhere."

"How can making me bark like a dog while I'm unconscious help?"

"Being in a hypnotic state is a form of *enhanced* consciousness, Web. You'll be aware of everything going on around you. You will be in complete control. I can't make you do anything you don't want to."

"It won't help."

"You can't know that. It can allow you to address some issues you ordinarily would be inhibited from doing."

"There are some things in my head maybe I don't want to figure out."

"You never know, Web, until you try. Please think about it. Please."

"Look, Claire, I'm sure you've got lots of crazy people to help. Why don't you think about them for a while." He clicked off.

Web pulled his car into the driveway, went inside, packed a duffel of clothes and then hesitated at the bottom of the attic stairs, holding the Harry Sullivan box under one arm. This really shouldn't be so hard, he told himself. An attic was an attic. Though he had told Claire otherwise, there was something about this house that had rattled him somewhere deep in his soul. Yet he reached up, gripped the cord and pulled down the stairs.

When he got to the attic, he put the box down and reached for the light cord but then drew his hand back. He looked to the various corners, seeking out threats, an endeavor that was now more instinct than habit. He drew his gaze across the plywood floor and then to all the blackened shapes of his family's bleak history, in the form of clothes racks, piles of books, heaps of junk left to rot. The stack of burgundy-colored rug remnants near the stairway held his attention. They were tightly rolled and bound with tape. He picked one up. It was heavy and very hard, stiff as it was with both cold and age. The remnants matched the rug on the floor below and Web wondered why his mother had kept them.

Off to the side there once had been a large pile of clothes. Now the space was empty. Web had sometimes come up here, pulled the attic door closed after him and hidden under the clothes pile during his stepfather's many rampages. His stepfather had also kept his stash of drugs and special liquor up here too, because he feared his wife getting her hands on them. He would stumble up here in the middle of the night, already wasted, and seek out additional means to do his mind further damage. It was the early seventies, the country still digging itself out from Vietnam, and people like his stepfather, who had never taken up arms for his country or for any other cause, used the general angst and indifference of the times as an excuse to live life on a perpetual high. Part of the attic floor was also over the ceiling of Web's bedroom. When he was young and in bed, Web would hear his stepfather's footsteps overhead as the man sought out his mood-altering substances. Young Web would be terrified that Stockton might come crashing down through the ceiling, to land on top of him, and beat the hell out of him. A cobra in your bed, kill or be killed. When Stockton did beat him Web would have gone to his mother, but most of the time she was not there to console him. She often took long drives at night and came home in the morning, hours after Web had dressed and fed himself and rushed off to school so he wouldn't have to confront the old man across the breakfast table. The creak of steps still bothered him to this day. He closed his eyes and breathed in the chilly air, and in his mind that old, vanished pile of clothes rose high into the air. And then right on cue there was a slash of red and then sounds flooded him that made Web open his eyes and rush back down the stairs and close the attic door. He had had this vision a thousand times and could never figure it out. He had gotten to the point where he didn't want to decipher it, but for now, for some reason, he felt like he was closer to its true meaning than ever before.

He sat in the Mercury and pulled out his cell phone and the piece of paper Big F had given him the night before. He checked his watch. It was right at the time the paper said to call. He punched in the numbers and the phone was immediately answered. He was given a set of instructions and then the line went dead. At least they were an efficient bunch. Well, he was going to have a busy night.

As he drove off, he paraphrased the immortal words of TOC:

"Web London to the rest of the human race, *nobody* has control."

30

Web drove to Romano's house and picked him up. Angie was standing in the doorway when Romano came out with his bags and she didn't look very happy. At least, Web deduced this when he waved to Angie and got the finger in return for his troubles. Romano loaded two sniper rifles, an MP-5, a set of Kevlar and four semiautomatic pistols along with ammo clips for each into the trunk.

"Christ, we're not going after Saddam, Paulie."

"You do it your way and I'll do it mine. The guy who blew away Chris Miller is still out there and if he's getting off thousand-yard shots at yours truly, then I want to be able to shoot the son of a bitch back. Capeesh?" He turned and waved to Angie. "Bye-bye, sweetie-pie."

Angie flipped him the bird too before slamming the door behind her.

"I take it she's upset," said Web.

"I had some leave time. We were supposed to go see her mother in bayou country. Slidell, Louisiana, to be exact."

"I'm sorry, Paulie."

Romano looked at him and smiled, before pulling his Yankees cap over his eyes and settling back in his seat. "I'm not."

They drove to East Winds, where they were met at the gate by a pair of FBI agents. They showed their creds and were allowed in. The Bureau presence was here in its full glory after the attempted murder of Billy Canfield via exploding cell phone. The Bureau's bomb squad van passed them going out, no doubt with every bit of evidence they could scrounge from the debris. Web felt sure that Bureau agents were interviewing everyone on the farm who might be remotely connected with where that phone might have come from. Web was also sure Billy Canfield would be less than thrilled with all that activity. Yet at least he had saved the man's life. That had gotten them entry into the farm.

He had just finished this thought when a horse and rider came into view. It was a big, glossy Thoroughbred with a perfect blending of shimmering muscle, tendon and bone, all moving in a delicate synchronicity that made it seem more machine than animal. Web had ridden a few times but had never really gotten into it, and yet he had to admit, the sight was really something to behold. The rider was dressed in brown riding britches, high, polished black boots and a light-blue cotton sweater. The hands were gloved. The black riding helmet failed to fully cover the long blond hair.

He rolled his window down as the woman rode the horse over to the car.

"I'm Gwen Canfield. You must be Web."

"I am. This is Paul Romano. Did your husband tell you the arrangement?"

"Yes. He asked me to show you to where you'll be staying," said Gwen.

She took off her helmet, pulled back her blond hair and it fell across her shoulders.

Web looked at the horse and said, "She's a beauty."

"It's a he."

"Sorry, didn't check the equipment. Didn't want to embarrass anybody."

She patted the horse's neck. "Baron doesn't mind, do you? Secure in your masculinity, aren't you?"

"We should all be so lucky."

Gwen eased a bit back on the small English-style riding saddle, one hand firmly holding on to the double loop of reins, and looked around. "Billy told me what happened in the Rover. I want to thank you for what you did. Billy probably forgot to."

"Just doing my job." Though he had never met Gwen, other HRT members at the trial in Richmond had described her as high strung and emotional. This woman was very calm, almost detached in a way; despite her words of gratitude her tone was subdued. Maybe she had just used up all the emotions she had back then.

Web had seen pictures of Gwen Canfield taken by the media at the trial. Unlike her husband, Gwen had aged very well. She was, he figured, in her mid- to late thirties. Her blond hair was still long. Her figure was that of a woman ten years younger, with curves where men enjoyed seeing them and a bosom that would never fail to draw stares. Her features were lovely, with high cheekbones and full lips. If she had been an actress, the camera would have fallen in love with her. She was also tall and carried herself very erect. The horse rider's posture, Web assumed.

"We're going to the carriage house. It's right down this road."

Gwen turned Baron around, punched the horse in the sides with her boots, gave a loud call that sounded indecipherable to Web yet in horse language must have meant gallop like holy hell, because that's exactly what old Baron did. Horse and rider flew down the road. Then Gwen leaned forward, actually blending in with the horse's torso as Baron lifted off the ground, clearing the three-foot slanted jump-in fence line—a breach in the fence designed to allow horse and rider to pass through—landing in one of the paddocks and galloping on without missing a step. Or hoof. Web honked his horn in applause, and Gwen waved without looking back.

The carriage house, as it turned out, was the place with the big Palladian windows and patinaed weather vane Web had seen earlier. Gwen dismounted from Baron and tethered him to a post. As they were unloading their stuff from the car, Web gave Romano a sign not to unpack his weapons in front of the woman.

Web looked at the location of the carriage house and its relation to the main house, which he could barely see down the long, tree-lined road. He turned to Gwen. "I don't mean to sound ungrateful, but would it be possible for us to stay in the main house? If anything goes down, it might take us a little too long to get to you."

"Billy said the carriage house. If you have a problem with that, you'll have to take it up with him."

Well, I guess I will, Web told himself. To her he said, "I'm sorry about all this, Mrs. Canfield. You shouldn't have to go through this again."

"I never assume the world is fair anymore." She looked at him closely. "I'm sorry, Billy said that we know you, but I don't remember from where."

"I was part of the Hostage Rescue Team that was at the school that day."

She looked down for a moment. "I see. And now that man is loose again. The one who killed David."

"Unfortunately, yes. But hopefully not for long."

"He should have been put to death."

"I'm not arguing with you, Mrs. Canfield."

"Just make it Gwen. We're not too formal out here."

"Okay, Gwen. And you can make it Web and Paulie. But we're here to make sure that you and your husband are safe."

She glanced at him. "I haven't felt safe in years, Web. I don't think things are going to change now."

She led them inside. The ground floor of the carriage house was filled with restored antique cars. Web looked at car-happy Romano and thought his partner was going to have a coronary.

Gwen explained, "Billy collects them. His little private car museum, I guess."

"Geez," exclaimed Romano, "that's a right-hand drive Stutz Bearcat." He walked around the space in wonder, like a boy at the Baseball Hall of Fame. "And that's a 1939 Lincoln LeBaron. Only nine of them were ever made. And omigod." He rushed over to the far corner of the room and stopped dead. "Web, this, this is a 1936 Duesenberg SSJ Speedster." He looked at Gwen. "Am I wrong, or were there only two of these ever built, one for Clark Gable and the other for Gary Cooper? Please tell me I'm not wrong."

Gwen nodded. "You know your cars. That's Coop's."

Romano looked to Web like he was going to faint.

"This is beautiful," said Romano. He turned to the woman. "I want you to know, Gwen, that I am truly honored to be under the same roof with these legendary machines."

Web thought he was going to be sick to his stomach.

Gwen looked at Web and shook her head, a tiny smile clutching at the corners of her mouth. "Men and their toys. Do you have any toys, Web?"

"Not really. Didn't have any as a kid either."

She gave him a penetrating stare and then said, "Upstairs are two bedrooms, each with its own bath and a fully stocked kitchen and living area. This used to be the estate's carriage house back in Colonial times. It's a very historical property. In the 1940s the owner set it up as the firehouse. Billy reconfigured it as guest quarters when he bought the place, although with twenty bedrooms in the main house, I always thought a guest house was a bit superfluous."

"Twenty bedrooms!" said Romano.

"I know," said Gwen. "I grew up on a farm outside of Louisville. We had two bedrooms for seven people."

"Billy didn't come from money either that I remember," said Web. "Trucking is not an easy business, but he did it."

"He was complaining that this farm is sucking every cent of his down the drain," commented Romano. "But those cars don't come cheap."

Gwen really smiled for the first time and Web felt himself smiling at her. "You'll soon learn that Billy Canfield likes to complain. About everything. But especially about money. I'm sure he told you we sank every cent we had into this place, and we did. But what he probably didn't tell you is that the first colt we ever sold won the Kentucky Derby and was third in the Preakness."

"What was that horse's name?"

"King David," Gwen answered quietly. "Now, we didn't get any of that purse, of course, but it put us on the map, and we have the brood mare here that had the King. The stallion that we had her studded with wasn't all that great, which means that our mare's bloodlines got a lot of the credit for the King's prowess."

"Seems sort of right, though, considering the female does all the real work," said Web.

Gwen shot him a glance. "I like your way of thinking. So with the King to our credit, everybody in this country who knows anything about horse racing knows about East Winds and our horses generally fetch a nice premium. Now, we do have some race winners here and the stud fees are impressive. On top of that we've got a good crop of yearlings the past two years and we run a tight ship. Don't get me wrong, it is amazingly expensive to run a breeding farm. But as much as Billy complains, I think we'll be okay."

"That's good to know," said Web. "I guess you came up here soon after the trial."

She said curtly, "If you need anything, just call the house and we'll take care of it. The number's on the wall next to the phone upstairs." She left before they could even thank her.

They went upstairs and looked around. The furnishings were all antique, the appointments refined and elegant and Web was sure that Gwen Canfield's touches had been felt heavily here. Billy Canfield just didn't seem the interior decorator type.

"Man, this is some place," said Romano.

"Yeah, some place that's a long way from the people we're supposed to be protecting, and that I don't like."

"So call Bates and have him call Canfield and they can yell at each other. We're just the foot soldiers, we do what we're told."

"So what do you make of Gwen Canfield?"

"Seems nice enough. She's a real looker too. A lady. Canfield's a lucky guy."

"Don't get any ideas, Paulie."

"Yeah, like Angie would let me live to enjoy it."

"Unpack your stuff and let's make rounds. I want to hook up with Canfield. If we're going to protect him, we need to at least be near the guy. And we're probably going to have to go in shifts, Paulie, so we'll alternate sleep."

"Hey, just like the good old sniper days."

"Yeah, just like the good old sniper days, except you snore like a damn freight train."

"Not anymore; Angie had me fixed."

"How'd she do that?"

"I really don't want to get into it, Web."

They went outside and immediately ran into Percy Bates.

"Any luck on the bomb?" asked Web.

"It was a pretty sophisticated device, from what the techs told me. We're talking to everybody who might know something, but so far nothing. But that phone didn't get in there by itself."

"So maybe we have an inside job. A Free Society member on the premises, maybe?" added Web.

Bates nodded and he looked very worried. "They recruit people from areas just like this. Rural white guys who like guns and land and the old ways and have a big chip on their shoulder because they see the world changing fast and they're no longer on top of it."

"Anything happening with the Frees in southern Virginia?"

"We've got people watching them but nothing so far. Now they might just be lying low after all this activity. That would be the smart thing to do. And they're not dumb. They have to know they're suspected in this and that we're watching. All we need is one link and we can go after them."

"Where's Canfield? I sort of like to keep track of the man I'm supposed to be protecting."

Bates said, "And Gwen too. She received the same death threats that her husband did."

Web thought about this. "Well, Paulie and I can split up, but it'd be nice to have more men on this. East Winds looks to be a pretty big place."

"Two thousand acres and sixty-eight buildings, actually. I talked to Canfield about that and he said if I wanted to bring more guys out here, he'd see me in court and then see me in hell, and I'm taking the guy at face value. It's up to you two, but listen, Web, we're not going to be very far away."

"I'm counting on that, Perce."

"Oh, and Web?"

"Yeah?"

"Thanks for saving my life."

They found Billy Canfield down at the equestrian center examining the foreleg of a stallion while Nemo Strait and two young men dressed in riding clothes looked on.

Canfield said to one of the young men, "Better call the vet; might only be a sprain, but maybe a fracture. Hope to hell it's not." As the man walked off, Canfield called after him, "And tell that damn farrier that unless he comes up with a better shoe, I'm changing shops. We got some stock with soft hooves and the glue-ons are pretty damn good for that and he doesn't even carry 'em."

"Yes, sir."

Canfield patted the horse's flank, wiped off his hands and walked over to the HRT men.

"Farrier?" asked Romano.

"The horseshoer man," answered Canfield. "A glorified black-smith. In the old days horse farms would keep one on full-time. Now they come around once a week in their truck with a forge in the bed and their anvil and hammer and prestamped shoes and do their work. They're not cheap, but who'd want to do that kind of work? It's hard, hot and dangerous, what with crazy horses trying to kick your brains out."

"What are those glue-ons you mentioned?" Web wanted to know.

Strait answered, "Sometimes a horse's hoof walls get too thin for the nails and they break up, especially horses imported from Europe, because of the climate and soil differences; their hooves get brittle. A soft shoe doesn't require any nails, it's like a little bag over the hooves. It lasts a couple of months if done right. And the glue-ons are just what they sound like. Shoes glued on, no nails."

"Sound like a lot to learn about this business."

"Well, I've always been a quick learner," said Billy with a glance at Strait. Next he stared over at Bates. "You guys done talking to my boys? I've got a farm to run."

"We'll be out of here pretty soon."

Canfield looked at Web then pointed at Bates. "He told me about the phone killings and all. But that was still pretty quick thinking on your part."

"I'm a fast learner too," said Web.

Canfield studied him curiously. "Well, what's the next thing you'd like to learn about?"

"East Winds. I'd like to go over every inch of it."

"Have to get Gwen to do that. I've got things requiring my attention."

Web looked at Romano. "Paulie here will go with you."

Canfield looked like he was going to erupt but then seemed to pull it back in. "All right." He looked at Romano. "Paul, how are you on a horse?"

Romano jerked, blinked and looked at Web and then at Canfield. "I've never been on one."

Canfield put an arm around the HRT man and smiled. "Well, I hope you're as fast a learner as your partner."

31

Gwen was at the equestrian center with Baron when her husband asked her to show Web around the place. She led Web to the horse stalls.

"The best way to see the farm is on horseback. Do you ride?" she asked.

"A little. I'm certainly not in your league."

"Then I've got just the horse for you."

Boo, Gwen told him, was a Trakehner, a German breed, a warm-blooded horse bred to be superior warhorses and a cross between a hot-blooded, high-spirited and temperamental Arabian and a cold-blooded, calm and hardworking draft. The horse weighed about seventeen hundred pounds, stood almost eighteen hands high and looked at Web like he wanted to take a bite out of his skull as they stood next to Boo in the stall.

"Boo was a great dressage horse, but now his work is done and he doesn't really like to move all that much. He's gotten fat and happy. We call him 'old grump' because that's what he pretty much is. But deep down he's a sweetheart, and he's very flexible too. You can ride him English or western saddle."

"Yeah, I'm sure," said Web as he stared up at the beast. Boo didn't look the least bit happy that Web was in his personal space.

Gwen put the square saddle pad over the horse's back and next had Web help her place the heavy Western-style saddle over the pad. "Now watch while I cinch the saddle, he'll hold his breath and push out his belly." Web watched in fascination as the horse did exactly that.

"When you think it's tight, he'll let out his breath and it loosens. Then you try and climb on and the saddle slides over his withers. The horse gets a good laugh and the rider gets a few bruises."

"Good to know dumb animals are that smart," said Web.

Gwen showed Web how to transfer from the halter to the bridle and how to slip the latter over Boo's head, seat it correctly and then buckle it. They led Boo outside and over to a stone mounting block.

Web adjusted the chaps Gwen had given him to prevent the saddle from chafing his legs and to allow Web to get a better grip, stepped onto the block and climbed aboard, while Boo just stood there patiently.

"So what do you think?" asked Gwen.

"It's a long way down."

She noted the pistol in his holster. "Do you have to bring the gun?"

"Yes," Web said firmly.

They went to the riding ring and Gwen led horse and rider around the ring. Next Gwen showed Web neck-reining to brake, turn and back the horse up, and sounds and leg pressure to make the animal go and stop. "Boo's been all over the farm, so if you let him, he'll go where he's supposed to. Nice and easy."

Hired help had brought Baron around while they were working with Boo. Gwen mounted up on her horse. "Now, Boo is the patriarch of this place and he and Baron have never ridden together before. So Boo may try and establish his dominance over Baron to show him who's boss."

"Sort of like guys with too much testosterone," opined Web.

Gwen looked at him in a strange way. "Boo's a gelding, Web." He looked at her blankly, not getting it. "If he were a man, we'd call him a eunuch."

"Poor Boo."

The two horses seemed to establish a grudging truce, and Web watched as Gwen slipped a Motorola walkie-talkie radio out of her back pocket and turned it on. "Just in case there's a problem," she said.

"Smart to keep in communication," said Web. "I've got my cell phone too."

"After what happened today with Billy, I'm not sure I'll ever use one again," she said.

Web looked down at his phone and started having some doubts.

They started off, trailed by a golden retriever named Opie, and another compact but strongly built canine Gwen called Tuff. "Strait has a dog running around here too," she said. "Calls him Old Cuss, and it's an apt description because he's nothing but trouble." The sky was clear, and as they went up and down the small hills on the property, it seemed to Web that he could see almost all the way to Charlottesville. Boo was content to follow Baron and kept up a sedate pace that didn't tax Web.

Gwen reined Baron to a halt. Web eased Boo next to her.

"As I said, East Winds has been around a very long time. The King of England gave Lord Culpeper a land grant consisting of millions of acres in the 1600s. A descendant of Lord Culpeper's gave a thousand acres of this land grant to his eldest daughter upon her marriage to a man named Adam Rolfe. The central part of the house was started in 1765 and completed in 1781 by Rolfe, who was an expert builder and also a merchant. You've seen the outside of the main house?" Web nodded. "Well, it was constructed in the Georgian style. And the millwork, particularly the dentil moldings, are some of the best I have ever seen."

"Georgian, that's what I would have guessed." Web was lying; he wouldn't have known a Georgian style if it leapt up and bit him in his dentil moldings.

"The estate remained in the Rolfe family until the early 1900s. During that time it was a true working plantation and crops were raised here: tobacco, soybeans, hemp, that sort of thing."

"And slaves to work it, I guess," said Web. "At least until the end of the Civil War."

"Actually, no, the plantation was close enough to Washington that its owners were Northern sympathizers. In fact, East Winds was part of the Underground Railroad.

"In 1910," Gwen continued, "the estate was sold out of the family. It passed through a series of hands until Walter Sennick bought it at the end of World War II. He was an inventor and made a huge fortune selling his ideas to the automobile manufacturers. He made East Winds into a small self-contained town, and at its peak he had over three hundred full-time employees here. There was also a company store, phone exchange, firehouse, those sorts of things."

"Nothing like never having to leave home." The whole time Gwen was talking, Web had been surveying the grounds, judging where possible attacks might come from and how best to defend against them. Yet if there was a rat on the inside, that sort of strategy might be futile. A Trojan horse worked as well now as it had thousands of years ago.

Gwen nodded. "Now there are sixty-eight buildings in total with twenty-seven miles of board fencing. Nineteen paddocks. Fifteen full-time employees. And we still farm here—corn, mostly—although our main interest is breeding Thoroughbreds. Next year we have twenty-two foals due. And we've got a great crop of yearlings going to sale very soon. It's all very exciting."

They rode on and soon came to a high-banked water crossing, where Gwen instructed Web on how to let the horse choose its own footing when going down into the mud. She had Web lean back very far, so that his head was almost resting on Boo's rump when the horse was going down the bank. Then she had Web meld his body into the horse's neck and grasp Boo's mane when the horse was heading up the bank on the other side. Web successfully navigated the stream and earned high praise from Gwen.

They passed an old stone and wood building that Gwen told him was an old Civil War–era hospital that they were thinking of turning into a museum. "We've rehabbed it, put in central air and heat, it's got a kitchen, bedroom, so the curator could live in there," Gwen told him. "An operating table and surgical instruments from the time period are there as well."

"From what I know of that, a Civil War soldier would've taken a minié ball any day over a trip to the hospital."

They rode by a two-hundred-year-old bank barn, so named because it was two stories and built on such a steep grade that it had two entrances on separate levels. There was also a riding ring where horse and rider practiced their dressage. Dressage, Gwen explained, consisted of specialized steps and movements of a horse and rider, akin to a figure skater's routine. They passed a tall wooden tower with a stone foundation that Gwen told him had been used for both observation of wildfires and also for the horse races that had been held here a century ago.

Web studied the place and the surrounding countryside. As a

former sniper constantly on the lookout for the best ground, Web concluded that the tower would definitely be a good observation post, yet he didn't have the manpower to utilize it properly.

They rode past a two-story frame building that Gwen identified as the farm manager's house.

"Nemo Strait seems to do a good job for you."

"He's experienced and knows what he's doing, and he brought a full handpicked crew with him, so that was a plus," Gwen said with what Web perceived as little interest.

They examined entry and exit points in the rear grounds and Web made mental notes of each. Once, a deer broke clear of the tree line and Opie and Tuff took off after it. Neither horse reacted to this clamor, although Web was so startled by the deer flashing in front of him that he had almost fallen off Boo.

Next she led him into a little tree-shaded glen. Web could hear water running nearby and he was not prepared, as they rounded a short curve, to see a small, open building, painted white and with a cedar shake roof, that looked like a gazebo until Web saw the cross on top and the small altar inside with a kneeling pad and a small statue of Jesus on the cross.

He looked over at Gwen for an explanation. She was staring at the small temple as though in a trance and then she glanced over at him.

"This is my chapel, I guess you'd call it. I'm Catholic. My father was a Eucharistic minister, and two of my uncles are priests. Religion runs pretty deep in my life."

"So you had this built?"

"Yes, for my son. I come out here and pray for him just about every day, rain or cold. Do you mind?"

"Please."

"Are you a religious person?"

"In my own way, I guess," Web answered vaguely.

"I used to be a lot more than I am now, actually. I've tried to understand why what happened could happen to someone so innocent. I've never been able to find an answer."

She dismounted and went inside the chapel, crossed herself, took out her rosary from her pocket and then knelt down and started to pray while Web watched her in silence.

After a few minutes she rose and rejoined him.

They rode on and finally came to a large building that had clearly been abandoned for some time.

"The old Monkey House," said Gwen. "Sennick built it and kept all sorts of chimps, baboons, even gorillas there. Why, I don't know. Legend has it that when some of the animals would escape from their cages they'd be chased through the trees by beer-drinking local yokels with shotguns, who didn't want the monkeys around anyway. For that reason they called the forest around here the monkey jungle. The thought of those poor animals being gunned down by a pack of drunken morons makes me sick."

They dismounted and went into the building. Web could see through the roof where large holes had been worn in by time and the elements. The old cages, rusted and broken, were still lined up against the walls, and there were trenches presumably for catching animal waste and other disgusting things. Trash and old broken machinery littered the concrete floor, along with tree branches and rotted leaves. Tree roots clung to the outside walls and there was what looked to be a loading dock. Web tried to imagine what an inventor of auto accessories would want with a pack of monkeys. None of his theories were pleasant ones. All Web could think of was animals strapped to gurneys, electrical lines capturing the power of lightning bolts and old man Sennick in surgical garb ready to do his dirty work on the terrified simians. The place had a distinct feeling of melancholy, of hopelessness, of death, even, and Web was glad to leave it.

They continued their ride and Gwen dutifully pointed out all the buildings and their associated history until Web was having a hard time keeping track of everything. He was very surprised to look at his watch and see that three hours had passed.

"We should probably head back," said Gwen. "For your first ride, three hours is plenty. You're going to find yourself a little sore."

"I'm good," said Web. "I really enjoyed it." The ride had been peaceful, tranquil, relaxing, everything he hadn't been experiencing for practically all of his life. However, when they got back to the equestrian center and Web climbed off Boo, he was surprised to find that his legs and back were so stiff he could barely walk upright once his feet hit the ground. Gwen noted this and smiled wryly. "Tomorrow it'll be another part of your body that hurts."

Web was already rubbing his buttocks. "I *feel* what you mean."

A couple of hired help came out and took the horses from them. Gwen told Web that they would take off the gear and scrub and wash down the horses. That was usually the job of the person riding the horse, Gwen said. It helped you bond with the animal. "You take care of the horse, and the horse takes care of you," she said.

"Kind of like having a partner."

"Exactly like having a partner." Gwen looked over at the complex's small office and said, "I'll be back in a minute, Web, I want to check on a few things."

As she walked off, Web started taking off his chaps.

"First time on a horse in a while?" Web looked up and saw Nemo Strait heading his way. A couple of other guys in baseball caps were sitting in the cab of a pickup truck that had large hay bales in the back. They were watching Web closely.

"Damn, how could you tell?"

Strait came up next to Web and leaned against the stone mounting block. He looked off in the direction where Gwen had gone.

"She's a good rider."

"I'd say she is too. But then, what do I know?"

"She pushes the horses sometimes further than she should, though."

Web looked at him curiously. "She seems to really love them."

"You can love something and still hurt it, now, can't you?"

Web had not anticipated this sort of mental process from Strait. He thought he had the big, dumb Neanderthal figured out, and here the guy was being thoughtful and maybe even sensitive. "I take it you've been around horses a long time."

"All my life. Folks think they can figure them out. You can't. You just have to go with the flow and never make the mistake of thinking you have them pegged. That's when you get yourself hurt."

"Sounds like a good formula for people too." Strait almost smiled, Web noted. *Almost.*

Strait glanced over at the truck where his men still were watching the two closely. "You really think Mr. Canfield might be in danger?"

"I can't be a hundred percent sure, but I'd rather be safe than sorry."

"He's a tough old cuss, but we all respect him. He didn't inherit his money like most folks around here; man earned it with his sweat. Got to respect that."

"Yes, you do. You have any ideas on how that phone might have got into his truck?"

"Been thinking about that. See, thing is, nobody drives that car 'cept him and Mrs. Canfield. We all got our own vehicles."

"When he got in it, it was unlocked. And do they keep their vehicles in the garage at night?"

"They got lots of cars and trucks, and the garage at the house is only two bays, and one of them is filled with supplies."

"So somebody, particularly at night, could have accessed the Rover, left the phone and probably nobody would have seen him."

Strait scratched the back of his neck. "I guess so. You got to understand, out here lots of folks don't even bother to lock the doors to their homes."

"Well, until this is over, tell everybody to lock everything they can. You have to understand that threat can come from everywhere, inside and out."

Strait stared at him for a long moment. "This Free Society thing, I've heard of it."

"You know anybody who might be a member or a former member?"

"No, but I could ask around."

"Well, if you do, keep it low-key. We don't want to spook anybody."

"We all got a good gig here, don't want to see nothing happen to the Canfields."

"Good. Anything else you think I need to know?"

"Look, if somebody here is in on this, you got to understand that a farm can be a real dangerous place. Big tractors, sharp tools, propane gas tanks, welding equipment, horses that'll kick your brains out if you let down your guard, snakes, steep slopes. Lot of ways to get killed and make it look like an accident."

"That's real good to know too. Thanks, Nemo." Actually, Web didn't know if that was advice or a threat.

Strait spit on the ground. "Hey, you keep up that riding, you'll be Roy Rogers in no time."

Gwen rejoined Web and showed him through the equestrian center. There were eleven buildings in total.

The foaling stalls were their first stop and Gwen showed Web how they were equipped with closed-circuit television to monitor the expectant mares. The floors were rubber-matted and had a covering of straw to keep the dust down.

"We have really high hopes for some of the foals coming next year. We had several mares bred out in Kentucky by stallions with remarkable bloodlines."

"How much does that stuff run?"

"It can run six figures a pop."

"That's expensive sex."

"There are a lot of conditions attached to that payment, of course, the most important being that the foal is actually born alive and can also stand and nurse. But a great-looking yearling sired by a successful racehorse can bring enormous amounts of money. It's a very picky business, though. You have to think of every contingency, and yet simple bad luck can still ruin your chances."

Web thought that sounded very much like being an HRT man. "Yeah, the way Billy described it to us, it doesn't sound like a business for the faint of heart."

"Well, the money is nice, Web, but that's not why I do it. It's the rush you get from seeing a horse you raised, nurtured and trained thundering around that track; the most beautiful, the most perfect racing machine every created. And seeing the finish line, watching this truly noble animal prance into the winner's circle, knowing that for at least a few minutes everything in your life is absolutely perfect. Well, there's no other feeling quite like that."

Web wondered if the nurturing of horses had replaced the lost son. If it had, he was glad that Gwen Canfield had found something in her life she could feel good about.

"I guess you probably feel the same way about your work."

"Maybe I used to," he replied.

"I didn't put two and two together before," she said. "I didn't know you were part of what happened to those men in Washington. I'm very sorry."

"Thanks. It's a pretty sorry situation all around, actually."

"I never really understood how men could do that sort of job."

"Well, I guess the easiest way to look at it, Gwen, is that we do that job because there are people in the world who make us do it."

"People like Ernest Free?"

"People just like him."

As they finished at the center, Gwen asked him what Strait had wanted.

"Just some friendly neighborly advice. By the way, did he come with the farm or did you hire him?"

"Billy did. He and his crew came with good references." She looked around. "So what now?"

"How about the main house?"

As they drove up to the mansion in an open Jeep, Web heard a roaring overhead and looked up. A small chopper was coming in low and fast. It flew past and disappeared over the treetops.

Web looked over Gwen. "Where is that going?"

She frowned. "The neighboring farm. Southern Belle. In addition to the chopper pad, they also have an airstrip. When their jet comes over, it scares the horses to death. Billy's talked to them about it, but they go their own way."

"Who are they?"

"*What* are they is more like it—a company of some sort. They run a horse farm too but a pretty strange one."

"What do you mean?"

"I mean they don't have all that many horses, and the men they have working for them don't look to me to know the difference between a colt and a filly. But they must be doing something right. The house at Southern Belle is even bigger than ours."

"I guess they have a lot of buildings, like you."

"Yes, although the ones we have came with the spread. They've built a bunch of new ones there, massive ones, almost like warehouses, though I don't know what they'd be storing in that sort of quantity. They only came here about two and a half years ago."

"So you've been over there?"

"Twice. Once to be neighborly and they weren't. The second time to complain about their low-flying aircraft. We weren't thrown off the place, but it was pretty awkward, even for Billy, and he's usually the one making people feel uncomfortable."

Web sat back and thought about all this even as he glanced in the direction where the chopper had disappeared.

It took them a while, but they covered the stone mansion from top to bottom. The lower level held a billiard room, a wine cellar and a dressing area to change into swimsuits. The pool itself was thirty by sixty feet and made entirely of steel from a World War II–era battleship that had been decommissioned, she said. There was a lower kitchen with a Vulcan stove that had a big chrome hood dating from 1912, working dumbwaiters and a laundry room. In the boiler room Web got to see big McLain units kicking out radiant steam heat, and there was a room containing nothing except wooden bins for storing firewood. Each woodbin was labeled for a particular room.

The main-level dining room had the heads of English stags on the walls and an antler chandelier. The kitchen was impressively large, with delft wall tile and a genuine silver closet. There were three ballrooms, assorted studies, parlors and living rooms and an exercise room. On the upper floors there were seventeen bathrooms, twenty bedrooms, a library that seemed to have no end and numerous other spaces. The place was truly enormous, and Web knew he was incapable of making it totally secure.

As they ended the tour, Gwen looked around with a wistful air. "I've really come to love this place. I know it's too big and grandiose in parts, but it's also very healing, you know?"

"I guess I can see that. How many staff do you have in the house?"

"Well, we have three women who come and clean and do laundry and look after things and then they leave, unless we're having a lot of guests of dinner and then they'll stay and help. They're all local folks."

"Who does the cooking?"

"I do. It's something else I enjoy. We have a handyman of sorts. He looks like he's a million years old, but he's just lived life really hard. He comes most days. Nemo and his men run the rest of the farm. Racehorses have to be exercised every day, so we also have riders, three young women and one man. All of them live at the equestrian center."

"And there is a security system. I noted the alarm pad as we came in."

"We never use it."

"You will now."

Gwen said nothing to this. She showed Web into the last room.

The master bedroom was vast but curiously sparsely furnished. Web also noticed the anteroom off the master bedroom that also had a bed.

"Billy works late a lot and doesn't want to disturb me when he comes to bed," explained Gwen. "He's always considerate that way."

The way she looked when she said this made Web think Billy wasn't all that considerate.

She continued, "Most people only see the hard side of Billy, and I guess there were more than a few people that were a little skeptical of our getting married. I guess half of them thought I was marrying Billy for money and the other half thought he was robbing the cradle. But the fact is, we just clicked. We enjoy each other's company. My mother was in the last stages of lung cancer when we started dating, and Billy came to the hospice every day for four months. And he didn't just sit there and stare at my mother dying. He brought her things, talked with her, argued with her about politics and sports and made her feel like she was still living, I suppose. It made it a lot easier for all of us and I'll never forget that. He's had a rough life and he's rough around the edges because of it. But he's been everything in a husband that a woman could ask for. He left Richmond, a place he loved, and gave up the only business he's ever known to start over on a horse farm because I asked him to. And I think he knew we had to get away from it all, too many bad memories.

"And he was a wonderful father to David, did everything with him. He didn't spoil him because he thought that would make David weak, but he loved that boy with every ounce of his being. If anything, I think losing him destroyed Billy more than it did me because, while he had children from his first marriage, David was his only son. But if he considers you a friend, there is absolutely nothing he wouldn't do for you. He'd spend his last nickel to help you. There aren't many people like that left."

Web noted the photos on the wall and on a built-in cabinet. There were many pictures of David. He was a handsome boy who had taken after his mother more than his father. Web turned and found Gwen at his shoulder looking at her son.

"It's been a long time now," she said.

"I know. I guess time really doesn't stop for anyone or anything."

"Time's also supposed to help. But it doesn't."

"He was your only child?"

She nodded. "Billy has grown kids from his first marriage, but David was my only one. Funny, when I was a little girl I was certain I'd have a big family. I was one of five. Hard to believe my little boy would be in high school now." She suddenly turned away and Web saw a hand go up to her face.

"I think that's enough for now, Gwen. I really appreciate your taking the time."

She turned back to him and he could see her damp cheeks. "Billy wanted me to invite you and your friend up for drinks and dinner tonight."

"You don't have to do that."

"Well, we want to. You saved his life, after all, and if we're going to be spending time together, we probably should get to know each other a little better. Say five-thirty?"

"Only if you're sure."

"I'm sure, Web, but thanks for asking."

"Just so you know, we didn't bring any fancy clothes."

"We're not fancy people."

32

Claire was walking to her car in the underground garage of her office building when a well-built man in a suit approached her.

"Dr. Daniels?"

She looked at him cautiously. "Yes."

He held out his identification. "I'm Agent Phillips with the FBI. We'd like to talk to you—right now, if that's convenient."

Claire looked bewildered. "*Who* wants to talk to me?"

Agent Phillips turned and pointed past the garage gate, where a black limousine with tinted windows was waiting, its engine running.

"It'll all be explained, ma'am." He gently put a hand on her elbow. "Just right this way, Doctor, it won't take long at all and we'll bring you right back here."

Claire allowed herself to be led out of the garage. Phillips held the door for her and then climbed in the front passenger seat. Before Claire was even settled against the cushion, the limo sped off.

Claire was startled when the man sitting across from her in the rear-facing seats leaned forward.

"Thank you for agreeing to talk to us, Dr. Daniels."

"I didn't agree to talk with anyone. I don't even know why I'm here."

She noted that a glass partition that separated the back of the car from the front had been raised. "Who are you?"

"My name is John Winters. I'm head of the FBI's Washington Field Office."

"Well, Mr. Winters—" Claire began.

"My friends call me Buck."

"Well, Mr. Winters, I don't know why you'd want to talk to me."

Winters sat back. "Oh, I think you have an idea. You're a very smart woman." He tapped a large file next to him. "Quite an impressive C.V."

Claire stared at the file. "I'm not sure whether I should be flattered or deeply annoyed that you've been investigating me."

Winters smiled. "For now, we'll just assume you're flattered. But you also have to realize that in your position you see quite a few members of the Bureau, their spouses, support people."

"All my security clearances are up to date. And it's not like I'm exposed to anything that's top secret. All files are thoroughly censored before they get to me."

"But how do you censor the human mind, Dr. Daniels?"

"What my patients tell me is absolutely confidential."

"Oh, I'm sure it is. And I'm also certain that stressed-out people, folks with serious mental and emotional issues, probably pour out their hearts to you."

"Some more than others. Exactly where is this going, Mr. Winters?"

"The fact is, Dr. Daniels, you are in a position to hear some pretty important information given to you by some very vulnerable people."

"I am well aware of that. And it goes no farther than my office."

Winters leaned forward again. "One of your current patients is Web London. Is that right?"

"I can't answer that."

Winters smiled. "Come on, Doctor."

"When I said that I do not reveal confidences, I meant it. That includes whether someone is a patient of mine."

"Well, just so you're aware, as head of WFO, I'm privy to who at the Bureau is seeing a shrink, okay?"

"We prefer 'psychiatrist,' or at least 'mental health professional.'"

"So I know that Web London is seeing you," Winters said. "And I know that he's seen another psychiatrist there several times in the past. An Ed O'Bannon." Again Claire said nothing. "So one thing I want to know is why the switch to you?"

"And again, I can't answer those—"

She watched as Winters pulled a slip of paper out of the file next to him. He handed it to her. She looked down at it. It was a release form signed by Web London and notarized. It stated, among other things, that anyone providing psychiatric care to Web London could discuss the parameters of the diagnosis and treatment with one John Winters, director of WFO. Claire had never seen a form like this before, but it was an original document on official Bureau stationery.

"Now we can dispense with the reluctance."

"Where did this document come from and why haven't I seen it before?"

"It's a new policy. In fact, Web's case is the first time we've used it. My idea."

"It's an invasion of doctor-and-patient confidentiality."

"Not if the patient has waived it."

Claire read the document very carefully—so carefully, in fact, and she took such a long time doing it, that Winters finally started to fume. She handed it back to him.

"Okay, let me see some ID," she said.

"Excuse me?"

"It says I can reveal certain information to John Winters, head of WFO. All I know about you is you drive around in a limo and say you're John Winters."

"I thought my aide identified himself."

"He did. But *you* haven't."

Winters smiled, pulled out his creds and showed them to Claire. She spent longer than necessary going over them, just to put the man on notice that she didn't like this one bit and that she was not going to make this easy.

He sat back. "Now, about Web London."

"He selected me because Dr. O'Bannon wasn't available. We had a good session and he decided to stay with me."

"What's his diagnosis?"

"I'm not sure I've made one yet."

"Have you suggested any treatment to him?"

"That would be a little premature," she said dryly, "since I haven't made a diagnosis yet. That would sort of be like operating on someone before you've even done a physical."

"Sorry, but most shrinks—excuse me—psychiatrists I know just prescribe some pills."

"Well, I guess I'm not like any psychiatrists you know, then."

"Can you tell me what happened to him in that courtyard?"

"No, I cannot."

"Can't or won't?" He held up the release form. "We can make this smooth for you or extremely difficult."

"That form also states that I may withhold any information told to me in confidence by a patient and also any conclusions of mine based on such information, if, using my professional discretion, such disclosure would do harm to the patient."

Winters moved across and sat next to Claire. "Dr. Daniels, are you aware of what happened in that courtyard?"

"Yes. I've read the papers, and I've talked to Web about it."

"You see, it goes beyond the murder of six agents, horrific as that is. It strikes right at the fundamental integrity of the Bureau. And without that, you have nothing."

"I'm not sure how someone ambushing a team of FBI agents diminishes the integrity of the FBI. If anything, it should evoke sympathy."

"Unfortunately, that's not the world we work in. Let me tell you what this ambush has done. First, by taking out our elite strike force, criminal elements now believe we are vulnerable at all levels. Second, the press has blown this unfortunate incident to such extraordinary heights, using such incendiary language, that the public confidence in us has been badly shaken and even the lawmakers on Capitol Hill who should know better are doubting us. And lastly, the morale of the Bureau as a whole is at an all-time low over this. It really is a triple whammy."

"I guess I can see that," Claire said cautiously.

"So the sooner the matter is resolved, the sooner we understand how it happened in the first place, the sooner we can make matters right again. I'm sure you don't want the criminals in this country thinking they can run roughshod over honest citizens."

"I'm certain that won't happen."

"Are you?" He stared hard at her. "Well, I'm right in the middle of it, and I'm not nearly so certain as you seem to be."

Claire felt a chill go up her back at the man's words.

He patted her on the shoulder. "Now, what can you tell me about Web without, *in your discretion,* violating any professional standards?"

Claire began slowly, the whole process loathsome to her. "He has some issues. I believe they go back to his childhood, as such issues often do. He froze in that alley. I'm sure he's told the investigators at the FBI that." She looked at him for affirmation of this, but Winters didn't take the bait.

"Go on," he said simply.

Claire went through the details of what Web had seen and heard in the alley, including the words spoken to him by Kevin Westbrook, how they affected him, his subsequent feelings of paralysis and how he had fought against them and ultimately won.

"Yes, he won," said Winters. "He dropped right before the guns fired and he managed to walk away alive."

"I can tell you that he feels enormous guilt for having been the sole survivor."

"And so he should."

"He didn't suddenly turn coward, if that's what you were wondering. He's one of the bravest men I've ever met. In fact, he might be too brave, too much of a risk-taker."

"I wasn't thinking he had become a coward; not even his own worst enemy could say that Web London was a coward."

She looked at him curiously. "What, then?"

"There are worse things than being a coward." He paused. "Like being a traitor."

"My professional opinion is that that is not the case. His freezing in that alley represents deep-rooted problems stemming from a very challenging childhood that Web is trying to cope with."

"I see. So perhaps he shouldn't be with HRT, then. Perhaps not in the Bureau at all."

Now Claire could feel herself freeze. *What had she just done?*

"That's not what I said."

"No, Doctor, that's what *I* said."

As promised, they dropped her back off at the garage. As she was getting out, Buck Winters leaned forward and gripped her arm. Claire felt herself instinctively drawing back.

"I certainly can't stop you from telling Web about our meeting,

Doctor, but I'm asking you not to. This is an ongoing FBI investigation and the results, whatever they happen to be, will rock the Bureau more than it's ever been. So I'm asking you, as a good citizen, to keep all this on the QT for now."

"I can't guarantee you that. And I trust Web."

"I'm sure you do. There's a lot about him to trust. Do you know how many men he's killed in his career?"

"No, is that important to know?"

"I'm sure the relatives of those people would think it important."

"You're making it sound like he's the criminal. I'm assuming that if he's killed people, it was part of his job, the job you expect him to do."

"Well, I guess that's always open to interpretation, isn't it?" He let go of her arm and added a parting shot. "I'm sure we'll be seeing each other again."

W hen Romano and Web left for dinner at the mansion, Romano was walking a little funny. He told Web that Billy had gotten him on a horse and Romano had immediately fallen off.

"I don't know why the hell I can't follow the guy in a truck. Horses just ain't my thing."

"Well, I rode over most of the property today and a lot of it you can't get to even by truck."

"Did you fall off too?"

"Yeah, twice," Web said. Why tell the truth and get Romano's hair up again? he figured.

"So who'd you ride with?" asked Romano.

"Gwen. Had a nice time. How about you? Have any fun?"

"Yeah, I never knew how much fun mucking a stall could be. You should try it sometime."

Billy met Web and Romano at the front door of the stone house. He was wearing an old corduroy jacket with patched elbows, a pair of khaki pants, a wrinkled white button-down shirt and loafers without socks. And he already had a drink in hand. He led them through the front hall and down a curving staircase of walnut that looked old enough to have arrived in the Colonies as a gift from a long-dead king or queen. Though he'd been through the place earlier, Web still caught himself occasionally ogling the large rooms, elaborate millwork, heavy draperies and enormous artwork that looked museum-quality and probably was, and then they arrived at the lower level. Romano looked around and kept muttering, "Holy shit," under his breath.

Web again noted Billy's limp. "You have an accident?" he asked, pointing to the man's leg.

"Yeah, a one-ton draft horse decided to take a roll while I was on the sumbitch."

The floor in the lower level was flagstone, the exposed walls stone and twelve-by-twelve beams had the task of holding up the ceiling. There were large leather couches and chairs placed precisely, probably to encourage several conversation groups, or perhaps even conspiratorial factions, for this definitely looked like that sort of place to Web, though the Canfields didn't seem the type. If they didn't like you, they probably weren't bashful about showing it, especially Billy. The walls were festooned with the racks of yet more English stags along with numerous mounted heads of deer, a cheetah, a lion, a rhino, a moose and mounted full bodies of a large variety of birds and fish. Mounted on another wall was a very large walleyed pike. There was also a full-sized grizzly in a charging pose and an enormous swordfish in perpetual soar. On one display table was a coiled diamondback rattler and a king cobra, with eyes seemingly ablaze and fangs showing and ready to do some serious damage. Web gave both stuffed reptiles a wide berth. He had never cared much for snakes after almost being bitten by an enraged water moccasin on a mission in Alabama.

There was a well-stocked gun cabinet against one wall. Web and Romano enviously checked out the array of Churchill, Rizzini and Piotti firearms, weapons that would easily set you back five figures. You really couldn't be a member of HRT and not be an aficionado of showpieces like these, though most FBI agents lacked the financial wherewithal to do more than press their noses to the glass. Web wondered if the weapons were for show only or whether anybody here ever actually used them. Billy looked like he would be comfortable around guns, maybe even Gwen too. If the man had killed all these animals, he would damn well have to be handy with firearms.

A full bar of dark cherry sat against another wall. It looked like it had been yanked straight from a London pub. Web's strong impression when he had first seen this room was that it had the feel of an English club spiked with a bit of the Wild West.

Gwen was sitting on a couch that looked substantial enough to sail in across the Atlantic. She rose when they entered the room. She was wearing a beige sundress that went down to her ankles and that had a scooped neckline showing a good portion of cleavage. A bit of her white bra strap showed from under the sundress's thin shoulder straps. Her bare arms were browned by the sun and were tight and firm. Probably from horse-reining, Web assumed, since his arms were aching a little from doing just that for three hours. Black leather flats were on her feet. Still, she was only a couple inches shorter than Romano. As she sat back down and crossed her legs, the sundress slipped back an inch or so and Web was a little surprised to see that she wore a gold ankle chain, because it seemed a bit out of sync with her refined bearing. Her face was nicely tanned too and the contrast of the blond hair was striking. Billy Canfield was indeed a fortunate man, thought Web, though he wondered how much of the life in their marriage had died with their son.

Web was surprised to see Nemo Strait sitting in one of the chairs. The farm manager had cleaned up and was wearing a Polo shirt that showed off his muscular physique, with chino pants and loafers. He was a striking man, Web had to admit.

Strait raised his glass to Web and Romano.

"Welcome to Casa Canfield," he said with a big grin.

Web looked at the numerous animal trophies. "They come with the house?" he asked Billy.

"Hell, no," said the man. "About four years ago I had me a calling, I guess you'd say, to go off and shoot things. Became a big-game hunter and a deep-sea fisherman. Was even on TV a few times on some sporting shows. Went round the world bagging stuff like that." He pointed to the tusked head of a wild boar on one wall and then over at the grizzly, which stood at least nine feet tall on a specially built display unit, its fangs bared and its long claws looking ready to shred somebody.

He went over and rubbed the thick neck of the enormous bear. "Now, this thing did its best to kill me, twice. Second time it almost did, but I got it." He pointed over at the rhino. "Those damn things look slow and heavy-footed. That is, they do until they're coming at you about thirty miles an hour with nothing between you and your Maker but your nerves, good aim and a steady trigger finger. You aim for the brain. Now, if you miss and hit the rhino's horn, you're a dead man."

"Poor animals," said Gwen.

"Hell, the damn things cost me a fortune," replied her husband dryly. He looked at one of the stags and then nodded at Web. "You know, the stag is the old symbol of virility, wisdom and life. And there it is hanging on my wall, dead as a doornail. I kind of like the irony in that. Now, I do all my own stuffing. Got to be a pretty damn good taxidermist, if I do say so myself."

Web was wondering about the timing of Billy's desire to kill. It must have occurred soon after the trial had ended in Ernest Free's plea bargain that had most certainly let him live.

Billy continued, "Here, let me show you. You want to come, Nemo?"

"No way. I've already seen your little operation and I ain't had my dinner yet."

Billy led them down a hallway and unlocked a door there. Gwen did not accompany them either. They went inside and Web looked around. The place was large and crammed with worktables and shelves and on the these surfaces were cans of liquids and pastes and sharp knives and scalpels, dozens of other tools, large vises, ropes and complicated pulley systems hanging from the ceiling. In one corner was the skin of an elk partially stretched over a form, and in another corner stood a wild turkey in all its dead glory. In other corners were stuffed birds and fish and some large and small animals Web couldn't even recognize. Web had smelled rotted corpses and it wasn't that bad in here, but, all the same, Web wouldn't want to breathe it every day.

"You killed all these?" asked Romano.

"Every one," said Billy with delight. "I only stuff what I kill. I don't do nobody any favors on that score." He picked up a rag and squirted some liquid on it and started rubbing on one of the tools. "Other folks golf for relaxation, I kill and stuff."

"I guess it's all relative," opined Web.

"It's therapeutic, I've found. But Gwen don't see it that way. She's never come in here and I suspect she never will. Now, taxidermy has come a long way. You don't have to build your forms anymore, you can buy real good ones made out of compressed cork, laminated paper and such, and then fit it to what you're mounting. It's still quite a process, a lot of planning and measuring and you got to have a bit of both the butcher and the artist in you. The basic steps are you gut the body and then prep the skin. A lot of folks use borax, but the purists like myself still poison the skin with arsenic. You get your best longevity there. And I even do some of my own tanning."

"You keep arsenic around here?" asked Romano.

"Tons of it." Billy eyed the man. "Don't worry, I always wash my hands after working down here, and I don't do none of the cooking." He laughed and Romano joined him, albeit a little nervously.

"Then you prep the skull, assemble your wires and such and then do your filling and final assembling."

Web eyed the room's equipment. It seemed one bare step removed from a slaughterhouse. "Lots of stuff in here."

"Well, you need a lot of stuff to do the job right." He pointed out various pieces. "Like I said, you got your anatomically correct urethane forms for the animals, but I still make some of my own using plaster of paris, modeling clay, cord-wrapped excelsior and the like. Ain't got to have everything handed to you, right?"

"Right," said Romano.

"Then you got your chemicals, poisons and salt, lots of salt to preserve the skin. Then you need your measurite and calipers for linear measurements and achieving symmetry. Scalpels for the obvious reason; I use what's called a perfect knife, German-made, those damn Germans know how to make the knives. It's for skinning and caping—you know, severing the neck from the body hide, for example—the detail work around the eyes and mouth and the like. You got your skinning knives, paring knives, bone saw, shavers, skifes for leather, even a fleshing machine. Now, that is a damn fine invention."

Under his breath Web said, "Lucky, lucky world."

"Got me Kevlar fleshing gloves so I don't chop off one of my fingers. Scissors, hide pullers, lip tuckers, nippers, forceps, probes and surgical needles. Sounds like a cross between a mortician and a plastic surgeon, don't it?" He pointed to mixing bowls, paintbrushes, an air compressor and a number of tins.

"That's the artistic part of the business. The finishing touches to do justice to the animal."

"Funny thing," said Web, "thinking about doing justice to something you've killed."

"I guess that separates folks like me from sons of bitches that kill and keep on walking," Billy shot back.

"I guess so," said Web.

Billy walked over to a deerskin that was drying on a large table. "You know what's the first thing you cut off when you're gutting a deer?" he asked looking directly at Web.

"What's that?"

"Its penis."

"Good to know," said Web dryly.

"Deer die like people," continued Billy. "With their eyes open. Glazing takes place almost immediately. If the eyes are closed or blinking, you better shoot 'em again." He looked at Web again. "I suppose you run across that a lot in your line of work."

"Sometimes that's not an option with human beings."

"I guess not, though I'd take any one of the animals I got on display here over the human scum you got to deal with." He took a sip of his drink. "I think that's one of the reasons I like this place so much," said Billy. "Damn contradictions, since I seem to be a living breathing one myself. Born dirt poor, barely finished ninth grade, made a lot of money in the unglamorous business of hauling cigarettes and other junk up and down the highways of this fine country and married me a beautiful, intelligent young woman with a college degree. And now here I am, the master of an estate smack in the middle of fancy-ass Virginia hunt country stuffing animals. One lucky man. Makes me want to get drunk, so let's go do something about that."

He led them back and they rejoined Gwen. She gave Web a weak smile as if to say, *I know and I'm sorry.*

Bill went behind the bar and pointed at his wife. "Scotch, honey?"
She nodded. "I'll join you in another," he said. "Boys? And don't
hand me that bullshit that you're on duty. If you don't drink with
me, I'm throwing your butts out of here."

"Beer, if you have it."

"We have everything here, Web."

Web made a mental note that the man said it like he damn well
meant it.

"Same for me," said Romano.

"I'll have one too, Billy," said Strait. He walked over and took a
bottle of beer from his boss and then joined Web and Romano.

"I'm a lot more used to beer than I am fancy mixed drinks."

"Country boy?" asked Romano.

"Yes, sir, I grew up at the foothills of the Blue Ridge on a horse
farm," said Strait. "But I wanted to see the world." He rolled up his
sleeve and showed them his Marine Corps insignia. "Well, I did, on
Uncle Sam's dime. Actually, I only saw a little slice of it called
Southeast Asia, and it's hard to enjoy something like that when
people are shooting at you."

"You don't look old enough to have been in Vietnam," commented
Web.

Strait smiled broadly. "All my clean living, I guess." He added,
"Truth is, I got drafted right near the end, only eighteen years old
and change. First year in the jungle, I just kept my head down and
tried my best to keep it on my shoulders. Then I got my ass caught
and spent three months as a POW. Damn Viet Cong were into some
sick stuff, messing with your mind, trying to turn you traitor."

"I didn't know that about you, Strait," said Billy.

"Well, it's not something I put on my résumé." He laughed. "But
I finally escaped and an Army shrink helped me to straighten out
myself. That and a lot of booze and other stuff I can't mention," he
added, grinning. "Got discharged, came back to the States and
pulled a little duty as a guard at a juvenile detention center. Now, let
me tell you, some of the kids I was guarding, they'd make the damn
Viet Cong look like a bunch of wimps. Then I got married, but my
ex didn't like my pay scale of six bucks an hour, so I got me a desk
job for a while, but that just wasn't me. Like I said, I grew up in the

outdoors, around horses all my life. It's in your blood." He looked over at Billy. "It better be, because it ain't in your bank account."

They all laughed at that one, except Gwen. She looked annoyed that the cowpoke was even in her home, thought Web, who was watching her closely.

"So anyway," Strait continued, "I went back to horses and my wife walked out on me and took my boy and girl."

"You see them much?" asked Web.

"Used to, not anymore." He grinned. "Thought my son would follow in his old man's footsteps and be either a military grunt or maybe even get into the horses." He slapped his thigh. "Hell, you know what?"

"What's that?" asked Romano.

"Found out he was allergic to the damn things. Life sure is funny sometimes."

As Web studied the man, it didn't seem to him that Strait thought life was humorous at all. He had initially pegged Strait as a slow-witted fellow who did what he was told. He was going to have to re-think that.

"Then Billy come along, and now I'm helping him"—he glanced at Gwen—"and Ms. Canfield build their little empire right here."

Billy raised his beer to the man. "And doing a fine job of it, Strait."

On that, Web noted, Gwen looked away, and despite Billy's words of praise it seemed that he was not all that enamored of his foreman. Web decided to change the flow of conversation.

"Lower levels are usually cold," Web said to Billy. "Especially with all this stone. And yet it feels warmer down here than it did upstairs."

"We have the best heat in the world here," replied Billy, who worked the bar like he had been born to it. "Radiant steam. Gwen said she showed you around. Well, those three Weil McLain boilers you saw heat the water to two-twelve and turn it into steam, of course. The steam flows through the pipes and into the cast-iron Gurney radiators that are in each room in the house. Then the steam cools back to water, runs through the system again, is turned into steam once more and on it goes. And you have not only warmth, but a built-in humidifier." He handed Web his beer. "A lot of the steam pipes run under this floor, that's why it's so nice down here. I love it. And this time of year, it can get to be eighty-five in the day and forty at night. But McLain boilers is why Gwen can go bare-armed down here and still feel nice and toasty, ain't that right, honey?"

"Actually, I've felt hot all day."

Web rubbed his hand against the bar. "Nice setup with this thing."

"Dates from 1910," said Billy. "The owner back then put a lot of work into the place. It needed it, though. Unfortunately, it needed a lot more by the time we got to it. Story of my life." He carried the drinks over on a serving platter and handed them out. They all sat down.

"Gwen tells me you've got some promising yearlings."

"Yeah, maybe a Triple Crown winner in there," said Billy. "Now, that would be nice. Pay at least a month's worth of bills on this damn place."

Gwen and Web exchanged smiles at this comment.

"We can always hope," said Gwen. "But being one step from the poorhouse all the time at least is exciting."

"Well, we do okay here," said Strait, looking at her.

Web thought the choice of pronouns interesting. He was starting to wonder who actually owned the place.

Billy took a pull on his scotch. "Yeah, this ain't such a bad place. Even got fox hunting around here."

Gwen looked repulsed. "That's disgusting."

"Well, this *is* fox-hunting country, and in Virginia you got to do like the snooty Virginians do." Billy smiled at Web. "Actually, our damn neighbors can be kind of a pain in the ass. They got ticked at me because I wouldn't let them ride across my land while they were chasing that damn fox. I told them they didn't fox-hunt down Richmond way and it seemed like the deck was stacked against the little feller anyway and I've always tended to root for the underdog. Well, those pricks took me to court. And won. There were some old covenant in my chain of title that said fox hunting apparently runs with the land."

Romano looked disgusted. "Now, that's a bitch. Talk about your unfree country."

"Well, they don't come across East Winds anymore," said Strait.

"Why's that?" asked Web.

"Billy shot one of their dogs—excuse me, hounds." He slapped his leg and laughed.

Billy was nodding as though remembering a pleasant memory. "He took after one of my horses. That particular horse was worth about three hundred thousand dollars. Damn hound dog's a dime a dozen. So damn right I shot him."

"Did they take you to court again?" asked Web.

"They did, and this time I kicked their ass." He smiled, took another drink and looked at Web. "So did you enjoy the fifty-cent tour Gwen gave you?"

"She'd make a great tour guide, actually. I was interested in the farm being a stop on the Underground Railroad during the Civil War."

Billy pointed to the gun cabinet. "And that stop's right over there."

Web looked at the gun cabinet and said, "I'm not getting it."

"Go ahead and show him, Billy," said Strait.

Billy motioned for Web and Romano to follow him. He went over and pushed down on what Web figured must be a lever concealed in the cabinet's frame. Web heard a click and the cabinet swung toward him, revealing a small opening.

"There's no electricity or windows in there, just a couple of rough bunks, but when you're running for your freedom, you can't be too picky," said Billy. He picked up a flashlight that was hanging on a wall peg and handed it to Web. "Have a look."

Web took the flashlight, poked his head inside and swung the light around. He almost dropped the flashlight when the light caught on a man sitting there in a bentwood rocker. As his eyes adjusted to the poor light, he saw it was actually a mannequin dressed as a male slave, with a hat and muttonchop whiskers, the whites of its eyes in unsettling contrast to the painted black skin.

Billy laughed and said, "You've got some damn strong nerves. Most people scream."

"Billy put that in there, not me, Web," said Gwen quickly, with a trace of disgust in her voice.

"It's one of my sick little jokes," added Billy. "But hell, if you can't laugh at life, what are you gonna laugh at?"

On that they finished their drinks and went in to dinner.

They didn't eat in the formal dining room. As Billy explained it, the room was so big that when you wanted to talk to one another you had to scream to be heard and he was a little hard of hearing as it was. They ate in a small room off the kitchen. Gwen gave the blessing and made the sign of the cross, as did Romano. Strait, Web, and Billy just looked on.

Gwen had made a Caesar salad, sirloin tips, fresh asparagus in a cream sauce and what smelled and tasted like homemade rolls. Cherry pie and coffee finished off the meal, and Romano sat back, rubbing his flat, hard stomach.

"A lot better than MREs," he said, referring to the U.S. military's meals-ready-to-eat.

"Thanks, Gwen, it was great," said Web.

"We used to entertain quite a bit in Richmond," she said. "We don't do a lot of that anymore." She shot a quick glance at her husband as she said this.

"Lots of things we don't do anymore," said Billy Canfield. "But it was a fine meal and my toast to the chef." He went over to the sideboard and brought back a decanter of brandy and four cut-crystal glasses. "Now, I'm partial to my Jim Beam, like any good southern gentleman, but a proper toast requires a proper libation." He poured out the brandy and filled his glass with Beam, and they toasted Gwen.

She smiled and raised her glass to them. "Well, it's nice to be so popular with so many men."

As they took their leave, Web drew Billy aside.

"I just want to get the ground rules clear. Be sure to set the alarm when we leave, and set it every night before you go to bed. There are so many ways in and out of this place, I want you and Gwen to come and go the same way. That way you won't inadvertently leave a door unlocked. If you're thinking of going out, even if it's just a stroll, you call us first and we go with you. If anything spooks you or Gwen, you call us. Nothing is too small, okay? Here's my cell phone number. It'll be on twenty-four hours a day. And I want you to strongly consider letting Romano and me stay in the house. If something goes down, seconds do count."

Billy looked at the slip of paper with Web's number on it. "Pris-

oners in our own home, I guess it's come to that. Those bastards."
He shook his head wearily.

"Those guns in your cabinet, they just for show or you use them
in your hunting?"

"Most of them are shotguns. Couldn't use them on game you
want to mount because shotgun ammo ruins the skin and takes off
heads. I keep my big-game weapons in a locked cabinet upstairs.
I've also got me a twelve-gauge and a .357 Magnum too. Both
loaded. They're for two-legged sumbitches trespassing on my land.
Gwen's a damn fine shot too. Probably better'n me."

"Good, just remember to shoot only the bad guys. Now, you got
any travel plans coming up?"

"Just a shipment of horses we're taking up to Kentucky in a few
days. I'm going with Strait and some of the boys."

"Talk to Bates, he may see it differently."

"Listen to Web," said Nemo, who walked over after overhearing
their conversation. "Somebody's looking to get to you, Billy. Stay
put so the Feds can protect you."

"Going soft on me, Nemo?" asked Billy.

"Hell no. Something happens to you, I'm out of a job."

"Any visitors you expecting out of the ordinary?" Web asked.

Billy shook his head. "Most of our friends in Richmond aren't
our friends anymore. Maybe it's mostly our fault. We keep to ourselves here."

"These neighbors of yours, at the Southern Belle, what do you
know about them?"

"Only that they're ruder than me." He laughed. "To tell you the
truth, I don't know much about them. They don't join in much local stuff, not that I do either. I've only seen what I guess was the
foreman."

"How about that chopper and their plane?"

Billy made a face. "That is damn aggravating. Scares the horses."

"How often do you see the plane and the chopper go out?"

Billy considered this. "A lot."

"What's a lot? Nightly, weekly?"

"Not nightly, but more often than weekly."

"Same direction each time or different?"

"Different." He looked at Web warily. "What're you thinking?"

Web gave a tight smile. "I'm thinking we'll just keep an eye on that airline next door."

When Romano and Web got back to the carriage house, Web filled him in on the talk he had had with Billy.

"You think something's going down on the property next door?" said Romano.

"No, I think something going's *up*."

"Well, that was an interesting evening. I gotta tell you, that hobby of Canfield's is kind of spooky."

"Yeah, it's not exactly like building model planes. And what's your take on Nemo Strait?"

"Seems like a regular enough fellow."

"I was sort of surprised he was invited to the big house for dinner with the boss."

"Well, look at where Billy came from. He's probably more comfortable around people like Strait than a bunch of rich fat cats fox hunting."

"You're probably right. Gwen didn't seem to care for him, though."

"She's more of a lady. And he's kind of crude." He added with a smile, "Like me. I didn't know she was Catholic."

"Yeah, she's got a little chapel in the woods where she goes to pray every day for her son, the one I let die."

"You didn't let the kid die, Web. Hell, if the negotiators had let you guys do your thing from the get-go, the boy probably would be alive."

"Look, Paulie, I got an appointment tonight, so you're going to have to go it alone. I don't have to leave for a while, so you can get some shut-eye. Bates is keeping agents at the rear and front gates for the next couple of days, though, so you're not really all by your lonesome."

"Appointment, what kind of appointment?"

"I'll tell you all about it when I get back."

"This have something to do with what happened to Charlie Team?"

"Maybe."

"Well, damn, Web, I'd like to be in on that."

And I'd like you to be covering my back. "Can't desert the old post. I should be back before morning. Now, if I were you, I'd patrol around a little bit. I wouldn't be surprised if Canfield started off by testing us and so he might slip out. Although I think almost dying this morning put the fear of God in him, but we can't take that chance."

"Not to worry, I'll do some snooping."

"If you see that plane or chopper go over, log it in. And I brought a bunch of night optics, help yourself."

"Those damn things always give me a headache and they screw with your depth perception too much."

"Yeah, well, you remember those 'damn things' saved our necks in Kosovo."

"Okay, okay. I'm gonna hit the sack."

"And Paulie?"

"Yeah?"

"Just because there aren't a bunch of guys with big guns surrounding us doesn't mean it's not dangerous. Be extra careful. I don't want to lose anybody else, okay?"

"Hey, Web, remember who you're talking to."

"You and me have had our differences over the years, but we've also been to hell and back together. I kind of like having you around. You hear me?"

"Gee, Web, you really do care."

"You're a real prick, Romano, you know that?"

33

When Web had called the number on the slip of paper Big F had given him, the voice that had answered was a man's. Web didn't know if it belonged to Big F, since his initial encounter with the giant had involved concussions rather than words. Web had hoped it was Big F on the line because the voice was high and shrill. What a wonderful joke for God to play on the man by giving him a squeaky set of pipes. Yet a silly voice wasn't going to lessen the fear of doing the two-step with the walking oak again. Big F didn't hit with his tonsils.

The man had told Web to be driving north across the Woodrow Wilson Bridge at exactly eleven o'clock that night. Web would receive additional instructions at that time; by cell phone, Web figured. His number was unlisted, but it seemed nothing was sacred these days.

Web, of course, had sensibly questioned why he should even go.

"If you want to know what happened to your buddies, you'll be there," the man had said. "And if you want to keep on living," he added. Appropriately enough, the phone line had gone dead after that.

Web thought about running down to Quantico and snagging a Barrett .50 rifle and a couple thousand rounds of ammo from the equipment cage. One of the great things about HRT was that it purchased for its operators the very latest weapons and then let them do with them what they wanted. It was like a giant candy store for the violence-minded. Yet he finally decided that even at gun-happy HRT, it might raise some eyebrows—his checking out a .50 and enough ammo to shoot up a good-sized city. He did briefly think about calling in Bates as backup but then realized that might hold disastrous consequences. Big F hadn't survived on the streets this long by being stupid or impossibly lucky. He would smell the Bureau boys for sure, and wouldn't that just royally piss off the big guy. But if he had information about who had set up his team, Web had to find out what it was.

He had driven past the entrance to the Southern Belle farm. The opening was not as ornate at East Winds. And Web noted that the gates were closed and locked. He thought he could see a man patrolling near the entrance, but he wasn't certain of that or whether the man was armed. An interesting place. Even as he was thinking this, he heard the chopper coming overhead. He looked up, saw it passing by and then it disappeared from his sight. Maybe it was landing at Southern Belle. Maybe terrorists had landed in America. Web was only half kidding.

He had stopped to fill the car with gas. He thought about calling Claire but then decided against it. What would he say? *Maybe I'll see you tomorrow, and maybe I won't.*

The Woodrow Wilson Bridge had long been the single worst traffic bottleneck in the United States interstate highway system. To most local drivers, mentioning the name of the twenty-eighth President of the United States sent them into fits of rage. What a legacy, Web thought, for a life of selfless public service. Better to have your name attached to a rest stop. At least then people would think of you in connection with badly needed bodily relief.

He rolled onto the aging bridge and checked his watch. Thirty seconds to eleven. The Potomac was calm tonight, with no boat traffic apparent. The thick line of trees on the Maryland side contrasted sharply with the bright lights of Old Town Alexandria on the Virginia side and the Capitol dome and national monuments to the north. He passed the halfway point on the bridge. Traffic was relatively light and flowing well. A Virginia state police car passed Web heading in the opposite direction. Web felt like yelling after him, *Hey, wanta be my friend tonight? Got an appointment with Doctor Death.*

Web left the bridge and kept driving. He looked around. Nothing. So much for exact timing. Then a chilling thought hit him. Was he being set up to take a hit? Was there a sniper out there somewhere drawing a bead on him right now with his scope? Was the guy dialing in the drop compensation right now, seating the shell, settling his finger on the trigger, exhaling one last breath before he fired? Was Web London the world's biggest idiot?

"Take the next right. NOW! NOW!"

The voice seemed to come from everywhere and nowhere and startled Web so badly he almost pulled the Mercury into a one-eighty.

"Shit!" Web cried out even as he shot the car across three lanes of traffic while horns blared at him and cars dodged around him. He cut it so close the sedan skimmed the guardrail.

Web was now on the entry ramp onto Interstate 295.

"Take it to D.C.," the voice said in a calmer tone.

"Damn it, give me a little more notice next time," Web shot back, and then wondered if the guy could even hear him. He also wondered how they had managed to plant a communications device in his car without anyone seeing them. Web pointed the car north to D.C. He took deep breaths to calm himself. Right now he wished to never again hear another voice without a face to go with it.

"Keep going," the voice said. "I'll tell you where to turn."

Well, so much for what one wished for. It wasn't Squeaky Voice. Maybe this was Big F. It seemed to be a Big F voice, thought Web, for it was deep, blunt, threatening. Figured.

Web was very familiar with the area he was now in. The low-down on this stretch of lonely, woods-bracketed highway was that if one's car broke down, it would not be there when the owner came back for it. And if the owner stayed with his broken-down car, he wouldn't be coming back either. The boys that hunted here were the AAA of felony. Also down this way was St. Elizabeth's, the mental hospital for celebrity maniacs like John Hinckley and for those who kept trying to go over the fence at the White House, among many others.

The voice said, "Take the next exit. Turn left at the light, go one-point-one miles and take a right."

"Should I be writing this down or can you fax it to me?" asked Web, because he just felt like it.

"Shut the hell up!"

Well, at least they could hear him. And *see* him. He looked in his rearview mirror, but there were quite a few headlights back there. And yet if there was one thing Web couldn't stand, it was a criminal who lacked a good sense of humor. He slipped that one away in his payback file. He followed the directions and soon was smack in the middle of the death zones of Northeast and Southeast D.C. that bordered the Anacostia River and where over a thousand people had been murdered in the last seven years. By comparison, across the river and seemingly several universes away the affluent Northwest area had suffered a little over twenty homicides in the same time span. However, there was some sense of perverse balance because the Northwest quadrant had far more larcenies and thefts committed, for a very simple reason: the poor rarely had things criminals wanted to steal while the wealthy, of course, had an abundance of them. The Frederick Douglas National Historical Site was along where Web was traveling, and Web figured that the Martin Luther King, Jr., of his time would not be at all pleased with how things had turned out.

Web was given another set of directions and soon was pulling down a dirt road winding between nothing but trees and dense foliage. Web had been around here before. It was a favorite dumping ground for those in the more violent stretches of the city who didn't like to mess up their neighborhoods with body parts. HRT had done a couple of ops down here, in fact. One had gone textbook, without one shot fired. The other had left three men dead. All bad guys who just couldn't accept the fact that they were so outclassed and thus had stupidly pulled guns instead of putting up their hands. Maybe they thought there would be warning shots fired. Well, there was no chapter in the HRT manual on warning shots. Whenever Web had pulled his trigger, somebody ended up dead.

"Stop the car," said the voice, "and get out. Lay your gun on the front seat."

"How do you know I have a gun?"

"If you don't, you got horseshit for brains."

"And if I give my gun up, what exactly do I have for brains?"

"If you don't, you ain't gonna have no brains left."

Web placed the pistol on the front seat and slowly got out of the car and looked around. He saw nothing except trees and a moonless sky. He could smell the river water, and it was hardly comforting. The few movements he heard were assuredly not Big F–like, most likely squirrels, foxes or minor-grade criminals trolling for their supper. Right now the only thing Web wished he had done was stash Romano in the trunk. *Well, now you think of that.*

He stiffened slightly when he heard them coming. As they appeared from the cover of trees, Web could make out three large men in a row. They were all taller than Web, and they all had some serious hardware pointed at him. Web wasn't really focusing on them, though, for the far larger man was right behind them. Web had felt sure he was going to see the giant tonight, and yet the sight of Big F was still a little unnerving. He had on different clothes, but the same Club Med style. The shirt, though, wasn't open this time. All of Web's wounds inflicted by the giant criminal seemed to tingle in the man's presence as though some chemical interaction had just been triggered. Next to Big F was a white guy, which surprised Web until he recognized Clyde Macy in the flesh. He resembled a skeleton more in person than he did in the photo. Web recalled his talk with Bates when they had speculated who Cove's inside person might be. Macy? Peebles? Macy didn't look like a snitch, but who really knew? As Web kept his gaze on the man, he noted that the suit Macy wore and the ear radio made him look like Secret Service. Maybe he'd had aspirations to join the Service once, until he realized he liked killing people more. Peebles was nowhere in sight. The new breed of criminal entrepreneurs apparently didn't like to get their fingernails dirty.

The three underlings circled Web while Big F stood there and watched. Macy hung off to the side. He looked alert and relaxed at the same time. But it was easy to tell the man took his work very seriously. To Web, the other men looked a little bored, as though they were the varsity called in to scrimmage with the JV. Well, that was a real confidence booster. One man drew a short object from his coat pocket that looked like a microphone. He ran it up and down Web's body while another man checked Web for additional weapons. He found none but did confiscate Web's cell phone. Another of the men, with what Web knew now was an electronic wand designed to ferret out nosey surveillance devices, did the once-over on Web's car. The wand only sounded once, near the rear seat, but the man seemed unconcerned by this. He turned and nodded at Big F. Web understood this silent exchange: The man had detected the electronic device they had planted in Web's car. The men stepped back and Big F came forward and leaned his bulk on the hood of Web's car. Web thought he could hear the car groaning, and who could blame it?

"How's the face?"

The man's voice was neither squeaky high nor brutally deep. It was middle-of-the-road, calm, nonthreatening. It wasn't the faceless voice inside Web's car. Web could be talking to his stockbroker—if he had a stockbroker, that is.

"Only thing hurt was my pride. I take it you're Big F."

The man smiled at that and then slapped his thigh. To Web it sounded like the ominous smack of thunder. Everything this guy did was big. The other men laughed too, obviously cueing off their boss.

"Shit. Big F. Damn right I'm Big F. That's good. Ain't that good, boys?"

They all nodded and said it was good. Damn good. Macy didn't even crack a smile. He just stood there and stared at Web like he was trying to will him to die.

"Because if there was somebody bigger than you coming down the pike, then I don't think I want to make his acquaintance." Web knew it was always good to get on the bad guy's good side, show you weren't afraid. Violent criminals just loved fear. And they just loved to cut the throats of fearful people.

Big F laughed again. Yet when he stopped and looked serious, so did everybody else. Instantly, Web noted.

"I got me a problem."

"I'm here to help." Web eased forward just a notch. Now he could take out two of the guys with kicks. Big F was something else altogether, sort of like punching Mount Rushmore, but you went with the point of least resistance first.

"Somebody's setting me up to take a fall for something I ain't done."

"You know what happened to my team?"

"I don't need that shit, you understand me?" He stood, towering over them all, and the look in his eyes made Web's heart race. "How old you think I am?"

Web gave him the once-over. "Twenty-two."

"Thirty-two," Big F said proudly. "Now, that in black years." He turned to Macy. "What that be in tidy whitey time?"

"A hundred and twenty," said Macy in a learned tone, as though he were the Ph.D. of this illustrious group.

Big F looked back at Web. "I'm a hundred and twenty. I'm an old man in a young man's bizness. I don't need this shit. You go tell your crew that. Don't come hunting my ass down, 'cause I ain't done it."

Web nodded. "Then I need to know whose business it is. Without that, I can guarantee you squat."

Big F eased himself back down on the car and slid out a Beretta nine-millimeter, with a muzzle suppressor attached, Web noted. Things were definitely not looking good.

"Messengers a dime a dozen," said Big F, eyeing Web calmly.

"It'll mean a lot more coming from me. I've got a lot invested in this one." Web took one tiny step forward as he pretended to be merely shifting his weight. Now he could tag Big F with a spin kick right on the cerebellum. If the man could shake that off, then crown him king of the world. "And maybe you figure you owe me one for saving Kevin. Him being your little brother and all."

"He ain't my brother."

Web tried hard not to show his surprise. "Is that right?"

"He my son." Big F rubbed his nose, coughed and then spit. "Course, we got the same mama."

Web started for a moment and then looked at the other men. They obviously already knew this and seemed to accept it as mainstream, at least their version of mainstream. Yet why shouldn't they? Web thought. What was a little incest among family? You couldn't exactly do it with strangers. Grandma had said Kevin was a little slow. Well, with that twisted family tree, Web could see why.

"Well, I hope Kevin's okay," said Web.

"The boy's got nothing to do with you," Big F said sharply.

Okay, thought Web, so Kevin did mean something to the man. That was valuable intelligence. "Who took out my team? Tell me, and we go our separate ways. No hard feelings."

"Ain't that easy."

"Sure it is," Web prompted. "Names. That's all I want."

Big F studied his pistol. "You know what my biggest problem is?"

Web eyed the Beretta and wondered if *he* was Big F's biggest problem. He prepared to launch himself.

"Economy's too hot. I can't keep good people." He looked over at his men. "Toona-man, front and center."

Web watched as one of the men stepped forward. He was six-foot-four and broad-shouldered and wore what looked to Web to be a very expensive suit and enough gold and silver on his neck, wrists and fingers to start his own precious metals exchange.

"You think you can take this little dude with just your hands, Toona?"

Toona smirked. "Ain't be needing both hands for that boy."

"Don't know 'bout that," said Big F. "Way this boy kicked me, I felt that shit. Well, if you think you can, lay your gun down and get to it."

Toona slipped his gun out of his waistband and placed it on the ground. He was at least fifteen years younger than Web and much larger. And yet he moved so gracefully that Web was certain the man was as nimble as he was strong. And when Toona assumed a classic martial arts stance, Web knew he was in for something serious, and he hadn't even recovered from last night.

Web held up his hand. "Look, we don't have to do this. You think you can kick my ass, I think I can kick yours. Let's just call it a draw."

Big F shook his head. "Uh-uh, little dude. Either fight or take the bullet."

Web stared at the man and his gun, sighed, then put up his fists.

The two men circled each other for a few moments. Web sized his opponent up and saw few weaknesses, yet he did see something else that might be helpful. He tried a kick and Toona easily caught Web's leg and held on to it for a moment before twisting the limb and throwing Web down. Web quickly rose and took a side kick on the forearm. It stung like hell, but better his arm than his head. The two feinted and parried a few times more before

Toona caught Web with a flying spinner and he went down again, but he bounced right back up.

"Is that all the shit you got, Toona?" taunted Web. "Man, you got me by fifty pounds and fifteen years. If I was you, your ass would be out for the count by now."

Toona dropped his smirk and hit Web with an old-fashioned right jab but ate a hard left cross to the head in return. Toona didn't seem to like his face getting marked, something Web was quick to pick up on.

"Hey, Toona, a screwed-up face isn't the end of the world. With no ladies eating up your paycheck, you can probably really put some bucks away for retirement."

"You going down, man," said Toona. "And you staying down."

"Not from some pussy like you, I'm not."

An enraged Toona lunged at Web and caught him with a sharp punch right to the kidney. Web almost went down from the blow, but he wrapped his arms around Toona's middle and started to squeeze. Toona hit him with two more shots to the head, but Web held on. Like a constrictor, each time Toona took a breath, Web would squeeze a little bit more, not letting the man's diaphragm return to its original position.

More head shots and more squeezes and Web could start to feel the bigger man wavering, his gasps of breath so pleasant to hear. And then Web loosened his grip just a little, and it was enough for Toona to get his own clench on Web, which was what Web had intended. The two men swung each other around, panting heavily, their rivulets of sweat meeting each time their bodies did.

Toona tried to throw Web off, but Web held on, because he had other plans. Finally, Toona swung Web around and Web's grip was broken and he went sprawling. Actually, he did a controlled forward roll, grabbed Toona's pistol where he had left it on the ground, came upright, lunged forward, put a neck lock on the stunned Toona and placed the gun to his head, all in a blur of motion.

"You have to get yourself some better security," Web said to Big F. "Ain't that right, Toona?"

Big F raised his pistol and fired. His shot hit Toona dead center in the forehead. The man dropped and died without making one sound. Most gunshots to the head had that effect, Web knew, the ability of the victim to speak gone before the brain could dial up the scream. Bullets and flesh were like ex-wives. They just never mixed that well.

Web stared as Big F casually slipped the gun back in his waistband as though he had just disposed of an irksome mole in a vegetable garden. Big F's men looked as stunned as Web. Toona's demise had obviously been on only Big F's agenda. Macy, however, just stood there, his gun trained on Web; the sudden violent death of a colleague didn't seem to interest him at all. He was all cool and professional, standing there in a classic Weaver firing stance, his gaze riveted on the gun in Web's hand. Web wondered where the guy had received his training. Probably some paramilitary outfit staffed by ex-good-guys who, for some reason or other, had slid to the dark side.

With his hostage gone and multiple guns pointing at him, Web dropped the pistol.

"Good help," said Big F to Web, "I can't find it. I give my crew cash, clothes, cars and bitches. Show 'em the ropes, teach 'em the bizness, 'cause I ain't be doing this shit all my life. Cash in my chips, lose myself till I kick living. And you think that makes 'em loyal? Shit, no. They just keep biting the hand that feeds 'em. Toona making his own action on the side and think I ain't know it. Skimming dollars and dope off all the time. And he thinking I stupid and don't check that shit. But that ain't the dumbest thing he done. Dumbest thing the boy done is he be using the products. You put that shit in you, you talk to anybody 'bout anything. He be high on that shit and he be mouthing off to a whole crew a DEA and his ass not even know it. Sell us all down the river. Well, I ain't going down no river. I ain't being no drug kingpin working my bizness from the inside with no chance in hell of ever getting on the outside again. Uh-uh. No way, baby. No way. That ain't how it ending for me. I eat me some bullets before I go to mighty whitey's house."

He glanced sharply at his men. "You just gonna leave Toona there or what? Show some *damn* respect for the dead."

"What the hell you want us to do with him?" said one of them, his arms spread wide, his features angry, though Web easily sensed the fear he held for his boss. Web was certain Big F could smell that fear too. He no doubt counted on it in running his "bizness." If he wanted to teach his people loyalty, they had one very compelling reason lying right there in a growing red pond. And taking out Toona had probably been meant as a warning to Web too. Well, he felt incredibly warned.

Big F shook his head in obvious disgust. "I got to tell you every damn thing to do like you a little baby or something? I smell me water and so can you. Throw his ass in the river. And tie something to it, so it ain't come up!"

The men gingerly picked up their fallen comrade, bitching the whole time about getting blood and other Toona bits on their fine Versace. Macy stood in exactly the same spot. Apparently, Web thought, he was inner circle and thus was allowed to stay for extra innings.

When the others had disappeared down the trail, Big F eyed Web. "See what I mean 'bout good help? Can't get none. Everybody wants to get rich overnight. Nobody wants to work for a damn thing no more. Start at the top. They all wanta start at the top. I started at eight years old running dollar bags of white rock. Worked my ass off for over twenty years and these brothers today be thinking they deserve every dime I got 'cause they be doing this shit for a coupla months. New economy, my ass!"

If Big F had been sitting in a maximum-security prison cell wearing Hannibal Lecter ready-to-wear and Web was safely on the other side of the bars, Web might have started laughing his guts out at this capitalistic tirade. Yet right now all he was wondering was when Big F would finally focus on the fact that Web was an eyewitness to murder.

"Now, Toona, he must've killed five or six people. So I just saved you the trouble of frying his ass. Ain't gotta thank me."

Web didn't. In fact, he said nothing. He probably could have made some smart remark, but witnessing the cold-blooded murder of another human being, no matter how much he might have deserved it, was not a great lead-in to humor for Web.

"I guess everybody got trouble." Big F wiped at one of his eyes. "But the Lord done showered me with some extra helpings. I got me family coming out my ass and every one of them looking for cash. Got me a ninety-year-old great-aunt I ain't even know I had coming round talking like this." His voice rose higher. "'Now, Francis, can't you take care of my eyes? Got me the cataracts, honey, can't see to play the Bingo no mo'. Do something about it for me, will you, honey? Used to bounce you on my knee. Used to change your shitty diaper.' And I peel off some cash and there you go. And she back a week later 'bout her damn cat what got female problems." He looked at Web incredulously. "A fucking cat with female problems. 'And it only be a thousand dollars, Francis,' she says, 'that all it be, honey, and remember I wiped your shitty diaper while your mama was down the river or else shooting herself up with that little needle of hers.' And you know what I do? I peel off ten hundreds and give it to her and her cat."

"The *F* stands for Francis?"

Big F grinned. And it seemed to Web that he saw for the first time signs of little Kevin in this hulking, murderous adult.

"Yeah, what'd you think it stood for?"

Web shook his head. "No clue."

Big F took out a small box, unwrapped a pill and put it in his mouth. He offered one to Web, who declined.

"Tagamet, Pepcid AC, Zantac," said Big F. "I eat 'em like peanuts. Had me an upper GI done. Damn belly looks like a mole's been through it. This shit's getting to me, ain't no lie."

"So why don't you retire?"

"Easy to say, not so easy to do. Ain't like they give me a going-away lunch and a gold watch in my line a work."

"Sorry to tell you, but the cops never stop looking."

"The cops I can deal with. It's some folks in the bizness what giving me the pain in the ass. They think if you want to quit working you gonna rat 'em out. They can't understand why'd you walk away from a life like mine. Money out the ass, 'cept you got to keep hiding it, and you got to keep moving around, and you're still always wondering when somebody, like maybe your bitch or your brother or your cat-loving great-aunt, is gonna put a hole in your head while you sleeping." He grinned. "Now, don't you worry 'bout me. I be fine." He popped another pill and then closely eyed Web. "You one of them guys from HRT?"

"I am."

"I hear you dudes are some serious shit. When you hit me the other night, boy, that hurt. That's rare, little man, let me tell you, that's rare. You guys must be some bad shit."

"We're actually really lovable when you get to know us."

Big F didn't crack a smile at Web's remark. "So how come you ain't dead?"

"Guardian angel."

Now Big F smiled broadly. "Right, that's good shit. Tell me where I can get me one."

Big F shifted his bulk along with the direction of the conversation. "You want to know how them guns got in that building?"

Web stiffened. "You willing to testify to it?"

"Yeah. I come on down to the courthouse. You go on ahead and wait for me."

"Okay, how'd they get the guns in there?"

"You know how old them buildings are?"

Web's eyes narrowed. "Old? No. Why?"

"The 1950s. I ain't old 'nough to remember, but my mama was. She told me."

"Was?"

"Too much coke. Not the soda pop. Yeah, 1950s. Think, HRT. Think."

"I'm not getting it."

He shook his head and looked over at Macy and then back at Web. "I thought you damn Feds all went to college."

"Some colleges are better than others."

"If you can't fly the shit in through the roof and you can't take it in the front door, what you got left?"

Web thought for a moment before it hit him. "Under. The 1950s. Cold War. Underground bomb shelters. Tunnels?"

"Damn, you smart after all. There you go."

"That's still not much to go on."

"That's your problem. I gave you something, now you tell your folks to back off my ass. I ain't got no reason in the world to waste a buncha Feds. You go back and make sure they understand that." He paused and rubbed some pine needles with his huge foot, and then he looked directly at Web. "You guys ain't playing games on me and got Kevin but ain't saying, are you?"

Web considered how best to answer that. Ironically, given his present company, he decided that the truth was the best approach. "We don't have Kevin."

"See, local cops I don't trust as far as I can throw 'em. Too many brothers end up dead when the local cops get to 'em. Now, Feds ain't worth too much in my book neither, but you guys ain't killing people for no reason."

"Thanks."

"So other things being equal, see, if you guys got Kevin, then I know he be all right. And maybe you boys just hold on to him for a while till this shit blows over."

The way the man was half looking at him, Web could tell Big F really wanted Kevin to be in the custody of the FBI, where he would be reasonably safe.

"I wish we did have him, but we don't. I'm playing it straight with you." Then he added, "But I think Kevin might have been involved somehow."

"Bullshit," roared Big F. "He a kid. He ain't done nothing. He ain't going to no jail, no way is he. Not Kevin."

"I didn't say he knew what he was doing. You're right: He's just a kid, a scared kid. But whoever took him is behind what happened. At least that's what I think. I don't know why Kevin was in that alley, but his being there wasn't a coincidence. I want him just as bad as you do. And I want him safe too. I saved him once in that alley, I don't want it to be for naught."

"Right, so he can testify and then spend the rest of his life in witness protection. Some life."

"At least it's a life," Web shot back.

Big F and he had a prolonged stare-down until the big man finally looked away.

"I'm going to do everything I can to get Kevin back safe and sound, Francis. I promise you that. But if he knows something, he's going to have to tell us. We'll protect him."

"Yeah, sure you will. Done a real good job of that so far, ain't you?"

They heard the other men returning. "A name would be nice to go with the tunnels," said Web, but Big F was already shaking his head.

"Ain't got none to give."

When the two men came into sight, Big F motioned to one of them. "Make sure the two-way in the car ain't working."

The man nodded, slid into the front seat of Web's car and fired two bullets into the government-issued radio and then ripped out the hand-held microphone. He also popped the ammo clip out of Web's gun, fired the round that was chambered into the dirt and handed it back to him. The other man pulled out Web's cell phone from his pocket, ceremoniously smashed it against a tree and then handed it back to Web with a broad smile. "Ain't making 'em like they used to."

"We got to be going now," said Big F. "And in case you thinking 'bout coming after my ass for pulling the trigger on Toona, think 'bout this." He paused and stared grimly at Web. "Anytime I want you dead, you dead. Anytime I want any of your friends dead, they dead. You got a pet and I want it dead, it dead."

Web eyed the man steadily. "You don't want to go down that road, Francis. You really don't."

"What? You gonna kick my ass? You gonna hurt me bad? You gonna kill me?" He unbuttoned his shirt and stepped closer to Web. Web had seen a lot in his line of work, yet he had never seen anything quite like this.

The man's chest and belly were covered with knife wounds, bullets holes, thick, angry-looking scars, burn marks and what looked to be tunnels of ripped flesh badly healed. To Web it seemed a painting collectively produced by an insane world.

"One hundred and twenty in nice little tidy-whitey years," Big F said quietly. He closed the shirt and his face held, to Web's thinking, a look of obvious pride at surviving all that those scars represented. And right now, Web couldn't deny the man that.

Big F said, "You come after me, you better bring something to do the job right. And I'll still cut off your dick and stuff it down your throat."

Big F turned away and it was all Web could do not to leap on the man's back. Now was not Web's time to settle this, yet he couldn't just leave it like this.

He called after Big F. "So I guess you're grooming Kevin to inherit your empire. Your brother-son. I'm sure he's real proud of you."

Big F turned back. "I said Kevin's not your bizness."

"We shared a lot back in that alley. He told me lots of stuff." It was all a bluff, but a calculated one, if Web was reading the signals right. Whoever had switched Kevin out might be Big F's enemy. If that was the case, then playing one against the other might not be such a bad idea. Web was thinking that Big F was not above lying about not being involved, but that didn't mean the street capitalist hadn't done a joint venture with somebody else to knock off Charlie Team. If so, Web wanted everybody. Everybody.

Big F walked up to Web and looked him over, as though gauging either his guts or his stupidity.

"If you want Kevin back, I expect some cooperation," said Web. He hadn't mentioned what Big F had told him. He figured Big F wanted to keep the information about the tunnels under the target building between him and Web, which was why Big F had sent the two men off to give Toona a burial in the river.

"Expect this," said Big F.

Web managed to partially block the blow with his forearm, but the impact of Big F's bowling-ball fist and his own arm against his jaw still knocked him on top of the hood of the car, where his head smacked against the windshield, cracking it.

Web woke up a half hour later, slowly slid off the car hood and staggered around holding his arm and rubbing his jaw and head and cursing. Calming down, he discovered that his jaw, arm and head did not appear broken and he wondered how that was possible. He also wondered how many more concussions he could endure before his brain fell out of his head.

And then Web whirled and pointed his gun at the man who had just emerged from behind a stand of trees. The man was pointing his own gun at Web.

"Nice try," said the man, "but your gun doesn't have any bullets." He stepped forward and Web got a better look at him.

"Cove?"

Randall Cove put his gun away and leaned up against the car. He said, "That dude is one seriously dangerous person. Him blowing away his own guy like that, that was a new one even for me." He looked at Web's face. "You're gonna have some good bruises tomorrow, but it's better than a visit with the coroner."

Web put his empty gun away and rubbed the back of his head. "I take it you had a ringside seat. Thanks for the assist."

Cove looked at him grimly. "Look, man, I'm a fellow agent, undercover or not. Carry the same creds, took the same oath, work through the same bullshit you do at the Bureau. If they'd tried to take you out, you would have known my presence. But they didn't and so I didn't. If it makes you feel any better, while you were unconscious, I shooed away some brothers who came sniffing around your carcass."

"Thanks, because I'm not done with this carcass yet."

"We need to talk, but not here. Some of Big F's boys might still be hanging around. And this place ain't safe, not even for armed lawmen."

Web looked around. "Where, then? They knocked your old office down."

Cove smiled. "You been talking to Sonny, I know. I guess if old Sonny Venables thinks you're all right, you're all right. Boy's got a nose for bad meat like the best hound dog I ever had me in Mississippi."

"There's a lot of shit going on. You been in touch with Bates lately?"

"We talk, but neither one of us is telling the other everything, and that's cool. I know where Perce is coming from and he knows where I'm standing." He handed Web a slip of paper. "Meet me here in thirty minutes."

Web looked at his watch. "I'm on special assignment. I've got to get back."

"Don't worry, it won't take long. Oh, one more thing." He climbed inside Web's car and searched for a few moments before coming back out holding something.

"Satellite-based tracking device. Good as the stuff we use," said Cove.

"They've got a satellite," said Web. "That's comforting."

"It's got a wireless communicator too."

So Web had been correct in deducing how they had relayed the directions to him after crossing over the Wilson Bridge.

Cove switched the device off and pocketed it. "Evidence is evidence. Surprised they didn't take it," he added before disappearing into the woods.

Sufficiently recovered to keep both eyes open at the same time and seeing only double instead of in gauzy triplicate, Web put the car in gear and headed out. He met Cove at the Mall downtown, at a bench near the Smithsonian Castle. When Web sat down there, he heard a voice but didn't react. All that had been on the paper. Web reasoned that Cove was behind a set of bushes near the bench.

"So Bates said he filled you in on me."

"He did. I'm sorry what happened to your family."

"Yeah," was all Cove said to that.

"I found the news clipping at your house, about you and Bates."

"You are good. That hiding place has worked for years."

"Why hide it?"

"Red herring. Somebody searching your house, it gives them something to find that really means nothing. Anything really important I keep in my head."

"So the clipping was just a dodge? Nothing important?"

Cove didn't respond, so Web said, "Bates said you were on the butts of some big-time dealers, that they might have set up my team."

"That's right. But this story is a long way from over. And I heard Westbrook tell you about the tunnels. I never figured that one. Good way to get the computers out and the guns in."

"I'm going to fill in Bates on that one ASAP and we'll go take a look. You want in?"

Cove didn't answer and it took a second for Web to figure out why. Across the street a man was walking by. He was dressed like a homeless person, was staggering slightly as though he were drunk and he could very well have been both. However, Web couldn't take any chances and obviously neither could Cove. Web reached for his gun and realized again that it was empty. He had a spare mag in the trunk of the car, but that was parked a good hundred feet away and he had forgotten to get the ammo out, idiot that he was. As though in answer to his thoughts, Web felt something slide next to him through the back support of the bench. He gripped the pistol that Cove had just handed him, whispered a thank-you and sat there, the gun held at his side, its muzzle following each move of the man across the street until he moved off.

"You just never know what riffraff's going to come on by," Cove said.

"Bates said that you might have been working through one of Westbrook's guys, maybe Peebles or Macy, and that they might've set you up."

"Macy and Peebles weren't my inside connection. I think my guy was dealing straight with me, at least mostly, but I think *he* was set up."

"So if the guy was shooting straight with you, any chance we can use him to get to the truth?"

"Not anymore."

"How come?"

"Because my inside guy was Toona."

"You're kidding me."

"Big F's guys skim all the time. That was just bullshit he was feeding you. He killed Toona for the ultimate sin, working with the cops."

"Did Toona think there were others involved besides Westbrook?"

"Toona was basically muscle, but he had some brains. I've been working with him for about six months. We nailed him on some small stuff, but he'd already done four years in prison early on in his career and didn't want to do any more. He told me about this new group coming in that was handling some of the local crew's distribution and even cleaning up their dirty money through some legit operations. The service didn't come cheap, but most of the crews apparently signed on—except Westbrook. He doesn't trust anybody that much. But even drug crews get tired of shooting each other up. And consolidation of operations and cost-cutting works just as well in illegal businesses as it does legitimate ones. I'd been digging deep on this group but couldn't crack it. My undercover identity was as a point man for a drug crew looking to relocate from Arizona to rural Virginia. We'd heard about this group and I got myself invited to look over their operation. At first I thought it was connected to Westbrook's piece. But when I saw what was there, I knew it was big-time stuff."

"Bates mentioned the Oxycontin piece."

"That's what makes this one special. I think the product this group was principally supplying the locals with were prescription drugs like Oxy, Percocet and the like. Low risk and huge profit margins. Now, Toona wasn't in the ops side of the business, but he seemed to think that too. It'd be a whole new paradigm in the District's drug trade. And this new group wasn't stopping at D.C. I believe they're moving the stuff up and down the East Coast."

"Oxy started out rural."

"Yeah, you heard of Rocky Mountain high? Well this is Appalachian high. But the Appalachian Mountains touch on about twenty states, from Alabama all the way up to the Canadian border. And there's lots of room there to carve out a new homegrown drug empire on the backs of legitimate drugs. That's why I called in WFO as soon as I realized the operation in that warehouse was a lot bigger than Westbrook. Now, I could have kept digging and maybe got some more stuff, but I ran the risk of them pulling out. I figured if we could get the bean counters to testify, we could bring this whole Oxy crew down. Man, I look back at it now, and you know what I think?"

"That it was too good to be true?"

"You got it." Cove stopped talking for a moment. "Look, Web, I'm sorry what happened to your guys. I never in a million years smelled the setup. But I'll take the responsibility because it was my screwup. And I'll sacrifice everything I got left, even my life, to make it right."

"What you do for a living, I never could. I don't know how you guys do it."

"Funny, I was thinking the same thing about you. Now you go to those tunnels and figure out how they got that stuff in and out. And maybe you'll see something that'll tell you who. And I'm not thinking that it's Westbrook. There's somebody else out there, having a nice laugh at our expense."

"You got any firmer thoughts on that?"

"I'm still feeling my way. Whoever it is, they are wired in tight somewhere important, because they seem to be able to keep one step ahead of everybody."

"Wired tight to who, somebody at the Bureau?"

"You said it, I didn't."

"You got proof of that?"

"My gut. You listen to yours?"

"All the time. I take it you feel like the odd man out."

"What, you mean everybody and their brother thinking I turned traitor and helped burn a bunch of my own? Yeah, it has occupied my thoughts of late."

"You're not alone there, Cove."

"Hey, Web, we're blood brothers in a way. Branded traitors for something we didn't do, and some people just don't want to hear it."

"Is that why you're not coming in?"

"See, the bottom line is, I got taken, snookered, suckered, whatever you want to call it. I'm no traitor, but I messed up, that's almost as bad as jumping sides in my line of work."

"We are blood brothers, then, because I did the same damn thing."

"Well, maybe we'll both be standing at the end of this dance, what do you say?"

"I say I'll give it my best shot."

"Keep your head down, London, these mothers shoot low."

"Hey, Cove?"

"Yeah?"

"Apology accepted."

Web drove to DuPont Circle. He grabbed a spare mag for his pistol from the trunk and put the gun Cove had given him in the rear of his waistband and then took a cab to the WFO. Bates had long since gone home and Web decided he would wait until morning to contact him. The guy could probably use a good night's sleep and those tunnels weren't going anywhere. Instead of checking out another set of Bucar wheels, Web decided to do something really crazy. He was going to go get his very own car.

The press army wasn't parked outside his house anymore, yet Web still did not take any chances. He entered the house from the rear, slipped inside the Mach, opened the garage doors and eased the car out, its lights off. He waited until he was down the street before he turned on the lights, then he stepped on the gas, all the while looking in his rearview mirror. Nothing. He headed back to East Winds.

34

When Web got back to the carriage house, Romano wasn't there; Web even checked the antique cars downstairs in case his partner had crawled into one to admire it and had fallen asleep. It was almost four o'clock in the morning and his partner was probably prowling around outside. As a sniper, Romano had been restless with too much natural energy despite all their training to take things slow and methodically unless drastic circumstances dictated otherwise. Yet when it was time for action, just about everybody took a backseat to Paul Romano. Since Web's cell phone was out of operation, he used the phone in the house to call Romano and breathed a sigh of relief when the man answered.

"So how'd your appointment go?" asked Romano.

"Boring. I'll fill you in later. Where are you?"

"Everything was secure, so I've been poking around the place. There's an old watchtower on the west side. See for miles in every direction."

"I know; I've been there."

"Well, I'm there right now. Felt like a little jog."

"That's a bit of a hike, Paulie."

"Walk in the park. You might want to come out here and bring out a pair of NVs."

"What are you spying on?"

"You'll see."

Web left the carriage house from the rear, slipped on his headgear, attached his ambient light source night-vision binoculars to it, powered up and fixed the relief to his eyes. The world instantly became an ethereal, fluid green. You couldn't use the contraption for very long because the goggles were heavy enough that you would get a piercing pain in your neck, followed by a headache that would make you forget the neck ache. Web always kept one eye closed when scanning through the goggles even though this distorted your depth perception even more; if you didn't keep one eye closed, when you stopped looking through the goggles all you'd see would be a brilliant orange ball in each eye. And at that point a ninety-year-old in a wheelchair could get the drop on you.

As a sniper, one had to use various pieces of equipment to get the job done, from high-tech to the lowest tech of all: camouflage. Web coveted his Ghillie suit, a concoction of burlap and cordura material that he had patiently covered with animal excrement and other foul substances to allow it to blend into a rugged forest or jungle environment. Each HRT sniper gave his Ghillie his own personal stamp and Web had spent years improving on his by defiling it even more. The Ghillie had been originally designed by the Scots over four hundred years ago in the course of waging countless guerrilla wars against those seeking to conquer them. It worked just as well now as it had then. Web had lain under his Ghillie in the middle of a jungle in Central America with dope dealers toting submachine guns walking all around him, and they never knew Web was there until he stuck his gun in their backs and read them their rights.

He moved forward again and pushed and then clicked the NV to IR status, which caused an internal light source to come on and vastly intensified the field of vision. Web wanted to make sure the equipment worked, for NV goggles batteries were notorious for failing right when you needed them to work. He didn't like to use the IR for very long, because it had one major drawback. For anyone watching *him* with night-vision goggles, the IR magnifier gave off a light beacon, like a large flashlight in one's face. Web would be a sitting duck. He clicked off the IR and put the headgear away in his backpack. He would rely on merely his eyes from now on, something he had done with every shot he had ever taken. Sometimes you couldn't improve on nature.

The air was crisp and the sounds of the farm and surrounding woods many and varied. Web set a good pace and he covered the ground to the watchtower in enviable time. It was good to know he was still in decent shape. After eight years of relentless training you didn't lose it all in a short period of time, he reasoned. He liked the forest in the darkness; it felt as comfortable to him as a La-Z-Boy and a big-screen TV would to the average American male.

He sighted the watchtower and stopped. Since he didn't have a cell phone, Web put his hands up to his face, formed a rude bugle of sorts and let out a call, the same signal he and Romano had used when they were sniping. It could either be a gust of wind or a bird commonly found just about anywhere. Web was sure Romano would remember, and a few seconds later he heard the answering message. All clear.

Web broke from the tree line and hustled to the watchtower, gripped the wooden rungs and climbed silently up. Romano greeted him at the little hinged door in the floor of the observation space. Web knew Romano couldn't see Web's fresh injuries courtesy of Toona and Big F, and that was just as well, because he didn't want to waste breath right now explaining them. And of course Romano would give him a hard time about it. He could just hear the words *Shit, you let them do that to you?* passing through the man's lips.

Web looked at Romano as he pulled out a ten-power Litton scope that was normally attached to a .308 sniper rifle.

"Anything good on?" asked Web.

"Check this out, right through that break in the trees to the northwest."

Web looked through the scope. "I take it I'm looking at the Southern Belle."

"Interesting stuff going on, for a horse farm."

Web adjusted the scope to his eye and sighted through it. There was indeed a nice break in the trees, which revealed a fine view of the neighboring spread.

There were two sizable buildings that looked relatively new. Large trucks were parked next to them and Web watched as men with walkie-talkies raced in different directions. A door opened on the side of one of the buildings and Web saw that whatever was going on inside required a lot of light. A tractor-trailer was backed up to a warehouse-type roll-up door and men were bringing large boxes out on hand trucks and rolling them up inside the truck's trailer.

"Something big is going on," said Web. "Auto chop shop, drugs, stolen aviation parts, spies, technology pirates or lots of other things. Damn."

"Fascinating neighborhood. And here I was, thinking Virginia horse country was just a bunch of old duffers riding around drunk chasing little foxes while the little women had tea in the afternoon. Boy, have I got a lot to learn." He looked at Web. "So what do you think?"

"I think with all we got going on, the Southern Belle will have to keep. But if something pops at least we'll be right here to do something about it."

Romano grinned, obviously happy with the thought of coming action and possible mayhem. "Now you're talking my language."

35

Kevin Westbrook had filled up all his sketchbooks and was now sitting and staring at the walls. He wondered if he would ever stand under sunlight again. He had grown used to the sounds of the machinery and the water running. It no longer affected his sleep, though he regretted growing used to this condition of his imprisonment, as though it were an omen that those conditions would become permanent.

The footsteps reached his ears over the other sounds and he retreated to his bed like an animal in a zoo cage as visitors approached.

The door opened and the same man who'd visited him earlier came in. Kevin didn't know who he was and the man had never bothered to tell Kevin his name.

"How you doing, Kevin?"

"Got a headache."

The man reached in his pocket and pulled out a bottle of Tylenol. "In my line of work, I always got some of this handy." He gave two pills to the boy and poured him out a glass of water from the bottle on the table.

"Probably lack of sunlight," added Kevin.

The man smiled at this. "Well, we'll see if we can do something about that soon."

"That mean I be getting out of here soon?"

"It might mean just that. Things are rolling along."

"So you won't be needing me no more." As soon as Kevin said this he regretted it. That statement could certainly cut both ways.

The man stared at him. "You did a pretty good job, Kev. Real good, considering you're just a kid. We'll remember that."

"Can I go home soon?"

"Not up to me, actually."

"I ain't say nothing to nobody."

"Nobody like Francis?"

"Nobody means nobody."

"Well, it won't matter, really."

Kevin instantly looked suspicious. "You ain't hurting my brother."

The man held up his hands in mock surrender. "I didn't say we were. In fact, if things go okay, only people who need to get hurt are going to get hurt, okay?"

"You hurt all them men in that courtyard. You hurt them dead."

The fellow perched on the table and crossed his arms over his chest. Though the man's movements weren't threatening, Kevin drew back a bit.

"Like I said, the people who deserve to be hurt are the ones who get hurt. It's not always that way, you know that, lots of innocent people get hurt all the time. I had me enough lessons on that, and looks like you have too." He eyed the wounds on the boy's face.

Kevin had nothing to say to this. The man opened one of the sketchbooks and looked at some of the drawings.

"This the Last Supper?" he asked.

"Yep. Jesus. Before they crucified him. He's the one in the middle," said Kevin.

"I went to Sunday school," the man said with another big smile. "I know all about Jesus, son."

Kevin had drawn the painting from memory. He had done it for two reasons: to pass the time and for the sheer comfort of having the Son of God close right now. Maybe the Lord would get the message and send some guardian angels down to help one Kevin Westbrook, who desperately needed some type of intervention, divine or otherwise.

"This is good stuff, Kevin. You're real talented."

He looked at another picture and held it up. "What's this of?"

"My brother reading to me."

His pistol on the nightstand, his men outside the room with their own guns, his brother Francis would put a big arm around Kevin and draw him close to his massive chest and they would sit and read far into the night, until Kevin would fall asleep. He would awake in the morning and all the men would be gone and so would his brother. But the place they had stopped in the book would be marked; it was a sure sign that his brother intended to come back and finish reading it to him.

The man looked surprised. "He'd read to you?"

Kevin nodded. "Yeah, why not? Ain't nobody ever read to you when you was little?"

"No," he replied. He put the sketchbook back on the table. "How old are you, Kevin?"

"Ten."

"That's a good age, your whole life ahead of you. Wish I had me that."

"You ever gonna let me go?" asked Kevin.

The man's look managed to cut Kevin's hopes right to nothing.

"I like you, Kevin. You kind of remind me of me when I was little. I didn't really have any family to speak of neither."

"I got my brother!"

"I know you do. But I'm talking about a normal life, you know, Mommy and Daddy and sisters and brothers living in the same place."

"What's normal for some folks ain't normal for everybody."

The man grinned and shook his head. "You got a lot of wisdom in that little head. I guess nothing about life is normal when you get down to it."

"You know my brother. He ain't somebody you fool around with."

"I don't know him personally, but me and him do some business together. And I'm sure he ain't somebody you want to fool around with, and thank you for the advice. But the thing is, we're working together right now, sort of. I asked him real nicely to do something for me having to do with that Web London fellow, and he did it."

"I bet he done it 'cause you told him you had me. He doing it 'cause he don't want nothing to happen to me."

"I'm sure he did, Kevin. But just so you know, we're going to return the favor. Some folks real close to your brother want to cut in on his business. We're going to help him out there."

"Why you gonna help him?" Kevin asked suspiciously. "What's in it for you?"

He laughed. "Man, if you were just a little bit older, I'd make you my partner. Well, let's just put it this way, it's a win-win for everybody."

"So you ain't answered my question. You gonna let me go?"

The man rose and went over to the door. "You just hang in there, Kev. Good things tend to happen to patient folks."

36

When he got back to the carriage house, Web called Bates at home, waking him up, and told him about his violent encounter with Big F. He also told him about his meeting with Cove. He rendezvoused with Bates and a team of agents at the courtyard in southeast D.C. an hour later. The sun was just starting its rise and Web could only shake his head. He hadn't even been to sleep yet and it was time to start a new workday. Bates gave him another phone to replace the one Westbrook's guy had smashed; same phone number, so that was convenient.

Web thanked Bates, who didn't comment on the fresh injuries to Web's face, though Bates clearly was not in a good mood.

"You keep going through government equipment like that, it's coming out of your damn paycheck. And I left you messages on your old phone that you never returned."

"Well, damn, Perce. I get voice-mail messages popping up on my screen sometimes a day after I get them."

"I never had a problem."

"Well, that really helps me, doesn't it?"

They had left one agent to watch their cars. In this neighborhood, nothing was safe or sacred, least of all Uncle Sam's property. In fact, some enterprising young fellows would like nothing better than to chop-shop a Bucar and make a tidy profit in the bargain.

As they walked, Bates's temper seemed to grow. "You're lucky you're alive, Web," he snapped, not seeming happy at all that Web had been so lucky. "That's what you get for going off on your own.

I can't believe you went into that with no backup. You disobeyed my orders. I could have your ass, all of it."

"But you won't because I'm giving you what you need. A break."

Bates finally calmed down and shook his head. "Did he really blow the guy away right in front of you for being a snitch?"

"That's not something one tends to get wrong."

"Jesus, the balls the guy must have."

"Bowling balls, if they fit the rest of him."

They all went inside the target building and down to the basement level. It was dark and damp, and it stank. Going from a stone mansion in Virginia horse country to a dungeon in Anacostia made Web want to laugh. Yet he really had to concede that he was more of a dungeon guy.

"Tunnels, the man said," commented Bates, looking around. There were no working lights down here, so each agent had brought a searchlight. "See, the thing is, we checked for things like that, Web."

"Well, we need to check again, because he seemed to know what he was talking about, and there's really no other way those guns could have been brought in with no one seeing anything. Don't they have plans down at the Department of Public Works that would show the location of the tunnels?"

"This is D.C., okay? If you want to go and try and find anything at a city agency, be my guest. Stuff from yesterday is hard enough to track down, much less from half a century ago."

They searched everywhere until Web came to a large collection of fifty-gallon oil drums in a far corner. They were ten abreast and ten deep. "What's with all this?"

"Furnace system was oil-based. Supply just got left when the place was shut down. Too costly to move it."

"Anybody check under them?"

In answer, one of the agents went over to the pile and pushed against one of the drums. It didn't budge. "Nothing's under here, Web. You wouldn't park a million tons of oil on top of a tunnel you had to get in and out of."

"Is that right?" Web eyed the drum the man had tried to move. He put his foot against it and it was indeed full. Web pushed the one next to it and the one next to that. Then he pushed against drums in the second row. All full.

"Okay, are you convinced?" asked Bates.

"Humor me."

As Bates and the other agents watched, Web climbed on top of the drums and started stepping from one to another. With each one he would stop and rock his weight back and forth. When he reached the middle of the cluster of oil drums, he rocked on top of one can and almost fell over. "This one's empty." He stepped over to the drum next to it. "This one too." He marched out a four-drum-by-four-drum grid. "These are all empty. Give me a hand."

The other agents scampered up to help and very quickly they had cleared away the empty drums and their lights shone on a door in the floor.

Bates stared at it and then looked at Web. "Son of a bitch. How'd you figure that one out?"

"I did a case when I worked in the Kansas City Field Office. Guy scammed a bunch of bankers by filling up a warehouse with drums that were supposed to contain heating oil the guy was using for collateral for this huge loan. The bankers sent their inspectors out and sure enough, they opened a few drums and they were all filled with heating oil. But they only checked the front fringes because guys in suits don't like to climb over dirty oil drums. Turns out ninety percent of the drums were empty. I know because I checked every damn one after we were called in when the guy skipped town."

Bates looked chagrined. "I owe you one, Web."

"And believe me I'll hold you to that."

Guns drawn, they opened the door, climbed down into the tunnel and followed its straight and then sharply angled path.

Web flashed his light on the floor. "Somebody's been through here recently. Look at all those tracks."

The tunnel ended in a stairwell. They headed quietly up, every man alert and ready to fire. They eased the unlocked door open and found themselves in another building much like the one they had just left. The area they were in had a lot of abandoned property. They moved stealthily upstairs. The room they found there was large and empty. They moved back downstairs, exited the building and looked around.

"I figure we went west about two blocks," said one of the agents, and Web agreed with that. They all looked at the building where the tunnel had led. Faded lettering on one wall identified it as once having been a food distribution company, and it came complete with a loading dock where trucks could deliver bananas. Or machine guns. At the loading dock were a couple of abandoned trucks, tires gone, doors missing.

"In the middle of the night you pull up with a truck and squeeze it right between these two, off-load your crates, take 'em through the tunnel and that's it," said Web. His gaze swept the area. "And there are no residences around here, no one to see anything, that's probably why they used it."

"Okay, but we got Big F on murder one. With your testimony he goes away forever."

"You have to find him first, and from what I've seen he's pretty good at what he does."

"We're going to need to put you in protective custody."

"No, you don't. I'm good on that."

"What the hell do you mean, you're good on that? This guy has every incentive to blow you away."

"If he had wanted to do that, he would've done it last night. I was just a tad helpless then. Besides, I've got a job to do—protect Billy and Gwen Canfield—and I'm going to finish that job."

"That's what I don't get. He murders a guy right in front of you and lets you walk."

"So I could deliver the message about the tunnels."

"What, he's never heard of a damn phone? I'm not kidding, Web, I want you in protection."

"You said you owed me, I'm calling in my chit."

"What the hell is more important than staying alive?"

"I don't know, Perce, in my line of work I've never really thought about it very much. And I'm not going in."

"I'm your superior, I can make you."

"Yeah, I guess you can," said Web, looking at the man evenly.

"Aw, shit, you're more trouble than you're worth, London."

"Figured you learned that a long time ago."

Bates looked around the loading dock. "The thing is, there's nothing tying the Frees to this warehouse or those guns. Without something to go on, we can't hit them. Right now they're being little angels, giving us no excuse to pay a visit."

"Nothing has turned up with the killings in Richmond to connect them to the Frees? That's a lot of tracks to cover."

"From the angle of the shot on Judge Leadbetter we traced it to a building across the street that's under construction. Hundreds of people work there all the time, laborers who come and go."

"What about the phone call he got?"

"Pay phone in southside Richmond. No trace."

"But the judge was downtown. So at least two people were involved and they had communication links so the timing of the call was right."

"That's right. I never thought we were dealing with amateurs here."

"What about Watkins and Wingo?"

"All the people in Wingo's office have been checked out."

"Cleaning people? One of them could have applied the atropine to the phone receiver."

"Again, we checked. Those people come and go, but we found no leads."

"Watkins?"

"Gas leak. It was an old house."

"Come on, he gets a phone call right as he walks in. Again, it's split-second timing. And by somebody who knew all three men's routines. And he just happened to have a solenoid in his phone that would make the spark necessary to blow him to heaven?"

"I know, Web, but these guys also had lots of other people with incentives to kill them. One or two of the murders might be related, but maybe all of them aren't. At least right now all we have to link them are the phones and the Ernest Free case."

"They're connected, Percc, trust me."

"Right, but we have to convince a jury, and that's getting almost impossible to do these days."

"Anything on the bomb out at East Winds?"

"Very sophisticated C4 device. We've checked the backgrounds of all the people working out there. Most of the farmhands came with Strait when the place they were working at closed down. They're all pretty much clean. A few had misdemeanors, mostly for drunk and disorderly, stuff you'd expect from a bunch of rednecks."

"What about Nemo Strait?"

"Like he told you. Grew up on a small horse farm that his father managed. That's how he learned the business. He fought in Vietnam and was a superb soldier. Lots of medals and lots of hard fighting. He spent three months as a POW."

"One tough dude, to be able to survive that. The Cong weren't known for their hospitality."

"He did some odd jobs when he got back to the States, prison guard, computer sales. Along the way he married, had some kids, started working again with horses and got divorced. He came to the Canfields just about the time they bought East Winds."

"What about old Ernest B. Free?"

"Not one damn sighting, and that's got me amazed, frankly. Usually we have thousands of phone calls, ninety-nine percent of them wrong, but usually we get one or two legit leads. This time, nothing."

A very frustrated Web looked around. His gaze went past the device and then came back to it and was riveted. "Damn," he said.

"What? What is it, Web?" said Bates.

Web pointed. "I think maybe we've got another eyewitness of sorts."

Bates looked over at the traffic signal at the corner diagonal from the warehouse loading dock. Like other signals in the area, on top of it was mounted a surveillance camera. And like the other cameras Web had seen in the area on his last trip through, this one had been pointed in another direction, presumably by mischievous hands, and that direction happened to be right at the loading dock.

"Damn," echoed Bates. "You thinking what I'm thinking?"

"Yeah," said Web. "That looks like one of the older models on video loops that run twenty-four hours a day. The newer ones only activate when they're triggered by the speed of a car and take a still photo of the rear license plate."

"Well, let's hope the District police haven't taped over a certain segment."

Bates signaled for one of his men to make that call immediately.

Web said, "I've got to get back to the farm. Romano's probably starting to feel lonely."

"I really don't like this, Web. What if you end up dead between now and then?"

"You got Cove. He saw it too."

"What if *he* ends up dead too? That's just as likely, with everything that's been going down."

"Got a pen and some paper?"

Web wrote out the entire account of Toona's murder. Toona's real name was Charles Towson, Web had found out from Bates, and no one knew where the nickname had come from, yet everyone working the streets seemed to have one. Well, whoever pulled Charlie Towson's body out of the river, if anyone ever did, was going to lose whatever was in his stomach. Web positively identified the killer as Francis "Big F" Westbrook. He signed it with a flourish and two other agents witnessed his signature.

"Are you kidding me? A defense attorney will tear that apart," raged Bates.

"It's the best I can do right now." Web walked away.

37

When he returned to East Winds, Web checked in with Romano and then went to the carriage house and eased into a hot bath. A catnap while he was soaking and he'd be as good as new, he figured. He'd gotten by on a lot less sleep over the years.

Romano had seen Web's fresh wounds and his comment had been predictable.

"You let somebody beat the crap out of you *again*? You're giving HRT a bad name, Web."

Web had told him that next time he'd make sure he was beaten in places that didn't show.

For the next several days, his and Romano's routine was just that—routine. When Gwen and Billy had seen his injuries from the encounter with Big F, Gwen exclaimed, "My God, are you all right?"

"Looks like old Boo kicked you in the face," commented Billy as he sucked on an unlit cigarette.

"Actually, I would have preferred Boo," replied Web.

Gwen had insisted on putting some medicine on Web's cuts. Her fingers felt very nice against his-skin. As she tended to him, Billy had said, "Never a dull moment for you federal types, I guess."

"I guess," replied Web.

He and Romano got to know the Canfields better and saw how much work it took to run a farm. As promised, they both pitched in, although Romano bitched and complained every evening to Web about it. East Winds was vast and wondrous, and Web actually started to feel that maybe he should try something else for a living. He figured those feelings would disappear as soon as he left

East Winds permanently. Gwen Canfield was an interesting woman, fascinating in many ways and as intelligent and reserved as she was beautiful and mannered. She and Billy were like the proverbial fire and ice.

Web had ridden with her every day, as much to protect her as to understand the lay of the land better. And, he had to admit, there were far worse ways to spend one's time than riding around a beautiful place with a beautiful woman. She had stopped and prayed at the chapel each day and Web had sat on Boo and watched her. She never invited him to join her and he never suggested that he should. The fact that David Canfield had died on his watch was enough reason for him to keep his distance around the woman.

Each evening the FBI agents had gone to the large house and spent time with them. Billy had led a fascinating life and loved to share stories from it. Each time Nemo Strait had attended and Web found he had more in common with the ex-Marine than he would have thought. Strait had done a lot in his life, everything from soldiering to bronco busting.

"Live by my brains and my brawn, though I seem to have less of both as time goes by."

"We're sort of in the same boat," said Web. "You see yourself doing the horse thing until you drop?"

"Well, I have to say I think about the day I walk away from all the manure and ornery animals." He glanced at the Canfields, lowered his voice and added, grinning, "I'm talking about the two- *and* four-legged varieties." In a normal tone he said, "But like I said, it gets in your blood. Some days I see myself getting my own little spread and running it right."

"Nice dream," said Romano. "Some days I want to have my own NASCAR team."

Web looked at his partner. "I didn't know that, Paulie."

"Hey, a guy's got to have some secrets."

"You got that right," said Strait. "My ex told me once that she never knew what I was thinking. You know what I told her? I told her that was the difference between men and women. Women tell you exactly what they think of you. Men just hold it in." He glanced over at Billy Canfield, who was across the large room examining his stuffed grizzly and downing his third beer in the last half hour. Gwen had gone upstairs to check on dinner. "Although sometimes the reverse is true, you know," said Strait.

Web looked at Canfield and then back at Strait. "Is that right?"

What was becoming more apparent also was that Gwen and Billy spent a lot of time apart. Web never directly asked Gwen about this, but her occasional comments made it seem as though that was more Billy's choice than Gwen's. The blame game over David, perhaps, thought Web.

And despite what Gwen had suggested earlier, it was also clear that Nemo Strait was an integral part of the operation at East Winds. Several times Web had seen Billy turn to the foreman for a definitive answer on matters related to the horses or the running of the farm.

"Been doing this since I was a baby," Strait told Web once. "Ain't much I haven't seen when it comes to horses and farms and such. But Billy, he's picking it up fast."

"And Gwen?"

"She knows more than Billy, but she's sort of set in her ways too. Been trying to put a soft shoe on Baron because that animal has got some brittle hooves, but she won't have no part of it. 'I know my horse,' she tells me. Stubborn. Probably one of the reasons Billy married her."

"*One* of them, anyway," said Web.

Strait sighed. "You got that right, she's a looker. But you know what, lookers make a man's life miserable. Know why? 'Cause some other guy's always trying to take her away. My ex wouldn't of won no beauty contests on her best day, but hell, I didn't sit around worrying about some other fox in the chicken coop either."

"Billy doesn't seem worried about that."

"Fellow's hard to read sometimes. But he's a thinker, all right. A lot going on in that old head of his."

"That one I agree with," replied Web.

Web had been in contact with Bates every day, but nothing, as yet, had come through on the surveillance tape.

Early one morning, Web had just got out of the shower when his phone rang. He reached over and snagged it off the toilet. It was Claire Daniels.

"Have you thought any more about the hypnosis?"

"Look, Claire, I'm on a job."

"Web, if you really want to make some progress, then I feel hypnosis is the key."

"Nobody is looking around in my head."

She persisted. "We can start and if you're uncomfortable in any way, we'll stop. Fair enough?"

"Claire, I'm busy. I can't deal with this right now."

"Web, you came to me for help. I'm doing my best to help you, but I need your cooperation. Trust me, you've been through a lot worse than anything hypnosis will throw at you."

"Right. Sorry, no sell."

She paused and then said, "Listen, Web, I met with someone that you might want to know about."

He didn't answer.

"Buck Winters? Name ring a bell?"

"What did he want?"

"You signed a release that allowed him to ask me about your treatment. Do you remember doing that?"

"I guess. I signed a lot of papers around that time."

"I'm sure. They really took advantage of you."

"What did he want and what did you tell him?"

"Well, there was a big difference between the two. He tried to make a convincing case for why I should tell him everything, but the release form gave me enough wiggle room to stall him. I'll probably hear about it later, but that's just the way it goes."

He thought about this for a few seconds. "You stuck out your neck for me, Claire. I appreciate that."

"But that's one of the reasons I'm calling you. Winters seemed dead set on nailing you to the wall on what happened. He even used the word 'traitor.'"

"That's actually not such a big surprise. Buck and I haven't really seen eye to eye since Waco."

"But if we can get to the root of your issues, Web, and show him and everyone else very clearly that you're not a traitor, well, I can't see how that would be a bad thing. Can you?"

Web sighed. He didn't want to waive on this, but Web also didn't want people to have doubts about him forever. *He* didn't want to have doubts about his ability to do his job at HRT. "Do you really think the hypnosis will help?"

"We won't know, Web, until we try. But I've had great success with hypnosis in other patients."

He finally said, "Okay, maybe we can talk about this some more. Face to face."

"Here at my office?"

"I'm on an assignment."

"Can I come to where you are?"

Web thought about this. Did he really want to do this? The smart thing would be to tell Claire Daniels to go to hell and get on with his life. The problem with that was, he had never really gotten the help he was now coming to believe he actually needed. At some point he would have to pay the piper. And he was coming to understand that Claire really did want to help him. "I'll send somebody for you."

"Who?"

"His name's Romano, Paul Romano. He's HRT. Don't tell him anything, okay, because sometimes he's got a big mouth."

"Fine, Web. Where are you?"

"You'll see, Doc. You'll see."

"I'm free in about an hour. Do you need more time?"

"That's plenty of time."

Web dried off, dressed, found Romano and told him what he wanted him to do.

"Who is the woman?" he asked suspiciously. "Is this your shrink?"

"They like to be called psychiatrists."

"I'm not your chauffeur. I'm on a job, Web."

"Paulie, come on. I want to check in with Billy and Gwen. And you've been carrying the full load out here, let me take it for a while. If you leave now, she'll be ready to go by the time you get there."

"And what if something goes down while I'm gone?"

"Then I'll handle it."

"And what if you get popped?"

"What, you worrying about me all of a sudden?"

"No, I don't want to get my butt in a ringer over it. I got a family to think of."

"You mean Angie will kill you."

"That's exactly what I mean."

"Look, just do it and I swear to you I'll be grafted to the Canfields' souls until you get back."

Romano didn't look happy about it, but he finally agreed and got Claire's name and address from Web. "But listen up: The real reason I'm doing this is so I can go get my own wheels."

"You mean the 'Vette?"

"Yeah, I mean the 'Vette. I bet Billy would love to see it, him and me being automotive aficionados."

"Just go, Paulie, before I throw up."

Romano had told him that the Canfields were at the main house, so Web jogged up there and knocked on the door. An older woman dressed in jeans and a T-shirt and wearing a brightly colored bandanna answered the door and escorted him back to the small sunlit breakfast area off the kitchen where Gwen and Billy were eating.

Gwen rose and said, "Would you like some coffee or something to eat?"

Web accepted some coffee, eggs and toast. "Romano and I were patrolling the place the other night and saw some interesting activity going on next door," he said.

Gwen and Billy exchanged glances and Billy said, "At the Southern Belle? Damn right it's interesting."

"So you've seen some things too?"

"Billy," said Gwen, "you have no proof."

"Proof of what?" asked Web quickly.

"Maybe I ain't got any proof, but I got my common sense," said Billy, "and the goings-on over there make about as much sense with running a horse farm as me running a convent."

"So what have you seen?"

"You tell me first."

Web did so and Billy acknowledged that all of it jived with what he had seen. "See, what gets me," said Billy, "are the semis. Now, I was in trucking for twenty years, and you only use those over-the-road rigs to haul some serious cargo long distances."

"Have any of the other neighbors complained?" asked Web.

He shook his head. "I'm by far the closest one they got. The place on the other side, the owners are at their home in Naples or their other one in Nantucket. They just bought the farm so they can ride when they want to. Can you imagine that, shell out eight million dollars for nine hundred acres just so you can ride twice a year? What, the dumb shits never heard of a stable?" He shook his head and continued, "And the trucks only come and go at night. A little tricky, driving those beasts in the dark on these narrow windy roads. It's not like we have streetlights out here. And there's something else."

Web perked up. "What's that?"

"Remember I told you that a company had bought the place?"

"Right."

"Well, a while back, after all the planes and choppers and such, I went over to the courthouse and did a little digging. The company—it's an LLC, by the way, a limited liability company—is owned by two gents from California. Harvey and Giles Ransome, I guess they're brothers, or maybe they're married, you know, being from California and all." He shook his head.

"You know anything about them?"

"Nope. But you're the detective, figured you could dig something up fast if you wanted to."

"I'll look into it."

"I invited them over once I found out their names. Walked right over there and everything."

"What happened?"

"This time their *people* thanked me real polite-like but said they weren't in. Said they'd pass along the invite. Yeah, right! And I'm a Chinaman."

Gwen poured herself another cup of coffee. She had on jeans, a light brown pullover sweater and low-heeled boots. Before returning to her seat, she pinned up her hair and revealed a very long neck that for a few moments Web found he couldn't take his eyes off of. She sat back down and looked anxiously back and forth at the two men before coming to rest her gaze on Web.

"What do you think it might be, Web?"

"I've got my suspicions, but that's all they are."

Billy eyed him keenly as he took a last bite of toast and wiped his mouth with his napkin. "You're thinking it's maybe the mafioso running stolen goods or something. Believe me, that crap went on in the trucking business. If I had a dollar for every I-talian come through my door with a suitcase full of money in exchange for hauling their stuff in my trucks, well, I wouldn't need to be working my ass off on this farm."

"God," said Gwen, as she pounded the table with her hand, "we leave Richmond to get away from murderous white supremacists and move next door to a bunch of criminals." She stood, went over to the sink and stared out the window.

Billy said, "Look here, Gwen, whoever is next to us, it don't matter in our lives, okay? They do their thing and we do ours. If they got something illegal, it's not our problem, 'cause Web is gonna bust 'em, okay? We're running a horse farm, just like you wanted. Okay?"

She turned and looked at him anxiously. "But not what you wanted?"

He grinned. "Oh, sure. Hell, I even kind of like mucking the stalls." He glanced at Web for a moment. "Pushing manure is sort of therapeutic." To Web, the man didn't look like he meant it. Billy looked away and said, "Well, look what the cat dragged in."

Web glanced over at the doorway and saw Nemo Strait standing there, his Stetson in his hands. He was staring at Billy and his features were a little unkind, it seemed to Web.

Billy said, "Y'all ready to go?"

"Yes, sir, just come up to let you know before we hit the road."

They all went outside and down to the main road, where Web saw a caravan of ten horse trailers, some bumper-pulled, others fifth wheels hooked to heavy-duty trucks, and each emblazoned with the East Winds logo.

"Most of those are brand-new trailers," said Billy. "Cost a damn fortune 'cause we had to customize some, but I guess you got to look good, at least that's what folks keep telling me. Ain't that right, Nemo?"

"If you say so, Billy."

Billy pointed to the trailers. "Now, those three are custom fab three-horse slant loads." He continued pointing. "Then we got two Sundowner Pro Stock MPs, a straight-load gooseneck with horse dressing room, a ten-foot Townsmand bumper pull with young Bobby Lee all by his lonesome inside, two Sunlite 760s and that big-ass one over there." He pointed to the last trailer, an elaborate-looking contraption that resembled more of a people coach than one for horses. "Now, that's the little jewel in this group, though it sure ain't little. That's a Classic Coach Silverado. Living compartment for the boys in front, tack space and other equipment and such in the middle and then space for two horses in the back. It's a beaut. All self-contained."

"Where are they heading?" asked Web.

"Kentucky," answered Gwen. "They have a big yearling sale up there." She pointed to the trailers. "These are our best yearlings, nineteen of them in all."

She sounded a little sad, thought Web. Maybe for her it was like more children going away.

Billy said, "This is what separates the men from the boys. This sale goes well, we have a good year. I normally go too, but the FBI has persuaded me otherwise." He shot a glance at Web. "So if the sales aren't like they should be, I guess you guys can make up the difference."

"That's not my call," said Web.

Billy shook his head. "Yeah, I bet. Those bastard buyers pick the horses apart and lowball us, then we're selling pencils on the sidewalk. Now, these yearlings are some of our best ever. But those folks will hem and haw and find every little flaw they can, and then try to buy 'em for pennies on a dollar, and next thing you know, they got the next Secretariat. Well, that's not going to happen. I been down that road before. You haul their asses back here, Strait, if they don't fetch the reserves I gave you. Screw 'em."

Nemo nodded. "Yes, sir."

Web watched as Gwen went over to one of the smaller trailers and looked inside it.

"That's Bobby Lee," said Billy, pointing to the horse inside the trailer Gwen was looking at. "Now, if things go right, that horse will bring us a nice little bundle. He's special, so he doesn't have to share his ride with another horse. Damn, wish I had me a deal like that. That's my problem, too many people around."

Web wondered whom, if anyone, the man was referring to. "How come you don't keep the horses and race them yourself?" asked Web.

"It takes mountains of money to raise and maintain Thorough-breds for racing, that's why the most successful farms are run by corporations and syndicates primarily. They have lots of capital behind them, so they can weather bad times. We can't compete with that. East Winds is a breeding farm and that's all we really want to be. Believe me, that's a big enough pain in the ass. Ain't that right, Gwen?"

She said nothing and moved away when Web went over to Bobby Lee and looked inside the Townsmand ten-foot trailer. The rear windows of the trailer were open and Web could see the horse inside, starting with the top of his bushy tail. Strait came over and stood next to him.

"Hate to see Bobby Lee go, he's a good horse. Fifteen hands already, beautiful chestnut coat, glossy, damn impressive musculature, look at that chest, and he's got a lot of growing left to do."

"He is a nice-looking animal." Web looked at the heavy-duty equipment boxes welded on the interior walls of the horse trailer. "What are those for?"

Strait opened the trailer and went inside, coaxing Bobby Lee over to the side. He opened one of the boxes. "Horses are worse than women when it comes to traveling." He grinned and stepped aside. Inside the box Web saw halters and bridles and blankets and every other piece of equipment a horse might need.

Strait ran his hand along the soft rubber that lined the outside of the boxes. "We pad the sides so the horse doesn't hurt itself against the edges."

"Not a lot of room for error," Web said as Strait closed up the box.

"There's a lot of little details that might not seem so obvious to nonhorse folks. For example, you riding with a single horse in a two-staller, you got to keep the animal on the driver's side so the extra weight don't keep pulling you to the side of the road. These trailers are real versatile. All the dividers swing out and you can re-configure them. Keep a mare in the back and the foal up front, for example." He tapped the walls. "Galvaneal metal, and that lasts a lot longer than people." He pointed to the long, open space directly in front of the horse. "And up here is their feeding and water trough. And over there"—he pointed to the door on the side—"is the escape hatch if you got to get the horse out fast and don't want to get kicked in the process."

"Where's the TV?"

Strait laughed. "Tell me about it. I wished I traveled half as good as these animals, although I tell you, with the Silverado over there, we're going to be living in style now. Even got its own toilet and kitchen, so no more Porta Potties and fast food for yours truly. Billy really outdid himself with that one, and me and the boys sure appreciate it."

Web looked at the roof of the trailer. Bobby Lee's head was close to it.

Strait was watching him and smiled. "Bobby Lee is a big yearling and we can't make the roof any higher."

"How come?"

"Give horses enough room, they'll take advantage of it. Hell, I watched one horse that didn't like to be trailered do a backward somersault, if you can believe it, and jump out the rear onto the highway, where he got hit by a truck. It wasn't a pretty sight and almost cost me my job. That's why horses are situated facing the front of the trailer, or else they'll try and jump right out. And we got a side access door and side ramp on all the trailers so you can take the horses out frontways if there's an emergency. It's faster, and you try taking a frightened horse out from the back on a highway, you might just get your head handed to you if it decides to kick. See what I mean?"

"Gotcha."

"Yep, they're complicated machines. Sort of like my ex-wife." Strait laughed again.

Web fanned the air in front of his nose. "Boy, these trailers get pretty ripe."

"Huh," said Strait as he patted Bobby Lee's neck, came back out and secured the trailer latch, "just wait until that horse has been in there a few hours, then you'll really smell something. Now, dogs love the smell of horse manure, but humans don't. I guess that's why we're called civilized. That's why we replaced the aluminum floors with wooden ones, they drain better; and also why we spread the sawdust on the floors. You just sweep it clean, manure and all. Better than the straw."

They left Bobby Lee and went back over to Billy.

"Now, you got all the trailer stickers for state inspection and the horse papers?" asked Billy.

"Yes, sir." Strait looked at Web. "You cross state lines with a bunch of animals, the police stop you at random, and they ain't gonna let you go one step farther until they check your commercial license and the horse's vet certificates and such. They're worried about spreading equine diseases and such."

"And who can blame them?" said Gwen as she rejoined them.

"No, ma'am," said Strait. He tipped his hat. "Well, here's to making East Winds some big bucks."

Strait climbed in one of the trucks and Web and the Canfields watched as the caravan of trailers started up and passed down the main road and out of East Winds. Web glanced over at Gwen, who looked very upset. Billy walked back up to the house.

"You okay?" he asked her.

"I'm as okay as I'm ever going to be, Web." She crossed her arms over her chest and walked off, away from the house.

Web just stood there, looking at husband and wife going their separate ways.

38

Romano picked up Claire and was driving her back to East Winds, taking great care that they weren't followed.

Claire glanced at the man's hand and said, "When did you graduate from Columbia?"

Romano looked at her in surprise and then saw that she was staring at the ring on his finger. "Good eye. I graduated longer ago than I'd like to admit."

"I went there too. Pretty nice, going to college in New York."

"Nothing like it," agreed Romano.

"What was your major?"

"Who cares? I barely got in and I barely graduated."

"Actually, Paul Amadeo Romano, Junior, you entered Columbia at the age of seventeen and graduated in three years near the top of your class with a degree in political science. Your senior thesis was titled 'The Derivative Political Philosophies of Plato, Hobbes, John Stuart Mills and Francis Bacon.' And you were accepted into the Kennedy School of Government at Harvard but didn't attend."

Romano's gaze was chilling. "I don't appreciate people checking me out."

"Part of a therapist's job is not only to understand the patient but also to become familiar with significant people in his life. Web must trust you and think highly of you for him to send you to bring me back here. So I did a few mouse clicks and looked you up. Nothing classified, of course."

Romano still looked at her suspiciously.

"Not many people would have turned down Harvard."

"Well, nobody ever accused me of being most people."

"You were awarded a scholarship, so it wasn't money."

"I didn't go because I'd had enough of school."

"And you joined the military."

"Lots of people do."

"Lots of people out of high school do, but not those near the top of their class at Columbia with a free ticket to Harvard."

"Look, I'm from a big Italian family, okay, we got priorities. Traditions." He added quietly, "Sometimes people get around to them a little too late. That's all."

"So you're the oldest son?"

He shot her another suspicious glance. "Another mouse click? Damn, I hate computers."

"No, but you are a junior, and that normally goes to the oldest son. And your father's deceased and he wasn't a college man?"

Romano almost pulled the car over. "You're freaking me, lady, and you better knock it off."

"I'm not a magician, Mr. Romano, just a humble psychiatrist. You mentioned large Italian family, traditions and priorities. But you didn't mention expectations. The oldest sons in such families usually face expectations they have to live up to. You said people get around to these traditions sometimes too late. So I'm thinking that you went to college against your father's wishes, he died, and you left academia to pursue the occupation your father envisioned for you. And yet you still wear your college ring. That's probably your way of showing you didn't totally capitualate to living out your father's plans for you. It's just observation and deduction, Mr. Romano, just the sorts of tools law enforcement people use every day."

"That don't make it any easier to take."

She studied him. "Do you realize that you talk like an uneducated man at times?"

"You're pushing my buttons all the wrong way."

"I'm sorry. But you're extremely interesting. In fact, you and Web are both interesting. I suppose it comes with the territory. What you do for a living takes a very, very special sort of person."

"Don't try and brown-nose your way out of this, Doc."

"I guess innate curiosity about my fellow human beings comes with what I do for a living. I meant no offense."

They drove in silence for a while.

"My old man," said Romano, "wanted only one thing in life. He wanted to be one of New York's finest."

"NYPD?"

Romano nodded. "Only he never finished high school and he had a bad ticker. He spent his life on the docks hauling crates of fish and hating every second of it. But he wanted that uniform, man, like nothing else in life."

"And because he couldn't, he wanted you to wear it for him?"

Romano looked over at her and nodded. "Only my ma didn't see it that way. She didn't want me working on the docks and she sure as hell didn't want me strapping on a gun for a living. I was a smart student, aced the college boards, got into Columbia, did great there and had my sights on maybe even teaching."

"And then your father died?"

"Ticker finally quit on him. I made it to the hospital right before he died." Romano stopped and looked out the window. "He said I'd shamed him. He said I'd shamed him and then he died."

"And with him died your dreams of teaching?"

"I never could bring myself to go out for NYPD. I could've made it, easy. I hooked on to the military, made Delta, jumped to FBI and then on to HRT. None of it was too much for me. The harder they tried to hurt me, the more I thrived."

"So you eventually did become a policeman of sorts."

He stared at her. "But I did it my way." He paused. "I loved my old man, don't get me wrong. But I never shamed him. And every day I think about that being his dying thought. And it either makes me want to start bawling or killing somebody."

"I can understand that."

"Can you? I sure as hell never could."

"You're not my patient, obviously, but just a friendly piece of advice: At some point you have to live your life the way you want to. Otherwise the building up of resentment and other negative factors can do great damage psychologically. You'll find that not only will you hurt yourself, but those you love."

He looked at her with a level of sadness that touched her deeply.

"I think it might be a little too late for that." Then he added, "But you're right about the ring."

So, talk to me about this hypnosis," said Web.

Romano had dropped Claire off at the carriage house and gone on to watch over the Canfields. Claire and Web were sitting in the living room staring at each other.

"I know that you didn't agree to do it with him, but didn't O'Bannon explain it to you when he offered to hypnotize you?"

"I guess I forgot."

"Just relax and go with the flow, Web. You know, seat-of-the-pants kind of guy. You're one of those types."

"Oh, you think so?"

She smiled at him over the rim of the cup of tea he had made for her. "I don't have to be a psychiatrist, Web, to see that." She looked out the window. "This is some place."

"Yes, it is."

"I suppose you can't tell me what you're doing out here?"

"I'm probably breaking every rule in the book just by having you out here, but I figured Romano would know if anyone was following him." And it's not like whoever was behind the killings didn't know where the Canfields lived, thought Web, because they had gotten the phone bomb in here.

"Romano would make an interesting case study. I identified about five major psychoses, classic passive-aggressive posturing and an unhealthy appetite for pain and violence just in the car ride here."

"Really? I would have guessed more."

"And he's also intelligent, sensitive, deeply emotional, incredibly independent but amazingly loyal. Quite a smorgasbord."

"If you need somebody to cover your back, there's nobody better than Paulie. He's got this rough outside, but the guy has a big heart. But man, if he doesn't like you, watch out. His wife Angie is even more of a piece of work, though. I found out recently that she's seeing O'Bannon. So are some of the other wives. I even saw Deb Riner there. She's the widow of Teddy Riner—he was our team leader."

"We have a large number of FBI and other law enforcement clientele. Years ago Dr. O'Bannon worked in-house at the Bureau.

When he went into private practice, he brought quite a few patients with him. It is a specialty practice because law enforcement people have unique jobs and the stress and personal issues associated with that occupation can be devastating if left untreated. I personally find it all fascinating. And I admire what all of you do very much. I hope you know that."

Web looked over at her, his expression searching and pained.

"Is there something else bothering you?" she asked quietly.

"My Bureau file you were given. Did it by chance have the background interview with Harry Sullivan in it?"

She took a moment to answer. "Yes. I thought about telling you, but I thought it better for you to find out for yourself. I take it you did."

"Yeah," he said in a tight voice. "About fourteen years too late."

"Your father had no reason to say anything good about you. He was going to be in prison for the next twenty years. He hadn't seen you in forever. And yet—"

"And yet he said I'd make the best damn FBI agent there ever was or ever would be and you could quote him on that."

"Yes," she said quietly.

"Maybe some day he and I should meet," said Web.

Claire met his gaze. "I think, Web, that that might be traumatic, but I also think it might be a good idea."

"A voice out of the past?"

"Something like that."

"Speaking of voices, I was thinking about what Kevin Westbrook said to me in that alley."

Claire sat up straighter. "'Damn to hell'?"

"What do you know about voodoo?"

"Not much. You think Kevin put a curse on you?"

"No, the people behind him. I don't know, I'm just thinking out loud."

Claire looked doubtful. "I guess it's possible, Web, though I wouldn't count on that being the answer."

Web cracked his knuckles. "You're probably right. Okay, Doc, pull out your watch and start swinging."

"I use a blue pen, if you don't mind. However, first I want you to sit in the recliner over there and lean back. You don't undergo hypnosis while standing at attention, Web. You need to relax and I'm going to help you do that."

Web sat in the recliner and Claire positioned herself across from him on an ottoman.

"Now, the first thing we need to address are the myths surrounding hypnosis. As I told you, it's not a state of unconsciousness, it's an altered state of *consciousness*. Your brain, in fact, will experience the same brain wave activity it would in a relaxed state, which is alpha rhythm. While in the trance you'll be incredibly relaxed, but it's also a heightened state of awareness and of suggestibility and you are in complete control of what goes on. All hypnosis, in fact, is self-hypnosis, and I'm merely here to help guide you to the point where you are relaxed enough to reach that state. No one can hypnotize anyone who doesn't really want to be hypnotized, and you can't be forced to do something you really don't want to do. So you are completely safe. No barking dogs need apply." She smiled reassuringly. "Are you with me?"

Web nodded.

She held up the pen. "Would you believe this is a pen that Freud himself used?"

"No, I wouldn't."

She smiled again. "Good, because he didn't. We use an object like this when hypnotizing patients. Now I want you to become totally focused with your eyes on the tip of this pen." She held it about six inches from Web's face and above his natural line of sight. Web raised his head to look at it. "No, Web, you can only use your eyes." She placed a hand on top of his head to keep it level. Now Web had to direct his gaze nearly straight up to see the tip.

"That's very good, Web, very good. Most people get tired very quickly, but I'm sure you won't. I know you're very strong and very determined, just keep staring, staring at the tip of the pen." Without seeming to, Claire's voice had dropped to an even level without being a monotone, her words coming steadily and always in the same soothing manner as she offered him encouragement.

A minute passed. Then, as Web continued to stare at the tip of the pen, Claire said, "And blink." And Web blinked. Claire could see that his eyes were becoming strained staring from that very uncomfortable angle, and then they started to water. And he had actually blinked first and then she had instantly said, "And blink." But he wouldn't be sure of the sequence of events. He was too busy concentrating on the pen's tip, on keeping his eyes open. But it made him believe something had happened, that she was slowly assuming control over him. Even if he'd been through it before he would still be wondering whether this hypnosis thing actually worked. First came eye fatigue, and next came mind confusion. All to get him relaxed enough to open up.

"You are doing so well, Web," she said, "better than just about anyone. You're getting more and more relaxed. Just keep staring at that tip." And she could tell he was so determined to keep staring, to keep getting that encouragement. He was a classic overachiever, she easily deduced; he was eager to please and receive praise. He needed attention and love because he obviously had not gotten much of either as a child.

"And blink." And he did so again and she knew it felt so good to him, relieved the strain. She knew the tip of the pen was starting to grow larger and larger for him, and that he was beginning not to want to look at it anymore.

"And it seems you really want to close your eyes," Claire said. "And your eyelids are getting heavier and heavier. It's hard to keep them open and it seems you really want to close them. Close your eyes." And Web did, but he immediately reopened them. That almost always happened, Claire knew. "Keep staring at the pen, Web, just keep staring at the tip, you're doing really well. Outstanding. Just let your eyes close naturally when they're ready to close."

Web's eyes slowly drifted closed and stayed that way.

"I want you to say out loud the word 'ten' ten times fast. Go ahead and do that."

Web did so and then Claire asked. "What are aluminum cans made from?"

"Tin," Web said in a proud voice, and smiled.

"Aluminum."

His smile faded.

Claire continued in her soothing voice, "You know what a strop is? It's a rough leather strap that men used to use in the Old West to sharpen their razors. I want you to say the word 'strop' ten times very fast. Go ahead and do it."

Obviously very wary now, Web said the word ten times.

"What do you do at a green light?"

"STOP!" he said loudly.

"Actually, at a green light, you go." Web's shoulders collapsed in obvious frustration, but Claire was quick to praise him.

"You're doing really well. Almost nobody gets those answers right. But you look so relaxed. Now I want you to count out loud backward from three hundred by threes."

Web started to do so. He had counted back to 279 when she told him to start counting backward by fives. He did so until she had him do it by sevens and then by nines.

Claire interrupted and told him, "Stop counting and just relax. Now you're at the top of the escalator, and that point represents more relaxation. And the bottom of the escalator is the deepest relaxation there is. You're going to take the escalator down, okay? You're going to be more relaxed than you've ever been. Okay?" Web nodded. Claire's voice was as welcome and as gentle as a wispy summer breeze.

"You're going slowly down the escalator. You're gliding down, as if on air. Deeper into relaxation." Claire started counting backward from ten and offered soothing words as she did so. At the count of one she said, "You appear to be very relaxed."

Claire studied Web's features and his skin color. His body had gone from tense to loose. His face was red, evidencing enhanced blood flow there. His eyelids were closed yet fluttering. She told him that she was going to pick up one of his hands—before she did so, to avoid startling him. She gently took it. The hand was limp. She let it go.

"You're near the bottom of the escalator. You're just about to get off. Deepest relaxation, like nothing you've ever felt. It's perfect."

She once more picked up his hand after warning him first that she was going to do so. "What's your favorite color?"

"Green," Web said softly.

"Green, a nice soothing color. Like grass. I'm putting a balloon, a green balloon, in your hand. I'm doing that right now. Do you feel that?" Web nodded. "Now I'm going to pump it up with helium. As you know, helium is lighter than air. I'm pumping up the green balloon. It's getting more full. It's beginning to rise. It's getting fuller."

Claire watched as Web's hand rose from the arm of the recliner as if buoyed by the imaginary balloon.

"Now, on the count of three, your hand will drop back to the chair." She counted to three and Web's hand returned to the chair. She waited about thirty seconds and then said, "Your hand is now getting cold, very cold, I think I see frostbite."

She watched as Web's hand curled and shook. "All right, it's gone now, all normal, all warm." The hand relaxed.

Typically, Claire would not have been as elaborate in putting Web through these paces, the deepening of relaxation techniques. Normally she would have stopped with the balloon. However, she had been curious about something, and that curiosity had been answered because Claire concluded that Web was probably a somnambule. Most people in the field would agree that between five and ten percent of the general population was highly susceptible to hypnosis, with the same percentage highly resistant to it. Somnambules went a step further. They were so susceptible to hypnosis that they could be compelled to experience physical sensations hypnotically, as Web had just done. They could also be expected to reliably execute posthypnotic suggestions. And, surprisingly, very intelligent people often were the easiest to hypnotize.

"Web, can you hear me?" He nodded. "Web, listen very carefully to my voice. Focus on my voice. The balloon is now gone. Just keep on relaxing. Now you're holding a video camera in your hand. You're the cameraman. What you see through your lens is all that you and I can see, do you understand, Mr. Cameraman?" Another nod. "Okay, my only role is to point you around in time, but you control everything else. Through the camera you'll be looking in on other people, to see what they're up to. The camera has a microphone, so we'll be able to hear too. All right?" He nodded. "You're doing so well, Mr. Cameraman. I'm so proud of you."

Claire sat back and thought for a moment. As a therapist who had studied Web's background, she knew exactly the area she should be focusing on in his past to help him. His most severe psychological problems did not stem from the death of his HRT col-

leagues. They came directly from the triangular relationship between his mother, stepfather and himself. And yet her first stop in
Web London's past would be earlier.

"I want you to go back to March eighth, 1969, Mr. Cameraman.
Can you get me back there?"

Web didn't respond for a bit. Then he said, "Yes."

"Tell me what you see, Mr. Cameraman." She knew that his
birthday was March 8. In 1969, Web would be turning six years old.
That was probably the last year he would have been with Harry Sullivan. She wanted to establish a baseline for Web with the man, a
pleasant memory, and a birthday party for a little boy would set that
tone perfectly. "The relaxed Mr. Cameraman will focus and swing
his camera around. Whom do you see?" she prompted again.

"I see a house. I see a room, a room with no one in it."

"Concentrate and focus, swing your camera around. Don't you
see anyone? March eighth, 1969." She suddenly feared that there
had been no party for Web.

"Wait a minute," said Web. "Wait a minute, I see something."

"What do you see?"

"A man—no, a woman. She's pretty, very pretty. She has a hat
on, a funny hat, and she's carrying a cake with candles."

"Sounds like somebody must be having a party. Is it a boy or a
girl, Mr. Cameraman?"

"A boy's. Yes, and now there are other people coming out, like
they were hiding. They're yelling something, they're yelling, 'Happy
birthday.'"

"That's great, Web, a little boy's having a birthday party. What
does he look like?"

"He has dark hair, sort of tall. He's blowing out the candles on
the cake. Everybody's singing happy birthday."

"Does this boy hear a daddy singing? How about daddy, Mr.
Cameraman?"

"I see him. I see him." Web's face was turning red and his breathing had accelerated. Claire watched his physical signs closely. She
would not put Web at risk physically or emotionally. She would not
go that far.

"What does he look like?"

"He's big, really big, bigger than anybody else there. A giant."

"And what is happening between the boy and his giant daddy, Mr. Cameraman?"

"The boy is running to him. And the man's lifting him up on his shoulders, like he doesn't weigh anything."

"Oh, a strong daddy."

"He's kissing the boy, they're dancing around the room and they're singing some song."

"Listen carefully, Mr. Cameraman, turn up the sound control on the microphone. Can you hear any of the words?"

Web first shook his head and then nodded. "Eyes, shining eyes."

Claire searched her memory and then it hit her: Harry Sullivan, the Irishman. "Irish eyes. Irish eyes are smiling?"

"That's it! But no, he's made up his own words to the song, and they're funny, everyone's laughing. And now the man's giving the boy something."

"A present? Is it a birthday present?"

Web's face contorted and he lurched forward. Claire looked alarmed and she sat forward too. "Relax, Mr. Cameraman. It's just a picture you're looking at, that's all. Just a picture. What do you see?"

"I see men. Men have come in the house."

"What men? What do they look like?"

"They're in brown, dressed in brown with cowboy hats. They have guns."

Now Claire's heart skipped a beat. Should she pull the plug on this? She studied Web closely. He appeared to be calming down. "What are the men doing, Mr. Cameraman? What do they want?"

"They're taking him, they're taking the man away. He's yelling. He's screaming, they're all screaming. The cowboys are putting shiny things on the man's hands. The mommy is screaming, she's grabbed the little boy."

Web covered his ears with his hands and was rocking back and forth so violently he was close to tipping the recliner over. "They're yelling, they're yelling. The little boy's yelling, 'Daddy! Daddy!'" Web was now screaming himself.

Oh, shit, Claire thought. *Shiny things on his hands?* The police had come to arrest Harry Sullivan right in the middle of Web's sixth birthday party. Good God!

Claire looked back at Web. "Okay, Mr. Cameraman," she said in her smoothest, most comforting voice, "just relax, we're going somewhere else. Take your camera and turn it off for right now until we decide where to go. Okay, your camera is going dark now, relaxed Mr. Cameraman. You see nothing. You're relaxed and seeing nothing at all. Everyone is gone. There's no one left yelling. All gone. All dark."

Web slowly calmed and put his hands down and leaned back.

Claire sat back and tried to relax as well. She had been through some intense hypnosis sessions before and discovered some surprising things about patients' pasts, but each time was still new, still emotional. For a minute or more Claire wavered. Should she move forward? There was the very real possibility she would never get Web in a hypnotic state again.

"Okay, Mr. Cameraman, we're moving forward." She glanced at the notes she had pulled from the file she had placed under a couch pillow. She had waited until Web was under hypnosis before taking them out. She had noted from their previous sessions that the use of files bothered him. That wasn't unusual, for who would want their life set forth on paper for all to see and scrutinize? And she remembered how she had felt when Buck Winters had pulled the same tactic on her. The pages had dates scribbled on them. She had gotten them from Web's file and discussions with him. "We're moving on to . . ." She hesitated. Could he handle this? Could *she* handle this? She made up her mind and told Web the new date to move on to. It was the date his stepfather had died. "What do you see, Mr. Cameraman?"

"Nothing."

"Nothing?" Claire remembered. "Turn your camera back on. Now what do you see?"

"Still nothing. It's dark, totally black."

That was odd, thought Claire. "Is it nighttime? Turn on the light on your video recorder, Mr. Cameraman."

"No, there are no lights. I don't want a light."

Claire leaned forward, as Web was now referring to himself. This was tricky. This now placed the patient right in the bull's-eye of his very own unconscious. Still, she decided to press forward.

"Why doesn't the Cameraman want a light?"

"Because I'm scared."

"Why is the *little boy* scared?" She had to keep the objectivity here even as Web continued to wander to the cliff of subjectivity. It could be a long way down, Claire well knew.

"Because he's out there."

"Who, Raymond Stockton?"

"Raymond Stockton," Web repeated.

"Where is the little boy's mother?"

Web's chest started to heave again. He was gripping the sides of the recliner so tightly his fingers were shaking.

"Where is your mother?"

Web's voice was high, like a boy still a ways from puberty. "Gone. No, she's back. Fighting. Always fighting."

"Your mother and father are fighting?"

"Always. Shhh!" Web hissed. "He's coming. He's coming."

"How do you know, what do you see?"

"The door's coming down. It always squeaks. Always. Just like that. He's coming up the steps. He keeps it up here. His drugs. I've seen him. I've seen him."

"Relax, Web, it's all right. It's all right." Claire didn't want to touch him, for fear she would startle him, but she was so close to Web there was practically no discernible space between them. She watched over Web as she would have over her mother if it were the woman's last minute on earth. Claire prepared herself to end this before it got out of control, yet if they could just get a little further. Just a little further.

"He's up at the top of the stairs. I hear him. I hear my mother. She's down there. Waiting."

"But you can't see. You're still in darkness."

"I can see." The tone of voice took Claire by surprise, for it was deep and menacing, no longer the cry of a terribly frightened boy.

"How can you see, Mr. Cameraman? What do you see?"

Web screamed the next words out so suddenly that Claire nearly fell to the floor.

"Damn it, you already know this."

For a split second she was sure he was talking directly to her. That had never happened before in a hypnotic session. What did he

mean? That she already knew this information? But then he
calmed and continued.

"I lifted up the pile of clothes a little. I'm under the pile of
clothes. Hiding."

"From the little boy's stepfather?"

"I don't want him to see me."

"Because the little boy is scared?"

"No, I'm not scared. I don't want him to see me. He can't see me,
not yet."

"Why, what do you mean?"

"He's right in front of me, but his back is to me. His stash is right
over there. He's bending down to get it."

Web's voice was growing deeper, as though he were growing
from a boy to a man right in front of her.

"I'm coming out of hiding, I don't have to hide anymore. The
clothes are rising up with me. They're my mother's clothes. She
put this pile up here for me."

"She did? Why?"

"To hide under, for when he came. I'm up. I'm standing up. I'm
taller than he is. I'm bigger than he is."

There was a tone to Web's voice now that made Claire very nervous. She realized that her own breath was coming in gasps even
as Web had calmed. She had a cold dread of where this was going.
She should pull him out. Every professional instinct she had told
her to stop this, and yet she just couldn't.

"The carpet rolls. Hard as iron," Web said in his deep-man voice.
"I've got one, had it under the clothes. I'm up now, bigger than he
is. He's a little man. So little."

"Web," began Claire. She dropped all pretense of the cameraman. This was getting out of hand.

"I've got it in my hand. Like a bat. I'm a great baseball player.
Can hit it a mile. Swing harder than anyone. I'm big and strong.
Like my dad. My *real* dad."

"Web, please."

"He's not even looking. Doesn't know I'm there. Batter up."

She changed tactics again. "Mr. Cameraman, I want you to turn
off your camera."

"Pitch is coming. Fastball. I see it. Easy. I'm getting ready."

"Mr. Cameraman, I want you—"

"It's almost here. He's turning. I want him to. I want him to see this. See me."

"Web! Turn it off."

"He sees me. He sees me. I'm swinging for the fences."

"Turn off the camera. Stop, you don't see this. Stop!"

"I'm swinging. He sees me, he knows how hard I can hit. He's scared now. He's scared! He's scared, I'm not! No more! No more!"

Claire watched helplessly as he gripped an imaginary bat and swung for the fences.

"It's a hit. It's a hit. Slash of red, slash of red. The ball's going down. It's going down. It's a home run, a country mile. It's outta here. Outta here. Good-bye, good-bye, mister asshole." He grew quiet for a long moment while Claire studied him carefully.

"He's getting up. He's getting back up." He paused. "Yes, Mom," he said. "Here's the bat, Mom." He reached out his hand as though handing off something. Claire almost reached out her hand to take it before she caught herself.

"Mom's hitting him. In the head. Lots of blood. He's not moving anymore. He's not. It's over."

He became silent and slumped back in the recliner. Claire slumped down too, her heart beating so hard she put a hand over her chest as though to prevent it from bursting through. All she could envision was Raymond Stockton plunging down the attic stairs after being hit by a hard roll of carpet and hitting his head on the way down and then being finished off by his wife with the same roll of carpet.

"I want you to completely relax, Web. I want you to sleep, to sleep, that's all."

She watched as his body dissolved even farther into the chair. As Claire looked up, she received another shock. Romano was standing there, staring at her, his hand near his gun.

"What the hell's going on?" he demanded.

"He's under hypnosis, Mr. Romano. He's all right."

"How do I know that?"

"I guess you'll just have to trust me." She was still too stricken to argue with the man. "How much did you hear?"

"I was coming back here to check on him when I heard Web screaming."

"He's reliving some very delicate memories of the past. I'm not sure what it all means yet, but it was a big step to get to this point."

Claire's experiences in forensics had prompted several theories to consider. It had obviously been planned that the blows had been struck with the rolled-up carpet. Stockton presumably would have had carpet fibers in his head wound when he hit the floor. And if the carpet on the floor were the same carpet as the remnant in the attic, then the police would just assume that the fibers became embedded in his head wound when he hit the floor. They would not suspect that someone had slugged him with a rolled-up remnant in the attic. After all the complaints of abuse against the man, everyone, including the police, had probably been grateful he was finally dead. Finished with the stepfather, Claire moved on to the mother.

Web had said Charlotte London had placed the pile of clothes there. Had she also supplied the rolled-up carpet? Had she coached her tall, strong teenage son on how to do away with the abusive husband? Was that how the woman had decided to handle it? And then stepped in to finish the job, leaving Web to later pick up the pieces, allowing him to repress guilt so deep he couldn't even remember the event except under hypnosis? But such an extraordinary repressed memory would taint every aspect of his being and of his future. It would manifest itself in many ways, none of them positive. Claire could now clearly understand why Web was like he was. He had become a lawman not to make up for Harry Sullivan's felonious ways but because of his own guilt. A boy helping to kill his stepfather at the instruction of his natural mother; from a mental health perspective it didn't get more screwed up than that.

Claire looked over at Web, who just sat there so peacefully, with his eyes closed, awaiting her next instruction. She also now understood his somnambulism. Children from homes of terrible abuse often withdrew into fantasy worlds as protection from the horrors of reality. Such children created imaginary friends to combat loneliness and also invented wonderful lives and adventures to ward off feelings of insecurity and depression. Claire had treated somnambules who could control their higher brain functions to such an extent that they could either embellish or completely wipe out whole sections of their memories, just as Web had done. Though a dynamic, independent, self-reliant sort on the outside, Web London, she concluded, was obedient and relied upon others on the inside; hence, his dependence on his HRT team and his exceptional ability to carry out orders. He was eager to please, to be accepted.

She shook her head. The man was a mess inside. And yet he had withstood the psychological battering of both the Bureau and HRT. Web had said he had figured out the MMPI test and had managed to lie his way right through it. He did not know how right he was about that.

She looked at Romano as something new occurred to her. She would have to craft the question delicately because she couldn't reveal any patient confidences. Web had told her previously that he wasn't taking any medications, and she had accepted his word on that. With what she had just learned, though, she wondered if he were taking something that would help combat the internal traumas that were clearly eating away at him. She motioned Romano over to a far corner, out of Web's hearing. "Do you know anything about any medications Web might be taking?"

"Did Web say he was taking any pills?"

"I was just wondering. It's sort of standard operating procedure for shrinks to ask," she answered evasively.

"Lots of people take pills to help them sleep," Romano said defensively.

She hadn't said they were sleeping pills. So Romano did know about them, thought Claire. "I'm not saying it's wrong, I was just wondering if he ever mentioned to you if he took anything, and if so, what he took."

"You think he might be addicted, is that it? Well, I'm telling you you're nuts."

"I'm not implying that at all. It's just important that I know in case I want to prescribe something for him. I don't want any dangerous drug interactions."

Romano still was not buying it. "So why don't you ask him?"

"Well, I'm sure you're well aware that people don't always tell their doctors the truth, particularly the kind of doctor I am. I just want to make sure there are no problems."

Romano looked over at Web, apparently to make sure he was still out. He looked back at Claire and seemed to be having trouble getting the words out. "I saw him holding what looked like a prescription bottle the other day. But look, he's hurting right now and he's probably a little screwed up about things and maybe needs a little help pill wise, but the Bureau's real stiff on that crap. They throw you overboard and let you sink or swim on your own. Well, guys have to look out for each other, then." Romano stopped, looked over at Web and said a little wistfully, "He's the best HRT's ever had."

"You know he thinks very highly of you too."

"I guess I did know."

Romano left the room. Claire went to the window and watched as he crossed the road and was soon out of sight. It would have been very hard for him to reveal a confidence like that about his friend, and he probably felt himself a traitor for doing it. But in the end it would help Web far more than hurt him.

She sat across from Web, leaned forward and spoke slowly so that he wouldn't miss a word. Ordinarily hypnosis was used to pare away the inhibitions and layers covering repressed memories that prevented patients from really talking about their troubles. Typically the patient was brought out of hypnosis fully remembering everything that had happened while he was under. Here, Claire could not do that. It would be too traumatic. Instead, she gave Web a posthypnotic suggestion. It instructed him that when he came out of the hypnotic state he would remember only enough to allow him to deal adequately with the situation. What would control what, if anything, he remembered would be his unconscious. Under the circumstances, Claire felt certain he would remember almost nothing. He was not prepared to deal with this, so buried was it within his unconscious. She slowly brought him up the escalator, step by step. Before he came fully out of it, she finished composing herself, prepared herself to face him.

When he finally opened his eyes, he looked around the room and then at her. He smiled. "Anything good?"

"First I need to ask you a question, Web." She paused to collect herself again before saying, "Are you taking any medication?"

His eyes narrowed. "Didn't you already ask me that?"

"I'm asking you now."

"Why?"

"You mentioned voodoo as an explanation for why you froze. Let me offer another one: negative drug interaction."

"I wasn't taking any medication before we went into that alley, Claire. I would never do that."

"Drug interactions are funny," replied Claire. "Depending on what you're taking, the effects can materialize some time after you've stopped taking them." She paused once again and added, "It's important for you to be entirely truthful on this point, Web. It really is, if you want to get to the truth."

They stared at each other for a long moment, and then Web rose and went into his bathroom. A minute later he came back and handed her a small vial with pills in it. He sat back down as she examined the contents.

"Since you have them with you, should I assume you've been taking them recently?"

"I'm on a job, Claire. No pills. So I deal with the insomnia and the pain you sometimes get with two big holes in you and half a face."

"So why do you have them?"

"Security blanket. You're a psychiatrist—you understand that and thumb-sucking, don't you?"

Claire took out the pills and examined them one by one. They were all different. Most she recognized, some she didn't. She held up one of the pills. "Do you know where you got this?"

"Why?" he asked suspiciously. "Is there something wrong with it?"

"Perhaps. Did you get these pills from O'Bannon?" she said doubtfully.

"It's possible, I guess. Although I thought I finished his prescription a long time ago."

"Well, if not O'Bannon, who, then?"

Web became defensive. "Look, I had to get off the painkillers they were giving me for my *injuries*, because I was growing dependent on them. And then I couldn't sleep, for like a year. Some HRT guys have the same problem. It's not like we're doing illegal drugs or crap like that, but you can only go so long without sleep, even at HRT. Some of the guys have given me pills over the years. I just collect them in a bottle and take them when I need them. That pill might have come from one of them. What's the big deal?"

"I'm not blaming you for taking medication to help you sleep, Web. But it's stupid and dangerous for you to take an oddball assortment of pills, even from friends, when you have no idea what drug interactions might occur from their use. You're very lucky something serious hasn't happened to you. And maybe it did. In the alley. Maybe this odd method of pill taking is the reason you froze." Claire was also thinking that the traumatic events surrounding Raymond Stockton's death might have bubbled to the surface at the worst possible time—when Web was in that alley. Perhaps, as she had thought earlier, seeing Kevin Westbrook had triggered something in Web, disabling him.

Web covered his face with his hands. "Shit! This is unbelievable. Unbelievable!"

"I can't say for sure that's the case, Web." She looked at him sympathetically, but there was something else she needed to know. "Have you reported the medication you've been taking to your supervisor?"

He uncovered his face but didn't look at her.

"Okay," she said slowly.

"Are you going to say anything?"

"Are you still taking them?"

"No. As best I can recall, the last time I took one prior to the mission in the alley was a week before. That's it."

"Then I have nothing to report." She held up the same pill again. "I don't recognize this medication, and as a psychiatrist I've seen just about all of them. I'd like to get it analyzed. It'll be on the QT," she quickly added, as he looked alarmed. "I have a friend. Your name will never come up."

"Do you really think it was the pills, Claire?"

She stared at the pill before pocketing the vial and looking back at him. "Web, I'm afraid we'll never know for certain."

"So was the hypnosis a bust?" Web asked finally, though Claire could tell his mind was clearly on the pills and their possible implication in what had happened to Charlie Team.

"No, it wasn't. I learned a lot."

"Like what?"

"Like Harry Sullivan was arrested during your sixth-year birthday party. Do you remember talking about that?" She was reasonably certain he might recall that from the hypnosis session. But *not* the event with Stockton.

Web slowly nodded. "Actually, I do. Some of it, anyway."

"For what it's worth, before the arrest, you and Harry were having a great time. He clearly loved you very much."

"That's good to know," Web said, without enthusiasm.

"Often situations that are traumatic are repressed, Web, sort of a safety valve. Your psyche can't handle it, that level of confrontation, and you basically bury it so you don't need to face it."

"But that's like burying toxic waste," he said in a low voice.

"That's right. And it sometimes seeps out and does considerable damage."

"Anything else?" he asked.

"Do you recall anything else?"

He shook his head.

Claire looked away for a moment. Web, she knew, was in no shape to hear the truth about his stepfather's death. She looked back at him and managed a tiny smile. "Well, I think that's enough."

She looked at her watch. "And I need to get back."

"So my dad and me were really getting along?"

"You were singing songs, he was carrying you on his shoulders. Yes, you were having a great time."

"It's starting to come back to me. So there's still hope for me, right?" Web smiled, perhaps to show he was partly kidding.

"There's always hope, Web," Claire replied.

39

Sonny Venables was off duty and out of uniform as he sat in an unmarked car and surveyed the area. There was stirring in the backseat as the big man who was lying on the floorboard stretched out his long legs.

"Don't get antsy, Randy," said Venables. "We got some time to go yet."

"Trust me, I've waited dudes out a lot longer than this, and from places a lot shittier than the backseat of a car."

Venables nudged out a cigarette from the pack in his pocket, lit it, cracked his window and blew smoke out.

"So you were telling me about your meeting with London."

"I covered his backside even though he didn't know it at the time. Good thing too, though I don't think Westbrook would have really killed him."

"I heard about that guy, but I've never run into him."

"Lucky you. But let me tell you there's a lot worse than him out there. At least Westbrook's got a little code of honor. Most dudes out there are just flat-out nuts. Kill you just to kill you and brag about it. Westbrook does everything for a real good reason."

"Like maybe take out HRT?"

"Don't think so. But he delivered a message to London about the tunnels under the building that was HRT's target. That's apparently how the guns came in. London checked it out with Bates. And I heard that he was right."

"From what you've told me about Westbrook, he doesn't sound like a message boy."

"He is if the person he delivered the message for has somebody he cares about, like his son."

"Gotcha. So *that* person was behind what happened to HRT?"

"That's my thinking."

"So where's the Oxy come into to all this?"

"That's the op I saw in the building that night. They even had some of the product there. No coke bricks, just bags of pills. And I saw computerized records that laid it all out. Millions of bucks in business. And in two days it was cleared out."

"Why all that trouble to set you up? Why wipe out HRT? That just brings the Bureau down on them like a ton of bricks."

"It doesn't make a lot of sense," Cove agreed, "but that seems to be what happened."

Venables stiffened and flicked his cigarette out the window. "Show time, Randy."

Venables watched as a man left the building they'd been watching, walked along the street, turned right and headed down an alley. Venables started the car and it moved slowly forward.

"Is it the guy you were expecting?" asked Cove.

"Yep. You want some info on new drugs coming to town, this boy will know it. Name's Tyrone Walker, but he goes by T. Real imaginative. Belonged to three or four different crews over the years. Time in jail, time in the hospital, time in drug rehab. He's about twenty-six and looks ten years older than me and *I* don't look all that good for my age."

"Funny I never ran across T before."

"Hey, you don't have a monopoly on information in this town. I might just be a lowly street cop, but I get around."

"Good thing, Sonny, because I'm tainted goods right now. Nobody will talk to me."

"Well, old T will, with the right persuasion."

Venables pulled around the corner, hit the gas, then turned right onto a street that ran parallel to the one where they had been parked. As soon as they turned the corner, T emerged from the alley, which cut through to this street.

Venables looked around. "Coast looks clear. You want to do your thing?"

Cove was already out of the car. Before he knew what was hap-

pening, T had been searched expertly and was lying facedown in
the backseat of Venables's car, with one of Cove's big hands on the
back of his neck, keeping him there. Venables drove off while T
loudly cursed them. By the time he calmed, they were two miles
away and in a better part of town. Cove pulled T to a sitting position. The man looked first at Cove and then at Venables.

"Hey, T," said Venables. "You looking good. Been taking care of
yourself?"

Cove could sense T was about to make a lunge out the other
door, so he clamped his arm around T's shoulders. "Hey, we just
want to talk to you, T. Just talk."

"What if I don't wanta talk?"

"Then you can just get out of the car," said Cove.

"Is that right? Okay, stop the car and I'm getting out."

"Whoa, there, T, he didn't say anything about me stopping the
car *before* you got out." Venables cut the wheel, entered an on-
ramp, and they pulled onto Interstate 395, crossed the Fourteenth
Street Bridge and they were in Virginia. Venables pushed the accelerator to sixty.

T stared out the window at the traffic streaming by and then sat
back, his arms folded across his chest.

"Now, my friend here—" began Venables.

"Your damn friend got a name?"

Cove tightened his grip on T's shoulders. "Yeah, I got a name.
You call me T-Rex. Tell him why, Sonny."

"'Cause he eats little T's for breakfast, lunch and dinner," said
Sonny.

"And I just want some information about some new product
in town. Crews buying it up and stuff like that. No problems.
Just a couple of names and we let you off right where we picked
you up."

"And trust me, T, you don't want to piss this man off," added
Venables.

"You cops, you ain't doing nothing to me 'less you want to get
your ass sued off."

Cove stared at the man for a moment and then said, "Right now,
T, you better be real nice to me. I'm not feeling good about things,
and I don't give a shit if somebody sues me or not."

"Fuck off."

"Sonny, take the next right. Head to the GW Parkway. Lot of quiet places there," he added ominously.

"You got it."

In a few minutes, they were on the George Washington, or GW, Parkway, heading north.

"Take the next turnoff," Cove said.

They pulled into a sightseeing lot that provided a beautiful view of Georgetown and, far below, the Potomac River. A stone wall served as a buffer from the steep drop. Day had turned to dusk and there were no other cars parked in the lot. Cove looked around, opened the door and pulled T out with him.

"If you dudes arresting me, I want my lawyer."

Venables got out too and looked around. He eyed the drop, glanced back at Cove and shrugged.

Cove grabbed the smallish T around the waist and lifted him up.

"What the hell you doing, man?"

Cove climbed over the stone wall and down on the other side while T struggled in vain. There was a narrow strip of ground and then a drop of about a hundred feet into the river, which was filled with rocks. Down the river and on the opposite bank were a number of buildings housing local boating clubs. They were painted bright colors and their members rowed the waters in canoes, sculls, kayaks and other assorted watercraft that required muscle rather than combustion engines to make them move. There were several of them on the water right now and T was given an inverted view of that picturesque scene because Cove was holding him upside down, by the legs, over the drop.

"Holy shit," screamed out the flailing T as he looked down to oblivion.

"Now, we can do this the easy way or the hard way, and you're gonna have to decide real quick, because I'm out of time and patience," said Cove.

Venables squatted on top of the wall and kept a lookout for other cars. "Better listen to him, T, the man doesn't lie."

"But you guys are cops," wailed T. "You can't do this shit. It's fucking unconstitutional."

"I never said I was a cop," said Cove.

T stiffened and then glanced over at Venables. "But, damn it, *he* is."

"Hey, I'm not my brother's keeper," said Venables. "And I'm getting ready to retire anyway. I don't give a shit."

"Oxy," said Cove calmly. "I want to know who's buying it in D.C."

"Are you one crazy-ass mother or what?" screamed T.

"Yes, I am." Cove let his grip slip a bit and T went down about six inches. Now Cove had hold of only the man's ankles.

"Oh, God, oh, sweet Jesus, help me," whimpered T.

"Don't be talking to Jesus, T, not after the life you've led," answered Venables. "He might just send a lightning bolt, and I'm standing way too close."

"Talk to me," said Cove in his calm voice. "Oxy."

"I can't tell you nothing. Then folks come after my ass."

Cove let his grip slip again. Now he was holding on only to the man's feet. "You're wearing loafers, T," he said. "Loafers slip right off."

"Go to hell."

Cove let go of one of the feet and now was holding T by one foot with both hands. He looked back at Venables. "Sonny, I think we better drop this one and go get us somebody else who's a little smarter."

"I got just the person. Let's go."

Cove started to let go of the foot.

"No!" screamed T. "I'll talk. I'll tell you."

Cove remained motionless.

"No, I mean put me down and I'll tell you."

"Sonny, go start the car while I throw this piece of crap in the Potomac."

"*No!* I'll talk, right here. I swear."

"Oxy," prompted Cove again.

"Oxy," repeated T, and he started talking fast, telling Cove all he needed to know.

Claire pulled her Volvo into her driveway and cut the engine. It was a nice neighborhood, not too far away from her office and she had been fortunate enough to buy into it before housing prices soared. She made a good enough income, but the cost of living in northern Virginia had become ridiculous. Builders were cramming places on any scrap of land they could find and yet there were more than enough people willing to buy them.

Her house was a three-bedroom Cape Cod with a nice patch of lawn in front, flowers in window boxes, a cedar shake roof and a two-car garage attached to the house by a breezeway. The street was tree-lined and the neighborhood contained a nice mixture of young and old as well as professional and working-class people.

After being divorced for so long, Claire was close to accepting that she would forever remain single. There were few eligible men in the social circles where she mingled and none of them had captured her interest. She had girlfriends always on the lookout to fix her up with yet another tech mini-mogul or lawyer, but she found them to be so egotistical and self-centered that she figured marrying one of them wouldn't be all that different from remaining single. As a rebuke, she had asked one very self-involved high-tech chap at a party if he had ever heard of Narcissus. He had wanted to know if it was a new type of Internet software and then gone right on talking about how fabulous he was.

She pulled her briefcase out of the car and headed up to the front steps. She hadn't pulled the car into the garage because she intended to go out again. The man coming out of her backyard startled Claire. He was black and large, with a head that appeared shaven, though he wore a cap. Claire focused on his gas company uniform and the electronic gas gauge he held in his hand. He passed her, smiled and went across the street. She felt embarrassed for her automatic suspicion of a black man, though she had to admit, also with some embarrassment, that there were few people of color in her neighborhood. Yet who could blame her for being paranoid, after spending time with Web London and men like him?

She unlocked the door and went inside, her mind on her session with Web. It had been shocking in many ways but at least more revealing than shocking. She put her briefcase down and headed to her bedroom to change. It was still light out and she thought she would take advantage of the nice weather and go for a walk. She remembered the pills in her pocket, pulled them out and examined them. The unfamiliar one intrigued her greatly. She had a friend who worked in the pharmacy department at Fairfax Hospital. He could run it through some tests and tell her what this was. It didn't look like any sleep medication she had ever seen, but she could be mistaken. She also hoped she was mistaken about a drug interaction having made Web freeze up in that alley. That might be something he could never recover from. As crazy as Web's theory on voodoo was, she would take a curse over something Web had inadvertently put into his body that caused his friends to die without him. No, the answer had to lie in his past, she was convinced of that.

She sat on the bed and took off her shoes, went into her small walk-in closet, disrobed and pulled on a T-shirt and shorts because the heat had returned. Barefoot, she came back out and looked at the phone. Maybe she should call Web and talk to him. At some point she had to tell him what she had learned about Stockton's death. The timing of it, though, was critical. Too early or too late a disclosure and the consequences could be disastrous. She decided to take the chicken's way out and figure it out later. Maybe the walk would help her decide. She went over to her drawer and pulled out a baseball cap. She was about to put it on when a hand went around her mouth. She dropped the cap and instinctively began to struggle until she felt the gun barrel against her cheek and she stopped, her eyes wide with fear, breaths suddenly coming in heaves. She remembered she hadn't locked the door on the way in. It was such a safe neighborhood, or at least it had been. Her racing mind wondered if the gas man was an impostor and he had come back and was now about to rape her and then kill her.

"What do you want?" she asked in a voice that was so muffled by the hand over her mouth that it didn't sound like her own. She could tell it was a man, though his hand was gloved, because of the strength in it. The hand left her mouth and encircled her neck.

The man didn't answer and Claire saw the blindfold coming toward her, and the next moment she was in total darkness. She felt herself being led over to the bed and she was terrified the rape was about to happen. Should she scream or fight? And yet the gun was still pressed to her right cheek. And the silence of her attacker was more unnerving than hearing his voice.

"Just be cool," the man said, "all we want is information. Nothing else from you." His words seemed clear enough to her. Her body was safe. At least she could hope that.

He guided her down so that she was sitting on the edge of the bed. She told herself that if he pushed her back and climbed on her, she would fight, gun or not.

And yet she sensed him moving away from her. And at the same time she sensed the entrance of another person. She tensed as this person sat next to her on the bed. A heavy man, she deduced, for the bed went down quite a bit with his weight. But he didn't touch her, though even through the blindfold she could feel his gaze upon her.

"You seeing Web London?"

She jerked a bit at this question, for it hadn't occurred to her that this was about Web, though she wondered why it hadn't. Her life was fairly ordinary, routine, no guns and men killed. That was Web's life. Like it or not, she was now part of that life.

"What do you mean?" she managed to say.

She heard the man let out a grunt, one of annoyance, she thought.

"You're a psychiatrist and he's your patient, isn't that true?"

Claire wanted to say that ethically she couldn't reveal that information, but she felt certain that if she did, this man would kill her. As though he would care about her ethical constraints. To add credence to her belief, she heard what clearly sounded like the hammer of a gun being cocked. She had been around guns as a consulting forensic psychiatrist and knew that sound pretty well. A large cold mass formed in her stomach and her limbs became rigid, and she wondered how Web could deal with people like this every day of his life.

"I'm seeing him, yes."

"Now we getting somewhere. Did he mention a boy to you, a boy named Kevin?"

She nodded because her mouth had dried up so much she didn't think she could speak.

"He happen to know where that boy is now?"

Claire shook her head and tensed as he lightly squeezed her shoulder.

"Relax, lady, ain't nobody gonna hurt you long as you cooperate.

If you don't cooperate, then we have quite a problem," he added ominously.

Claire heard him snap his fingers and about a minute passed in silence, and then she felt something touch her lips. She drew back.

"Water," the man said. "You got dry mouth. People scared shitless get that all the time. Drink."

The last word was an order and Claire immediately obeyed it.

"Now talk, no more nods or shakes, you understand me?"

She started to nod and then caught herself. "Yes."

"What'd he say about Kevin? Everything, I have to know it all."

"Why?" She wasn't exactly sure where that bold question had come from.

"I got my reasons."

"Do you want to hurt the boy?"

"No," the man said quietly. "I just want him back nice and safe."

He sounded sincere, but then criminals often did, she reminded herself. Ted Bundy had been the king of smooth talkers while he methodically killed scores of women, smiling all the way.

"I have no reason to believe you, you know."

"Kevin, he my son."

She tensed at this and then relaxed. Could this be the Big F person Web had told her about? But he had said the man was Kevin's brother, not father. The man *sounded* like a concerned parent, yet there was something not quite right. Claire would just have to go with her professional gut on this one. What she sensed very clearly was that these men would kill her. "Web said he saw Kevin in the alley. He said Kevin said something to him and it affected him in a weird way. He saw him later, while the guns were firing. He gave him a note and sent him off. He didn't see him after that. But he's been looking for him."

"Is that all?"

She nodded and then caught herself. She could feel him move closer, and even though she wore the blindfold, she closed her eyes. She could feel tears forming there.

"Ground rules are no more nods or shakes, I need to hear words, last time I'm telling you, you got me?"

"Yes." She fought back the tears.

"Now, did he say anything else, about anything peculiar happening when he saw Kevin the second time?"

She said, "No," but she had hesitated a second too long. She could clearly feel it, as though the pause had been a day long in duration. And she thought that he had noticed it, as well. She was correct in that assumption, for she instantly felt the cold muzzle of a pistol against her cheek.

"We having a serious misunderstanding here, like maybe I ain't making myself clear. Just so we are clear, let me lay this out for you, bitch. To get my boy back, I'll blow your brains out and everybody you ever cared about in your whole life. I see pictures all over the place of this cute-looking girl. Bet that's your daughter, ain't it?" Claire didn't answer and she felt his hand wrap around her neck. His hand was gloved, which surprised her until she thought of fingerprints and DNA that machines could detect off of corpses. Her corpse! This thought made her feel faint.

"Ain't it?"

"Yes!"

He kept his hand on her neck. "See, you got you your little girl nice and safe. Perfect little house in a perfect little place. But see, I don't got me my boy and he's all I have. Why you get your girl and I ain't get my boy? You think that's fair? Do you?" He squeezed her neck a little and Claire felt herself start to gag.

"No."

"No, what?"

"No, I don't think that's fair," she managed to say in a garbled voice.

"Yeah? Well, it's a little late for that, baby."

The next thing she felt was being pushed back on the bed. Her earlier promise to fight if they attempted to rape her seemed ridiculous now. She was so frightened she could barely breathe. She felt a pillow being placed over her face and then something hard jammed into the center of the pillow. It took her a few seconds to realize that the hard object was the pistol and the pillow would serve as a crude silencer.

She thought of her daughter, Maggie, and she thought of how

her body would be found. The tears streamed down her cheeks. And then for one miraculous second her wits came back to her.

"He said that somebody had switched the kids in the alley."

The pillow did not move for some seconds and Claire thought she had lost after all.

Then it was slowly removed and she was jerked up so hard she thought her arm had been dislocated.

"Say again?"

"He said that Kevin had been switched in the alley for another boy. The boy who went to the police wasn't Kevin. He was taken in the alley before he got to the police."

"Does he know why?"

"No. And he doesn't know who did it. Only that it happened."

She felt the pistol against her cheek again. For some reason it wasn't as frightening the second time around.

"You lying, you ain't gonna like what I'm gonna do to you."

"That's what he said." She felt like she had betrayed Web to save herself and she wondered if he would have rather died than done such a thing. He probably would have. The tears started coming again, and not out of fear this time but from her own weakness.

"He thinks that Kevin being in that alley was planned by whoever was behind what happened. He thinks Kevin was somehow involved." She quickly added, "But unwittingly. He's only a child."

The pistol was removed from her cheek and her interrogator's large presence also moved away.

"That it?"

"That's all I know."

"You tell anybody we here, you know what I'll do to you. And I can find your daughter. We been through your house, we know all there is to know about you and her. Do we understand each other?"

"Yes," she managed to get out.

"I'm just doing this to get my son back, that's all. I ain't like busting in people's homes and roughing 'em up, that ain't my style, especially women, but what I got to do to get my boy back, I'll do."

She felt herself nodding at this and then stopped.

She never heard them go, although her hearing could not have been any more acute.

She waited a few minutes to make sure, then she said, "Hello?" And then she said it again. She reached up slowly to undo the blindfold. She was waiting for hands to stop her, but none came. She finally pulled off the blindfold and she quickly looked around the room, half expecting someone to leap out at her. She would have liked to collapse on the bed and cry for the rest of the day and night, but she couldn't stay here. They said they had been everywhere in her house. She threw some clothes in an overnight bag, grabbed her purse and a pair of tennis shoes and went to the front door. She looked out but saw no one. She quickly went to her car and got in. As she drove off, she kept her gaze on the rearview mirror to see if anyone was following her. She was no expert in that, but there didn't seem to be anyone there. Claire entered the Capital Beltway and sped up, unsure of exactly where she would go.

40

Antoine Peebles pulled off the gloves and sat back, a broad smile on his intelligent features. He looked over at Macy, who was driving. The man's face was inscrutable, as always.

"Damn good performance, if I do say so myself," said Peebles. "I think I got the man's voice and diction just right. I haven't said 'ain't' that many times in my whole life. So what do you think?"

"You sounded like the boss," agreed Macy.

"And the lady gets all pissed off and she goes to Web London and the cops and they go looking for Francis."

"And maybe us."

"No, I explained all that to you. You have to think at the macro and micro level, Mace," said Peebles as though lecturing a student. "We've already distanced ourselves from him. And on top of that he's got no product and half his crew is already gone because of that. His cash flow is down to almost nothing. In this business you have two-day inventory levels, tops. He had some stuff hidden, I'll give him credit for that, but that's gone. And when he shot Toona he lost four more guys just from that." Peebles shook his head. "And with all that happening, what does he do? He spends every second thinking about the kid. Every night he's looking for him, roughing people up, burning bridges, not trusting anybody."

"Guess he's smart not to trust anybody," said Macy, glancing at Peebles. "Especially you and me."

Peebles ignored this. "He could write a book on stupid management techniques, killing one of your own guys like that in front of everybody. In front of an FBI agent! He's got a death wish."

"You have to keep your guys in line," said Macy evenly. "You have to lead from strength." He looked over at Peebles with an expression that clearly showed he thought his companion lacked that attribute, but Peebles didn't notice because he was still obviously reveling in his triumph. "And you can't blame the guy for trying to find his son."

Peebles said, "You can't mix business and personal. He's screwed himself already, burning political capital, over what? Something that is never going to happen. That kid is never coming back. Whoever took him, that boy is six feet under if there was anything left of him. Now I've already got new supply lines set up and his defectors have joined me." He looked at Macy. "You probably don't know this, but my maneuver is classic Machiavelli. And I've been skimming the best crew members from other gangs over the last six months. We're just about ready to go and this time we do it all my way. We run it like a real business. Accountability, pay and promotion for merit, bonuses for exemplary performance and rewards for innovation that go right to the corporate bottom line. We're going to take over our own money-laundering efforts and cut costs where they need to be cut. Not every crew has to have jewelry and five-hundred-dollar-a-night hookers. I'm even envisioning a retirement plan instead of the brothers throwing their money after cars and carats and having nothing when they're too old to do this anymore. And I'm implementing a dress code for management level, no more of this looking like crap. A professional has to have a professional image. Look at you, you look slick, that's what I want."

Macy released a rare smile. "Some of the boys aren't going to like that."

"They have to grow up sometime." He looked over at Macy. "I gotta tell you, it was an awesome feeling having that gun in my hand."

"Would you have shot her?"

"Are you nuts? I was just scaring her."

"Well, you pull a gun, some point you may have to use it," said Macy.

"That's your job. You're head of security, Mace. My right-hand guy. You showed your stuff when you came up with the plan to nab Kevin. And you did the down-and-dirty work rounding up the other crews to join forces. Now we're going to go places, my man; a lot farther than Francis was taking us, and a lot faster. He's old school, the new ways are the best ways. That's why the dinosaurs died."

They pulled down an alley and Peebles checked his watch. "Okay, you got the meeting place all set up?"

"They're all there, just like you wanted."

"Mood?"

"Good, but suspicious. You got them worried but definitely interested."

"That's what I wanted to hear. This is where we stake out our territory, Mace, and where we let the others know that Francis is no longer the force. This is *our* time. Let's do it." He paused as a sudden thought hit him.

"What the hell was that woman talking about, somebody switching Kevin for another kid in that alley?"

Macy shrugged. "No clue."

"You got the kid, right?"

"Safe and sound. For now. You want to see him?"

"I don't want to go anywhere near that kid. He knows me, something goes wrong and he gets to Francis . . ." The fear was palpable on Peebles's features.

The car stopped and Macy got out and scanned the alley in both directions and then looked up to the rooftops. He finally signaled the all-clear to his new boss. Peebles climbed out, adjusted his tie and buttoned up his double-breasted suit. Macy held the building's door open for him and Peebles walked briskly through. They climbed the steps and with each one Peebles seemed to transform into a larger and larger presence. This was his moment and he had been waiting for it for years. Out with the old and in with the new.

He reached the top and waited for Macy to open the door for him. There would be seven men waiting for him in here, each representing a slice of the District's illegal drug distribution. They had never worked together; instead, each had grabbed his little share and overseen his own little fiefdom. They shared neither information nor resources. When disagreements came up, they resolved them by shooting each other. They fed information to the police about other crews when it suited them and the cops came in and cherry-picked them. Francis had done the same thing, and while it was a short-term fix that seemed to have merit, Peebles knew it could not have been more of a management disaster from a long-term perspective. And it was time for Antoine Peebles to step in and take charge.

He opened the door and walked into the room where he would start his own legend.

Peebles looked around. And saw no one there.

Peebles didn't even have a chance to turn before the pistol was at his head and the shot was fired into his brain. He dropped to the floor, blood running down his fine tie and over his very professional attire.

Macy put the pistol away and bent over the dead man. "I read Machiavelli, Twan," he said without a trace of conceit. He turned out the light and walked back down the stairs. He had a plane to catch because things were really going to start rocking now.

Web guided Boo up the small hill and reined up next to Gwen, who was on Baron.

Romano was covering Billy down at the equestrian center; actually, Web had left the two admiring Romano's Corvette. With most of the farm's men gone to the horse sale, Web had felt particularly vulnerable and had gotten Canfield to okay some more agents coming on the farm to patrol the grounds and keep watch, at least until the men returned.

"It's so beautiful this time of year," said Gwen. She looked over at Web. "I guess you think we have a pretty easy life here. Big house, lots of help, just ride around all day admiring the view."

She smiled, yet Web sensed she was being serious. He wondered why a woman like Gwen Canfield, with all she'd been through, would have the need to seek approval from anyone, especially a stranger like him. "I think you've both been through a lot, you've worked hard and now you're enjoying the fruits of that labor. That's supposed to be the American dream, isn't it?"

"I suppose so," she answered without conviction. She looked

at the sun overhead. "It's hot today." Web could tell the woman wanted to talk to him about something but didn't quite know how to broach it.

"I've been an FBI agent for so long, Gwen, I've heard just about everything and I tend to be a very good listener."

She shot him a glance. "I don't spill my heart even to people I know *well*, Web, at least not anymore."

"I'm not asking you to. But if you want to talk, I'm here."

They rode some more and then she stopped. "I've been thinking about the trial in Richmond. Those awful people even sued the FBI, didn't they?"

"Tried to, but it got thrown out. The lawyer, Scott Wingo, the one who was recently killed, he tried to make some hay out of that during Ernest Free's trial, but the judge saw right through it and put a stop to it. But it probably caused enough doubt in the jury's eyes that the prosecutor got scared and did a plea bargain." He paused and then added, "Of course he's dead too now, and the judge."

Gwen stared over at him with her large, sad eyes. "And yet Ernest Free is alive and free, after everything he did."

"Life makes no sense sometimes, Gwen."

"Billy and I had a wonderful life before all that happened. I love him very much. But ever since David was killed, it hasn't been the same. The fault probably lies more with me than him. It was my idea to put David in that school. I wanted him to get a first-rate education and I wanted him to be exposed to lots of different types of people—translation, people of color and ethnicity. Billy is a good man, but he was born and raised in Richmond, not with any sort of wealth or privilege but in a neighborhood where you'd never see anyone but those of your own kind." She added quickly, "He's not a racist or anything like that. Half the drivers and dockworkers at his trucking company were black and he treated them all the same. If you worked hard, you had a job at fair wages. I've even gone with him to drivers' homes when they'd fallen off the wagon. He would bring food and money to the families, counsel the men, get them professional help and pay for it, or AA meetings, get them back on their feet. And even though he could have fired them, even under union rules, he didn't. He told me once his lot on earth was to be the King of Second Chances, because he'd had enough of his. I know some people might look at him and me and not see the attraction, but I know there's nothing he wouldn't do for me and he's stood right next to me through good and bad times and we've both had our share of those."

"Hey, Gwen, you don't have to convince me. But if you're having problems, have you sought counseling? I actually know someone."

She gave Web a hopeless look, gazed up at the hot sun again and said, "I'm going for a swim."

They rode back to the stables and Web drove Gwen back to the house in one of the farm trucks. She changed into her swimsuit and met Web at the pool area. He wasn't swimming, he told her, because his gun would get wet. She smiled at this remark and went over and turned a key that was set in a device built into a stone wall next to the pool. The gray automatic pool cover slid back on its tracks.

"We put this in because we kept finding turtles, frogs and even the occasional black snake in the pool," she explained.

As the cover slid into its holding trench at the far end of the pool, Web squatted down and examined the current-machine built into the deep end of the pool. He looked up in time to see Gwen step out of her sandals and slip out of her robe. She had on a one-piece suit that was cut a little low at the bosom and a little high at the hips and buttocks. Her body had a nice tan, and the muscles in her thighs and calves matched those he had already seen in her arms and shoulders. Forget the butt-burners and thigh-masters, women should just go horseback riding.

"How's this thing work?" asked Web.

Gwen tucked her long hair under a swim cap and walked over to him. "Water's pumped from the pool and through the cannon that you see there. It shoots out the water at a certain rate providing a resistance that you can increase or decrease, as you want. We had a portable machine for a while that was very cumbersome. And then I was using it so much that it made sense to have it built in. The pool's heated, so I use it pretty much year-round."

"I guess that's why you're in such great shape."

"Thank you, kind sir. Sure you don't want to swim with me?"

"I'd probably just slow you down."

"Right. There's not an ounce of fat on you." She went over to a control panel that was bolted to the stone wall that was set against the side of the pool nearest the house, opened the box and pushed some buttons.

Web heard water pressure building up and then he looked into the pool and saw white frothing water pouring out of the underwater cannon, creating the current Gwen was going to swim against.

She put on a pair of swim goggles and dove in. Web watched as she came to the surface and started her strokes. He watched for about ten minutes. The woman never varied her pace or stroke. She was like a machine herself and Web was actually glad he had declined the woman's offer to join her in the pool. Every HRT man had to be able to swim and know how to use diving equipment, and Web was a strong swimmer, but he wasn't sure he could have kept up with Gwen Canfield.

After about twenty minutes the frothing water stopped and Gwen came over to the side of the pool.

"Done?" asked Web.

"No, I had it set for forty-five minutes. The circuit might have tripped."

"Where's the power box?"

She pointed to the double doors set in a stone wall that was built up against a small slope. "In the pool equipment room."

With the grade of land the way it was here, Web figured the room was partly underground. He headed over and turned the knob. "It's locked."

"That's odd, we never lock it."

"You know where the key is?"

"No. Like I said, we never lock it, I just assumed there wasn't a key. I guess I'll have to cut my swim short."

"No, you won't." He smiled. "The FBI is a full-service agency and a happy client is our best customer." He pulled out his key ring, on which he always carried a very slim piece of metal that could pick ninety-nine percent of the world's locks in about thirty seconds. He opened the pool equipment room in half that time.

He went in, found the light switch and turned on the lights, which was a good thing, because even with the lights, he almost took a tumble down a short flight of steps just inside the doorway. Well, he thought, that was a lawyer's dream case. The place was noisy, with water running and machinery clanking and pumping. He went down the stairs. There were shelves filled with pool stuff, big canisters of powdered chlorine, skimmers, scrubbers, an aquatic robot to clean the pool and assorted junk that probably no one had used in years. It was cool down here and Web calculated that he was about ten feet underground at this point because the floor had continued to gently slope downward once he had gone down the stairs.

Web found the power box and sure enough the circuit had tripped. Since the current machine was a new addition, unless they had upgraded their wiring, it might be throwing too much electrical strain on the system. They should probably have that looked at before it blew and started a fire. He made a mental note to tell Gwen this. As he threw the breaker back on, he heard the machine start up again. There was really quite a racket down here. As he turned to go back outside, Web didn't notice another door down a short hallway. He turned and walked back out, turning off the light.

On the other side of that door and down another short hallway was another door, for there was quite the little maze down here. Inside that room Kevin Westbrook held his breath. First he had heard footsteps and then he hadn't. He had heard the damn machine go on and then off and then on again. And the chlorine smell, for he had long ago deduced what it was and grown used to it. But the footsteps going away had surprised him. Whenever people had come down here before, they had come to see him. He wondered why they hadn't this time.

41

While Gwen showered, Web waited in the library. One wall of the room consisted of built-in cabinetry with a large-screen TV. There were also five shelves filled with videocassettes and Web idly ran his gaze along them until the handwritten numbers on one of them made him freeze. He reached out and took it off the shelf. The numbers he had seen were only a date, yet the date was one that Web would never forget. He looked around, but there was no one about.

Web popped the tape in the VCR. The scene was one he had played over and over in his head. The Richmond school was filled with smart, willing children from all types of socioeconomic backgrounds. It was quite symbolic, the newspapers had said at the time, that the former capital of the Confederacy was trying a bold program to reintegrate its schools after most federal courts and most states had thrown up their hands and said what was there was the best that could be done. Well, Richmond had tried to do more and was succeeding, drawing national attention to its programs. Then Ernest B. Free and several of his homicidal gang had walked in the front doors with body armor and enough automatic weaponry to defeat the Union in the Civil War.

Chaos had followed as the two teachers were gunned down and over forty hostages, including thirty children, ages six to sixteen, were forced to take part in an event not one of them wanted anything to do with. The negotiators had worked the phones nonstop with the men inside, trying to keep them calm, to see what they wanted and whether it could be gotten for them. And all the time Web and his Charlie Team were standing by along with Zulu Team sniper guns trained on every available point of attack. Then there were sounds of gunfire inside and Web and his men were called up to the front lines. Each man had the battle plan firmly in mind, though it had been concocted on the fly on the way down from Quantico. Web remembered that they had gotten so close to getting the call to hit the target that he had even rubbed his .45s for luck.

What little Web knew about the Frees had not made him feel any better. They were violent but disciplined and well armed. And they were entrenched and had lots of innocent lives in their control.

The Frees had contacted the negotiators through a phone system that they had jerry-rigged. The shots were merely a misfire, they had said. Right away Web hadn't liked that. He could sense something bad coming, for the very simple fact that men like the Frees didn't operate under good faith. Yet Charlie Team had been called off. After Waco, the FBI's position on hostage rescue had changed. Basically it was a sit-and-wait game and the Bureau had shown that it was willing to wait until a new year had dawned before forcing the issue, so deeply ingrained was the starkly brutal image of lost children burning in Texas. But after the Frees had broken off negotiations, HRT had been called up again and this time Web knew they were going in.

With the TV cameras out front letting the whole world watch this drama unfold frame by frame, Web and Charlie Team had inched toward a little-used entrance at the rear of the building. To maximize surprise, since the precise location of the hostages and the Frees was not known, they had decided against using a breach charge to blow the exterior door and had opted for stealth. They had gotten inside quietly and made their way down the corridor and toward the gymnasium, where the best intelligence available said the hostages probably were.

HRT had crept to the double door, where Web had peered through the glass on the door and methodically counted hostages and hostage takers. They all appeared to be there. Just before ducking down, Web had made eye contact with the boy; he tried to keep him calm so he wouldn't give Web and company away, even giving him a thumbs-up. At the time Web didn't know that the young man was David Canfield.

HRT had begun its countdown. Each operator knew exactly where to shoot and they were confident that they could take out each of the Frees without losing any more hostages, though each of them also knew that things could go to hell quickly through the unexpected.

And they did.

Right before they burst into the room, there came a loud, high-pitched sound. It could not have come at a more inopportune time. And to this day Web didn't know its source.

HRT came in firing, but the Frees, now forewarned, instantly returned it.

And the shots were carefully placed. David Canfield had been shot through his left lung, the round exiting out of his chest. He dropped to the floor. With every breath the boy was jettisoning his blood through the large hole in his body. Though it couldn't have been more than a couple of seconds, David Canfield had stared at Web with an expression the man would never forget. It was as though the boy had put his entire faith in Web, his touchstone against all the madness, and Web had let him down. Thumbs-up.

That's when the real fighting started, and Web had to forget about David Canfield and concentrate on the other hostages and the men trying to kill him. He had taken the flamer after saving Lou Patterson, then eaten the rounds in his neck and torso. After that he had been a one-man wrecking crew and none of the Frees were left standing. Web couldn't believe that Ernest Free had managed to survive.

Reliving this was sickening, yet Web hunched forward as the cameras captured him once more. He was being brought out on a stretcher, paramedics surrounding him. To his left was Lou Patterson. On his right was a sheet over a body. David Canfield was the only hostage to have died with HRT on the case. Web continued to watch himself on the TV as the cameras alternated between him fighting for his life and David Canfield's still body. A light from one of the TV cameras continued to shine on the boy until somebody actually shot it out. Web often wondered who had done it. And then the tape went dark.

"I was the one who shot out that camera light."

Web whirled around and saw Billy Canfield standing there, staring at the TV and seemingly having been privy to Web's thoughts. He moved forward, his steps halting, his finger pointing at the screen.

Web rose from the couch. "God, Billy, I'm sorry, I shouldn't have—"

"See," Billy continued, "that damn light was shining right on my boy. They didn't have to do that." He finally focused on Web. "They didn't have to do that, it wasn't right. My little Davy was always sensitive to bright lights."

It was then that Gwen came in, dressed in jeans and a pink blouse, her feet bare and her hair still wet. Web shot her an apologetic look and she quickly deduced what had happened. She took her husband by the arm, but he immediately pulled away from her. Web read something close to hate for her in his eyes.

"Why don't you two sit in here and watch it?" he shouted at Gwen. "Damn you. I know, Gwen. Don't think I don't."

He stalked out of the room, while Gwen, without even looking at Web, fled in the other direction.

Feeling tremendous guilt, Web popped the tape out and started to put it on the shelf; and then he stopped. He glanced toward the door, slid the tape in his jacket pocket and went back to the carriage house. He put the tape in the VCR there and turned on the TV. He watched the tape five more times and something was there that he just couldn't quite get, a sound in the background. He turned up the volume and got very close to the screen, yet that didn't work. Finally he called Bates and explained what he was thinking. "I've got the tape here," he said.

Bates said, "I know the one you're talking about. It was shot by a network affiliate in Richmond. We've got one in archives. I'll have our guys give it a close look."

Web clicked the TV off and took the tape out of the VCR. It had also been discovered later that two black teenage females had been raped by the Frees; apparently their hatred for those of color did not prevent them from having forcible sex with them.

But what had Billy meant when he told Gwen that he knew? Knew what?

His ringing cell phone interrupted Web's thoughts. He answered it. The woman was nearly hysterical.

"Claire, what's wrong?"

He listened to her frightened tones and then said, "Stay right where you are. I'll be there as fast as I can." He hung up, called Romano, filled him in and was on the road in a few minutes.

42

Claire had gone to a very safe and public place, a police sub-station at a suburban mall. She hadn't filed a report with the police, she told Web when he showed up.

"Why the hell not?"

"I wanted to talk to you first."

"Look, Claire, from how you described it, it sounds like my buddy Francis Westbrook and one of his sidekicks, probably Clyde Macy. The last time I saw them, somebody died. You don't realize how lucky you are."

"But I can't tell for sure it was them, I was blindfolded."

"But you would recognize their voices?"

"Probably." She paused and looked puzzled.

"What is it, Claire, what's bugging you?"

"This Francis, how educated would you say he is?"

"In street smarts, he's a Ph.D. In book learning, nil. Why?"

"The man who threatened me had an odd way of talking. He would alternate between slang and ghetto talk, and the diction and vocabulary of an educated man. I could sense he was uncomfortable with what he was saying, because it felt forced sometimes, as though he were trying to think of appropriate words as he went along, suppressing his natural choices but occasionally erring, and using words that, you know—"

"Would be more along the lines of the person he was trying to impersonate?"

"Impersonate, exactly."

Web took a deep breath. Well, this was getting interesting. He was thinking about a second-in-command trying to pull a coup on his boss or push the knife in a little deeper, depending on how one looked at it. Antoine Peebles, the wannabe drug king with a sheepskin. He looked at her with new admiration. "You've got a good pair of ears, Claire, always waiting for those cues from us poor screwed-up head cases."

"I'm scared, Web. I'm really scared. I've counseled people for years about facing what frightens them, being proactive instead of reactive, and this happens to me and I feel paralyzed."

He found his arm going protectively around her as he led her to his car. "Well, you have a right to be scared. What happened to you would scare most people."

"But not you." She said this, he noted, almost enviously.

As they climbed in his Mach, Web told her, "It's not that I don't ever get scared, Claire, because I do."

"Well, you certainly don't show it."

"Yes, I do, just in a different way." He closed the car door and thought for a moment before glancing at her and actually gripping her hand. "You can deal with your fear in two different ways. Close up like a clam and hide from the world or do something about it."

"Now you sound like the psychiatrist," she said wearily.

"Well, I learned from the best." He squeezed her hand. "What do you say, want to help me crack this thing?"

"I trust you, Web."

This surprised him, chiefly because that wasn't what he had asked her.

He put the car in gear. "Well, let's go see if we can find a little boy named Kevin."

Web parked in the alley behind the duplex where Kevin had lived, and he and Claire went to the rear door just in case somebody was watching the front, like Bates's men. He definitely didn't want to run afoul of the Bureau right now. Web knocked.

"Yeah, who is it?" The voice was a man's, not Grandma's, and it definitely wasn't friendly.

"Jerome, is that you?"

Web could sense a presence just on the other side of the door.

"Who the hell wants to know?"

"Web London, FBI. And how are you today, Jerome?"

Web and Claire heard the word "Shit" muttered loudly, but the door did not open.

"Jerome, I'm still here and I'll stay here until you open the door. And don't try running out the front like you did last time. We've got that covered."

He heard chains sliding back and locks popping open and he was eye to eye with Jerome. Web was very surprised to see that he had on a white shirt, nice slacks and a tie to go with his sullen look.

"Got a date?"

"Damn, you real funny for a Fed. What do you want?"

"Just talk. You alone?"

Jerome stepped back. "Not anymore. Look, we told you all we know. Man, can't you stop bugging us?"

Web ushered Claire inside, followed her and then closed the door behind them. They looked around the small kitchen. "Just trying to find Kevin. You want that, don't you?" Web asked.

"What's that supposed to mean?"

"It means I don't tend to trust anyone. I just want to talk, that's all."

"Look, I'm busy. You want to talk to somebody, you can talk to my lawyer." Jerome looked at Claire. "What is she, *your* date?"

"No, she's my shrink."

"Yeah, that's a good one."

"No, really, Jerome, I am," said Claire as she stepped forward. "And I'm afraid that Mr. London has some issues."

"What does his issues have to do with me?"

"Well, he's been devoting so much time to this case that I believe he's becoming almost obsessed with it. That sort of obsession can reach dangerous, sometimes violent levels if not dealt with in a reasonable period of time."

Jerome looked over at Web and took as step back. "If this man is crazy, I had nothing to do with it. He was crazy the first time he came here."

"But you don't want anything to happen to someone, like yourself or others. Mr. London is only trying to find the truth, and in my professional opinion finding the truth, for someone with his particular set of issues, is very important. And to those who help him find it, he would, psychologically speaking, be very grateful. The flip side of that is somewhere you really don't want to go." She looked at Web with an expression of sorrow mixed with just the right touch of fear. "I've seen the results of that before with Mr. London; that's one reason why I'm here. To prevent another tragedy."

Web just had to admire the woman's work.

Jerome stared back and forth at Claire and Web. Then he said in a far more calm tone, "Look, I told you all I know. I really have."

Web spoke very firmly. "No, Jerome, you haven't. I want to know stuff about Kevin maybe you've never even thought about. Now let's cut the shit and get down to it."

Jerome motioned them to follow and turned and walked down the hallway into the small living room where Web had first spoken to them. Before he left the kitchen, Web noted that it was very clean, the sinks spotless, the floor scrubbed. As he and Claire followed Jerome down the hallway and into the living room, he saw that the trash had been picked up, the floors mopped, the walls scrubbed. Web could smell disinfectant everywhere. A door was leaning against the wall next to the bathroom, and the sheet had been taken down. The openings in the ceiling had been shored up and braced. Grandma's doing, he thought, at least he did until Jerome picked up a broom and started sweeping a pile of trash into a large garbage bag.

Web looked around at the "new" home. "Your doing?"

"We don't have to be living in no pigsty."

"Where's your grandma?"

"At work. Over at the hospital. In the cafeteria."

"How come you're not at work?"

"I will be in an hour, hope you ain't plan on keeping me long."

"You look too nice to be planning to knock over a bank."

"Man, you are a riot."

"So where's work?" *You don't have a job, Jerome, just admit it.*

Jerome finished filling the bag, tied it closed and tossed it to Web. "You mind throwing that out the front door?"

Claire opened the door and Web did so, setting the bag on the front stoop along with quite a few others. When he closed the door, Jerome had pulled a toolbox out of a closet. He took out a screw-driver, Vise-Grips and a hammer. He laid the tools next to the bath-room opening and gripped the door.

"Give me a hand, here, will you?"

Web helped him lift the door closer to the opening and then held on to it and watched as Jerome tightened the sagging hinges and used the Vise-Grips to pop out the door pins. They lifted the door up, worked it into place and Jerome tapped the hinges in with the hammer. He closed and opened the door several times to see that it was aligned properly.

"A handy guy. But that's not your job, unless carpenters wear ties to work."

Jerome put his tools away before answering. "I work nights at a company servicing their computer system. Just got the position a few months ago."

"So you know computers?" asked Claire.

"Got my AS in computer science at the community college. Yeah, I know my way around 'em."

Web was unimpressed. "Uh-huh. You know computers?"

"You got a hearing problem? That's what I said."

"Last time I was here, you didn't look gainfully employed."

"Like I said, I work nights."

"Right."

Jerome stared at Web and then went over and slid a computer case out from under the couch. He flipped it open and fired it up.

"You on-line, man?" asked Jerome.

"We talking skates or what?"

"Ha-ha. Computers. Internet. You know what that is, don't you?"

"Nah, I've been traveling around the galaxy the last ten years, I'm so behind."

Jerome punched a few keys and they listened as it was an-nounced to Jerome that "You've got mail" on AOL.

"Wait a minute, how can you access the Internet without a phone?" said Web.

"My computer has wireless technology, a card that lets me do that. It's like having a built-in cell phone." He smiled at Web and shook his head in obvious amazement. "Man, I hope most Feds aren't as ignorant as you are about computers."

"Don't push it, Jerome."

"You know what a cookie is?"

"Sugary thing that gives you love handles."

"You just never quit, do you? A cookie is a simple piece of text. An HTTP header with a text-only string. The string has the domain, the path, value variable that a website sets and a lifetime. Lots of companies use cookies to personalize information, track popular links or for demographics. It keeps site content fresh and of interest to users. For example." He hit a few keys and the screen changed. "I've been on this site a lot recently and it knows that. So it doesn't show me the same stuff unless I specifically request it. And they're starting to use cookies in back-end interactions, like storing personal data a user has given to the site, like passwords and such."

"Storing personal data. That sounds sort of Big Brotherish," said Claire.

"Well, it can be, but cookies are just text, no program, they're not virus-susceptible. It can't even access your hard drive, although your browser can save cookie values there if necessary, but that's about it. Some people think cookies will fill up their hard drive, but that's pretty much impossible. Most ISPs put limits on cookies. Netscape limits them to three hundred, so you get up to that number and it automatically discards the older ones. Microsoft puts them in your TIF folder with a max default setting of two percent of your hard drive. And cookies are usually so small that you'd need about ten million cookies to fill up a gig hard drive. In fact, I'm writing a few million lines of code that will take cookies to a new level, taking out the bad stuff and making them a lot more useful. And maybe I'll make myself a few million bucks in the process." He grinned. "The ultimate cookie."

He shut down his computer and looked at Web. "Any more questions?"

The admiration was clear on Web's features. "Okay, you convinced me, you know computers."

"Yeah, I bust my ass in school, finally get a job that doesn't require me to wear a hair net and the fine folks at Social Services tell

us we make too much damn money and we got to leave our home
we been at for the last five years."

"System sucks."

"No, people who have never been on it think the system sucks.
For people on it, we wouldn't have had anyplace to live without it.
But it still ticks me off that I'm making a little more than damn
Burger King pays and we get kicked out. It's not like my employer
dropped any stock options on somebody like me."

"Look, it's still a start, Jerome. And better than the alternative
around here, you know that."

"I'm gonna keep moving up. Work my ass off and then we are
out of here and we're never looking back."

"You and your grandmother?"

"She took me in when my mama died. Brain tumor and no
health insurance, that ain't a real good combo. My daddy bit it on
a .45 he stuck in his own mouth when he was high on something.
You damn right I'll take care of her, just like she took care of me."

"And Kevin?"

"I take care of Kevin too." He glowered at Web. "If you people
can find him."

"We're trying. I know a little about his family. His relation to
Big—I mean, Francis."

"He's Kevin's father. So what?"

"A little more than that. I've met Francis up close. Too close, actually." Web pointed out the remnants of his assorted facial injuries inflicted by the man.

Jerome looked at him curiously. "You lucky that's all he done
to you."

"Yeah, I'm getting that feeling. He told me how Kevin came into
this world. With his mother and all."

"Stepmother."

"What?"

"She was Francis's stepmother. Strung out most of the time.
Don't know what happened to his real mama."

Web let out a relieved breath. It wasn't incest. He glanced at
Claire, who said, "So they're actually not brothers. They're father
and son. Does Kevin know that?"

"I never told him."

"But he thinks Francis is his brother? Is that how Francis wanted it?" asked Claire, while Web watched her closely.

"What Francis wants, he gets, that answer enough for you?"

"Why would Francis want Kevin to believe they were brothers?"

"Maybe he didn't want Kevin to know he was screwing his step-mom and Kevin's mom. Her name was Roxy. She was into drugs and all that, but she was good to Kevin before she died."

"How did Kevin get shot?" asked Web

"He was with Francis, got caught in some gang shootout. Francis brought him here, only time I ever seen that man cry. I took him to the hospital myself 'cause cops just arrest his ass if Francis took him. Kevin never cried, not one time, and bleeding like a son of a bitch. But he's never been the same since. Other kids tease him, call him a retard."

"Kids can be cruel, and then they grow up and get even more cruel, they're just a lot more subtle about it," commented Claire.

"Kevin ain't stupid. Smart as a whip. And he can draw, man, draw like you can't believe."

Claire looked interested. "Care to show me?"

Jerome checked his watch. "I can't be late for work. And I got to take the bus."

"To your big cookie shop?" asked Web.

For the very first time Jerome and Web exchanged a smile. "I tell you what, Jerome, you show us Kevin's stuff and talk to us a little bit more and I'll personally drive you to work in one bitching machine that'll have all your friends envious as hell. How about that?"

Jerome led them upstairs and down a short hallway that ended with a very small room. When Jerome turned on the light, Web and Claire looked around in amazement. Every inch of the walls and even the ceiling was covered with drawings on paper, some in charcoal, others in colored pencil and still others in pen and ink. And on a small table next to a mattress on the floor were stacks of sketchbooks. Claire picked up one and started going through it, while Web continued to gaze at the drawings on the wall. Some of them were things Web could recognize, landscapes and people; Jerome and his grandmother were reproduced in amazing detail.

Other drawings were abstract in content and Web couldn't make sense of them.

Claire looked up from the sketchbook and her gaze swept around the room before focusing on Jerome. "I know a little something about art, Jerome, because my daughter is majoring in art history. Kevin has serious talent."

Jerome looked to Web like the proud father. "Kevin says that how he sees things sometimes. 'Just drawing what I'm seeing,' he tells me."

Web looked at the art supplies and sketchbooks piled on the table. There was also a small easel in the corner with a blank canvas on it.

"All this stuff costs money. Francis contributing?"

"I buy Kevin his art stuff. He gets Kevin other stuff, clothes, shoes, basic things."

"He offer to ever help you and your grandmother?"

"He offered. But we ain't taking that money. We know where it comes from. Kevin's another matter. It's his daddy. Father's got a right to provide for his son."

"Daddy come around much?"

Jerome shrugged. "When he wants to."

"You think he might be the one who has Kevin? Give it to me straight."

Jerome shook his head. "As much as I don't like Francis, if you ask me, he'd cut off his own head before he'd let anything happen to that boy. I mean, he'll kill you so much as look at you. But around Kevin he was gentle. A gentle giant, I guess you could say. He didn't want Kevin living with him because he knew it'd be too dangerous."

"I imagine that was a big sacrifice for Francis, giving up something that he loved so much. But that's the true test of love, really: sacrifice," said Web.

"Well, man changes where he sleeps all the time 'cause people looking to kill him. Hell of a way to live. But he had people watching Kevin, making sure nobody got to Francis by going after him. It ain't like everybody knew of the connection, but he wasn't taking any chances."

"You seen him since Kevin disappeared?" asked Web.

Jerome stepped back on that one and put his hands in his pockets, and Web instantly sensed the wall going back up.

"I'm not looking to get you in trouble, Jerome. Just tell me straight and I promise you it won't go any further. You're doing really well, keep your string going."

Jerome seemed to think about this, one hand playing with his tie, as though wondering what the thing was doing around his neck.

"The night Kevin didn't come home. It was late, maybe three in the morning. I had just got home from work and Granny was up and all a mess. She told me Kevin was missing. I was upstairs changing and getting ready to go looking for Kevin and wondering whether we should call the cops. I hear my granny downstairs talking to somebody, or *he* was talking—yelling, that is—at her. It was Francis. He was mad like I ain't heard him mad ever before." He paused and looked for a moment like he might bolt again. "He was looking for Kevin too. Was sure Granny had him hid somewhere, at least maybe he was hoping that was it. The way he was talking, I thought he be going after Granny. I almost come down the stairs. Now, I ain't no coward, and I ain't stupid either; hell, that man probably take only a second to kill me, but it ain't like I'm letting him or anybody come in here and hurt her without trying to do something about it. You understand me?"

"I do, Jerome."

"Francis, he finally calmed down, he was getting it that Kevin wasn't here. So he left. Last time we've seen him. That's the truth."

"I appreciate you telling me. I guess it's probably hard to trust people right now."

Jerome looked Web up and down. "You saved Kevin's life. That's worth something."

Web looked at him warily.

"I read the papers, Mr. Web London, Hostage Rescue Team. Kevin be dead, wasn't for you. Maybe that's why Francis didn't bust your skull."

"Hadn't really thought about it that way."

Web looked at the stack of sketchbooks again. "The other agents who came here, did you tell them any of this?"

"They didn't really ask."

"How about Kevin's room? They search up here?"

"Couple of them looked around, didn't take very long."

Web looked at Claire. They seemed to read each other's thoughts. She said, "Do you mind if I borrow those sketchbooks? I'd like to show them to my daughter."

Jerome looked at the books and then at Web. "You gotta promise to bring them back. That's Kevin whole life, right there," he said.

"I promise. I promise I'll do everything I can to bring Kevin back too." He gathered up the sketchbooks and then put a hand on Jerome's shoulder. "Now it's time to get you to work. You'll find my chauffeuring fees are very reasonable."

As they walked downstairs, Web had one more question. "Kevin was in that alley alone in the middle of the night. Did he do that a lot?"

Jerome looked away and said nothing.

"Come on, Jerome, don't get tongue-tied on me now."

"Hell, Kevin wanted to help us out, you know, make some money and we get out of this place. It bothered him that he never could do much like that. He was just a kid, but he thought like a grown-up on some things."

"I guess a particular environment might do that for you."

"Well, Kevin, he be out on the streets sometimes. Granny too old to keep up with him. I don't know who he was hanging with, and whenever I caught him out there, I brought his butt home. But maybe he might be trying to make a little cash on the side. And around here you can get that money, no matter how young you are, you hear me?"

They dropped Jerome off at work and headed back to Claire's house.

"By the way, you handled yourself like a pro back there," he said.

"I guess it's more mental than physical, and that's my jurisdiction." She glanced at Web. "You know, you were pretty rough on Jerome."

"It's probably because I've seen a million guys just like him in my life."

"Stereotyping is dangerous, Web, not to mention unfair to the person being categorized. The fact is, you can only know one Jerome at a time. And I could tell this Jerome busted your preconception all apart."

"He did," admitted Web. "I guess when you've been doing my kind of work for so long, it's easier to lump folks together."

"Like fathers?"

Web didn't answer that one.

Claire said, "It is sad about Francis and Kevin. From what Jerome said, he must love his son very much. And to have to lead such a life."

"I don't doubt the big guy loves Kevin either, but I've seen that same big guy kill a man in cold blood right in front of him, and he's also cleaned my clock twice, so my sympathy has its limits," said Web very firmly.

"One's environment does tend to dictate one's choices, Web."

"I can accept a little of that argument, but I've seen too many guys from even worse backgrounds make it just fine."

"Including maybe yourself?"

He ignored her question and instead said, "I figure you pack some things and we find you a safe house with some agents there to make sure those folks don't come back."

"I'm not so sure that's a good idea."

"I want you to be safe."

"I want to be safe too, trust me, I have no death wish. But if you're right and that person was just pretending to be Francis to scare me and throw suspicion on him, I'm probably not in any real danger."

"*Probably* is right. That's only one theory, Claire, and it might be the wrong one."

"I think if my routine remains the same, they have no reason to think I'm a threat. And I have something I really need to work on."

"What?"

She glanced over at him and Web had never seen her look so troubled. "I'm thinking about a very brave man going into an alley, listening to a little boy say something quite extraordinary and then being unable to do his job."

He shot her a look. "You can't be sure there's a connection."

She held up a page of the sketchbook for him to see. "Oh, I'm pretty sure there's a connection."

The drawing was stark, exacting, possessing a powerful clarity that seemed beyond a young boy. A figure that looked so like Kevin it could have been a self-portrait was standing in what looked to be a high-walled alley. A man who could have been Web in complete combat gear was in full running stride next to Kevin. The boy's hand was extended. What was in the boy's hand had Web fixated. The device was small, easily secreted in a trouser pocket. The stream of light that shot out from it reached across the page and ended at the margin. It was as though the boy held some sort of futuristic weapon that shot light beams, à la *Star Wars* or *Star Trek*. Actually, it was a device that all people, especially kids, would be familiar with these days. It was a remote control, and this one was sending out a beam of light. It could have been to a TV, stereo or some other electronic equipment. But Web knew that it wasn't. He hadn't even seen a TV in Kevin's house and there was certainly not one in his room. This remote control, Web felt sure, had activated the laser in the courtyard that, in turn, had triggered the miniguns when Web and Charlie Team had come thundering into the space. The kid had kick-started it all. And somebody had prepared the boy for exactly what he would see that night, namely men in body armor with guns, for it wasn't like Kevin Westbrook had come back to his house to make this drawing after the fact.

Who was that someone?

Two cars behind Web's Mach, Francis Westbrook drove the Lincoln Navigator himself. Without product to sell, a large part of his crew had already jumped ship. Folks didn't let the grass grow under their feet in the drug trade, and the grass always seemed to be greener someplace else. Of course, when you got to the new place, it was just the same old crap. You lived and died by your wits and the stupid did not survive for very long, yet for every dealer that was killed, a dozen were ready to take his place; the lure of the drug business was strong despite its high mortality rate, because people in Francis Westbrook's world weren't exactly loaded down with options. Forget the social scientists with their little charts and graphs, Westbrook could vividly teach the mother of all courses on that subject.

He shook his head as his thoughts returned to his dilemma. Peebles was nowhere to be found, and even the once-loyal Macy had disappeared. The men he had left were not ones Westbrook really trusted, thus he had gone it alone on this mission. He had been watching Jerome's place in the hopes that Kevin might come wandering up. Instead he had gotten a nice prize in the interim. HRT London and the woman. She was the shrink, he at least had learned that before his men deserted him. He steered with his fingertip, his right hand on the grip of the pistol lying on the front seat. He had watched London and the woman go in and then come out with Jerome. The lady had been carrying Kevin's sketchbooks, and Francis wondered why. Did the books have a clue to the boy's whereabouts? He had personally searched this city high and low looking for his son, threatened people, broken bones and overinflated egos in the process, shelled out thousands in cash for snitch work, and with all that, nothing. The Feds sure as hell didn't have him; they weren't playing games with him, perhaps trying to get Kevin to testify against the father, of that he was sure. Francis had been real careful on that; Kevin knew nothing about what his old man did, at least not the sort of details that were required on the witness stand. But if he did, Francis would just bite the bullet and take the fall. Above all, he had to do what was best for Kevin. In many ways he had already led a full, rich life, about as much as someone like him could reasonably expect. But Kevin had a lot more living to do. London was a smart guy. Francis's plan was to follow him and see where that took him. Where he hoped it took him, of course, was to Kevin.

43

Web drove Claire home, where she packed some clothes and other things, and then he took her to her car and followed her to a hotel, where she checked in. After they'd promised each other to keep in touch with fresh developments, Web rushed back to East Winds.

Romano was at the carriage house. "The Canfields are in the house. I don't know what happened, but something's shook them up. White as sheets, both of them."

"I know what did it, Paulie," and Web explained about the videotape.

"You know there was nothing you could do, Web. I'm just pissed I was overseas at the time, I would've loved to hit those guys." He snapped his fingers. "Oh, before I forget, Ann Lyle called and said she really needed to talk to you."

"How come she didn't call me directly?"

"I talked to her a couple of days ago. Just checking in. I gave her the phone number here, just in case we needed a hard-line contact."

Web pulled out his phone, and while he was dialing Ann he asked Romano, "So, how'd Billy like your 'Vette?"

"Sweet, man, sweet. Said he had an opportunity to buy one a couple of years ago for—are you ready for this?—for fifty thousand dollars. Fifty big ones."

"Better not let Angie find out about that. I see four wheels and a ragtop becoming new furniture and college accounts."

Romano paled. "Shit, I never thought of that. You gotta swear you won't tell her, Web. You gotta swear."

"Hold on, Paulie." Web spoke into the phone. "Ann, it's Web, what's up?"

Ann's voice was very low. "There's something going down here. That's why I'm here so late."

Web tensed. He knew what that meant. "An op?"

"The guys built a new target in the practice area two days ago and have been going over it like crazy. The assaulters have been going through their equipment today seven ways from Sunday and the commander's doors been closed all morning, and some of the snipers have already been deployed. You know how it is, Web."

"Yeah, I know. You have any idea what the target might be?"

Ann's voice dropped even lower. "A tape from a surveillance camera came in a few days ago. It shows that a truck was parked at the loading dock of an abandoned building near where the shooting occurred. The tape wasn't at the best angle, I understand, but I believe it shows the guns being unloaded from the truck."

Web nearly tore the phone in half. Bates had kept this from him. "Who was the truck registered to, Ann?"

"Silas Free. He's one of the founders of the Free Society, Web. Pretty stupid of him to use his real name."

Son of a bitch. They were hitting the Frees. "How are they getting there?"

"Military aircraft from Andrews to an old Marine Corps airfield near Danville. They're heading out at O-twelve-hundred. The trucks have already been sent down via semi."

"What's the assault force?"

"Hotel, Gulf, X-Ray and Whiskey."

"That's it? That's not full strength."

"Echo, Yankee and Zulu are out of the country on VIP protection detail. There's no Charlie Team. And on top of that, one of the Hotel assaulters broke his leg during a training exercise and Romano's with you on special assignment. We're a little thin right now."

"I'm on my way. Don't let the train leave without me."

He looked at Romano. "Get the guys at the gates to collapse around the house and take over protection detail."

"Where are we going?"

"It's time to bang 'em and hang 'em, Paulie."

While Romano called the perimeter guards, Web ran outside,

popped the trunk of his Mach and checked what he had. The answer was he had plenty. The life of an HRT operator required that he keep several days' worth of clothes in his trunk along with a variety of other items essential for when you were called out of the country for a week or a month with virtually no notice. Web had supplemented this "normal" allotment with lots of goodies he had taken from the HRT equipment cage and the stash he kept at home, which included a formidable arsenal. Even with his FBI creds, he'd have a tough time explaining this cache to a state trooper on a routine traffic stop.

When Romano came back, Web said, "Bates kept it from me, the little shit. They found direct evidence tying the Frees to the hit on Charlie, using the damn tip *I* gave him. And he wasn't even going to invite us to the party. Probably thinks we'll freak and pop people unnecessarily."

"You know," said Romano, "that really offends my sense of professionalism."

"Well, tell your sense of professionalism to shake a leg, we don't have much time."

"Well, why didn't you say so?" He grabbed Web's arm. "If speed is what we need, we ain't taking that hunk of junk."

"What the hell are you talking about?"

Five minutes later the big-block 'Vette loaded down with weaponry blew through the open gates at East Winds and hit the main strip.

It was mostly back roads down to Quantico, but Romano kept the 'Vette on seventy pretty much the whole way, going around curves so fast Web felt himself grabbing the edge of his seat and hoping Romano didn't notice. When they got to Interstate 95, Romano smoothly shifted gears and popped the clutch. Web watched the speedometer swiftly move to triple digits. Romano slid in an eight-track tape, of all things, and revved up the music. The best of Bachman-Turner Overdrive was soon shattering the night air, because they were driving with the top down. While Romano drove, Web checked their guns. Even with the highway lights, it was very dark, but his fingers knew every inch of the things.

He looked over at Romano, who was smiling and singing along with BTO as they were "taking care of business." The guy was bobbing his head like he was back in high school and banging at a Springsteen concert.

"You gotta strange way of preparing yourself for combat, Paulie."

"What, like you and the rubbing you give your pistols for luck?" Web looked at him in surprise. "Riner told me. He thought it was a hoot."

"I guess nothing's sacred," muttered Web.

They cruised into Quantico in record time. They both knew the sentry posted at the east entrance off the Bureau Parkway, and Romano didn't bother to slow down.

"Triple eight, Jimbo," he yelled out as he roared by, referring to the crisis page of three eights that told HRT members to get the hell to Quantico.

"Go get 'em, guys!" yelled back Jimbo.

Romano parked the car; they pulled their gear and hauled it to the admin building. Romano used his security card to open the gate, and they headed to the front door, where a video surveillance camera was watching them. In front of the entrance, six trees had been planted in memory of the fallen members of Charlie Team. Inside, they passed Ann Lyle's office. She came to the door, and she and Web exchanged a glance but not more than that. Strictly from the rule book, Ann shouldn't have called and told Web about the assault. And he would never do anything to get her in trouble. But they both knew that what she had done was the right thing to do, rule book be damned.

Web met his commander, Jack Pritchard, in the hallway. The man looked in astonishment at Web and Romano with all their gear.

"Reporting for duty, sir," said Web.

"How the hell did you even know about it?" demanded Pritchard.

"I'm still a member of HRT. I can smell these things a mile away."

Pritchard didn't push it, though he did glance in the direction of Ann Lyle's office.

"I want in," said Web.

"That's impossible," said Pritchard. "You're still on SRB leave, and he"—he pointed at Romano—"got his ass taken off on special assignment that I wasn't even made privy to. Now shove off."

The commander turned on his heel and headed back to the equipment room. Web and Romano shoved off, right after the man. The assaulters and snipers who hadn't already been deployed on the mission were gathered here, going over last-minute details. The

snipers were checking to make sure they each had restocked a numbered lot of match-grade ammo. They were updating logbooks,
tightening trigger assemblies and cleaning scopes and barrels. The
assaulters were inspecting their own weapons and breaking out
their breaching gear, tactical bags and body armor. The personnel in
the logistics cell of HRT were running around loading gear into the
trucks and trying to remember everything the mini-invasion would
need to succeed. They all stopped doing what they were doing when
Pritchard and then Web and Romano barged into their space.

"Come on, Jack," said Web, "you got teams all over the damned
place, and not even counting Paulie, you're short a guy on Hotel,
you can use the extra hands."

Pritchard whirled around. "How the hell did you know we were
short a guy?" The HRT chief obviously had had enough of leaks.

Web looked around the room. "I can count. And I count five assaulters on Hotel. Add me and Paulie and you're at full strength."

"You haven't been briefed, you haven't worked the mock target
and you haven't even been training for a while. You're *not* going."

Web moved in front of the man and blocked his way. Jack
Pritchard was about five-ten and Web had him by at least thirty
pounds and about five years, but Web knew if it came to a fight
that he would be in for one. But he didn't want to fight, not his
own man anyway.

"Brief us on the way over. Show us the attack points. We've got
our own equipment and all we need are Kevlar, a flight suit and a
helmet. How many of these have Paulie and me done, Jack? Don't
treat us like some clueless bastard right out of NOTS. We don't deserve that."

Pritchard stepped back and stared at Web for a very long minute.
The longer it went on the more Web thought Pritchard might actually throw him out of the place. HRT, like other quasi-military
units, frowned on such insubordination.

"I tell you what, Web, I'll leave it up to them." He pointed at the
assaulters.

Web hadn't been expecting that sort of decision. But he stepped
forward and looked at each of the Hotel and Gulf guys one by one.
He had fought side-by-side with most of them, first as a sniper and
then as one of their own, an assaulter. His gaze finally settled on

Romano. The men would accept Paulie back without question. But Web was damaged goods, the guy who had frozen at the worst possible moment, and every man in this room was wondering if he would do it again and cost them their lives.

Web had saved Romano's life during a raid on a Montana militiamen site. Romano had returned the favor a year later during a VIP protection detail in the Middle East when a foot soldier from a fringe rebel group had tried to run their party down with an empty bus he had stolen. The rebel would have succeeded in getting at least Web, but Romano had pushed Web out of the way and popped the driver between the eyes with a round from his .45. Yet despite all that, and their recent time together, Web had never really been able to read the man. As he looked around the room, it seemed that the men were looking to Romano to settle the issue, and despite the guy having driven Web here to take part in the assault, Web had no clue what he would say now.

He watched as Romano put a hand on Web's shoulder. Looking at his teammates, Romano said, "Web London can cover my back anytime, anyplace."

And in the alpha male society of HRT, a man like Paul Romano—who was feared even by some of his teammates—saying that was all it took. After they finished suiting up, Pritchard called all the men into the small meeting room. He stood at the front staring at them, and they stared back. It seemed to Web that the commander spent more time gazing at him than at any of the others.

"It goes without saying," began Pritchard, "that this mission is critical. All our missions are critical. I know that each man here will conduct himself in the utmost professional manner while still doing his job to the best of his ability." Pritchard's tone was stilted, the man looked nervous, and he had done enough dangerous things in his life that Web had long assumed the man had no nerves.

Web and Romano exchanged glances. This sort of pep talk was a little out of the ordinary. They weren't a bunch of high school kids getting ready to play football.

Pritchard's stern demeanor collapsed. "Okay, let me cut the official crap. The folks we're going after tonight are suspected of doing in Charlie Team. You all know that. We hope we're going to hit them by surprise. Short and sweet and no shots fired." He paused and looked up and down the ranks once more. "You know the orders of engagement. This Free Society has come our way before, down in Richmond. That was Charlie Team too, and some think that what happened in that courtyard was an act of revenge by the Frees.

"There are no known hostages. The ground logistics are a little tricky, but we've handled far worse. We fly in, the trucks will be waiting and we execute." Pritchard was pacing now, and then he stopped. "If you have to take a shot tonight, you do it. If they fire back, I don't have to tell any of you what to do. But don't be stupid about this. The last thing we need is for the media to be screaming tomorrow morning about HRT wiping out guys who don't need to be wiped out. If they were involved in Charlie's getting ripped, let's bag them and let the legal process work its course. Don't, and I repeat don't, fire because you're thinking about what these guys might have done to six men who belonged to us. You're better than that. You deserve better than that. And I know you'll come through." He paused once more and seemed to search each of his men's faces, once again lingering the longest, it seemed, on Web.

Pritchard finished with, "Let's hit it."

As the men filed out, Web walked up next to Pritchard.

"Jack, I hear where you're coming from, but if you're that concerned about somebody going off the deep end, why have HRT do this hit at all? You said there aren't any hostages, so an FBI SWAT team could handle this with backup from the locals. Why us?"

"We're still part of the FBI, Web, although you wouldn't know it from the way some people act around here."

"Meaning orders from uptown for HRT to do this gig?"

"That's the procedure, and you know that as well as I do."

"Because of the circumstances, did you request a pass on this one?"

"Actually, I did, because I personally don't think we should be doing it. Not this soon after losing our guys. And I agree with you, a SWAT team could go easy enough."

"And they turned you down?"

"Like I said, we're part of the FBI and I do what I'm told. Now you wanted in on this, are you backing out now?"

"See you at the O.K. Corral."

A few minutes later they were on their way to Andrews Air Force Base, ready to go to war.

The Bureau, Web had learned from one of his HRT colleagues, had contemplated executing a search warrant on the Frees' compound but had decided that they would let HRT secure the place first and then execute the search. The last thing the Bureau wanted was a couple of agents getting killed while trying to serve the search warrant. Besides, video of machine guns used to kill federal agents being unloaded from a truck rented by Silas Free was pretty damning.

On the short bumpy flight down in a military transport jet, Web went over the five-paragraph operations order and he and Romano were filled in on specific details. There would be no negotiation with the Frees and no warnings to come out with their hands up. The memories of the school incident in Richmond and the massacre of Charlie Team had precluded those options. Fewer people would die tonight if HRT just hit them without warning, at least that's what the powers-that-be had decided, and Web was perfectly fine with that decision. The fact that there were no known hostages made things easier and also more complicated. Complicated in that Web was still wondering why an FBI SWAT team hadn't been called in to handle this. He hoped it was a combination of the reputation the Frees had for being extremely dangerous and well armed, and the fact that even the good guys were entitled to exact sweet justice some of the time. But something just didn't feel right about this.

Intelligence gathered by WFO over the last several months put the Frees at a compound they had created a decade earlier about forty miles west of Danville, Virginia, in a very remote part of the state with woods on three sides. Snipers from Whiskey and X-Ray had set up surveillance twenty-four hours before with WFO agents and had been feeding valuable intelligence back ever since. The plans for the target had actually been in the HRT database for a while now. HRT had rebuilt the interior of the school on its back lot and practiced with something more than the unit's usual vigor and determination. While there wasn't an HRT member who would consciously open fire unless he, another team member or an innocent person was in danger, there wasn't a single HRT operator who wasn't at least partly wishing that the Frees would try and fight back. Maybe, Web thought, that group would include Commander Jack Pritchard too, despite his passionate speech to the contrary.

They landed, climbed in their trucks, which had just been off-loaded from a special truck transport, and drove to the preliminary staging area and interfaced with the local police and folks from WFO who were spearheading the effort. Web turned his back and fiddled with some of his gear when he saw Percy Bates appear from one of the Bucars and talk to Pritchard. Web didn't really need a run-in with Bates right now for a lot of reasons, the main one being he didn't know if he could trust himself not to punch the guy's lights out for not telling him about the assault. Bates was probably just trying to protect Web, maybe from himself, but Web would have preferred to make that decision on his own.

They drove to the last staging point and received a final set of orders. Now it was time to hit the road to the target. They moved quickly through the darkened rural roads. Hotel Team was in one Suburban and was approaching the Frees' compound from the rear, while Gulf was going in the left side. The topography would require the assault teams to navigate through the dark, dense woods. That wasn't really a problem, since they had night-vision optics. Just before the truck doors popped open, Romano crossed himself. Web almost said what he had always said to Danny Garcia, that God didn't come around here and that they were on their own, but he didn't. Yet he wished Romano hadn't done the sign of the cross. This was all beginning to seem way too familiar, and for the first time Web started to wonder if he was in any shape to participate in the assault. The doors popped open before he could think any more on this and they poured into the woods and then came to a stop, crouching and surveying the terrain ahead.

Through his bone mic Web listened as the snipers filled them in on what lay ahead. Web recognized Ken McCarthy's voice from X-Ray. McCarthy's call sign was Sierra One, meaning he held the snipers' highest observation post. He was probably straddling a thick branch of one of the big oaks that ringed the perimeter around the compound, Web figured. That would allow him to see

the entire area, get a good firing lane and provide maximum de-
filade, or position of cover and concealment. The Frees were definitely inside the compound. Most of them lived there, in fact. The
snipers had counted at least ten of them inside. There were four
buildings constituting the fenced compound. Three were living
quarters and one was a large warehouse-style building where the
men held their meetings and did whatever work they did while
there, such as making bombs and plotting how to kill innocent people, no doubt, thought Web. There were often dogs at outposts like
this. Canines were always a problem—not so much a personal danger to HRT members, since even the fiercest dog couldn't bite
through Kevlar or withstand a bullet, but they were terrific early
warning sentrics. Fortunately—thus far, at least—there were no
dogs here; maybe some of the Frees were allergic. The weaponry
they'd seen were mostly pistols and shotguns, although one young
lad of about seventeen, McCarthy said, was carrying an MP-5.

There were two sentries outside, one in the front and one in the
rear, armed with pistols only and bored expressions, McCarthy
wryly noted. As was customary with HRT, the sentries were given
identification names by the sniper that had first spotted them. The
guard in front was named Pale Shaq, because he bore a passing resemblance to the big basketball center but, of course, was white,
since the Frees were definitely not going to have persons of another
color around. The one in the rear was christened Gameboy, because
McCarthy had noted a Gameboy player sticking out of his front
pocket. The snipers had also observed that both sentries carried cell
phones that had a walkie-talkie feature. That posed a problem,
since they could quickly signal trouble to their confederates inside.

Hotel Team spread out and moved through the woods with great
caution. Over their flight suits they wore IR camouflage, green
smocks with visual patterns that broke up each man's night profile. Thus, even if the Frees had night-vision optics, they wouldn't
get a clean visual. Though the compound was not yet in sight, in
the dense foliage the Frees might have posted either additional
pickets or even booby traps that had escaped the eyes of the
snipers, unlikely as that might be. Web's NV goggles made night
into day, but he kept one eye closed still and assumed all the oth-

ers were doing the same thing to avoid the orange burn later. They hit another stop spot and Web pulled the goggles up and blinked quickly to reduce the effects of the high-tech optics. His head was already starting to hurt. On the actual assault Romano would be point man and Web would bring up the rear. Though Romano hadn't practiced this hit with the team, he was still the best assaulter they had. Web slid his hand down the short barrel of the MP-5 subgun he was carrying. He wasn't toting his usual SR75 rifle because, after using it in that courtyard, he had found he couldn't pick the damn thing up again. He first touched the .45 pistol in his tactical holster and next the twin gun riding in his cross-draw shoulder rig that hung across his trauma plate, and he smiled tightly when he saw Romano watching him do this and giving him a thumbs-up.

"Now we're bulletproof, big guy," said Romano. The man was probably still doing BTO turns in his head, thought Web.

Web's heartbeat was not yet at sixty-four and he was striving mightily to get it there. He rubbed his fingers against his palm and was surprised to feel sweat, for it was a chilly night. Yet sixty pounds of gear and body armor made for a nice little personal sauna. He had pistol mags hanging from his gun belt and spare MP-5 ammo in his thigh pads, along with flash bangs, slap charges and other goodies that he might or might not need tonight, you just never knew. Still, he hoped the sweat didn't signal nerves that could cause him to screw up right at the moment he needed to be perfect.

They moved forward again and neared the edge of the woods. Through his goggles Web could clearly make out the Frees' compound. To ensure that communications were short and that everyone was working off the same page, the first floor of a target, in HRT parlance, was always designated Alpha, the second, Bravo. The front of the building was white; the right, red; the left, green; and the rear, black. All the doors, windows and other openings was given sequential numbers beginning with the farthest port to the left. Thus Gameboy was stationed on the outside of the fence at roughly Alpha level black port three, while Pale Shaq was at Alpha level white port four. Web checked out Gameboy through his goggles and quickly summed the guy up as untrained as well as downright careless. The accuracy of this opinion was reinforced when the guy pulled the Gameboy from his pocket and actually started playing it.

There were lights on in the main building of the compound. The lights must have been powered by portable generators, because there were no overhead electrical lines evident. If there had been, HRT would have found the transformer supplying the power and shut it off just before the assault. Going from light to dark was disorienting and would have given HRT the slight edge it needed to prevail without loss of life.

Since there were only two assault teams, snipers were standing by to jump into their blacks, or Nomex flight suits, and help in the attack. Each sniper carried, in addition to his sniper rifle, a CAR-16 auto assault rifle with a three-power Litton night scope. The plan was to hit from the front and the side in blitzkrieg style and contain the Frees in the main building. At that point the regular FBI would come in, read rights, execute search warrants and the next stop for the Frees would be court and then prison.

There was just enough to make this interesting, thought Web. The Frees had to know that the FBI was watching them. This was a very rural area and word of strangers got around, and the Bureau had had them under surveillance for a while now. HRT had to assume that their chief weapon, the element of surprise, would at least be diminished in this case.

Having learned something from the Charlie Team debacle, they had brought along two very bulky but very powerful thermal imagers. Romano fired one up and performed a sweep of each building on their side of the compound. Gulf was doing the same from the front. This thermal imager could look through darkened glass and even walls and nail the heat-filled image of any person lurking there with a slingshot or a mini-gun. Romano completed his surveillance and gave the all-clear. No automated sniper nest this time. All buildings except the main one were empty. It might go very clean.

Through his NV goggles Web looked around and noted the lights winking through the jumble of trees. These light pulses represented snipers who were wearing fireflies, infrared glow plugs the size of a cigarette lighter. The flies would blink every two seconds in a light spectrum visible only with night optics. This way the snipers could keep in touch with one another without giving away their position. If a target was suspected of having night optics as well, the flies weren't used, for obvious reasons. Assaulters never used them. Each wink of light represented a friendly body with a .308 suppressed rifle backing him up. It was comforting when you weren't sure whether you were walking into an ice-cream parlor or a hornet's nest. Web assumed tonight that it would be the latter.

With a flick of his thumb, Web put the fire selector on his MP-5 to multiple-round bursts and then worked on getting his pulse rate down to the proper zone. There were the sounds of wildlife all around—squirrels, mostly—and birds flitting from tree limb to tree limb, disturbed by the men crouched in their space with all this fancy gear. The padding of animal paws and the flapping of bird wings was somehow comforting, if only to reassure Web that he was still on planet earth, still connected to living, breathing things, though he had potential killing on his mind.

The plan here was a little dicey. The snipers were not going to open fire on the sentries. Gunning down folks in cold blood who had yet to be convicted of anything was not something law enforcement types got to do very often; Web certainly never had. It would take a very high-stakes hostage situation to justify that sort of approval from Washington. The director and probably the attorney general would have to bless that sort of operation. Here they were going to flank the guards, jump them and make sure they had no time or opportunity to warn their comrades inside of the coming attack. The assaulters could have employed a diversionary explosive, or perhaps drawn the guards into the woods somehow to be met by assaulters in Ghillies waiting to jump them, but the flanking plan had been devised based on prior intelligence gathered on the Frees. That intel had proved correct in the careless nature of the sentries. It might just work, thought Web.

If the exterior breach points were locked, they would be blown, of course. That would warn the rest of the Frees, but by then HRT would be inside and the battle would pretty much be over, barring something extraordinary occurring, which Web could no longer rule out, ever again. Hotel was going to hit from the rear, Gulf from the side, in a very explosive way. Assault teams always tried to hit from angles, never front-back or side-side, to avoid friendly fire casualties.

Web tensed as Romano asked TOC for compromise authority and

quickly got it. Now Web took one last cleansing breath and assumed the total focus of an assaulter with one of the most elite law enforcement teams ever put together. Pulse at sixty-four, Web really did just know his body's inner workings.

Romano gave the high sign and he and Web went to the left and the other two operators slid to the right. A minute later they were on both flanks of Gameboy, who was still intent on his video screen, apparently having a great time whipping the computer's ass. By the time he looked up, there were .45 pistols stuck in both of his ears. Before he even had a chance to say, "Shit," he was down on the ground, Peerless cuffs around his hands and ankles, and a plastic chain strap tied the cuffs together so that he was fully immobilized like a tethered calf during a roping contest. At the same time a strip of adhesive was placed over his mouth. They took his pistol, cell phone and a knife they found in a sheath tied to his ankle. Web did leave the man his precious Gameboy.

They passed the living quarters of the group and moved to the crisis site, the exterior rear door of the main building, and crouched low. Romano touched the door gingerly, then grasped the door handle and tried it. Through his mask, Web could see him grimace. It was locked. Romano called up the breacher, who quickly moved forward, laid his four-hundred-grain flex linear charge, rolled out his cable and readied the detonator, while the rest of the team watched his back even as they took cover.

At that point Romano informed TOC that they were at phase line green and Web listened to TOC's confirmatory response. Thirty seconds later, members of Gulf did the same thing, so Web knew they had successfully bagged Pale Shaq out front and then gone to the side of the building for their very special assault. TOC stated that it had control, and the line rankled Web even more now than it had before. *Yeah, that's what you said to Charlie, wasn't it?*

Three snipers joined the Gulf boys on the side and Ken McCarthy had come down from his Sierra One position and become an instant assaulter, along with two other Whiskey snipers who joined Web and Hotel Team. When Ken saw Web, Web couldn't see the man's expression, but Web was sure it was a surprised one. They all took off their NV goggles, since muzzle flashes and explosives made them useless anyway and would actually leave you blind and defenseless in such a light-filled environment. From here on, everyone had to simply use their ordinary five senses, and that was okay by Web.

The countdown began. Web's heartbeat seemed to slow even more with each number. When TOC reached three, Web was fully in the zone. At the count of two, every HRT operator looked away from the crisis site so that the blast wouldn't blind them. At the same moment each man's fingers also slipped off his weapon's safety once more; and then index fingers slid to triggers. *Here we go, boys,* Web thought.

The charge blew and the doors fell inward and Web and company roared through.

"Banging," called out Romano as he drew a flash bang from his stretch cordura holder, pulled the pin and lobbed. Three seconds later a hundred-and-eighty-decibel explosion screamed through the hallway with a million-candlepower flash in its wake.

Web was to the right of Romano, looking for threats from any source, his gaze going first to distant corners, then pulling back. There was a small interior room with a hallway heading left off that. Their intelligence, confirmed by their thermal imagery, had told them that the Frees were gathered in the main room in the left rear of the building. It was a large space, maybe forty-by-forty, and mostly open, so they didn't have to worry about lots of nooks and crannies for resistance to hole up in, but it was still a large space to secure, and there would no doubt be furniture and other equipment to hide behind. They dropped off one guy to hold the room they had first entered. The rules of engagement were that you never gave back ground you had taken, and you never allowed yourself to be rear-flanked. The rest of the strike force raced on.

So far, they had seen no one, although there were shouts up ahead. Web and the rest of Hotel flew down the hallway. One more turn and they'd hit the double doors to the target space.

"Banging," yelled Web. He pulled the pin, lobbed the flash bang around this last turn. Now anybody looking to ambush them from up there would have to do so while blind and deaf.

When they reached the double doors, no one bothered to check whether they were locked. Romano quickly placed a slap charge on the doorjamb. The explosive consisted of a length of tire rubber one inch wide and six inches long with a strip of C4 explosive called a Detasheet. At the bottom of the device were a shock tube and a blasting cap. The men stood back, and Romano whispered into his mic. A few seconds went by and the slap charge blew and the doors collapsed inward.

At the exact same moment the side wall of the main room exploded inward and Gulf Team charged through the opening. They had placed a flex-linear charge—a V-shaped strip of lead and foam, loaded with explosives—around the wall. It had completely taken out the wall, throwing debris into the room. One of the Frees was already on the floor, holding his bloodied head and screaming.

Hotel charged in from the main doors and blitzed the danger zones that were basically any space where somebody with a gun could take cover and do HRT harm.

"Banging," called out Romano as he raced down the right side of the room. The flash bang explosion sounded seconds later. The room was filled with smoke and blinding light and the shouts and screams were deafening as the Frees fell over each other trying to escape. However, there were no shots and Web began to think that this might just end peacefully, at least by HRT standards. Web followed Romano, his gaze sweeping the area, looking to the farthest corners for threats and then reeling back. He saw both young and old men hiding under overturned chairs, prone on the floor or pushed against the walls, all covering their eyes and holding their ears, all of them stunned by the carefully crafted assault. The overhead lights had been shot out by HRT as soon as they entered the room. They were all operating in darkness now except for the occasional flash bang.

"FBI! On the floor. Hands behind your head. Fingers interlocked. Do it! *Now!* Or you're fucking dead!" Romano screamed all this out in a Brooklyn-accented, staccato roar.

That mouthful even got Web's attention.

Most of the Frees in Web's line of sight began to obey the instruction, semi-incapacitated as they were. That's when he heard the first shot. And that was followed by another shot that hit the wall right next to Web's head. From the corner of his eye Web saw a Free coming up from the floor holding an MP-5 and pointing it his way. Romano must have seen the same thing. They fired together, both their MP-5s on multiple-round bursts. All eight shots hit the man either in the head or torso and he and his gun went back down to the floor and stayed there.

The other Frees, blinded and disoriented but also angered by the death of one of their members, pulled their weapons and opened fire from behind whatever bulwarks they could find. HRT did the same. However, it was pistols, shotguns, flesh and overmatched men playing soldier against body armor, subguns and men trained for battle and killing. The gunfight did not last very long. The Frees foolishly looked at the eyes of their opponents. Web and his men calmly keyed on the hands and the weapons held there as they fired round after round, moving forward, staying on their marks. Aim-point red laser dots from the finders bolted to their subguns were directly on their targets. They maintained their fields of fire, shooting around and over each other as though they were performing a superbly choreographed dance. The frantic Frees shot wildly and with no discipline and missed badly. HRT aimed with precision and scored hit after hit. Twice HRT operators were shot, more out of luck than skill, but they were torso hits, ordinary pistol ammo running right into the latest-generation Kevlar; and while the impacts of the bullets stung like a bitch, the only result was a deep bruise. HRT aimed for the head and chest and each time a round impacted, another Free died.

With the rout clearly on, Web had had enough of this carnage and he flipped his MP-5 to full auto and raked the tops of the cheap tables and chairs, blowing chips of particle board and wood veneer and strips of metal into the air and filling the opposite walls with lead as his weapon threw out slugs at the rate of almost nine hundred a minute. HRT did not fire warning shots, but there was nothing in the manuals or in any other training Web had done that said you had to slaughter an outclassed enemy for no reason. The remaining Frees were no danger to anyone anymore; they just needed some extra persuasion to officially give up. Romano did likewise with spray from his gun. The resulting blizzard of destruction had the opposition flat on their bellies, hands over their heads, their thoughts of fighting and perhaps winning obviously gone. In unison Web and Romano slapped in fresh ten-millimeter ammo stacks with machinelike movements and speed.

They opened fire again, once more aiming just over the heads of the cowering enemy, and poured it on until the last of the Frees still alive finally made the only sensible choice. Two crawled out from the debris of dead bodies and destroyed chairs and tables, their hands in the air, their weapons on the floor. They looked shell-shocked and were sobbing. Another Free just sat there staring at his hands, bloody from touching a large, seeping wound on his leg, and there was vomit on his shirt. An operator went over to him, cuffed him and then laid him gently back, slapped on surgical gloves and mask and started ministering to the wound; a gunman suddenly turned lifesaver of his enemy. Paramedics were called up from the medic truck that accompanied every HRT assault to tend to the wounded. The guy would probably live, Web concluded, after checking out the bloody leg, if only to spend the rest of his life in prison.

As Romano and another assaulter cuffed the first two Frees to surrender, several other operators went quickly around the room making sure that the dead actually were. The men on the floor were just bodies now, Web felt certain. Humans were not built to withstand one shot to the head, much less half a dozen.

Web finally lowered his gun and took a deep breath. He surveyed the battlefield, looked over the survivors. Some didn't even appear old enough to drive, dressed in oversized farm jeans, T-shirts and dirty boots. One of them had a peach-fuzz goatee; another even had acne. Two of the dead men looked old enough to be grandfathers and maybe had recruited their grandsons to join the Frees; and die as one. They hardly qualified as worthy opponents. They were just a bunch of stupid people with guns and screwed-up lives who had run into the realization of their worst nightmares and foolishly chosen the wrong course of action. Web counted eight dead bodies, the blood flowing thick and absorbing fast into the cheap carpet. And, though the Frees would contest it, all blood, re-

gardless of ethnic or racial background, flowed red out of the body.
At that level, everybody was the same.

He leaned against the wall even as he heard the sirens coming.
It hadn't been a fair fight. Yet it had not been a fair fight last time
either. A part of him should have at least felt some level of satisfaction. However, the only thing Web London felt was sick to his
stomach. Killing was never an easy business and maybe that's
what separated him from men like the Ernest B. Frees of the
world.

Romano came up to him. "Where the hell did those shots come
from?"

Web just shook his head.

"Well, shit," said Romano, "it ain't exactly how I figured this going down."

Web noted the large bullet hole in Romano's cammie smock that
revealed the Kevlar underneath. The hole was near his belly button. Romano followed Web's gaze and shrugged it off like it was a
mosquito bite.

"Another inch lower and Angie'd have to get her kicks somewhere else," said Romano.

Web struggled to recall exactly what he had seen and what he
had heard and exactly when. Web knew one thing for certain:
they were all in for a lot of questions and none of those questions
held easy answers. Pritchard's warning came hurtling back to
him. They had just annihilated numerous members of the Frees,
the group suspected of wiping out a team of HRT. What Web and
the others had really done was open fire and wasted a bunch of
young boys and old men because shots had come from a source
they weren't sure of and because Web had seen one of them lifting up his gun and pointing it his way. Web was completely justified in doing what he did, but it wouldn't take a master spin
doctor to whip that set of facts into something that smelled to
high heaven. And in Washington, D.C., they had more spinmeis-
ters per capita than anywhere else on the planet.

Web could hear feet pounding toward them. The regulars would
be showing up soon, the Bates's of the world. They would take
over the task of figuring out what the hell had happened. Like Ro-

mano had said, HRT was just in the business of banging and hanging. Well, they just might have hung themselves this time. Web started to feel something he never had when the bullets were flying: fear.

There was movement over a thousand yards away in the woods to the rear of the compound and behind the perimeter set up by HRT. The ground seemed to rise up and a man crouched there, his sniper rifle with attached scope held in his right hand. It was the same rifle he had used to kill Chris Miller outside Randall Cove's house in Fredericksburg. The FBI probably thought that Web London had been the target, but they would be wrong. Miller's death was just another way to bring further misery to Web London. And what the man had just done, instigating the fight between the hapless Frees and HRT, was simply another method of adding to London's mounting troubles. The man laid aside the cloth that was covered with dirt, mud, animal feces, leaves and other things designed to help him blend in with the surroundings, his very own Ghillie suit. He had long ago concluded that one should only copy from the best. And, at least for now, HRT was the best. And Web London was supposed to be the best of this elite group. That distinction put him squarely in the man's sights. This was personal to him. Very personal. He folded the material and hooked it to his backpack, and Clyde Macy quietly made his escape. Despite his normally stoic nature, the man just had to smile. Mission accomplished.

44

Since he hadn't been able to get a handle on the origin of the group supplying Oxy and other prescription drugs to the D.C. area, Randall Cove had changed strategies and decided to hit it from the receiving instead of the supply end. He had used what the informant T had told him to latch on to a drug crew, who T had told him had lately been dealing these narcotics. It was amazing the results you could get from a snitch when you held him upside down over a hundred-foot drop. Cove figured at some point they would have to pick up more of the product. This new tactic had brought him here tonight, and he hoped it would produce some huge dividends.

The woods were thick and Cove moved through them as quietly as a human being was equipped to do. He stopped near the tree line, squatted low and surveyed the terrain. The vehicles were parked on a dirt road that snaked through these woods near the Kentucky–West Virginia border. If Cove had had any backup to call, he would have. He had thought about bringing Venables, but Sonny had done enough and he also had a wife and kids and was getting ready to retire. Cove was not going to mess with that. Cove was a brave man, well used to being in dangerous situations, but still there was a fine line between courage and idiocy and Cove had always kept on the right side of that flimsy divider.

Cove ducked down as several men gathered around one of the vehicles. He slipped out his NV monocular for a closer look. The plastic-wrapped items the men were carrying confirmed Cove's suspicions. Not coke bricks but what looked to be tens of thousands of pills. He pulled his flashless camera and took some pictures, and then Cove debated what to do next. There were at least five men that he could see, and all of them were armed. He couldn't really execute an arrest without putting himself in serious jeopardy. While he was contemplating his next act, Cove didn't notice, but the wind changed slightly. He didn't realize it, in fact, until the dog that had been lying on the other side of the truck, and out of Cove's line of sight, came tearing around the vehicle and directly at his position.

Cove swore under his breath, turned and fled through the woods. The dog was gaining, though, with each step, and Cove's battered knees just weren't up to this anymore. And he heard something else that didn't provide him with much hope either. There were two-legged animals coming his way.

They cornered him in a swampy section of earth. The dog came at Cove, fangs bared, and Cove aimed his pistol and shot it dead. That was the last time he would fire, as an array of pistols were leveled at him. He put his gun up in the air in surrender.

"Drop it," said one of the pursuers, and Cove dropped it.

The men came forward and one of them frisked Cove and found the other gun he kept stashed in his coat sleeve and also took his camera.

Nemo Strait knelt next to the dog and touched it gently. Then he looked up at Cove like the man had just slit his mother's throat. Strait raised his pistol and stepped forward.

"I had Old Cuss for six years. Damn good dog."

Cove said nothing. Another man punched him in the back with his gun but only got a grunt from Cove.

Strait drew closer and spit in Cove's face. "Damn me for not making sure you were dead when we shoved your car down that slope. You should've just called that your luckiest day on earth and got yourself out of town."

Cove said nothing, but he took one tiny step closer to Strait. He glanced at some of the other men. The buyers of those prescription drugs were from the city and all were black. Cove didn't look to his own race for help here. Money trumped everything else in the criminal world.

Strait looked over his shoulder, toward where the horse trailer with Bobby Lee was, and then looked back at his prisoner and smiled.

"Man, you always got to be in other people's business? Huh?" He tapped his gun against Cove's cheek and then slapped it hard with the metal. "Answer me when I ask you a question."

Cove's response was to spit in the man's face.

Strait wiped off his face and put his gun against Cove's temple. "You can just kiss your ass good-bye."

The knife came out of the same sleeve that Cove's second gun had. He had never had anyone check for weapons in the same spot where one had already been found. He aimed for the heart, but Cove's foot slipped in the mud, and Strait was a bit quicker than Cove had anticipated, and the knife plunged deeply into Strait's shoulder. Strait fell back into the swampy water, the knife still in his shoulder.

Cove stood there staring at the men surrounding him.

For a split second every sound in the world seemed to stop for Cove. In his mind he could see his wife and children running to him from across a field of nothing but beautiful flowers, and their smiles and anticipated hugs carried away every foul thing that had ever happened to him in his whole life. And there was a great deal to wash away.

And then the guns opened fire. Cove was struck several times and went down. At the same instant all the men looked to the sky because they could hear the drone of a chopper. Seconds later, lights appeared over the treetops.

Strait jumped up. "Let's get the hell out of here."

Even with his injury, the powerful Strait was able to cradle his dead dog and carry it off. In less than a minute the place was empty. The chopper soared on, its crew apparently unaware of what had happened down below. Strait had been wrong—the chopper was merely ferrying a group of businessmen back from a very late meeting.

As the sounds of the night resumed, there came a groan out of the darkness. Randall Cove tried to get up, but as strong as he was, he couldn't make it. The body armor he was wearing had absorbed three of the five shots. The two shots that had hit him directly had taken their toll though. He dropped back to the ground as his blood turned the water red.

Claire Daniels was in her office, working very late. The outer door was locked and the building had security, so she actually felt safer here than at the hotel where she was staying. Her pharmacist friend had gotten back to her on the odd looking pill that she had taken from Web. Claire had assumed it was some powerful barbiturate because she still thought it possible that a bad drug interaction with a delayed effect had incapacitated Web in that alley. At some level it might seem far-fetched, but it did cover the facts as she knew them, and right now nothing else came close. The phone call had changed all that.

"It's a placebo," her friend had told her. "Like they use for control groups in drug tests."

A placebo? Claire was stunned. All the other pills were what they had appeared to be.

As she sat in her office now, Claire tried to figure it all out. If it wasn't a drug interaction, what could it be? She refused to believe that Kevin Westbrook had placed a curse on Web with the words "damn to hell." And yet, clearly, the words had had an effect on him. Had he just cracked?

Claire looked at some of Kevin's sketchbooks that Web had allowed her to keep. The one with Kevin pointing the remote control had gone right to the FBI, and there were no other drawings like that in any of the other sketchbooks. Claire studied the drawings she had, many of them quite expertly done. The boy had considerable artistic talent.

Nowhere in the sketchbooks were the words "damn to hell" written. It couldn't be that easy, Claire supposed. She wondered again about the words. Old-sounding—Civil War, maybe before. "Damn the torpedoes, full steam ahead," or something like that Admiral Farragut had reportedly said during a naval battle in the War Between the States.

Claire wrote the words on a piece of paper. Civil War–era, Web had thought. Slavery. Black and white. White supremacists. Her brow wrinkled as she thought about it, but then it dawned upon her. Yet Claire's next thought was that it couldn't be.

The Free Society? Damn to hell. She looked at her computer. It was just possible. A few clicks of the mouse and a few minutes gave her the answer. The Free Society had a website. A disgusting, hate-filled propaganda tool that they presumably used to recruit the ignorant and demonic into their ranks. When she saw it, the breath froze in her throat.

At that very moment her office went completely dark. The timing of the blackout coupled with what she had just learned caused her to cry out. She immediately picked up the phone and called the front security desk.

The reassuring voice of the guard came on the line and she explained what had happened. "It's not the building, Dr. Daniels. We've got lights down here. Probably a tripped circuit breaker. You want me to come up?"

She looked out her window and saw that surrounding buildings were also lit. "No, that's all right. I think I've got a flashlight. If it's just that, I can turn it back on."

She hung up, rummaged through her desk and finally found a flashlight, then felt here way out of her office and into the darkened reception area. She made her way to the closet where the power box was and turned the handle. It was locked. That was a little strange, she thought, but then she remembered that the closet also housed the phone and security system lines for the office, and those lines needed to be protected from interference. But how was she supposed to trip the breaker back, then? She contemplated packing up and going to the hotel, but all of her notes were here and she didn't have a laptop computer on which she could access the Internet from the hotel.

She shone the light on the lock. It looked pretty simple. She went into the small kitchen and found a screwdriver. She went back to the door, held the light under her armpit and worked on the lock. It took about five minutes, and resulting from more luck than skill, the lock finally gave and she opened the door. She shone the light inside and looked around. She quickly found the power

box, and the main circuit had indeed tripped. She popped it back
and the lights came on. She was about to close the door when
something caught her attention. A small device was wired into the
power lines that ran up the wall. Claire didn't know much about
such things, but it still looked out of place to her, almost like a bug.

Perhaps it was because of what she had just discovered, or that
she had suddenly become unduly paranoid, but in a flash it hit her.
She raced from the room, never noticing the tiny wireless trip button on the doorjamb that was activated whenever someone opened
the door to the power closet.

She ran to her office and looked around. Her gaze went from
floor to walls and finally to the ceiling and stopped. She grabbed
her desk chair, slipped off her shoes and stood on the chair to reach
the smoke detector. She had been working with law enforcement
folks for enough years to know that smoke detectors were favorite
places to house listening devices. She pulled the piece off the ceiling, and there appeared to be wiring there that shouldn't have
been. Was it only her office, or were others bugged as well?

She left the detector dangling from the ceiling, jumped off the
chair and ran to the office next to hers, which was O'Bannon's. It
was locked; however, it was the same lock as on the power closet.
Using the screwdriver, she was able once again to pop it. She went
in, flicked on the light and looked up. There was another smoke detector. She ripped it down and found the same suspicious wiring.
She was about to race to another office when she saw the open file
on the desk.

It went against all of her professional instincts to examine a colleague's files, but the circumstances were particularly extenuating,
she told herself.

She picked up the file. The name on it was Deborah Riner. Web
had mentioned her, the widow of one of the men from his team.
She ran her gaze through the many pages. Riner had been coming
to see O'Bannon for quite some time and at frequent intervals.
What surprised Claire was the number of notations for hypnosis
sessions that they had engaged in. O'Bannon had hypnotized the
woman almost every time she had come to see him.

Something truly awful dawned on Claire as she noted some of

the dates that Riner had come in. Three days before the slaughter of Web's team in the courtyard had occurred was one date that popped out at Claire.

She put the papers down and went over to the filing cabinet. It was locked too, yet cheaply constructed, and she quickly levered it open with the screwdriver, no longer caring about professional etiquette. She started pulling out files. There were many agents and spouses of FBI agents represented in here from many parts of the Bureau. She scanned some of the files. Like Riner's, they involved an inordinate number of hypnosis sessions.

Claire's thoughts raced. Hypnosis was a funny thing. You could, in very rare circumstances, use it to get someone to do something he or she ordinarily wouldn't do. But what you also could do was put a person under, get him or her relaxed and comfortable and trusting and then subtly pry information on what this person as agent was doing—or, in the cases of a spouse of the agent, what the husband or wife was doing. Claire could envision O'Bannon coaxing out from a hypnotized and vulnerable and perhaps distressed Debbie Riner whatever details she knew of her husband's work. Including what target was going to be visited by HRT and exactly when, if Teddy Riner shared that with his wife. And some men would, despite professional rules that prohibited it. Many marriages, Claire knew, trumped all such policies, if just to keep domestic peace. Or it could be as simple as a slip of the tongue by one of the HRT men, which a hypnotized wife would then unwittingly pass on.

It would all be fairly simple for someone as experienced as Ed O'Bannon. And, as she had done with Web, O'Bannon could always give a carefully crafted posthypnotic suggestion that would swab away from the person's memory anything suspicious that might have occurred during hypnosis—even the fact that they had been hypnotized at all. *My God,* Claire thought, *Debbie Riner might have unwittingly aided in her husband's murder.*

And on top of that, the listening devices recorded all of the confidential information that was given by the patients who came here. Valuable information that could later be used to blackmail them or set others up, as Web's team had been. Without going into detail, Web had mentioned that things were going wrong at the Bureau. If Claire was right about what O'Bannon was doing the psychiatrist could be behind many of these problems.

As she stared at the file cabinet, Claire's gaze settled on something that wasn't there. Under the letter *L* there were several files for people with a last name that started with that letter. But there was a large and empty hanging file. Claire wondered if that was where Web's file had been. Yet the one O'Bannon had given her wasn't nearly as large as the space she was looking at, unless he had not given her the whole file. Would the man have kept part of the file away from her? O'Bannon was a supremely confident, even arrogant man, she knew. In his mind no one was smarter or more experienced. It was just possible he was withholding information to keep her in the dark. Perhaps he had had an even more powerful reason, beyond professional vanity, to keep Web as a patient.

She immediately started scouring the office. She worked through the man's desk and any other space where the missing information could be hidden and found nothing. Then she looked up once more. The ceiling was a drop-down. She climbed on the chair again, holding her flashlight, and popped up one of the ceiling panels. On her tiptoes she could see above the ceiling. She shone her light around and almost immediately saw a small box that had been placed on the metal framework holding up the ceiling. She moved her chair over there and quickly pulled the box down. Inside was the rest of Web's file, and as she sat down to examine it she discovered it was a treasure trove. Claire kept shaking her head as each new page held a stunning revelation.

O'Bannon, she knew, was organized to the point of obsession, something the two had laughed about before. And he kept meticulous notes. Those notes, though cryptic and indecipherable to a layperson, revealed to Claire that he had hypnotized Web numerous times, even more than Debbie Riner, when Web had come to him after his mother's death. Each time O'Bannon had employed a posthypnotic suggestion, much as Claire had done, to suppress the session from Web's consciousness. Claire jolted upright as she discovered that during one of the hypnotic sessions, Web had revealed to O'Bannon the entire episode about his stepfather's death. The notes were almost in code, but Claire saw references to "Stockton," "attic" and "DADDY DEAREST" written in all caps, enough to convince her that O'Bannon had gotten the same story she had from Web. Now Web's shouting at her during the hypnotic session, "You already know this!" made complete sense. His subconscious *had* revealed it all once, only to O'Bannon and not to her. The use of the placebos was also discussed in the notes. Claire figured they were probably to gauge how firmly O'Bannon had insinuated his commands into Web's subconscious. And in fact, as she read further, O'Bannon had noted that the placebo had been coupled with his hypnotic suggestion to Web that these were the most powerful sleeping pills on the market, and Web had duly reported that the pills were working. Web had also told O'Bannon about the contest among HRT members with the Taser guns.

The truth of what had happened to Web in that alley finally hit her. It was ingenious, she thought, because it didn't have the problematic issue of making Web do something he didn't want to do, like kill someone in cold blood, which Claire did not believe was possible, but rather commanded Web *not* to do something.

She contemplated calling Web to tell him what she had figured out and to enlist his help, but she couldn't from here, not with all the listening devices around. She would have to leave the office and call him.

She continued leafing through the material. The cruelest aspect of this doctor-patient relationship was revealed on the very last page, and showed that O'Bannon had built in a level of certainty that Web would perform as instructed. O'Bannon had written in his cryptic manner that he had established an excellent rapport of trust with Web. And O'Bannon had noted that a psychiatrist (O'Bannon wisely was not claiming to have done so himself) could build into his hypnotic suggestion that he was a father figure to a patient such as Web and would protect him against his stepfather. And that if Web failed to carry out the psychiatrist's commands, then the stepfather would come back and kill Web; in effect, his only safety lay in doing exactly as he was instructed. O'Bannon had concluded that Web would make an excellent candidate for posthypnotic suggestion, and thus posed a security risk. It was only Claire's special knowledge and her familiarity with Web's case that allowed her to read between the lines of O'Bannon's report. Claire, with her clear understanding of Web's psychological makeup, knew it would have been impossible for Web to counteract that command. And yet, with all that, Web had still managed to temporarily overcome the posthypnotic suggestion, go into that courtyard and fire at those guns, despite a potent mental barrage telling him not to. That had to have been Web's most remarkable performance of the night.

Claire had to concede that O'Bannon had written his report very craftily and was obviously covering his tracks, another reason for her to be careful. O'Bannon had foreseen just about every contingency, except for Claire's treating Web, finding out for herself what O'Bannon already had from plumbing the depths of Web's subconscious, and now her discovering both the bugs and this file. No wonder O'Bannon had tried so hard to keep Web as his patient.

It was time to call in the people who knew how to handle these things. She was way out of her league.

Claire turned to go back to her office, to grab her things and leave. The man was standing there watching her. She held up her screwdriver, but he pointed a gun at her.

And Ed O'Bannon looked as though he would have no problem using it.

45

Back at Quantico, Web put away his gear and gave his debriefing along with the rest of the crew. They couldn't explain much. Web believed the shots could have come from outside the building. If so, those bullets would have to be in the room somewhere, though there were lots of slugs embedded in the walls that would have to be sorted through and matched to their respective weapons. The snipers were being debriefed as well, but Web didn't know what they had seen or heard. If the shots had come from outside, then the snipers must have noticed something; they had the place pretty much surrounded. No one had come out of the building, so far as Web knew. Yet if the shots had originated from outside, the shooter was already there when HRT had shown up—and that, once more, meant a probable leak of HRT's assault. None of it was good news.

WFO was combing though the compound looking for additional clues further linking the Frees to the hit on Charlie Team. Web hoped they could find enough to explain it all, though he doubted they could. How could you explain young kids and old men with that much hate in their hearts?

Showered and changed, Web and Romano were walking down the hallway of the admin building to leave when Bates appeared in front of them, motioned them to follow him into an empty office.

"I guess I'm bad luck, Perce," said Web, only half jokingly. He really was wondering if he was suddenly jinxed somehow.

Romano piped up. "No, really bad luck would've had us losing guys, not them. I'm never going to apologize for walking out of a place alive. Like flying a plane, man, any landing is a good landing."

"Both of you shut up," said Bates, and they did. "The press will rip us on this, but we can handle it," the man said. "What I can't handle are two guys disobeying orders."

"They were short-handed, Perce," said Web, "and I can't believe you never told me. I was the one who put you on to that camera."

Bates got right in his face. "I didn't tell you, Web, precisely to prevent what did happen from happening."

Web didn't back down an inch. "Whether I was there or not, the result would've been the same. If you get shot at, you shoot back. And I wasn't going to let my guys go in weak. You can run me out of the Bureau if you want, but I'd do the same damn thing again."

Both men stared at each other until their features grew calmer.

Bates sat down and shook his head. He looked up at the men and motioned them to sit too. "What the hell," said Bates, "it can't get any worse, so why should I worry?"

"If you were so concerned about something like this happening, why didn't you send a SWAT team instead?" asked Web.

"It wasn't my call. Orders came from higher up."

"How high up?"

"That's not your concern."

"It is if my ass is going to be in the ringer over this."

Bates just stubbornly shook his head.

"If the shots came from outside, somebody knew we were hitting the place," said Romano.

"That's brilliant, Romano, remind me to put you in for a promotion," snapped Bates.

"Leaks can come from anywhere," said Web, "from the bottom up or the top down, right, Perce?"

"Stow it, Web."

"Is there anything you can tell us, then?"

"Actually, the night wasn't a total waste." He turned and opened a file on the desk behind him. "Found some interesting stuff on the Frees. Silas Free was among the dead. And with him were several gents in their sixties and four men who weren't old enough to vote yet. I guess the Frees had really fallen out of favor after the school shooting—recruiting problems."

"But no Ernest B. Free," said Web. "I checked."

"No. No Ernie." Bates pulled some papers out of the file. "But hidden in a space in the floor of one of the houses we did find a quantity of bomb-making materials and three intelligence files on Judge Leadbetter, Scott Wingo and Fred Watkins."

"Pretty clean trail," said Romano.

"And that's not all. We also found Oxycontin, Percocet and Percodan with a street value of about ten thousand dollars."

Web looked surprised. "The Frees working the black market for prescription drugs?"

"Membership down, probably funds running low. Oxy is a big-time moneymaker in rural areas. It makes sense," said Bates.

"Damn, do you think that's the tie-in to what Cove was investigating? Frees set up a bogus drug op center in D.C., snooker Cove and HRT gets called in and then wiped out."

Bates was already nodding. "And maybe they're the ones putting the muscle on Westbrook and the other drug crews to get them to combine," added Bates.

Though Web also nodded his head in agreement at this, something just didn't feel right.

"We also found this," continued Bates. "A roster of past and present members of the Free Society." He looked at Web. "Want to take a guess who was once a Free?"

Web shook his head. "I'm too tired to think. Tell me."

"Clyde Macy."

Web forgot all about Oxycontin. "You're kidding me."

"From ten years ago, until about two months after the shooting in Richmond. The Frees kept good records; maybe to use as black-mail on ex-members later when their cash flow ran low. KKK probably does something like that."

"Macy a Free, and then he jumps to being muscle for a black guy in ghetto D.C. Epiphany, or the man just looking for work where he can get it?"

"Don't know. And we've now lost track of him. And of course there's the other body."

"What other body?"

"Antoine Peebles. Gunshot wound to the head. We found him last night."

"You think Westbrook was behind it?"

"It makes sense, though nothing in this case has made sense so far."

Web debated whether to tell Bates about Claire's run-in with someone impersonating Big F but then finally decided against it. Web didn't think the giant had been behind Peebles's death. But he had no reason to help Big F, and he might just confuse things by telling Bates.

Web held out his hand for the file. "Mind if I take a look?"

Bates stared at him for a long moment. "Sure. But if you see anything that hits you funny, I'd appreciate knowing about it before you walk out of this office."

While Romano stepped out of the room to speak to another Hotel Team member who passed by, Web turned through the pages. There was a posed photo of a younger Clyde Macy in combat garb holding a machine gun in one hand and a shotgun in the other and with a scowl that would probably scare off bears. As he read through the file, Web saw the speeding tickets Macy had gotten and that Bates had mentioned earlier. He glanced at the tickets and looked up. "A guy like this, and all he's got are speeding tickets?"

"Hey, such is life. He's one lucky or careful bastard or both," said Bates.

"How about the rental truck that the machine guns came off?"

"Silas Free *did* rent it. We checked with the rental agency. They remembered him. But about a week after he rented it, he filed a stolen vehicle report."

"Pretty convenient," said Web.

"No, it's SOP for people plotting some serious stuff. Rent the vehicle and then say it was stolen. And you hide it somewhere and fill it full of explosives or, in this case, machine guns."

"The rental truck is direct evidence of the Frees' connection to what happened to Charlie Team," said Web.

"And after last night, we are going to need it," commented Bates ominously.

The next thing Web turned to made his mouth go dry. He looked up at Bates and showed him the pages. "What's this?"

"Oh, that's real cute. That's the Frees' newsletter. I guess they want to keep members informed on their various murders and mayhem. It's a fairly recent thing, because I'd never heard of it before. They even have a website now, if you can believe it."

Web didn't hear Bates's remark. He just stared at the name of the newsletter emblazoned across the top of the front page.

Damn to Hell. That was the name of the Free Society's newsletter. And they were also the exact words Kevin Westbrook had spoken to him in the alley.

Web and Romano walked over to the 'Vette. Web was still deep in thought over what he had learned. It was all so murky, though, like the edges of a nightmare. You knew something formidable was lurking nearby, yet you couldn't get a comfortable handle on it.

Web stowed his gear in the 'Vette and started to climb in the passenger side.

Romano was looking at him with an expression that was probably as close to sympathy as the man ever got. "Hey, Web, you know, all the years we've been working together I've never once let you drive this thing."

Web looked confused. "What?"

"How about you drive us back to the farm? Trust me, when you're feeling shitty, there's nothing like a ride in this machine to get you back."

"Thanks, Paulie, but I don't think so."

In response, Romano tossed the keys to Web, who caught them. "It's like a bottle of great wine, Web, you have to sit back and just let the experience happen." Romano climbed in the passenger side and looked at him. "You don't keep a beautiful woman waiting, Web."

"Don't tell me you gave this thing a name too, like your guns."

"Just get in." He winked at Web and added, "If you think you're man enough."

They drove out to the main road. Before they hit the highway,

Romano said, "Okay, rule number one, you get one scratch on her and your ass is mine."

"You'd think after eight years of jumping out of choppers with me in the middle of the night with explosives tied to our butts that you'd trust me to drive your stupid car."

"Rule number two, you call her a stupid car again and I'll break your face. Her name is Destiny."

"Destiny?"

"Destiny."

When they reached Interstate 95, Web headed south and passed a state trooper writing a ticket. The hour was still early enough and they were heading against traffic, so they were pretty much alone.

"Okay, we got some breathing space now and a long straight-away. So punch it now or forever hold your gonads," said Romano.

Web glanced at him and then hit the accelerator. The car roared to a hundred so fast Web could feel himself being held against the seat by the force of the acceleration. They flew past the only other car on the road as if it had been parked. "Not bad, Paulie, and I've only got it halfway to the floor. Let's see what it really can do."

Web punched the gas again and the car rocketed even faster. They were now coming up to a curve in the highway. From the corner of his eye Web watched Romano. The guy looked calmly ahead, as though he drove this fast every day. Hell, maybe he did. Web cranked the car to a hundred and thirty and then a hundred and forty. The trees on either side were one green blur and the curve was directly ahead. There was no way Web could navigate it at this speed. Web glanced at Romano again and he saw a small bead of sweat appear on the man's forehead. That alone was worth about ten million bucks.

They were two seconds from kissing a wall of pines.

"Okay, okay," said Romano, "slow the damn thing down."

"You mean slow Destiny down?"

"Just do it!"

Web hit the brakes and they soared around the long curve at a mere eighty miles an hour.

"Slow it down some more, I just changed the oil."

"I'll bet Destiny loved you being inside her. Was it good for you too?" Web cut it to seventy, found an exit and they pulled in front of a diner. Inside, they ordered coffee.

As the waitress walked off, Web leaned forward. "I hope you're prepared for the heat we're going to take about the Frees." Romano shrugged but said nothing. "It's going to come, you know."

"Let it. Those pricks had it coming. Wasting Charlie."

"They haven't been convicted yet, Paulie."

"The brass at the Bureau wouldn't have authorized the hit unless they were damn sure they knew those punks had done it." He added in a less confident tone, "At least I sure as hell hope so."

Web leaned back. "What's bothering me about this whole scenario is the fact that we're expected to believe that the guys we just wiped out were sophisticated enough to put together an automated sniper nest using mini-guns stolen from the Army and they did it so well that nobody saw it coming. And on top of that, they murdered a judge, prosecutor and attorney using cutting-edge bomb materials and came within a whisker of taking out Billy Canfield and you and me as well? And now they're supposed to be orchestrating a large-scale drug operation that's reached into the District? And this is supposed to be revenge for something that happened years ago? Hell, most of the guys we just shot were still in sixth grade back when Ernie and his buddies hit that school. Their stupid sentries were playing video games and they had one subgun in the whole group. This shit does not compute, Paulie, or am I missing something?"

"No, it doesn't add up," he agreed. "But you got direct evidence, Web, enough to go to court with and win. And who gives a shit about the Frees? They're scum."

"That's right. Who cares about the Frees? They make a perfect patsy. And everybody's figuring they busted Ernest Free out of a maximum-security prison two thousand miles from here, but he wasn't in that compound. And I'm thinking those losers would have as much chance of knocking over the White House as they would getting Ernie out of jail."

Romano stared at Web. "Okay, you've got my attention. What are you thinking?"

"I'm thinking why a real tough street-drug dealer would bother to tell me about those tunnels. And I'm also wondering why a truck registered to Silas B. Free and later reported stolen is videotaped at the exact spot where we think the guns are going in once we know about the tunnels. You didn't hear Bates say that because you had stepped out of the room. Maybe Silas was telling the truth. Maybe the truck *was* stolen. But you're right, it's connect-the-dots time, everything seems to fit. That may be nice and clean from a prosecutor's point of view, but I don't think even old Silas was that stupid, and I don't think my good buddy Francis Westbrook is that charitable." Web looked out the dirty window of the diner as sunlight started to stream in. Wouldn't it be nice if things could clear up so pristinely in his head? He looked back at Romano. "Were you born with a silver spoon in your mouth, Paulie?"

"Yeah, right, one of ten kids in tenement housing in Brooklyn? Hell, I had my own butler."

"Well, I wasn't born with one either, but my gut tells me we were just spoonfed the sweetest damn concoction you ever saw and we swallowed every drop. I think somebody wanted the Frees wiped out, and we just did it for them."

46

When they got back to East Winds, Web called Claire on her cell phone, but she didn't answer. He tried her at work and got no answer. Web called the hotel where she was staying. No luck there either. He put the phone down, not liking any of that one bit. He mulled whether to go to the hotel or not. She might simply be in the shower. He decided to try later.

The next thing he and Romano did was something neither of them could avoid: They grabbed a few hours of sleep. After that they drove up to the main house and relieved the agents patrolling there. Gwen met them at the door, her face pale.

"We've seen the news," she said. She led them inside to a sitting room off the main hallway.

"Where's Billy?" asked Web.

"Upstairs. He's just been lying in the bed. He hadn't seen that tape in years. I didn't even know it was on the damn shelf." Web could see that her face was damp with tears.

"It was my fault, Gwen, I don't know what the hell I was thinking, playing that tape in your house."

"It didn't matter, Web, it was bound to happen sometime."

"Is there anything we can do?"

"You've damn well done enough."

They all turned and looked at the doorway, where Billy stood in old jeans, bare feet, with his shirttail hanging out. His hair was in disarray and he basically looked like hell, observed Web. Billy lit up a cigarette and cupped his hand for an ashtray as he came forward. Web noted that Gwen made no move to stop him from smoking.

He sat down across from the two men, his piercing eyes watching them from behind the drifts of smoke. Web could smell the alcohol from where he stood and assumed Gwen could too. She rose from her chair to go to her husband, but he motioned her back down.

"We saw the TV," said Billy.

"That's what Gwen said," replied Web.

Billy squinted at him, as though he were having trouble seeing over the one foot that separated them. "You killed them all?"

"Not all. Most." Web kept his gaze on the man. Part of him thought Billy might toast the demise of the Frees, and part of him thought the man might throw him and Romano out for leaving any of them alive.

"How'd it feel?"

"Billy!" said Gwen. "You have no right to ask that. We're talking about people being killed."

"I know all about people being killed, honey," said Billy as he shot her a smile that had nothing in it. He looked back at Web, awaiting an answer.

"It felt like shit. It always feels like shit. Most of them were high school age or grandfathers."

"My son was ten." He said this without emotion, just stating it as a clear, indisputable fact.

"I know that."

"But I hear what you're saying. It ain't easy killing somebody, unless you're way screwed up to begin with. It's only hard for the good guys." He pointed at Web and then at Romano. "For men like you."

Gwen swiftly went to her husband before he could stop her again. She put an arm around his shoulders. "Let's go back upstairs."

Billy ignored her. "TV says old Ernest B. Free wasn't among the dead. That right?"

Web nodded and Billy smiled. "Sumbitch's luck just keeps holding, doesn't it?"

"Looks that way. But if he was planning to come home to his little group, he'll have to find somewhere else to live."

Billy considered this. "Well, that's something." He looked at Gwen. "Where's Strait?"

Gwen seemed very relieved by the change in subject. "On his

way back from the sale. He'll be here tonight. He called from the road. It went really well. Every yearling sold and we got the price we wanted on every one."

"Well, damn, that's something to celebrate." He eyed Web and Romano. "You fellows want to celebrate? I tell you what, we'll wait until old Nemo gets back tonight and then we'll have us a little party right here. What do you say?"

"I doubt that they feel much like celebrating, Billy," said Gwen.

"Well, I sure as hell do. We got yearlings sold, Frees dead and we got to give Web and Paul here a going-away party, 'cause with those boys dead, we don't need protection anymore, do we? Y'all can pack up and get out right now," he said in a loud voice.

"Billy, please," said Gwen.

Web was about to say that the jury was still out on Gwen and Billy being safe, but he stopped himself. "I tell you what, Billy, you let us stay on a couple more days and we'll come to your party tonight."

Gwen looked at him in astonishment while Billy merely nodded and grinned, sucking down the rest of his cigarette with a long pull. He put it out in his leathery palm without even wincing. Web noted the man's hands for the first time. They were large, muscular and stained with what looked to be acid or something like it. Then he recalled the taxidermy workshop. Killing and stuffing.

"See you tonight, gents," said Billy.

Gwen led them out and told Web in a low voice that he didn't have to do this.

"I'll see you tonight, Gwen," was all he said in response, and she closed the door slowly after them.

W hat the hell was all that about?" said Romano. "I mean, talk about your freaky shit."

Before Web could answer, his phone rang. He whipped it out, hoping it was Claire, but it was Bates.

"I guess it's time to pull the pole on the East Winds tent," Bates said.

"You can call your guys off, but the Canfields have asked Romano and me to stay."

"Are you kidding me?"

"No, and I think it's a good idea, actually. The Frees who were at that compound are gone, but who's to say they don't have more members out there? And Ernie's still at large."

"That's true. Okay, look, you hang there, but let me know if anything goes down, and I mean the second it happens, not Web London time."

"You got it. Anything from Cove?"

"Nothing. It's like he's disappeared from the face of the earth."

Web thought about Claire. "Yeah, I got one of those too."

About the time that Web was wiping out the Free Society in southern Virginia, Claire Daniels sat blindfolded with a gag stuffed painfully in her mouth. She could hear men in the background discussing, or rather arguing, presumably about her. She recognized Ed O'Bannon's voice and she bristled each time she heard it. The bastard had kept the gun on her all the way down to the parking garage and then duct-taped her arms and legs and thrown her in his trunk. She had no idea where she was. As she blinked back tears, she still couldn't believe she had worked next to the man all this time and never suspected what was going on.

The voices stopped and she felt people moving toward her. All she could think was that another pistol was going to be placed against her head, and this time the person would surely fire and kill her. Claire was suddenly pulled up so roughly she thought they had popped her arm out of place. She felt herself being lifted up and put over a shoulder. Whoever was carrying her was strong; the man wasn't even breathing hard, and where her stomach was pressing against him, he felt hard as iron.

A few minutes went by and she was laid down and then she felt the plink of metal against metal. Another car trunk. Blindfolded and shuttled from place to place, Claire had lost her sense of balance and also felt nauseous. The car started and they were soon on the move. She tried listening for sounds that would provide some clue as to where they were, but she soon gave up, there were just too many confusing noises, and they were all muffled. She judged they had been driving for about an hour when the movement of the car seemed to indicate that they had gone from straight, level roads to winding, rolling ones. Had they gone into the country? Were they driving her to some isolated wooded area to kill her and leave her body for the animals, insects and elements to slowly destroy? In her work with law enforcement, Claire had seen the remains of a woman who had been raped and murdered and left in the forest for two weeks. Other than bone, there was virtually nothing left of her. She had become sick at the sight of it. Was that how she would be found?

The car slowed and then she felt a sharp turn and then it decreased its speed again. Now they were going over rough dirt roads and she was pitched around in the trunk, hitting her head twice, once hard enough to bring tears. The car stopped again and then she heard the engine cut off and the doors open. She braced herself. She heard footsteps moving to the rear. She tensed even more, the feeling of despair and helplessness far worse than she had ever endured before. What did it feel like to die? A bullet to the head, would there be any sensation of pain? Web had been shot, twice. He knew what it was like to think he was dying. He had survived, though, because he was a survivor. He had it much tougher in life than she had. She counseled folks over their troubles, and except for a divorce that was fairly amicable, Claire had had no significant disruptions in her own life. For the first time ever, she wondered what gave her the right, other than her fancy degrees, to tell people how to get through their *issues*. Yes, Web had survived much; Claire didn't think she was that strong. She took a deep breath as the trunk was opened and strong hands closed around her and lifted her up. It wasn't O'Bannon. Claire knew he was a man of very little physical strength. From all around she heard the sounds of the forest and animals that lived there, predators that might soon be visiting her remains. She initially fought back the tears and then just decided to let them go. These people wouldn't care.

She felt the man moving over uneven ground, stumbling a few times but then righting himself. His feet went from dirt to something else, wood, brick, or perhaps stone, she wasn't sure, but she had heard the change in sounds, and then a door was unlocked and opened. This surprised her because she had assumed they were in the middle of nowhere. Perhaps it was a cabin, but then she heard noises of machinery going and what she thought was the flow of water. Were they near a stream or river? Was there a dam nearby or a water treatment plant? Was that where her body was going to end up? Then she had a sense of either going up or down, she wasn't sure about that either, for with her ruined sense of balance she had also lost her sense of direction. In fact, she thought she might be sick, and her stomach pushing into the man's hard, bony shoulder didn't help much. And there was also a strong chemical odor that seemed familiar but that she couldn't quite identify, so out of whack were all her senses. For an instant she thought that vomiting on him would give her some small sense of pleasure, of triumph, but it also might prompt him to accelerate the timing of her death.

Another door opened and they passed through, presumably into another room. He squatted and laid her down on something soft, perhaps a bed. Her skirt had risen up embarrassingly high while she'd been riding on the man's shoulders, and with her hands bound she had no way to pull it down. She tensed when she felt his hands go up her legs to a point where she thought he was going to pull down her underpants and add rape to his list of felonies. However, all he did was tug her skirt down to its normal position.

The next thing he did was pull her bound hands over her head and the clink of metal made her think that he had handcuffed her hands to something, perhaps the bed or a ring bolted to the wall. As soon as he moved away, she tried to pull her hands down, but couldn't budge them. Whatever she was handcuffed to, she wouldn't be able to escape it.

"You'll get some food and water later. For now, just try to relax." She didn't recognize the voice. The man didn't laugh at his insane words, but Claire could easily sense the mirth behind them.

The door closed and she was once again alone. Alone, that is, until she sensed movement from across the room.

"You okay, lady?" asked Kevin Westbrook.

47

W eb was now getting worried. Claire had not called back, and he had phoned the hotel but gotten no answer. He called her house and there was no answer there either. Her office hadn't seen her; she had no patients scheduled because it was her normal day off. Maybe she had just gone out for a drive along the Blue Ridge or something, he thought. She hadn't mentioned a trip to him, and even if she had gone, why didn't she answer her cell phone? Every professional instinct he had was telling him something was wrong.

He left Romano at East Winds and drove to the hotel. It was not the sort of place where anyone would necessarily note the coming and going of guests, but Web figured he'd try. However, the staff that possibly would have seen her come in the previous evening was not on duty yet. And no one he talked to remembered anyone resembling Claire coming through the lobby the day before. Her car wasn't in the parking lot either. He drove to her house, found a back window open and crawled through. Web went through her house thoroughly but found nothing that could tell him where she might have gone. He did find a book with her daughter's phone number and address in it. She went to school in California, so it wasn't like Claire could have popped in to see her for the day. Web contemplated calling the daughter, but a call from the FBI might throw the girl into needless hysterics if it turned out nothing was wrong. He left and went to Claire's office. O'Bannon was not in, but another person who worked there was. She hadn't talked to Claire and didn't know where she might be.

"Three strikes and you're out," muttered Web.

He went downstairs to the security desk, flashed his badge and asked if anything unusual had happened the previous night. The rental cop snapped to attention at the sight of the FBI shield and flipped through the notes left by the night shift. Web had gone through the security check before when he had come to see Claire because guests had to sign in, but he didn't recognize this guard. They probably rotated them throughout lots of buildings.

"Yeah, the log shows a call from Dr. Daniels at twelve-thirty A.M. She said the lights had gone out in her office and the guard informed her that all electrical systems were a go and that it might be her circuit breaker and asked if she needed assistance." The young man read this all in a stilted yet quavering voice probably not all that far removed from puberty. "She replied in the negative and that was all." He looked up from the paper. "You want me to do anything?"

The kid's big eyes were just begging Web to send him into action. The guy was armed and probably shouldn't have been, Web noted.

"I know you keep a record of visitors entering and leaving the building. I just signed in on my way in."

"That's right."

Web waited patiently for a few seconds, but the kid just wasn't getting it.

"Can I *see* the register?" Web finally said.

The fellow almost jumped out of his chair. Web had noted that the kid had checked out his face and might have recognized him from all the TV stuff lately. He was probably thinking that Web was half insane and needed to be humored at all costs if one wanted to avoid a violent death. And right now Web was perfectly fine with that perception.

"Yes, sir."

He pulled the book out and Web quickly searched through the pages. There had been lots of guests during business hours the day before, but they ended at six o'clock. He looked at the guard.

"What about after hours? What's the sign-in procedure?"

"Well, it's a keycard system and the doors automatically lock at six. If you want to get in after six, a tenant has to call down and let security know, and when the guest gets here we call up and the tenant has to come down and get the person when they show up. Or the guest may use the exterior phone, identify themselves and who they're here to see. We call up, and the tenant comes down. If the tenant doesn't answer or isn't expecting the visitor, they don't come in, that's the rule. There are some government offices in here and such. I think maybe something to do with the Pentagon, even," he added, with a small measure of pride. "It's a very secure facility."

"I'm sure," said Web absently as he continued to study the pages. "This place have an underground garage?" Web had always parked out front.

"Yes, sir, but it's on a keycard system twenty-four hours a day, tenants only."

Web made a mental note to check and see if Claire's Volvo was there. "So tenants can come and go through the garage elevator and bypass security?"

"That's right, but tenants only."

"Regular lift gate on the garage?"

The guard nodded.

"How about someone slipping into the garage without a car? Can they take the elevator up without a keycard?"

"Not after hours."

"But how about during business hours?" persisted Web.

"Um, that might be possible," said the guard in a small voice, as though Web's observation had just blown his whole professional life.

"Right. Look, is there any way I can talk to the guy who was on duty last night, the one who spoke with Claire?"

"Tommy Gaines. He's a friend of mine; we actually joined up at the same time, right out of high school. He's working the ten-to-six shift." He grinned. "Tommy's probably home dead asleep."

"Call him," said Web in a tone that made the kid grab the phone and start dialing.

Tommy was reached and Web took the phone and identified himself. He could hear the sleepy Gaines become instantly alert. "How can I help you?"

Web explained what he was looking for. "I take it you didn't see Claire Daniels leave?"

"No, I figured she just went out through the garage like she always does. I worked the day shift there for a year and so I knew who she was. She was a real nice lady."

"She's not dead yet, son," said Web.

"No, sir, I didn't mean that."

"It says she called you at twelve-thirty last night. Did she often work that late?"

"Well, I wouldn't necessarily know that, since she didn't have to come and go through the front lobby."

"I understand that; I was trying to find out if you had ever seen her here that late before."

"No, I hadn't."

"Did she sound strange when she called?"

"She sounded scared, but I guess if the lights went out on me I would be too, and she was a woman by herself and all."

"Right." Web knew female FBI, Secret Service and DEA agents who could bite young Mr. Gaines in half and never break a sweat. "Did she *say* that she was all by herself?"

"What? Well, actually, come to think of it, no, she didn't. But I sort of got that impression because she called down and all."

"And the lights down here were fine?"

"Yep. And I could see some of the other buildings out the front. The lights were all right there too. That's why I told her the breaker might have popped. See, this building is set up that each unit has control boxes for their space. That way if one office is doing renovation or has to cut the power for some reason, it doesn't affect the rest of the building. There is a main power switch for the whole building, but that's locked up and the building engineer has the key."

"And you told her you'd come up, but she said that was all right and she said she'd check the circuit breaker box herself."

"That's right."

"And you didn't hear anything else from her?"

"That's right."

Web thought for a moment. The lights were working in Claire's office now. But it might be worth another check.

"Oh, Agent London," Gaines said. "Now that I think about it, about twenty minutes after Claire called I did notice something."

Web tensed. "What? And give it to me exactly as you remember it, Tommy."

"Well, an elevator started up. That can only happen after hours if somebody has a keycard and activates it."

"Where did the elevator originate?"

"From the garage, heading up. I could see it on the floor indicator. It was on P2 and then was coming back up. I was doing rounds and got a clear view of it."

The other guard piped up to Web, "Maybe that was Claire Daniels leaving."

Web shook his head. "Most elevators, especially after hours, are programmed to return to the lobby level. If Claire had hit the button for the elevator, it would have originated from the lobby, not the garage level."

"Oh, that's right," said the crestfallen kid.

Tommy Gaines obviously had heard this exchange and said, "I guess I was thinking it was Ms. Daniels too, because she had called so recently, and I was thinking the lights going out had freaked her out and she had decided to go on home. But you're right about the elevators. The car must have been called from someone on the P2 level and I happened to pass by it when it was heading back up and got it in my head that Ms. Daniels had called it up."

Web said, "But did you see where it stopped at? If I remember correctly, the office where she works takes up most of that floor."

"No, I just kept making my rounds. So I didn't see that or when it came back down either. But whoever it was didn't come out the lobby, I would have seen them." He added, "Sorry, that's all I know."

"No, that's okay, Tommy, you've helped me a lot." He looked at the kid at the desk. "And you too."

As Web hit the elevator button and headed back up, he had a lot to think about. Either it was coincidental that somebody had gone up about twenty minutes after Claire called down, perhaps just another tenant burning the midnight oil, or something else was going on. Under the circumstances, Web just had to assume it was the latter.

When Web got to Claire's offices, he asked the same woman who had helped him before if he could see the electrical closet.

"It's over there, I think," she said uncertainly.

"Thanks."

"Do you think something's happened to Claire?" the woman asked nervously.

"I'm sure she's fine."

Web went to the closet and found it locked. He looked around, but the woman had gone back into her office. He pulled out his little picklock kit and soon had the closet open. He looked around. The first thing that struck him was that something had been pulled out of the wall. There was a clear gap on the power board and wire insulation and other bits of debris were on the floor. Web had no idea whether it had been done recently or long ago. He hoped it hadn't happened last night. As he swung his head around, his experienced eyes picked up what Claire's had missed: the wireless button trip on the inside of the doorjamb, similar to those installed in homes that would trigger an alarm if the door was opened and the contacts broken. Web had seen lots of these devices but never on an electrical closet in an office building. He walked to the front door of the office and opened it. There was no trip button there; in fact, he saw no security panel at all. Why have a security system on your electrical closet and not your office? A cold sense of dread hit Web as he looked at all the closed doors of this space. Claire had told him that a great number of FBI agents, spouses and other law enforcement types sought professional help here. A lot of intimate, confidential information was being revealed behind those portals.

"Shit!" Web ran to Claire's office. The door was locked. He picked it and went in. He saw the flashlight on the floor and was about to search her desk when he happened to look up and saw the smoke detector dangling there. He reached for it and drew back as his FBI training took over. Potential crime scene, fingerprints; don't contaminate the evidence. He called Bates, explained the situation to him and the FBI put out an APB on Claire; and Bates and a tech team showed up thirty minutes later.

Within three hours the entire office had been meticulously gone over and the people questioned. Web was sitting out in the waiting room the whole time. Bates came out, looking pale.

"I don't believe this, Web, I really don't."

"The smoke detectors were listening devices, weren't they?"

Bates nodded. "And video. Pinhole cameras."

"PLC technology?"

Bates nodded again. "Like the spooks use. Sophisticated stuff."

"Well, I guess we just found our leak."

Bates looked down at a list he held. "I guess, you look at it singly, and it's like an agent here, a spouse there, no big deal. But we checked uptown, where they keep records on this because the Bureau's insurance foots the bill. Can you believe that almost two hundred agents, spouses and other personnel connected with the Bureau are patients here? I'm talking people at the bottom all the way to people at the top. And who knows how many at other agencies like DEA, Secret Service, Capitol Police?"

"Well, going to shrinks wasn't real popular with agents before this. Now I guess you can just kiss it good-bye."

"O'Bannon had high-level clearances. Ex-Army, worked in-house at the Bureau as a counselor, solid as a rock. Or so we thought."

"An ocean of intelligence." Web just shook his head. "Debbie Riner, Angie Romano and others. Guys aren't supposed to really talk to their wives about work, but it happens. I mean, everybody's human."

"That must be how they knew you guys were hitting the place that night and even which team was going to be where. It was a planned assault, lots of lead time. One of the guys could have told the missus and she lets it slip to O'Bannon and, *bam*, the bugs pick it up." Bates covered his face with his hand. "Damn, how do I tell Debbie Riner she might have helped kill her husband?"

"You don't, Perce. You don't," Web said firmly.

"But if I don't, she'll find out from some source. And, God, think of the blackmail potential. How do we know *that* hasn't happened already?"

"Face it, Perce, this is an octopus with tentacles that never stops growing." Web looked around the office. "All personnel accounted for here?"

"All except Claire Daniels."

"And O'Bannon?"

Bates sat down. "It looks like he was definitely involved. His files have been cleared out. We checked his house. That's been cleared out too. We've got APBs out, but if this all went down last night, he's got a big head start. By private plane he could already be out of the country." Bates rubbed his head. "This is a nightmare. Do you know what will happen when the media gets hold of this? The Bureau's credibility will be wrecked."

"Well, if we can nail the people behind this, we might be able to get some of it back."

"O'Bannon's not sticking around for us to come and arrest him, Web."

"I'm not talking about O'Bannon."

"Who, then?"

"First of all, let me ask you a question that'll probably make you wanta take a swing at me, but I need a straight answer if I'm going to be able to help you."

"Ask it, Web."

"Is there any possibility that O'Bannon was working with the Bureau to bug the offices so management would know what the foot soldiers' problems were?"

"That crossed my mind, actually. And the answer is no. Thing is, there are some real higher-ups who come her too, it's not just rank-and-filers. And I'm talking the kind of heavyweights—and their wives, by the way—who could bring down just about everybody at the Bureau if that sort of crap was going on."

"Okay, then let's assume that O'Bannon orchestrated this whole intelligence-gathering scheme. Why? Not for kicks. For profit. It always comes down to the bucks. He sells information to lots of different people and law enforcement operations everywhere get blown as a result. And maybe somebody bought info from O'Bannon to execute the hit on Charlie. Like you said, he could have gotten details from one of the wives he was seeing as a patient. Whoever's behind *that*, I want them."

"Well, I thought we *did* know. The Frees. We already nailed them."

"Oh, you really think so?"

"Don't you?"

"It seems to fit, almost too perfectly. Do we have any more information about what might have happened to Claire?"

"Yeah, and it's not good. Less than half an hour after the lights went out in Claire's office, O'Bannon arrived at the garage. He used his keycard to get in and that gave us both his identity and the time of entry."

Web nodded and his spirits fell even more. "She trips the alarm, O'Bannon probably had a remote unit at his house and got the signal. He hightails it over here."

"And finds Claire."

"Yeah."

"I'm sorry, Web."

Web drove back to East Winds, as depressed as he'd ever been in his life. As bad as things looked for the Bureau right now, he didn't even care. All he cared about was finding Claire alive.

Romano was cleaning one of his pistols and looked over when Web came up the stairs of the carriage house. "Man, you look bummed."

Web sat down across from him.

"I screwed up, Paulie."

"Hell, it's not the first time." Romano smiled, but Web obviously wasn't in the mood. Romano put down the gun and looked at his friend. "So talk to me."

"Claire Daniels."

"Your shrink."

"My *psychiatrist*." He paused and then added, "And my friend. Some guys threatened her but then let her go. They're connected with my case, so she was put in danger because of me. She comes to me for help, and what do I do? I don't help."

"Did you offer her protection?"

"Yes, but she didn't want to take it. She thought the threat wasn't real; she made it sound very logical. Now it turns out this O'Bannon guy she worked with was bugging all the psychiatrists' offices and getting information from patients during sessions. Lots of those patients were people who worked at the Bureau. And folks connected to them," he added. He didn't know if Romano was aware that Angie was seeing O'Bannon. And if he didn't know, Web did not want to be the one to tell him. "Then he's probably been selling the info to the highest bidder to use in knocking out law enforcement operations all over the place."

"Holy shit! Do you think Claire was in on it?"

"No! It looks like she stumbled on the truth and now she's disappeared."

"Maybe she's hiding out."

"She would've called." Web's hands balled to fists. "Damn, I'm an idiot for not putting her on around-the-clock protection. Now it's too late."

"Don't be so sure. From the little I saw of her, she can take care of herself. On the drive to the farm, I was talking to her some, and the lady is sharp."

"You mean you were trying to get some free psychiatric advice."

"I wasn't looking for any, but hey, everybody's got problems, okay? Talking to Claire, she made me see some things. Take me and Angie."

Web stared at him with great interest, if only to get his mind off Claire's plight for a few moments. "Okay, what about you and Angie?"

Romano looked vastly uncomfortable now that he had raised the subject. "She doesn't want me to do HRT anymore. She's tired of me being gone all the time. I guess no big surprise there." He added quietly, "And the boys are getting older and they deserve a father who's around more than a month out of every year."

"Is that what she said?"

Romano looked away, "No, that's what *I* said."

"So you really thinking of hanging up your .45s?"

Romano shot him a glance. "Don't you ever think about it?"

Web sat back. "I talked to Debbie Riner recently and she said more or less the same thing about Teddy. But it's different for me, I don't have a wife or kids, Paulie."

Romano hunched forward. "See, the things is, in the last eight years I've missed four Christmases, both my boys' First Communions, every damn Halloween, a couple of Thanksgivings and my son Robbie being born! And on top of that I can't tell you how many birthdays, baseball games and soccer matches, special stuff like that. Hell, it's like my boys are surprised when I'm home, Web, not when I'm gone, because me gone is like normal to them."

He touched the spot near his belly button. "And that hit I took last night? Got a nasty bruise and it hurt like hell for a while, but what if it *had* been an inch lower, or two feet higher and through my head? I'm gone. But you know what? It wouldn't have been that much different than when I was alive, at least for Angie and the boys. And then what happens? Angie's gonna get remarried, you know that, and the boys will maybe get a real dad and forget

all about Paul Romano even being their old man. I'd take a damn
Barrett round in the head over that, Web, I really would. Every
time I think about it—shit!"

Web could actually see wetness in Romano's eyes, and the sight
of one of the toughest men he had ever known being brought to
his knees over love for his family hit Web harder than even Francis
Westbrook ever could. Romano quickly looked away and swiped at
his face.

Web gripped Romano's shoulder. "That's not going to happen,
Paulie; you're a good dad. Your kids would never forget you." As
soon as he said this, it struck Web. He had forgotten his father, totally and completely. A birthday party, six years old. Claire had said
Web and his old man were having a really good time. Until the
cops showed up. "And you're doing good for your country too,
don't forget that," he added. "Nobody gives a damn about serving
their country anymore. Everybody just complains about how rotten it is without doing anything to make it better. But man, the
second they need you, you better be there."

"Yeah, serving my country. And wiping out a bunch of hick kids
and old farts who couldn't hit the Statue of Liberty from three feet
away with a bazooka."

Web sat back and said nothing because he had nothing more to
say on that subject.

Romano looked up at him. "Claire will turn up, Web, and who
knows, maybe you and her can be more than friends. Get a real life."

"You don't think it's too late?" It all sounded impossible to
achieve.

"Hell, if it ain't too late for me, it sure ain't too late for you," said
Romano.

Web didn't think he sounded too confident and the men looked
miserably at each other.

Web stood. "You know, Paulie, both of us are in sorry-ass shape.
And you know what else?"

"What?"

"Now I'm really looking forward to this party tonight."

48

Percy Bates was sitting in the strategic ops center at WFO when the man walked in. Buck Winters wasn't alone. He had his usual twin escorts and also several others with him. Bates recognized one as a young Bureau lawyer and another as an investigator from the Bureau's Office of Professional Responsibility, which looked into any wrongdoing by members of the FBI. With exaggerated solemnity, they all sat down across from Bates.

Winters tapped the tabletop with one of his long fingers. "How's the investigation coming, Perce?"

"It's coming real well," answered Bates. He looked at the other people. "So what's all this? Are you starting an investigation of your own?"

"Heard from Randall Cove lately?" asked Winters.

Bates once more glanced at the others. "You know, Buck, with all due respect, is it okay for these people to be hearing that name?"

"They're all cleared for it, Perce. Trust me. They've been cleared for a lot." Winters stared directly at him now. "This is a total disaster, you know."

"Look, HRT got sent in and they were fired upon and they fired back. Those rules of engagement are about as clean as you can get. Nothing in the Constitution says our guys have to stand there and get gunned down."

"I wasn't specifically talking about the Free Society massacre."

"Damn it, Buck, it wasn't a massacre. The Frees had guns too, and they were using them."

"Eight dead, old men and young boys, and not one loss on HRT's side. Now, how do you think the press will play out that one?"

Bates dropped the file he was holding along with any shred of patience he had left. "Well, if the Bureau does its usual head-in-the-sand and lets everybody else control the facts and the spin, I guess not real well. What do we have to do to make our 'image' look okay, lose a few guys on every mission?"

"Another Waco," said the fresh-faced lawyer, shaking her head.

"Like hell it is," yelled Bates. "You don't know what you're talking about. You were still in law school with your thumb up your ass when Waco went down."

"Like I was saying," said Winters calmly, "I wasn't specifically talking about the Frees."

"What, then?" asked Bates.

"Oh, I don't know, maybe the fact that the entire security of the FBI has been compromised."

Bates took a long breath. "Because of the psychiatrist's office?"

Winters exploded. "Yeah, Perce, that's right, because for God knows how long, agents and secretaries and technicians and who the hell knows who else, but apparently everybody who has a head problem in the Bureau, has spilled their guts in that place. And somebody's been vacuuming it up and using it for God knows what. I'd call that a compromise of security."

"We're out looking for O'Bannon right now."

"The damage has already been done."

"It's better than us never having found out about it."

"Not by a wide margin it's not. I guess you know that I was on record a long time ago against using outside psychiatrists and psychologists, for this very security reason."

Bates studied the man warily. *And so you're going to use this disaster to move your career a few pegs higher, right, Buck? Like maybe the director's office?*

"No, Buck, actually, I wasn't aware of that."

"It's all in the paper trail," Winters said confidently. "Check it."

"I'm sure it is, Buck. You were always the best of the best with the old paper trail." *And not much else having to do with being a real FBI agent.*

"Well, heads are going to roll on this one."

But not yours.

"So what's this I read about London participating in the assault? Please tell me that's just an enormous typo."

"He was there," admitted Bates.

Winters looked like he was ready to erupt again. Then Bates sensed a very small indication of satisfaction on the man's features, and he finally understood where this conversation was going.

"Well, the press can just go ahead and crucify us now," said Winters. "HRT takes out its revenge on old men and young boys. That'll be the lead headline on the wires tomorrow. Now hear this, Bates and hear it good, London is through, effective immediately." For effect, Winters picked up a pencil off the table and snapped it in half.

"Buck, you can't do that. It's still under review."

"Yes, I can do that. He was on official leave of absence pending an SRB inquiry." Winters motioned to one of his aides, who handed him a file. Winters took his time slipping on a pair of reading glasses and then glanced over the file. "And now I've also discovered that while on paid leave he was assigned to protection duty regarding one William Canfield who operates a horse farm in Fauquier County. Who authorized that?"

"I did. Canfield's son was killed by the Frees in Richmond. Three people connected with that incident have been murdered, we believe by the Frees. You know all that. We didn't want Canfield to become number four. Web was available and Canfield trusts him. In fact, Web saved his life. And mine. So it seemed a good fit."

"Can't say much for Canfield's judgment, then."

"And we had direct evidence connecting a truck, rented by Silas Free, to the machine guns that were used to ambush HRT. We had every right to hit them. And the assault was okayed by all appropriate parties. Check the paper trail."

"I realize that. I actually signed off on it myself."

"You did?" Bates asked, with a curious expression. "I actually wanted a SWAT team, Buck. You didn't insist on HRT going in, did you?" Winters didn't answer, and right then and Bates realized exactly why HRT had been sent in. Winters had wanted something like this to happen to fuel his crusade against Hostage Rescue. And

Bates also knew that, as wily as Winters was, he'd never be able to prove it.

"I was not made aware that Web London was part of the assault," Winters continued.

"Well, that came later," Bates said slowly. He was defenseless on that one and he knew it.

"Oh, thanks for the explanation, that really clears it all up. And who authorized London being in on the assault?"

"His commander, Jack Pritchard, would've had to give the okay."

"Then he's gone. Effective now."

Bates stood. "My God, Buck, you can't do that. Pritchard's pulled twenty-three years at the Bureau. He's one of the best we've ever had."

"Not anymore he's not. As of now, he's one of the worst. And it will be duly noted for the official record. And I'm going to recommend that he be stripped of everything, including his pension, for insubordination, action detrimental to the Bureau and about a half dozen other things. Believe me, it'll be an easy sell once all this breaks. There will be an enormous need for scapegoats."

"Buck, please don't do this. Okay, maybe he stepped out of bounds a little on this one, but he's got a list of commendations taller than I am. He's risked his life more times than I can count. And he's got a wife and five kids, two of them in college. This'll ruin him. This will kill him."

Winters put the file down. "I tell you what, Perce, I'll make a deal with you, because I like you and I respect you."

Bates sat down, instantly suspicious as the cobra moved in for the kill. "What sort of deal?"

"If Pritchard stays, London goes. No questions asked. No fight, no defenses. He just goes. What's it going to be?"

Percy Bates just sat there while Buck Winters watched him, waiting for his answer.

For years Claire had been a tooth grinder, to such an extent, in fact, that her dentist had made her a mouth guard that she wore at night to save her teeth from being worn down to the gums. She had wondered where this symptom of anxiety came from, perhaps from listening to her patients' problems. Now she was thankful for her grinding because she had worn the gag down such that it had finally ripped apart and she spit it out. The way her hands were bound over her head, however, made removing the blindfold impossible. She had tried to rub her head against the wall to pry it off that way, until it felt like she had worn off most of her hair. Exhausted, she slumped over.

"It's okay, lady, I'll be your eyes," said Kevin. "They got me locked up too, but I'm working on that."

With her gag off, they had started talking and Claire had learned who Kevin was.

"Web London told me about you," she said. "And I've been to your house. We spoke to Jerome."

Kevin looked anxious. "I bet they worried. I bet Granny about to die from worry."

"They're okay, Kevin. But they *are* worried. Jerome loves you very much."

"He always good to me. He and Granny."

"Do you know where we are?"

"Nope."

Claire took a deep breath. "It smells like chemicals. Like we're near a dry cleaner's shop or some type of manufacturing plant." She struggled to recall the details of how she had gotten here. The roads and the terrain the man had carried her over seemed more reminiscent of the country than the city.

"How long have you been here?"

"Ain't know. Days sort of run together."

"Has anyone been in to see you?"

"Same man. Ain't know who he is. He treats me nice. But he gonna kill me, I can see that in his eyes. It's the nice ones you got to watch out for. Folks who scream and shake their fist, I'll take them any day over the quiet ones."

If she hadn't been so unnerved at the thought of being murdered, Claire might have smiled at the boy's mature insight into human nature.

"How did you get hooked up with all this?"

"Money," Kevin said plainly.

"We saw the sketch you did, with the remote control."

"I ain't know what was gonna happen. Nobody told me that. They just give me it and told me what to say."

"Damn to hell?"

"Yep. Then I was supposed to trail 'em going down that alley and then, when I got close enough to the courtyard, hit the remote button. I seen that man, Web, he all froze up, and the rest of his buddies went running into that courtyard. Web, he ain't never see me behind him. He got up and followed his buddies, but he was walking like he was drunk or something. I hit the button and then hung back."

"Because you wanted to see what happened?"

"Those people ain't never tell me about no guns. I swear that on my mama's grave, I swear!"

"I believe you, Kevin."

"I was supposed to go back to where I was, but I couldn't. Seeing all them folks die like that. And then Web, he yelled at me. About give me a heart attack. He saved my butt. I would've run out there if it ain't for him and then I be dead too."

"Web said that somebody switched you for another boy."

"That's right. I ain't know why."

Claire took a deep breath and the strong chemical smell invaded her lungs again. Now she too was able to identify it as chlorine, but she had no idea what its source was. She felt totally helpless.

49

Web and Romano met Nemo Strait on their way up to the mansion to attend the party.

"What happened to you?" asked Romano. Strait's arm was in a sling.

"Let a damn horse get the drop on me. Thing kicked me. Felt like my collarbone was in my throat."

"Anything broken?" asked Web.

"They x-rayed it up at the hospital in Kentucky and they didn't see anything, but they put me in this thing for the time being. Now I'm a one-armed farm manager and Billy's probably going to be pissed at that."

They were welcomed at the house by Billy. Web was surprised at how he was dressed. He had on nice, pressed slacks and a blue blazer, his hair was neatly combed and he had even shaved. Yet as they passed through, Web could smell on the man's breath that he had begun the party a while back.

Billy led them down to the lower level.

Next to the bar were two men Web didn't know. They were dressed expensively if casually in Armani, Bruno Magli with no socks, Tag Heuer watches, and gold necklaces that were visible because the men's shirts were open about two buttons too many. They were deeply tanned, fit and trim, nails professionally manicured and hair perfectly coifed, and for many reasons Web's initial impression was that they were gay.

Billy led Romano and Web over to them. "Wanta introduce y'all to a couple new friends of mine. Giles and Harvey Ransome, they're brothers, now, they ain't married." Billy was the only one to laugh at that remark. "They're my neighbors from next door. Finally got them to come over for a drink."

Web and Romano exchanged a quick glance.

"This is Web London and Paul—no, make that Paulie," Billy added with a wink. "From the Federal Bureau of Investigation."

The Ransome brothers both looked ready to run at that. Harvey Ransome, Web thought, appeared as though he might faint.

Web put out his hand. "We're off duty tonight."

The Ransome brothers cautiously extended their hands, as though they feared that there was a real threat of handcuffs being placed on them.

"Billy didn't tell us the FBI would be here tonight," Giles said, giving his host an unfriendly stare.

"I love surprises," said Billy. "Ever since I was a kid." He looked over at Strait. "What in the hell happened to you?"

"Horse got the better of me."

"This is my farm manager, Nemo Strait," said Billy to the Ransome brothers. "He just made me a small fortune up in Kentucky selling a bunch of horse meat to some new suckers."

"We did real well," said Strait quietly.

"Where the hell are my manners?" said Billy. "You boys need some drinks." He pointed at Web and Romano. "I know you boys are beer drinkers. How 'bout you, Nemo?"

"Whiskey and water, best kind of painkiller there is."

Billy went behind the bar. "I'll join you in that one." He looked toward the stairs. "Well, come on down and join the party."

Web looked toward the stairs, expecting to see Gwen. Instead there was Percy Bates.

"Billy was nice enough to give me an invite," he explained as he joined them. He smiled at Web, but in that smile Web could see something that he didn't particularly like.

Once they all had drinks in hand, they broke up into small groups. Web went over to the Ransome brothers and began subtly probing them as to what was going on at the Southern Belle, but the men were being exceptionally guarded, which made Web even more suspicious. Nemo and Romano were looking over Canfield's collection of shotguns, while Billy was standing all alone and scowling back at the grizzly bear in the corner.

One by one all their heads turned when she came down the stairs. If Billy was more overdressed than usual, his wife looked ready to attend a Hollywood premiere; she was as far removed from her normal boots-and-jeans horse-rider persona as it was possible to be. The red gown was long, body-hugging and ran down to her ankles; the slit came to midthigh, right at the precise point where decency was still maintained but where male fantasy was compelled to sprint. The shoes were open-toed, with ankle straps that, to Web, at least, suggested the concept of bondage if one hadn't already been thinking about it. The gown was strapless, her bare shoulders tanned and muscular but retaining much feminine allure despite the ripples. The gown's bodice was cut low enough to make maneuvering difficult without revealing too much, and perhaps that was the intent. Her hair was piled high on her head, her jewelry tasteful and the woman required very little makeup.

There was complete silence as she descended to them until Web heard Romano whisper, *"Amore,"* and then he took a gulp of beer.

"Now the party can really get started," said Billy. "What you having, Gwen?"

"Ginger ale."

Billy filled this order. He looked over at the Ransome brothers.

"She's stunning," said Harvey.

"A goddess," echoed Giles.

"She's also my wife." He brought the drink over to her. "Nemo got himself all banged up with a horse."

Web noted that she barely glanced in the man's direction. "So I see." She nodded toward the Ransomes. "I don't believe we've met," she said coolly.

Harvey and Giles fell over themselves to see which of them she would meet first.

Web just stood back and watched all this happen. The woman was, without doubt, exceptionally beautiful, yet the way she was dressed, the magisterial way that she was acting, seemed totally out of sync with Gwen Canfield, at least as he had pegged her. Perhaps he had been wrong.

He didn't notice Bates at his elbow until the man spoke.

"A going-away party, I understand."

"Yeah, case closed. Good guys win again," Web added dryly. "Time to get drunk and pat ourselves on the back, at least until all the shit comes back tomorrow."

"We need to talk later. It's important."

Web glanced at him. To someone who didn't know the man well, Bates looked like he didn't have a care in the world. To Web, who did know him about as well as anybody, the man seemed ready to implode with whatever he was carrying around inside.

"Don't tell me I won the lottery?"

"I guess it's all in how you look at it. I'll let you decide. You want to slip outside and discuss it now?"

Web eyed the man steadily. So it *was* pretty bad. "No, Perce, right now I just want to enjoy my drink and go over and talk to a very beautiful woman."

He left Bates and managed to extract Gwen from the fawning Ransome brothers. They settled in twin club leather chairs, and Gwen cradled her drink in her lap and looked over at her husband.

"He's already been partying hard for about six hours."

"So I see." He looked her over without seeming to. At least he thought so until she shot him a glance.

"A little different attire than you're used to, I know," she said. Her cheeks reddened slightly at this remark.

"Hey, you got it, flaunt it. I'm just glad there aren't any other women here, because they'd really be out of their league. They wouldn't just be wallflowers, they'd be part of the wall, as far as the men here are concerned."

She patted his hand. "You're sweet. The fact is, I'm about as uncomfortable in this dress as I can be; worried that I'm going to fall out any second and embarrass myself, and my feet are already killing me. These Italian shoes are pretty to look at and absolutely impossible to wear if your feet are over a size four."

"So why the getup, then?"

"Billy picked it out for me. He's not the sort of man who tells his wife what to do or wear," she added quickly. "Quite the contrary. I usually pick his clothes out. But he wanted me to look really knock-'em-dead, he said."

Web raised his glass. "Consider your mission accomplished. But why?"

"I don't know, Web, I really don't know what's going through his head right now."

"Maybe it has something to do with that damn tape. Again, I'm sorry."

Gwen just shook her head. "It's not just that. This has been brewing for some time. Billy's been changing over the last few months or so, and I'm not sure why."

To Web it seemed like the woman did know why but wasn't to the point where she was going to reveal it to a semi-stranger like him.

"His behavior has been becoming more and more bizarre."

He looked at her curiously. "How so?"

"Well, he's become obsessed with his stuffed animals, always down there messing around. My God, that is the most repulsive thing."

"It is pretty gruesome."

"And he's been drinking hard, even for him." She looked at Web and spoke in a lower voice. "Do you know what he told me while we were getting dressed?" She took a sip of her ginger ale. "He said that they should put all the heads of the Free Society members up on poles and parade them around, like they used to do hundred of years ago."

"Why? To send a message?"

"No."

They both looked up and saw Billy standing there.

He downed the rest of his whiskey. "No, you do it because the best place to put your enemies is right in front of you, so you know exactly where they are all the time."

"That's not always easy to do," commented Web.

Billy smiled through his drink glass. "That's right. And that's why folks' enemies get the drop on 'em more often than not." It was just a quick glance, but Web was almost certain that Billy looked at Nemo Strait when he said this.

Billy held up his glass. "Ready for a fresh one?"

"I'm still working on this one."

"Well, let me know. Gwen, you ready for a real libation?"

"Dressed this way in a room full of men, I think I need to keep my wits about me tonight," she said with a coy smile.

For the record, Web noted, her husband didn't return the smile.

Right before they went up to dinner, Web heard a scream and looked over to its source. The gun cabinet was swung open, revealing the secret room. And Harvey and Giles were both holding their chests after having been surprised by Billy's slave mannequin. And the man himself was leaning against the wall laughing so hard he was gagging. Web just had to smile.

After dinner, coffee and snifters of brandy that Billy insisted everybody try, they all took their leave. Gwen gave Web a hug and he felt her soft breasts push into his own hard chest. Her fingers seemed to cling to him a beat too long. He didn't know exactly how to take that and so all he managed to say was good-bye.

They went outside and Strait climbed in his truck and one-armed it back to his house. A limo pulled up in the front circle and Harvey and Giles Ransome piled inside. They had both made fools of themselves over Gwen, Web had thought, but she had taken it with good graces. She was no doubt upstairs right this minute slipping out of the painful shoes and the uncomfortable dress. In fact, she was probably naked right now, and Web felt himself glancing toward the upstairs windows—in hopes of what? he asked himself. A glimpse? It didn't happen.

Bates came up to him and Romano.

"Romano, Web and I need to talk."

The man said it in such a tone that all Romano did was turn and walk toward the carriage house.

Web and Bates faced off. "Okay," Web said, "what's the deal?"

Bates told him and Web took it silently until the man finished.

"What about Romano?" asked Web.

"Buck didn't mention him, so I'm assuming he's okay."

"Let's keep it that way."

"I don't know what to do, Web. I'm caught between a rock and a hard place."

"No, you're not. I'll make it easy for you. I'll resign."

"Are you shitting me?"

"It's time for me to move on, Perce, do something else. I'm not getting any younger, and to tell you the truth, I'd like to find out what it's like having a job where people aren't shooting at you."

"We can fight this, Web. Winters doesn't have the final say on this."

"I'm tired of fighting, Perce."

Bates just looked at the man helplessly. "I didn't want it to end this way."

"Me and Romano will finish up here and then I'll be moving on."

"You know the heat this is going to generate, with what happened with the Frees. And with you leaving HRT, the timing of that will make everyone assume you're the scapegoat. It's going to get dicey. The media will come after you. In fact, it's already starting."

"There was a time when that would've bothered me. But not now."

The men stood there quietly for a few seconds as many years of fighting the good fight together suddenly had abruptly come to an end for them and it seemed neither of them was prepared for it. Web finally turned and walked away.

50

It was around two o'clock in the morning. The only movements at East Winds were the horses in the pastures and the wildlife in the encroaching forest. Then came footsteps that crept along the path leading through the trees.

There was one light on in the house and a man's silhouette was stark in the outline of the window. Nemo Strait held a cold beer can against his injured shoulder, grimacing as the frosty metal hit the damaged skin. He wore a T-shirt and boxer shorts; his thick, muscular legs had split the fabric at the thigh. He lay on his bed, picked up the semiautomatic pistol there and deftly loaded the gun's magazine, but with only one hand he had trouble sliding the bolt back to chamber a round. Frustrated, he finally put the gun on the nightstand, lay back on the bed and sipped his beer.

Nemo Strait, by nature, was a worrier. And right now he had a lot to concern him. He was still thinking about the chopper that had come out of nowhere in the dark woods. Strait had watched the flight of the aircraft. It had not landed in the woods, and it did not appear to be the police. Strait had thought about going back to where they had shot Cove to make certain the guy was dead. Yet he had to be. They had fired five shots into him, no one could shake that, and even if the man somehow managed to live, he'd be a vegetable, incapable of telling anyone what had happened. Still, Strait didn't like it and he had scanned every news program he could find in the hopes of learning that an FBI undercover agent had been found dead. And he also wanted to hear that there were no clues to the killers. He rubbed his shoulder. Strait's blood was out there, of course, but they had to have something to match his DNA to, and his was not on file anywhere that he could remember. Except the Army! But after more than twenty-five years, would they still have it? Would the stuff be any good? He doubted it. Still, he could feel it was getting close to the time he would be moving on. He had accomplished everything he had set out to do, and last night's transaction had left him with enough money to retire to just about anywhere he wanted. At first he had thought about buying a place up in the Ozarks and passing the rest of his life doing nothing more than fishing and spending his money in increments that would arouse no suspicions. Now he was rethinking that strategy. Now he was thinking that another country might be a far better retirement venue. Well, he had heard the fishing was terrific in Greece.

If Strait heard the back door open, he made no indication. It had been a long day and his painkiller was wearing off. He took another slug of it and wiped his lips.

The door to his bedroom slowly opened. Again, Strait seemed not to notice. The person moved into the room. Strait turned on some music on the radio next to his bed. The figure moved closer to the bed. Finally Strait stopped what he was doing and slowly looked around.

"I didn't think you were going to come tonight," he said. "Thinking with one arm I wasn't good enough anymore." He took a drink of his beer and then put it down.

Gwen stood looking down at him. She wore the red dress she had had on at the party, but her high heels had been replaced with flats; her gold anklet glittered a bit in the wash of light.

She moved closer to him, her gaze drifting to his shoulder. "Does it hurt much?"

"Just every time I breathe."

"Which horse did it?"

"Bobby Lee."

"He's not known as a kicker."

"Every horse can be a kicker."

"I forgot, you're the expert." She smiled demurely, but there was something behind the look that was not nearly so playful.

"No, but I grew up with the damn things. I mean, you don't learn this stuff in a year or even in ten years. Look at Billy, he's a fast learner, but he still basically knows shit about running a horse farm."

"You're right. That's why we hired you and your good old boys." She paused. "You're our white knight, Nemo."

Strait lit up a cigarette. "Yeah, that's a good one." She surprised him by reaching over and taking a drink of his beer.

"Don't you have anything stronger than this?" she asked.

"Bourbon."

"Get it."

While he pulled out the bottle and glasses, she perched on the bed and rubbed her calf. She touched the anklet, a gift from Billy. It had both their names engraved on it. Strait handed her a full glass and she downed it in one pass and handed it back to him for a refill.

"Take it easy on that stuff, Gwen. It's not candy."

"It is to me. Besides, I didn't drink at the party. I was a good girl."

Strait's gaze ran down her long body, took in her bare legs, her ample bosom. "Every man in the place wanted to jump your bones."

Gwen did not smile at this compliment. "Not every man."

"Hey, Billy's getting up there, can't do it on demand anymore. Hell, I'm getting to that point myself faster than I'd like."

"It has nothing to do with age." She reached over and took a puff of the cigarette and then handed it back. "And when your husband hasn't touched you in years, it tends to drive a woman to other sources." She glanced at him. "I hope you recognize your limited role here."

He shrugged. "A man has to take what he can get. But it ain't right that he still blames you for what happened to your son."

"He has every right. I was the reason David was at that school."

"You didn't order them crazy Frees in there to shoot up the place, now, did you?"

"No, and I didn't ask the FBI to send down a bunch of men who were too cowardly or incompetent to save my son either."

"Kind of strange, having the FBI right here on the farm."

"We knew that was a very real possibility."

Strait smiled. "Come here to protect you."

Gwen said dryly, "From ourselves."

"Well, the little bomb in Billy's phone that I detonated when Web tossed it out the car, that threw them off the scent for good. They're not looking in our direction."

"Web London is a lot smarter than you probably think."

"Oh, I know he's real smart. I ain't going around underestimating anybody on this one."

Gwen took a sip of her second bourbon, slipped off her flats and slid back on the bed.

He caressed her hair. "I been missing you, lady."

"Billy could care less, but it's a little difficult to move around with the FBI patrolling your property."

"Well," said Strait, "now it's just Web and Romano. He's another one to watch. Ex-SWAT and Delta, that dude can be bad news. See it in his eyes."

Gwen rolled over on her stomach, propped up on her elbows and stared at him. His eyes were locked on her cleavage, which was now spilling out of her dress. She noted his gaze, but apparently his attention did not interest her.

"I wanted to ask you about the horse trailers."

Gwen's question caused his gaze to lift from her breasts to her face.

"What about 'em?"

"I grew up on a horse farm too, Nemo. You had some of those rigs customized in a very special way, and I want you to tell me why."

He grinned. "Can't a man have any secrets?"

She got up on her knees and slid closer to him. She started kissing his neck, and his hand went first to her chest and then moved to her bottom. He hiked her dress up to her waist and discovered she had on no underwear.

"Good thinking. With me as horny as I am, you would've just gotten those panties ripped off anyway."

She moaned into his ear as his fingers moved over her. One of her hands went to his face and then down to the neckline of his T-shirt. And then with a flash she had ripped the shirt down the front and sat back.

Her movement surprised Strait so much that he almost fell off the bed.

He followed her gaze to the bloodstained bandage on his shoulder.

"Mighty odd bruise from a horse kick," said Gwen.

The two stared at each other. And before he could stop her, Gwen picked up Strait's pistol, chambered a round and drew aims at various points in the room. She looked at the gun.

"The balance on this is off. And you really should get some lithium sights, Nemo. They do make a difference with night fire."

A bead of sweat appeared on Strait's forehead. "You handle that thing real good."

"Horses weren't the only thing I grew up with in Kentucky. My father and brothers were very active members of the NRA. I would've joined too, only it wasn't deemed ladylike by my parents."

"Hey, that's real good to know. I'm a member too." He breathed a sigh of relief when she set the safety, yet she still didn't put the gun down.

"So what is it?" she asked. "Drugs?"

"Look, baby, why don't we just have a drink and get to—"

The pistol came up and the safety went off. "I came here to screw you, Nemo, not to be screwed *with.* It's late and I'm starting to get tired. If you want any candy tonight, you better cut the bullshit."

"Okay, okay. Damn, you are something." He took a quick belt of his drink and wiped his mouth with his hand. "It's drugs, but not the kind you think. Prescription stuff with a kick twice that of morphine. No lab, no border problem. Just steal 'em or work a deal with a pharmacy assistant making eight bills an hour. This Oxycontin stuff started rural. But I'm taking it to the big cities. About damn time us country folks got a piece of the pie. It's sweet."

"And you're using East Winds as your base and our trailers to move your product."

"Well, we've been distributing the drugs, mostly in pickup trucks, prearranged drop spots and even through the mail. Then I got the idea to use the horse trailers. We move horses across state lines all the time. And if the cops stop us for permits and papers on the trailers or the horses, the smell's gonna keep them away from where the stuff is, and I don't know of many dogs trained to sniff out prescription drugs. I've been shuffling men and trailers around so you and Billy wouldn't notice. The run we made to Kentucky was our biggest yet."

He raised his beer in salute, apparently to himself.

Gwen eyed his wound. "But not a complete success."

"Well, you do something illegal, you got to be prepared to face some risk."

"Did this risk come from your demand chain or maybe the cops?"

"Come on, now, honey, what does it matter?"

"You're right. I guess either way it means you've put us at risk. You were supposed to be working for us, Nemo, full-time."

"Well, a person's got to look out for himself. And it was too good a deal to pass up. And I ain't breaking my back on horse farms the rest of my life, okay?"

"I hired you for a specific purpose, because of your unique qualities and experience."

"Right, the fact that I got a damn good head on my shoulders, know folks who don't mind killing people and I can put together some pretty slick explosives. Well, I done that, baby." He ticked the points off his fingers. "A federal judge, a U.S. attorney, a defense counsel."

"Leadbetter, Watkins and Wingo. A judge with no backbone, a prosecutor with no guts and a defense counsel who would gladly defend his own mother's killer if the guy had enough money. I consider that we did society a service by ending their pathetic lives."

"Right, and we took out HRT and then suckered them into wiping out the damn Frees. Man, we tricked a veteran undercover into thinking that he'd come upon the drug operation to end all drug operations. We set that place up like something straight out of the movie *The Sting*." He looked at her and his features grew grim. "So I delivered for you, lady. So what I do on my time is *my* business. I ain't your damn slave, Gwen."

She kept the pistol pointed at him. "Web London is still standing."

"Well, hell, you said to keep him that way. Make him look like a coward. We got lucky when I found out the shrink he was seeing was an old acquaintance of mine from Vietnam. So everybody thinks Web's rotten to the core. This whole thing took a lot of planning, had a lot of risk, and let me tell you we executed it to damn near perfection, and you got it for pennies on the dollar 'cause I think what happened to your son stinks." He looked at her with a hurt expression. "And I don't even remember you saying thank you."

Her tone was businesslike, her expression unreadable. "Thank you. How much money have you made off the drugs?"

Surprised, he lowered his drink. "Why?"

"After what I've paid you and what we've sunk into this place, Billy and I are in the hole. They'll be coming to take his antique car collection pretty soon because we borrowed against that too. We could use some free cash flow, because we're going to be selling out and moving on too, especially since however you got that injury tells me that one day somebody's going to come knocking on our door with questions I don't have answers for. And frankly, I've had enough of Virginia hunt country. I'm thinking our next stop is a small island where it never gets cold and there are no damn phones."

"You want me to give you a share of *my* drug money?" he asked incredulously.

"Actually, demand would be more accurate."

Nemo spread his hands. "Well, I wasn't kidding, darlin', we got some good prices for those fine yearlings," he said in a very sincere tone.

She laughed at him. "This place never made any money before we bought it and it's not going to make any money now. Fine yearlings or not."

"Well, what do you want from me?"

"It's very simple. I want you to tell me how much you have made from the drugs."

He hesitated for a moment before answering. "Not that much, actually."

She raised the pistol and pointed it in his direction. "How much?"

"Okay, 'bout a million. There, you satisfied?"

She gripped the pistol with both hands and took very careful aim at his head. "Last chance. How *much*, Nemo?"

"Okay, okay, don't get your panties all twisted." He let out a deep breath. "Tens of millions."

"Then I want twenty percent. And then we go our separate ways."

"Twenty damn percent!"

"Wired to an offshore account. I'm assuming that a great businessman like yourself has set up some secret accounts somewhere to hide your millions. Excuse me, *tens* of millions."

"But look, I got expenses."

"Right, you probably paid your help off in pills, since most of them are too stupid to know better. And since running prescription drugs means low cost, lower risk, I imagine your profit margins are pretty nice, and I don't think you've been paying taxes on the income. And on top of that, you use our equipment that we paid for to move your product and also the manpower we're paying to work the farm to do it for you. So there was very little capital out of your pocket, and that makes for an even greater return on investment. And so, yes, I want my share. We'll call it rental fees for equipment and labor. And you're lucky it's only twenty percent." She slid a hand enticingly down her front. "In fact, you're fortunate that I'm in a generous mood right now."

Strait just shook his head. "What, was your dad a damn MBA too?"

"Billy and I have gotten the wrong end of the deal for long enough. At least we're still alive. My son only had ten years. Does that sound fair to you?"

"And if I say no?"

"I'll shoot you."

"In cold blood. A religious woman like yourself?"

"I pray for my son every day, but I can't say that my faith in God is absolute anymore. And I can always call the cops."

Nemo smiled and shook his head. "And tell them what? I'm dealing drugs? And oh, yeah, I killed a bunch of people for you? What's your leverage?"

"My leverage, Nemo, is that I don't give a damn anymore what happens to me. That's the best leverage of all. I have nothing more to lose because I've already lost everything."

"What about Billy?"

"He knows nothing about this. And now it's twenty-five percent."

"Well, hell."

Keeping the gun trained on him, she stood, unzipped her dress and let it fall to the floor, then stepped out of it completely naked.

"And here's the sweetener," she said. "Going once, going twice . . ."

"Deal!" said Nemo Strait as he held his arms out for her.

The sex was hard and left them both breathless. Strait collapsed on his back nursing his aching arm, while Gwen let her legs down and stretched them out. Strait had almost driven her right through the box springs and twisted her legs back into positions they were never meant to go. She would be hurting for a couple days, but it was a wonderful pain, something her husband had withheld from her for so long. And not just the sex, but also the love, which was far worse. In public he made a pretense of affection; in private he bothered not at all. He had never been abusive to her—on the contrary it was extreme diffidence coupled with irreversible melancholy; being ignored had never been so painful.

Gwen sat back against the headboard, lit a cigarette and blew fat rings to the ceiling. She lay there for about an hour and then reached over and put a hand on Strait's hairy chest, slowly rousing him.

"That was wonderful, Nemo."

"Uh-huh," he grunted back.

"Think you can do it again before sunrise?"

He opened one eye. "Damn it, woman, I ain't nineteen, and I got a bad wing. You get me some of that Viagra crap, maybe I can."

"In your line of work I'd think you'd be tired of pills."

He raised his head slightly and looked at her. "Hey, you wouldn't entertain the notion of moving to Greece with me, would you? It'd be a hell of a lot of fun. Guaranteed."

"I have no doubt, but my place is with my husband whether he knows it or not."

He slumped back down. "Yeah, I thought you'd say that."

"And you're really just looking to cut me out of my twenty-five percent."

"Okay, I give up."

"Nemo?"

"Yeah?"

"What do you think happened to Ernest B. Free?"

He sat up, used her cigarette to light his, then sat back next to her and put an arm around her.

"Hell if I know. That one's really got me stumped. I thought he'd be at the compound HRT hit, but he wasn't. Unless the Feds are lying, but why would they? They bag him, they'd be screaming that to the world. And the guy I used to set up the Frees also planted the drugs and other stuff down there, including some made-up files on the judge and two lawyers. He actually knows old Ernie, so he would've seen and recognized him if he was down there. Even if they had him real well hidden."

She ran her fingers through his hair. "Web and Romano are leaving soon."

"Yeah, I know. Good riddance. They're cramping my style, although it was pretty sweet driving fifty thousand stolen pills right out under the Feds' noses. But to tell you the truth, I kind of like those guys. If they found out what we've done, they'd try and put us on death row, but except for that, I wouldn't mind popping back a few brews with them from time to time."

Strait glanced over at Gwen, and the look on her face startled him. "I loathe Web London," she said.

"Look, Gwen, I know what happened with your son and all—"

She exploded and beat the mattress with her fists. "It makes me sick to see his face. They're worse than the Frees. They come rushing in to save the world and innocent people start dying. Those people swore to me that once HRT was called in, no one else would die. And then they paraded around Web London as this big hero while my son lies dead in his grave. I'd love to shoot them all down myself."

Strait swallowed nervously at her wild tone and words as she knelt there on the bed, her hair in her face. Her lean, naked body, every muscle tensed, made her look like a panther about to spring. He eyed the gun where she'd put it on the nightstand and was ready to make a lunge for it, but she was quicker. She pointed the gun all around the room as Strait looked on nervously. Finally the barrel ended up pointed at Gwen herself. She looked down at it, as though she wasn't sure what it was. Her finger eased closer to the trigger.

"Then why don't you do it yourself?" he said, eyeing the gun. "Kill Web, I mean. Like you said, accidents happen. Especially on horse farms."

Gwen thought about this and finally dropped her angry look and smiled at him, putting down the gun.

"Maybe I will."

"Just don't blow it, though, 'cause we're in the home stretch."

She got under the covers, snuggled against him, kissed his cheek and put her hand under the sheet, rubbed him down there. "Just one more time," she said in a low, throaty voice, her gaze holding his. She slid the sheet off them both and looked down and smiled.

"My goodness, who needs Viagra, Nemo?"

"Woman, you are playing me like Charlie Daniels plays the fiddle."

Even without the potency drug, Strait managed to satisfy her one more time though it about killed him.

Later, as Gwen dressed, he watched her.

"Damn, you are a hellcat."

She zipped up her dress and held her shoes in one hand. Strait got up and started gingerly pulling his shirt over his bad arm. She looked at him. "Early morning plans?"

"Aw, you know how the life on a horse farm is, there's always something to do."

She turned to leave.

"You know, nothing personal or anything, Gwen, but it ain't good for a person to carry that much hate around. You just got to let it go at some point or else it'll ruin you. I was like that when my ex took the kids. At some point you just got to let it go."

She slowly turned and looked at him. "When you've seen your only child lying dead right in front of you with a bloody hole in his chest, Nemo, and then you lose the only other person you love because of it; when you've reached the lowest point of despair a person can reach and then watch yourself drop even lower—*then* you can come and talk to me about letting go of the hate."

51

Claire jerked up from a deep sleep that she had fallen into from exhaustion and despite her terror. She felt the fingers against her skin and she was about to strike out at her attacker when the voice made her stop.

"It's just me, Claire," said Kevin as he lifted off her blindfold.

There was no light, so Claire had to let her eyes adjust to the darkness. She looked down at Kevin, who was sitting next to her, his hands around the cuffs that held her to the wall.

"I thought you were tied up too."

He smiled and held up a small bit of metal. "I was. But I took this off one of the markers they give me to draw with. Picked the lock. I'm good with my hands."

"I can see that."

"Give me just one more minute and I get you loose too."

In less time than that, Kevin had her free. She rubbed her wrists and sat up, looked around and eyed the door. "I take it the door's locked?"

"Always has been. Maybe not now, if they think we chained up."

"Good point." She stood, taking a moment to get her balance after being off her feet for so long, a condition that was compounded by the darkness. She looked around again. "Anything we can use for a weapon, in case someone's on the other side of that door?" she whispered.

Kevin went over to the cot, turned it over on its side and unscrewed two of the metal legs. He kept one and handed the other to Claire.

"You hit 'em high and I hit 'em low," he said.

Claire nodded, without a lot of confidence, though. She wasn't sure she could hit anybody.

Kevin seemed to sense her trepidation, because he added, "We only hit 'em if they trying to hurt us, right?"

"Right," said Claire a lot more firmly.

They inched over to the door and tried it. It was locked. They listened intently for a bit yet could hear no one on the other side, even though the machinelike sounds were not as loud now. "I guess we're not getting out of here until they want us to," said Claire.

Kevin eyed the door and stepped back. "I ain't never noticed that before."

"What?"

"That the door hinges are on the inside."

Claire looked hopeful, but only for an instant. "But we'd need a screwdriver and hammer to get them out."

"Well, we got the hammer." He held up the metal table leg. "And right here is the screwdriver."

He went over to where the cuffs that had held Claire were attached to a bolt in the wall. With Claire's help, they finally managed to unscrew the bolt from the wall and Kevin slid off the cuffs. He held up one of the cuffs. "It got an nice edge to it, like a screwdriver."

"Good thinking again, Kevin," said Claire with considerable admiration. Here she was, feeling totally helpless, and Kevin was pulling one miracle after another out of his hat.

It took them some time and they kept stopping and listening for anyone coming, but the hinge pins finally came out. They were able to pry open the door and step through. It was dark here too, and they stumbled along, touching the walls of the narrow corridor for guidance. The smell of chlorine was very strong now. They were confronted with another locked door that Kevin was able to pick with his pen clasp. They encountered yet another door that, thankfully, was unlocked.

Claire took in a long breath, as did Kevin. He smiled at her. "Feels good to finally be outside.

"Well, let's get going before they come and lock us back up."

They moved past the covered pool, crept through the bushes and then down a winding grass path. As they neared the end of the path, Claire could see a building far up ahead. It was the mansion. She had glimpsed it on her visit. They were at East Winds Farm!

"Omigod," she exclaimed.

"Shhh," said Kevin.

She whispered into his ear, "I know where we are. I have friends who are here, we just have to get to them." The problem was that, in the darkness, it was hard to tell in which direction was the house that Web and Romano were using, even with the mansion as a marker.

"If they at the place where we been locked up, how you know they really your friends?"

"I just know. Come on." She took his hand and they made their way in what Claire thought was the direction of the carriage house. Long before they could reach it, however, both stiffened when they heard a vehicle coming. They ran back into the bushes and peered out. Claire's spirits plummeted. It was a truck, not the Mach or Romano's Corvette. She gasped when the truck pulled to a stop and several men with guns climbed out. Their escape had apparently been detected. She and Kevin ran deeper into the woods, such that Claire totally lost her bearings.

They finally stopped, caught their breath. Kevin looked around. "I ain't never seen so many trees in one place. Can't tell which way's out."

Claire breathed deeply, attempting to get her lungs and her nerves under control. She nodded. "I know." She studied the lay of the unfamiliar land and was attempting to make a decision on which direction they should go when they heard footsteps. Claire pulled Kevin to her and they squatted low in the underbrush.

The person was on the path and walked right past them, obviously unaware of Claire's and Kevin's presence. Claire peeked out. She didn't know Gwen Canfield and thus had no idea why a woman in a long red dress was walking barefoot through thick woods at this hour. Claire thought about calling out to her but finally decided against it. She had no idea who their captors were. This woman could be part of that group.

Once Gwen was out of sight, Claire and Kevin started moving again. They came to a darkened house, but that had a truck parked out front. Claire was debating whether to try and slip inside the place and use the phone to call the police when a man charged out of the house, jumped in his truck and roared off.

"I think that person just found out we got loose," she whispered to Kevin. "Come on."

They ran to the house. Claire had noted that in his haste the man had left the door open. They were about to go inside when they heard a sound that made Claire's stomach lurch.

"He's coming back," cried out Kevin. They raced back into the woods even as the truck bore down on them.

Pushing their way through the thick undergrowth, Claire quickly lost her shoes, and her and Kevin's clothes were being shredded by thorny vines and hard branches. They reached an open bit of ground, paused to catch their breath but took off running again when they heard the sounds of feet crashing through the underbrush.

They raced through to an open space and Claire saw a building loom up out of the darkness.

"Quick," she said to Kevin, "in there."

They climbed up on a loading dock and entered the Monkey House through a hole in the wall. Claire and Kevin looked around at the ruined insides of the place. Claire shivered when she observed the rusted cages. Kevin held his nose.

"Damn, it stinks in here," he said.

The sounds of men, and now the baying of dogs, were growing closer. "Over there," Claire said frantically. She climbed onto a box, boosted Kevin up and into a hole in the wall that probably once housed a ventilator fan. "Stay down and keep quiet," she told him.

"Where you going?"

"Not far," she said. "But if they find me, don't come out; whatever they say they'll do to me, don't come out. Do you understand?"

Kevin nodded slowly. "Claire," he said. She turned back. "Please be careful."

She smiled weakly, squeezed his hand and climbed back down. She looked around for a moment and then crept out through a gash in the rear wall. Once she was outside, the sounds of the dogs was even more terrifying. They must have given the animals something with her and Kevin's scent on it. She tore off a bit of her dress, grabbed a small rock, tied it inside the strip of material and threw it as far away from the Monkey House as she could. Then she ran off in the opposite direction. She reached the woods again, slid down an embankment and halted at the bottom. She looked around, trying to gauge the direction the sounds of men and dogs were coming from. Unfortunately, because of the topography, the noises were echoing all around. She forded a small creek, falling down halfway across and soaking herself. She struggled up and managed to scale a small embankment on the other side, then found herself on flat land. She was so tired now, part of her just wanted to lie here and wait for them to find her. Yet Claire pushed herself up and ran. When she reached another steep climb, she gripped a sapling and used it to thrust herself up. At the top she surveyed the land. Off in the distance she saw a light, and then another and another, all in pairs. A road. She took several deep breaths and took off at a steady jog. Her feet were torn and bleeding, but she didn't allow the pain to slow her down. She had to get help. She had to get help for Kevin.

The sounds of the men and dogs were gone now and she allowed herself the small hope that she might actually manage to succeed in escaping. She crawled the last few feet to the road and sat in the ditch for a moment, the tears spilling from her, partly from exhaustion, fear and having gained her freedom. She heard a car coming, stood and ran into the road, waving her arms and screaming for help.

At first it didn't appear the vehicle was going to stop at all. And Claire realized that she must look like some lunatic. But the vehicle finally slowed and then stopped. She ran to the passenger door and pulled it open. Her first sight was of Kevin sitting in the front seat, his mouth gagged, his arms and legs bound. The second sight was of Nemo Strait pointing a gun at her.

"Hey, Doc," he said. "You need a ride?"

He stretched his long body and then involuntarily shivered. The night had been a little cool and the dampness seemed to have settled into him. He wrapped the blanket tighter around him.

Francis Westbrook was not accustomed to camping out. What he was doing was about as close to camping as he was probably ever going to get, and he was not enjoying it. He drank some water and then edged his head out from his hiding place. The sun would be rising soon, he gauged. He hadn't slept particularly well; hell, he hadn't really slept since Kevin had disappeared. One lousy phone call, that was all he had been given. He had met with London, like they had told him to, and filled him in on the tunnels, again like they had told him to. He had undertaken a little unfinished business along the way with Toona, sure. Contrary to what Westbrook had told Web, he could abide skimmers and even those who used the product because if you didn't you wouldn't have anyone willing to come to work for you in the drug trade, it was as simple as that. But what he would never tolerate was a snitch. Macy had tipped him off to what Toona was doing and he had checked it out himself and found out Macy had been correct. So Toona was, appropriately enough, fish food. Sometimes life *was* fair, he thought.

Through the street grapevine he had learned that Peebles had been killed. The boy just didn't have what it took. But Westbrook had also learned, albeit too late, that Peebles had been orchestrating a takeover of his crew and consolidation of other crews in the area. That one had caught him off guard. He hadn't thought that old Twan had that in him. Macy had simply disappeared. That disloyalty had really ticked him off. Westbrook shrugged. Served him right for putting any trust in a white boy.

Now whoever had killed Twan might be gunning for him. Westbrook would just have to lie low and rely only upon himself until things worked out. Relying only on himself—it was just like old times. He had a couple of pistols, a few mags of ammo, about a thousand dollars in his pocket. He had abandoned the Navigator when he had come here, and the cops were still looking for him. Well, let them look. He had seen the Feds patrolling the place, but he had spent enough time dodging the cops to know how to hide even his very large carcass so that he blended right in with where he was. He had seen some strange things going on here. And he had heard the sounds of dogs barking off in the distance. The dogs were bad news. He had hunkered down farther into his hiding place and pulled over him a blanket he had covered with branches and leaves until the sounds had receded. As best as he could figure, London was still close by, and if London thought this place was important, then Westbrook did too. He checked his gun and settled back, took another drink of water, listened to the crickets and wondered what the new day would bring. Maybe it would bring Kevin.

Ed O'Bannon paced around the small, bare space. He hadn't smoked in years, yet he had gone through almost a pack in the last two hours. Discovery was something that he had always contemplated, but as time went on and things went smoothly, his fears had receded, even as his bank account had swollen. He heard someone coming and turned to the door. It was locked, and thus he was surprised when he heard the knob turning. O'Bannon backed away. When the man came in, he breathed a sigh of relief.

"Long time no see, Doc."

O'Bannon put out his hand and Nemo Strait shook it.

"I wasn't sure you were going to make it, Nemo."

"When have I ever let you down?"

"I've got to get going. The Feds are bottling the country up."

"Don't get yourself all bent out of shape. We got lots of ways for you to go and the planes, papers and the people to get you there." Strait held up a packet of documents. "Through Mexico to Rio and then on to Johannesburg. From there you got your option of Australia, New Zealand, lots of fugitives go there. Or maybe hit our old stomping grounds in Southeast Asia."

O'Bannon eyed the packet and breathed another sigh of relief. He smiled and lit another cigarette. "That seems like a hundred years ago."

"Hey, I'll never forget. You saved my ass after the Viet Cong screwed with my mind."

"Deprogramming, not so difficult for someone who knows what he's doing."

"Lucky for me you did," said Strait. He paused and grinned.

"And catching a little drug action on the side. That was a nice little side benefit for your practice."

O'Bannon shrugged. "Everyone was doing that back then."

"Hell, yes, they were, myself included, though it was just for my personal use."

"I have to hand it to you, when you looked me up with your idea of bugging my offices and selling the information on the streets, that was pure genius."

Strait grinned. "Well, the Feds got all these resources, we had to level the playing field a little bit. But it was a win-win. You got the info, I got folks who need that stuff to conduct their business, myself included. You make money, I make money and the Feds get the short end of the stick. What could be better?"

When Gwen had brought Strait in on her plan to exact revenge on the people involved with her son's death, he had started investigating both Hostage Rescue and Web London. Growing up on a horse farm just made a person methodical like that, Strait had long ago realized. You got all the information you could, formed a plan and executed that plan. Until he had been captured by the Viet Cong, Strait had been an excellent soldier, leading his company in and out of many hellish situations, and he had a chest full of medals to prove it, not that that had ever mattered to him. Then he discovered that the Ed O'Bannon he had known in Vietnam was the same O'Bannon treating Web London. That had given him the idea to both set up London and HRT because he knew firsthand what Ed O'Bannon could do with someone's mind. Initially, however, O'Bannon wanted no part of it. But when Strait had learned how many law enforcement people he had as patients, he had approached O'Bannon again and repeated his offer to bug the premises, sell the information to criminals and split the proceeds fifty-fifty with the good doctor. With that inducement O'Bannon had signed on immediately. The passage of years had not lessened the man's greed. Some of the bugged psychiatrist sessions had also provided Strait with all the information he needed to set up HRT. He had never told O'Bannon about his Oxycontin drug trade because the man no doubt would've wanted a cut of that too. And now Strait already had a partner in Gwen Canfield. Twenty-five percent, damn! But he had to admit, last night had been worth it.

Nemo said, "I was one surprised pup when you brought Claire Daniels to us. Although I guess I shouldn't have been. When you told me London was seeing her, I knew it'd be a problem down the road."

"I tried to get him to stay with me. But like I said, I couldn't push too hard without raising suspicions. I kept most of his file from her, of course. And you were the only ones I could turn to."

"You did the right thing. I can guarantee you this: She'll never testify against you in court."

O'Bannon shook his head. "It's hard to believe it's over."

"Well, we had us one sweet operation going."

"'Had' is right," O'Bannon said mournfully.

"I guess you got no love for our federal government either."

"After what I saw in Vietnam? No. And working for the Bureau in-house didn't do much to change that opinion."

"Well, I'm betting you got you a nice little nest egg to last you the rest of your days."

O'Bannon nodded. "I've been smart about it. Now I just hope I get to enjoy it."

"I want to thank you, Doc, for all your help. You did London perfect."

"With his background, believe me, he was an easy case. Didn't even need any drugs." He smiled. "The man trusted me. What does that say for the mighty FBI?"

Strait yawned and rubbed at his eyes.

"Late night?" asked O'Bannon.

"You could say that. Sort of burning the candle at both ends and in the middle too."

There was a quiet knock at the door.

Strait said, "Come on in." He looked at O'Bannon. "Here's your ride. This is my best guy. He'll take care of everything."

Clyde Macy walked in and stared first at O'Bannon and then at Strait.

"I go way back with this boy. Showed him the error of his ways, I guess, ain't that right?"

Macy said, "The old man I never had."

Strait laughed. "You got that right. If you can believe it, this boy infiltrated a black drug crew in D.C. Set 'em up to take the heat for what we did. One of 'em, dude named Antoine Peebles, was trying to take over this fellow Westbrook's turf. So Mace played along with this little plan, Peebles helped us when we needed it, and then Mace killed Peebles."

O'Bannon looked puzzled. "Why'd you do that?"

"Because I wanted to," said Macy, his remorseless eyes dead on O'Bannon. "It was a mission I put together for myself. And I successfully completed it."

Strait chuckled. "Then he made sure HRT and the Free Society shot it out. The man is invaluable. Okay, Mace, this is Ed O'Bannon, the friend I told you about." He handed O'Bannon the documents and slapped him on the shoulder and shook his hand.

"I meant what I said, Doc, you did right by us. Thanks again, and you make yourself one fun-loving fugitive from justice."

Strait turned and left. As he closed the door behind him, he heard the first muffled shot and then one more. Damn, that Macy was efficient. He'd taught the boy real well. He did have some faults, though. Macy's competition thing with the FBI was sometimes inconvenient. One of the concessions he had made to keep the boy happy had been pretty risky, but all in all Strait could not have pulled this off without Clyde Macy.

Strait had nothing against Ed O'Bannon, but loose ends were loose ends. And Nemo Strait didn't trust Ed O'Bannon or anyone else. Okay, one problem down, now just two more to go: Kevin Westbrook and Claire Daniels. They had escaped once, but they wouldn't have a chance to do it again. And then it was time to call it a career. The Greek islands were sounding better and better. Not bad for a boy who had grown up dirt poor and who had lived by his wits ever since. America was the land of opportunity indeed.

As he got in his truck, Nemo Strait wondered if there were any horse farms in Greece. He hoped not.

In the carriage house Web opened his eyes and looked around. He didn't hear Romano stirring, and when he glanced at his watch he knew why. It was not yet six. He got up, opened the window and inhaled an early morning breeze. He had slept unusually heavily.

He would be gone from here soon and part of him was glad about that and part of him wasn't.

What he was thinking about mostly, though, was Claire. His experience told him that there was very little chance that the woman was still alive. It was numbing, the thought of never seeing her again.

As he continued to gaze outside, he saw Gwen driving down the road from the mansion in a Jeep with its top off. She pulled into the cobblestone courtyard in front of the carriage house and got out. She was dressed to ride in jeans, boots and a sweater; her long hair gracefully framed her face. She wore no hat.

As she walked to the door, he called out. "Rent check's in the mail, call off the eviction."

She looked up, smiled and waved. "I thought we might go for one last ride." She looked at the lightening sky. "By the time we saddle up, it'll be the best time of the day to cruise the trails. You with me, Mr. London?" She flashed a smile that seemed to push away just about every concern Web had.

They saddled their mounts, Gwen on Baron and Web on a smaller roan horse named Comet. Gwen explained that Boo had an infected leg.

"Hope the big fellow will be all right."

"Not to worry, horses are very resilient," answered Gwen.

They covered a good deal of ground over about an hour and a half, and as they rode along all Gwen could think was that she had never killed anyone before. Yes, she had bluffed Nemo Strait the night before, but when it came down to it, could she do it? She looked at Web riding next to her and tried her best to cast him in the form of her worst enemy, her most terrifying nightmare. Yet it was difficult to do. For years she had dreamed about killing each and every member of this so-called heroic band of federal agents whom everyone had assured here were the best there was. That they would get her son and all the other hostages out alive; that was what they had drilled into her, until Gwen's fears had receded and her expectations had soared. It was like being told you had cancer but that it was absolutely curable, and you believed this until they closed your coffin and put you in the ground. Well, they had almost accomplished their goal of rescuing every hostage, allowing only her son to perish. And then she had watched, seething, as Web London's face graced newspaper, magazines, TV shows, his heroic deeds outlined in nauseating detail, ending with a medal given to him personally by the President himself. She could not think of his horrible injuries. She did not know of the grueling ordeals he had endured as he fought his way back on to HRT. Not that any of that would have mattered to her. All she could think of was that Web was alive and her son was dead. Some hero.

Yes, the sight of her son lying dead next to Web London had popped something in her brain. She could actually remember the crackle that seemed to go through every nerve in her body, like lightning had struck; and she had never been the same since. She had never had a day since when she did not see the bloody body of her son lying there on the ground. Nor could she ever forget the image of men in battle gear going in to rescue her son and somehow managing to bring everyone out alive except him. She looked back at Web and he slowly took on hues of black, of evil. He was the last man. Yes, she could kill him. And maybe her nightmare would finally be over.

"I suppose you and Romano will be leaving today?"

"Looks that way."

Gwen smiled and flicked at her hair. She kept a tight grip on her reins, for she felt her hand might start shaking. "Your good work done?"

"Something like that. How's Billy?"

"All right. He goes through moods, like we all do."

"You don't strike me as moody. You seem the type to roll with the punches."

"You'd be surprised sometimes."

"That was some party last night."

"Billy can really throw them. The Ransome brothers were not exactly what I expected."

"You don't believe that's their real name, do you?"

"Not for a second."

"When I first met them I thought they were gay. That is, until you walked into the room, and then their sexual orientation became pretty clear."

Gwen laughed. "I'll take that as a compliment."

They rode past the opening to the small glen where Gwen's chapel was.

"Aren't you going to the chapel today?"

"Not today." Gwen looked away from the opening in the trees. Today was not a day for prayer. While Web wasn't looking, though, she crossed herself. *Forgive me, God, for what I am about to do.* Even as she silently mouthed the words, she never really expected that prayer to be answered.

They reached a steep slope of earth that at the top was covered with trees. She had never taken Web this way before. Perhaps in the back of her mind she had known this day would come.

Gwen whipped up Baron and charged toward the slope, Web and Comet right on their heels. They galloped up the slope, Web almost nosing ahead of Gwen. When they got to the top, they stopped their mounts and gazed out over the countryside while the horses sucked in huge amounts of air.

Gwen looked at Web with genuine admiration. "I'm impressed."

"Hey, I had a great teacher."

"The watchtower is close by. The view's even better from there."

Web didn't tell her he'd already been up there with Romano when they had checked out the Ransomes' spread. "Sounds good."

They rode to the tower, tethered the horses to a wooden post and let them graze. Gwen led Web up to the top of the tower and they watched the sun rising and the woods coming to life down below.

"I guess it doesn't get much better than this," said Web.

"You'd think not," said Gwen.

He leaned against the belly-high wall and looked at her.

"Problems with you and Billy?"

"It's that obvious?"

"I've seen worse."

"Have you? What if I told you that you have no damn idea what you're talking about?" she said with sudden anger.

Web's tone remained calm. "You know, we've never really done that. Talked."

She avoided his gaze. "Actually, I've talked to you more than I do to most people. And I barely know *you*."

"Chitchat, maybe. And I'm not that hard to get to know."

500   DAVID BALDACCI

"I'm not totally comfortable with you yet, Web."

"Well, we're running out of time. I don't think our worlds will come together again. But I guess that's a good thing."

"I suppose," she said. "I'm not sure Billy and I will be at East Winds much longer."

Web looked surprised. "I thought this was it for you two. Why go anywhere else? You may have your problems, but you're happy here. Aren't you? This is the life you wanted, right?"

She spoke slowly. "There's a lot of factors that go into the equation of happiness. Some are more apparent than others."

"I guess I can't help you there. I'm not an expert on happiness, Gwen."

She shot him a curious glance. "Neither am I." They stared at each other awkwardly for a long moment.

"Well, you deserve to be happy, Gwen."

"Why?" she asked quickly. For some reason, she actually wanted to hear his reasoning.

"Because you've suffered so much. It's only fair—that is, if anything in this life is fair."

"Have *you* suffered?" There was a harsh bite to her words, but she covered it quickly with a sympathetic expression. She wanted to hear that he had. But it couldn't come close to what she had endured.

"I've had my share of bad times. My childhood wasn't exactly the American dream. And my adulthood hasn't really made up for that."

"I always wondered why people do what you do. The good guys." She said this with a completely straight face.

"I do the things I do because they need doing and most people can't or won't do them. I'd much prefer that my occupation become obsolete, but I just don't see that happening." He looked down. "I never had a chance to tell you this, but I might not get another one." He drew in a long breath. "What happened in Richmond, that was about my first time as an assaulter, the guys who go in and get the hostages." He paused again. "After Waco the FBI was really spooked and got ultraconservative in those situations. I'm not saying that that was right or wrong, just that it was different. We wait around for the negotiators listening to all the lies on the phone. It seemed like it always took someone dying before they let us do what we do, and by then we were always playing catch-up. But those were the new rules and we had to play by them." He shook his head. "I knew something was up when the Frees broke off negotiations. I could feel it. I'd been a sniper for a lot of years, and watching things unfold all that time, you get a sixth sense for what's coming. You just do." He looked at Gwen. "I've never told you about this. Do you want to hear it?"

"Yes." Gwen said this so fast, she had no time to even think about it.

"Billy knows some of it. When he came to see me in the hospital."

"I'm sorry I never was able to."

"I didn't expect you to. I was stunned to see Billy, actually." Web seemed to take a few moments to compose his thoughts. While he did so, Gwen stared out at the foothills of the Blue Ridge in the distance. Now that she thought about it, she really didn't want to hear this, but she couldn't tell him no.

Web said, "We got to the gymnasium entrance clean. I looked through the window. Your son saw me. We made eye contact."

This clearly surprised her. "I didn't know that."

"Well, I never told anyone before, not even Billy. The time never seemed right."

"What did he look like?" she said slowly. Her pulse was pounding in her ears as she waited for his answer.

"He looked scared, Gwen. But he also looked stubborn, defiant. Not an easy thing when you're ten years old and facing a bunch of psychos with guns. I guess now I see where David got that spirit."

"Go on," she said in a small voice.

"I motioned to him to keep calm. I gave him the thumbs-up be-cause I wanted him to stay cool. If he got spooked and reacted or something, they probably would have shot him instantly."

"Did he?"

Web nodded. "He was smart. He knew what I was trying to do. He was right with me, Gwen. With all that stuff going down, he was as brave as anyone could be."

Gwen could see that there were tears in his eyes. She tried to say something but found she couldn't speak. The terrible years of her life started to seem erased by his words.

"We were about to go in. Quiet, no explosive. We'd seen through the window where each of the Frees was positioned. We were just going to pop them all at once. We got our countdown and then it happened."

"What? What happened?"

"A sound from inside. It was like a damn bird or whistle, or alarm or something. It was loud, high-pitched and it couldn't have come at a worse time. The Frees were instantly on alert and when we came through the door, they opened fire. I don't know why they shot David, but he was the first to go down."

Gwen wasn't looking at Web now. Her gaze seemed frozen on the hills. *A whistle?*

"I saw the shot hit him." Web's voice was now very shaky. "I saw his face. His eyes." Web closed his and the tears dribbled out from under the lids. "They were still looking at me."

Gwen's eyes were filled with tears now too, yet she still wasn't looking at Web. "What did he look like then?"

He turned and stared at her. "He looked betrayed," Web said. He touched his damaged face. "My face, and the two bullet holes I have in my body, none of it hurt me more than the look on your son's face." He said again, "Betrayed."

Gwen was trembling so badly now that she had to support herself against the railing as the tears poured from her. Still, she couldn't look at him. *A whistle.*

"Maybe that's why I disobeyed orders when I joined the attack on the Frees." He stared at her. "It cost me my career, Gwen, I've been kicked out of the Bureau for it. But I'd do it again. Maybe it was my way of atoning for things. See, your son deserved better than I could give him. I live with that every day. And I'm sorry that I let him and you down. I don't expect forgiveness, but I just wanted you to know."

She said quietly, "We probably should get back."

Gwen went down first and walked over to Comet instead of Baron. She lifted the horse's foreleg. Every nerve in Gwen's body was now on fire, her pulse still banging in her ears. She could barely stand, but she had to do this, despite all that had just been revealed, she had to do this. She had waited long enough. She closed her eyes and then reopened them.

"Is there a problem?" asked Web.

She couldn't look at the man. "It seemed like he was a bit off in front. But it looks all right. I'll have to keep an eye on it."

She reached up and patted Comet's neck, and while Web wasn't looking she slipped the object she held in her hand under the saddle.

"Okay, now this is your big test," she said. "We're going to gallop hard down that slope toward those trees, but then you have to rein in the horse quickly because the path through the trees is too narrow to do much more than a walk. Understand?"

"I'm game." Web patted Comet's neck.

"I'm sure you are. Let's ride," she said with finality.

They both swung into the saddle and started toward the trees.

"You want to lead?" asked Web as he settled into the saddle.

"You go ahead. I want to watch Comet's leg—"

The horse bolted and Web wasn't ready for it. Comet accelerated and headed at full gallop down the slope and straight for the thick trees.

"Web!" screamed Gwen, and she rode after him, but she was subtly reining Baron in and was falling behind. As she watched, Web lost a stirrup and then almost fell off. The reins dropped from his hands and he clutched the saddle horn in desperation even as the ground between him and trees was closing fast. He didn't know it, but every bounce in the saddle was driving the small tack Gwen had placed under the saddle further into the horse's body.

Web never looked back. But if he had, he would have seen a woman suddenly in terrible conflict. Gwen Canfield wanted so desperately to see horse and rider slam into those trees. She wanted to see Web London die right in front of her, to be vanquished forever. She wanted to be released from the pain that had tormented her for so long. She just couldn't endure it anymore. She was beyond her limit. Something had to give. All she had to do was sit back. Instead she whipped up Baron and thundered after Web. Fifty feet separated Web from those trees, and Comet was living up to his name. At forty feet, Gwen slipped a little to the side of her horse. At thirty feet she started reaching out, poising her hand at just the right angle. They were twenty feet from the trees and now Gwen had thrown her fate in with Web's, for if she couldn't stop Comet, she and Baron would be hitting those trees too.

At ten feet she managed to lean far enough over to grab the reins. And she pulled with a strength that came from all the agony bottled up inside her for all those years, for she almost single-handedly pulled down a thousand-pound horse going at break-neck speed barely five feet from the tree line.

Breathless, she looked over at Web, who just sat there, slumped over. He finally glanced at her but still said nothing. And yet Gwen felt like the load of the collective misery of the world had been lifted from her shoulders. She had long envisioned it as akin to barnacles against her soul, impossible to remove; and yet now it had disappeared like sand in a breeze. And she marveled that finally letting go of all the hate could actually feel this wonderful. Yet the cruelty of life had not finished with her, because now Gwen's hate had been replaced with something even more corrosive: guilt.

52

When Gwen dropped Web off at the carriage house, she was strangely silent. He tried to thank her for saving his life, but she had cut him off and driven away. A very curious woman was Gwen Canfield. Maybe she blamed herself somehow for what had happened with Comet.

Yet at least Web had accomplished his goal of finally telling the woman what he had been holding in all these years. He thought about going up and telling Billy too, but maybe it would be better coming from Gwen—that is, if she bothered to tell her husband at all.

He went inside and Romano was eating breakfast. "You look a little whipped," commented Romano.

"Hard ride."

"So we are officially done here, aren't we? See, Angie's back and she is one ticked-off lady. I'm going to need to head home sometime and face the music."

"Yeah, I guess we're done here."

"Hey, Web, I'll race you back to Quantico, we'll find out what your Mach is really made of."

"Look, Paulie, the last thing I need is a speeding . . ." He froze and Romano looked at him curiously.

"What? It's not the end of the world getting stopped for speeding. You flash your creds and they let you go. Professional courtesy."

Web pulled out his cell phone and punched in the numbers. He asked for Percy Bates, but he wasn't in.

"Where is he? This is Web London."

Web knew Bates's secretary, June, and she recognized his voice. "I know it's you, Web. I'm so sorry what happened."

"So Perce isn't around?"

"The truth is, he took a couple days off. The media relations people are going nuts. They wanted to bring you in to get some quotes, but Perce said no. Have you seen the TV or the papers?"

"No."

"Well, someone would've thought we killed the Pope by mistake, for the fuss people are making over what happened."

"Well, a lot of people did die, June."

"People with guns shooting at other people take that risk, Web," she said, steadfastly toeing the Bureau line. "Anyway, Perce said he had to get away for a couple of days. I know he felt horrible about what happened with you."

"I know, June, but maybe there's a silver lining in there for me."

"I hope so, I really do. Now, can I help you with anything?"

"Clyde Macy, he worked as a foot soldier for one of the local drug crews. I saw some speeding tickets in his file. I just wanted to find out exactly where he had gotten them and when."

"I'll have to call somebody for that, but it should only take a few minutes."

Web gave her his number to call back. As promised, she did shortly. She gave him the information and Web thanked her and clicked off. He looked over at Romano with a dumbfounded expression.

"What?" asked Romano as he swallowed the last bite of his pastrami-on-rye breakfast.

"Clyde Macy got three speeding tickets over a six-month period. Almost lost his license."

"Big whoop. So he drives too fast."

"Guess where he got all three?"

"Where?"

"All within one mile of the Southern Belle farm, and one of them less than a hundred yards from the entrance. The entrance was actually noted as a landmark on the Fauquier County police officer's report. That's why I picked up on it."

"Okay, so I guess I'm not going home to Angie today?"

"Sure you are. But tonight we're hitting the Southern Belle."

They packed their gear and got in their cars.

"You tell them we're heading out?" He motioned toward the mansion.

"They know." Web glanced back at the stone house and said quietly, "Good luck, Gwen."

As they were driving out, they saw Nemo heading toward them in his truck. He slowed and stopped. He looked, Web noted, very surprised to see him.

"Hey, you boys wanta have a beer?" Nemo asked.

The 'Vette's top was down, and Romano was seated up on the top of the seat back. "Give me a rain check on that."

Strait pointed at him and grinned. "You got it, Delta."

"Thanks for your help, Nemo," said Web.

"I guess you guys are closing up shop."

"Looks that way, but keep an eye out on the Canfields. Old Ernie is still at large."

"That I will."

As Web and Romano drove off, Nemo looked thoughtfully after them and then stared up ahead at the mansion. Apparently the hellcat had lost her nerve.

Angie Romano was not in a good mood. She'd had her sons by herself all this time and the trip to Bayou Country apparently had not been all that pleasant. Web tried to give her a friendly hug when he came to pick up Romano but stopped when she glared at him like she might break his arms if he tried.

And so the toughest member of Hotel Team and the sole survivor of Charlie Team fled the Romano household late at night and climbed in the Mach for what might well be their final gig together. Web had not told Romano about him resigning from the Bureau, but the word had gotten around and Romano had found out when he got back home. He had been really upset at Web for not telling him, but now he was more upset at the Bureau.

"You give 'em everything you got, and this . . . this is how they thank you. Man, it almost makes me want to go and work for a cartel in Colombia. At least you know where you stand with those guys."

"Forget it, Paulie. Hell, if things work out right, I'll start my own protection company and you can come and work for me."

"Yeah, and I'm wearing a bra under my Kevlar."

The men were prepared to go to war, with their .45s and MP-5s and body armor and even their .308 sniper rifles, because they weren't exactly sure what they would find at the Southern Belle. They couldn't call the Bureau in because they had nothing to tell them except some speeding tickets and a few conspiracy theories. But the bright side to Web's not being officially with the Bureau anymore was that sometimes an honest citizen could get into places and do things a cop never could. Web had had second thoughts about taking Romano, but when he voiced those concerns with Romano, the man had told him that if he didn't go, neither would Web, because Romano said he'd shoot Web in a place no man would want to be shot. And Web chose not to test Romano's resolve.

Web parked the Mach on a dirt road that ran along the property line between East Winds and the Southern Belle. As they were making their way through the dense forest, Romano was complaining. "These damn NV goggles are already giving me a headache. I hate the sons of bitches. They weigh a ton. And you can't even shoot anyone when you're wearing 'em. So what the hell good is that?"

"Then take the damn things off, Paulie, or stop complaining, before *you* give *me* a headache." However, Web slid his off too and rubbed his neck.

As forest sounds came at them from all directions, Romano said, "No snipers to cover our butt. I'm feeling kind of nervous and lonely, Web."

The man was just kidding, Web knew. There was nothing on this earth that really scared Paul Romano, at least that Web knew of. Well, except for Angie.

"You'll get over it."

"Hey, Web, you still haven't told me what you expect to find tonight."

"Whatever it is, it'll be more than we know right now." Without Bureau resources behind him, Web had not been able to send the FBI's fact-digging machine into gear to discover what it could about Harvey and Giles Ransome. He could have called Ann Lyle, but he just didn't want to talk to the woman right now. With him out of HRT, it would've been too hard because she would no doubt break down and then so would he.

The two men made their way forward through the trees until they could make out the buildings they had seen from the watchtower. Web signaled for Romano to hold up while Web crept forward. Web smiled when he reached the edge of the tree line. There was a lot of activity at the old Southern Belle tonight. A large truck was parked at one of the warehouse-style buildings, its ramp down. Men were carrying equipment out of the truck and Web's gaze went over each of them looking for weaponry, yet he saw none. A large crate on a forklift was being driven to the warehouse. When the door slid open, Web tried to make out what was going on inside, but he couldn't. All he could see were blinding lights before the door closed. Off to one side Web did see a horse trailer with a man working around it. From his angle Web couldn't see if there was actually a horse in it or not.

He spoke into his walkie-talkie and called Romano up to his position. Romano joined him a minute later and squatted next to him. He surveyed what Web had been looking at and whispered to him, "So, what's your take?"

"Could be anything from drugs to a chop shop, I don't know."

At that moment the door to the building opened and the forklift came back out. And that's when they heard the woman's scream. It rose higher and higher. Web and Romano looked at each other.

"Or maybe a slavery ring," hissed Romano.

They put their MP-5s on automatic fire and slid out from the woods. Each held the butt of his weapon against his right pec, the muzzle gripped with the index and forefinger.

They made it to the side of the warehouse without being seen. Web spotted a side door and pointed it out to Romano, who nodded. Web made more hand signals, telling Romano with his fingers in the special language of the assaulter what he was planning. In a way it was like the communication between a baseball pitcher and his catcher. However, the big difference was they would be facing something a lot more ominous than a Louisville Slugger.

Web tried the door. Surprisingly, it was unlocked. He opened it a notch farther. Then they heard the woman scream again in a garbled manner, like someone was driving something right down her throat.

Web and Romano burst in, guns ready, took in the scene in sec-

onds. From the corner of his eye Web could see Giles Ransome sitting in a chair.

Web bellowed out, "FBI, on the floor, fingers interlocked behind
your head. Do it or you're fucking dead." Romano would be proud,
thought Web.

There were more screams from all corners as people hit the floor.
Web caught a glimpse of somebody flying by to his left and he
pointed his gun that way. Romano was charging straight ahead
and then stopped.

Harvey Ransome was standing in the middle of what looked like
a bedroom, a bunch of papers in one hand. On the bed were three
beautiful, surgically enhanced and totally naked women and one
young man, fully aroused.

"What in the hell is going on here?" yelled Harvey. When he saw
that it was Web, he paled.

Web and Romano were looking around now and they both noted
the film cameras, banks of lights, generators, grips, gaffers, cam-
eramen, props and the mock bedroom suite, which was one of four
different sets, the others resembling an office, the inside of a limo
and, Web noted with surprise, a church. That's what this was? The
Southern Belle was the cover for a porno studio? The screams had
been ones of false ecstasy?

Web lowered his weapon as Harvey advanced toward him, script
in hand.

"What the hell is going on, Web?"

Web shook his head clear and stared fiercely at the man. "You
tell me."

"This is a perfectly legit business. You can look it up. We have all
the permits and approvals." He motioned toward the naked people
in the large bed. "And all of these people are professional actors, of
legal age. You can check them out."

Romano went over to the bed, where Web joined him.

The young women looked at the two men with defiant expressions, while the man tried to hide under the sheet, his most
prominent feature now long since deflated.

The women didn't make a move to cover themselves up in the
presence of strange men with guns.

"All you people here voluntarily?" asked Romano.

"You bet, sugar," said one whose bosom was so large it almost covered her stomach. "Hey, you want a part in the movie? I'd like to show you how *voluntarily* I can be." When Romano blushed, the women all started laughing.

"You got a gun that big in your pants?" said another woman.

"Web?" Romano asked helplessly. "What do you want to do here?"

Giles joined his brother. "This is First Amendment territory, Web. You don't want to go there. We'll have you and the Bureau in court for years and we'll win."

"Well, if it's so legit, why the farm cover?"

"We have to think of the neighbors. If they knew what we were really doing, they could make trouble for us. They're wealthy and they know powerful people in public office who could make our lives miserable."

"All we want," said Harvey, "is to be left alone to create our art."

"Art?" said Web. He waved his hand at the naked bodies. "Is that what you call screwing on a two-bit set with inflated Barbie dolls? Art?"

One of the women stood up in all her naked and pumped-up glory. She barely looked twenty. "Who the hell do you think you are?"

"No offense, lady, but I'm just calling it like I see it."

"You don't know what the hell you're talking about."

"Yeah, you're right, and I bet your mommy's real proud of you too, isn't she?" said Web.

Harvey put a hand on Web's shoulder. "Listen, Web, we *are* legit. We pay our taxes, we do things by the book. Check it out; we're not going anywhere. My brother and I have been doing this for thirty years out in California."

"So why'd you move here?"

"We got tired of the LA scene," answered Giles. "And this is such pretty country."

Romano looked at the naked actors. "Well, I doubt they ever see it."

"We don't want trouble, Web," said Harvey. "Like I said, we'll win in court, but we don't want it to go to court. We're not hurting anybody here. And lots of people, whether they admit it or not, use our product. And not just flakes on the fringes, but moms and dads smack in the middle of mainstream USA. You know what they say, sex is good for the soul, and watching professional sex can be even better."

"It's fantasy, man, all fantasy," added Giles. "We just give people what they want."

"Okay, okay, I get your point." No wonder the two brothers had been all over Gwen Canfield. They probably wanted to hire her for their next production.

"Listen, is there anything we can do for you? You know, to say thank you for keeping this on the QT?" asked Harvey anxiously.

"Just so we understand each other, Harv, I *will* check you out. And if you're lying to me, or any of these 'actors' are underage, I'll be back. And if you're thinking of sneaking out in the meantime, don't try, because we'll have people posted."

"All right. I guess that's fair."

"Oh, and there is something you can do for me."

"Just name it."

"Stop flying your aircraft over East Winds. It's bothering some friends of mine."

Harvey put out his hand. "You have my word."

Web didn't shake his hand. Instead he looked at the young women. "And you ladies have my sympathy."

Romano and Web made their way out, laughter following in their wake.

"Gee," said Romano, "I'd call that mission a sterling success."

"Shut up, Paulie."

As they were heading back to the woods, Web saw the same man standing by the horse trailer that he had observed earlier. Web walked over. The fellow was dressed like a farmhand. He looked alarmed when he saw their guns until Romano flashed his badge.

"Look, I don't want any trouble," said the man, who looked to be about fifty. "Serves me right, though, for hiring on to this outfit."

"I guess you help provide the legitimate cover."

The man looked toward the warehouse—or, as Web now knew, film soundstage. "Lots of things need covering up around here. If my poor wife were still with us, she'd skin me alive, but they're paying twice the going rate."

"That should've told you something," said Web.

"I know, I know, but I guess everybody gets greedy and I been doing this work a long time. Too long, I suppose."

Web looked over at the trailer. There was a horse in it. Web could see the top of its head.

"You going somewhere?"

"Yep. Got a long ride. Taking that horse up for sale. Got to put on a pretense that we know what we're doing here. And that yearling is actually pretty nice."

Web went over to the trailer. "Really? He looks kind of small to me."

The man looked at Web like he was crazy. "Small? He's fifteen hands. That ain't small for a yearling."

Web looked inside the trailer. The top of it was a good eighteen inches above the horse's head. He looked at the man. "Is this a special trailer?"

"Special . . . what do you mean?"

"Sizewise. Is it particularly big?"

"Nope, it's your standard seven-foot Townsmand bumper pull."

"*This* is a standard Townsmand? And that yearling is fifteen hands high? You're sure?"

"As sure as I'm standing here."

Web shone his light around the interior.

"If this is a standard trailer, how come you don't have your tack boxes down there?" He looked at the man suspiciously and shone his light at the sides of the trailer's interior.

The man looked at where the light was shining. "Well, the first point, son, is you don't never put anything like that where a horse can nick its leg on 'em. A nicked leg can blow a sale."

"You can pad them," Web shot back.

"And the second point is . . ." He pointed up to the front of the trailer, where Web could see a large compartment filled with tack, medicine bottles, ropes, blankets and the like. "And the second point is, you got all that tack room right there, so why do you need to put something special in that might just tear up your horse's legs?" The man looked at Web like he really was insane.

Web wasn't paying attention because something was starting to seep into his brain that, if true, would put a whole new face on everything that had been happening. He fumbled in his pocket and pulled out some photos he had kept in an envelope, photos Bates had given him. Web picked one out and held it in front of Romano as he shone his light on it. "The guy who you gave the kid to that night?" he said. "Is this him? Think of him with a blond crew cut, not bald. I know it's hard because he was wearing shades. But try."

Romano studied the photo and then gaped at Web. "I think that's him."

Web immediately took off running for the tree line, Romano right behind him.

"What the hell's got into you, Web?"

Web didn't answer. He just kept running.

53

The door to the underground room opened and Nemo Strait walked in. Claire and Kevin were each cuffed to a large iron bolt in the wall, and their arms and legs were also bound with thick rope. Strait had ordered them gagged but not blindfolded. "You've already seen way too much, Doc," he had explained to Claire, "but it won't matter none." His chilling meaning had been absolutely clear.

His men poured in behind Strait and came at her and Kevin with blankets and more ropes.

"Help us, help us," Claire tried to scream out, but her words were barely audible because of the gag. She struggled vainly against the men. Kevin just stared silently at his captors, as though his expectation of death had finally been realized.

"Let's move it," said Nemo Strait. "We don't have all night, and we got a lot to do."

As they carried Kevin out, Strait affectionately patted the boy on the head.

Web looked in each of the back windows of Nemo Strait's house. The man's truck wasn't parked out front, but Web was taking no chances. Romano was checking the sides and the front. They hooked up and Romano shook his head. "Nothing. Place is empty."

"Not for long," said Web.

It took all of twenty seconds to pick the back door lock and they were inside. They methodically searched the place until they came to the man's bedroom.

"What exactly are we looking for, Web?"

Web was in the bedroom closet and didn't answer right away. He finally backed out with an old shoebox. "This might be a start."

He sat on a chair next to the bed and started going through the old photos. He held one up. "Here we go. Remember Strait said he was a guard at a juvenile detention center when he got back from Nam?"

"So?"

"So, guess who was an inmate at that same juvie center for putting a meat cleaver in his grandma's head? I saw the file when I met with Bates at WFO."

"Who are you talking about?"

"Clyde Macy. He's the guy in the photo I showed you, the guy who impersonated an FBI agent. Damn, I wish I'd shown you his photo before. Now I'm betting if we looked at the dates it'll show Macy and Strait were there at the same time."

"But Macy was with the Frees after that."

"And maybe Strait finds him and convinces him to come and work for him."

"But you said Macy was muscle for Westbrook."

"What Macy is, is a cop wannabe. I'm thinking he was undercover and was infiltrating Westbrook's organization as part of Strait's drug ring."

"Strait's drug ring!"

"Oxycontin. Horse trailers, the perfect way to move the stuff. The trailer at the Southern Belle was how a Townsmand is really set up. Strait had the one at East Winds put in with a false bottom that raised the floor so much a fifteen-hands-high yearling's head almost touched the roof. And he had storage boxes put in to carry even more drugs. And the speeding tickets? Macy wasn't going to the Southern Belle, he was coming here. And I bet he was the one who found out Toona was snitching for Cove. He used that information to set up Cove and us and then told Westbrook, who eliminated Toona."

"You think maybe Macy was the one who fired the shots at the Free compound and started the slaughter?"

"And planted the drugs there and all the other 'evidence' for us to conveniently find. And he probably stole Silas's truck. I'm betting he was also the one who shot Chris Miller outside of Cove's house. And Strait is ex-Army and maybe that's how he got hold of those machine guns, and he probably knows something about making bombs."

"But that means they were both tied in somehow to the hit on HRT. Why?"

All this time Web had been going through the photos until he stopped and pulled another one out. "Son of a bitch."

"What?"

Web turned the photo around. It was a picture of Strait in uniform in Vietnam. Next to him was a man that Romano didn't recognize, but Web certainly did. Even though the guy was much younger in the photo, he really hadn't changed all that much.

"Ed O'Bannon. He was the army shrink who helped Strait after he escaped from the Viet Cong."

"Jesus."

"And that means that they may have Claire, and even Kevin, around here somewhere. The farm would be a perfect place to hide them."

"But I still don't get it, Web, why would Strait and O'Bannon and Macy want to take out Charlie Team? It makes no sense."

Web thought hard, but that answer wasn't coming to him. At least it didn't until he glanced down and saw it. He put the shoebox aside and slowly reached down and plucked the object up from where it had fallen partially under the bed.

He held the anklet up and shone his light on it. Yet Web already knew to whom it belonged. He ripped the bedspread off and examined the pillows with his flashlight. It only took him a few moments to find the long blond hairs.

He looked at Romano in disbelief. "Gwen."

The trailer was backed up to the pool equipment room. The horse ramp was down and one of Strait's men had slid out the long piece of metal revealing the false bottom space that was easily big enough for a large shipment of pills . . . or the bodies of a woman and a little boy.

Strait was overseeing the transfer of Claire and Kevin to this compartment. They were struggling mightily and making noise—too much noise.

"Open the pool," he ordered. "Be easier if we drown 'em first. And cleaner than shooting them here."

The cover over the pool cranked back and then the men partially slipped the ropes and blankets off Claire and Kevin and started dragging them over to the water.

That's when the voice called out.

"What the hell are you doing?"

Strait and his men whirled around. Gwen was standing there, holding a pistol.

"Hey, Gwen, what are you doing up?" asked Strait innocently.

She looked at Claire and Kevin.

"Who are they, Nemo?"

"Just a couple of issues I got to deal with and then we can all ride off into the sunset."

"You're going to kill them?"

"No, I'm going to let them testify and put me on death row."

Several of Strait's men laughed at this. Strait drew closer to Gwen, never taking his eyes off her.

"Let me ask you a question, Gwen. You said you were going to take care of London. But I saw him ride off today and the man was breathing just fine."

"I changed my mind."

"Oh, that's good, you changed your mind. You mean you got cold feet. I figured. When you get right down to it, Gwen, you ain't got the stuff to do this. The killing. That's why you need men like me to do it for you."

"I want you to leave now. You and all your people."

"Well, I'm planning to do that."

"No, I mean without your *issues.*"

Strait smiled and drew still closer to the woman. "Now sweetie, you know I can't do that."

"I'll let you have a head start of twelve hours before I release them."

"And then what? That's a lot of explaining to do. And you'll take the heat for it?"

"I'm not going to let you kill them, Nemo. Enough people have died already. And it's my fault. You were right, I should have let go of the hate a long time ago, but whenever I tried all I could see was my son, dead."

"See, the problem is, if I leave them here and they talk, the cops will never stop looking for me. But if I kill them, then when I exit stage left, nobody gives a crap. And that's a big difference, because once I settle down in a place, I like to stay there, and I'm not spending my retirement running from the FBI."

He glanced toward one of his men; he was circling around behind Gwen.

Gwen gripped her pistol and aimed it at Strait's head. "I'm telling you for the last time, leave!"

"And what about your cut of the drug money?"

"That was all your doing. And I don't want it. I'll take the heat for everything. Just go!"

"Damn, woman, what got into you, you see God or something?"

"Get the hell off my land, Strait, now!"

"Look out, Gwen!" screamed Web.

The voice caught all of them off guard, but the man circling behind Gwen still fired his gun, which missed because she had ducked down at Web's warning. The shot hit behind her.

Web's sniper rifle barked and the man fell dead into the pool, the chlorinated water instantly turning red.

Nemo and his men took cover behind the horse trailer and opened fire, while Gwen disappeared into the bushes.

After they had left Strait's place, Web and Romano had gone to the equestrian center because Web wanted to check something; sure enough, he found the small wound on Comet's back. Gwen had plotted to kill him and then had a change of heart. Because of their talk? If so, Web wished he had had it years ago with the woman. He didn't have proof of it all, but it seemed clear to him that Gwen had enlisted Nemo and his men to exact her revenge for her son's death. Whether it was Billy Canfield's neglect that had driven her to Strait's bed, he didn't know.

They were headed to the mansion next when they had heard the noise at the pool area and come running in time to hear the exchange between Gwen and Strait, in time to hear Gwen admit that the people killed had been her fault, her revenge. Now they

were in a full-fledged firefight with no way to call in reinforcements. And the big problem was that Claire and Kevin were
caught in the middle.

It seemed that Strait realized this because he called out, "Hey,
Web, why don't you come on out now? 'Cause if you don't, I'm
gonna put a bullet into the woman and the kid."

Web and Romano looked at each other. Strait didn't know Romano was there. Romano turned and headed to the left. Web
headed right and then stopped.

"Come on, Nemo, you've got no chance, and the cavalry's on the
way."

"That's right, I'm a desperate man with not a damn thing to
lose." He fired a shot very close to Claire's head where she and
Kevin lay on the pool deck.

"Look, Nemo," said Web, "two more killings aren't going to help
you any."

Strait laughed. "Hell, Web, they ain't gonna *hurt* me none either."

"Okay, Nemo, tell me the one thing I haven't been able to figure
out," Web called out. "Why the kid switch in the alley?"

"What? You want me to incriminate myself?" Strait yelled back
and laughed again.

"Look around, Nemo—I got all the evidence I need."

"So if I do like you say, you'll put in a good word for me with the
judge, right?" Strait laughed again.

"Couldn't hurt."

"Well, Web, in my line of work you tend to congregate with some
interesting folks. And one particular fellow had some right definite
demands, and he's the sort of fellow you got to accommodate. This
is definitely a fellow you got to keep happy, you know what I'm
saying?"

"Clyde Macy?"

"Now, I ain't naming no names, Web. I ain't no squealer."

"Let me help you then. Macy is a wannabe cop. He's just itching
to prove he's better. He was dying to dress like an FBI agent, waltz
in and take the kid right out of our hands. Just to show himself
that he could pull it off."

"Damn, Web, you'd make a good detective."

"But maybe you weren't as confident. You needed Kevin, and

you couldn't risk Macy not pulling it off and getting Kevin back. You had to use Kevin in the first place in that alley to throw suspicion on Big F, and you needed Kevin later as leverage over him. So you substituted the other kid for Kevin. That way, Macy gets to have his fun at the Bureau's expense, and if he fails you still have Kevin. Am I right?"

"Hell, I guess we'll never know."

"So where's the other kid?"

"Like I said, I guess we'll never know."

Web's walkie-talkie crackled. Romano was in position.

"Okay, one more chance, Nemo, you got five seconds to surrender."

Web didn't bother counting to five. He slipped his MP-5 to full auto and opened fire, strafing the horse trailer behind which Nemo and his men had taken cover.

Strait and his men dropped flat to the ground at the same time Romano came up behind them.

One of the men saw him and turned to fire and took two MP-5 rounds between his eyes for his trouble.

"Guns on the ground. Now!" ordered Romano.

Web saw it, but Romano didn't because his back was to it: a small bit of condensation that was rising into the air off in the woods. Condensation caused by the cold coming up from a gun barrel. It was a classic mistake by someone who knew something about fieldcraft and sniping, but not the small, critical details that really made the difference. As a sniper Web would use his breath to heat his barrel and eliminate the condensation.

"Six o'clock, Romano," he screamed.

But it was too late. The shot hit Romano at the base of his spine and the impact from the high-speed round knocked him down.

"Paulie!" yelled Web.

Another man rolled out and took aim at the fallen HRT, but Web dropped him with his .308. He wedged the MP-5 against his pec with one hand and pulled out one of his .45s with the other.

"Romano!"

He breathed a sigh of relief as Romano started to rise. While it had penetrated his armor, the slug could not get through Link, the third .45 he kept back there in a special holster.

Another shot hit near Web and he dropped to the ground even as

Romano threw himself into the bushes. Strait took this opportunity to race out and grab Claire and half carry, half drag her to the truck hooked to the trailer.

Web looked up and saw what Strait was trying to do. Web shot out the truck tires. Cursing loudly, Strait dragged Claire off into the darkness.

Web snagged his walkie-talkie. "Paulie, Paulie, you okay?" Several anxious seconds went by and then Romano answered. His voice was a little shaky, but he was the same old Romano.

"Whoever shot me doesn't know jack-shit about bullet drop over distance. Fired too low."

"Lucky for you. I didn't see the barrel condensation until it was too late. I'm betting it's Macy out there somewhere. Strait's got Claire. I'm going after them. Kevin Westbrook is still by the pool."

"I got things covered here, Web."

"You sure?"

"Hell, it's only four against one. Go!"

Web turned and raced after Claire and Strait.

Romano had lost his MP-5 and his sniper rifle was not going to be very efficient at such close quarters. He pulled out his .45s and, taking a page from Web's book, actually rubbed one of them for luck. Despite his bravado, four against one were not good odds. He could get three of them and still be undone by number four. And there was still the shooter who had nailed him to worry about. He squatted low and edged along the bushes that surrounded the pool area. Shots were fired, but he didn't fire back, because they were way off, and muzzle flashes told him where his adversaries were. He kept moving and watching. Each time a shot was fired, he duly noted it. These guys were amateurs, but even amateurs got lucky, especially with superior numbers. He crouched low and saw the kid by the pool. He wasn't moving and Romano was thinking that maybe one of the shots had found its mark. But then the kid raised his head slightly. Romano slipped on his NV goggles and now he could see what the boy's problem was. His legs were still tightly bound.

Romano kept moving, putting distance between himself and the enemy. He wanted to get some range so that he could use his rifle. He had his night scope on and all he would need was a sliver of head to work with. Reduce the enemy to three or maybe even one and then he would move in with his pistols. One on one, Romano would win every time.

His plan was textbook. Read their muzzle signatures. Keep moving. Outflank them. Then move in, pop one or two, the others would lose their nerve and give themselves away, maybe start running and he would use his sniper rifle, wait for them to enter the kill zone and then it would all be over.

A voice called out, "Hey, Romano, come on out now, and without the gun."

Romano said nothing. He was spending his time getting a fix on the exact location of that voice so he could silence it. He thought it was the farmhand he had dropped on his first day at the farm, but he wasn't sure.

"Romano, I hope you're listening to me. Because you got five seconds to come out or I'm going to put a bullet into the kid's head."

Romano muttered under his breath as he drew closer to the source of the voice. He had no desire to let the boy die, but if he came out of cover, the reality was that both he and Kevin Westbrook would die. Romano never played that game and his only course of action was to try and kill them all before they got to the boy, which was going to be pretty much impossible.

"I'm sorry, kid," he muttered under his breath as he moved forward and took up his firing position.

The man who had spoken was indeed the fellow Romano had knocked down at the equestrian center. He was crawling forward on his belly, holding his pistol. He stopped, silently counted to five and called out once more. "Last chance, HRT." He waited a moment, shrugged, stood and took direct aim at Kevin Westbrook's head from the cover of the bushes. The man was not a great shot, but this execution would not require a high level of skill.

All of the air left the man's body as the enormous man burst from cover and hit him so hard he landed about seven feet away and on the pool deck. The big man raced to the boy and swooped him up in one massive arm. Then Francis Westbrook turned and ran off into the night with his son, even as he fired his pistol back over his shoulder.

Another man jumped out from cover and took aim at Westbrook's broad back. He was about to fire when Romano came out from cover and shot him down. He didn't know that the large man was Francis Westbrook, but Romano wasn't going to sit back and let anyone take it in the back. The only problem was that he revealed his position and he took a round in the leg for being such a nice guy. Romano tried to drag himself off but soon found an array of guns pointed at him. He was hauled down to the pool deck and three men stood over him.

"Well, shit, HRTs ain't so hot after all," said one. That one started getting Romano worked up.

"Just shoot his ass," said another. Romano's face turned red and his hands turned to fists.

"I say we stick his head in the water and drown the mother, nice and slow."

Romano looked up and saw that this came from the gent whom Westbrook had drop-kicked on to the pool deck, the same guy Romano had floored his first day at East Winds. His big gut was still sucking in huge amounts of air and there was blood around his nose where he had skidded across the stone.

"What do you say to that, Romano?" the man asked, even as he prodded Romano in the side with his boot.

"Sounds good to me," Romano said. He exploded forward and laid his shoulder into the man's quivering gut and they both went into the water. Romano took a huge breath and then dragged the man under. The two men on the pool deck did what Romano thought they would. They fired into the water. But Romano and the other man were too deep for the bullets to do any damage.

One of the guys had a seemingly brilliant idea. He raced over and hit the button to close the pool cover. As it settled over Romano and the man he was still struggling with, Romano, far from being concerned, knew that now he had the means to actually survive this. He slipped out his knife and cut the man's throat. Blood filled the water. Romano then grabbed the body around the legs and pushed it up until he could feel the man's head slam against the cover, as though he were bursting to the surface for air. Then he heard what he expected to hear, the guns firing into the head. He lowered the body, moved his position and then lifted the body up again. Again the guns fired, sending little jets of propelled water by him on either side. Now, they no doubt thought both of them were dead. At least Romano hoped they did; in fact, he was counting on it to survive.

He lowered the body again and then let go of it. It slowly sank to the bottom of the pool to join the one already there, the man Web had shot earlier. Now Romano had to undertake the riskiest part of this plan. He let out most of his remaining air, floated to the top and hooked his arm into the filter opening as though he had been caught there after getting his head blown off. As the cover opened, he was really hoping these guys did not understand the physics of freshly killed bodies in water, namely that they sank rather than floated on the surface. If they opened fire on him now, he was dead. But they didn't. The cover dragged his body some and Romano didn't move a muscle. It wasn't time yet. When the hands reached down and pulled him out, he still didn't move. They laid him on the pool deck facedown. He could sense them on either side. And then he heard it. They all did. Sirens. Somebody had called the cops.

One of the men said, "Let's get the hell out of here."

That was the last thing he would ever say. Romano erupted to his feet and hit both men dead center of their chests with backward thrusts of the two knives he had hidden in both of his hands. The blades went in up to their hilts, piercing each of their hearts.

They stared at him even as they dropped into the water. Romano stood up straight, surveyed the battlefield, ripped off his shirt and used a small tree branch to put a tourniquet on his leg, fished Link, the pistol that had blocked the bullet from hitting his back, out of the water and held up the ruined gun.

"Well, hell," he said.

54

Web was trailing Strait and Claire as best as he could. He was alternating with his NV goggles and his own eyes, but it was very dark here and even NVs needed some ambient light to work properly. He was relying more on his hearing than his eyes, actually, but he couldn't fire at anything based on that, because he could as easily hit Claire as Strait.

He approached the Monkey House, slowed his pace and finally stopped. The ruined building looked ominous during the day; now it was completely unnerving. The problem was, if Strait was inside and Web moved past without clearing the building first, Strait could rear-flank him.

Web kept a tight grip on his MP-5 and quietly moved forward. He entered the place from the south end and stepped over the debris that littered the former animal prison. Shafts of moonlight came through the holes in the roof as the clouds overhead moved past. The light eerily washed over the wrecked cages and the sight was a test even for Web's hardened nerves.

Moving through the space without making a sound was impossible and Web's gaze kept darting in all directions in hope that he would see something that would give him the instant he needed to save his and Claire's lives and end Strait's in the bargain. There was the issue of Macy being out there too, and that was troublesome because the man did have some tactical skill.

Web immediately sank to the floor as he heard a creak to his left. He slipped on his NV goggles and scanned the space grid by grid.

He looked overhead too because there was a catwalk up there. That's when the garbled scream rang out.

He rolled and the shot hit right where he had been lying. He came up, his gun ready to fire. That had sounded like Claire's voice warning him. He heard shuffling at the far end of the building and then feet running away. He was about to race after them when he saw the same thing he had seen before, gun barrel condensation. He dropped just before the gun fired, and the bullet hit one of the cages and ricocheted harmlessly into a wall.

Well, that was good to know—Macy, if that's who it really was, wasn't smart enough to realize his earlier error.

Web did a sweep of the space in the direction where the shot had come from with his MP-5, blowing junk in the air and rattling empty cages. When he stopped and put in a fresh clip he heard another pair of feet running away. He slipped out and took up the chase again grateful to be leaving the Monkey House behind.

He felt like he was closing in when Web sensed something to his left and hit the ground again. The shot smacked into a tree directly behind where he'd been standing.

Rifle shot, not pistol, he judged. It was Macy again, then, not Strait. He had probably dropped back again and was covering for his boss. "The wannabe against the real thing," Web said softly. "Well, bring it on."

As a sniper, Web would remain totally motionless when he was on duty. The rule was that in a standoff, the first man to move and give himself away died. Thus he could lie completely still while waiting to kill someone. He was able to slow down his pulse and even regulate the efficiency of his bladder so that he could go long intervals without having to urinate. He was like an anaconda lying in wait in the grass for a jaguar. When it came, the snake exploded, and no more jaguar.

As he lay there, Web wondered how Macy was able to track him as effectively as he had. That made Web start thinking about the equipment the guy might be carrying. Bates had given him an additional piece of information about the attack on the Frees' compound. Two .308 slugs had been dug out of the walls. If Macy was carrying the same ordnance that HRT used, maybe he was carrying other equipment similar to what Web was using. Web recalled the photo of Macy in his paramilitary regalia. All those elements definitely fit the profile of a wannabe.

Web slithered forward on his belly, making only minimal noise. He wanted to test something, and giving away his position seemed to be the best way to do it.

A shot hit close to him.

Okay, that confirmed that, thought Web. The guy had night optics too.

He slipped on his NV goggles and did a sweep of the area. That's when he saw it; only for an instant, but it was enough. It was just enough.

Clyde Macy was feeling good about his strategy. He knew that HRT members were very skilled, but he had always suspected they were also overrated. He had, after all, breached their perimeter at the Frees' compound. And he had shot one of them down at the pool area. He hadn't stuck around long enough to see Romano get back up. When Strait had grabbed Claire and run, Macy, ever the loyal lieutenant, had left to cover his boss's back. Strait had been good to him, taking him under his wing at the detention center. And when Macy had gotten out and strayed into the world of the Frees, Strait had tracked him down and made him see the light. The Frees were amateurs. The debacle in Richmond showed him that. And, Strait had pointed out, they don't pay you a dime, yet they expect you to help support them. And for what? Strait had pointedly asked him. For the privilege of associating with stupid people.

He had taken the sound advice and had worked with Strait for several years. The current gig had been the most lucrative. They had made a fortune with the drug running, and Macy had even gotten to set up the Free Society in the bargain. That and gunning down old Twan—it was all worth it. Now that the plan was disappearing as quickly as the sirens were heading their way, Macy had one more goal left. To kill London. That would prove his ultimate superiority. In a way, Macy had been training his entire adult life for this very moment.

He slipped on his NV goggles, fired them up and scanned the area where he had last seen London. The man was obviously losing it, moving around like that. He was overconfident and had suddenly found himself matched against a foe who was actually better than he was. And now it was time to finish it. Just as he thought this, he locked onto the green beacon blaring at him. For a second Macy was stunned, for he didn't know what it was. And then he realized it must be a reflection from London's night optics. He aimed, exhaled all his breath; muscle on muscle his finger slid to the trigger. He became absolutely motionless. And then he fired. The shot hit the beacon dead center and the light went out. It was only then that Macy realized his own night optics, turned on full power as they were, were probably giving off the same beacon. But one had to be looking through his own night optics to see the light, and he had just finished off London. He was just a split second quicker, and because of that he was alive and London wasn't. That's what it often came down to.

Before Macy could draw another breath, the bullet hit him squarely in the forehead. For a millisecond his mind didn't react to the fact that half of his head was now missing. Then the gun fell from his hands and Clyde Macy slumped to the dirt.

Web rose from behind a small berm about three ticks on the clock away from where he had propped up his goggles on a stump and turned them on full power. He hadn't had to rely on the green beacon coming from Macy's night optics. As soon as Macy fired at what he thought was Web's head, his muzzle flash had revealed his position. A second later, it was over. Final score: professional, one; wannabe, dead.

He didn't have time to reflect further on his victory because the crash of feet rushing through the underbrush made Web hit the ground and aim his .308. When the pair cleared the tree line and stepped into his kill zone, Web hesitated and then rose on his knees, his rifle pointed directly at the man's enormous chest.

"Put down the gun, Francis!"

Westbrook jerked and looked around in the darkness. Through his rifle scope Web could clearly see the giant push Kevin behind him, shielding the boy from this new threat.

"It's Web London, Francis. Put the weapon down. Now!"

"Stay behind me, Kev," said Westbrook as he edged away from the sound of Web's voice.

"Last time, Francis; gun down and then you. Or you'll be going down another way."

"I getting Kevin out of here, little man. That all I want to do. No problems, no problems."

Web aimed his shot at a tree branch ten feet above Westbrook's head. The limb was cleanly cut in two and fell behind them. That was the first warning shot Web had ever fired in his career, and he wondered why he had even bothered. Kevin yelled out, but Westbrook said nothing. He just kept backing up. Then he did something that surprised even Web. He dropped his gun, knelt down and pulled Kevin up on his back. At first Web thought he was going to use Kevin as a shield, but Westbrook kept his body between Web and the boy. And he kept retreating.

"No problems, HRT. Just heading on out. Got things to do."

Web put another shot in the dirt to the left of him. A second warning. Shit. What the hell was wrong with him? Take the guy. He's a criminal. A murderer.

"No problems," said Westbrook again. "Just heading out, me and the kid."

Web aimed the next shot at the man's head. Then he realized that, with the ammo he was chambering he couldn't shoot Westbrook, because the bullet might pass through even the big man's thick body and hit Kevin. He could aim for the legs and drop the giant. He contemplated this and was aiming for the best possible location when he heard Kevin.

"Web, please, don't shoot my brother. Please. He just helping me."

Through his scope Web could see the boy's face next to his father's. He was holding on to the thick neck with both hands, his face filled with fear, tears running down his cheeks. Francis Westbrook looked calm, as though he were ready to face his death. Web recalled all the scars on the man's belly. He had obviously faced down death many times. He was 120 in whitey years. Web's finger slid to the trigger. If Web shot him in the leg, at least Kevin would be able to visit him in prison. It was the right thing to do. He was a cop. The man was a criminal. That's how things worked. No exceptions. No involved internal deliberations. Just shoot.

And yet Web allowed the pair to slide off into the woods and disappear. Web's finger moved away from the trigger. He screamed out, "Take him back to his home, Francis. And then you better run like hell, because I'll be coming for you, you son of a bitch."

55

Strait had heard the sirens too and he couldn't believe how quickly everything had gone to hell. Story of his life. He put his gun against Claire's head and pulled out her gag. He had already untied her so he wouldn't have to carry her.

"Afraid you're my ticket out of here, lady. And even that might not be enough. But just so you don't get your hopes up, if it looks like they're going to take me, I'm gonna shoot you."

"Why?" wailed Claire helplessly.

"'Cause I'm pissed off, that's why. 'Cause I worked my ass off for nothing, that's why. Now come on." He jerked her along as they made their way toward the equestrian center. There were trucks there that maybe, just maybe he could use to get out of here. They were approaching the center from the east and when he saw the peak of the big hay barn, Strait actually smiled. The farm was vast and its topography complex, and the cops would come in the front, no doubt, while Strait left from the rear. By the time they realized what was going on, he would have ditched the truck, gotten to the little safe house he had set up just for this contingency and then quietly disappeared, not with all his money, but with some of it.

They cleared a rise in the land and started down toward the horse stalls. The man came at them from out of the darkness. At first Strait thought it was Macy, but then the clouds moved past and the moonlight revealed Billy Canfield standing there, shotgun in hand. Strait instantly held Claire in front of him, the gun to her temple.

"Get out the way, old man, I ain't got no time for you."

"Why, because the cops are coming? You damn right they are, 'cause I called 'em."

Strait shook his head, a vicious look on his features. "And why'd you do that?"

"I don't know what the hell you been doing on my farm, but I do know you been sleeping with my wife. You must think I'm stupid or something."

"Well, somebody had to be screwing her, Billy, 'cause you sure as hell weren't."

"That's my business," roared Canfield, "not yours."

"Oh, it's my business, all right, and let me tell you it was some damn fine business. You didn't know what you were missing, old man."

Canfield raised his shotgun.

"Yeah, go on and fire, Billy, and with that scattergun you'll kill this nice lady too."

The men silently stared at each other until Strait completely realized his advantage.

Still using Claire as a shield, he pointed his pistol at Billy and prepared to fire.

"Billy!"

Strait looked over in time to see Gwen and Baron charging straight at him. He yelled, pushed Claire away and got off two quick shots. And then a bullet hit him in the head, instantly crumpling him.

Web had rushed out of the woods, quickly taken in what was happening and fired, killing Strait. Baron reared up and his front hooves came down on Strait's body.

Web quickly ran to Claire's side. He didn't have to check Strait. He knew the man was dead.

"Are you okay?" he asked Claire.

She nodded, then sat up and started crying. Web hugged her and then looked over and saw that Billy Canfield had shuffled over to a dark mass and then dropped to his knees. Web rose, and went over to him and looked at where Gwen lay on the ground, her chest covered by a pool of blood where at least one of Strait's shots had hit its mark. She looked up at them both, her breath coming in painful gasps. Web dropped to his knees, ripped open her shirt and saw the wound. He slowly covered her chest back up and looked at her. His expression obviously told her the truth.

She gripped his hand. "I'm so scared, Web."

Web knelt down closer as Billy just squatted there, staring at his dying wife.

"You're not alone, Gwen." That was all he could think to say. He wanted to hate this woman for what she had done to him, to Teddy Riner and all the rest. But he couldn't. And it wasn't just because she had saved his life, and Claire's and Kevin's. It was because Web didn't know what he would have done had he been in the woman's shoes, with all that rage and hatred building up over the years. Maybe he would have done the same; he just hoped not.

"I'm not scared of dying, Web. I'm scared I won't see David." Blood dribbled from her mouth and her words were a little garbled, but Web understood her.

Heaven and hell; that was it? With maybe purgatory not even an option.

Her eyes were starting to lose focus and Web could feel her grip loosening.

"David," she said weakly. "David." She looked to the sky. "Forgive me, Father, for I have sinned . . ." Her voice trailed off and she started sobbing.

Web assumed the woman would have crawled to her little chapel if she'd had the strength. He looked around for something, anything. And then it appeared in the form of Paul Romano walking stiffly over to them. He had driven off in the truck that had been hooked to the trailer by the pool, flat tires and all, thanks to Web.

Web rushed over to him, looked at his bloody leg. "You okay?"

"Just a scratch. Thanks for asking."

"Paulie, can you take Gwen's Last Confession?"

"What?"

Web pointed to where Gwen lay in the grass. "Gwen's dying. I want you to hear her Last Confession."

Romano took a step back. "Are you nuts? Do I look like a priest?"

"She's dying, Paulie, she won't know. She believes she's going to hell and she won't see her son."

"This is the same woman who masterminded wiping out Charlie Team and you want me to forgive her too for all the stuff she's done?"

"Yes, it's important."

"No way am I doing that."

"Come on, Romano, it won't kill you."

Romano looked to the sky for an instant. "How do you know?"

"Paulie, please, I know I have no right to ask you, but please, there's not much time. It's the right thing to do." He added in desperation, "God will understand."

The men stared at each other for a long moment and then Romano shook his head, limped over and knelt down beside Gwen. He took her hand in his, made the sign of the cross over her and asked her if she wanted to make her Last Confession. In weakening tones she said she did.

Finished, Romano rose and stepped away.

Web again knelt down beside Gwen. Her eyes were starting to glaze over, but for a brief moment she was able to focus on him and even gave him a weak smile as though to thank him, as with each breath she pumped more blood out of her body. The resemblance to the wound that had claimed her son was striking.

She clutched Web's hand with renewed strength and mouthed the words, "I'm so sorry, Web, can you forgive me?"

Web looked at the beautiful eyes that were growing dimmer by the second. In those eyes and the woman's features he saw a different image, that of a young boy who had trusted Web and who had then been failed by him.

"I forgive you," he said to the dying woman, and he hoped that somewhere, somehow, David Canfield was doing the same for him.

With that, Web stepped back and passed her hand over to Billy, who took it and knelt down beside his wife. Web watched as the chest rose and fell with greater and greater speed, and then, finally, it just stopped and the hand went limp. As Billy quietly sobbed over the body of his wife, Web helped Claire stand, put his arm under Romano to assist him, and the three started to walk off together.

The shotgun blast made them all jump. When they turned around, Billy was just then walking away from Strait's body, a curl of smoke rising from his shotgun.

56

For the next few days, the police and the FBI had poured all over East Winds, collecting evidence, wrapping up bodies and generally trying to figure everything out, although that, under even the best circumstances, would take some time. On a very somber note, the body of the boy who had been substituted for Kevin in the alley had been found in a grave deep in the woods at East Winds. They boy had been identified as a runaway from Ohio who had somehow had the great misfortune to run into Nemo Strait and Clyde Macy, no doubt with promises of some fast money.

As Web walked over the grounds, he could only shake his head at how quickly the pastoral setting of the farm had turned into a battlefield. Bates had cut short his vacation and was now here overseeing things. Romano was in the hospital getting his leg wound treated, but the bullet had hit neither bone nor major artery and the doctors predicted a quick and full recovery for someone as fit as Paul Romano. However, Web was certain that Angie was giving her husband a really hard time about almost getting killed. No doubt if someone was going to do Romano in, she wanted the honors.

As Web was walking up the drive to the mansion, he saw Bates coming out the front door. Billy Canfield stood on the porch and stared at seemingly nothing. The man had nothing left, Web thought. Bates saw Web and came over.

"Damn, what a mess," Bates said.

"Well, it's pretty clear now that it was a mess for a long time before this."

"Actually, you're right. We discovered records at Strait's house

and chased down his suppliers. The shot that killed Antoine Peebles was traced to a gun we found on Macy. Ed O'Bannon's turned
up too, in a Dumpster. Same gun killed him. And the rifle Macy
was carrying when you shot him, we matched that to the hits on
Judge Leadbetter and Chris Miller."

"A ballistics hat trick. Don't you just love it when the pieces start
falling into place?"

"Oh, and we also checked the tape of the shooting in Richmond
like you asked us to."

Web shot him a glance. "What'd you find?"

"You were right, there was something there. A phone ringing."

"It wasn't a ringing sound. It was more like a—"

"A whistle? That's right. It was a cellular phone. You know, you
can do just about any ringing sound you want. This one was a bird
whistle. Nobody ever thought much about it before. It's not like we
needed it as evidence to nail Ernie Free."

"Whose phone was it?"

"David Canfield's. A cell phone his mother had given him in case
of emergency."

Web looked stunned, even as Bates nodded sadly.

"It was Gwen calling him. He never answered. Probably the only
way she thought she could talk to him at that point. She just
picked the worst time to do it. She didn't know when HRT was going in, of course."

"So you think that's why the phones were the theme with the
killings?"

"Well, we'll never know for sure, but it looks that way. Maybe
she felt since she couldn't talk to her son, she wanted the phones
to be the last things those three guys ever saw. She also left a written statement that exonerated Billy. I guess Gwen was thinking
she wouldn't survive this, and she turned out to be right. We've
confirmed Billy's innocence from other sources. And we were also
able to nab a few of Strait's men who weren't at the farm that
night. They spilled their guts."

"Good. The man's suffered enough."

Bates shook his head. "Those guys confirmed that Gwen wasn't
in on the drug stuff. But I guess she found out later and wanted a
cut of it. God, and she looked so normal."

"She was normal," snapped Web. "But what happened to her son just took over her life." He sighed deeply. "You know, I have every reason to hate the woman, and the only thing I feel is sorry for her. Sorry that she couldn't have gone on. And part of me is thinking that if I had saved her son, none of this would have happened. That maybe I do a lot more harm than good."

"You can't carry that burden, Web. That's not fair to you."

"Well, life wasn't very fair to Gwen Canfield, now, was it?"

The two men walked along.

"Well, if you want some good news, you're reinstated with the Bureau, and if you so request, Buck Winters will give you a personal apology. And I'm counting on you so requesting."

Web shook his head. "I need some time to think about it, Perce."

"Buck's apology?"

"Coming back to the Bureau."

Bates gaped at him. "You're kidding. Come on, Web, you got your whole life tied up in it."

"I know, that's the problem."

"Well, take all the time that you want. After all this, the official word at the Bureau is that anything you want, you got."

"Gee, that's really nice of them."

"How's Romano?"

"Bitching and complaining, so he's just fine."

They stopped and looked back at the mansion, where Billy Canfield was just now turning and going into the house.

Bates pointed at him. "Now, there's the guy I really feel sorry for. He's lost it all."

Web nodded in agreement.

"You remember he said at the party, you keep your enemies out in the open, right where you can see them all the time?" Bates shook his head and looked around. "Well, his enemies were all around him and the poor guy never knew it.'

"Yeah."

"You need a ride back?"

"I'm gonna hang here awhile longer."

Bates and Web shook hands. "Thanks, Web, for everything."

Bates turned and walked off, while Web ambled along. And then he stopped, turned and looked in Bates's direction and then at the mansion. Web suddenly took off at a dead run to the stone house. He raced through the front door and down the stairs to the lower level, where he made a beeline for Billy's taxidermy room. It was locked. Web easily broke open the lock, went inside and quickly found what he was searching for. He carried the small jar in one hand and ran over to the gun cabinet. He found and hit the hidden latch and the door swung open. He pulled the flashlight off the wall and went inside. The mannequin peered back at him. Web hung the light on a peg on the wall so that the beam shone on the dummy. He took off the mannequin's hairpiece and carefully peeled off the whiskers. Next he opened the jar and carefully applied the paint remover to the face. It came off quickly. Web kept working away until the dark skin became white. With the hair and whiskers gone and the original skin color, Web stood back. He had seen the face so many times he would have recognized it in his sleep, and yet the few devices Canfield had used to disguise the face had worked to perfection. The man *had* been true to his word: He had kept his real enemy right where he could always find him.

Web knew he was looking upon Ernest B. Free for the first time since the shootout in Richmond.

"You know those I-talians I told you about?"

Web whipped around and there was Billy Canfield.

"Those I-talians," Billy continued, "who'd offer me all that money to move their stolen property? Remember I was telling you about them?"

"I remember."

Canfield seemed to be in a fog. He wasn't even looking at Web; he was staring at Ernie, maybe admiring his handiwork, Web thought.

"Well, contrary to what I told you, I accepted one of those offers and did a real good job for them. Then, after what happened to my son and all, they came to me one day about four months ago and offered to do me a favor in appreciation for all my years of loyalty to the family."

"Break Ernest Free out of prison and deliver him to you?"

"See, them I-talians are strong on family, and after what that man did to my son . . ." Billy stopped and rubbed at his eyes. "Anyway, Gwen probably showed you the little building what used to be a Civil War hospital at the farm."

"She did."

"Well, that's where I did him. I sent Strait and his men off to pick up some horses and put Gwen on a plane to see her family in Kentucky, so I could work uninterrupted. I used some of the same surgical instruments the folks back in the Civil War did." He went over and touched Free's shoulder. "Cut his tongue out first 'cause he was making such a ruckus. I expected that from a little worm like him. Love to make others suffer but can't take a drop of pain themselves. And then you know what I did?"

"Tell me."

Billy smiled proudly. "I gutted him just the way you would a deer. Cut his balls off first. See, I figured somebody what done something like that to a little boy, he can't call himself no man, so why would he need any balls? You see my reasoning?"

Web said nothing, but though Billy did not appear to be armed, Web's hand slipped to the grip of his pistol. Canfield did not seem to notice, or if he did, he didn't seem to care.

He cocked his head and surveyed his work from different angles. "Now, I'm not an educated man or anything, ain't read many books and such, but it seemed sort of poetic justice, I guess you'd say, that old Ernie B. Free would sit locked in a little room where slaves came through hunting for their freedom. But he ain't never gonna get his. Freedom, that is. And I'd know right where the son of a bitch was every minute of every day and show people to frighten them, like he was some little carnival freak." He looked at Web with the expression of a man no longer part of the sane world. "Don't that seem right to you?"

Again Web said nothing.

Billy stared at him and nodded. "I'd do it again, you know. In a minute I would."

"Tell me, Billy, what did it feel like, killing a man?"

Canfield studied him for a very long moment. "It felt like shit."

"Did it take any of the hurt away?"

"Not a damn drop. And now I got nothing left." He paused, his lips trembling. "I shut her out of my life, you know. My own wife.

Drove her to Strait's bed, ignored her. She knew I knew and I didn't say nothing about it, and that probably hurt more than if I'd beaten her for it. Right when she needed me most I wasn't there. Maybe if I had been, she could've got herself through this."

Web stared at him. "Maybe she could have, Billy. But now we'll never know."

They heard footsteps coming down the stairs and both men walked outside the room. It was Bates. He looked surprised to see Web.

"I forgot I needed to ask you a few more things, Billy." Bates looked at Web's pale face. "Are you okay?" He glanced at the stricken Billy and then back at Web. "What's going on here?"

Web looked at Billy and then said to Bates, "Everything's just fine. Why don't you ask Billy the questions later? I think he needs some time to himself." Web looked once more at Canfield, and then he put his arm around Bates and led him up the stairs.

They had just reached the main floor when they heard the blast. It was the fancy Churchill shotgun.

Web just knew.

57

Web dropped in on Kevin Westbrook two days after Billy Canfield killed himself. The boy was back with Jerome and his granny, thanks to his father. Part of Web hoped Francis "Big F" Westbrook made it to his retirement. At least he had left his son out of it. The grandmother, whose name Web learned was Rosa, was in wonderful spirits and had made them all lunch. As promised, Web had brought back the photo of Kevin and given it to Rosa, returned the sketchbooks Claire had taken previously to Kevin and also had a long talk with Jerome.

"Never saw the man," said Jerome of Big F. "One minute Kevin wasn't here, and now he is."

"How's the big cookie coming?" asked Web.

Jerome smiled and said, "It's in the oven and I'm about to turn on the heat."

Before Web left, Kevin gave him a sketch he had done. It showed a little boy and a large man side by side.

"Is that you and your brother?" Web asked.

"Nope, that's me and you," Kevin answered, and then gave Web a hug.

When he went back to his car, Web got quite a shock. On his windshield was a piece of paper. What was written on the paper made Web look in all directions, one hand on his pistol grip. Yet the man was long gone. He looked at the paper again. It simply read, "I owe you. Big F."

Some other good news was that Randall Cove had been found.

Some kids playing in the woods had come across him. He had been admitted into a local hospital as a John Doe, since he was carrying no identification. He had been unconscious for several days but had finally come to, and the Bureau had been notified. He was also expected to fully recover from his wounds.

Web went to see him after Cove was flown back to Washington. The man was covered in bandages, had lost a lot of weight and wasn't in the best of moods, but he was alive. That was something to feel good about, Web told him, and got a growl in return.

"I've been right where you are," Web told him, "except I was missing half my face. You got off easy."

"None of it feels easy. Not a damn bit."

"They say bullet wounds give you character."

"I got enough character to last the rest of my life, then."

Web had glanced around the room. "So how long you in for?"

"Hell if I know. I'm just the patient. But if they stick me with one more needle, somebody around here besides me is gonna be hurting."

"I don't like hospitals much either."

"Well, if I hadn't been wearing my Kevlar, I'd be at the morgue. Got two bruises on my chest I think are with me permanently."

"First rule of engagement, always place one in the head."

"I'm glad they didn't read your rules of engagement. So you broke the Oxy ring?"

"I'd say *we* did it."

"And you popped Strait?"

Web nodded. "And then Billy Canfield added a layer of buckshot. I don't think it was necessary, but it probably made him feel better. But then again, not that much better."

Cove nodded. "I guess I can see that." Web got up to leave. "Hey, Web, I owe you. I mean, I really owe you a lot."

"No, you don't. Nobody owes me a damn thing."

"Hey, HRT, you brought the whole house of cards down."

"What I did was my job. And to tell you the truth, I'm getting a little tired of doing it." The men shook hands.

"Take it easy, Cove. And when they cut you loose from here, let the Bureau give you a nice, safe desk job where the only nasty things people are shooting at you are memos."

"Memos? Sounds pretty boring."

"Yeah, it does, doesn't it?"

Web parked the Mach at the curb and walked up the sidewalk. Claire Daniels was not dressed in work clothes on this warm evening but rather a pretty sundress and sandals. The dinner was tasty, the wine a nice companion to the meal and the lights low and inviting, and Web had no idea why he was here as Claire sat across from him on the couch by the empty fireplace and tucked her legs under her.

"Fully recovered?" he asked.

"Not that I ever will be. Business-wise, I'm great. I thought this thing with O'Bannon would've wrecked my practice, but the phone hasn't stopped ringing."

"Hey, lots of people are in need of a good shrink—excuse me, psychiatrist."

"Actually, I've been taking a fair amount of time off."

"Different priorities?"

"Something like that. I did see Romano."

"He's out of the hospital now. Did you go to his house?"

"No. At my office. He came with Angie. I guess she told him about her seeing a psychiatrist. I'm helping them work through some issues together. They said they didn't mind you knowing."

Web took a sip of wine. "Well, everybody sure as hell has issues, don't they?"

"I wouldn't be surprised if Romano left HRT."

"We'll see."

She eyed him. "So, are you leaving HRT?"

"We'll see."

She put down the wineglass she'd been holding. "I wanted to thank you for saving my life, Web. That's one of the reasons I invited you for dinner tonight."

He tried to keep it light. "Hey, that's what I do, rescue hostages." But then his jovial look faded. "You're welcome, Claire. I'm just glad I was there." He looked at her curiously. "One of the reasons. So, what are the others?"

"Cueing on my body language? Reading between the lines?" She refused to catch his gaze, and Web could sense the nervousness underneath the joking manner.

"What is it, Claire?"

"I'm filing my report with the FBI soon. The report detailing what I believe happened to you in the alley when you froze. I wanted to discuss it with you first."

Web sat forward. "Okay, let me have it."

"I think O'Bannon gave you a posthypnotic suggestion. A command, an instruction of sorts to stop you from doing your job."

"But you said that you can't make someone do something they don't want to do, or wouldn't do normally, while under hypnosis."

"That's right, but there are always exceptions to such rules. If the person being hypnotized has a very strong relationship with the person doing the hypnotizing or that person is a powerful authority figure, the person may do something outside his normal range of action, even hurting someone else. The rationale may be that he feels this authority figure would not make anyone do something really wrong. It really comes down to issues of trust. And according to his notes, O'Bannon had established a trusting relationship with you."

"How do you get from trust to me freezing? Did he brainwash me? Like the *Manchurian Candidate*?"

"Brainwashing is something very different from hypnotizing. It takes time and is more of an indoctrination in which, through sleep deprivation, physical torture and mental manipulation, you change the personality of someone, make him wholly different, you break his will, his spirit and then you recast it as you wish. What O'Bannon did was build an order into your unconscious. When you heard the phrase 'Damn to hell' the reaction would start.

"The phrase was coupled with a safety valve of some sort, in case you heard the phrase or something similar to it elsewhere. In your case I think that safety valve was hearing communications over your wireless receiver when you were in the alley. Remember, that's when you said you actually froze. In O'Bannon's notes was a record of the Taser gun story you also told me. So the physical reaction he programmed in was one he knew would paralyze you. 'Damn to hell' plus communications over the radio would cause you to freeze, like you had been hit with a Taser dart."

Web shook his head. "And O'Bannon could do all that to my mind?"

Claire said, "I believe you to be a somnabule, Web, a person very susceptible to hypnotic suggestion. But you were almost able to override that suggestion. I'm certain you weren't supposed to be able to rise and walk in that courtyard. That was your pure will coming through, if that makes you feel any better. It was probably your most remarkable feat of the night, machine guns notwithstanding."

"And they used the phrase 'Damn to hell' to further incriminate the Free Society because it was the name of their newsletter."

"Yes. When I saw that on their website lots of things started making sense."

"That's a lot to take in, Claire."

She sat forward, her hands in her lap. Suddenly Web felt like he was back in her office, enduring another session. "Web, I have something else to tell you, something even more disconcerting. I should have told you before, but I wasn't sure you were ready to deal with it, and with everything that happened, well, I was just afraid to, I guess. Compared to you, I'm not very brave. Compared to you, nobody's brave, actually."

He ignored the compliment and simply stared at her. "Tell me what?"

She looked directly at him. "When I hypnotized you, I learned a lot more than that your father was arrested at your sixth-year birthday party." She added quickly, "But I couldn't tell you about it then. It would have been too traumatic."

"Tell me what? I don't remember a damn thing happening other than the party, and even that was a little fuzzy."

"Web, please listen very carefully to me."

He rose in his distress. "I thought you said I was in complete control. That it was a heightened state of awareness. Damn it, that's what you said, Claire. Did you lie to me?"

"It's usually that way, Web, but I had to do it differently. For a very good reason."

"The only *reason* I let you play around in my mind, lady, was because you said I'd be there running the show." Web sat down and clenched his hands together so they'd stop shaking. *What the hell had he told her while he was under other than the birthday fiasco?*

"There are times, Web, when I have to make the decision not to allow the patient under hypnosis to remember what occurred. I don't take that step lightly, and I certainly didn't do it lightly with you."

He had to admire her. In voice and manner, she was in control. He didn't know whether to lean across and kiss her or slap her face.

"What, exactly, Claire, did you do to me?"

"I gave you a posthypnotic suggestion." She looked down. "The same technique O'Bannon used on you to make you freeze in the alley, so you wouldn't remember some things from our hypnosis session."

"Great, Claire, I'm easy, I'm a frigging somnabule so it's easy to screw with my mind, right?"

"Web, I did what I thought was best—"

"Claire, just tell me!" snapped Web impatiently.

"It has to do with your mother and your stepfather. How he died, actually."

His face flushed for an instant. Web was suddenly fearful. He suddenly hated her guts. "I already told you how he died. He fell. It's in your precious little file. Go read it again."

"You're right. He did fall. But he wasn't alone. You told me about a pile of clothes near the attic entrance?"

He stared at her. "They're gone, they've been gone a long time."

"They were a great hiding place for a terrified and abused young man to hide."

"What? Meaning me?"

"A great hiding place at the behest of your mother. She knew that Stockton went up there to get his drugs."

"So what? I knew that too. I told you that when I *wasn't* hypnotized."

"You also told me about some rolls of old carpet." She added very quietly, "That they were as hard as iron."

Web stood and backed away from her like a frightened child. "Okay, Claire, this is officially nuts."

"She got you to do it, Web. That was her way of taking care of the abusive father."

Web sat down on the floor and put his head in his hands. "I'm not understanding any of this, Claire. None of it!"

Claire took a deep breath. "You didn't kill him, Web. You struck him with the carpet and he fell. But your mother—"

"Stop it!" he shouted. "Just stop it! This is the biggest bunch of bullshit I've ever heard."

"Web, I'm telling you the truth. Otherwise how would I know these things?"

"I don't know!" he shouted. "I don't know anything!"

Claire knelt down in front of him, reached out and took his hand. "After all you've done for me, I feel terrible about all of it. But please believe me that I only did it to help you. This was so hard for me too. Can you understand that? Can you believe that? Can you trust me?"

He stood so abruptly she almost fell backward in surprise. Web headed for the door.

She called after him. "Web, please."

He walked outside and she followed him, the tears falling freely from her now.

Web climbed in the car and fired up the Mach. Claire walked unsteadily down the sidewalk toward him.

"Web, we can't leave it like this."

He rolled down the window and looked at her even as Claire's eyes searched his.

"I'm going away for a while, Claire."

She looked bewildered. "Going away? Where?"

"I'm going to see my father. Why don't you analyze that one while I'm gone."

He gunned the car and drove off under a sky dominated by a gathering storm, the black Mach quickly vanishing into the darkness. Web glanced back once, his gaze catching Claire Daniels standing there, illuminated by the wash of light from her cozy house. And then Web looked ahead and kept going.

Acknowledgments

To my good friends Philip Edney and Neal Schiff at the FBI for all their help and counsel. Thanks for always being there for me.

Thanks to Special Agent W. K. Walker for his help and advice.

To Dr. Steve Sobelman for his invaluable assistance with the psychological aspects of the novel and for being a great guy and dear friend. Steve, we'd love you anyway, even if you weren't married to your fabulous wife, Sloane Brown.

To my wonderful friends Kelly and Scott Adams for all their help and advice with the equestrian and horse farm aspects of the novel, and for tramping through the snow with me over a couple thousand acres. Kelly, thanks also for teaching me to ride Boo. I'll be back for more!

To my new friend Dr. Stephen P. Long for help on the Oxycontin portion of the book. Steve, your comments were insightful and right on the mark.

To Lisa Vance and Lucy Childs for keeping my literary life straight.

To Art and Lynette for all they do for us.

To Steve Jennings for again reading every page with his eagle eye.

To Dr. Catherine Broome for patiently explaining complicated medical matters to me in a way even I could understand.

To Aaron Priest for all your great advice on this one. I owe you.

To Frances Jalet-Miller for another superb editing job. You outdid yourself this time, Francie. And to Rob McMahon for his very thoughtful comments.

To Deborah Hocutt for making my life so much better. And to her husband, Daniel, for designing an incredible website.

To Michelle for keeping our crazy world straight on course.

To all those wonderful souls at the Warner Books family, including Larry, Maureen, Jamie, Tina, Emi, Martha, Karen, Jackie Joiner and Jackie Meyer, Bob Castillo, Susanna Einstein, Kelly Leonard and Maja Thomas: You're the best.

And, finally, to my friend Chris Whitcomb, Hostage Rescue Team operator, who also happens to be a wonderful writer and one of the most extraordinary individuals I've ever met. Chris, I couldn't have done this novel without you. You went far beyond the call of duty in helping me and I will never forget it. I wish you every success in your writing career, you deserve it.

split second

David Baldacci
Published December 2003

DON'T BLINK your life might depend on it . . .

'He was the only one in the room who could see it. His attention stayed there for one beat, two beats, three beats, far too long. Yet who could blame him for not being able to pull his gaze away from *that*?'

When something distracts Secret Agent Sean King for a split second, it costs him his career and presidential candidate Clyde Ritter his life. What stole his attention? Why was Ritter shot? Where were the other detail leaders?

Eight years later Michelle Maxwell is on the fast track through the ranks of the Secret Service when her career is stopped short: presidential candidate John Bruno is abducted from a funeral home while under her protection.

The similarity between the two cases drives Michelle to re-open investigations into the Ritter fiasco and join forces with attractive ex-agent, King. The pair are determined to get to the bottom of what happened in those critical moments.

Meanwhile, high-ranking members of the legal system and key witnesses from both cases are going missing. King is losing friends, colleagues and clients fast and his ex-lover, Joan Dillinger, is play-ing curious games – she wants Sean back, but she also owes him for something . . .

AN EXTRACT FROM THIS STUNNING THRILLER FOLLOWS . . .

PROLOGUE

September, 1996

It only took a split second. Although, it seemed like the longest split second ever.

They were on the campaign trail at a nondescript hotel meet-and-greet in a place so far out you had to use long distance to reach the boonies. Standing behind his protectee, he had scanned the crowd, while his ear mike buzzed sporadically with unremarkable information. It had been muggy in the large room filled with excited people waving "Elect Clyde Ritter" pennants. There were more than a few infants being thrust toward the smiling candidate. He hated this because the babies could so easily shield a gun until it was too late. Yet the little ones just kept coming and Clyde kissed them all, and ulcers seemed to form in his belly as he observed this potentially dangerous spectacle.

The crowd drew closer, right up to the velvet rope on stanchions that had been placed as a line in the sand. In response, he had moved closer to Ritter. The palm of his outstretched hand rested lightly on the candidate's sweaty, coatless back, so that he could pull him down in an instant if something happened. He couldn't very well stand in front of the man, for the candidate belonged to the *people*. His catechism was set in stone: shake hands, wave, smile, nail a sound bite in time for the six o'clock news, then pucker up and kiss a fat baby. And all the time he silently watched the crowd, keeping his hand on Ritter's soaked shirt and looked for threats, he hoped in all the right places.

Someone called out from the rear of the space. Ritter answered the jibe back with his own bit of humor and the crowd laughed good-naturedly, or at least most of them did. There were people here who hated Ritter and all he stood for. Faces didn't lie, not for those trained to read them, and he could read a face, as well as he could shoot a gun. That's what he spent all his working life doing: reading the hearts and souls of men and women through their eyes, their physical tics.

He keyed on two men in particular, ten feet away, on the right. They looked like potential trouble although each wore a short sleeve shirt and tight pants with no place to house a weapon, which dropped them several pegs on the danger meter. Assassins tended to favor bulky clothing and small handguns. Still, he mumbled a few words into his mic, telling others of his concern. Then his gaze flitted to the clock on the back of the wall. It was 10:32 in the morning. Five more minutes and then they were on to the next town where the handshakes, the sound bites, the baby kisses and the face reading would continue.

His gaze had turned in the direction of the new sound, and then the new sight, something totally unexpected. Standing facing the crowd and behind the hard-politicking Ritter, he was the only one in the room who could see it. His attention stayed there for one beat, two beats, three beats, far too long. Yet who could blame him for not being able to pull his gaze away from *that*? Everyone, as it turned out, including himself.

He heard the bang, like the sound of a dropped book. He could feel the moisture on his hand where it had touched Ritter's back. And now the moisture wasn't just sweat. His hand stung, where the slug had come out the body and taken a chunk off his middle finger before hitting the wall behind him. As Ritter dropped, the split second moved into maximum overdrive akin to a comet going hell-bent and still taking a billion light years to get where it was actually going.

Shrieks from the crowd poured out and then seemed to dissolve into one long, soulless moan. Faces stretched into images one only saw in carnival fun houses. Then the blur hit him like the force of an exploding grenade as feet moved and bodies gyrated and the screams came at him from all directions. People pushed, pulled and ducked to get out of the way. He remembered thinking that there was no greater chaos than when swift, violent death knocks on the door of an unsuspecting crowd.

And the now ex-presidential candidate Clyde Ritter was lying by his feet on the hardwood floor shot right through the heart. His gaze left the newly deceased and was now on the shooter, a tall, handsome man in a tweed jacket and wearing glasses. The killer's Smith & Wesson .44 was still pointing at the spot where Ritter had been standing, as though waiting for the target to get back up so he could be shot all over again. The mass of panicked people held back the guards who were fighting to get through, so that he and the killer were the only ones at the party.

He pointed his pistol at the chest of the assassin. He gave no warning, called out not one constitutional right accorded the assassin under American jurisprudence. His duty now clear, he fired once, and then again, though the first time was enough. It dropped the man right where he stood. He never said a word, as though he had expected to die for what he'd done, and accepted the terms

stoically like a good martyr should. And all mar-
tyrs left behind people like him, the ones who
were blamed for letting it happen in the first place.
Three men had actually died that day, and he had
been one of them.

Sean Ignatius King, Born August 1, 1960 –
Died September 21, 1996 in a place he had never
even heard of until the final day of his life. And yet
he had it far worse than the other fallen. They
went tidily into their coffins and were forever
mourned by those who loved them or at least
loved what they stood for. The soon to be ex-
Secret Service agent King had no such luck. After
his death, his unlikely burden was to keep right on
living.

saving faith

To Aaron Priest,
my friend

ONE

The somber group of men sat in a large room that rested far belowground, accessed by only a single, high-speed elevator. The chamber had been secretly built during the early 1960s under the guise of renovating the private building that squatted over it. The original plan, of course, was to use this "super-bunker" as a refuge during a nuclear attack. This facility was not for the top leaders of American government, it was for those whose level of relative "unimportance" dictated that they probably wouldn't be able to get out in time but who still rated protection afforded no ordinary citizen. Politically, even in the context of total destruction, there must be order.

The bunker was built at a time when people believed it possible to survive a direct nuclear hit by burrowing into the earth inside a steel cocoon. After the holocaust that would annihilate the rest of the country, leaders would emerge from the rubble with absolutely nothing left to lead, unless you counted vapor.

The original, aboveground building had been leveled long ago, but the subterranean room remained under what was now a small strip mall that had been vacant for years. Forgotten by virtually all, the chamber was now used as a meeting place for certain people in the country's primary intelligence-gathering agency. There was some risk involved, since the meetings were not related to the men's

1

official duties. The matters discussed at these gatherings were illegal, and tonight even murderous. Thus additional precautions had been necessary.

The super-thick steel walls had been supplemented by a copper coating. That measure, along with tons of dirt overhead, protected against prying electronic ears lurking in space and elsewhere. These men didn't particularly like coming to this underground room. It was inconvenient, and ironically, it seemed a little too James Bondish even for their admittedly cloak-and-dagger tastes. However, the truth was the earth was now encircled with so much advanced surveillance technology that virtually no conversation taking place on its surface was safe from interception. One had to dig into the dirt to escape his enemies, and if there was a place where people could meet with reasonable confidence that their conversations would not be overheard even in their world of ultrasophisticated peekaboo, this was it.

The gray-headed people present at the meeting were all white males, and most were nearing their agency's mandatory retirement age of sixty. Dressed quietly and professionally, they could have been doctors, lawyers or investment bankers. One would probably not remember any of the group a day after seeing them. This anonymity was their stock-in-trade. These sorts of people lived and died, sometimes violently, over such details.

Collectively, this cabal possessed thousands of secrets that could never be known by the general public because the public would certainly condemn rather than applaud the actions giving rise to these secrets. However, America often demanded results – economic, political, social and otherwise – that could be obtained only by smashing certain parts of the world to a bloody pulp. It was the job of these men

2

to figure out how to do so in a clandestine manner that would not reflect poorly on the United States, yet would still keep the country safe from the pesky, international terrorists and other foreigners unhappy with these global developments.

The purpose of tonight's gathering was to plot the killing of Faith Lockhart. Technically, the CIA was prohibited by presidential executive order from engaging in assassination. However, these men, though employed by the Agency, were not representing the CIA tonight. This was their private agenda, and there was little disagreement that the woman had to die, and soon; it was critical for the well-being of the country. These men knew this, even if American presidents did not. However, because of another life that was involved, the meeting had become acrimonious, the group resembling a cadre of posturing members fighting on Capitol Hill over billion-dollar slices of pork.

"What you're saying, then," one of the white-haired men said as he poked the smoke-filled air with a slender finger, "is that along with Lockhart we have to kill a federal agent." This man shook his head incredulously. "Why kill one of our own? It can only lead to disaster."

The gentleman at the head of the table nodded thoughtfully. Robert Thornhill was the CIA's most distinguished Cold War soldier, a man whose status at the Agency was unique. His reputation was unassailable, his compilation of professional victories unmatched. As associate deputy director of Operations, he was the Agency's ultimate free safety. The DDO, or deputy director of operations, was responsible for running the field operations that undertook the secret collection of foreign intelligence. The operations directorate of the CIA was also unofficially known as the "spy shop," and the

3

deputy director was still not even publicly identified. It was the perfect place to get meaningful work
done.

Thornhill had organized this select group, who
were as upset as he about the state of affairs at the
CIA. It was he who had remembered that this
bloated underground time capsule existed. And it
was Thornhill who had found the money to secretly
bring the chamber back to working condition and
upgrade its facilities. There were thousands of little
taxpayer-funded toys like that sprinkled around the
country, many of them gone to complete waste.
Thornhill joked to himself, *Well, if governments didn't
waste their citizens' hard-earned money, then what would
be left for governments to do?*

Even now, as he ran his hand over the stainless
steel console with its quaint built-in ashtrays, sniffed
the filtered air and felt the protective coolness of the
earth all around, Thornhill's mind wandered back
for a moment to the Cold War period. At least there
was a measure of certainty with the hammer and
sickle. In truth, Thornhill would take the lumbering
Russian bull over the agile sand snake that you
never knew was out there until it flung its venom
into you. There were many who wanted nothing
more in life than to topple the United States. It was
his job to ensure that never happened.

Gazing around the table, Thornhill gauged each
man's devotion to his country and was satisfied. He
had wanted to serve America for as long as he could
remember. His father had been with the OSS, the
World War II-era predecessor to the CIA. He had
known little of what his father did at the time, but
the man had instilled in his son the philosophy that
there was no greater thing to do with one's life than
to serve one's country. Thornhill had joined the
Agency right out of Yale. Right up until the day he

died, his father had been proud of his son. But no prouder than the son had been of the old man.

Thornhill's hair was a shining silver, which lent him a distinguished air. His eyes were gray and active, the angle of his chin blunt. His voice was deep, cultured; technical jargon and the poetry of Longfellow flowed from his mouth with equal ease. The man still wore three-piece suits and favored pipe smoking over cigarettes. The fifty-eight-year-old Thornhill could have quietly finished out his time at the CIA and led the pleasant life of a former public servant, well traveled, erudite. He had no thought of going out quietly, and the reason was very clear.

For the last ten years, the CIA's responsibilities and budgets had been decimated. It was a disastrous development, for the firestorms that were popping up across the world now often involved fanatical minds accountable to no political body and possessing the capability to obtain weapons of mass destruction. And while just about everyone thought high-tech was the answer for all the ills of the world, the best satellites in the world couldn't stroll down alleys in Baghdad, Seoul or Belgrade and take the emotional temperature of the people there. Computers in space could never capture what people were thinking, what devilish thoughts were lurking in their hearts. Thornhill would always choose a smart field operative willing to risk his or her life over the best hardware money could buy.

Thornhill had just such a small group of skilled operatives within the CIA, completely loyal to him and his private agenda. They had all worked hard to regain for the Agency its former prominence. Now Thornhill finally had the vehicle to do that. He would very soon have under his thumb powerful congressmen, senators, even the vice president

5

himself, and enough high-ranking bureaucrats to choke an independent counsel. Thornhill would see his budgets revive, his manpower skyrocket, his agency's scope of responsibility in the world return to its rightful place.

The strategy had worked for J. Edgar Hoover and the FBI. It was no coincidence, Thornhill believed, that the Bureau's budget and influence had flourished under the late director and his allegedly "secret" files on powerful politicians. If there was one organization in the world that Robert Thornhill hated with all his soul, it was the FBI. But he would use whatever tactics he could to bring his agency back to the forefront, even if it meant stealing a page from his most bitter foe. *Well, watch me do you one better, Ed.*

Thornhill focused again on the men clustered around him. "Not having to kill one of our own would, of course, be ideal," he said. "However, the fact is, the FBI have her under 'round-the-clock stealth security. The only time she's truly vulnerable is when she goes to the cottage. They may place her in Witness Protection without warning, so we have to hit them at the cottage."

Another man spoke up. "Okay, we kill Lockhart, but let the FBI agent live, for God's sake, Bob."

Thornhill shook his head. "The risk is too great. I know that killing a fellow agent is deplorable. But to shirk our duty now would be a catastrophic mistake. You know what we've invested in this operation. We cannot fail."

"Dammit, Bob," the first man to protest said, "do you know what will happen if the FBI learns we took out one of their people?"

"If we can't keep a secret like that, we have no business doing what we do," Thornhill snapped. "This is not the first time lives have been sacrificed."

Another member of the group leaned forward in his chair. He was the youngest of them. He had, however, earned the respect of the group with his intelligence and his ability to exercise extreme, focused ruthlessness.

"We've only really looked at the scenario of killing Lockhart to forestall the FBI's investigation into Buchanan. Why not appeal to the FBI director and have him order his team to give up the investigation? Then no one has to die."

Thornhill gave his younger colleague a disappointed look. "And how would you propose going about explaining to the FBI director why we wish him to do so?"

"How about some semblance of the truth?" the younger man said. "Even in the intelligence business there's sometimes room for that, isn't there?"

Thornhill smiled warmly. "So I should say to the FBI director – who, by the way, would love to see us all permanently interred in a museum – that we wish him to call off his potentially blockbuster investigation so that the CIA can use illegal means to trump his agency. Brilliant. Why didn't I think of that? And where would you like to serve *your* prison term?"

"For chrissakes, Bob, we *work* with the FBI now. This isn't 1960 anymore. Don't forget about CTC."

CTC stood for the Counter Terrorism Center, a cooperative effort between the CIA and the FBI to fight terrorism by sharing intelligence and resources. It had been generally deemed a success by those involved. To Thornhill, it was simply another way for the FBI to stick its greedy fingers into his business.

"I happen to be involved in CTC in a modest way," Thornhill said. "I find it an ideal perch on which to keep tabs on the Bureau and what they're

7

up to, which is usually no good, as far as we're concerned."

"Come on, we're all on the same team, Bob."

Thornhill's eyes focused on the younger man in such a way that everyone in the room froze. "I request that you never say those words in my presence again," Thornhill said.

The man paled and sat back in his chair.

Thornhill clenched his pipe between his teeth. "Would you like me to give you concrete examples of the FBI taking the credit, the glory for work done by our agency? For the blood spilled by our field agents? For the countless times we've saved the world from annihilation? How they manipulate investigations in order to crush everyone else, to beef up their already bloated budget? Would you like me to give you instances in my thirty-six-year career where the FBI did all it could to discredit our mission, our people? Would you?" The man slowly shook his head as Thornhill's gaze bored into him. "I don't give a damn if the FBI director himself came down here and kissed my shoes and swore his undying allegiance to me – I will not be swayed. Ever! Have I made my position clear?"

"I understand." As he said this, the younger man managed not to shake his head in bewilderment. Everyone in this room other than Robert Thornhill knew that the FBI and CIA actually got along well. Though they could be ham-handed at times in joint investigations because they had more resources than anyone else, the FBI was not on a witch hunt to bring down the Agency. But the men in this room also understood quite clearly that Robert Thornhill believed the FBI was their worst enemy. And they also knew that Thornhill had, decades ago, orchestrated a number of Agency-authorized assassinations with cunning and zeal. Why cross such a man?

8

Another colleague said, "But if we kill the agent, don't you think the FBI will go on a crusade to find out the truth? They have the resources to scorch the earth. No matter how good we are, we can't match their strength. Then where are we?"

Some grumbling rose from the others. Thornhill looked around warily. The collection of men here represented an uneasy alliance. They were paranoid, inscrutable fellows long used to keeping their own counsel. It had truly been a miracle to forge them together in the first place.

"The FBI *will* do everything they can to solve the murder of one of their agents and the chief witness to one of their most ambitious investigations ever. So what I would propose doing is to give them the solution we desire them to have." They looked curiously at him. He sipped water from his glass and then took a minute to prime his pipe.

"After years of helping Buchanan run his operation, Faith Lockhart's conscience or good sense or paranoia got the better of her. She went to the FBI and has now begun telling them everything she knows. Through a little foresight on my part, we were able to discover this development. Buchanan, however, is completely unaware that his partner has turned against him. He also doesn't know that we intend to kill her. Only we know." Thornhill inwardly congratulated himself for this last remark. It felt good, omniscience; it was the business he was in, after all.

"The FBI, however, may suspect that he does know about her betrayal or may find out at some point. Thus, to the outside observer, no one in the world has greater motivation to kill Faith Lockhart than Danny Buchanan."

"And your point?" the questioner persisted.

"My point," said Thornhill tersely, "is quite

simple. Instead of allowing Buchanan to disappear, we tip off the FBI that he and his clients discovered Lockhart's duplicity and had her and the agent murdered."

"But once they get hold of Buchanan, he'll tell them everything," the man quickly responded.

Thornhill looked at him as a disappointed teacher to pupil. Over the last year, Buchanan had given them everything they needed; he was now officially expendable.

The truth slowly dawned on the group. "So we tip the FBI about Buchanan *posthumously*. Three deaths. Correction, three murders," another man said.

Thornhill looked around the room, silently gauging the reaction of the others to this exchange, to his plan. Despite their protestations about killing an FBI agent he knew that three deaths meant nothing to these men. They were from the old school, which quite clearly understood that sacrifices of that nature were sometimes necessary. Certainly what they did for a living sometimes cost people their lives; however, their operations had also avoided open war. Kill three to save three million, who could possibly argue with that? Even if the victims were relatively innocent. Every soldier who ever died in battle was innocent too. Covert action, quaintly referred to as the "third option" in intelligence circles, the one between diplomacy and open war, was where the CIA could really prove its worth, Thornhill believed. Although it was also at the heart of some of the Agency's worst disasters. Well, without risk there was never the possibility for glory. That epitaph could be put on his tombstone.

No formal vote was taken by Thornhill; none was needed.

"Thank you, gentlemen," Thornhill said. "I'll take care of everything." He adjourned the meeting.

TWO

The small, wood-shingled cottage stood alone at the end of a short, hard-packed gravel road, its dirt shoulders laced with the tangled sprawl of dandelion, curly dock and chickweed. The ramshackle structure rested on an acre of cleared flat land, but was surrounded on three sides by woods where each tree struggled to find sunlight at the expense of its neighbor. Because of wetlands and other development problems, the eighty-year-old home had never had any neighbors. The nearest community was about three miles away by car, but less than half that distance if one had the backbone to challenge the dense woods.

For much of the last twenty years the rustic cottage had been used for impromptu teen parties, and on occasion by the wandering homeless looking for the comfort and relative safety of four walls and a roof, however porous. The cottage's discouraged current owner, who had recently inherited the beast, had finally opted to rent it out. He had found a willing tenant who had paid the full year's rent in advance, in cash.

Tonight the calf-high grass in the front yard was pushed low and then straightened in the face of a strengthening wind. Behind the house a line of thick oaks seemed to mimic the movements of the grass as they swayed back and forth. It hardly seemed possible, yet except for the wind, there were no other sounds.

Save one.

In the woods, several hundred yards directly behind the house, a pair of feet splashed through a shallow creek bed. The man's dirty trousers and soaked boots attested to the difficulty with which he had navigated the congested terrain in the dark, even with the aid of a three-quarters-full moon. He paused to scrape his muddy boots against the trunk of a fallen tree.

Lee Adams was both sweaty and chilled after the punishing trek. At forty-one years of age, his six-foot-two body was exceptionally strong. He worked out regularly, and his biceps and delts showed it. Keeping in reasonably good shape was a necessity in his line of work. While he was often required to sit in a car for days on end, or in a library or courthouse reviewing microfiche records, he also, on occasion, had to climb trees, subdue men even larger than he was or, like now, slog through gully-filled woods in the dead of night. A little extra muscle never hurt. However, he wasn't twenty anymore either, and his body was letting him know it.

Lee had thick, wavy brown hair that seemed perpetually in his face, a quick, infectious smile, pronounced cheekbones and an engaging set of blue eyes that had caused female hearts spontaneously to flutter from fifth grade onward. He had suffered enough broken bones during his career, though, and other assorted injuries, that his body felt far older than it looked. And that's what hit him every morning when he rose. The creaks, the little pains. Cancerous tumor or merely arthritis? he sometimes wondered. What the hell did it really matter? When God punched your ticket, He did so with authority. A good diet and messing around with weights or pitter-pattering on the treadmill wasn't going to change the Man's decision to pull your string.

Lee looked up ahead. He couldn't see the cottage just yet; the forest clutter was too thick. He fussed with the controls of the camera he had pulled from his knapsack while he took a series of replenishing breaths. Lee had made this same trek several times before but had never gone inside the cottage. He had seen things, though – peculiar things. That's why he was back. It was time to learn the secret of this place.

His wind having returned, Lee trudged on, his only companions the scurrying wildlife. Deer, rabbit, squirrel and even beaver were plentiful in this still-rural part of northern Virginia. As he walked along, Lee listened to the flit of flying creatures. All he could envision were rabid, foaming bats blindly cleaving the air around his head. And it seemed that every few steps he would run straight into a twister of mosquitoes. Though he had been paid a large amount of cash up front, he was seriously considering increasing his daily fee on this one.

When he approached the edge of the woods, Lee stopped. He had a great deal of experience spying on the haunts of people and their activities. Slow and methodical was the best way, like a pilot's checklist. You just had to hope nothing happened to make you improvise.

Lee's bent nose was a permanent badge of honor from his time as an amateur boxer in the Navy, where he had taken out his youthful aggression in a square of roped canvas against an opponent of like weight and ability. A pair of stout gloves, quick hands and nimble feet, cagey mind and a strong heart had constituted his arsenal of weapons. The majority of the time, they had been enough for victory.

After his military stint, things had worked out mostly okay for him. Never rich, never actually poor despite being mostly self-employed over the years,

13

usually free; never quite alone, though he had been divorced for almost fifteen years. The only good thing from that marriage had just turned twenty. His daughter was tall, blond and brainy, as well as the proud bearer of a full academic scholarship to the University of Virginia and a star on the women's soccer team. And for the last ten years, Renee Adams had no interest whatsoever in having anything to do with her old man. A decision that had her mother's full blessing, if not her insistence, Lee well knew. And his ex had seemed so kind on those first few dates, so infatuated with his Navy uniform, so enthusiastic in tearing up his bed.

His ex-wife, a former stripper named Trish Bardoe, had married on the rebound a fellow by the name of Eddie Stipowicz, an unemployed engineer with a drinking problem. Lee thought she was heading for disaster and had tried to get custody of Renee on the grounds that her mom and stepfather could not provide for her. Well, about that time, Eddie, a sneaky runt Lee despised, invented, mostly by accident, some microchip piece of crap that had made him a gazillionaire. Lee's custody battle had lost its juice after that. To add insult to injury, there had been stories on Eddie in the *Wall Street Journal*, *Time*, *Newsweek* and a number of other publications. He was famous. Their house had even been featured in *Architectural Digest*.

Lee had gotten that issue of the *Digest*. Trish's new home was grossly huge, mostly crimson red or eggplant so dark it made Lee think of the inside of a coffin. The windows were cathedral-size, the furniture large enough to become lost in and there were enough wood moldings, paneling and staircases to heat a typical midwestern town for an entire year. There were also stone fountains sculpted with naked people. What a kicker! A photo of the happy couple

14

was included in the spread. In Lee's opinion they might as well have captioned it "The Nerd and the Bombshell strike it rich in poor taste."

One photo had captured Lee's complete attention, however. Renee had been poised on the most magnificent stallion Lee had ever seen, on a field of grass that was so green and perfectly trimmed that it looked like a pond of sea glass. Lee had carefully cut that photo out and put it away in a safe spot – his family album of sorts. The article, of course, made no mention of him; no reason that it should. The one thing that had ticked him off, though, was the reference to Renee as Ed's daughter.

"Stepdaughter," Lee had said out loud when he read that line. "Stepdaughter. That one you can't take away, Trish." Most of the time he felt no envy for the wealth his ex-wife now had, for it meant that his daughter would never want. But it still hurt.

When you had something for all those years, something you had made with a part of yourself, and loved more than it was probably good to love anything, and then lost it – well, Lee tried never to dwell for long on that loss. Big tough guy that he was, when he did let himself think about the massive hole dead center in his chest, he ended up blubbering like a baby.

Life was so funny sometimes. Funny like when you get a clean bill of health one day and drop dead the next.

Lee looked down at his muddy pants and worked a painful cramp out of his weary leg at the same time he swatted a mosquito out of his eye. Hotel-size house. Servants. Fountains. Big horses. Sleek private jet. . . . Probably all a real pain in the ass.

Lee hugged the camera to his chest. It was loaded with 400-speed film that Lee was "turbocharging" by setting the camera's ISO speed to 1600. Fast film required less light, and with the shutter opening for shorter periods of time, there was far less likelihood that camera wobble or vibration would distort any photos. He slipped on a 600mm telephoto lens and flipped down the lens' attached tripod.

Peering between the branches of a wild dogwood, Lee focused on the rear of the cottage. Scattered clouds drifted past the moon and deepened the darkness around him. He took a series of shots and then put the camera away.

As he stared at the house, the problem was he couldn't tell from here if the place was occupied or not. It was true he couldn't see a light on, but the place might have an interior room not visible from here. Added to that, he couldn't see the front of the house, and there might be a car parked there, for all he knew. He had observed the traffic and foot patterns on his other trips here. There hadn't been much to see. Few cars came down this road, and no walkers or joggers did. All the cars he had seen had turned around, obviously having made a wrong turn. All, that is, except one.

He glanced up at the sky. The wind had died down. Lee roughly calculated that the clouds would obscure the moonlight for a few minutes more. He slung the pack across his back, tensed for a moment, as though marshaling all of his energy, and then slid out of the woods.

Lee glided noiselessly until he reached a spot where he could squat behind a copse of overgrown bushes and still observe the front and back of the house. While he watched the house, the shades of darkness grew lighter as the moon reappeared. It seemed to be lazily watching him, curious as to what he was doing here.

Though isolated, the cottage was only a forty-minute drive from downtown D.C. That made it very convenient for any number of things. Lee had made inquiries about the owner and found him to be squeaky clean. The renter, however, had been a little tougher to pin down.

Lee pulled out a device that looked like a cassette recorder but was actually a battery-powered lock-pick gun, along with a zippered case, which he opened. He felt the different lock picks inside, then selected the one he wanted. Using an Allen wrench, he secured the pick into the machine. Lee's fingers moved quickly, confidently, even as another bank of cloud passed over, deepening the darkness once more. Lee had done this so many times that he could have closed his eyes and his fingers would carry on, manipulating his tools of felony with enviable precision.

Lee had already checked out the locks on the cottage with his spotting scope during daylight. That had also disturbed him. Deadbolt locks on all the exterior doors. Sash locks on both the first- *and* second-story windows. All the hardware looked new too. On a falling-down rental in the middle of nowhere.

Despite the cool weather, a bead of nervous sweat surfaced on Lee's forehead as he thought about this. He touched the 9mm in his belt clip holster; the metal was comforting. He took a moment to put the single-action pistol in a cocked-and-locked position – a round in the firing chamber, the hammer cocked and the safety set.

The cottage also had a security system. That had been a real stunner. If he was smart, Lee would pack his tools of criminality and go home, reporting failure to his employer. However, he took pride in his work. He would see it through at least until something happened to make him change his mind. And Lee could run very fast when he needed to.

Getting into the house wouldn't be all that difficult, particularly since Lee had the pass-code. He'd managed to get it the third time he'd been there, when the two people had come to the cottage. He had already confirmed the place was wired, so he had come prepared. He had beat the couple here and waited while they did whatever they were doing inside. When they had come out, the woman had entered the pass-code to arm the system. Lee, hiding in the same copse he was in now, just happened to have a bit of electronic wizardry that snatched that code right out of the air like a fly ball neatly falling into a glove. All electrical current produces a magnetic field, like a little transmitter. When the tall woman had punched in the numbers, the security system had thrown off a discrete signal for each digit, right into Lee's electronic mitt.

Lee checked the cloud cover once more, slapped on a pair of latex gloves with reinforced fingertip and palm pads, readied his flashlight and took another deep breath. A minute later he moved out from the cover of the bushes and made it quietly to the back door. He slipped off his muddy boots and set them next to the door. He didn't want to leave traces of his visit. Good private investigators were invisible. Lee held the light under his arm while he inserted the pick in the door lock and activated the device.

He used the pick gun partly for speed and partly because he didn't crack enough locks to be that proficient at it. A pick and tension tool required constant use to allow the fingers the level of sensitivity required to detect the proximity of the shear line, the subtle descent of the tension tool as the lock's tumblers began to do their little jig. Using a pick and tension tool, an experienced locksmith could pick the lock faster than Lee could with his pick gun. It was a true art and Lee knew his limitations. Soon, he felt the dead bolt sliding back.

When he eased open the door, the silence was broken by the low beeping sound of the security system. He quickly found the control pad, punched in six numbers and the beeping sound immediately stopped. As Lee closed the door softly behind him, he knew he was now a felon.

The man lowered his rifle and the red dot emanating from the weapon's laser scope disappeared from the wide back of an unsuspecting Lee Adams. The man holding the rifle was Leonid Serov, a former KGB officer specializing in assassination. Serov had found himself without gainful employment after the breakup of the Soviet Union. However, his ability to efficiently kill human beings was much in demand in the "civilized" world. Fairly well pampered as a communist for many years, with his own apartment and car, Serov had grown wealthy literally over-night as a capitalist. If he had only known.

Serov didn't know Lee Adams and had no idea why he was here. He had not noticed him until Lee had made his break for the bushes near the house, because Lee had come through the woods on the side farthest from the Russian. The sounds of his presence, Serov correctly surmised, had been covered by the wind.

Serov checked his watch. They would be coming soon. He inspected the elongated suppressor attached to the rifle. He rubbed its long snout gently, like a favorite pet, as though bestowing the notion of infallibility on to the polished metal. The rifle's stock was a special composite of Kevlar, fiberglass and graphite that provided remarkable stability. And the weapon's bore was not rifled in the conventional way. Instead it had a rounded rectangular profile,

19

known as polygonal boring, with a right-hand twist. This type of rifling was supposed to increase muzzle velocity by upward of eight percent, and, more important, a ballistics match on a bullet fired from this gun was virtually impossible because there were no lands or grooves in the barrel that would make distinctive markings on the bullet as it exploded from the weapon. Success really was all in the details. Serov had built his entire career on that one philosophy.

The place was so isolated that Serov had mulled over perhaps removing the suppressor and relying on his skill as a marksman, his high-tech scope and his well-conceived exit plan. His confidence was justified, he believed. Just like the tree falling, when you kill someone in the middle of nowhere, who can hear him die? And he had known some suppressors to greatly distort the flight path of a bullet, with the unacceptable result that no one had died, except for the would-be assassin once his client had learned of the failure. Still, Serov had personally supervised this device's construction and was confident it would perform as designed.

The Russian shifted quietly, working out a cramp in his shoulder. He had been here since nightfall but was used to lengthy vigils. He never tired during these assignments. He took life seriously enough that preparing to extinguish another's kept his adrenaline high. With risk always came invigoration, it seemed. Whether you were mountain climbing or contemplating murder, it ironically made you feel more alive to have the possibility of death so close.

His escape route through the woods would take him to a quiet road where a car would be waiting to whisk him to nearby Dulles Airport. He would go on to other assignments, other places probably far more exotic than this. However, for his particular purpose, this setting had its virtues.

Killing someone in the city was the most difficult. Setting up where you would shoot, pulling the trigger and then escaping, all were vastly complicated by the fact that witnesses and the police were only a few anxious steps away in any direction. Give him the country, the isolation of the rural life, the cover of trees, the separation of homes, and like a tiger in a cattle pen he would kill with numbing efficiency every day of the week.

Serov sat on a stump a few feet from the tree line and only about thirty yards from the house. Despite the thickness of the woods, this spot allowed a clear field of fire: A bullet only needed an inch or so of free space. The man and woman, he had been told, would enter the house from the rear door. Only they would never make it that far. Whatever the laser touched, the bullet would destroy. He was confident he could hit a lightning bug from twice the distance he was confronted with here.

Things were set up so perfectly that Serov's instincts told him to be on high alert. Now he had an excellent reason not to fall into that trap: the man in the house. He was not the police. Law enforcement types didn't slink through the bushes and break into people's homes. Since he had not been made aware beforehand of the man's presence tonight, he concluded that the man was not on his side. However, Serov did not like to deviate from an established plan. He decided that if the man remained in the house after the bodies fell, he would follow through on his original plan and escape through the woods. If the man interfered in any way or came outside after the shots were fired – well, Serov had plenty of ammo, and the result would be three bodies instead of two.

21

THREE

Daniel Buchanan sat in his darkened office and sipped black coffee of such strength that he could almost feel his pulse rise with each swallow. After another long day of trying to convince legislators that his causes were worthy of their attention, the level of exhaustion was intense, and enormous amounts of caffeine were increasingly becoming the only remedy. A full night of sleep was not typically an option. A catnap here or there, closing his eyes while being driven around to the next meeting, the next flight, occasionally blanking out during an interminably long congressional hearing, even an hour or two in his bed at home – that was his official rest. Otherwise, he was working the Hill in all its near-mystical facets.

Sitting in the chambers of various congressmen, Buchanan would hear the voting buzzer go off and watch the TV every member had in his or her office. The monitor gave them the current bill up for vote, the tally for and against and the time they had left to scurry like ants to the floor and cast their ballot. With about five minutes remaining on a vote, Buchanan would conclude his meeting and hurry down the corridors looking for other members he needed to talk to, the Whip Wind-up Report clutched in his hand. It gave the daily voting schedules, which helped Buchanan determine where certain members might be – critical information when you were tracking dozens of moving targets who probably didn't want to talk to you.

Today Buchanan had managed to grab the ear of an important senator by riding the private underground subway to the Capitol for a floor vote. Buchanan left the man feeling fairly confident of help. He wasn't one of Buchanan's "special" people, but Buchanan was aware that you never knew where help could come from. He didn't care that his clients weren't popular or that they lacked a constituency that would hook a member's attention. He would just keep hammering away. The cause was a virtuous one; the means were therefore susceptible to a lower standard of conduct.

Buchanan's office was sparsely furnished and lacked many of the normal accoutrements of a busy lobbyist. Danny, as he liked to be called, kept no computer, no diskettes, no files, no records of anything of importance here. Paper files could be stolen, computers could be hacked into. Telephone conversations were bugged all the time. Spies were listening with everything from drinking glasses pressed to walls, to the latest gadgets that a year before hadn't even been invented but that could suck up streams of valuable information right out of the air. A typical organization bled confidential information the way a torpedoed ship shed its sailors. And Buchanan had a lot to hide.

For over two decades Buchanan had been the top influence peddler of them all. In some important ways he had laid the groundwork for lobbying in Washington. It had evolved from highly paid lawyers dozing at congressional hearings to a world of numbing complexity where the stakes couldn't possibly be higher. As a Capitol Hill hired gun, he had successfully represented environmental polluters in battles with the EPA, allowing them to spread death to an unsuspecting public; he had

23

been the lead political strategist for pharmaceutical giants who had killed moms and their kids; next a passionate advocate for gun makers who didn't care if their weapons were safe; then a behind-the-scenes player for automobile manufacturers who would rather fight than admit they were wrong on safety issues; and finally, in the mother of all cash cows, he had spearheaded the efforts of tobacco companies in bloody wars with everyone. Back then Washington could not afford to ignore him or his clients. And Buchanan had earned an enormous fortune.

Many of the strategies he had concocted during that time had become staples of current legislative manipulation. He had had congressmen float bills on the House floor he knew would be defeated, in order to rip away platforms for change later. Buchanan's clients hated change. He had constantly fought rearguard actions as those who wanted what his clients had nipped at his heels. How many times had he avoided outright political disaster by flooding members' offices with letters, propaganda, thinly veiled threats to drop financial support. "My client will support you for reelection, Senator, because we know you'll do right by us. And, by the way, the contribution check is already in your campaign account." How many times had he said those words.

Ironically, it was the spoils of lobbying for the powerful that had led to a dramatic change in Buchanan's life over ten years ago. His original plan had been to build his career first and then settle down with a wife and raise a family. Deciding to see the world before he took on the responsibilities of marriage and family, Buchanan had driven through western Africa in a sixty-thousand-dollar Range Rover on a photography safari. In addition to the beautiful animals, he had seen squalor and human suffering of unmatched depth. On another trip, to a remote region of the Sudan, he had witnessed a mass burial of children. An epidemic had swept the village earlier, he was told. It was one of the devastating diseases that routinely afflicted the area, killing off the young and elderly. What was the disease? Buchanan had asked. Something like measles, he was told.

Another trip he had watched as billions of American-produced cigarettes were unloaded on Chinese docks, to be consumed by people who already spent their lives wearing masks because of abysmal air pollution. He was witness to birth-control devices that had been banned in the United States being dumped by the hundreds of thousands in South America with one set of instructions written only in English. He had viewed shacks next to skyscrapers in Mexico City, starvation next to crooked capitalists in Russia. Though he had never been able to go there, North Korea, he knew, was a certified gangster state where it was believed that ten percent of the population had starved to death in the last five years. Every country had its schizo-phrenic story to tell.

After two years of this "pilgrimage," Buchanan's passion for marriage, having a family of his own, had evaporated. All the dying children he had seen became his children, his family. Fresh graves would still come by the millions for the young, the old, the starving of the world, but not without a fight that had become his. And he brought to it all that he had, more than he had ever given to the tobacco, chemical and gun behemoths. To this day he recalled in precise detail how this revelation of sorts had come: returning from a trip to South America, an airplane lavatory, him on his knees, his stomach sickened. It was as though he had personally murdered every dying child he had seen on that continent.

With eyes freshly opened, Buchanan started marching to these places to see precisely how he could help. He had personally brought a shipment of food and medicine to one country, only to discover there was no way to transport it to the interior regions. He had watched, helpless, as looters stripped his "care" package clean. Then he started working as an unpaid fund-raiser for humanitarian organizations ranging from CARE to Catholic Relief Services. He had done well, but the dollars amounted to a drip into a bottomless bucket. The numbers were not in their favor; the problem was only getting worse.

That's when Buchanan turned to his mastery of Washington. He had left the firm he had founded, taking only one person with him: Faith Lockhart. For the last decade his clients, his wards, were the most impoverished countries in the world. In truth, it was difficult for Buchanan to regard them as geopolitical units; he saw them as fragile clusters of devastated people under various flags who had no voice. He had dedicated the remainder of his life to solving the unsolvable problem of the global have-nots.

He had used all of his immense lobbying skills and contacts in Washington, only to find that these new causes paled in popularity to those he had represented before. When he had gone to Capitol Hill as an advocate of the powerful, the politicians had greeted him with smiles, no doubt with visions of campaign contributions and PAC dollars dancing in their heads. Now they gave him nothing. Some members of Congress bragged that they didn't even have passports, that the United States already spent far too much on foreign aid. Charity starts at home, they had said, and let's damn well keep it there.

But by far the most common retort was, "Where's the constituency, Danny? How does feeding the Ethiopians get me reelected in Illinois?" As he was quickly ushered from office after office, he sensed that they all looked at him with pity: Danny Buchanan, perhaps the greatest lobbyist ever, was now muddled, senile. It was so sad. Sure, it was a good cause and all, who can doubt that, but get real. Africa? Starving babies in Latin America? I've got my own problems right here.

"Look, if it ain't trade, troops or oil, Danny, why the hell are you here wasting my time?" one highly regarded senator had told him. That could be the quintessential statement on America foreign policy.

Could they be that blind? Buchanan had asked himself over and over. Or was he the utter fool?

Finally, Buchanan decided he had only one option. It was completely illegal, but a man pushed to the precipice could not afford allegiance to pristine ethics. Using the fortune he had amassed over the years, he had taken to bribing, in very special ways, certain key politicians for their assistance. It had worked wonderfully. The aid to his clients had grown, in so many different ways. Even as his own wealth was dissipated, things were looking up, Buchanan believed. Or at least things were not getting worse; he would count holding of precious, hard-won ground as a success. It had all worked well, until about a year ago.

As if on cue, the knock on his office door startled him from his reverie. The building was closed, supposedly secure, the cleaning crews long since departed. He didn't get up from his desk. He simply watched as the door swung inward, the silhouette of a tall man framed against the opening. The man's hand reached out and flicked on the light.

Buchanan squinted as the glare of the overheads

hit him. When his eyes adjusted to the brightness, he watched as Robert Thornhill took off his trench coat, smoothed down his jacket and shirt and sat down across from him. The man's movements were graceful, unhurried, as though he had plopped down for a leisurely drink at his country club.

"How did you get in here?" Buchanan asked sharply. "The building is supposed to be secure." For some reason Buchanan could sense that others lurked right outside the door.

"And it is, Danny. It is. For *most* people."

"I don't like you coming here, Thornhill."

"I'm courteous enough to use your given name. I'd appreciate reciprocity on that point. A small thing, to be sure, but at least I'm not demanding that you address me as *Mister* Thornhill. That's the norm between master and servant, isn't it, Danny? You see, I'm not so bad to work for."

The man's smug look was designed, Buchanan knew, to drive him to such distraction that he couldn't think clearly. Instead he leaned back in his chair and settled his hands across his middle.

"To what do I owe the pleasure of your visit, *Bob*?"

"Your meeting with Senator Milstead."

"I could easily have met him in town. I'm not sure why you insisted that I go to Pennsylvania."

"But this way you get one more opportunity to make your pitch for all those starving masses. You see, I do have a heart."

"Does it even make a dent in whatever you call a conscience that you're using the plight of millions of men, women and children who consider it a miracle to see the sun rise, to further your own selfish agenda?"

"I'm not paid to have a conscience. I'm paid to protect the interests of this country. *Your* interests. Besides, if having a conscience were the criteria, there would be no one left in this town. In fact, I applaud your efforts. I have nothing against the poor and helpless. Good for you, Danny!"

"Sorry if I don't buy that."

Thornhill smiled. "Every country in the world has people like me. That is, they do if they're smart. We get the results everybody wants, because most 'everybody' lacks the courage to do it himself."

"So you play God? Interesting line of work."

"God is conceptual. I deal in facts. Speaking of which, you powered your agenda by illegal means; who are you to deny me the same right?"

In truth, Buchanan had no response to this statement. And Thornhill's intractably calm demeanor only reinforced the helplessness he felt.

"Any questions about the meeting with Milstead?" Thornhill asked.

"You have enough on Harvey Milstead to put him away for three lives. What are you really after?"

Thornhill chuckled. "I hope you're not accusing me of having a hidden agenda."

"You can tell me, Bob, we're partners."

"Maybe it's as simple as wanting you to jump when I snap my fingers."

"Fine, but a year from now, if you pop up like this, you may not leave under your own power."

"Threats from a solitary lobbyist to *me*." Thornhill sighed. "But not so solitary. You have an army of one. How is Faith? Doing well?"

"Faith is not a part of this. Faith will never be a part of this."

Thornhill nodded. "You're the only one in the crosshairs. You and your fine group of felonious politicians. America's best and brightest."

Buchanan stared coldly at his antagonist and said nothing.

"Things are coming to a head, Danny. As you said,

the show will be coming to a close soon. I hope you're ready to exit cleanly."

"When I leave, my trail will be so clean, not even your spy satellites will be able to pick it up."

"Confidence is inspiring. Yet so often misplaced."

"Is that all you wanted to tell me? Be prepared to escape? I've been ready to do that since the first minute I met you."

Thornhill stood. "You focus on Senator Milstead. Get us some good, juicy stuff. Get him to talk about the income he'll have when he retires, the nominal tasks he'll have to perform as window dressing. The more specific, the better."

"It heartens me to see you enjoying this so much. Probably a lot more fun than the Bay of Pigs."

"Before my time."

"Well, I'm sure you've made your mark in other ways."

Thornhill bristled for a moment and then his calm returned. "You'd make a fine poker player, Danny. But try to remember that a bluff when one is holding no face cards is still a bluff." Thornhill put on his trench coat. "Don't trouble yourself, I can find my way out."

In the next instant Thornhill was gone. The man appeared and disappeared at will, it seemed. Buchanan leaned back in his chair and let out a quick breath. His hands were trembling and he pressed them hard against the desk until the quivering stopped.

Thornhill had thundered into his life like an exploding torpedo. Buchanan had become, essentially, a lackey, now spying on those he had been bribing for years with his own money, now collecting a wealth of material for this ogre to use as blackmail. And Buchanan was powerless to stop the man.

30

Ironically, this decline in his material assets and now his work in the service of another had brought Buchanan directly back from whence he had come. He had grown up on the illustrious Philadelphia Main Line. He had lived on one of the most magnificent estates in that area. Stacked fieldstone walls – like thick gray brushstrokes of paint – outlined the grass perimeters of the vast, perfect lawns, on which was situated a sprawling twelve-thousand-square-foot house with broad, covered porches, and a detached quadruple-car garage with an apartment overhead. The house had more bedrooms than a dormitory, and lavish baths with costly tile and the luster of gold on something as commonplace as a faucet.

It was the world of the American blue bloods, where pampered lifestyles and crushing expectations existed side by side. Buchanan had observed this complex universe from an intimate perspective, yet he was not one of its privileged inhabitants. Buchanan's family had been the chauffeurs and maids and gardeners, the handymen, nannies and cooks to these blue bloods. Having survived the Canadian border winters, the Buchanans had migrated south, en masse, to a gentler climate, to less demanding work than that required by ax and spade, boat and hook. Up there they had hunted for food and cut wood for warmth, only to watch helplessly as nature mercilessly culled their ranks in a natural process that had made the survivors stronger, their descendants stronger still. And Danny Buchanan was perhaps the strongest of them all.

Young Danny Buchanan had watered the lawn and cleaned the pool, swept and repainted the tennis court, picked the flowers and vegetables and played, in a properly respectful manner, with the children.

As he had gotten older, Buchanan had huddled with the younger generation of the spoiled rich, deep in the privacy of the complex flower gardens, smoking, drinking and exploring each other sexually. Buchanan had even acted as pallbearer, weeping sincerely as he bore two of the young and the rich who had wasted their privileged lives, mixing too much whisky with a racing sports car, driving too fast for impaired motor skills. When you lived life that fast, often you died fast as well. Right now Buchanan could see his own end rushing headlong at him.

Buchanan had never felt comfortable in either group – the rich or the poor – since then. The rich he would never be a part of, no matter how much his bank account swelled. He had played with the wealthy heirs, but when mealtime came, they went to the formal dining room while he trudged to the kitchen to break his bread with the other servants. The baby blues had attended Harvard, Yale and Princeton; he had worked his way through night school at an institution his betters would openly mock.

Buchanan's own family was now equally foreign to him. He sent his relatives money. They sent it back. When he went to visit, he had found they had nothing to talk about. They neither understood nor cared about what he did. However, they made him feel that there was nothing honest about his life's occupation; he could see that in their tightly drawn faces, their mumbled words. Washington was as foreign as hell itself to all that they believed in. He lied for money, large sums of it. Better he had followed in their tread; honest if simple work. By rising above them, he had fallen far below what they represented: fairness, integrity, character.

The path he had chosen during the last ten years

had only deepened this solitary confinement. He had few friends. Nevertheless, he did have millions of strangers across the world who deeply depended on him for something as basic as survival. Even Buchanan had to admit, it was a bizarre existence.

And now, with the coming of Thornhill, Buchanan's foothold had dropped another rung on the ladder leading to the abyss. Now he could no longer even confide in his one indisputable soul mate, Faith Lockhart. She knew nothing about Thornhill, and she never would know of the man from the CIA; this was all that was keeping her safe. It had cost him his last thread of real human contact.

Danny Buchanan was now truly alone.

He stepped to the window of his office and looked out at majestic monuments known around the world. Some might argue that their beautiful facades were just that: Like the magician's hand, they were designed to guide the eyes away from the truly important business of this city, transacted usually for the benefit of a select few.

Buchanan had learned that effective, long-term power came essentially from the gentle force of rule of the few over the many, for most people were not political beasts. A delicate balance was called for, the few over the many, *gently*, civilly; and Buchanan knew that the most perfect example of it in the history of the world existed right here.

Closing his eyes, he let the darkness envelop him, let new energy spill into his body for the fight tomorrow. It promised to be a very long night, however, for in truth, his life had now become one long tunnel to nowhere. If he could only ensure Thornhill's destruction as well, it would all be worth it. One small crack in the darkness, that would be all Buchanan needed. If only it could be so.

FOUR

The car moved down the highway at precisely the speed limit. The man was driving, the woman next to him. Both sat rigidly, as though one feared a sudden attack from the other.

As a jet, landing gear down, roared over them like a swooping hawk on its way in to Dulles Airport, Faith Lockhart closed her eyes and pretended for a moment that she was on that plane, and instead of landing, it was beginning some far-flung journey. As she slowly opened her eyes, the car took an exit off the highway and they left the unsettling glare of sodium lights behind. They were soon sailing past jagged rows of trees on both sides of the road, the wide, grassy ditches deep and soggy; the dull pulse of flat-looking stars was now their only source of light other than the car's twin beams stabbing the darkness.

"I don't understand why Agent Reynolds couldn't come tonight," she said.

"The simple answer is, you're not the only investigation she has going, Faith," Special Agent Ken Newman replied. "But I'm not exactly a stranger, am I? We're just going to talk, like the other times. Pretend I'm Brooke Reynolds. We're all on the same team."

The car turned on to another, even more isolated road. On this stretch the trees were replaced by denuded fields awaiting the final scrape of the bulldozers. In a year's time there would be almost as many homes here as there had been trees before, as suburban sprawl continued its push. Now the land simply looked ravaged, naked. And bleak, perhaps because of what was to come. In that regard, the land and Faith Lockhart were as one.

Newman glanced over at her. Although he didn't like to admit it, he felt uneasy around Faith Lockhart, as though he were seated next to a ball of wired C-4 with no idea when it might explode. He shifted in his seat. His skin was a little raw where the leather of his shoulder holster usually rubbed against his skin. Most people developed a callus at that spot, but his skin just kept blistering and then peeling off. Ironically, he felt that the twinge of pain gave him an edge because he never relaxed; it was a clear warning that if he let down his guard, that small discomfort could become a fatal one. Tonight, however, because he was wearing body armor, the holster wasn't scraping his skin; the pain and heightened sense of awareness were not nearly as strong.

Faith could feel the blood rush through her ears, all senses elevated, the way they were when you were lying in bed late at night and hearing a strange, troubling sound. When you were a child and that happened, you raced to your parents' bed and climbed in, to be wrapped up, consoled by loving, understanding arms. Her parents were dead and she was now thirty-six years old. Who was out there for Faith Lockhart?

"And after tonight, it'll be Agent Reynolds instead of me," Newman said. "You're comfortable with her, aren't you?"

"I'm not sure 'comfort' applies to situations like this."

"Sure it does. It's very important, in fact. Reynolds is a straight shooter. Believe me, if it weren't for her, this thing would be going nowhere. You haven't exactly given us much to go on. But she believes in you. So long as you don't do anything to destroy that confidence, you have a powerful ally in Brooke Reynolds. She cares about you."

Faith crossed her legs and folded her arms across her chest. She was about five-five, and her torso was short. Her bosom was flatter than she would have liked, but her legs were long and well shaped. If nothing else, she could always count on her legs to get attention. The defined muscles in her calves and thighs, visible through her sheer stockings, were enough to cause Newman's gaze to flicker over them several times with what appeared to be mild interest, she noted.

Faith swatted her long auburn hair out of her face and rested her hand on the bridge of her nose. A few white strands of hair floated among the darker. They were not yet noticeable, but that would change with time. In fact, the pressure she was under would undoubtedly accelerate the aging process. Besides her hard work, agile wits and poise, Faith's good looks, she knew, had helped her career. It was shallow to believe that one's features made a difference. Yet the truth was they did, particularly when one dealt with an overwhelmingly male audience, as she had for her entire career.

The broad smiles she received when entering a senator's office were not so much due to her gray matter, she knew, as to the above-the-knee skirts she favored. Sometimes it was as simple as dangling a shoe. She was talking about children dying, families living in sewers in far-off lands, and these men were fixated on toe cleavage. God, testosterone was a man's greatest weakness and a woman's most powerful advantage. At least it helped to level a playing field that had always been tilted in favor of the males.

"It's nice to be so well loved," said Faith. "But picking me up in an alley. Coming out here in the middle of nowhere in the dead of night. That's a little much, don't you think?"

"Your walking into the Washington Field Office just wasn't an option. You're the star witness in what could be a very important investigation. This place is safe."

"You mean it's perfect for an ambush. How do you know we haven't been followed?"

"We've been followed, all right. By our people. If anyone else had been around, believe me, our people would've noticed it before sending us on. We had a tail car until we turned off the highway. There's nobody back there."

"So your people are infallible. I wish I had that kind of people working for me. Where do you find them?"

"Look, we know what we're doing, okay? Relax." Even as he said this, though, he checked the mirror again.

He glanced at the cell phone lying on the front seat, and Faith could easily read his thoughts. "Suddenly wanting backup?" Newman glanced sharply at her but said nothing. "Okay, so let's get to the principal terms," she said. "What do I really get out of all this? We've never quite nailed it down." When Newman still didn't respond, she studied his profile for a minute, sizing up his nerve. She reached over and touched his arm.

"I took a lot of risk to do what I'm doing," she said. She felt him tense through his suit jacket where her fingers rested. She kept her fingers there, applied slightly more pressure. Her fingertips could now distinguish the material of his jacket from that of his shirt. As he turned slightly toward her, Faith was able to see the bulletproof vest he was wearing. The

37

saliva in her mouth suddenly evaporated, along with her composure.

Newman glanced at her. "I'll give it to you straight. What exactly your deal will be, that's not up to me. So far, you haven't really given us anything. But play by the rules and everything will be okay. You'll cut your deal, you'll give us what we need and pretty soon you'll have a new identity selling seashells on Fiji, while your partner and his playmates become long-term guests of the government. Don't revel in it, don't think too much about it, just try to survive it. Remember, we're on your side here. We're the only friends you have."

Faith sat back, finally drawing her gaze from the body armor. She decided it was time to drop her bombshell. She may as well try it out on Newman instead of Reynolds. In some ways, Reynolds and she had hit it off. Two women in a sea of men. In many subtle ways, the female agent had understood things a man never would have. In other ways, however, they had been like two alley cats circling around fish bones.

"I want to bring in Buchanan. I know I can get him to do it. If we work together, your case will be much stronger." She said all of this quickly, vastly relieved to have it finally out.

Newman's face betrayed his astonishment. "Faith, we're pretty flexible, but we're not cutting a deal with the guy who, according to you, masterminded this whole thing."

"You don't understand all the facts. Why he did it. He's not the bad person in all this. He's a good guy."

"He broke the law. According to you, he corrupted government officials. That's enough for me."

"When you understand why he did it, you won't think that way."

38

"Don't pin your hopes on that strategy, Faith. Don't do that to yourself."

"What if I say it's both or none?"

"Then you're making the biggest mistake of your life."

"So it's either me or him?"

"And it shouldn't be that tough a choice."

"I'll just have to talk to Reynolds, then."

"She'll tell you the same thing I just did."

"Don't be so sure. I can be pretty persuasive. And I also happen to be right."

"Faith, you have no idea what's involved here. FBI agents don't decide who to prosecute. The U.S. Attorney's Office does. Even if Reynolds sided with you, and I doubt she will, I can tell you there's no way in hell the lawyers will go along. If they try to take down all these powerful politicos and cut a sweetheart deal with the guy who got them into it in the first place, they're gonna lose their asses, and then their jobs. This is Washington, these are eight-hundred-pound gorillas we're dealing with here. There'll be phones ringing off the hook, a media frenzy, behind-the-scenes deals going a mile a minute, and at the end of the day, we'll all be toast. Trust me, I've been doing this for twenty years. It's Buchanan or nothing."

Faith sat back and stared at the sky. For a moment, amid the clouds, she envisioned Danny Buchanan slumped over in a dark, hopeless prison cell. She could never let it come to that. She would have to talk to Reynolds and the attorneys, make them see that Buchanan had to be given immunity too. That was the only way it could work. But Newman sounded so sure of himself. What he had just said made perfect sense. This was Washington. As suddenly as the strike of a match, her confidence completely deserted her. Had she, the consummate

39

lobbyist, who had been tallying political scorecards for God knew how long, failed to account for the political situation here?

"I need a bathroom," Faith said.

"We'll be at the cottage in about fifteen minutes."

"Actually, if you take the next left, there's a twenty-four-hour gas station about a mile down the road."

He looked at her in surprise. "How do you know that?"

She looked back with a look of confidence that masked a rising panic. "I like to know what I'm getting into. That includes the people and the geography."

He didn't answer, but hung the left, and they were soon at the well-lit Exxon, which had a convenience store component. The highway had to be nearby, despite the isolation of the surroundings, because semis were parked up and down the lot. The Exxon obviously catered to open-road truckers. Men in boots and cowboy hats, Wrangler jeans and windbreakers, with trucking- and automotive-parts' logos stenciled across them, strode across the lot. Some patiently filled their rigs with fuel; others sipped hot coffee, tiny wisps of steam heat rising past tired, leathery faces. No one paid attention to the sedan as it pulled up next to the rest room located on the far side of the building.

Faith locked the bathroom door behind her, put the toilet lid down and sat on it. She didn't need to use the facilities; she needed time to think, to control the panic hitting her from all sides. She looked around, her eyes absently taking in the handwritten scribbles on the chipping yellow paint covering the block walls. Some of the obscene language almost made her blush. Some of the writings were witty – belly-rocking funny, even – in their crudeness. They probably surpassed anything the men had composed to decorate their rest room next door, although most males would never concede this possibility. Men were always underestimating women.

She stood, splashed cold tap water on her face and dried it with a paper towel. About that time her knees decided to give, and she locked them, her fingers curling tightly around the stained porcelain of the sink. She had had nightmares about doing that at her wedding: locking her knees and then passing out because of it. Well, one less thing to worry about now. She'd never had a lasting relationship in her life, unless one counted a certain young man in fifth grade whose name she couldn't remember but whose sky-blue eyes she would never forget.

Danny Buchanan had given her lasting friendship. He'd been her mentor and substitute father for the last fifteen years. He had seen potential in her where no one else had. He had given her a chance when she so desperately needed one. She had come to Washington with boundless ambition and enthusiasm and absolutely no focus. Lobbying? She knew nothing about it, but it sounded exciting. And lucrative. Her father had been a good-natured if aimless wanderer, dragging his wife and daughter from one get-rich scheme to the next. He was one of nature's cruelest concoctions: a visionary lacking the skills to implement that vision. He measured gainful employment in days instead of years. They all lived one nervous week to the next. When his plans went awry and he was losing other people's money, he would pack up Faith and her mother and flee. They'd been homeless on occasion, hungry more often than not; still, her father had always gotten back on his feet, however totteringly. Until the day he died. Poverty was a lasting, powerful memory for her.

41

Faith wanted a good, stable life, and she wanted to be dependent on no one for it. Buchanan had given her the opportunity, the skills to accomplish her dream, and much more than that. He had not only vision, but also the tools to execute his sweeping ideas. She could never betray him. She was in breathless awe of what he had done and was still trying so hard to do. He was the rock she needed at that stage of her life. In the last year their relationship had changed. Ever more reclusive, he had stopped talking to her. Danny was irritable, snapping for little reason. When she pressed him to tell her what was troubling him, he withdrew even more. Their relationship had been so close that the change had been even harder for her to accept. He became stealthy, stopped inviting her to travel with him; they no longer even engaged in their lengthy strategy sessions.

And then he had done something entirely original and personally devastating: He had lied to her. The matter had been purely trivial, but the implications were serious. If he spun lies in small areas, what was he holding from her of importance? They had one final confrontation and Buchanan had told her that no possible good could come from him sharing what troubled him. And then he dropped the real stunner.

If she wanted to leave his employ, she was free to do so, and maybe it was time she did, he had strongly intimated. His employ! The father telling his precocious daughter to get the hell out of the house was more the effect upon her.

Why did he want her to go away? And then it finally dawned on her. How could she have been so blind? They were on to Danny. Somebody was on to him, and he didn't want her to share his fate. She had point-blank confronted him on that issue. And he had point-blank denied it. And then insisted that she leave. Noble to the end.

And yet if he wouldn't confide in her, she would map a separate course for them. After much deliberation she had gone to the FBI. She knew there was a chance it was the FBI that had somehow discovered Danny's secret, but this might make it easier, Faith had thought. Now a thousand doubts assailed her for the decision to approach the Bureau. Did she really believe the Bureau would just fall all over themselves inviting Buchanan into the prosecution's fold? She cursed herself for giving them Danny's name, although he was very famous in a town of famous people; the FBI would not have failed to make the connection. They wanted Danny to go to prison. Her for Danny. That was supposed to be her choice? She had never felt more alone.

She looked at herself in the cracked mirror. The bones of her face seemed to be pushing through her skin, her eye sockets hollowing right in front of her. A centimeter of skin between her and nothing. Her grand vision, the way out for them both, had suddenly become a free fall of insane, dizzying proportion. Her father would have just packed up and fled into the night. What was his daughter supposed to do?

43

FIVE

Lee pulled out his pistol and pointed it ahead of him as he moved through the hallway. With his other hand he swung the flashlight in slow, steady arcs.

The first room he peered into was the kitchen, containing a small 1950s-era refrigerator, GE electric range and tattered black-and-yellow-checked linoleum flooring. The walls were discolored in places by water damage. The ceiling was unfinished, the joists and the subfloor above clearly visible. Lee gazed at the old copper pipes and the newer grafts of PVC as they made a series of right angles through the exposed, darkened wall studs.

There was no aroma of food here, only a smell of grease, presumably hardened in the stove-top burners and in the bowels of the vent, along with probably a few trillion bacteria. A chipped Formica table and four bent-metal, vinyl-backed chairs stood in the center of the kitchen. The counters were barren, no dishes visible. There were also no towels, coffeemaker or condiment canisters, nor any other item or personal touch that might have suggested the kitchen had been used in the last decade or so. It was as though he had stepped back in time, or happened upon a bomb shelter put into service during the hysteria of the fifties.

The small dining room was across the hallway from the kitchen. Lee looked at the waist-high wood paneling, darkened and cracked over the years. He had a sudden chill, though the air was stale and oppressive inside. The house apparently had no central heating, nor had Lee seen any wall-mounted air conditioners. There had been no heating oil tank outside either, at least aboveground. Lee eyed the chill-chasers bolted along the bottom of the walls, their power cords plugged into electrical outlets. As in the kitchen, the ceiling here was unfinished. The electrical line to the dust-ridden chandelier ran through holes bored in the exposed joists. Electricity, Lee deduced, must have come to the home after it was first built.

As he moved down the hallway toward the front of the house, Lee was unable to see the invisible trip beam, positioned at knee height, that stretched across the hall. He pierced this security perimeter, and from somewhere in the house a barely audible click was heard. Lee jerked for a moment, pointing his gun in wide circles, and then relaxed. It was an old house, and old houses made lots of noises. He was just being jumpy, yet he had a right to be. The cottage and its location were right the hell out of a *Friday the 13th* movie.

Lee entered one of the front rooms. There, under the sweep of his flashlight, he saw that the furniture had been moved up against the walls, and there were footprints and drag patterns in the layers of dust on the floor. In the center of the room were a number of folding chairs and a rectangular-shaped table. A stack of Styrofoam coffee cups rested at one end of the table next to a coffeemaker. Packets of coffee, creamer and sugar lay next to the coffeemaker.

Lee took all this in and jerked when he saw the windows. Not only were the heavy drapes drawn tight, but also the windows had been boarded over with big sheets of plywood, the drapes dangling from underneath the wood.

45

"Shit," Lee muttered. He quickly discovered that the small square windows set in the front door had been covered over with cardboard. He pulled out his camera and snapped some shots of all these puzzling items.

Wanting to complete his search as soon as possible, Lee hurried up the stairs to the second floor. He cautiously opened the door to the first bedroom and peered in. The bed was small and made, and its smell of mildew hit him immediately. The walls here were unfinished as well. Lee put his hand against the exposed wall and immediately felt air from the outside coming through the cracks. He was startled for a moment when he saw a slender line of light coming from the top of the wall. Then he realized it was the moonlight coming through a gap where wall was supposed to meet roof.

Lee carefully nudged open the closet door. It still let out a prolonged squeak that made him catch a breath. No clothes, not even a single hanger. He shook his head and went into the small connecting bathroom. Here, there was a more modern, drop-down ceiling, linoleum floor with pebble design and plasterboard walls covered with peeling flower-patterned wallpaper. The shower was a one-piece fiberglass unit. However, there were no towels, toilet paper or soap. No way to shower or even freshen up.

He went through into the other, adjoining bed-room. Here, the smell of mildew on the bedcovers was so strong he almost had to hold his nose. The closet here was empty as well.

None of this was making sense. He stood in the pool of moonlight coming through the window, felt his neck tickled by the drafts of air pushing through the cracks in the walls and shook his head. What was Faith Lockhart doing here if not using it as some kind of love nest? That was what his initial conclusion had been, even though he had only seen her with the tall woman. People swung lots of ways. But not even with concrete up their noses could they have been having sex on these sheets.

Returning downstairs, he went across the hallway and into the other front space, which Lee assumed was the living room. The windows here had been boarded over as well. There was a bookshelf notched into one of the walls, although no books were on it As in the kitchen, the ceiling was unfinished. As Lee swung his light upward, he spied the short pieces of wood tacked between the joists at forty-five-degree angles, forming a line of X's across the ceiling. The wood was clearly different from that used for the original construction; it was lighter and of a different grain. Additional support? Why had that been necessary?

He shook his head in the manner of a man resigned to his fate. Now added to Lee's list of worries was the possibility that the damn second floor would collapse at any minute on his head. He envisioned his obit headlined something like: LUCKLESS PI FELLED BY BATHTUB/SHOWER COMBO; WEALTHY EX-WIFE REFUSES COMMENT.

As Lee shone his light around, he froze. Set into one wall was a door. A closet, most likely. Nothing unusual about that, except that this door was secured by a deadbolt. He went over and examined the lock more closely, glancing at the small pile of wood dust on the floor directly under the lock. Lee knew it had been left over when the person installing the lock had drilled the hole through the wooden door. Exterior deadbolts. A security system. A deadbolt recently installed on an *interior* closet door in a crappy rental in the boonies. What could be so valuable here to go to all this trouble?

"Shit," Lee said again. He wanted to leave this

place, but he could not take his eyes off the lock. If Lee Adams had one fault – and it could hardly be considered a fault for someone in his line of work – it was that he was a very curious man. Secrets plagued him. People attempting to hide things came close to infuriating him. As a "lunch pail" kind of guy utterly convinced that great monied forces stalked the earth creating all kinds of havoc for ordinary folk like him, Lee believed in the principle of full and fair disclosure with all his substantial heart. Putting action to that belief, he wedged the flashlight under his armpit, holstered his gun and pulled out his lock-pick kit. His fingers worked nimbly as he slipped a fresh pick into the lock-pick gun. He took a deep breath, inserted the pick in the lock and turned on the machine.

When the deadbolt slid back, Lee took another deep breath, pulled his pistol and pointed it at the door as he turned the knob. He didn't really believe that anyone had locked himself in a closet and was about to jump him, but then again, he had seen stranger things happen. Someone might be on the other side of this door.

When he saw what was in the closet, a part of him wished the problem were as simple as someone preparing to ambush him. He swore under his breath, holstered his pistol and ran.

In the closet the blink of red lights from the stacks of electronic equipment shone forth now in the open doorway.

Lee raced into the other front room and shone his light around the walls in even patterns, moving higher and higher. Then he saw it. There was a camera lens in the wall next to the molding. Probably a pinhole lens, designed specifically for covert surveillance. It was impossible to see in the poor lighting, but the beam from the flashlight was reflecting off it. As he moved the beam around, he hit a total of four camera lenses.

Holy shit. The sound he had heard earlier. He must have tripped some device that had triggered the cameras. He raced back to the living room closet, flashed his light on the front of the video machine.

Eject! Where the hell was eject? He found the button, hit it and nothing happened. He punched it again and again. He hit the other buttons. Nothing. Then Lee's gaze closed on the *second* small infrared portal in the front of the machine, and the answer hit him. The machine was controlled by a special remote, its function buttons overridden. His blood ran cold with the possibilities this sort of arrangement suggested. He thought about putting a bullet into the thing, to make it cough up the precious tape. But for all he knew, the damn thing was armored and he'd end up eating his own slug off the ricochet. And what if it had a real-time satellite link and the tape was only a backup? Was there a camera in here? People could be looking at him right now. For one ridiculous second, he thought about giving them the finger.

Lee was about to run again but then had a sudden inspiration. He fumbled in his knapsack, his usually steady fingers now not quite so dexterous. His hands closed around the small case. He whipped it out, fought with the lid for an instant and then managed to pull out the small but powerful magnet.

Magnets were a popular burglary tool because they were ideal for locating and popping window pins once you had cut through the glass. Otherwise, the pins would defeat the most accomplished burglar. Now the magnet would play the reverse role: not helping him break in, but rather assisting him in making what he hoped would be an invisible exit.

He palmed the magnet and then ran it in front of the video machine and then over the top. He did it as many times as he could in the one minute he had allowed himself before fleeing for his life. He prayed that the magnetic field would obliterate the images on the tape. *His* images.

He threw the magnet back in his bag, turned and ran for the door. God only knew who might be on their way here. Lee suddenly stopped. Should he go back to the closet, rip the VCR out and take it with him? The next sound Lee heard drove all thoughts of the VCR from his mind.

A car was coming.

"Sonofabitch!" hissed Lee. Was it Lockhart and her escort? They had come here every *other* evening. So much for a pattern. He raced back down the hall, threw open the back door, burst through and hurdled the concrete stoop. He landed heavily in the slick grass, his shoeless feet slipped and he fell hard. The impact knocked the breath out of him and he felt a sharp pain where his elbow had struck at an odd angle. But fear was a great painkiller. Within a few seconds he was up and chugging for the tree line.

He was halfway to the woods when the car pulled into the driveway, its light beams bouncing a little as the car moved from flat road to uneven ground. Lee took another few strides, hit the tree line and dove under cover.

The red dot had lingered for a few moments on Lee's chest. Serov could have taken the man so easily. But that would warn the people in the car. The former KGB man aimed the rifle at the driver's-side door. He hoped the man who had now made it to the woods would not be stupid enough to try anything. He had been very lucky up until now. He had escaped death not once, but twice. One should not waste that much luck. It would be in such poor taste, Serov thought as he once more sighted through the laser scope.

Lee should have kept running, but he stopped, his chest heaving, and crept back to the tree line. His curiosity had always been his strongest trait, sometimes too strong. Besides, the people behind all the electronic equipment probably had already identified him. Hell, they probably knew the dentist he used and his preference for Coke over Pepsi, so he might as well stick around and see what was coming next. If the people in the car started for the woods, he would do his best impersonation of an Olympic marathoner, shoeless feet and all, and dare anyone to catch him.

He crouched down and took out his night-vision monocular. It utilized forward-looking infrared, or FLIR, technology, which was a vast improvement over the ambient light intensifier, or I-squareds, Lee had used in the past. FLIR worked by detecting, in essence, heat. It needed no light to operate, and unlike the I-squareds, it could distinguish dark images against dark backgrounds, with the heat transferred into crystal-clear video images.

As Lee focused the contraption, his field of vision was now a green screen with red images. The car appeared so close that Lee had the sense that he could reach out and touch it. The engine area glowed particularly brightly, since it was still very hot. He watched the man as he climbed out of the driver's side. Lee didn't recognize him, but the private investigator tensed as he watched Faith Lockhart climb out of the car and join the man. They were side by side at this point. The man hesitated as though he had forgotten something.

"Damn," Lee hissed between clenched teeth. "The

door." Lee focused for a moment on the back door to the cottage. It was standing wide open.

The man had obviously seen this. He turned, facing the woman, and reached inside his coat.

*

In the woods, Serov fixed his laser point on the base of the man's neck. He smiled contentedly. The man and woman were lined up nicely. The ammo the Russian was chambering was highly customized, military-style ordnance with full metal jackets. Serov was a careful student of both weapons and the wounds they caused. With its high velocity, the bullet would have minimal projectile deformity as it passed through its target. However, it would still cause devastating injury when the kinetic energy the bullet carried was released and then rapidly lost in the body. The initial wound track and cavity would be many times larger than the size of the bullet before it partially closed. And the destruction to tissue and bone would occur radially, akin to the epicenter of an earthquake, with terrible damage resulting a great distance away. It was quite beautiful, in its own way, Serov felt.

Velocity was the key to kinetic energy levels – the Russian was well aware – which, in turn, determined damage force on the target. Double the weight of a bullet and it doubled the kinetic energy. However, Serov had long ago learned that when you doubled the velocity at which the bullet was fired, the kinetic energy was *quadrupled*. And Serov's weapon and ammo were at the top end of the scale on velocity. Yes, beautiful indeed.

However, because of its full metal jacket, the bullet could also easily pass through one person and then strike and kill another. This was not an unpopular result for soldiers who were going at it in combat. And for hired killers with two targets.

However, if another bullet was required to kill the woman, so be it. Ammo was relatively cheap. Consequently, so were humans.

Serov took a slight breath, became absolutely still and lightly squeezed the trigger.

"Omigod!" Lee shouted as he watched the man's body twist and then pitch violently against the woman. They both dropped to the ground as though sewn together.

Lee instinctively started to race out of the woods to help. A shot hit the tree right next to his head. Lee instantly dropped to the ground and sought cover as another shot hit near him. Lying on his back, his body shaking so hard he could barely focus the damn monocular, Lee scanned the area where he thought the shots had come from.

Another shot hit close to him, kicking up wet dirt in his face, stinging his eyes. Whoever was out there knew what he was doing and was loaded for dinosaur. Lee could sense the shooter methodically closing in on him grid by grid.

Lee could tell that the shooter was using a suppressor, because each shot sounded like someone slapping a wall hard with the palm of his hand. *Splat. Splat. Splat.* They could have been balloons exploding at a children's party, not cone-shaped pieces of metal flying at a million Mach seeking to wipe out a certain PI.

Other than the hand holding his monocular, Lee tried not to move, tried not to breathe. For one terrifying instant he saw the red line of the laser dart near his leg like a curious snake, and then it was gone. He didn't have much time. If he just stayed here, he was a dead man.

Laying his gun on his chest, Lee stretched his fingers out and carefully groped for a moment in the dirt until his hand closed around a stone. Using just the flick of his wrist, he tossed the stone about five feet away, waited; and when it hit a tree, a bullet struck the same spot a few seconds later.

With his infrared eye, Lee instantly zeroed in on the heat of this last muzzle flash, as oxygen-deprived, super-hot gas escaping from the rifle barrel collided with the outside air. This simple reaction of physical elements had cost many a soldier his life as it revealed his position. Lee could only hope for the same result now.

Lee used the muzzle flash to fix on the man's thermal image amid the cover of trees. The shooter wasn't that far away, well within range of Lee's SIG. Realizing he would probably get only one attempt, Lee slowly gripped his gun and raised his arm, trying to locate a clear line of fire. Keeping his gaze on his target through the monocular, Lee clicked off the safety, said a silent prayer and fired eight shots from his fifteen-round mag. They were all aimed fairly close together, increasing his chances of a hit. His pistol shots were much louder than the rifle's suppressed ones. On all sides of him wildlife fled the human conflict.

One of Lee's shots miraculously found its mark, mainly because Serov had moved right into the path of the shot as he was attempting to shift to a closer position. The Russian grunted in pain as the bullet entered his left forearm. For a split second it stung, then the dull throbbing came as the bullet ripped through soft tissue and veins, shattered his humerus and finally came to rest in his clavicle. His left arm immediately became heavy and useless. After killing a dozen people in his career, always with a gun, Leonid Serov finally knew what it felt like to be shot. Clutching the rifle in his good hand, the ex-KGB agent took the professional way out. He turned and ran, blood splattering on the ground with each step.

Through the FLIR, Lee watched him run for a few moments. From the way the man was retreating, Lee was pretty certain that at least one of his shots had scored a hit. He decided it would be both stupid and unnecessary to chase an armed and wounded man. Besides, he had something else to do. He grabbed his bag and ran toward the cottage.

SIX

While Lee and Serov were exchanging fire, Faith struggled to get her breath back. The collision with Newman had taken most of her wind and left a throbbing pain in her shoulder. With convulsive strength she was able to roll him off. She felt a warm and sticky substance on her dress. For a terrifying moment she thought she had been shot. Faith couldn't have known it, but the agent's Glock had acted as a mini-shield, deflecting the bullet as it left his body. It was the only reason she was still alive. For a moment she stared at what was left of Newman's face and felt herself growing sick.

Pulling her gaze away, Faith managed to squat low in the driveway and slide her hand into Newman's pocket, then pulled out his car keys. Faith's heart was pumping so frantically that it was difficult for her mind to focus. She could barely hold the damn car keys. Still crouching, she eased open the driver's-side door.

Her body was shaking so hard she didn't even know if she could drive the car once she got in it. Then she was inside, slammed the door shut and locked it. When the engine caught, she put the car in gear, hit the gas and the engine flooded and died on her. Swearing loudly, she turned the key again; the engine caught. She made a more cautious movement on the gas pedal and the engine remained purring.

She was about to hit the gas when her breath

caught in her throat. A man stood at the driver's-side window. He was breathing heavily and looked as scared as she felt. What really held her attention, though, was the gun pointed directly at her. He motioned for her to roll the window down. She contemplated hitting the gas.

"Don't try it," he said, seemingly reading her thoughts. "I'm not the one who shot at you," he said through the glass. He added, "If I were, you'd already be dead."

Finally Faith edged down the window.

"Unlock the door," he said, "and move over."

"Who are you?"

"Let's go, lady. I don't know about you, but I don't want to be here when someone else shows up. They might be a better shot."

Faith unlocked the door and slid over. Lee holstered his gun, threw his bag in the back, got in, slammed the door shut and backed out. Right at that instant the cell phone rang, causing them to both jump. He stopped the car and they looked down at the phone and then at each other.

"It's not my phone," he said.

"It's not mine either," replied Faith.

When the ringing stopped, he asked, "Who's the dead guy?"

"I'm not telling you anything."

The car hit the road and he shifted to drive and punched the gas. "You might regret that decision."

"I don't think so."

He appeared confused by her confident tone.

She slipped her seat belt on as he took a curve a little fast. "If you shot that man back there, then you'll shoot me regardless of what I tell you or not. If you're telling the truth and you didn't shoot him, then I don't think you'll kill me simply because I won't talk."

"You have a very naive perspective of good and bad. Even good guys have to kill on occasion," he said.

"Are you speaking from experience?" Faith edged closer against the door.

He hit the auto door lock. "Now, don't go and throw yourself out the car. I just want to know what's going on. Starting with who's the dead guy."

Faith stared at him, her nerves completely shattered. When she finally spoke, her voice was very weak. "Do you mind if we just go somewhere, anywhere, so I can just sit and think for a bit?" She curled her fingers and added hoarsely, "I've never seen anyone killed before. I've never almost been . . ." Her voice rose as she said this last part and she started to tremble. "Please pull over. For God's sake, pull over! I'm going to be sick."

He skidded the car to a stop on the shoulder and hit the auto unlock button. Faith threw open the door, leaned out and vomited.

He reached across and put his hand on her shoulder, squeezing tightly until she stopped shaking. He spoke in a slow, steady tone. "You're gonna be okay." He paused and waited until she was able to sit back up and close the door before continuing. "First we need to ditch this car. Mine's on the other side of the woods. It'll only take a few minutes to get there. Then I know a place where you can be safe. Okay?"

"Okay," Faith managed to say.

SEVEN

Barely twenty minutes later, a sedan pulled into the cottage's driveway and a man and woman got out. The metal of their weapons reflected off the light thrown from the car's headlights. Approaching the dead man, the woman knelt down and looked at the body. If she hadn't known Ken Newman very well, she might not have recognized him. She had seen human death before, yet she still felt something rising from her stomach to her throat. She quickly stood and turned away. The pair searched the cottage thoroughly and then did a quick sweep of the tree line before coming back to the body.

The large, barrel-chested fellow looked down at Ken Newman's body and uttered a curse. Howard Constantinople was "Connie" to all who knew him. A veteran FBI agent, he had seen just about everything in his career. However, tonight was new territory even for him. Ken Newman was a good friend of his. Connie looked as though he might burst into sobs.

The woman stood next to him. At six feet one, she matched Connie's height. Her brunette hair was cut very short, curving over her ears. Her face was long, narrow and intelligent, and she was dressed in a stylishly fitting pantsuit. Both the years and the stress of her occupation had hammered fine lines around her mouth and around her dark, sad eyes. Her gaze swept the surrounding

59

area with the ease of someone accustomed not only to observing but also to making accurate deductions from what she observed. There was an edge to her features that clearly demonstrated a powerful internal anger.

At age thirty-nine, Brooke Reynolds's attractive features and tall, lean physique would make her appealing to men for as long as she desired the attention. However, immersed as she was in the middle of a bitter divorce that had wreaked havoc on her two young children, she questioned whether she would ever again want the companionship of a man.

Reynolds had been christened, over the objections of her mother, Brooklyn Dodgers Reynolds by her overzealous baseball-fan father. Her old man had never been the same when his beloved ball club went to California. Almost from day one, her mother had insisted she be called Brooke.

"My God," Reynolds finally said, her gaze fixed on her dead colleague.

Connie looked over at her. "So what do we do now?"

She shook off the net of despair that had settled over her. Action was called for, swift but methodical. "We have a crime scene, Connie. We don't have much choice."

"Locals?"

"This is an AFO," she said, referring to an assault on a federal officer, "so the Bureau will be in the lead." She found she couldn't take her gaze from the body. "But we'll still have to work with the county and state people. I have contacts with them, so I'm reasonably sure we can control the information flow."

"With an AFO we have the Bureau's Violent Crime Unit. That breaks our Chinese wall."

Reynolds took a deep breath to quell the tears she felt rising to her eyes. "We'll do the best we can. The first thing we have to do is secure the crime scene, not that it's going to be too difficult out here. I'll call Paul Fisher at HQ and fill him in." Reynolds mentally went up her chain of command at the Bureau's Washington Field Office, or WFO. The ASAC, SAC and ADIC would have to be notified; the ADIC, or assistant director in charge, was the head of the WFO, really only a notch below the director of the FBI himself. Soon, she thought, there would be enough abbreviations here to sink a battleship.

"Dollars to donuts the director himself will be out here too," Connie added.

The walls of Reynolds's stomach started to burn. An agent being killed was a shock. An agent losing his life on her watch was a nightmare she would never wake up from.

An hour later, forces had converged on the scene, fortunately without any media. The state medical examiner verified what everyone who had even remotely seen the devastating wound already knew: namely, that Special Agent Ken Newman had died from a distant gunshot entry wound to the upper neck, exiting from his face. While the local police stood guard, the VCU, or Violent Crime Unit, agents methodically collected evidence.

Reynolds, Connie and their superiors gathered around her car. The ADIC was Fred Massey, the ranking agent at the scene. He was a small, humorless man who kept shaking his head in exaggerated motions. His white shirt collar was loose around a skinny neck, his bald head seeming to glow under the moonlight.

A VCU agent appeared with a videotape from the cottage and a pair of muddy boots. Reynolds and

Connie had noted the boots when they had searched the cottage, but had wisely opted against disturbing any evidence.

"Someone was in the house," he reported. "These boots were on the back stoop. No forced entry. The alarm was deactivated and the equipment closet was open. Looks like we maybe got the person on tape. They tripped the laser."

He handed the tape to Massey, who promptly handed it over to Reynolds. The act was far from subtle. All this was her responsibility. She would either get the credit or take the fall. The VCU agent put the boots in an evidence bag and went back into the house to continue searching.

Massey said, "Give me your observations, Agent Reynolds." His tone was curt, and everyone understood why.

Some of the other agents had openly shed tears and cursed loudly when they saw their colleague's body. As the only woman here, and Newman's squad supervisor to boot, Reynolds didn't feel she had the luxury of dissolving into tears in front of them. The vast majority of FBI agents went through their entire careers without ever even drawing their sidearms except for weapons recertification. Reynolds had sometimes wondered how she would react if such a catastrophe ever hit home. Now she knew: Not very well.

This was probably the most important case Reynolds would ever handle. A while back, she had been assigned to the Bureau's Public Corruption Unit, a component of the illustrious Criminal Investigation Division. After receiving a phone call from Faith Lockhart one night and secretly meeting the woman on several occasions, Reynolds had been named the squad supervisor of a unit detailed to a special. That "special" had the opportunity, if

62

Lockhart was telling the truth, to topple some of the biggest names in the United States government. Most agents would die for such a case during their careers. Well, one had tonight.

Reynolds held up the tape. "I'm hoping this tape will tell us something of what happened here. And what happened to Faith Lockhart."

"You think it's likely she shot Ken? If so, a nationwide APB goes out in about two seconds," Massey said.

Reynolds shook her head. "My gut tells me she had nothing to do with it. But the fact is we don't know enough. We'll check the blood type and other residue. If it only matches Ken's, then we know she wasn't hit as well. We know Ken hadn't fired his gun. And he had on his vest. Something took a chunk out of his Glock, though."

Connie nodded. "The bullet that killed him. Through the back of the neck and out the front. He had his weapon out, probably eye-height, the slug hit and deflected off it." Connie swallowed with difficulty. "The residue on Ken's pistol supports that conclusion."

Reynolds stared sadly at the man and continued the analysis. "So Ken might have been between Lockhart and the shooter?"

Connie slowly shook her head. "Human shield. I thought only the Secret Service did that crap."

Reynolds said, "I spoke with the ME. We won't know anything until the post and we can see the wound track, but I think it was most likely a rifle shot. Not the sort of weapon a woman ordinarily carries in her purse."

"So another person waiting for them?" Massey ventured.

"And why would that person kill and then go inside the house?" Connie asked.

"Maybe it was Newman and Lockhart who went in the house," Massey surmised.

Reynolds knew it had been years since Massey had worked a field investigation, but he was still her ADIC and she couldn't very well ignore him. She didn't have to agree with him, though.

Reynolds shook her head decisively. "If they had gone in the house, Ken wouldn't have been killed in the driveway. They'd still be in the house. We interview Lockhart for at least two hours each time. We got here a half hour after they would have, tops. And those weren't Ken's boots. But they are men's boots, about a size twelve. Odds are a big guy."

"If Newman and Lockhart didn't go in the house, and there are no signs of forced entry, then this third party had the passcode to the alarm." Massey's tone was clearly accusatory.

Reynolds looked miserable, but she had to keep going. "From where Ken fell, it looked like he had just gotten out of the car. Then something must have spooked Ken. He pulls his Glock and then takes the round."

Reynolds led them over to the driveway. "Look at the rut marks here. The ground around here is reasonably dry, but the tires really gouged the dirt. I think somebody was getting out of here in a hurry. Hell, fast enough that he ran out of his boots."

"And Lockhart?"

"Maybe the shooter took her with him," Connie said.

Reynolds thought about this. "It's possible, but I don't see why. They'd want her dead too."

"In the first place, how would a shooter know to come here?" Massey asked, and then answered his own question. "A leak?"

Reynolds had been considering this possibility from the moment she had seen Newman's body.

"With all due respect, sir, I don't see how that could be the case."

Massey coldly ticked off the points on his fingers. "We've got one dead man, a missing woman and a pair of boots. Put it all together and I'm looking at a third party being involved. Tell me how that third party got here without inside information."

Reynolds spoke in a very low tone. "It could be a random thing. Lonely place, possible armed robbery. It happens." She took a quick breath. "But if you're right and there is a leak, it's not complete." They all looked at her curiously. "The shooter obviously didn't know about our last-second change of plan. That Connie and I would be here tonight," Reynolds explained. "Ordinarily, I would've been with Faith, but I was working another case. It didn't pan out and I decided at the last minute to hook up with Connie and come out here."

Connie glanced over at the van. "You're right, no one could have known about that. Ken didn't even know."

"I *tried* to call Ken about twenty minutes before we got here. I didn't want to just suddenly appear. If he heard a car pull up to the safe house without prior warning, he might have gotten spooked, shot first and asked questions later. He must have already been dead when I tried to reach him."

Massey stepped toward her. "Agent Reynolds, I know you've been handling this investigation from the beginning. I know that your use of this safe house and the closed-circuit TV surveillance of Ms. Lockhart were all approved by the appropriate parties. I understand your difficulties in pursuing this case and gaining this witness's trust." Massey paused for a moment, seeming to select his words with great care. Newman's death had stunned them all, although agents were often in harm's way. Still, there would be definite blame assessed in this case, and everyone knew it.

Massey continued, "However, your approach was hardly textbook. And the fact is, an agent is dead."

Reynolds plunged right in. "We had to do this very quietly. We couldn't exactly have surrounded Lockhart with agents. Buchanan would've been gone before we had enough evidence for prosecution." She took a long breath. "Sir, you asked for my observations. Here they are. I don't think Lockhart killed Ken. I think Buchanan is behind it. We have to find her. But we have to do it quietly. If we put out an APB, then Ken Newman has probably died in vain. And if Lockhart is alive, she won't be for long if we go public."

Reynolds looked over at the van just as its doors closed on Newman's body. If she had been escorting Faith Lockhart instead of Ken, the odds were that she would have lost her life tonight. For any FBI agent, death was always a possibility, however remote. If she were killed, would Brooklyn Dodgers Reynolds fade in her children's memory? She was certain her six-year-old daughter would always remember "Mommy." She had doubts about three-year-old David, though. If she were killed, would David, years from now, only refer to Reynolds as his "birth" mother? The thought itself was nearly paralyzing.

One day she had actually taken the ridiculous step of having her palm read. The palm reader had warmly welcomed Reynolds, given her a cup of herbal tea, and chatted with her, asking her questions that tried to sound casual. These queries, Reynolds knew, were designed to gather background information to which the woman could add appropriate mumbo-jumbo as she "saw" into Reynolds's past, as well as her future.

After examining Reynolds's hand, the palm reader had told her that her life line was short. Significantly so, in fact. The worst she'd ever seen. The woman said this as she stared at what appeared to be a scar on Reynolds's palm. Reynolds knew it was the result of falling on a broken Coke bottle in her backyard when she was eight.

The reader had picked up her cup of tea, apparently waiting for Reynolds to plead for more information, presumably at an appropriate premium over the initial fee. Reynolds had informed her that she was strong as a horse with years in between even a simple bout of flu.

Death needn't be by natural causes, the palm reader had replied, her painted eyebrows rising to emphasize the obvious point.

On that, Reynolds had paid her five dollars and walked out the door.

Now she wondered.

Connie scuffed the dirt with his toe. "If Buchanan is behind this, he's probably long gone by now anyway."

"I don't think so," Reynolds replied. "If he runs right after this, then he's as good as admitting guilt. No, he'll play it cool."

"I don't like this," Massey said. "I say we APB Lockhart and bring her in, assuming she's still living."

"Sir," Reynolds said, her voice tight, edgy, "we can't name her as a subject in a homicide when we have reason to believe she wasn't involved in the murder, but may well be a victim herself. That opens the Bureau to a whole civil-action can of worms if she does turn up. You know that."

"Material witness, then. She damn well qualifies for that," said Massey.

Reynolds looked directly at him. "An APB is not

the answer. It's going to do more harm than good. For everybody involved."

"Buchanan has no reason to keep her alive."

"Lockhart is a smart woman," Reynolds said. "I spent time with her, got to know her. She's a survivor. If she can hang on for a few days, we have a shot. Buchanan can't possibly know what she's been telling us. But we do an APB naming her as a material witness, we just sign her death notice."

They were all silent for a bit. "All right, I see your point," Massey finally said. "You really think you can find her on the Q.T.?"

"Yes." What else could she say?

"Is that your gut talking, or your brain?"

"Both."

Massey studied her for a long moment. "For now, Agent Reynolds, you focus on finding Lockhart. The VCU people will investigate Newman's murder."

"I'd have them lockstep the yard looking for the slug that killed Ken. Then I'd search the woods," Reynolds said.

"Why the woods? The boots were on the stoop."

She glanced over at the tree line. "If I were here to ambush someone, that" – she pointed toward the woods – "would be my first tactical choice. Good cover, excellent line of fire and a hidden escape route. Car waiting, gun disposed of, a quick trip to Dulles Airport. In an hour the shooter's in another time zone. The shot that killed Ken entered the back of his neck. He's facing away from the woods. Ken must not have seen his attacker, or else he wouldn't have turned his back." She eyed the thick woods. "It all points there."

Another car pulled up and the director of the FBI himself climbed out. Massey and his aides hurried over, leaving Connie and Reynolds alone.

"So what's our plan of action?" Connie asked.

"Maybe I'll try to match those boots to my Cinderella," Reynolds said as she watched Massey talking to the director. The director was a former field agent who, Reynolds knew, would take this catastrophe extremely personally. Everybody and everything associated with it would be subject to intense scrutiny.

"We'll cover all the usual bases." She tapped her finger against the tape. "But this is really all we have. Whoever's on this tape we hit hard, like there's no tomorrow."

"Depending on how this turns out, we might not have many tomorrows left, Brooke," said Connie.

EIGHT

Lee gripped the steering wheel so hard his fingers were turning white. As the police car, lights blazing, raced past him going in the opposite direction, he let out an enormous breath and then pushed hard on the accelerator. They were in Lee's car after having ditched the other. He had scrubbed down the inside of the dead man's car, but he could have easily missed something. And nowadays equipment existed that could find things completely invisible to the naked eye. Not good.

As she watched the swirling lights disappear into the darkness, Faith wondered if the police were heading to the cottage. Did Ken Newman have a wife and kids? she wondered. There had been no wedding band on his finger. Like many women, Faith had the habit of making that quick observation. Yet he'd seemed like the fatherly type.

As Lee maneuvered the car through the back roads, Faith's hand moved up, down and then drew a vertical line across her chest as she finished crossing herself. The near-automatic movement conveyed a subtle sense of surprise to her. She added a silent prayer for the dead man. She whispered another prayer for any family he might have. "I'm so sorry you're dead," she said out loud, to help assuage her mounting feelings of guilt for simply having survived.

Lee looked over at her. "Friend of yours?"

She shook her head. "He was killed because of me. Isn't that enough?"

Faith was surprised at how easily the words of prayer and remorse had come back to her. Because of her nomadic father, her attendance at mass over the years had been sporadic. But her mother had insisted on Catholic schools wherever the family happened to venture, and her father had followed this rule after his wife had died. Catholic school must have ingrained something in her other than the constant bite of the ruler on her knuckles from Sister Something-or-other. The summer before her senior year, she had become an orphan, her travels with her father abruptly cut short by a heart attack. She was sent to live with a relative who did not want her and who took pains to show no attention to her. Faith had rebelled however she could. She smoked, she drank, she ceased to become virgin Faith long before it was fashionable to do so. At school the daily tugging down of her skirt to below her knees by the nuns only made her want to pull the damn thing up to her crotch. All in all, it was a truly forgettable year in her life, followed by several more as she struggled through college, tried to gain some direction in her life. Then for the past fifteen years she had thought her rudder was flawless, the grand movements of her life fluid. Now she was floundering, speeding toward the rocks.

Faith looked at Lee. "We need to call the police, tell somebody that he's back there."

Lee shook his head. "That opens a whole other can of worms. That is definitely not a good idea."

"We can't just leave him back there. It's not right."

"Do you suggest we go to the local precinct and try to explain this thing? They'll put us in strait-jackets."

71

"Dammit! If you won't do it, I will. I am *not* leaving him back there for the squirrels."

"All right, all right. Calm down." He sighed. "I guess we could place an anonymous call in a little while, get the cops to check it out."

"Fine," said Faith.

A few minutes later, Lee noticed that Faith was fidgeting.

"I have another request," she said.

The woman's demanding style was really starting to annoy him. Lee tried not to think about the hurt in his elbow, the irritating specks of cold dirt in his eyes, the unknown dangers that lay ahead.

"Like what?" he said wearily.

"There's a gas station near her. I'd like to wash up." She added quietly, "If that's okay."

Lee looked down at the stains on her clothes and his expression softened. "No problem," he said.

"It's down this road—"

"I know where it is," Lee said. "I like to get the lay of the land where I'm working."

Faith simply stared at him.

In the bathroom Faith tried not to focus on what she was doing as she painstakingly cleaned the blood off her clothing. Still, every couple of minutes she felt like ripping off all her clothes and scrubbing herself down using the soap from the dispenser and the stack of paper towels on the dirty sink.

When she climbed back in the car, her companion's look said what his mouth didn't.

"I'll make it, for now," she said.

"By the way, my name's Lee. Lee Adams."

Faith said nothing. He started the car and they left the gas station.

"You don't have to tell me your name," he said. "I

was hired to follow you, Ms. Lockhart."

She eyed him suspiciously. "Who hired you to do that?"

"Don't know."

"How could you possibly not know who hired you?"

"I admit it's a little unusual, but it happens, on occasion. Some people are embarrassed about hiring a private detective."

"So that's what you are, a private eye?" Her tone was one of contempt.

"It can be a very legit way of earning a buck. And I'm as legit as they come."

"And how did this person come to hire you?"

"Other than the fact that I've got a killer Yellow Pages ad, I don't have a clue."

"Do you have any idea what you're mixed up in, Mr. Adams?"

"Let's just say I have a better idea now than I did a little bit ago. Getting shot at is the one thing that has always captured my undivided attention."

"And who shot at you?"

"The same guy who nailed your friend. I think I winged him, but he got away."

Faith rubbed her temples and looked out into the darkness. His next words startled her.

"What are you, Witness Protection?" Lee waited. When she didn't answer, he continued. "I did a ten-second down-and-dirty on your friend while you were busy choking out the car. He had a Glock nine-millimeter and a Kevlar vest, for all the good it did him. The shield on his belt said FBI. I didn't have time to check for ID. So what was his name?"

"Does it matter?"

"It might."

"Why Witness Protection?" she asked.

"The cottage. Special locks, security system. It's a

73

safe house, of sorts. Nobody's living there, that's for sure."

"So you've been inside."

He nodded. "At first I thought you were having an affair. A couple minutes inside told me it wasn't a love nest. Strange house, though. Hidden cameras, tape-recording system. Did you know you were on stage, by the way?"

The astonished look on her face answered his question.

"If you didn't know who hired you, how were you engaged to follow me?"

"Easy enough. Phone message said a packet of information on you and an advance on my fee would be delivered to my office. They were. A file on you, and a big chunk of cash. It said to follow your movements, and I did."

"I was told I wasn't being followed."

"I've gotten pretty good at it."

"Apparently."

"Once I knew where you were going, I just got here ahead of you. Pretty simple."

"Was the voice a man's or woman's?"

"Couldn't tell; it was scrambled."

"Didn't that make you suspicious?"

"Everything makes me suspicious. One thing's for sure, whoever's after you, they ain't playing around. The ammo the guy was using back there could have wasted an elephant. I got to see it up close and personal."

He fell silent and Faith could not bring herself to say anything else. She had several credit cards in her purse, all with virtually limitless spending power. And they were all useless to her, because as soon as one went through the swipe machine, they would know where she was. She put her hand in her purse and touched the Tiffany pewter ring holding the keys to her beautiful home and her luxury car. Useless as well. In her wallet was the grand sum of fifty-five dollars and a few pennies. She had been stripped bare except for this cash and the clothes on her back. Her impoverished childhood had come roaring back in all its tarnished, hopeless memory.

She did have a large sum of cash, but it was in a safe-deposit box at her bank in D.C. The bank would not be open until tomorrow morning. And there were two other items she kept in that box that were even more critical to her: a driver's license and another credit card. They were both under a fake name. They had been relatively easy to set up, but she had hoped she would never have to use them. So much so that she had kept them in her bank instead of a more accessible place. Now she shook her head at such stupidity.

With those two cards she could go just about anywhere. If everything collapsed on top of her, she had often reminded herself, this would be her way out. *Well*, she thought now, *the roof's gone, the walls are creaking, the killer tornado's at the window and the fat lady is in the limo on the way back to the hotel. It's time to pull the tent and call it a life.*

She looked at Lee. What would she do with him? Faith knew that her most pressing challenge was surviving the rest of the night. Maybe he could help her do that. He seemed to know what he was doing, and he had a gun. If she could just get in and out of her bank without too much trouble, she would be okay. There were about seven hours between now and the bank's opening. They might as well have been seven years.

NINE

Thornhill sat in the small study of his lovely ivy-draped old home in a much-sought-after neighborhood in McLean, Virginia. His wife's family had money, and he enjoyed the luxuries that money could buy, as well as the freedom it gave him to be a public servant his entire career. Right now, though, he was not feeling much comfort.

The message he had just received was unbelievable to him, and yet all the plans had the potential for failure. He looked at the man sitting across from him. This person was also a veteran at the Agency, and a member of Thornhill's secret group. Philip Winslow shared Thornhill's ideals and concerns. They had spent many a night in Thornhill's study, both reminiscing about past glories and devising plans that would ensure there would be many future triumphs as well. They were both Yale graduates, two of the best and brightest. They had come along at a time when it was considered honorable to serve one's country. And the CIA had gotten its share of the Ivy League's best back then. They had also come from a generation in which a man did whatever it took to protect his country's interests. A man with vision, Thornhill believed with all his heart, had to be willing to take risks to achieve that vision.

"The FBI agent was killed," Thornhill said to his friend and colleague.

"And Lockhart?" Winslow asked.

Thornhill gave one brief shake of his head. "She's disappeared."

Winslow summed it up. "So we take out one of the Bureau's finest and let the real target get away." He clinked the ice in his drink. "Not good, Bob. The others won't be happy to hear that."

"Just to get all the good news out, our man was also shot in the process."

"By the agent?"

Thornhill shook his head. "No. There was someone else there tonight. Unknown as yet. Serov has been debriefed. He gave a description of the man who was at the cottage. We're doing computer generations of him right now. We should know his identity shortly."

"Could he tell us anything else?"

"Not at present. Mr. Serov is being detained, for now, in safe quarters."

"You know the Bureau will go after this tooth and nail, Bob."

"More precisely," Thornhill said, "they will do everything in their power to find Faith Lockhart."

"Who do they suspect?"

"Buchanan, of course. It's logical," Thornhill replied.

"So what do we do with Buchanan?"

"For now, nothing. We'll keep him informed. Of at least our version of the truth, that is. We'll keep him busy at the same time we keep close tabs on the FBI. He has a trip out of town this morning, so we're covered there. However, if the FBI's investigation gets too close to Buchanan, we'll provide him with an early death and provide our professional brethren with all the sordid facts of how Buchanan tried to have Lockhart murdered."

"And Lockhart?" Winslow asked.

"Oh, the FBI will find her. They're quite good at that sort of thing, in their limited way."

"I don't see how that helps us. She talks, and Buchanan goes down and takes us with him."

"I hardly think that," Thornhill said. "When the FBI finds her, we will be there as well, if we don't find her first. And this time we won't miss her. With Lockhart gone, Buchanan will soon follow. Then we can move forward with our original plan."

"God, if it could only work."

"Oh, it will work," said Thornhill with his usual optimism. To last as long as he had in this business, one had to have a positive attitude.

TEN

Lee pulled the car into the alleyway and stopped. His gaze swept over the darkened landscape. They had driven around for over two hours until he felt reasonably sure they had not been followed, and then he had made the phone call to the police from a pay phone. Although they seemed relatively safe now, Lee still kept one hand resting on the grip of his pistol, ready to pull it in an instant, to terminate their enemies with the salvos from his deadly SIG. That was a joke.

These days you could kill from a sky away, with a bomb smarter than a man, taking the most important thing men had without so much as a "Hello, you're dead." Lee wondered if, during the millisecond it took to cremate the poor bastards, the brain moved fast enough to spark the thought that the Hand of God had struck them down instead of something manufactured by man, the idiot. For a crazy moment, Lee scanned the sky looking for a guided missile. And depending on who was involved in all this, maybe it wasn't so crazy after all.

"What did you tell the police?" Faith asked.

"Short and sweet. The location of the place and what happened."

"And?"

"And the dispatcher was skeptical but did his best to keep me on the line."

Faith looked around the alley. "Is *this* the safe

79

place you mentioned?" She took in the darkness, the hidden crevices, the garbage can and the distant tap of footsteps on pavement.

"No, we leave the car here and walk to the safe place. Which, by the way, is my apartment."

"Where are we?"

"North Arlington. It's being yuppified, but it can still be dangerous, especially this time of night."

She stayed right next to him as they made their way down the alley and out on to the next street, which was an avenue of old but nicely kept-up attached rowhouses.

"Which one's yours?"

"The big one at the end there. Owner's retired, lives in Florida. He's got a couple of other properties. I troubleshoot for him, and he gives me a break on the rent."

Faith started to walk out of the alley, but Lee stopped her. "Give me a sec, I want to check things first."

She clutched his jacket. "You are not leaving me here alone."

"I'm just making sure there's nobody there waiting to throw us a surprise party. Anything looks weird, give a shout and I'm back in two shakes."

He disappeared and Faith edged into the crevice of the alley. Her heart was beating so loud, she half expected a window to open and a shoe to come sailing out at her. When she thought she could not take being alone anymore, Lee reappeared.

"Okay, it looks good. Let's go."

The outer door to the building was locked, but Lee opened it with his key. Faith noted the video camera bolted to the wall above her head.

Lee looked at her. "My idea. I like to know who's coming to see me."

They went up four flights of stairs to the top floor

and down the hallway to the last door on the right. Faith eyed the three locks on the door. Lee opened each of them with the same special key.

When the door opened, she heard a beeping sound. They went inside the apartment. On the wall was an alarm panel. Screwed into the wall above it was a piece of shiny copper on a hinge. Lee flipped the copper shield down so that it covered the alarm panel. He reached his hand underneath the copper plate and hit some buttons on the panel and the beeping sound stopped.

He looked over at Faith, who was watching him closely.

"Van Eck radiation. You probably wouldn't understand."

She hiked her eyebrows. "You're probably right."

Next to the alarm panel was a small video screen built into the wall. On the screen Faith could see the front stoop of the building. It was obviously the video link to the surveillance camera outside.

Lee locked the front door and then put his hand on it. "It's steel, set in a special metal frame I built myself. It doesn't matter how strong the lock is. What usually gives is the frame. A lousy two-by-four if you're lucky. A crook's Christmas present handed out by the building industry. I've also got pick-proof window locks, outside motion detectors, piggyback cellular on the alarm system's phone link. We'll be okay."

"I take it you're somewhat security-minded?" she said.

"No, I'm paranoid."

Faith heard something approaching from down the hall. She flinched, but relaxed when she saw Lee smile and move toward the sound. A second later an old German shepherd wandered around the corner. Lee squatted and played with the big dog, who

81

rolled over on his back. Lee accommodated the animal with a belly rub.

"Hey, Max, how you doing, boy?" Lee patted Max's head and the dog affectionately licked his owner's hand.

"Now, this thing is the best security device ever invented. Don't have to worry about electrical outages, batteries going dead or somebody turning his loyalties."

"So your plan is that we stay here?"

Lee looked up at her. "You want something to eat or drink? We might as well work on this over a full stomach."

"Hot tea would be nice. I couldn't really look at food right now."

A few minutes later they were sitting at the kitchen table. Faith sipped on herbal tea while Lee worked on a cup of coffee. Max dozed under the table.

"We have a problem," Lee began. "When I went in the cottage I tripped something. So I'm on the videotape."

Faith looked stricken. "My God, they could be on their way here right now."

"Maybe that's a good thing." Lee looked at her sharply.

"And why is that?"

"I'm not into helping criminals."

"So you think I'm a criminal?"

"Are you?"

Faith fingered her teacup. "I was working with the FBI, not against them."

"Okay, what were they doing with you?"

"I can't answer that."

"Then I can't help you. Come on, I'll give you a ride to your place." Lee started to rise from his chair.

She gripped his arm. "Wait, please wait." The thought of being left alone now was paralyzing.

He sat back down and waited expectantly.

"How much do I have to tell you before you'll help me?"

"Depends on what sort of help you want. I'm not doing anything against the law."

"I wouldn't ask you to."

"Then you've got no problem, other than somebody wanting to kill you."

Faith took a nervous sip of her tea while Lee watched her.

"If they know who you are from the video, should we be just sitting here?" she asked.

"I messed with the tape. Ran my magnet over it."

Faith looked at him, a glint of hope in her eyes. "You think you were able to erase it?"

"I can't tell for sure. I'm not an expert in that stuff."

"But at the very least it might take some time for them to reconstruct it?"

"That's what I'm hoping. But we're not exactly dealing with the Campfire Girls here. The recording equipment also had a security system built in. Chances are if the police try to force the tape out, it might self-destruct. Personally, I'd give the forty-seven bucks I have in the bank if that did happen. I'm a man who likes his privacy. But you still need to fill me in."

Faith didn't say anything. She just stared at him, like he had just made an unwanted pass at her.

Lee cocked his head at her. "I tell you what. I'm the detective, okay? I'll make some deductions and you tell me if I'm right or not, how's that?" When Faith still said nothing, he continued. "The cameras I saw were only in the living room. And the table, chairs, coffee and stuff were set up in the living room only. Now, I tripped the laser or whatever it was going in. That apparently set off the cameras."

"I guess that would make sense," Faith said.

"No, it doesn't. I had the access code to the alarm system," said Lee.

"So?"

"So I put in the code and disarmed the security system. So why have the trip device still operating? The way it was set up, even when the guy you were with disarmed the security system, he would still have engaged the cameras. Why would he want to record himself?"

Faith looked deeply confused. "I don't know."

"Hello, so they'd have you on film without you knowing it. Now the out-of-the-way place with the CIA-level security in place, the Feds, the cameras and taping equipment, all point to one thing." Lee paused as he thought about exactly how he was going to phrase this. "They brought you there to interrogate you. But maybe they're not sure of your level of cooperation, or they think somebody might try to pop you, so they film the interrogations just in case you turn up missing later on."

Faith looked at him with a resigned smile. "Terribly prescient of them, don't you think? The 'turning up missing' thing."

Lee stood and stared out the window as he thought things through. Something very important had just occurred to him. Something that he should have thought about a lot sooner. And even though he didn't know the woman, he was feeling kind of crappy about what he had to say. "I've got some bad news for you."

Faith looked startled. "What do you mean?"

"You're under interrogation by the FBI. Presumably you're also in their protective custody. One of their guys gets popped protecting you and I probably wounded the guy who killed him. The Feds have my face on their tape." He paused for a moment. "I've got to turn you in."

Faith jumped up. "You can't do that! You can't! You said you'd help me."

"If I don't, then I'm looking at some serious time in a place where guys get way too friendly with other guys. At the very least I lose my PI license. I'm sure if I knew you better I'd feel even worse about doing this, but at the end of the day I'm not sure even my grandma would be worth that much trouble." He slipped on his jacket. "Who's your principal handler?"

"I don't know his name," Faith said coldly.

"Do you have a phone number?"

"It wouldn't do any good. I doubt he'd be able to take the call now."

Lee eyed her dubiously. "Are you telling me the dead guy back there is your only contact?"

"That's it." Faith told this lie with a completely straight face.

"The guy was your handler and he never bothered to tell you his name? That's not exactly textbook FBI."

"Sorry, that's all I know."

"Is that right? Well, let me tell you what I know. I saw you at that cottage three other times with a woman. A tall brunette. What, did you sit around calling her Agent X?" He leaned right into her face. "Bullshit Rule Number One: Make damn sure the person you're lying to can't prove same." He hooked an arm around hers. "Let's go."

"You know, Mr. Adams, *you* have a problem you may not have thought about."

"Is that right? Care to share it?"

"What exactly are you going to tell the FBI when you bring me in?"

"I don't know, how about the truth?"

"Okay. Let's look at the truth. You were following

85

me because someone you don't know and can't identify instructed you to. Which means we only have your word for that. You were able to follow me even though the FBI assured me no one could. You were in that house tonight. Your face is on the tape. An FBI agent is dead. You fired your gun. You say you shot the other man, but you have no way to prove another man was even there. So the proven facts are we have you at the house and me at the house. You fired your gun and an FBI agent is dead."

"The ammo that killed that guy is not something my pistol happens to chamber," he said angrily, releasing her arm.

"So you threw the other gun away."

"Why would I snatch you from the place, then? If I was the shooter, why wouldn't I have killed you back there?"

"I'm not saying what *I* think, Mr. Adams. I'm just suggesting to you that the FBI might suspect you. I suppose if there's nothing in your past to make them suspicious, the FBI might believe you." She added offhandedly. "They'll probably just investigate you for a year and then drop it if nothing turns up."

Lee scowled at her. His recent past was squeaky clean. Going back a little further, the waters got a little murkier. When he was first starting out as a PI, he had done some things he would never even consider doing now. Not illegal, but still hard to explain to straightlaced federal agents.

And then there was the restraining order his ex had gotten right before Lucky Eddie had struck patent gold. Claimed Lee was stalking her, was perhaps violent. Lee would have become violent if he had gotten hold of the little shit. Every time Lee thought about the bruises on his daughter's arms and cheek when he had made an unexpected visit to their rat-trap apartment he almost had a stroke. Trish claimed Renee had fallen down the stairs. Stood there and lied to his face, when Lee could see the imprint of what he knew was a knuckle against his daughter's soft skin. He had taken a crowbar to Eddie's car and would've taken one to Eddie if the guy hadn't locked himself in the bathroom and called the cops.

So did he really want the FBI snooping around his life for the next twelve months? On the other hand, if he let the woman walk away and the Feds tracked him down, then where would he be? Everywhere he turned, he ran into a nest of snakes.

Faith spoke in a pleasant tone. "Do you want to drop me at the Washington Field Office? They're at Fourth and F Streets."

"Okay, okay, you've made your point," Lee said hotly. "But I didn't ask for this crap to be dropped in my lap."

"And I didn't ask for you to become involved in this either. But . . ."

"But what?"

"But if you weren't there tonight, I wouldn't be alive right now. I'm sorry I haven't thanked you before. I'm thanking you now."

Despite his suspicions, Lee felt his anger slowly receding. Either the woman was sincere or she was one of the slickest operators he'd come across. Or maybe it was a little slice of both. This was Washington, after all.

"Always glad to help a lady," he said dryly. "Okay, supposing I decide not to turn you in. What do you have in mind to pass the night away?"

"I need to get away from here. I need some time to think things through."

"The FBI is not going to just let you walk away. I'm assuming you've cut some sort of deal."

87

"Not yet. And even if I had, don't you think I have good grounds to declare them in default?"

"What about the people who tried to kill you?"

"Once I have some space, I can decide what to do. I'll probably end up just going back to the FBI. But I don't want to die. I don't want anyone else associated with me to die." She stared very deliberately at him.

"I appreciate your concern, but I can take care of myself. So where do you plan to run, and how do you plan to get there?"

Faith started to say something and then stopped. She looked down, suddenly wary.

"If you don't trust me, Faith, none of this works," Lee prodded gently. "If I let you walk, that means I'm going to bat for you big-time. But I haven't made that decision yet. A lot depends on what you're thinking. If the Feds need you to bring down some powerful people – and what I've seen so far clearly rules out this being shoplifting material – then I'm going to have to side with the Feds."

"What if I agreed to come back as long as they could give guarantees as to my safety?"

"I guess that sounds reasonable. But what guarantee is there that you'll come back at all?"

"What if you come with me?" she said quickly.

Lee stiffened so much that he accidentally kicked Max, who came out from under the table and looked at him pitifully.

Faith rushed on. "You said yourself that it's only a matter of time before they identify you on the tape. The person you shot, what if he identifies you to whoever hired him? It's obvious that you're in danger too."

"I'm not sure—"

"Lee," Faith said excitedly, "did it ever occur to you that the person who hired you to follow me had

88

you trailed as well? You could very well have been used to set up the shooting."

"Well, if they could follow me, they could follow you," he countered.

"But what if they wanted to frame you for all this somehow?"

Lee blew the air from his cheeks as the hopelessness of his situation set in. Sonofabitch, what a night. How the hell hadn't he seen it coming? Anonymous client. Bag full of cash. Mystery target. Lonely cottage. Had he been in a frigging coma or what? "I'm listening."

"I have a safe-deposit box in a bank in D.C. In that box I have cash, and some pieces of plastic with another name on them that'll let us go about as far as we need to. The only problem is they might be watching my bank. I need your help."

"*I* can't access your safe-deposit box."

"But you can help me scope the place out, see if anyone's watching. You're obviously better at that than I am. I go in, clean out the box and get out as fast as possible while you cover me. Anything looks suspicious, we run like hell."

"It sounds like we're planning to rob the place," he said angrily.

"I swear to God all the things in that box are mine."

Lee put a hand through his hair. "Okay, maybe that works. Then what?"

"Then we head south."

"South where?"

"The Carolina shore. Outer Banks. I have a place there."

"Are you listed as the owner? They can check that."

"I bought it in the name of a corporation and signed the papers under my other name, as an officer. But what about you? You can't travel under your own name."

"Don't worry about me. I've been more people in my life than Shirley MacLaine, and I've got the papers to prove it."

"Then we're all set."

Lee looked down at Max, who had settled his big head in his lap. Lee gently stroked the dog's nose.

"How long?"

Faith shook her head. "I don't know. A week, maybe."

Lee sighed. "I guess I can have the lady downstairs take care of Max."

"Then you'll do it?"

"Just so long as you understand that while I don't mind helping somebody who needs it, I'm not playing the world's greatest sucker either."

"You don't strike me as someone who would ever play that role."

"If you really want a laugh, tell my ex-wife that."

ELEVEN

Old Town Alexandria was located in northern Virginia next to the Potomac River, about a fifteen-minute drive south of Washington, D.C. The waters had been the primary reason the city had been established, and it had flourished as a seaport for a very long time. It was still an affluent and desirable place to live, although the river no longer played a prominent role in the town's economic future.

It was a setting of both old wealth and freshly monied families nestled within the graceful brick, stone and wood-frame structures of late eighteenth and early nineteenth century architecture. A few of the streets were covered in the very same rolling cobblestone that had supported the treads of Washington and Jefferson. And of the young Robert E. Lee at his two boyhood homes, which were set across from each other on Oronoco Street, itself named after a particular brand of long-ago Virginia-grown tobacco. Many of the town's sidewalks were brick and had buckled up around the numerous trees that had shaded the homes, streets and inhabitants for so long. A number of the wrought-iron fences that encircled the courtyards and gardens of the homes were painted the color of gold on their European-inspired spikes and finials.

At this early hour the streets of Old Town were quiet except for the drizzle of rain and the rush of wind among the branches of the aged, knobby trees whose shallow roots clutched at the hard Virginia clay. The street names reflected the colonial origins of the place. Driving through town, one would pass King, Queen, Duke and Prince Streets. Off-road parking was scarce here, so the narrow avenues were lined with virtually every make and model of vehicle. Placed against the two-hundred-year-old homes, the chrome, rubber and metal hulls seemed oddly out of place, as though a time warp had whisked the automobile back to the era of horse and buggy.

The narrow four-story brick townhouse that was wedged among a line of others along Duke Street was by no means the grandest in the area. There was a lone, tilting maple in the small front yard, its split trunk covered with leafy suckers. The wrought-iron fencing was in good but not superb condition. The home had a garden and courtyard out back, yet the plantings, dripping fountain and brickwork there were unremarkable when compared with others located but a few steps away.

Inside the home, the furnishings were far more elegant than the outside of the place would have led the observer to expect. There was a simple reason for this: The outside of the home was something Danny Buchanan could not hide from curious eyes.

The first traces of the pink dawn were just starting to nudge at the edges of the horizon as Buchanan sat, fully dressed, in the small oval-shaped library off the dining room. A car was waiting to take him to Reagan National Airport.

The senator he was meeting with was on the Appropriations Committee, arguably the Senate's most important committee, since it (and its subcommittees) controlled the government's purse strings. More importantly for Buchanan's purposes, the man also chaired the Subcommittee on Foreign

Operations, which determined where most foreign aid dollars went. The tall, distinguished senator with the smooth manners and confident tones was a longtime associate of Buchanan's. The man had always enjoyed the power that came with his position and he had consistently lived beyond his means. The retirement package he had waiting from Buchanan would be almost impossible for a human being to exhaust.

Buchanan's bribery scheme had started out cautiously at first. He had analyzed all the players in Washington who even remotely might further his goals, and whether they could be bribed. Many members of Congress were wealthy, but many others were not. It was often both a financial and familial nightmare for people to serve in Congress. Members had to maintain two residences, and the Washington metro area was not cheap. And their families often did not come with them. Buchanan approached the ones he figured he could corrupt and began a long process of feeling them out on possible involvement. The carrots he dangled were small at first but quickly grew in size if the targets showed any enthusiasm. Buchanan had selected well, because he had never had a target not agree to exchange votes and influence for rewards down the road. Perhaps they felt that the difference between what he proposed and what occurred in Washington every day was marginal at best. He didn't know if they cared that the goal was a worthy one. However, they hadn't gone out of their way to increase foreign aid to any of Buchanan's clients on their own.

And they had all seen colleagues leave office and grab the gold of lobbydom. But who wanted to work that hard then? Buchanan's experience was that ex-members made terrible lobbyists anyway. Going back hat in hand to lobby former colleagues over whom you no longer had any leverage was not appealing to these overly proud folk. Much smarter to use them when they were the most powerful they would ever be. Work them hard first. And then pay them grandly later. What could be better?

Buchanan wondered if he could really hold it together during the meeting with a man he had already betrayed. But then, betrayal was doled out in large doses in this town. Everyone was constantly scrambling for a chair before the music stopped. The senator would be understandably upset. Well, he would have to stand in line with the rest.

Buchanan suddenly felt tired. He didn't want to get in the car or climb on another plane, but he had no say in the matter. *Still a member of the Philadelphia servant class?*

The lobbyist focused his attention on the man who was standing before him.

"He sends his compliments," the burly man said. To the outside world he was Buchanan's driver. In reality he was one of Thornhill's men keeping close tabs on their most important charge.

"And please send Mr. Thornhill my sincerest wishes that God should decree he not grow one day older," said Buchanan.

"There have been important developments of which he would like you to be aware," the man said impassively.

"Such as?"

"Lockhart is working with the FBI to bring you down."

For a brief, dizzying moment Buchanan thought he would vomit all over himself. "What in the hell are you talking about?"

"This information was just discovered by our operative inside the Bureau."

"You mean they entrapped her? Made her work

94

for them?" *Just like you did to me.*

"She voluntarily went to them."

Buchanan slowly regained his composure. "Tell me everything," he said.

The man responded with a series of truths, half-truths and outright lies. He told them all with equal, practiced sincerity.

"Where is Faith now?"

"She's gone underground. The FBI is looking for her."

"How much has she told them? Should I be making plans to leave the country?"

"No. It's very early in the game. What she's told them thus far would not warrant prosecution of any kind. She's told them more of the process of how it was done, but not who was involved. However, that's not to say they can't follow up what she's told them. But they have to be careful. The targets aren't exactly flipping burgers at McDonald's."

"And the vaunted Mr. Thornhill doesn't know where Faith is? I hope his omniscience isn't failing him now."

"I have no information about that," said the man.

"A poor state of affairs for an intelligence-gathering agency," Buchanan said, even managing a smile. A log in the fireplace let out a loud pop, and a fat wad of sap shot out and hit the screen. Buchanan watched it dripping down the mesh face, its escape halted, its existence over. Why did he suddenly feel the remainder of his life had just been symbolically played out?

"Perhaps I should try to find her."

"It's really not your concern."

Buchanan stared at him. Had the idiot really said that? "*You* won't be the one going to prison."

"It'll work out. You just continue right on."

"I want to be kept informed. Clear?" Buchanan

turned to the window. In its reflection he studied the man's reaction to his sharply spoken words. But what were they really worth? Buchanan had clearly lost this round; he had no way of winning it, actually.

The street was dark, no visible movement, just the familiar sounds of squirrels corkscrewing up the trees and then leaping from branch to branch in their never-ending game of survival. Buchanan was engaged in a similar contest, but even more dangerous than hopping across the slippery bark of thirty-foot-tall trees. The wind had picked up some; the beginnings of a low howling sound could be heard in the chimney. A bit of smoke from the fire drifted into the room with the backdraft of air.

The man looked at his watch. "We need to leave in fifteen minutes to make your flight." He picked up Buchanan's briefcase, turned and left.

Robert Thornhill had always been careful in how he contacted Buchanan. No phone calls to the house or office. Face-to-face meetings only under conditions such as these where it would not raise suspicions, where surveillance by others could not be maintained. The first meeting between the two had been one of the few times in Buchanan's life that he had felt inadequate in the face of an opponent. Thornhill had calmly presented stark evidence of Buchanan's illegal dealings with members of Congress, high-ranking bureaucrats, even reaching inside the White House. Tapes of them going over voting schemes, strategies to defeat legislation, frank discussions of what their fake duties would be once they left office, how the payoffs would occur. The CIA man had uncovered Buchanan's web of slush funds and corporations designed to funnel money to his public officials.

"You now work for me," Thornhill had said

bluntly. "And you will go right on doing what you are doing until my net is as strong as steel. And then you will stand clear, and I will take over."

Buchanan had refused. "I'll go to prison," he had said. "I'll take that over indentured servitude."

Thornhill, Buchanan recalled, had looked slightly impatient. "I'm sorry if I wasn't clear. Prison isn't an option. You either work for me or you cease to live."

Buchanan had paled in the face of this threat, but still held firm. "A public servant embroiled in murder?"

"I'm a special type of public servant. I work in extremes. It tends to justify what I do."

"My answer's the same."

"Do you also speak for Faith Lockhart? Or should I consult her personally on the matter?"

That remark had struck Buchanan like a bullet to the brain. It was quite clear to Buchanan that Robert Thornhill was no bully. There was not a hint of bluster in the man. If he said something as innocuous as, "I'm sorry it's come to this," you would probably be dead the next day. Thornhill was a careful, deliberate, focused person, Buchanan had thought at the time. Not unlike himself. Buchanan had gone along. To save Faith.

Now Buchanan understood the relevance of Thornhill's safeguards. The FBI was watching him. Well, they had their work cut out for them, for Buchanan doubted they were in Thornhill's league when it came to clandestine operations. But everyone had an Achilles' heel. Thornhill had easily found his in Faith Lockhart. Buchanan had long wondered what Thornhill's weakness was.

Buchanan slumped in a chair and studied the painting hanging on the library wall. It was a portrait of a mother and child. It had hung in a private museum for almost eighty years. It was by one of the acknowledged – but lesser known – masters of the Renaissance period. The mother was clearly the protector, the infant boy unable to defend himself. The wondrous colors, the exquisitely painted profiles, the subtle brilliance of the hand that had invented this image so clearly evident in every brushstroke, never failed to enrapture anyone who saw it. The gentle curl of finger, the luminosity of the eyes, each detail still so vibrant almost four hundred years after the paint had hardened.

It was perfect love on both sides, uncomplicated by silent, corrosive agendas. As one level it was the simple thread of biological function. At another it was a phenomenon enhanced by the touch of God. This painting was his most prized possession. Unfortunately, it would soon have to be sold, and perhaps his home as well. He was running out of money to fund the "retirements" of his people. Indeed, he felt guilty for still owning the painting. The funds it could generate, the help it could bring to so many. And yet just to sit and gaze at it was so soothing, so uplifting. It was the height of selfishness, and brought him more pleasure than just about anything else.

But maybe it was all moot at this point. The end was coming for Buchanan. He knew that Thornhill would never let him walk away from all of this. And he had no illusions that he would let Buchanan's people enjoy any retirement whatsoever. They were his slaves-in-waiting. The CIA man, despite his refinement and pedigree, was a spy. What were spies but living lies? However, Buchanan would honor his agreement with his politicians. What he had promised them in return for helping him would be there, whether they would be able to enjoy it or not.

As the light of the fire played over the painting,

the woman's face, it seemed to Buchanan, took on the characteristics of Faith Lockhart – not the first time he had observed this. His gaze traced the set of full lips that could turn petulant or sensual without warning. As his eye ran down the long, gracefully formed face, the hair golden, not auburn, in just the right splash of angled light, he always thought of Faith. She had a pair of eyes that held you; the left pupil slightly off center added depth to make Faith's countenance truly remarkable. And it was as though this flaw of nature had empowered her to see right through anyone.

He remembered every detail of their very first meeting. Fresh out of college, she had bounded into his life with the enthusiasm of a newly minted missionary, ready to take on the world. She was raw, immature at certain levels, largely ignorant of the ways of Washington, astonishingly naive in various respects. And yet she could also command a room like a movie star. She could be funny and then turn serious on a dime. She could stroke egos with the best of them and still get her message across, without overtly pushing the issue. After five minutes talking to her, Buchanan knew she had what it took to flourish in his world. After her first month on the job, his intuition proved correct. She did her homework, worked tirelessly, learned the issues, dissected the players down to the level needed to do the job and then went deeper. She understood what everyone needed in order to walk away a winner. Burning bridges in this town meant you didn't survive. Sooner or later, you needed help from everyone, and memories were exceptionally long in the capital city. As tenacious as a wolverine, she had endured defeat after defeat on a number of fronts, but continued to pound away until she was victorious. He had never met anyone like her before or since. They had been through more together in fifteen years than couples married a lifetime. She was really all the family he had. The precocious daughter he was destined never to have. And now? How did he protect his little girl?

As the rain drifted across the roof and the wind strummed its peculiar sounds down the aged firebrick of his Old Town chimney, Buchanan forgot about his car and his flight and the dilemmas confronting him. The man continued to stare at the painting in the soft glow of the quietly crackling fire. And it was clearly not the work of the grand master that fascinated him so.

Faith had not betrayed him. Nothing Thornhill could ever tell him would change that belief. But now she was in Thornhill's way, which meant she was in mortal danger. He stared at the painting. "Run, Faith, run just as fast as you can," he said under his breath, with all the anguish of a desperate father seeing violent death racing after his child. In the face of the protector mother in the painting, Buchanan felt even more powerless.

TWELVE

B rooke Reynolds sat in rented office space about ten blocks from the Washington Field Office. The Bureau sometimes took off-site space for agents engaged in sensitive investigations, where something overheard even in the cafeteria or hallway could have disastrous effects. Virtually everything the Public Corruption Unit did was of a sensitive nature. The usual targets of the unit's investigation were not bank robbers wearing masks and waving guns. They were often people one read about on the front pages of the newspapers or saw being interviewed on the TV news.

Reynolds leaned forward and slipped out of her flats, rubbing her aching feet against the legs of her chair. Everything about her was tight, raw and hurting: Her sinuses were almost completely closed, her skin feverish, her throat scratchy. But at least she was alive. Unlike Ken Newman. She had driven straight to his home after first calling ahead to let his wife know she had to see her. Reynolds hadn't said why, but Anne Newman had known that her husband was dead. Reynolds had heard it in the tone of the few words the woman had managed to speak.

Normally, a person of a higher level than Reynolds would accompany her to the home of a bereaved spouse, to show that the Bureau did care, from top to bottom, when it lost one of its own. However, Reynolds had not waited for anyone else to volunteer to come with her. Ken was her responsibility, including telling his family that he was dead.

When she had arrived at the house, Reynolds had gotten right down to it, figuring a drawn-out monologue would only prolong the woman's obvious agony. Reynolds's compassion and empathy for the bereaved woman had been unhurried, however, and sincere. She had held Anne, consoled her as best she could, broken down in tears with her. Anne had taken the absence of information well, Reynolds had thought, far better than she probably would were the roles reversed.

Anne would be allowed to see her husband's body. Then it would be autopsied by the state's chief medical examiner. Connie and Reynolds would attend the post along with representatives from the Virginia State Police and the commonwealth's attorney office, all of whom were under strict confidentiality orders.

They would also have to count on Anne Newman to help keep angry and confused family members under control. It was a potentially weak link in the chain, expecting a woman in personal agony to help a government agency that couldn't even tell her all the circumstances of her husband's death. But it was all they had.

As she had left the stricken woman's home – the kids had been away with friends – Reynolds had the distinct feeling that Anne blamed her for Ken's death. And as Reynolds had walked back to her car she couldn't really disagree with that. The guilt Reynolds was feeling right now was like a crusty barnacle sunk into her skin, a free radical roaming inside her body, seeking a place to nest, grow and eventually kill her.

Outside the Newmans' home she had run into the

director of the FBI as he had come to offer his own condolences. He conveyed heartfelt sympathy to Reynolds for the loss of one of her men. He told her that he had been briefed on her conversation with Massey and that he concurred in her judgment. However, he made it clear that results had better be both quick and substantial.

As Reynolds now eyed the considerable clutter of her office, it occurred to her that the mess well symbolized the disorganization, some would say dysfunction, of her personal life. Matters of importance from many open cases lay across her desk and small conference table. They were wedged on to her shelves, had mutated into piles on her floor and even found their way on to the couch where she often slept, far away from her children.

But for her live-in nanny and the nanny's teenage daughter, Reynolds didn't know how should could possibly keep a halfway normal life for her kids. Rosemary, a wonderful woman from Central America who loved the children nearly as much as Reynolds did and was fanatical about keeping the house clean, the meals cooked and the clothes laundered, was costing Reynolds over a quarter of her entire salary and was more than worth every penny. But after the divorce was final it would be very tight. And Reynolds's ex would not be paying any alimony. His work as a fashion photographer, though lucrative, came in quick bursts followed by long periods of deliberate inactivity. Reynolds would be lucky if she didn't end up paying *him* alimony. And child support from him, while she would seek it, would be a joke. The man may as well have had "dead-beat dad" engraved on his forehead.

She looked at her watch. The FBI lab was working on the videotape right now. Because the existence of her "special" was unknown within the FBI except for very select personnel, any lab work that was required was supposed to be sent over under a dummy case name and file number. It would be nice to have separate laboratory facilities and personnel, but that would entail enormous expense that just didn't figure in the Bureau's budget. Even elite crime fighters had to live within the allowance Uncle Sam gave them. Normally a liaison agent at the main agency would work with Reynolds's team to coordinate any lab submissions and findings with Reynolds. However, Reynolds didn't have time for normal channels. She had personally delivered the tape to the lab and with her superior's blessing it had received a very high priority.

After meeting with Anne Newman she had gone home, cuddled for as long as she could with her sleeping kids, showered, changed and driven right back to work. All the time she had been thinking of that damn tape. As if in response to her thoughts, the phone rang.

"Yes?"

"You better come over," said the man. "And just so you know, it's not good news."

THIRTEEN

Faith awoke with a start. She looked at her watch. It was nearly seven. Lee had insisted that she get some rest, but she hadn't expected to be out so long. She sat up, feeling thickheaded. Her body was aching and when she swung her legs over the side of the bed, she felt a little sick to her stomach. She still had her suit on, but she had slipped off her shoes and pantyhose before lying down.

She got off the bed, padded into the adjoining bathroom and looked at herself in the mirror. "God," was all she could manage to say. Her hair was matted flat, her face a mess, her clothes filthy and her brain felt like cement. Such a pleasant way to begin the day.

She turned on the shower and stepped back into the bedroom to undress. She had taken off her clothes and was standing naked in the middle of the bedroom when Lee knocked on the door.

"Yes?" she said anxiously.

"Before you get in the shower, we need to do something," Lee said through the door.

"Is that right?" The odd tone of his words sent a chill up her spine. She quickly put her clothes back on and stood rigidly in the middle of the room.

"Can I come in?" He sounded impatient.

She went over and edged open the door. "What is—" Faith almost screamed when she saw him.

The man looking at her was not Lee Adams. This

man had a buzz cut, the hair dyed blond and damp, a matching short beard and mustache, and he wore glasses. And instead of dazzling blue, his eyes were brown.

The man smiled as he watched her reaction. "Good, it passed the test."

"Lee?"

"We can't exactly walk past the FBI as ourselves."

Lee held out his hands. Faith saw the scissors and a box of hair coloring.

"Short hair is easier to take care of, and personally I think it's a myth that blondes have more fun."

She looked at him dully. "You want me to cut my hair? And then color it?"

"No, I'll cut it. And if you want, I can color it for you too."

"I can't do that."

"You have to do that."

"I know it seems silly under the circumstances—"

"You're right, it does seem silly under the circumstances. Hair grows back, but once you're dead, you're dead," he said bluntly.

She started to protest but then realized he was right.

"How short?"

He cocked his head, examining her hair from different angles. "How about a short, Joan of Arc do? Boyish, but cute."

Faith just stared at him. "Wonderful. Boyish, but cute – my lifetime ambitions realized with a few snips and a bottle of hair color."

They went into the bathroom. Lee sat her down on the toilet and began to cut while Faith kept her eyes tightly shut.

"Want me to do the color too?" Lee asked when he was done.

"Please. I'm not sure I can look at it right now."

It took some time under the sink, and the smell of chemicals contained in the coloring mix was tough to take on an empty stomach, but when Faith finally managed to look in the mirror she was pleasantly surprised. It didn't look as bad as she would have thought. The outline of her head, now more fully revealed, was actually a nice shape. And the dark color went well with her skin tones.

"Now grab a shower," Lee said. "You can get your hair wet. Blow dryer's under the sink. There'll be some clean clothes on the bed."

She eyed his big frame. "I'm not your size."

"Not to worry. I run a full-service resort."

Thirty minutes later, Faith emerged from the bedroom in jeans and a flannel shirt, jacket and low-heeled boots that Lee had left for her. From power suit to college student. She felt years younger. The short black hair encircled her face, which she left au naturel. Faith had decided to forgo her usual makeup routine. Fresh start all around.

Lee sat at the kitchen table. He studied her new appearance. "Looks good," he said approvingly.

"You did it." She looked at his wet hair and a thought struck her. "Do you have a second bath-room?"

"Nope, just the one. I showered while you were sleeping. I didn't use the hair dryer because I was afraid it would wake you. You'll find I'm a very considerate soul."

She recoiled slightly. It was a creepy revelation, that he had been lurking around while she was asleep in his bed. She got this sudden image of a maniacal, scissors-toting Lee Adams leering while she lay there tied to the bed, naked and helpless.

"God, I must have really been out," she said as casually as she could.

"You were. I actually grabbed some shut-eye too."

107

He continued to study her appearance. "You know, you look better without makeup."

Faith smiled. "Your lies are very much appreciated." She smoothed down her shirt. "By the way, do you always keep women's clothes around your apartment?"

Lee pulled on a pair of socks and then some tennis shoes. He wore jeans and a white T-shirt that was spread taut across his chest. The veins in his biceps and smooth forearms rippled, and Faith hadn't really noticed before how thick his neck was. His torso narrowed dramatically at his waist, the pants slightly loose there, giving him a hard V-shape. His thighs looked ready to burst through the denim. He caught her staring and Faith quickly looked away.

"My niece Rachel," he said. "She goes to law school at Michigan. She clerked at the law firm here last year and stayed with me, rent-free. Only she earned more money in one summer than I do in about a year. She left some of her stuff. Lucky you're about the same size. She'll probably be back next summer."

"Tell her to be careful. This town has a way of destroying people."

"I don't think she'll have your problems. She wants to be a judge one day. No felons need apply."

Faith's face flushed. She took a mug from the sink rack and poured a cup of coffee.

Lee stood. "Look, that was out of line. I'm sorry."

"I deserve a lot worse than that, actually."

"Fine, I'll let other people do the honors."

Faith poured a cup of coffee for him and sat down at the table. Max came into the kitchen and nudged her hand. She smiled and petted the dog's broad head.

"Max taken care of?"

"All set." He checked his watch. "The bank opens

108

shortly. We'll have just enough time to pack. We'll get your stuff, head to the airport, get our tickets and fly, fly away."

"I can call down and arrange for the house from the airport. Or should I try from here?"

"No. Phone logs can be checked."

"I didn't think of that."

"You're going to have to start to." He took a sip of coffee. "Hope the place is available."

"It will be. I happen to own it. Or at least my other identity does."

"Small place?"

"Depends on what you call small. I think you'll be comfortable."

"I'm easy." He carried his coffee into the bedroom and came out a few minutes later wearing a navy blue sweater over his T-shirt. His mustache and beard were gone and he had a baseball cap on. He was carrying a small plastic bag.

"The evidence of our makeovers," he explained.

"And no disguise?"

"Mrs. Carter's used to me keeping odd hours, but if I barge in looking like somebody else, it'll be a little much for her this early in the morning. And I don't want her being able to give anyone a description later on."

"You are good at this," said Faith. "That's reassuring."

He called Max. The big dog obediently padded from the small living room into the kitchen, stretched his body and then sat next to Lee. "If the phone rings, don't answer it. And stay away from the windows."

Faith nodded and then he and Max were gone. She took her coffee and walked around the small apartment. It was a curious cross between a messy college dorm and a more mature person's home. In

109

what should have been the dining room, Faith found a home gym. Nothing fancy, no high-dollar, high-tech machines, just barbells, a weight bench and squat rack that were set up throughout the space. In one corner was a heavy punching bag and next to it a speed bag. Boxing and weight gloves, hand wraps and towels were neatly arranged on a small wooden table next to a box of white powder. A medicine ball sat in another corner.

On the walls were some photos of men in Navy whites. Faith picked out Lee quite easily. He looked pretty much the same at eighteen as he did now. However, the years had weathered his face, cut in lines and angles that made him even more attractive, even more seductive. Why was aging so damn tilted in favor of men? There were black and white photos of Lee in the boxing ring, and one of him with his hand raised in victory, a medal resting against his wide chest. His expression was calm, as though he had expected to win; in fact, as though he would not accept losing.

Faith gave the heavy bag a small punch with a loosely made fist, and her hand and wrist instantly throbbed. In that moment she recalled how big and thick Lee's hands were, the knuckles resembling a miniature mountain range. A very strong, resourceful, tough man. A man who could take punishment. She just hoped he would remain on her side.

She went into the bedroom. On the nightstand next to his bed was a cell phone and next to that a portable panic-button device. Faith had been too exhausted to notice them last night. She wondered if he slept with his pistol under his pillow. Was he really just paranoid or did he know something the rest of the world didn't?

It suddenly occurred to her: Wasn't he afraid she might make a run for it? She went back into the hallway. The front was covered; he would see her leave that way. But there was a back door off the kitchen that went down a fire escape. She went over to the door and tried to open it. It was locked. Deadbolted. The kind you could only open with a key even from inside. The windows also had key locks. It angered Faith, being trapped like this, but the truth was she had been trapped long before Lee Adams popped up in her life.

She continued looking through the apartment. Faith smiled at the collection of record albums housed in their original covers, and a framed poster from the movie *The Sting*. She doubted if the man had a CD player or even cable TV. She opened another door and went into the room. She started to turn on the light and then paused as a sound caught her attention. She stepped to the window, inched back the blinds and looked out. It was fully light outside now, although the sky was still gray and gloomy. She didn't see anyone, but that meant nothing. She could be encircled by an army and she'd never know it.

She turned the light on and looked around, surprised. A desk, file cabinets, a sophisticated phone system and shelves filled with manuals surrounded her. There were large pegboards on the wall with memo cards tacked to them. On the desk were neatly arranged files, a calendar and the usual desktop accessories. Apparently, Lee's home also served as his place of business.

If this was his office, maybe the file on her was here. Lee would probably be gone for a few more minutes. She started to sift carefully through the papers on his desk. Then she went through the desk drawers and then moved on to the file cabinets. Lee was very organized and he had a lot of clients – mostly business and law firms, from the file labels she was seeing. Defense lawyers, she assumed, since prosecutors had their own detective force.

The ringing phone made her almost leap out of her shoes. Trembling, she went over to it. The base unit had an LCD readout. Lee obviously had caller ID, because the number of the person calling him was displayed on the readout. It was long distance, with a 215 area code. Philadelphia, she recalled. Lee's voice came on and told the caller to leave a message after the beep. When that person started talking, Faith froze.

"Where is Faith Lockhart?" asked the voice of Danny Buchanan. Danny sounded very distressed as he fired more questions: What had Lee found out? He wanted answers and he wanted them immediately. Buchanan left a phone number, then hung up. Faith felt herself backing away from the phone. She stopped and stood still, transfixed by what she had just heard. A full minute passed as numbing thoughts of betrayal swirled through her mind like confetti in a parade. Then she heard a sound behind her and whirled around. Her scream was short, sharp, leaving her momentarily breathless. Lee was staring at her.

FOURTEEN

Buchanan looked around the crowded airport. He had taken a risk in calling Lee Adams directly, but his options now were few. As his eyes roamed the area, he wondered which of the people it was. The old lady in the corner with her big purse and hair in a bun? She had been on Buchanan's flight. A tall, middle-aged man had been pacing the aisle while Buchanan had been on the phone. He too had been on the flight from National.

The truth was Thornhill's people could be anywhere, anyone. It was like being attacked by nerve gas. You never saw the enemy. A sense of profound hopelessness gripped Buchanan.

Buchanan's greatest fear had been that Thornhill would either try to get Faith involved in his scheme, or suddenly find her a liability. He might have pushed Faith away, but would never abandon her. This was why he had hired Adams to follow her. As the end drew near, he had to make sure she remained safe.

Buchanan had looked in the phone book, of all places, and used the simplest logic he could think of. Lee Adams had been the first person listed under private investigators. Buchanan almost laughed out loud now at what he had done. But unlike Thornhill, he didn't have an army at his beck and call. For all he knew, Adams hadn't reported in because he was dead.

He paused for a moment. Should he just flee to the

ticket counter, book the first flight available to anywhere remote and then lose himself? Easy to fantasize about, quite another thing to implement. He envisioned trying to escape: Thornhill's heretofore invisible army would suddenly materialize and descend upon him from the shadows, displaying official-looking badges to anyone bold enough to intervene. Then Buchanan would be taken to a quiet room in the bowels of the Philadelphia airport. There Robert Thornhill would be calmly waiting with his pipe and his three-piece suit and his casual arrogance. He would calmly ask Buchanan, did he want to die right this very minute? Because Thornhill would certainly accommodate him if he did. And Buchanan would have absolutely no response.

Finally Danny Buchanan did the only thing he could do. He left the airport, climbed in his waiting car and drove to see his friend the senator, to put another nail in the man's coffin with his smiling, disarming manner and the listening device he was wearing, which looked exactly like skin and hair follicles and was so advanced that it wouldn't set off the most sophisticated of metal detectors. A surveillance van would follow him to his destination and record every word said by Buchanan and the senator.

As a backup, in case the transmission from his listening device was somehow interfered with, Buchanan's briefcase had a tape recorder built in to its frame. A slight twist on the briefcase handle activated the recorder. It too was undetectable by even the most sophisticated airport security. Thornhill really had thought of everything. *Damn the man.*

On the drive over, Buchanan comforted himself with a deliriously inspiring fantasy involving a pleading, broken Thornhill, an assortment of poisonous snakes, boiling oil and a rusted machete.

If only dreams could come true.

The person sitting in the airport was clean-cut, mid-thirties, dressed in a dark, conservatively cut suit and working on a laptop computer – meaning he mirrored about a thousand other business travelers all around him. He seemed busy and focused, even talking to himself at times. He gave the appearance, to the casual passersby, of a man preparing for a sales pitch or compiling a marketing report. He was actually quietly talking into the tiny microphone embedded in his necktie. What looked like infrared data ports on the backside of his computer were really sensors. One was designed to capture electronic signals. The other was a sound wand that collected words and posted them on to the screen. The first sensor quite easily snagged the phone number Buchanan had just called and automatically transmitted it to the screen. The voice sensor had been a little garbled, what with so many con-versations going on at the airport; but enough had come through to make the man excited. The words "Where is Faith Lockhart?" stared back at him from the screen.

The man conveyed the telephone number and other information to his colleagues back in Washington. Within seconds a computer at Langley had produced the account holder of the phone and the address to which the phone number was registered. Within minutes a very experienced team of professionals completely in the allegiance of Robert Thornhill – who had been waiting for just such a mission – was dispatched to Lee Adams's apartment.

Thornhill's instructions were simple. If Faith

Lockhart was there, they were to "terminate" her, as it was so benignly termed in official espionage parlance, as though she would simply be fired and asked to collect her personal belongings and leave the building, instead of a bullet fired into her head. Anyone with her would suffer the same fate. For the good of the country.

FIFTEEN

"You scared the hell out of me." Faith couldn't stop trembling.

Lee moved into the room and looked around. "What are you doing in my office?"

"Nothing! I was just wandering. I didn't even know you had your office here."

"That's because you didn't need to know that."

"I thought I heard a sound outside the window when I came in here."

"You did hear a sound, but it didn't come from the window." He pointed to the doorjamb.

Faith noted the rectangular piece of white plastic attached to the wood there.

"It's a sensor. Anybody opens the door to my office, it trips the sensor and triggers my beeper." He took the device out of his pocket. "If I hadn't had Max to calm down at Mrs. Carter's, I would've been up here a lot sooner." He scowled at her. "I don't appreciate this, Faith."

"Hey, I was just looking around, killing time."

"Interesting choice of words: 'killing.'"

"Lee, I'm not plotting against you. I swear it."

"Let's finish packing. Don't want to keep your bankers waiting."

Faith avoided looking at the phone again. Lee must not have heard the message. He had been hired by Buchanan to follow her. Had he killed the agent last night? When they got on the plane, would he somehow manage to push her out at thirty thousand

117

feet and laugh riotously while she plummeted screaming through the clouds?

But he could have killed her at any point from last night to now. Leaving her dead at the cottage would have been the easiest move. That's when it hit her: It would have been the easiest move unless Danny wanted to know how much she had told the FBI. That would explain why she was still alive. And also why Lee was so eager to get her to talk. Once she did, then he would kill her. And here they were flying off together to a North Carolina beach community that would be largely deserted this time of year. She slowly walked out of the room, a condemned woman on the way to her execution.

Twenty minutes later, Faith closed the small travel bag and slid her purse strap over her head and on to her shoulder. Lee came into the bedroom. He had put back on the mustache and beard, and the baseball cap was gone. In his right hand was his pistol, two boxes of ammo and his belt holster.

Faith watched as he loaded the items into a special hard-sided container. "You can't take a gun on a plane," she said.

"You're kidding, really? When did they start that shit?" He closed the container and locked it, pocketing the keys before looking at her. "You *can* take a gun on a plane if you disclose the weapon when you check in and fill out a declaration form. They ensure that the weapon is unloaded and in an approved case." He rapped his knuckles against the hard-sided aluminum case. "Which it is. They check that the ammo is a hundred rounds or fewer and is in the manufacturer's original or otherwise FAA-approved packaging. Again, I'm cool. Then they mark the bag with a special tag and it goes to the cargo bay, where it would be real hard for me to get to if I was thinking about skyjacking the plane, wouldn't you agree?"

"Thanks for the explanation," Faith said curtly.

"I'm not a damn amateur," he said hotly.

"I never said you were."

"Right."

"Okay, I'm sorry." She hesitated, intensely desiring to establish some sort of truce, for a number of reasons, her survival being chief among them. "Would you do me a favor?"

He looked at her suspiciously.

"Call me Faith."

The door buzzer startled them both.

Lee checked his watch. "Little early for visitors."

Faith watched in amazement as his hands moved like a machine. Within twenty seconds the pistol was out of the container and fully loaded. He put the container and the ammo boxes in his small travel bag and hoisted it over his shoulder. "Get your bag."

"Who do you think it is?" Faith felt her pulse throbbing in her ears.

"Let's go find out."

They stepped quietly into the hallway and Faith followed Lee to the front door.

He checked the TV screen. They both saw the man standing there on the front stoop of the building, a couple of packages in his arms. The familiar brown uniform was clearly visible. As they watched, he hit the buzzer once more.

"It's just the UPS man," Faith said, letting out a relieved breath.

Lee didn't take his eyes off the screen. "Is that right?" He hit a button on the screen that obviously moved the camera, as Faith found herself now staring at the street in front of the building. Something that should have been there wasn't.

"Where's his truck?" she said, her fear abruptly returning.

"Excellent question. And the fact is I know the UPS guy on this route real well, and that's not him."

"Maybe he's on vacation."

"Actually, he just got back from a week in the islands with his new bride. And he never comes at this time of the morning. Which means we've got a big problem."

"Maybe we can get out through the back."

"Yeah, I'm sure they forgot to cover the rear."

"There's only the one man."

"No, he's the only one we can see. He's got the front. They probably want to flush us out the back right into their arms."

"So we're trapped," she managed to whisper.

The buzzer rang again and Lee reached out his finger to hit the intercom button.

Faith grabbed his hand. "What the hell are you doing?"

"I'm going to ask what he wants: He'll say UPS and I'm going to let him in."

"You're going to let him in," Faith repeated dully. She glanced at his pistol. "What, and have a shoot-out in your apartment building?"

Lee's face hardened. "When I tell you to move, you move your ass like a T-Rex is breathing down your neck."

"Move? Move where?"

"Just follow me. And no more questions."

Lee hit the intercom button, the man identified himself and Lee touched the door release. As soon as he did, he activated the apartment's alarm system, whipped open the front door, grabbed Faith by the arm and pulled her out into the hallway. There was a door across from Lee's apartment. It had no apartment number on it. As Faith listened to the UPS man's footsteps echoing in the building down below, Lee already had unlocked the door. They

120

were through it in an instant and he quietly closed and locked the door behind them. The place was very dark, but Lee obviously knew his way around here. He led her to the back, through another door that opened up into what looked like a back bedroom, from the little Faith could see.

Lee opened another door in the room and motioned Faith in. She stepped through and almost immediately felt a wall against her. When Lee joined her, it was a very tight fit, like a telephone booth. He closed the door and the darkness became blacker than anything Faith had ever experienced before.

He startled her when he spoke, his breath tickling her ear. "Right in front of you there's a ladder. Here are the rungs." He gripped her hand and guided it until her fingers touched the rungs. "Okay?" She nodded. Lee continued whispering. "Give me your bag and start climbing. Take it slow. I'll sacrifice speed for silence right now. I'll be right behind you. When you get to the top, just stop. I'll take it from there."

As she began to climb, Faith started feeling severely claustrophobic. And, because she had lost her bearings, she was becoming queasy. Now would be such a perfect time to lose the contents of her stomach, little though it was.

She moved her hands and feet slowly as she went up. Then, gaining confidence, she started to pick up her pace. That was a mistake because her foot missed a rung, she slipped and her chin painfully clipped one of the rungs. But then Lee's strong arm was round her in an instant, holding her up. She took a moment to steady herself, tried to ignore the pain in her chin and kept climbing until she felt the ceiling above her head and then stopped.

Lee was still on the rung right below her. Then he

suddenly moved up on the same rung she was on, his legs on either side of hers so that her legs were pinched between his. He leaned against her with increasing force, and she wasn't sure what he was trying to do. It was becoming painful to breathe with her chest pushed up hard against the ladder rungs. For one terrifying moment she thought he had lured her in here to rape her. Suddenly a blast of light hit her from above and he moved away from her. She looked up, blinking rapidly. The view of the blue sky was so wonderful after the terror of the darkness that she felt like screaming in relief.

"Go up and on to the roof, but keep low. As low as you can," Lee whispered urgently into her ear.

She went up and through, dropping to her belly and looking around. The roof of the old building was flat, with a gravel and tar base. Bulky old heating units and newer air-conditioning machinery dotted the roof in various places. They made for good hiding places and Faith slid over and squatted next to the nearest one.

Lee was still on the ladder. He listened intently and then checked his watch. The guy would be at his door right about now. He would buzz, wait for Lee to answer. They had thirty seconds at most before the guy realized no one was coming to the door. It would be nice to have a little more time than that, and also a way to draw in the other forces Lee knew were out there. He pulled his cell phone from his pocket and hit a speed-dial number.

When the person answered, he said, "Mrs. Carter, it's Lee Adams. Listen to me, I want you to let Max out in the hallway. Right, I know I just dropped him off. I know he'll head up to my apartment. That's what I want. I, uh, I forgot to give him a shot he needs. Please hurry, I really need to get out of here."

He pocketed the phone and pushed the bags up

and out, then he hoisted himself through the opening and closed the hatch behind him. He scanned the roof and spotted Faith. Grabbing the bags, he slid over to her.

"Okay, we got a little time."

Down below they heard a dog start to bark loudly and Lee smiled. "Follow me." Squatting low, they made their way to the edge of the roof. The building attached to Lee's was a little shorter so that the roof was about five feet lower. Lee motioned for Faith to take his hands. She did so and he lowered her over the edge, holding tightly until her feet touched the roof. As soon as Lee joined her, they both heard shouts coming from Lee's building.

"Okay, they've made their all-out assault. They'll go through the door and that'll trip the alarm. I don't have a call-back option with the alarm company, so there's no delay in sending the cops. A few minutes and it'll be a big mess."

"What do we do in the meantime?" Faith asked.

"Three more buildings and then down the fire escape. Move!"

Five minutes later they were running through a back alley and then out on to another quiet suburban street flanked by a number of low-rise apartment buildings. The street was lined on both sides with parked cars. In the background Faith could hear the thump of a tennis ball being hit. She could make out a tennis court surrounded by several tall pine trees in a small park across from the apartment building.

She watched as Lee eyed a line of cars parked at the curb. Then he jogged across to the park area and bent down. When he straightened up, he was holding a tennis ball – one of many that had landed there from years of errant shots on the court. He walked back over to Faith. She could see that he was working a hole in the tennis ball with his pocketknife.

"What are you doing?" she asked.

"Go up on the sidewalk and walk as calmly as you can. And keep your eyes open."

"Lee—"

"Just do it, Faith!"

She spun around and went up on the sidewalk, paralleling his movements as he walked on the other side of the parked cars, his eyes scanning each of the vehicles. He finally stopped at a new-looking luxury model.

"See anybody watching us?" Lee asked.

Faith shook her head.

He walked over to the car and held the tennis ball against the key lock, the hole in the ball facing the lock's opening.

Faith looked at him as if he were insane. "What are you doing?"

In response, he slammed his fist against the tennis ball, driving all the air out of the ball and into the key lock. Faith watched in amazement as all four door locks popped open.

"How did you do that?"

"Get in."

Lee slid into the car, and Faith did the same.

He poked his head under the steering column and found the wires he needed.

"You can't hot-wire these new cars. The technology—" Faith stopped talking when the car started.

Lee sat up, put the car in gear and pulled away from the curb. He looked at Faith. "What?"

"All right, so how did the tennis ball unlock the car?"

"I've got my professional secrets."

Faith stared forward while he drove.

While Lee waited in the car with his eyes sharply on

the lookout, Faith entered her bank, explained what she wanted to the assistant manager and managed to sign her name, all without falling over in a dead faint. *Steady girl, one step at a time.* Fortunately, she knew the man.

The assistant manager looked curiously at her new appearance.

"Midlife crisis," she said, responding to his stare. "Decided to go for the youthful, streamlined look."

"It's very becoming, Ms. Lockhart," he said gallantly.

She closely watched him as he took her key, inserted it and the bank's duplicate key into the lock and pulled out her box. They left the vault and he set the box inside the private booth across from the vault reserved for safe-deposit box tenants. As he walked away, Faith continued to watch him.

Was he one of them? Was he going to slip away and call the police or the FBI or whoever was running around killing people? Instead he sat down at his desk, opened a white bag, extracted a glazed donut and proceeded to devour it.

Satisfied for the moment, Faith closed and locked the door. She opened the box and stared at the contents for a moment. Then she swept it all into her bag and closed the box. The young man put the safe-deposit box back in the vault and Faith walked out as calmly as she could.

Back in the car, Faith and Lee headed down Interstate 395, where they exited on to the GW Parkway and headed south to Reagan National Airport. Going against the morning rush hour, they made good time.

Faith looked over at Lee, who stared straight ahead, lost in thought.

"You did really well back there," she said.

"Actually, we cut it closer than I would have

liked." He paused and shook his head. "I'm really worried about Max, as stupid as that sounds under the circumstances."

"It doesn't sound stupid."

"Max and I have been together a long time. For years it's been only me and that old dog."

"I doubt they would have done anything to him with all those people around."

"Yeah, you'd like to think so, wouldn't you? But the fact is if they'll kill a man, a dog doesn't stand a chance."

"I'm sorry you had to do that for me."

He sat up straight. "Well, a dog is still a dog, Faith. And we've got other things to worry about, don't we?"

Faith found herself nodding. "Yes."

"I guess my magnet trick didn't work so well. They must have identified me through the video. Still, that was awfully fast." He shook his head, his expression a mix of admiration and fear. "Like scary fast."

Faith felt her spirits sink. If Lee was scared, at what level of sheer terror should she be operating? "Not very encouraging, is it?" she said.

"I might be a little better prepared if you tell me what's going on."

After the man's heroics, Faith found herself wanting to confide in him. But then the phone call from Buchanan came flashing back, ringing in her ears, like the shots last night.

"When we get to North Carolina, we'll have it all out. *Both* sides," Faith said.

126

SIXTEEN

Thornhill replaced the phone receiver and looked around his office, a disturbed expression on his face. His men had found the nest empty, and one of them had even been bitten by a dog. There had been reports of a man and woman running down the street. This was all just a little too much. Thornhill was a patient man, used to working on projects for many years, but still, there were limits to what he could tolerate. His men had listened to the message Buchanan had left on Lee's answering machine. They had taken the tape and played it back for Thornhill over his secure phone line.

"So you've hired a private investigator, Danny," Thornhill muttered to himself. "You'll pay for that one." He nodded thoughtfully. "I'll make you pay."

The police had responded to the burglar alarm, but when Thornhill's men had flashed official-looking IDs they had quickly backed off. Legally, the CIA had no authority to operate within the United States. Thus, Thornhill's team routinely carried several types of identification and would select one depending on who confronted them.

The patrolmen had been sent off with instructions to bury deeply all that they had seen. Still, Thornhill didn't like it. It was all too close to the edge. There were holes there, ways for people to gain an advantage over him.

He went to the window and looked outside. It was

127

a beautiful fall day, the colors starting to turn. As he studied the pleasing foliage, he primed his pipe, but unfortunately that was all he could do. CIA headquarters was a nonsmoking building. The deputy director had a balcony outside his office where Thornhill could sit and smoke, but it was not the same. During the Cold War, the CIA offices had been as foggy as steam baths. Tobacco helped one think, Thornhill believed. It was a minor thing, yet it symbolized all that had gone wrong with the place.

In Thornhill's opinion, the CIA's downfall had accelerated in 1994 with the Aldrich Ames' debacle. Thornhill still winced every time he thought of the former CIA counterintelligence officer being arrested for spying for the Soviets and later the Russians. And of course, as fate would have it, the FBI had broken the case. After that, the president had issued a directive ordering an FBI agent to be made a permanent employee of the CIA. From then on, this FBI agent oversaw the agency's counter-espionage efforts and had access to all CIA files. An FBI agent on the premises! His nose in all their secrets! Not to be outdone by the executive branch, the idiotic Congress had followed with a law requiring all government agencies, including the CIA, to notify the FBI whenever there was evidence that classified information might have been improperly disclosed to foreign powers. The result: The CIA took all the risk and gave the prize to the FBI. Thornhill seethed. It was a direct usurpation of the CIA's mission.

Thornhill's rage was building. The CIA could no longer even put people under surveillance or wiretap. If it had suspicions of someone, it had to go to the FBI and request surveillance, electronic or otherwise. If electronic surveillance was desired, then the FBI had to go to FISC, the Foreign Intelligence

Surveillance Court, and obtain authorization. The CIA couldn't even approach FISC on its own. It had to have its hand held by Big Brother. Everything was stacked in the FBI's favor.

Thornhill's thoughts went into a tailspin as he reminded himself that the shackles on the CIA weren't just domestic; the Agency had to get authorization from the president before commencing any covert operations overseas. The congressional oversight committees had to be told of any such operations in a timely fashion. And with the world of espionage becoming more and more complicated, the CIA and FBI found themselves continually running into each other over jurisdictional squabbles, use of witnesses and informants and the like. Though it was supposed to be a domestic agency only, the FBI, in reality, did considerable work abroad, where it focused on antiterrorism and anti-drug operations, including the collection and analysis of information. Again, that hit right at the CIA's home turf.

Was it any wonder Thornhill hated his federal counterparts? Like a cancer, the bastards were everywhere. And to drive the nail a little farther into the CIA's coffin, a former FBI agent now headed up the Center for CIA Security, which conducted internal background checks on all current and prospective personnel. And all CIA employees had to file annual financial disclosure forms that were damn well exhaustive in their current requirements.

Before he suffered a stroke thinking any more on this sore subject, Thornhill forced himself to turn his attention to other matters. If Buchanan had hired this PI person to follow Lockhart, then he very well could have been the man at the cottage last night and the person who had shot Serov. There had been permanent nerve damage to the man's arm from the

129

gunshot wound, and Thornhill had ordered the Russian to be finished off. A hired killer who could no longer hold a weapon steady enough to kill would look for other ways to make money and could pose a small threat. It was Serov's own fault, and if there was one thing Thornhill demanded from his people, it was accountability.

So this Lee Adams was now in the mix of things, he mused. Thornhill had already ordered a complete background search on the man. In these days of computerized files, he would have a full dossier in half an hour, if not sooner. Thornhill did have Adams's file on Faith Lockhart; his men had taken that from the apartment. The notes showed that the man was thorough, logical in his approach to investigation. That was both good and bad for Thornhill's purposes. Adams had also given Thornhill's men the slip. That was not an easy thing to do. On the good side, if Adams was logical, he should be amenable to a reasonable offer, meaning one that would allow him to live.

Presumably Adams had also escaped from the cottage with Faith Lockhart. He had not reported in to Buchanan about this, which was why Buchanan had left that phone message. Buchanan was obviously unaware of what had happened last night. Thornhill would do all he could to make sure this state of affairs continued.

How would they run? A train? Thornhill doubted it. Trains were slow. And you couldn't take a train overseas. Now, a train to an airport was a more intriguing possibility. Or a cab. That seemed certainly more likely.

Thornhill eased back into his chair as an assistant entered with some files he had requested. While everything at the CIA was computerized these days, Thornhill still liked the feel of paper in his hand. He could think much more clearly with paper than when he was simply staring at the pixeled screen.

So all the usual bases were covered. What about the unusual? With the added element of a professional investigator, Adams and Lockhart might be fleeing under false identities, even disguises. He had men at all three airports and the train stations. That would only go so far. The pair could easily rent a car and drive to New York and take a plane there. Or they could go south and do the same thing. It certainly was problematic.

Thornhill hated these sorts of chases. There were too many places to cover and he had limited manpower for these "extracurricular" activities of his. At least he had the advantage of operating more or less autonomously. No one from the director of central intelligence on down really questioned him as to what he was up to. Or if they did, he was able to dance around any issue they threw at him. He got results that made them all look good, and that was his biggest weapon.

It was much better to coax the runners out, bring them to you, which was certainly possible with the right sort of bait. Thornhill just had to come up with that bait. That would take some thinking. Lockhart had no family, no elderly parents or young children. He didn't know enough about Adams yet, but he would. If the man had just hooked up with the woman, he couldn't possibly be willing to sacrifice everything for her. Not just yet. Other things being equal, Adams was the one to focus on. And they had a communication link to him by virtue of knowing where he lived. If they needed to get a discreet message to him, they could.

Now Thornhill's thoughts turned to Buchanan. He was currently in Philadelphia meeting with a prominent senator on how best to further the agenda of one of Buchanan's clients. They had this particular fellow on enough felonious activity to make the man literally break down and plead for his miserable life. He had been a special pain in the ass to the CIA, nickle-and-diming them to death from the high perch of his Appropriations Committee seat. The payback would be so gratifying.

Thornhill envisioned walking into all these mighty politicians' offices and showing them the videos, the audiotapes, the paper trails. Of them and Buchanan plotting their little conspiracies, all the details of the future payoffs; they so eager to do Buchanan's bidding in return for all that money. How greedy they looked!

Good Senator, would you mind very much licking my boots, you whiny, squealing excuse for a human being. And then you will do exactly as I say, no more, no less, or I will crush you underfoot faster than you can say "vote for me."

Of course, Thornhill would never say that. These men demanded your respect even if they didn't deserve it. He would tell them that Danny Buchanan had disappeared and left these tapes with them. They weren't quite sure what to do with the evidence, but it appeared that the tapes should be turned over to the FBI. It seemed an awful thing to do; these fine men couldn't possibly be guilty of these sorts of things, but once the FBI started its feeding frenzy, they all knew where that would end: prison. And how could that possibly help the country? The world would laugh at us. Terrorists would be emboldened in the face of a supposedly weakened foe. And resources were so tight. Why, the CIA itself was understaffed and underfunded, it's responsibility unfairly curtailed. And could you fine people perhaps do something to change that? And would you please do so at the expense of the

FBI, the very bastards who would love to get their hands on these tapes so they could destroy you? Starting with getting them the hell off our backs? And we thank you very much, you fine public leaders. We knew you'd understand.

The first move in Thornhill's grand plan would be to have his new allies find a way to completely remove the FBI presence from the Agency. Next, the operations budget for the CIA would be increased by fifty percent. To start. In the next fiscal year he would get serious about the dollars. In the future, the CIA would only report to a joint intelligence committee instead of the separate House and Senate committees it was confronted with now. It was far easier to co-opt one committee. Then the hierarchy of the U.S. intelligence-gathering agencies needed to be straightened out once and for all. And the director of Central Intelligence would be at the very top of that pyramid. The FBI would be as far down the totem pole as Thornhill could bury it. And the tools of the CIA would be considerably strengthened. Domestic surveillance, the covert funding and arming of insurgency groups to overthrow enemies of the United States, even selective assassination, all would come back as weapons of choice for him and his colleagues. Right that minute Thornhill could think of five heads of state whose immediate deaths would leave the world a better, safer, more humane place. It was time to take the shackles off the best and brightest and let them do their jobs again. God, he was so close.

"Keep up the good work, Danny," Thornhill said out loud. "Pour it on until the end. That's a good man. Let them almost taste victory right before I take their lives away."

Grim-faced, he looked at his watch and rose from behind his desk. Thornhill was a man who loathed the press. He had, of course, never granted an interview in all his years at the Agency. But as senior as he was now, he occasionally had to undertake another sort of appearance, one that he equally detested. He had to testify before the House and Senate Select Committees on Intelligence on a series of matters involving the Agency.

In these "enlightened" times, CIA personnel gave more than one thousand substantive reports to Congress in a year's time. So much for covert operations. Thornhill was able to get through these briefings only by focusing on how easily he could manipulate the idiots who were supposed to be overseeing his agency. With their smug looks, they posed to him questions formulated by their very diligent staffs, who were more knowledgeable about most intelligence matters than the elected officials they served.

At least the hearing would be in camera, no public or press allowed. To Thornhill the First Amendment's rights to an unfettered press had been the biggest mistake the Founding Fathers had ever made. You had to be damn careful around the scribes; they looked for every advantage, any chance to put words in your mouth, trip you up, make the Agency look bad. It deeply hurt Thornhill that no one seemed to really trust them. Of course they lied about things; that was their job.

In Thornhill's mind the CIA was clearly the Hill's favorite whipping boy. The members loved to look tough in facing down the super-secret organization. That really played well back home: FARMER-TURNED-CONGRESSMAN STARES DOWN SPOOKS. By now Thornhill could write the headlines himself.

However, today's hearing actually promised to be positive because the Agency had scored some serious PR points lately in the most recent Middle

East peace talks. Indeed, largely through Thornhill's behind-the-scenes work, the Agency had overall fashioned a more benign, upstanding image, an image he would seek to bolster today.

Thornhill snapped his briefcase shut and put his pipe in his pocket. *Off to lie to a bunch of liars, and we both know it and we both win*, he thought. *Only in America.*

SEVENTEEN

"**S**enator," Buchanan said, shaking hands with the tall, elegant-looking gentleman. Senator Harvey Milstead was a proven leader with high morals and strong political instincts who offered thoughtful insight on the issues. A true statesman. That was the public perception. The reality was that Milstead was a womanizer of the first order and was addicted to painkillers for a chronically bad back, medications that sometimes left him incoherent. He also had a worsening drinking problem. It was years since he had sponsored any meaningful legislation of his own, although in his prime he had helped enact laws from which every American now benefited. These days when he spoke, it was in gobbledygook that no one ever bothered to check up on because he said it with such authority. Besides, the press loved the charming guy with such genteel manners, and he held a very powerful leadership position. He also fed the media machine with a flow of appropriately timed juicy leaks, and he was quotable to a fault. They loved him, Buchanan knew. How could they not?

There were five hundred and thirty-five members of Congress – a hundred senators plus the repre-sentatives in the House. Well over three-quarters of them, Buchanan estimated perhaps a little generously, were decent, hardworking, genuinely caring men and women who believed strongly in what they were doing both in Washington and for the people. Buchanan termed them, collectively, the "Believers." Buchanan stayed away from the Believers. Touching those folk would only have earned him a quick trip to prison.

The rest of the Washington leadership were like Harvey Milstead. Most were not drunks or womanizers or shells of their former selves, but, for various reasons, they were ripe for manipulation, easy targets for the lures Buchanan was tossing overboard.

There were two such groups that Buchanan had successfully recruited over the years. Forget Republicans and Democrats. The parties Buchanan was interested in were the members of the venerable "Townies," and the group Buchanan had labeled, only somewhat tongue-in-cheek, the "Zombies."

The Townies knew the system better than anyone. They *were* the system. Washington was their town, hence the nickname. They had all been here longer than God. If you cut them, their blood would run red, white and blue, or so they liked to tell you. There was another color Buchanan had added to that mix: green.

By contrast, the Zombies had come to Congress with nary a stitch of moral fiber or whiff of a political philosophy. They had won their place of leadership with the finest campaigns that media dollars could buy. They were fabulous on sound bite TV and in the confines of tightly controlled debates. They were, at best, mediocre in intellect and ability and yet delivered the sales pitch with the verve and enthusiasm of a JFK at his oratorical best. And when they were elected, they arrived in Washington with absolutely no idea what to do. Their only goal had already been achieved: They had won their campaign.

However, despite this, the Zombies tended to stay in Congress because they loved the power and access that came with being an incumbent. And with the cost of elections going through the stratosphere, it was still possible to defeat an entrenched incumbent . . . in the same way that it was still theoretically possible to climb Mount Everest without oxygen. One only had to hold his breath for several days.

Buchanan and Milstead sat down on a comfortable leather couch in the senator's spacious office. The shelves were filled with the usual spoils of a longtime politician: plaques and medals of appreciation, silver cups, awards made of crystal, hundreds of photographs of the senator standing with people even more famous than he; inscribed ceremonial gavels and bronzed miniature shovels symbolizing political pork brought to his state. As Buchanan looked around, it occurred to him that he had spent his entire professional life coming to places such as this, hat in hand, essentially begging.

It was early yet, but the man's staff was busy in the outer suite preparing for a hectic day with Keystone State constituents, a day laced with lunches, speeches, appearances and pop-in-and-out dinners, meet-and-greets, drinks and parties. The senator was not up for reelection, but it was always nice to put on a good show for the people back home.

"I appreciate your meeting with me on such short notice, Harvey."

"Hard to refuse you, Danny."

"I'll get right to it. Pickens's bill is looking to knock out my funding, along with about twenty other aid packages. We can't let that happen. The results speak for themselves. The infant mortality rate has been cut seventy percent. My God, the wonders of vaccine and antibiotics. Jobs are being created, the economy is moving from thuggery to legitimate business. Exports are up by a third, and imports from us are up twenty percent. So you see it's creating jobs here too. We can't let the plug be pulled now. Not only is it morally wrong, it's stupid from our side. If we can get countries like this on their feet, we won't have a trade imbalance. But you need reliable sources of electricity first. You need an educated population."

"AID has accomplished a lot," the senator pointed out.

Buchanan was intimately familiar with AID, or the Agency for International Development. Formerly an independent agency, it now reported to the Secretary of State, who also more or less controlled its very substantial budget. AID was the flagship of American foreign aid, with the vast majority of funds flowing through its long-standing programs. Every year it was like musical chairs to see where AID's limited budget dollars would end up. Buchanan had been caught without a seat many times, and he was so weary of it. The grant process was intensive and highly competitive, and unless you fit the template set up by AID for the programs it wanted to sponsor, you were out of luck.

"AID can't do it all. And my clients are too small a bite for IMF and the World Bank. Besides, now all I hear is 'sustainable development.' No dollars unless it goes for sustainable development. Hell, last time I looked, food and medicine were necessary for life. Doesn't that qualify?"

"You're preaching to the choir, Danny. But people count pennies around here too. The days of fat are over," Milstead said solemnly.

"My clients will take gristle. Just don't cut them off."

"Look, I just won't schedule the bill."

139

In the Senate, if a chairman didn't want a bill to get out of committee, he simply didn't schedule it for hearing, as Milstead was now suggesting. Buchanan had played that game many times before.

"But Pickens could end-run you on that," Buchanan said. "Word is he's dead set on getting this thing heard one way or another. And he might get a more sympathetic audience on the floor than he would in committee. Why not put a hold on the bill and run it out of session?" Buchanan suggested.

Danny Buchanan was the master at this technique. A hold was simply one senator objecting to a pending bill. The legislation would be in complete limbo until the hold was removed. Years ago, Buchanan and his allies on the Hill had used it to stunning effect in representing the most powerful special interests in the country. It took real power in Washington to make things not happen. And for Buchanan, that had always been the most fascinating aspect of the city. Why health care reform legislation or the tobacco settlement bills, propelled by intense media coverage and public clamor, simply disappeared into the yawning gulf of the Congress. And it was very often the case that special interests wanted to maintain the status quo they had worked so hard to erect. For them change was not good. Hence, a good deal of Buchanan's previous lobbying work had focused on burying any legislation that would harm his powerful clients.

The hold maneuver was also known as the "blind rolling" hold because, like the passing of the baton on a relay team, a different senator could place a new hold when the previous one had been released, and only the leadership knew who had placed the restriction. There was a lot more to it, but at the end of the day the blind rolling hold was an enormous waste of time, and hugely effective, which explained much of politics in a nutshell, Buchanan well knew.

The senator shook his head. "I found out Pickens has holds on two of my pieces, and I'm close to cutting a deal that'll make him let go. I hit him with another hold and the sonofabitch'll clamp down on my ass like a ferret on a cobra."

Buchanan sat back and sipped his coffee as a number of potential strategies rolled through his mind. "Look, let's go back to square one. If you have the votes to knock it out, schedule it and let the committee vote on it and kill the bastard for good. Then if he takes it to the floor I can't believe he'll have the support to carry it. Hell, once it's on the floor we can hold it up forever, ask for amendments, hit it in the cloak room, cut the crap out of it pretending to want to deal for some juice on one of your bills. In fact, we're so close to the elections now we can even play the quorum call game until he yells uncle."

Milstead nodded thoughtfully. "You know Archer and Simms are giving me a little trouble."

"Harvey, you've sent enough highway construction dollars to both those bastards' states to choke every man and woman and child there. Call them on it! They don't give a damn about this bill. They probably haven't even read the staff briefing materials."

Milstead looked suddenly confident. "One way or another, we'll get it done for you. In a one-point-seven-trillion-dollar budget, it's not that big a deal."

"It is for my client. A lot of people are counting on this one, Harvey. And most of them can't even walk yet."

"I hear you."

"You should take a fact-finding trip over there. I'll go with you. It's really beautiful country, you just can't use the land for shit. God might have blessed

141

America, but he forgot about a lot of the rest of the world. But they keep going. If you ever think you're having a bad day, it's a good memory to have."

Milstead coughed. "My schedule is really full, Danny. And you know I'm not running for re-election. Two more years and I'm out of here."

Okay, shop talk and humanitarian plea time is over, Buchanan thought. *Now let's play traitor.*

He leaned forward and casually moved his briefcase out of the way. One twist on the handle activated the recording device secreted inside. *This one's for you, Thornhill, you smug bastard.*

Buchanan cleared his throat. "Well, I guess it's never too early to talk about replacements. I need some people on Foreign Aid and Ops who'll participate in my little retirement program. I can promise them as good as I'll be paying you. They'll want for nothing. They just have to get my agenda done. I'm at the point now where I can't afford defeat on anything. They have to come through for me. That's the only way I can guarantee the payoff at the end. Just like you. You always come through for me, Harvey. Almost ten years and counting, and you always get it done. By hook or crook."

Milstead glanced at the door and then spoke in a very low voice, as though that made it all better. "I do have some people you might want to talk to." He looked nervous, uncomfortable. "About taking over some of my *duties*. I haven't broached the issue with them directly, of course, but I'd be surprised if they weren't amenable to some sort of arrangement."

"That's real good to hear."

"And you're right to plan ahead. The two years will go quickly."

"Hell, in two years I might not be here, Harvey."

The senator smiled warmly. "I didn't think you'd ever retire." He paused. "But I guess you have your

142

heir apparent. How is Faith, by the way? Vivacious as ever, I'm sure."

"Faith is Faith. You know that."

"Lucky to have someone like her backing you up."

"Very lucky," Buchanan said, frowning slightly.

"Give her my best when you see her. Tell her to come up and see old Harvey. Best mind and legs in the place," he added with a wink.

To this, Buchanan said nothing.

The senator sat back against the couch. "I've been in public service half my life. The pay is ridiculous – chickenshit, really, for somebody of my ability and stature. You know what I could earn on the outside. That's the trade-off when you serve your country."

"Absolutely, Harvey. Of course it is." *The bribe money is only your due. You earned it.*

"But I don't regret it. Any of it."

"No reason you should."

Milstead smiled wearily. "The dollars I've spent over the years rebuilding this country, shaping it for the future, for the next generation. And the next."

Now it was *his* money. *He* saved the country. "People never appreciate that," said Buchanan. "The media only goes after the dirt."

"Guess I'm just making up for it in my golden years."

After all these years a little humility, a little guilt remain. "You deserve it. You served your country well. It's all waiting for you. Just like we discussed. Better than we discussed. You and Louise will want for nothing. You'll live like a king and queen. You did your job, and you'll reap the rewards. The American way."

"I'm tired, Danny. Weary to the bones. Between you and me, I'm not sure I can last two more minutes, much less two more years. This place has sucked the life right out of me."

143

"You're a true statesman. A hero to us all."

Buchanan took a deep breath and wondered if Thornhill's boys parked in the van outside were enjoying this sappy exchange. In truth, Buchanan too was looking forward to getting out. He looked at his old friend. An expression of giddiness was on the man's features as he no doubt thought of a truly glorious retirement with his wife of thirty-five years, a woman he had cheated on many times, who had always allowed him back. And kept silent about it. The psychology of political wives would be a worthy college course, Buchanan believed.

In truth, Buchanan had a soft spot for his Townies. They actually had accomplished a lot, and in their own way were some of the most honorable people Buchanan had ever met. And yet the senator had no problem being bought.

Very soon Harvey Milstead would have a new master. The Thirteenth Amendment to the Constitution had outlawed slavery, but apparently no one had bothered telling Robert Thornhill that. He was turning his friends over to the Devil. That's what troubled Buchanan most of all. Thornhill, always Thornhill.

The men rose and Buchanan and the senator shook hands. "Thank you, Danny. Thank you for everything."

"Please, don't mention it," Buchanan said. "Please don't." He grabbed his spy briefcase and fled the room.

EIGHTEEN

"**D**egaussed?" Reynolds stared at the two technicians.

"My tape has been degaussed? Will someone please explain that to me?" She had watched the video twenty times now. From every angle possible. Or rather, she had watched jagged lines and dots swarm across the screen like a World War I aerial dogfight with heavy doses of ground flack thrown in. She had been sitting here for a very long time and knew no more than when she had first walked in.

"Without getting too technical—" one of the men started to say.

"Please don't," Reynolds interjected. Her head was pounding. If the tape was useless? Good God, it can't be.

"'Degaussing' is the reference term used for the erasure of a magnetic media. It's done for many reasons, some of the most common being so that the media can be used again, or to eliminate confidential information that was recorded on the media. A videotape is a form of magnetic media. What happened to the tape you gave us was an unwanted intrusional influence that has distorted and/or corrupted the media, preventing its proper utilization."

Reynolds stared in wonder at the man. What the hell would his technical answer have been?

"So you're saying someone intentionally screwed with the tape?" she said.

"That's right."

"But couldn't it be a problem with the tape itself? How can you be sure someone 'intruded' upon it?"

The other technician spoke up. "The level of corruption we've seen in the images so far would preclude that conclusion. We can't be one hundred percent sure, of course, but it really does look like third party interference. From what I understand, the surveillance system used was very sophisticated. A multiplexer with three or four cameras on line, so there was no dwell time gap. How were the units activated? Motion or trip?"

"Trip."

"Motion is better. The systems these days are so sensitive they can pick up a hand reaching for something on a desk in a one-foot-square-zone. Trips are obsolete."

"Thanks, I'll keep that in mind," she said dryly.

"We did a pixel zoom for detail enhancement, but still nothing. Definitely interference."

Reynolds remembered that the closet at the cottage containing the video equipment had been found open.

"Okay, how could they have done it?"

"Well, there's a wide variety of specialized equipment available."

Reynolds shook her head. "No, we're not talking a lab setting. We're looking at doing it on site, where the equipment was set up. And maybe whoever did it wouldn't have even known there was video recording equipment there. So assume that whatever they happened to have with them would have been what they used."

The techs thought for a moment. "Well," one of them said, "if the person had a powerful magnet and passed it over the recorder a number of times, that could distort the tape by rearranging the metallic

146

particles, which would, in turn, remove the previously recorded signals."

Reynolds took a deep, troubled breath. A simple magnet could have blown away her only clue. "Is there any way to get it back, the images on the tape?"

"It's possible, but it will take some time. We can't make any guarantees until we get in there."

"Do it. But let me make this real clear." She stood, towering over the two men. "I need to be able to see what's on that tape. I need to be able to see who was in that house. You have no higher priority than that. Check with the AD if you have a conflict, but whatever it takes, twenty-four hours a day. I need it. Understand?"

The men looked at each other briefly before nodding.

When Reynolds got back to her office, a man was waiting to see her.

"Paul." She nodded at him as she sat down.

Paul Fisher rose and closed the door to Reynolds's office. He was her liaison at Headquarters. He stepped over a pile of documents as he sat back down. "You look like you're overworked, Brooke. You always look like you're overworked. I guess that's what I love about you."

He smiled and Brooke caught herself smiling back.

Fisher was one of the few people at the FBI whom Reynolds looked up to, literally, as he was easily six-foot-five. They were about the same age, although Fisher was her superior in the chain of command and had been at the Bureau two years longer. He was competent and assured. He was also handsome, having retained the tousled blond hair and trim figure of his California days at UCLA. After her marriage had started to disintegrate, Reynolds had imagined having an affair with the divorced Fisher.

147

Even now, his unexpected visit made Reynolds feel fortunate she'd had the opportunity to go home, shower and change her clothes.

Fisher's jacket was off, his shirt draped gracefully over his long torso. He had just come on duty, she knew, although he tended to be around at all hours.

"I'm sorry about Ken," he said. "I was out of town, or I would've been there last night."

Reynolds played with a letter opener on her desk. "Not as sorry as I am. And neither of us is anywhere near where Anne Newman is on the sorry meter."

"I've talked to the SAC," Fisher said, referring to the special agent in charge, "but I want you to tell me about it."

After she told him what she knew, he rubbed his chin. "Obviously the targets know you're on to them."

"It would seem so."

"You're not that far along in the investigation, are you?"

"Nowhere near referring it to the U.S. attorney for indictment, if that's what you mean."

"So Ken's dead and your chief and only witness is MIA. Tell me about Faith Lockhart."

She glanced up sharply, being equally disturbed by his choice of words and the blunt tone he had used to say them.

He stared back at her, his hazel eyes holding a definable measure of unfriendliness, Reynolds concluded. But right now, she knew, he was not supposed to be her friend. He represented Headquarters.

"Is there something you want to tell *me*, Paul?"

"Brooke, we've always shot straight with each other." He paused and tapped his fingers against the arm of the chair as though trying to communicate

148

with her in Morse code. "I know Massey authorized some leeway for you last night, but they're all very concerned about you. You need to know that."

"I know that in light of recent developments—"

"They were concerned *before* this. Recent developments have only heightened that level of concern."

"Do they want me to just drop it? Christ, it could implicate people who have government buildings named after them."

"It's a question of proof. Without Lockhart what do you have?"

"It's there, Paul."

"What names has she given you, other than Buchanan?"

Reynolds looked momentarily flustered. The problem was Lockhart hadn't given them any names. Yet. She had been too smart for that. She was saving that for when her deal was completed.

"Nothing specific yet. But we'll get it. Buchanan didn't do business with local school board members. And she told us some of his scheme. They work for him while in power, and when they leave office he lines up jobs for them with no real duties and mega-dollars in compensation and other perks. It's simple. Simply brilliant. The level of detail she's provided us could not be made up."

"I'm not disputing her credibility. But again, can you prove your case? Right now?"

"We're doing everything we can to prove it. I was going to ask her to wear a wire for us when all this happened, but you can't rush these things, you know that. If I pushed too hard, or lost her confidence, we'd end up with nothing."

"Do you want my coldly reasoned analysis?" Fisher took her silence as assent. "You've got all these nameless but very powerful people, many of whom may have things lined up in the future or currently have nice post-public service careers. What's so unusual about that? It happens all the time. They get on the phone, have lunches, whisper in ears, call in some favors. That's America. So where are we?"

"This is more than that, Paul. A lot more."

"Are you saying you can trace the actual illegal activity, how the legislation was manipulated?"

"Not exactly."

"'Not exactly' is right. It's really like trying to prove a negative."

Reynolds knew he was right on that point. How did you prove someone *didn't* do something? Many of the tools Buchanan's people would have used to further his agenda were probably tools every politician used, legitimately. They were talking motivation here. *Why* somebody was doing something, not *how* they were doing it. The why was illegal, the how wasn't. Like a basketball player not trying his best because he'd been paid off.

"Is Buchanan a director in these unknown firms where the former, unknown politicians get jobs? A stockholder? Did he put up the money? Does he have any ongoing business with any of them?"

"You sound like a defense lawyer," she said hotly.

"That's exactly my intent. Because those are the sort of questions you'll need answers for."

"We have not been able to uncover evidence directly tying Buchanan to any of it."

"Then what are you basing your conclusion on? What's your evidence that there is a connection at all?"

Reynolds started to speak and then stopped. Her face flushed and in her agitation she broke in half the pencil she was holding.

"Let me answer that for you," said Fisher. "Faith Lockhart, your missing witness."

"We'll find her, Paul. And then we're back in business."

"And if you don't find her? What then?"

"We'll find another way."

"Can you determine the identities of the bribed officials independently?"

Reynolds desperately wanted to say yes to that question, but she couldn't. Buchanan had been in Washington for decades. He'd probably had dealings with just about every politician and bureaucrat in the city. It would be impossible to narrow down the list without Lockhart.

"Anything's possible," she said gamely.

He shook his head. "Actually, it's not, Brooke."

Reynolds erupted. "Buchanan and his cronies have broken the law. Doesn't that count for anything?"

"In a court of law it counts for zero without proof," he shot back.

She slammed her fist down on the desk. "I damn well refuse to believe that. Besides, the evidence is there; we just have to keep digging."

"You see, that's the problem. It would be one thing if you could do it in complete secrecy. But an investigation of this magnitude, with the sort of important targets we're talking about, can never remain completely secret. And now we have a homicide investigation to deal with as well."

"Meaning there will be leaks," Reynolds said, wondering if Fisher suspected that those leaks might have already occurred.

"Meaning that when you go after important people, you better be damn sure of your case before any leaks do occur. You can't target people like that unless you're loaded for bear. Right now, your gun's empty and I'm not sure where you go to reload. It pretty much says in the Bureau manual, you can't hunt down public officials based on rumor and innuendo."

She looked at him coolly when he finished saying this. "Okay, Paul, would you like to tell me exactly what it is you want me to do?"

"The Violent Crime Unit will keep you informed on its investigation. You have to find Lockhart. Since the two cases are inextricably connected, I suggest cooperation."

"I can't tell them anything about our investigation."

"I'm not asking you to. Just work with them to help clear Newman's murder. And find Lockhart."

"And beyond that? If we can't find her? What happens to my investigation?"

"I don't know, Brooke. The tea leaves are very hard to read right now."

Reynolds stood and looked out the window. Thick, dark clouds had turned day almost into night. She could see both her reflection and Fisher's in the window. He never took his eyes off her, and she doubted if he was all that interested at the moment in how her backside and long legs looked in the black knee-length skirt and matching stockings she was wearing.

As she stood there her ears picked up on a sound they usually didn't: the "white noise." At sensitive government facilities windows were potential outlets for valuable information, namely speech. To plug this leak, speakers were mounted at the windows in these facilities to filter out the sound of voices such that anyone lurking outside with the fanciest in surveillance equipment would end up with zip. The speakers accomplished this by emitting a sound akin to a small waterfall, hence the term "white noise." Reynolds, like most employees in such buildings, had tuned out the background noise; it was such a daily part of her life. Now she noticed it with stunning clarity. Was that a signal to her to notice other things as well? Things, people she saw every day and then thought no more of, accepting them for what they proclaimed to be? She turned to face Fisher.

"Thanks for the ringing vote of confidence, Paul."

"Your career has been nothing short of spectacular. But the public sector is often like the private in one regard: It's the 'what have you done for me lately?' syndrome. I'm not going to sugarcoat this, Brooke. I've already started to hear the rumblings."

She folded her arms across her chest. "I appreciate your complete bluntness," she said coldly. "If you'll excuse me, I'll see what I can do for you lately, Agent Fisher."

As Fisher rose to leave, he moved next to her, touching her lightly on the shoulder. Reynolds recoiled slightly from this, the bite of his words still weighing heavily upon her.

"I've always supported you, and I will continue to support you, Brooke. Don't read this as though I'm throwing you to the wolves. I'm not. I respect the hell out of you. I just didn't want you to be blindsided on this. You don't deserve that. This messenger is friendly."

"That's good to know, Paul," she said unenthusiastically.

When he reached the door, he turned back. "We're handling the media relations from WFO. We've already had inquiries from the press. For now, an agent was killed during an undercover operation. No other details were provided, including his identity. That won't last long. And when the dam breaks, I'm not sure who can keep dry."

As soon as the door closed behind him, a cold shudder hit Reynolds. She felt as though she were being suspended over a vat of boiling something. Was it her old paranoia kicking in? Or was it simply her reasoned judgment? She kicked her shoes off and paced her office, stepping over the paper land mines as she did so. She rocked on the balls of her feet, trying to guide the massive tension she was feeling throughout her body toward the floor. It didn't come close to working.

NINETEEN

T he recently named Ronald Reagan Washington National Airport, which everyone in the area still simply called "National," was very busy this morning. It was loved for its convenience to the city and its numerous daily flights, and hated for its congestion, short runways and stomach-jolting tight left turns to avoid restricted airspace. However, the airport's new sparkling terminal with its row of Jeffersonian-inspired domes and hulking, multi-tiered parking garages with skywalks to the terminal were very welcome to the hassled air traveler.

Lee and Faith entered the new terminal, where Lee eyed a police officer patrolling the corridor. They had left the car in one of the parking lots.

Faith watched the policeman's movements too. She was wearing "eyeglasses" that Lee had given her. The lenses were ordinary glass, but they helped to further change her look. She touched Lee's arm. "Nervous?"

"Always. It kind of gives me an edge. Makes up for a serious lack of formal schooling." He put their bags over his shoulder. "Let's grab a cup of coffee and let the line at the ticket counter die down a little, scope the place out." As they looked for a coffee shop, he asked, "Any idea of when we can get a flight out of here?"

"We fly through Norfolk and then take a com-muter to Pine Island, off the Outer Banks of North

Carolina. Flights to Norfolk are pretty frequent. The commuter to Pine Island you have to call ahead and schedule. Once we get the Norfolk flight scheduled, I'll call down and arrange that. They only fly during daylight."

"Why's that?"

"Because we won't be landing on a regular runway; it's more like a little road. No lights or tower or anything. Just a wind sock."

"That's comforting."

"Let me call down and check on the house."

They went over to the phone bank and Lee listened while Faith confirmed their arrival. She hung up. "All set. We can get a rental car once we get down there."

"So far, so good."

"It's a nice place to relax. You don't need to see or talk to anybody else if you don't want to."

"I don't want to," said Lee firmly.

"I'd like to ask you a question," Faith said as they walked toward a café.

"Shoot."

"How long had you been following me?"

"Six days," he promptly answered, "during which you made three trips to the cottage, including last night."

Last night, Faith thought. Was that all it had been? "And you haven't reported back to your employer yet?"

"No."

"Why not?"

"I like to do weekly reports, unless something really extraordinary happens. Believe me, if I'd had time, last night would have qualified for the mother of all reports."

"How were you to make these reports if you don't know who hired you?"

156

"I was given a phone number."

"And you never checked up on it?"

He looked at her with annoyance. "Nah, why should I care? Take the money and run."

She looked chastened. "I didn't mean it like that."

"Uh-huh, sure." He shifted the bags slightly and continued, "There's a special crisscross directory that'll give you the corresponding address if you have the phone number."

"And?"

"And in these days of satellite phones and nationwide cell networks and crap like that, nothing came up. I called the number. It must have been set up just to receive calls from me because it told Mr. Adams to leave any information on the tape. It also gave a P.O. box in D.C. Being the ever curious type I checked that out too, but it was listed in the name of a corporation I'd never heard of, with an address that turned out to be phony. Dead end." He looked down at her. "I take my work seriously, Faith. I don't like walking into traps. Famous last words, right?"

They stopped at the small café, bought their coffee and a couple of bagels and sat down in a vacant corner of the place.

Faith took a troubled breath as she sipped her coffee and nibbled on a poppyseed bagel oozing butter. Maybe he was being straight with her, but he still had a connection to Danny Buchanan. It was such a strange feeling suddenly being fearful of a man she had idolized. If things had not changed so much between them the last year, she would have been tempted to call Danny. But she was confused now, the horror of last night so crystal clear in her mind. Besides, what was she supposed to ask him: *Danny, did you try and have me killed last night? If you did, please stop, I'm working with the FBI to help you,*

really. And why did you hire Lee to follow me, Danny?
Yes, she had to part company with Lee, and soon.

"The report you were given, tell me what it said about me," Faith said.

"You're a lobbyist. You used to be with a big outfit, represented Fortune 500s. About ten years ago, you and a man named Daniel Buchanan started your own firm."

"Did it mention any of our current clients?"

He cocked his head. "No, is that important?"

"What do you know about Buchanan?"

"The report didn't say much about him, but I did some digging on my own, nothing you won't know. Buchanan is a legend on the Hill. Knows everybody and everybody knows him. Fought all the big battles, made a ton of money doing it. I assume you didn't do so badly yourself."

"I did well. What else?"

He stared at her strangely. "Why do you want to hear something you already know? Is Buchanan somehow mixed up in all this?"

Now it was Faith's turn to scrutinize Lee. If he was playing dumb, he was doing an exceptional job, she thought.

"Danny Buchanan is an honorable man. I owe him everything I have."

"Sounds like a good friend. But you didn't answer my question."

"People like Danny are rare. A true visionary."

"And you?"

"Me? I just help implement his vision. People like me are a dime a dozen."

"You don't strike me as so ordinary." Faith took a sip of coffee and didn't respond. "So how does one become a lobbyist?"

Faith stifled a yawn and sipped her coffee again. Her head was starting to pound. She had never

158

needed much rest, galloping the globe, catching only plane catnaps. But right now she felt like curling up under the table and sleeping for the next ten years. Maybe her body was reacting to the last twelve hours of horror by shutting itself down, throwing in the towel. *Please don't hurt me.*

"I could lie and say I wanted to change the world. That's what everyone says, isn't it?" She pulled a bottle of aspirin from her bag, popped two and washed them down with coffee. "Actually, I remember watching the Watergate hearings when I was a kid. All those very serious people in that room. All these middle-aged men with wide ugly tics, puffy faces, over-easy hair, talking into these clunky microphones, and all the lawyers whispering into their ears. All the media, the whole world focused right there. What the rest of the country apparently found appalling, I found extremely cool. All that power!" She smiled weakly into her coffee cup. "My demented soul. The nuns were right about me. One in particular, Sister Audrey Ann, truly believed my name was a blasphemy. 'Dear Faith,' she would say, 'live up to your Christian name, not down to your devilish urges.'"

"So you were a rabble rouser?"

"It's like if I saw a habit coming my way I just turned evil. My dad moved us around a lot, but I did well enough in school, even if I raised hell outside it. I went to a good college, ended up in Washington with all those memories of absolute power dancing in my head. I didn't have the faintest idea what to do with myself, but I knew desperately I wanted to get into the game. I did a stint on Capitol Hill for a freshman congressman and caught the eye of Danny Buchanan. He snatched me up, saw something in me, I guess. I think he liked my spirit – I was running the office with all of two months' experience behind me. The way I sort of refused to back down from anyone, even the Speaker of the House."

"I guess that is impressive for somebody right out of college."

"My philosophy was, after the nuns, politicians weren't much of a challenge."

Lee cracked a smile. "Makes me glad I went to public school." He glanced away for a second. "Don't look now, but the FBI is circling."

"What?" She whipped her head around, looking everywhere.

Lee rolled his eyes. "Oh, that was good."

"Where are they?"

He lightly smacked the tabletop. "They're nowhere. And they're everywhere. The Feds don't walk around with their badges pinned to their foreheads. You won't see them."

"So why the hell did you say they were circling?"

"It was a little test. And you failed. *I* can spot the Feds, sometimes, not always. If I ever say that to you again, I won't be kidding. They will be there. And you can't react the way you just did. Normal, slow movements. Just a pretty woman on a holiday with her boyfriend. Understand?"

"Okay, fine. But just don't pull that crap on me again. My nerves aren't well rested."

"How are you paying for the tickets?"

"How should I pay for them?"

"Your credit card. Under your other name. Don't want to flash a bunch of cash around. You buy a one-way ticket with cash leaving today, that might be a red flag for the airline. Right now, the less attention, the better. What is it, by the way? Your other name?"

"Suzanne Blake."

"Nice name."

"Suzanne was my mother's name."

"Was? Passed on?"

160

"Both my parents. My mother when I was eleven. My dad six years later. No brothers or sisters. I was a seventeen-year-old orphan."

"That must've been tough."

Faith didn't say anything for a long moment. Talking about her past was always hard, so she rarely did so. And she really didn't know this man. Still, there was something about Lee Adams that was comforting, solid. "I really loved my mother," she began. "She was a good woman, and long-suffering, because of my dad. He was a good person too, but one of those souls who always have an angle, a way to make a quick buck with these crazy ideas. And when his plan blew up, and it always did, we'd have to pack up and move on."

"Why was that?"

"Because other people always lost their money with my dad's grand schemes too. And they were understandably upset about it. We moved four times before my mother died. Five more times after that. We prayed for my dad every day, my mom and I. Right before she died, she told me to take care of him, and me all of eleven."

Lee shook his head. "I can't even relate to that. My parents have lived in the same house for fifty years. How did you manage to keep it together after your mother died?"

The words somehow came easier for Faith now. "It wasn't as tough as you'd think. Mom loved my dad, hated how he lived, his schemes, all the moving. But he wasn't going to change, so they weren't the happiest couple to live with. There were times I really thought she was going to kill him. When she died, it sort of became my dad and me against the world. He'd dress me up in the one nice outfit I had and show me off to all his prospective partners. I guess people would think, how can this guy be so bad, what with his little girl right there and all? When I got to be sixteen I'd even help him pitch his deals. I grew up fast. I guess that's where I got my motor mouth and my backbone. I learned to think on my feet."

"Quite an alternative education," Lee commented. "But I can see how it would serve you well as a lobbyist."

Her eyes grew moist. "On the way to every meeting, he'd say, 'This is the one, Faith, darling. I can feel it right here,' and he'd put his hand over his heart. 'It's all for you, baby girl. Daddy loves his Faith.' And I believed him every single damn time."

"Sounds like he really ended up hurting you," Lee said quietly.

Faith shook her head stubbornly. "It wasn't like he was trying to rip people off. We're not talking Ponzi schemes or anything. He sincerely believed his ideas would work. But they never did and we'd move on. And it wasn't like we ever made any money. God, we slept in our car enough times. How many times do I remember my dad strolling into the back door of restaurants and walking out a little later with dinner he had talked them into giving him. We'd sit in the backseat and eat. He'd stare at the sky, pointing out the constellations to me. He never even finished high school, but he knew all about the stars. Said he'd been chasing enough of them his whole life. We'd just sit there far into the night, and my dad would tell me things would get better. Just down the road."

"Sounds like a man who could talk his way into anywhere. Probably would've made a good PI."

Faith smiled as she thought back. "I'd walk into a bank with him, and within five minutes he'd know everybody by name, drinking coffee, talking with the bank manager like he'd known him all his whole life. And we'd walk out with a letter of recommendation and a list of local high-net-worth individuals for my dad to solicit. He just had that way about him. Everyone liked him. Until they lost their money. And we always lost what little we had too. Dad was a stickler about that. His money went in too. He was actually very honest."

"You sound like you still miss him."

"I do," she said proudly. "He named me Faith because he said with Faith beside him, how could he ever fail?" On this Faith closed her eyes, tears trickling down her cheeks.

Lee pulled a napkin out of the holder and slipped it into her hand. She wiped her eyes.

"I'm sorry," she said. "I've never really talked about this with anyone before."

"It's okay, Faith. I'm a good listener."

"I found my dad again in Danny," she said, clearing her throat, her eyes wide. "He has the same way about him. The pluck of the Irishman. He can talk his way into seeing anybody. Knows every angle, every issue. Refuses to back down from anyone. He's taught me a lot. And not just about lobbying. About life. He didn't have it easy growing up either. We had a lot in common."

Lee smiled. "So from scams with your dad to lobbying in D.C.?"

"And some would say my job description hasn't changed." Faith smiled at her own remark.

"And some would say that the nut didn't fall far from the tree."

She bit into her bagel. "Since we're into true confessions, how about your family?"

Lee settled back. "Four of each. I'm number six."

"God! Eight kids. Your mother must be a saint."

"We gave them both enough heartache to last ten lifetimes."

163

"So they're both still around."

"Going strong. We're all pretty close now, although we had some rough times growing up. Good support groups when things go haywire. Help's only a phone call away. Usually, that is. Not this time, though."

"That sounds nice. Real nice." Faith looked away.

Lee eyed her keenly, easily reading her thoughts. "Families have their problems too, Faith. Divorces, serious illnesses, depression, hard times, we've seen it all. I have to say sometimes I'd rather be an only child."

"No, you wouldn't," she said with authority. "You might think you would, but trust me, you wouldn't."

"I do."

She looked confused. "You do what?"

"Trust you."

She said slowly, "You know, for a paranoid PI, you sure make friends fast. I could be a mass murderer, for all you know."

"If you were really bad, the Feds would've had you in custody."

She put down her coffee and leaned toward him, her expression very serious. "I appreciate the observation. But just so we're very clear on this, I've never physically harmed even an ant in my entire life, and I still don't consider myself a criminal, but I guess if the FBI wanted to put me in jail, they could. Just so we're clear," she said again. "Now, you still want to get on that plane with me?"

"Absolutely. You've really got my curiosity up now."

She sighed and sat back, glancing down the terminal's corridor. "Don't look now, but here come a pair who look an awful lot like the FBI."

"Seriously?"

164

"Unlike you, I wouldn't even attempt to joke about something like that." She bent over and fiddled with something in her bag. After a few anxious moments, she sat back up as the pair passed by without looking at them.

"Lee, depending on what they've found out, they may be looking for a man and a woman. Why don't you stay here while I go buy the tickets? I'll meet you at the security gate."

Lee looked uncertain. "Let me think about that."

"I thought you said you trusted me."

"I do." For a moment he envisioned Faith's dad standing in front of him, asking for money. And damn if Lee wasn't reaching in his pocket for his wallet.

"But even trust has its limits, right? I tell you what, you keep the bags. I need to take my purse. If you're really worried, you have a clear view of the security entrance from here. If I try to give you the slip, you've got me dead on. And I'm sure you can run much faster than I can." She stood. "And you know I can't call in the FBI, now, can I?"

She eyed him for a moment longer, apparently daring him to challenge her logic.

"Okay."

"What's your new name? I'll need it for your ticket."

"Charles Wright."

She winked at him. "And your friends call you Chuck?"

He gave her an uneasy smile and then Faith turned and disappeared into the crowd.

As soon as she was gone, Lee regretted his decision. Sure she had left her bag, but it only had a few clothes in it, the ones he had given her! She had her purse with her, which meant she had what she really needed: her fake ID and her money. Yes, he could see the security gate from here, but what if she just walked out the front door? What if that's what she was doing right now? Without her, he had nothing. Except some really dangerous people who now knew where he lived. People who would take great pleasure in breaking his bones one by one until he told them what he knew, which was nothing. They wouldn't be thrilled to hear that. Next stop: your standard landfill burial. That did it. Lee jumped up, grabbed the bags and headed after her.

TWENTY

There was a knock on Reynolds's door. Connie popped his head in. Reynolds was on the phone but she waved him in.

Connie had two cups of coffee. He put one in front of Reynolds, together with two cream packets, a sugar and a swizzle stick. She thanked him with an appreciative smile. He sat down and sipped on his coffee while she finished her call.

Reynolds put down the phone and started mixing her coffee. "I would absolutely love some good news, Connie." She noted that he also had gone home, showered and changed. Rambling through the woods in the dark had probably done a real number on his suit, she assumed. His hair was still damp and the wetness made it seem more gray than usual. Reynolds kept forgetting that he was in his fifties. Connie just never seemed to change, always big, always craggy, the weatherbeaten rock upon which she clung when the riptide came calling. As it was right now.

"Do you want lies or the truth?"

Reynolds took a sip of the coffee, sighed and leaned back in her chair. "Right now, I'm not sure."

He sat forward, perching his coffee on her desk. "I worked the scene with the VCU boys. That's where I started at the Bureau, you know. Just like old times." He put his palms flat on his knees and flexed his thick neck to work out a kink. "Damn, my back feels

167

like Reggie White's been doing jumping jacks on it. I'm getting too old for this kind of work."

"You can't retire. I can't function without you."

Connie picked up his coffee cup. "The hell you say." It was obvious, though, that the remark had pleased him. He sat back, unbuttoned his jacket and let his belly push through. He let a minute or so pass as he presumably collected his thoughts.

Reynolds waited patiently. She knew Connie had not come down here to shoot the breeze with her. He rarely did that with anyone. Reynolds had learned that just about everything the man did had a specific purpose. Connie was a true veteran of the ways of bureaucracy and, consequently, he carried an agenda with him everywhere. While she thoroughly relied on him for his field expertise and his instincts, Reynolds never quite lost sight of the fact that she was younger, less experienced, yet was still his boss; it had to be a sore point with the man. And she was a woman, to boot, in a field that still didn't have many at her level of responsibility. She could not really blame Connie if he felt resentment toward her. And yet he had never said a negative word about her, nor had he ever dragged his feet on an assignment in order to make her look bad. On the contrary, he was methodical to a fault, and reliable as the sunrise. Still, she had to watch herself.

"I saw Anne Newman this morning. She appreciated your coming over last night. She said you were a real comfort."

This surprised Reynolds. Maybe the woman *didn't* blame her. "She took it about as well as anyone could."

"I understand the director went too. That was good of him. You know Ken and I go way back." The look on Connie's face was easily read. If the man caught up to the killer before the VCU did, there

168

might not be any need for a trial.

"I know. I never stopped to think how hard this must be for you."

"You have enough on your mind. Besides, I'm the last person you need to worry about." Connie took a swallow of coffee. "The shooter was hit. Least it looks that way."

Reynolds immediately sat forward. "Let me have everything."

Connie momentarily smiled. "Don't want to wait for the written report from VCU?" He crossed one thick leg over the other, hitching up his cuffed trousers as he did so. "You were right about the shooter's location. We found blood, a fair amount of it in the woods behind the house. Did a rough trajectory. The location jells with where the shot probably came from. We followed the trail as best we could, but lost it in the woods after a few hundred feet."

"Exactly how much blood? Life-threatening?"

"Hard to say. It was dark. A team's over there right now continuing the search. They're lock-stepping the lawn, looking for the slug that killed Ken. They're also canvassing the neighborhood, but the place was so isolated, I'm not sure that'll pay off."

Reynolds took a deep breath. "If we find a body, that would both simplify and complicate things."

Connie nodded thoughtfully. "I see where you're going with that."

"You got a blood sample?"

"Lab's running it as we speak. Don't know what it'll be worth."

"At the very least it'll confirm whether it's human or not."

"That's true. Maybe all we'll find is a deer carcass. But I don't think so." Reynolds perked up. "Nothing concrete," he said in response to her look, "just call it my gut."

"If the guy's wounded, that should make it a little easier to track him down."

"Maybe. If he required medical attention, he wouldn't be so stupid as to go to the local emergency room. They have to report gunshot wounds. And we don't know how badly he was hurt. Might have just been a flesh wound that bled like a bitch. If so, he bandages it up, gets on a plane and poof. Gone. I mean we've got all the bases covered, but if the guy was leaving on a private plane, then we got problems. The truth is he's probably already long gone."

"Or maybe dead. Apparently he missed his primary target. Whoever hired him won't be happy about that."

"Right."

Reynolds folded her hands in front of her as she thought of the next topic she wanted to discuss. "Connie, Ken's gun was unfired."

Connie had obviously given this line of inquiry some thought because he said, "Which means, if the blood is confirmed as human, we definitely have a *fourth* person at the cottage last night. And that party shot the shooter." He shook his head wearily. "Shit, listen to us, it all sounds crazy."

"Crazy but apparently true under the facts as we know them. Think about this: Could this fourth person have killed Ken? And not the guy who was wounded?"

"Don't think so. The VCUs are looking for shell cartridges in the woods where we think the other shot came from, as confirmation. If there was a gun battle between two unknown parties, then maybe we'll find another set of ejected shells as well."

"Well, this fourth person being present may

explain the door being unlocked and the cameras being tripped."

He sat up straight. "Anything on the tape yet? We had to get some faces or something."

"To put it simply, we have been degaussed."

"What?"

"Don't ask. For right now we can't count on the tape."

"Well, shit. That doesn't leave us with much "

"Specifically, it leaves us with Faith Lockhart."

"We've got all the airports, train and bus stations, rental car agencies covered. Her firm too, although I can't believe she'd go there."

"Agreed. Actually, that may be where the bullet came from," Reynolds said slowly.

"Buchanan?"

"Wish we could prove it."

"If we find Lockhart, we still may be able to. We'll have some leverage there."

"Don't count on it. Almost getting your head blown off can make you rethink loyalties," Reynolds said dryly.

"If Buchanan and his people are on to Lockhart, then they must be on to us as well."

"You said that before. A leak? From here?"

"A leak from somewhere. Here or at Lockhart's end. Maybe she did something to make Buchanan suspicious. From all accounts, the guy's cagey as hell. He had her followed somehow. They saw her meeting with you at the house. He dug a little more, hit the truth and contracted to take her out."

"I'd like to believe *that* more than someone here selling us down the river."

"So would I. But the fact is every law enforcement agency has some bad apples."

Reynolds briefly wondered for a moment if Connie was suspicious of her. Everyone who worked at the FBI, from special agents to support staff, had top-secret security clearance. When you applied for a job at the Bureau, teams of agents would show up investigating every single piece of your past, no matter how insignificant, talking to everyone who ever knew you. Every five years a full field investigation was conducted on on-board Bureau employees. In the interim any suspicious activity involving a bureau employee or any complaints of persons asking suspicious questions of an employee were to be reported to the security officer in the employee's division. That had never happened to Reynolds, thank God. Her record was clean.

If there were suspicions of a leak or other type of security breach, it might very well be investigated by the Office of Professional Responsibility, and a polygraph exam might be ordered for the suspect employee. Other than that, the Bureau was always on the lookout for any signs that an employee was having undue personal or professional problems that might make him or her susceptible to bribes or influence by third parties.

Reynolds knew Connie was doing okay financially. His wife had died years ago from a lengthy illness that had sapped their resources, but he lived in a nice house that was worth a lot more than he had paid for it. His kids' college educations were done, and he had his pension locked in. All in all, he had a nice retirement to look forward to.

On the other hand, Reynolds knew her personal life and finances were in abysmal shape. College funds? Hell, she'd be lucky if she could continue to afford the private school tuition for first grade. And pretty soon, she wouldn't have a house to call her own. That was being sold as part of the divorce. The condo she was eyeing was about the size of the one she had rented when she had finished college. It had seemed cozy with one person. An adult and two energetic kids would quickly turn cozy into cramped. And could she afford to keep her nanny? With her hours, how could she not? She couldn't leave the kids alone at night.

In any other occupation she would probably be on the top ten soon-to-crash-and-burn list. But in the FBI, the divorce rate was such that her mess of a marriage would not create a blip on the Bureau radar. A career in the FBI was often simply not conducive to a happy personal life.

She blinked for a moment as she found Connie's gaze still upon her. Did he really suspect her of being the leak? Of causing Ken Newman to die? She knew it looked bad. On the very night when she'd had Newman substitute for her with Lockhart, he was killed. She knew Paul Fisher had been thinking that, and she was reasonably sure Connie was right now.

She composed herself and said, "There's really nothing we can do about this theory of a leak right now. Let's concentrate on what we can do."

"Fine. So what's our next move?"

"Hit all our lines of investigation as hard as we can. Find Lockhart. Let's hope she uses a credit card for plane or train tickets. If she does that, we've got her. We need to at least make an effort to find the shooter. Shadow Buchanan. Unscramble that tape and see who was in the house. I want you to act as liaison with the VCU. We have a lot of threads, if we can only grab one or two of them and hold on."

"Hey, isn't that always the case?"

"We're in a *really* tight spot here, Connie."

He nodded thoughtfully. "I heard Fisher was here. Figured he'd been by to see you."

Reynolds didn't respond to this, and Connie plunged on.

"Thirteen years ago, I was heading up a joint undercover drug operation with the DEA in Brownsville, Texas." He paused for a moment as if deciding whether to go forward or not. "Our official goal was to disrupt the flow of cocaine over the Mexican border. Our unofficial goal was to accomplish our mission without making the Mexican government look bad. For that reason, we had open lines of communication with our counterparts in Mexico City. Perhaps too open, since there was rampant corruption south of the border at all levels. But it was done that way so the Mexican authorities could share in the glory after we did all the work and scored the perps heading up the cartel. After two years of work, a huge bust was planned. But our plans got leaked and my guys walked into an ambush that left two of them dead."

"Omigod. I heard about that case, but I didn't know you were involved in it."

"Hell, you were probably still cutting your teeth at Quantico."

Reynolds didn't know if this was a backdoor barb or not, but she chose not to respond.

"Anyway, after all that went down, I got a visit from one of the young ladder climbers at HQ who wouldn't know which end of his pistol to hold, and who politely informed me that if I didn't make things right, my ass was cooked. But there was one stipulation. If I found out our friends in Mexico sent us down the river, I couldn't use that as an excuse. International relations, I was told. I'd just have to fall on the sword for the good of the world." Connie's voice trembled a little as he said this last part.

Reynolds found she was holding her breath. It was not like Connie to talk this much. In the dictionary, the man's picture could well be found next to the word "taciturn."

He took a gulp of coffee and took a moment to wipe his lips with the back of his hand. "Well, you know what? I traced the leak right to the top of the Mexican police department and I put a big X on the bastards' foreheads and walked away from it. If my superiors didn't want to do anything about it, fine. But damn if I was going to take the fall for somebody else's shit." He eyed her steadily. "'International relations,'" he said, a bitter smile spreading across his lips as he did so. He rested his elbows on her desk.

Was this a challenge he was laying before her? Reynolds wondered. Was he expecting to leave an X on her forehead, or daring her to pin one on his?

"That's been my official motto ever since," he said.

"What's that?"

"Screw 'international relations.'"

TWENTY-ONE

Through the airport terminal drifted members of both the FBI and Central Intelligence, with the former group completely unaware of the latter's presence. Thornhill's men had the advantage of knowing that Lee Adams was probably traveling with Faith Lockhart. The FBI agents were only looking for the woman.

Lee unknowingly passed a couple of the FBI agents dressed as businessmen with briefcases and *Wall Street Journal*s. They were equally oblivious to him. Faith had passed by the agents a moment earlier.

Lee slowed when he got near to the main ticket counter. Faith was up there speaking with a clerk. This was starting to look okay. He had a sudden feeling of guilt for not having trusted her. He edged over to a corner and waited.

At the counter, Faith displayed her new ID and purchased three tickets. Two tickets were in the name of Suzanne Blake and Charles Wright. The woman barely looked at her photo. Thank God for that, although Faith supposed people rarely looked like their ID photos anyway. The flight to Norfolk International left in about forty-five minutes. The third ticket she purchased was in the name of Faith Lockhart. It was a flight heading to San Francisco with a stopover in Chicago. It left in forty minutes. She had spotted it on the monitors. West Coast, big city. She could lose herself, drive down the coast, maybe even sneak into Mexico. She wasn't sure how she would accomplish that, but she just had to take it one step at a time.

Faith had explained that she was buying the ticket to San Francisco for her boss, who would arrive shortly.

"She'll have to hurry," the clerk said. "She still has to check in. And they're going to begin boarding in about ten minutes."

"It won't be a problem," Faith assured her. "She doesn't have any luggage, so she can check in at the gate."

The clerk handed her the ticket. Faith figured she was safe using her real name on the ticket because she paid for all of them with her Suzanne Blake credit card. And the only other ID she had to check in with was her real one. It was Faith Lockhart or nothing. Everything would be okay.

She could not have been any more wrong.

As Lee watched Faith, a thought jolted him. His gun! He had to check it before going through security or all hell would break lose. He shot across to the counter and next to a startled Faith.

He put his arm around her and gave her a quick kiss on the cheek. "Hey, babe. Sorry, the phone call took longer than I thought." He looked at the ticket agent and said casually, "I have a pistol I need to check."

The ticket agent raised her eyes slightly at this. "You're Mr. Wright?"

Lee nodded. She went about processing the necessary documents. He showed her his fake ID and she stamped his passenger ticket appropriately and entered the information in the computer. He turned over the gun and ammo, and filled out the declaration form. The agent tagged the container and they left the ticket counter.

"Sorry, I forgot about the gun." Lee looked up ahead to the security gate. "Okay, they're going to have people posted at the gate. We'll go through separately. Be cool; you don't look anything like Faith Lockhart."

Although Faith felt her heart in her throat the entire time, they went through the security gate without incident.

As they passed the flight information monitors, Lee spotted their gate. "Down this way."

Faith nodded as she noted how the gates were configured here. The departure gate for the San Francisco flight was close enough to easily get to, but far enough away from the Norfolk gate. She hid a smile. Perfect.

As they walked along, she looked over at Lee. He had done a lot for her. She wasn't feeling good about what she was about to do, but had convinced herself it was for the best. For both of them.

They reached the gate for the flight to Norfolk. The plane would be boarding in about ten minutes, they were told. There was a good crowd waiting.

Lee looked at her. "You better call that commuter service for the flight to Pine Island."

Lee and Faith walked over to the phone bank and she made that call.

"All set," Faith said. "Now we can relax."

"Right," Lee said dryly.

Faith looked around. "I need to use the rest room."

"Better hurry."

She hustled off while Lee looked after her thoughtfully.

TWENTY-TWO

"**B**ingo!" The man sitting in front of the computer screen said. He was in a van outside of the airport. The FBI had a designated liaison with the airlines to monitor the travel of persons the Bureau was looking for. With more than one airline sharing reservation systems and data and the advent of code-sharing, the FBI's job had been made a little easier. The Bureau had requested that the name Faith Lockhart be marked with a tag in the major airlines' reservation systems. That request had just paid an enormous dividend.

"She just made a reservation for a flight to San Francisco that leaves in about half an hour," he said into his headset microphone. "United Airlines." He passed along the flight number and gate information. "Hit it," he ordered the men inside the terminal. He picked up the phone to notify Brooke Reynolds.

Lee was leafing through a magazine someone had left on the seat next to his when two men dressed in suits flew past. A few moments later, a pair of gents in jeans and windbreakers hurried past, heading in the same direction.

Lee immediately jumped up, looked around for anyone else hustling by, saw no one moving fast and then followed after the group.

The FBI agents, followed by the men in jeans, hurried past the women's room a minute before

Faith came out. The men had disappeared into the crowds by the time she emerged.

Lee slowed as he saw Faith come out from the women's room. Another false alarm? When she turned away from him and went in the opposite direction, he knew his fears were justified. As he kept his gaze on her, she looked at her watch and picked up her pace. Shit, he knew exactly what she was doing: going for another flight. And from the way she had checked her watch and started walking faster, it must be close to leaving. As he pushed through the crowds, he scanned the aisle ahead. There were ten gates remaining down here. He stopped for a second at the monitors, his gaze flying down the listings, checking the gates off one by one until he stopped at the flashing "boarding" message for a United flight to San Francisco. As his eye drifted farther, he saw that a flight to Toledo was also boarding. Which one was it? Well, there was one definite way to find out.

He sprinted ahead, cut through a waiting area and managed to get past Faith without her seeing him. He abruptly stopped within sight of the gate for the San Francisco flight. The men in suits who had sprinted past him were standing at the departure door talking to a nervous-looking United employee. Then the stone-faced men moved off and stood behind a partition, their gaze fixed on the crowd and departure area. FBI for sure. The San Francisco flight had to be the one Faith was going for.

But something didn't make sense. If Faith had used her phony name, how . . .? Then it hit Lee. She couldn't use her phony name for both tickets for flights leaving a few minutes apart. That would have been a big red flag for the ticket agent. She had used her real name because she needed ID to get on the flight. Shit! She was heading right for them. She'd show her ticket, the agent would signal the FBI and then it would be over.

Just as he was about to turn, he spotted the two men in windbreakers and jeans who had rushed past him earlier. To Lee's experienced eyes, they were watching the Feds intently, without seeming to do so. He edged closer, and with the gloomy weather outside he managed to catch their reflection in the window. One man held something in his hand. A chill went down Lee's back as he maneuvered some more and managed to spot what it was. Or what he thought it was. This case suddenly took on a whole other dimension.

Lee fought his way back down the aisle; seemingly everyone who lived in the Washington metropolitan area had decided to fly today. He saw Faith across the aisle. In another moment she'd be past him. He made a lunge across the wall of people and tripped over a garment bag someone had set down. He fell to the floor hard, his knee taking the brunt of the collision. When he sprang up, Faith was past him. He had a few seconds, if that.

"Suzanne? Suzanne Blake?" he called out.

At first it didn't register. But then she stopped, looked around. If she saw him, Lee knew she might run. But her stopping had given him the few seconds he needed. He circled and came up behind her.

Faith almost collapsed when he gripped her arm. "Turn around and walk with me," he said.

She pulled at his fingers. "Lee, you don't understand. Please, let me go."

"No, *you* don't understand. The FBI is waiting for you at the San Francisco gate."

The words made her freeze.

"You messed up bad. You made the second reservation in your name. They monitor stuff like that, Faith. They know you're here now."

They headed as quickly as they could back down the aisle to the original departure gate. The plane was boarding. Lee grabbed their bags, but instead of getting on the plane, Lee veered off, pulling Faith along with him. They went back through security and headed toward the elevator.

"Where are we going?" Faith said. "The plane to Norfolk is leaving."

"We're getting the hell out of here before they shut the whole terminal down looking for us."

They took the elevator down to the lower level, went outside and Lee signaled for a taxi. They got in one, Lee gave the man an address in Virginia and the cab pulled off. Only then did Lee look at her.

"We couldn't get on the plane to Norfolk."

"Why not? That ticket was in my other name."

Lee glanced at the driver, an old guy slumped down in his seat listening to country western on the radio.

Satisfied, Lee still spoke in low tones. "Because the first thing they'll do is check at the ticket counter to see who purchased the ticket for Faith Lockhart. Then they'll know Suzanne Blake did. And they'll know Charles Wright is traveling with you. And they'll be given descriptions of us both. And they'll check the reservations for Blake and Wright and the FBI will be waiting for us when we get off the plane in Norfolk."

Faith paled. "They move that fast?"

Lee trembled with rage. "Who the hell do you think you're dealing with here? Larry, Moe and Curly Joe?" He slapped his thigh in sudden anger. "Sonofabitch!"

"What?" Faith said frantically. "What?"

"They have my gun. It's registered in my name. My *real* name. Dammit! Now I've aided and abetted, and the Feds right on our ass." In his despair he rested his head in his hands. "This must be my birthday, things are going so good for me."

Faith started to touch him on the shoulder, but pulled her hand back. She looked out the window instead. "I'm sorry. I'm really, really sorry." She put a hand against the car window, letting the cold from the glass seep into her skin. "Look, just take me to the FBI. I'll tell them the truth."

"That would be great except the FBI's not going to take your word for it. And there's another thing."

"What?" Faith wondered if he was going to tell her about working for Buchanan.

"Not now." Lee was actually thinking of the other men at the gate, what he had seen in one of the men's hands. "Right now I'd like you to tell me what that was all about back there."

She stared out the window at the choppy gray Potomac. "I'm not sure I can," she said so softly he could barely hear her.

"Well, I'd like you to try," he said very firmly. "I'd like you to try very, very hard."

"I don't think you'd understand."

"I can understand with the best of them."

She finally turned to him, her face flushed, her gaze refusing to catch his. She nervously played with the edge of her jacket. "I just thought it would be better if you weren't with me. You see, I thought you'd be safer that way."

Lee looked away in disgust. "Bullshit!"

"It's true!"

He whirled back around and clutched her shoulder so tightly she winced in pain. "Listen, Faith, they were at my apartment, whoever *they* are. They know I'm involved. Whether I'm with you or not, the danger level really doesn't change for me, it actually gets worse. And you running around trying to ditch me isn't damn well helping."

183

"But they knew you were involved. Remember back at your apartment."

Lee shook his head. "Those weren't the Feds."

She looked stunned. "Who, then?"

"I don't know. But the Feds don't show up disguised as UPS men. FBI Rule Number One: Overwhelming force trumps all. They would've come with about a hundred guys and the Hostage Rescue Team and the dogs and body armor and shit like that. And they just come in and take your ass, case closed." Lee's voice grew calmer as he thought things through. "Now, the guys waiting for you at the gate were FBI." He nodded thoughtfully. "They weren't trying to hide who they were." The other two men at the departure gate? All bets were off. But he knew Faith was very lucky to be alive.

"Oh, and by the way, you're welcome for me saving your butt again. Another few seconds and you're back in FBI land with more questions than you have answers for. Maybe I should've just let them take you," he added wearily.

"Why didn't you?" she asked quietly.

Lee almost felt like laughing. The whole experience was like a dream. *But where do I go to wake up?*

"Right now, lunacy seems to be at the top of the list."

Faith attempted a smile. "Thank God for lunatics."

Lee didn't smile back. "From now on, we are Siamese twins. You better get used to seeing a man take a piss because, lady, we are inseparable from here on."

"Lee—"

"I don't want to hear it! Just don't say a damn thing." His voice was trembling. "I'm so close to punching the shit out of you, I swear to God." He made a big show of reaching over and clamping one big hand over her wrist, as though a living handcuff. Then he sat back, staring at nothing.

Faith didn't try to pull her hand away, not that she could have. And she was really terrified he might take a swing at her. This was probably about as angry as Lee Adams had ever gotten in his entire life, she thought. She finally sat back and tried to calm down. Her heart was beating so fast it seemed impossible for her blood vessels to survive the pressure. Maybe she'd save everyone a lot of trouble and just drop from a coronary.

In Washington you could lie about sex, money, power, loyalties. You could spin falsehoods into truths and simple facts into lies. She had seen it all. It was one of the most frustrating and cruelest places on earth, where one relied on old alliances and quick feet for survival and where every new day, every fresh relationship, could be the one that made you or destroyed you. And Faith had thrived in that world, loved it, in fact. Until now.

Faith could not look at Lee Adams, for fear of what she would see in his eyes. He was all she had. Although she barely knew the man, for some reason she craved his respect, his understanding. She knew she would get neither. She didn't deserve them.

Out of the car window she stared at a plane quickly gaining altitude. In another few seconds it would disappear into the clouds. Soon the passengers would only be able to see that layer of puffy cumulus beneath them, as though the world below had suddenly disappeared. Why couldn't she be on that plane and just keep climbing, to a place where she could start over? Why couldn't a place like that exist? Why?

TWENTY-THREE

B rooke Reynolds sat glumly at the small table, chin resting on her palm, and wondered if anything ever was going to go right on this case. They had found Ken Newman's car. It had been professionally cleansed such that her team of "experts" were unable to provide her with any real clues. She had just checked with the lab. They were still messing around with the tape. Worst of all, Faith Lockhart had slipped right through her fingers. At this rate she'd be FBI director in no time. She was certain there would be a stream of messages from the ADIC on down when she returned to her office, and none of them complimentary, she imagined.

Reynolds and Connie were in a private area at Reagan National. They had thoroughly questioned the airline employee who had sold Faith Lockhart her tickets. They had reviewed all the surveillance tapes and the agent had readily picked out Lockhart. Reynolds assumed the woman was Faith Lockhart. The ticket agent had been shown a picture of Lockhart and was reasonably sure she was the same woman.

If it was Lockhart, she had changed her appearance considerably: a haircut and dye job, from what Reynolds had seen on the airport surveillance tape. And now Lockhart had help. For also captured on the video was a tall, well-built man leaving with Lockhart. Reynolds had initiated the obvious inquiries including checking taxi pickups at the airport during that time. They also had colleagues checking in Norfolk in case the pair had made additional travel arrangements there. So far nothing had turned up. They did, however, have one very promising lead.

Reynolds opened the metal gun case and looked at the SIG-Sauer 9mm while Connie leaned against the wall and scowled at nothing. The gun had already been checked for prints, and they were running the results through the Bureau's databases, but they had something even better: The gun was registered. They had quickly gotten the name and address of the owner from the Virginia State Police.

Reynolds said, "Okay, so the gun's registered to this Lee Adams. We're getting a photo of the guy from DMV. I'm assuming he's the one with Lockhart. What do we know about him so far?"

Connie took a mouthful of Coke from the cup he was holding and popped two Advil. "PI. Been around awhile. Seems very legit. Some of the guys at the Bureau know him in fact. Say he's a good guy. We'll get his picture to the ticket agent. See if she can positive-ID him. That's all for right now. We'll have more soon." He glanced at the gun. "We found shell casings in the woods behind the cottage. They'd been fired from a pistol. Nine-millimeter. From the number we found, the person emptied half his mag at something."

"Think this is the pistol?"

"We haven't found any slugs to match it to, but ballistics will tell us if the pinprick on the shell casings we found match ones fired from that gun," Connie said, referring to the indentation a gun's firing pin makes on the bottom of the shell casing, a mark about as unique as a fingerprint. "And since we've got his ammo, we can test-fire from the source, which is ideal, you know. And we're running a print check on the casings. That won't definitely confirm if Adams was there, since he could've loaded the pistol earlier and someone else could have fired it at the cottage, but it's still something."

They both knew that shell casings were much better surfaces for getting usable prints than a pistol grip.

"It'd be nice if we could get his prints inside the cottage."

"VCU found nothing. Adams obviously knows how to do this stuff. Had to be wearing gloves."

"If ballistics does match, then Adams looks to be the one who wounded the shooter."

"He didn't fire all those times at Ken, that's for sure, and a SIG is for shit long-distance. If Adams was able to hit Ken with a pistol shot from that distance in the dark, then we've got to get him a job at Quantico on the firing range."

Reynolds looked unconvinced.

Connie went on. "And the lab confirmed that the blood in the woods is definitely human. We also found a slug near the spot where all the pistol shell casings were. Struck a tree and stayed there. We also turned up a number of shell casings near the blood. Rifle ordnance. Full metal jacket, heavy-caliber stuff. And customized, no manufacturer's code or caliber stamp on the casings. But the lab did say the ammo used a Berdan primer instead of an American Boxer."

Reynolds looked at him sharply. "Berdan? So European manufacture?"

"There are so many freaky variations these days, but it looks that way."

Reynolds was very familiar with the Berdan primer. It differed from the American version principally in that it had no integral anvil. The anvil was constructed right into the cartridge case, forming a miniature T-shaped projection in the primer pocket with two flash holes to allow the exploded primer to get to the powder. It was a clever, efficient design, Reynolds thought.

When you pulled the trigger of a weapon, Brooke had learned when she joined the Bureau, the firing pin hit the primer cup, compressing the primer between the cup and anvil and causing the primer to explode. This mini-explosion, in turn, shot through the flash holes and ignited the powder to temperatures in excess of five thousand degrees. A millisecond later the bullet went roaring down the gun barrel, and before you could blink, a human being was probably dead. Guns were by far the weapon of choice for murder in America, and Brooke knew that homicide events happened at the rate of fifty-five times a day in the United States. Consequently, Reynolds and her colleagues would never lack for work.

"European-manufactured shells might tie in to the foreign interest angle Lockhart was telling us about," Reynolds said almost to herself. "So Adams and the shooter were going at it and Adams gets the better of it." Reynolds stared thoughtfully at her partner. "Any connection between Adams and Lockhart?"

"None that we can see right now, but we've just started digging."

"Here's another theory, Connie: Adams came out of the woods, killed Ken and then went back through the woods. He could've fallen on something and cut himself. That would account for the blood. I know that doesn't explain the rifle slug, but it's a possibility we can't ignore. For all we know, he was carrying a rifle as well. Or it could have been from a hunter's gun. They hunt in those woods, I bet."

"Come on, Brooke. The guy can't have a gun battle with himself. Remember the two separate piles of different shell casings. And no hunter I know is going to stand there and pump shot after shot at something. They'll kill their buddy or maybe themselves. Most states require plugs in a rifle's magazine to limit shots for that very reason. And those shell casings hadn't been there very long."

"Okay, okay, but I'm just not willing to trust Adams at this point."

"And you think I am? I don't trust my own mother, God rest her soul. But I can't ignore facts either. Lockhart drives away in Ken's car? And Adams just leaves his boots behind before he takes his jaunt through the woods? Come on, you don't believe that."

"Look, Connie, I'm just pointing out the possibilities. I'm not saying I'm sold on any of them. The thing that keeps bugging me is, what spooked Ken? If the shooter's in the woods, it wasn't *him*."

Connie rubbed his jaw. "Now, that's true."

Reynolds suddenly snapped her fingers. "Dammit, the door. How could I have been so blind? When we got to the cottage the screen door was wide open. I remember it clearly. It opens out, so Ken would have seen it when he turned that way. What would he have done? Pull his gun."

"And he might have seen the boots too. It was dark, but the cottage's back porch isn't that big." Connie took another swallow of Coke and rubbed his left temple. "Come on, Advil, do your magic. Well, we'll know for certain if Adams was even there when the lab guys unscramble the video."

"*If* they unscramble it. But why would Adams have been at the cottage in the first place?"

"Maybe someone hired him to shadow Lockhart."

"Buchanan?"

190

"Probably first on my list."

"But if Buchanan hired the shooter to take out Lockhart, why have Adams there to witness it?"

Connie bunched up his thick shoulders and then let them collapse, like a bear scratching itself against a tree. "That for sure doesn't make a helluva lot of sense."

"Well, let me complicate things further for you. Two tickets were purchased by Lockhart for a trip to Norfolk. But only *one* in her real name for the trip to San Francisco."

"And you got Adams running after our guys on the airport surveillance video."

"Think Lockhart tried to give him the slip?"

"Ticket agent said Adams didn't come up to the counter until after Lockhart had purchased the tickets. And the video shows Adams leading her back from the vicinity of the San Francisco gate."

"So maybe an involuntary partnership of sorts," Reynolds said. She had a sudden thought as she looked at Connie. *Like ours, perhaps?* "You know what I'd really like?" Reynolds said. Connie raised his eyebrows. "I'd like to return Mr. Adams's boots. We have his home address?"

"North Arlington. Twenty minutes from here, tops."

Reynolds rose. "Let's go."

TWENTY-FOUR

While Connie parked the car at the curb, Reynolds stared up at the old brownstone. "Adams must do pretty well. This isn't a cheap area."

Connie looked around and said, "Maybe I should sell my house and buy an apartment around here. Stroll around the street, sit in the park, enjoy life."

"Thoughts of retirement creeping in?"

"Seeing Ken in a body bag isn't making me want to do this forever."

They walked up to the front door. Each of them noted the video camera, and then Connie rang the door buzzer.

"Who is it?" a voice fiercely demanded.

"FBI," Reynolds said. "Agents Reynolds and Constantinople."

The door didn't buzz open as they had expected.

"Show me your badges," the elderly voice proclaimed. "Hold them up to the camera."

The two agents looked at each other.

Reynolds smiled. "Let's play nice and do as we're told, Connie."

The pair held up their credentials, or "creds," to the camera. They both carried them the same way: gold badge pinned to the outside of the ID case, so you got the shield first and the picture ID card last. It was intended to be intimidating. And it was. A minute later they heard a door open from inside the building and a woman's face appeared at the glass of the old-fashioned double doors.

"Let me see them again," she said. "My eyes aren't all that good anymore."

"Ma'am—" Connie began hotly until Reynolds elbowed him. They held up their creds again.

The woman scrutinized them and then opened the door.

"I'm sorry," she said as they came in. "But after all the goings-on this morning, I'm about ready to pack my bags and leave for good. And this has been my home for twenty years."

"What goings-on?" Reynolds asked sharply.

The woman eyed her warily. "Who did you come here to see?"

"Lee Adams," Reynolds said.

"I thought so. Well, he's not here."

"Any idea where he might be, Mrs. . . .?"

"Carter. Angie Carter. And no, I don't have any idea where he's got to. Left this morning and I haven't seen him since."

"So what happened this morning?" Connie said. "It was this morning, right?"

Carter nodded. "Fairly early. Just having my coffee when Lee called down and said he wanted me to watch Max because he was going away." They looked at her curiously. "Max is Lee's German shepherd." Her mouth quivered for a moment. "Poor animal."

Reynolds said, "What happened to the dog?"

"They hit him. He'll be okay, but they hurt him."

Connie edged closer to the old woman. "Who hurt him?"

"Ms. Carter, why don't we go into your apartment and sit down?" Reynolds suggested.

The apartment contained old, comfortable furniture, tiny shelves with odd knickknacks placed just so and the aroma of burnt kale and onions.

193

After they were seated, Reynolds said, "Maybe it would be better if you just started at the beginning, and we'll ask questions along the way."

Carter told of how she had agreed to keep Lee's dog. "I do it a lot, Lee's gone a lot. He's a private investigator, you know."

"We know. So he didn't say where he was going? Nothing at all?" Connie prompted.

"Never does. *Private* investigator is just what it means, and Lee was a stickler for that."

"Does he have a separate office somewhere?"

"No, he uses his spare bedroom for an office. He also looks after the building. He's the one who put in the camera outside, sturdy locks on the doors, things like that. Never accepted one penny for it either. Anybody has a problem in the building – the tenants are mostly old, like me – they go to Lee, and he takes care of it."

Reynolds smiled warmly. "Sounds like a nice guy. Go on with your story."

"Well, I had just gotten Max settled when the UPS man came. Saw him out the window. And then Lee called me and said to let Max out."

Reynolds interrupted. "Did he call from the building?"

"Don't know. The connection was a little scratchy, like one of those cellular phones, maybe. But the thing is, I didn't see him leave the building. Guess he could have gone out the back and down the fire escape, though."

"How did he sound?"

Mrs. Carter patted her hands together while she thought. "Well, I guess I have to say he was agitated about something. I was surprised he wanted me to let Max back out. I mean, I had just gotten him settled, like I told you. Lee said he needed to give the dog a shot or something. Now that didn't make any sense to me, but I did what Lee told me and then all hell broke loose after that."

"This UPS man, did you see him?"

Mrs. Carter snorted. "He wasn't the UPS man. I mean, he had on the uniform and everything, but he wasn't our regular UPS person."

"Maybe a replacement. A substitute."

"I've never seen a UPS man carrying a gun before, have you?"

"So you saw a gun?"

She nodded. "When he came running back down the steps. He had a gun in one hand, and his other hand was bleeding. But I'm getting ahead of myself. Before that I heard Max barking like I've never heard him bark before. Then there was a scuffle, could hear it clear as day. Feet stomping, a man yelling, Max's claws on the wood floor. Then I heard a thud and then I heard poor old Max howl. Then somebody started beating on Lee's door. The next thing I know, I hear a bunch of feet going up the fire escape. I looked out the window of my kitchen and saw all these men running up the fire escape. It was like I was watching a TV show. I went back to the front door and looked out my peephole. That's when I saw the UPS man go out the front door. Guess he went around back and joined the others. I'm not sure."

Connie leaned forward in his chair. "Did these other men have any type of uniforms on?"

Mrs. Carter looked at him strangely. "Well, you of all people should know."

Reynolds looked at her, confused. "What do you mean?"

But Mrs. Carter hurried on with her story. "When they knocked the back door in, the alarm went off. The police came right off."

"What happened when the police came?"

"The men were still here. At least some of them were."

"Did the police arrest them?"

"Of course not. The police took Max away and let them keep searching the place."

Reynolds exclaimed, "Do you have any idea why the police let them stay?"

"Same reason I let you in the door."

Reynolds looked in shock at Connie and then back at Carter and said, "You mean—"

"I mean," Carter broke in testily, "they were the FBI."

TWENTY-FIVE

"What exactly are we doing here, Lee?" Faith asked. They had taken two other cabs after the one from the airport. The last taxi had dropped them off in what seemed like the middle of nowhere, and they had been walking along back streets now for what seemed like several miles.

Lee glanced at her. "Rule number one when running from the law: Assume they'll find the cabbie or cabbies who dropped you off. So you never let a cabbie drop you off at your real destination." He pointed up ahead. "We're almost there." As he walked along, Lee put his hands up to his eyes and popped out the contact lenses, returning his eyes to their normal blue. He put the lenses away in a special case in his bag. "Those suckers kill my eyes."

Faith stared ahead but saw nothing other than run-down homes, cracked sidewalks and sickly-looking trees and lawns. They were traveling parallel to U.S. Route 1 in Virginia, also known as Jefferson Davis Highway after the president of the Confederacy. It was ironic they were here, Faith thought, since Davis himself knew very well about being chased. In fact he had been chased all over the South after the war until the boys in blue had finally caught up with him and Davis had served a long prison term. Faith knew the history, she just didn't want the same result.

She didn't ordinarily come to this part of northern

Virginia. It was heavily industrialized, speckled with on-the-fringe small businesses, truck and boat repair shops, shady-looking car dealerships working out of rusted trailers, and a flea market housed in a decrepit building one failing support beam from condemnation. She was a little surprised when Lee turned and headed for Jeff Davis. She hurried to stay up with him.

"Shouldn't we be getting out of town? I mean, according to you, the FBI can do anything. And then there's the other people you refused to name who are on our track. I'm sure they're incredibly deadly in their own right. And here we are strolling through the suburbs." Lee said nothing and she finally grabbed his arm. "Lee, will you please tell me what's going on?"

He stopped so abruptly she bumped into him. It was like hitting a wall.

Lee glared at her. "Call me stupid, but I just can't shake the feeling that the more information you have, the more likely you'll get another harebrained idea in your head that'll end up getting us both checked into coffins."

"Look, I'm sorry about the airport. You're right, it was stupid. But I had my reasons."

"Your reasons are bullshit. Your whole life is bullshit," he said angrily, and started walking again.

She hurried up next to him, jerked on his arm and they squared off.

"Okay, if you really feel like that, what do you say we just go our separate ways? Here and now. Each take our chances."

He put his hands on his hips. "Because of you I can't go home and I can't use my credit card. I don't have my gun, the Feds are right on my butt and I've got four bucks in my wallet. Let me just jump right on that offer, lady."

"You can have half my cash."

"And where exactly are you going to go?"

"My whole life might be bullshit, and this may shock you, but I *can* take care of myself."

He shook his head. "We stick together. For a lot of reasons. Number one being when and if the Feds pick us up, I want you right there next to me swearing on your mother's grave that yours truly is just an innocent babe stuck in the middle of *your* nightmare."

"Lee!"

"Discussion closed."

He started walking fast and Faith decided against saying anything else. The truth was she didn't *want* to go it alone. She jogged up to him as they turned on to Route 1. At the light they hurried across the street.

"I want you to wait here," Lee said, putting the bags down. "There's a chance I might get recognized where I'm going, and I don't want you with me."

Faith looked around. Behind her was an eight-foot-high chain-link fence with barbed wire on the top. It housed a boat repair facility. Inside the fence a Doberman patrolled the area. Did boats really require that much security? she wondered. Maybe in this area everything did. The business on the next corner was located inside an ugly cinder-block building with big red banners across the windows proclaiming the best deals in town on new and used motorcycles. The parking lot was filled with the two-wheeled machines.

"Do I *have* to stay here by myself?" she said.

Lee pulled out a baseball cap from his bag and put on his sunglasses. "Yes," he said curtly. "Or was that a ghost back there telling me she can take care of herself?"

With no snappy reply coming to mind, Faith had to content herself with angrily watching as Lee hurried across the street and into the motorcycle shop. As she waited, she suddenly sensed a presence behind her. When she turned, she was staring directly at the large Doberman. It had wandered out of the yard. Apparently the boat yard's tight security didn't include closing the damn gate! When the animal showed its teeth and uttered a low, terrifying growl, Faith slowly reached down and gripped the bags. Holding them in front of her, she backed across the street and into the parking lot of the motorcycle shop. The Dobie lost interest in her and went back inside the boat yard.

Faith breathed a sigh of relief and put down the bags. She noted a couple of fleshy teenagers sporting sparse goatees checking out a used Yamaha at the same time they were ogling her. She pulled her baseball cap down farther, turned away and pretended to examine a shiny red Kawasaki that was, surprise, on sale. Across Jeff Davis was a business that leased heavy construction equipment. She looked at a crane that rose a good thirty feet in the air. Dangling from its cable was a small forklift that had a sign painted across it that read, RENT ME. Everywhere she looked was a world she no longer knew much about. She had traveled a much different circuit: capital cities of the world, high political stakes, demanding clients, enormous amounts of power and money, all perpetually shifting like the continental plates. Things got crushed in between these masses all the time, and no one even knew it. She suddenly realized that the *real* world was a two-ton forklift dangling like a guppy on a string. Rent me. Employ people. Build something.

But Danny had given her a shot at redemption. She was a dime a dozen, yet she had been doing some good in the world. For ten years now she had been helping people who desperately needed it. Perhaps also these ten years she'd been atoning for the vicarious guilt she'd felt growing up, watching her father's shenanigans, however well intentioned, and all the pain they had caused. She had actually been afraid to ever analyze that part of her life too deeply.

Faith heard footsteps behind her and turned around. The man was dressed in jeans, black boots and a sweatshirt with the logo of the motorcycle shop printed across it. He was young, early twenties, big, sleepy eyes, tall, slender and good-looking. And he knew it, she could readily tell, by his cocky manner. His expression clearly evidenced that his interest in Faith was deeper than her choice in two-wheeled transportation.

"Can I help you with anything, ma'am? Anything at all?"

"Just browsing. I'm waiting for my boyfriend."

"Hey, this is a pretty machine over here." He pointed to a BMW cycle that just reeked, even to Faith's untrained eye, of money. Wasted money, in her opinion. But then again, wasn't she the proud owner of a big BMW sedan, which sat in the garage of her very expensive digs in McLean?

He rubbed one hand slowly across the Beemer's gas tank. "Purrs like a kitten. You take care of beautiful things, they take good care of you. Real good." A big smile broke across his features as he said this. He looked her over and winked.

Faith wondered if this was his best pickup line.

"I don't drive them, I just ride on them," she said casually, and then regretted her choice of words.

He smiled broadly. "Well, that's the best news I've heard all day. In fact, you just made my whole year. Just ride 'em, huh?" The young man laughed and clapped his hands together. "Well, how about we go for a spin, sweet thing? You can check out *my* equipment. Just climb on."

Her face flashed. "I don't appreciate your—"

"Now, don't go getting mad. If you need anything, my name's Rick." He held out his card and winked at her again. He added in a low voice, "Home phone's on the back, babe."

She looked at the card in his hand with distaste. "Okay, Rick, but I like full disclosure. My boyfriend is inside. Are you man enough to meet him?"

Rick didn't look so comfortable now. "I'm man enough for anything, babe."

"Good to hear. My boyfriend is inside. He's about your height, but he's got a real man's body."

The hand holding the card dropped to Rick's side as he scowled at her. Faith easily sensed that his pat lines had been forgotten and his mind was too slow to think of new ones.

Faith eyed him closely. "Yeah, his shoulders are about the size of Nebraska, and did I mention he's an ex-Navy boxing champ?"

"Is that right?" Rick pocketed his card.

"Don't take my word for it; he's right there. Go ahead and ask him." She pointed behind him.

Rick whirled around and watched as Lee came out of the building carrying two helmets and two one-piece riding suits. A map was stuffed into his front jacket pocket. Even under the bulky clothes he was wearing, Lee's impressive build was very apparent. He glared suspiciously at Rick.

"Do I know you?" Lee asked him gruffly.

Rick smiled uneasily and then swallowed with difficulty as he looked Lee over. "N-no, sir," he stammered.

"Then what the hell do you want, kid?"

Faith piped in, "Oh, he was just asking me the sorts of things I liked in my riding equipment, right,

Ricky?" She smiled at the young salesman.

"That's right. Yep. Well, see ya." Rick practically ran toward the shop.

"Bye-bye, sweet thing," Faith called after him.

Lee scowled at her. "I told you to wait across the street. Can I not leave you alone for one damn minute?"

"I had an encounter with a Dobie. Retreat seemed the wisest course."

"Right. What, were you negotiating with the guy to jump me so you can get away?"

"Don't get crazy on me, Lee."

"I kind of wished you had. It'd give me an excuse to kick the shit out of somebody. What'd he really want?"

"Junior wanted to sell me something, and it wasn't a motorcycle. What's that?" she asked, pointing at what he was carrying.

"Necessary equipment for motorcycle riders this time of year. At sixty miles an hour, there's a tiny bite in the air."

"We don't have a motorcycle."

"We do now."

She followed him around back to where an enormous Honda Gold Wing SE road bike sat. With its slick chrome and futuristic design, high-tech equipment and full windshield, the motorcycle looked like something Batman might tool around on. It was painted pearl-gray-green with dark gray green trim and had a king and queen seat with a padded backrest. The passenger would fit snugly there, like a ball in a glove. It was so big and elaborately equipped that it looked like an open-air recreational vehicle.

Lee stuck a key in the ignition and started putting on his suit. He handed the other outfit to Faith.

"Just where are we going on this thing?"

Lee zipped up his suit. "*We* are going to your little place in North Carolina."

"All that way on a motorcycle?"

"We can't rent a car without a credit card and ID. Your car and mine are useless. We can't take a train, plane or bus. They'll cover all those places. Unless you can sprout wings, this is it."

"I've never even been on a motorcycle."

He took off his shades. "You don't have to drive it. That's what I'm here for. So what do you say? Want to go for a ride?" He flashed a grin at her.

Faith felt as though a brick had hit her in the head when he said those words. Her skin was afire as she looked at him perched on that machine. And at that exact moment, as though by the will of God, the sun broke through the gloom. A shaft of light came down and ignited those already dazzling blue eyes into flame-filled sapphires. She found she couldn't move. Lord, she could barely breathe; her knees began to quiver.

It was fifth grade, recess. The boy with the man-size eyes the exact color of Lee's had ridden his bike with the banana seat up to where she sat on the swing reading a book.

"Want to go for a ride?" he had asked her. "No," she had said, and then immediately dropped her book and climbed on back. They were an "item" for two months, planning their lives together, vowing their undying love for each other, even though they never exchanged so much as a peck on the lips. Then her mother died, and Faith's father moved them away. She briefly wondered if Lee and he could be one and the same. She had banished the memory so completely from her subconscious that she couldn't even remember the boy's name. It could be Lee, couldn't it? She thought this because the only other time in her entire life when her knees had gone weak was on that playground. The boy had said what Lee had just said, and the sun had hit those eyes just as it had smacked Lee's, and her heart felt as though it would explode if she didn't do exactly as he said. Just how it felt right now.

"Are you okay?" Lee asked.

Faith gripped one of the handlebars to steady herself, and said as calmly as she could, "And they're just going to let you drive off with it?"

"My brother runs the place. It's a demo. We're officially taking it for an extended test drive."

"I can't believe I'm doing this." Just like fifth grade, there was no way she could not get on that bike.

"Consider the alternative, and then the idea of your butt on this Honda starts looking beautiful." He slid his shades on and flipped his helmet's shield down as though putting an exclamation point on this statement.

Faith slipped on the suit, and with Lee's help managed to get the helmet on snugly. He loaded their bags into the Honda's spacious trunk and saddle pouches, and Faith climbed on behind him. He started the engine, gunned it for a moment or so and then hit the gas. When he released the clutch, the power of the Honda threw Faith back against the padded bar and she found herself clamping her arms and legs around Lee and the eight-hundred-pound motorcycle, respectively, as they rocketed on to Jeff Davis heading south.

She almost jumped off the bike when she heard the voice in her ear.

"Okay, calm down, it's a Chatterbox helmet-to-helmet audio link," Lee's voice said. He'd obviously felt her shock. "You ever driven down to your beach house?"

"No, I always flew."

"That's okay. I've got a map. We'll take 95 down and pick up Interstate 64 at Richmond. That'll get us to Norfolk. We'll figure out the best way from there. We'll grab something to eat on the way. We should make it before it gets too dark. Okay?"

She found herself nodding and then remembered to say, "Okay."

"Now, just sit back and relax. You're in good hands."

Instead, she leaned into him, circled her arms around his waist and held tightly. She was suddenly immersed in the recollection of those divine two months in fifth grade. This had to be an omen. Maybe they could drive off and never come back. Start at the Outer Banks, hire a boat and end up on a patch of soil somewhere in the Caribbean no one had ever been before, a place no one would ever see except for them. She could learn to keep a hut, cook with coconut milk or whatever they had there, be a good little homemaker while Lee was off catching fish. They could make love every night under the moonlight and there would be no one to complain. Or watch. She leaned farther into him. None of that sounded bad. Or too far-fetched, under the circumstances. None of it.

"Oh, and Faith?" Lee said into her ear.

She touched her helmet to his, felt the solid breadth of his torso against her breasts. She was twenty again, the wind was delicious, the warmth of the sun inspiring, her greatest worry a midterm exam. A sudden vision of them lying naked under the sky, skin brown, hair wet, limbs intertwined, made her wish they weren't in body suits with thick zippers, going sixty miles an hour over hard pavement.

"Yes?"

"If you even think about trying to pull another

206

stunt on me like at the airport, I'll use those good hands to wring your neck. Understand?"

She leaned away from him and rested her back against the sissy bar, pushing herself deep into the leather. And away from him. Her shining white knight with the bedeviling blue eyes.

So much for memories. So much for dreams.

TWENTY-SIX

The event was typical of Washington: A political fund-raising dinner at a downtown hotel. The chicken was stringy and cold, the wine cheap, the conversation high-powered, the stakes enormous, the protocol tricky, the egos often impossible. The attendees were either wealthy and/or well connected, or underpaid political staffers who worked long, frantic hours during the day and were rewarded for these prodigious efforts by being compelled to work these sorts of events at night. The Secretary of the Treasury was supposed to have attended, along with some other political heavyweights; even since he had become engaged to a well-known Hollywood actress with a thing about exhibiting her cleavage at the drop of an intern, the secretary had been more in demand than the keeper of the cash normally was. Then, at the last minute, he had gotten a better offer to speak at another event, which was often the case in the endless game of "where is the political grass greener?" An underling had been sent in his place, a gawky, nervous person no one really knew or cared about.

The event was another opportunity to see and be seen, to check the ever-changing pecking order of a certain subgroup of the political hierarchy. Most never even sat down to eat. They just dropped off their check and then it was off to another fundraiser. Networking flowed through the room as though from a well-fed spring. Or open wound, depending on how one looked at it.

Danny Buchanan surveyed the room. How many of these events had he attended over the years? During the frenzy of key fund-raising periods when he used to represent Big Business, Buchanan would attend breakfasts, luncheons, dinners and assorted parties nonstop for weeks. Exhausted, he had sometimes shown up at the wrong event – a reception for the senator from North Dakota instead of a dinner for the South Dakota congressman. After taking over for the world's poor, he had no such problems, for the simple fact that he now had no money to give members. However, Buchanan was well aware that if there was one truism in political fund-raising, it was that there was never enough money. And that meant that there would *always* be the opportunity for influence peddling. Always.

After he got back from Philly, his day had really started. He had met with half a dozen different members on the Hill and their staff on a myriad of matters, and set up appointments for future meetings. Staffs were important, particularly com-mittee staff, especially appropriations committee staff. Members came and went. The staff tended to stay forever; they knew the issues and process cold. And Danny knew that you never wanted to surprise a member by trying to dodge the staff. You might be successful once, but you were dead after that, as the angry aides took their revenge by shutting you completely out.

A late luncheon followed, with a paying client whom Faith had typically taken care of. Buchanan had had to make excuses for her absence, and he did so with his usual aplomb and humor. "Sorry, you get the second string today," he told the client. "But I'll try not to mess things up too badly for you."

Though there was no need to bolster Faith's

excellent reputation, Buchanan had recounted to this client the story of how Faith had once personally hand-delivered – in a gift box with a big red ribbon, no less – to all five hundred and thirty-five members of Congress detailed polling data that showed the American public was fully in support of funding for global vaccination of all children. She'd included in the gift box accompanying briefing materials and before-and-after photos of vaccinated children from distant lands. Sometimes pictures were the most important weapons Danny and she had. Then she had worked the phone for thirty-six hours straight enlisting support here and overseas and made exhaustive presentations with several of the larger international relief organizations over a two-week period on three continents to show just how such a thing could be accomplished. How important it was. The result: passage of a bill in Congress that supported a study to determine if such an endeavor could work. Now consultants would rack up millions of dollars in fees and kill several forests of trees for the mountains of paper the study would generate (to justify the enormous consulting fees, of course), with no assurances that a single child would receive a single dose of vaccine.

"A small success, to be sure, but a step forward," Buchanan had told the client. "When Faith goes after something, stay out of her way." The client already knew this about Faith, Buchanan was aware. Perhaps he was just saying it to bolster his own spirits. Perhaps he just wanted to talk about Faith. He had been hard on her the last year, very hard. Terrified that she would be drawn into his Thornhillian nightmare, he had outright pushed her away. Well, he had succeeded in driving her right into the arms of the FBI, it seemed. *I'm sorry, Faith.*

After the luncheon it was back to the Hill, where

Buchanan waited with a handful of Rolaids on a series of floor votes. He sent in his cards to the floor asking for time from some of the members. He would buttonhole others as they came off the elevator.

"Foreign debt relief is essential, Senator," he individually told more than a dozen members, hustling along beside them and their overly protective entourage. "They're spending more on debt payments than on health and education," Danny would plead. "What good is a strong balance sheet when the population is dying at the rate of ten percent a year? They'll have great credit and not a damn person left to use it. Let's spread the wealth here."

"Right, right, Danny, we'll get back to you. Send me some materials." Like the petals of a flower closing up for the night, the entourage would close ranks around the member, and Danny the bee would be off to gather other nectar.

Congress was an ecosystem just as complicated as the one existing in the oceans. As Danny trolled the corridors, he looked at the activity swirling all around. True to their titles, whips were everywhere prodding members to follow party line. Back in the whip's chamber, Buchanan knew the phones were constantly being worked with the same goal in mind. Gofers scurried down the corridors in search of people more important than themselves. Small groups of people huddled in pockets of the broad hallways, discussing matters of importance with solemn, downcast expressions. Men and women pushed on to crowded elevators with the hope of snaring a few precious seconds with a member whose support they desperately needed. Members talked with each other, laying the groundwork for future deals or reaffirming agreements already struck. It was all chaotic and yet possessed a certain order, as people coupled and uncoupled like robotic arms around hunks of metal on an assembly line. Give a touch here and on to the next one. Danny dared to think that his work might be as exhausting as childbirth; and he would swear it was more exhilarating than skydiving. Buchanan was thoroughly addicted to it. As crazy as it sounded, he would miss it.

"Get back to me?" was his typical closing to each member's aide.

"Of course, you can count on it," would be each aide's typical response.

And, of course, he'd never hear back. But they would hear from him. Again and again, until they got it. You just fired your shotgun pellets and hoped one stuck somewhere.

Next, Buchanan had spent a few minutes with one of his "chosen few," going over the language Buchanan wanted to insert in a line amendment in a bill's report. Almost no one ever read the report language, but it was in the monotonous details that important actions were accomplished. In this case, the language would tell the managers at AID precisely how funding approved by the underlying bill was to be spent.

With the verbiage in good shape, Buchanan mentally checked that off his list and went prowling again for other members. From years of practice, Buchanan navigated with ease the labyrinths of the Senate and House office buildings where even veterans of the Hill sometimes became lost. The only other place where he spent as much time was the Capitol itself. His eyes darted left and right, picking up on everyone he saw, staff members or other lobbyists, swiftly making a calculation as to whether a particular person could help the cause or not. And when you went into chambers with members or caught them in the halls, you had better be ready to roll. They were busy, often harassed, and thinking of five hundred things at once.

Fortunately, Buchanan could summarize the most complex issues in a matter of sentences, a talent for which he was legendary; members, besieged on all sides by special interests of every kind, absolutely demanded this skill. And he could pitch his client's position with passion. All in two minutes while walking down a crowded corridor or while packed inside an elevator or, if he was very lucky, on a long plane flight. Catching the really powerful members was important. If he could get the Speaker of the House to voice support for one of his bills, even informally, Buchanan would use that to leverage other members on the fence. Sometimes that was enough.

"He in, Doris?" Buchanan asked as he popped his head into a member's chambers and eyed the matronly appointments secretary, a veteran of the place.

"He's leaving in five minutes to catch a flight, Danny."

"That's great because I only need two minutes. I can use the other three to catch up with you. I like talking to you better anyway. And God bless Steve, but you're far easier on the eye, my dear."

Doris's heavy face crinkled into a smile. "You smoothie, you."

And he got his two minutes with Congressman Steve.

Buchanan next had stopped at the cloakroom and found out which Senate committees had been assigned to a series of bills he was interested in. There were committees of primary and sequential and, in rare cases, concurrent jurisdiction, depending on what was in a particular bill. Simply

213

determining who had what bill and in what priority of importance was a huge, ever-changing jigsaw puzzle that lobbyists had to constantly figure out. It was often a maddening challenge, and there was no one better at it than Danny Buchanan.

In the course of this day Buchanan had, as always, plied members' offices with his "leave behinds," information and summaries the staff would need to educate their members on the issues. If they had a question or concern, he would find an answer or an expert, promptly. And Buchanan had concluded every single meeting with the all-important question: "When can I follow up?" Without getting a date certain, he would never hear back from any of them. He would be forgotten, his place taken by a hundred others clamoring just as passionately for their clients.

Then he had spent the late afternoon covering other clients normally handled by Faith. He gave apologies and vague explanations for her absence. What else could he do?

After that he gave remarks at a think-tank-sponsored seminar on world hunger, and then it was back to his office to make phone calls ranging from reminding members' staffs of a variety of issues coming up for vote, to drumming up coalition support from other charitable organizations. A couple of dinners were arranged, future overseas travel booked, along with a visit in January to the White House, where he would personally introduce the President to the new head of an international children's right organization. It was a real coup that Buchanan and the organizations he supported hoped would generate some good publicity. They were constantly on the lookout for celebrity support. Faith had been particularly good at that. Journalists were rarely interested in the poor from faraway

214

lands, but throw in a Hollywood superstar and the media room would be bustling with scribes. Such was life.

Then Buchanan had spent some time doing his FARA – or Foreign Agent Registration Act – quarterly reports, which were a real pain in the ass, particularly since you had to stamp every page filed with Congress with the ominous label "foreign propaganda," as if you were Tokyo Rose calling for the overthrow of the U.S. government, instead of, in Danny's case, selling his soul to get crop seeds and powdered milk.

After bending a few more ears on the phone, then studying a few hundred pages of briefing materials, he had decided to call it a day. A glamorous day in the life of a typical Washington lobbyist, which usually ended with him collapsing into bed, except that today he did not have that luxury. Instead, he was here in this downtown hotel, attending yet another political fund-raiser, and the reason was standing in the far corner of the room sipping a glass of white wine and looking extremely bored. Buchanan headed over.

"You look like you could use something stronger than white wine."

Senator Russell Ward turned and a smile broke across his face as he looked at Buchanan. "It's good to see an honest face in this sea of iniquity, Danny."

"How about we trade this place for the Monocle?"

Ward put his glass down on a table. "Best offer I've had all day."

TWENTY-SEVEN

The Monocle was a restaurant of longstanding on Capitol Hill's Senate side. The restaurant, and the U.S. Capitol Police building, which itself used to be an Immigration and Naturalization building, were the only two structures left in this location that formerly housed a long row of buildings. The Monocle was a favorite place for politicians, lobbyists and VIPs to gather for lunch, dinner and drinks.

The maître d' welcomed Buchanan and Ward by name and ushered the pair to a private corner table. The decor was conservative, the walls adorned with enough photographs of past and present politicians to fill the Washington Monument. The food was good, yet people didn't come for the delights of the menus; they came to be seen, do business and talk shop. Ward and Buchanan were regulars here.

They ordered drinks and perused the menu for a moment.

As Ward studied his menu, Buchanan studied him.

Russell Ward had been called Rusty for as long as Buchanan could remember. And that was a long time, since the two had grown up together. As chairman of the Senate Select Committee on Intelligence, Ward was a powerful influence on the well-being – or not – of all the country's intelligence agencies. He was smart, politically savvy, honest, hard-working, and he came from a very wealthy

northeast family that had lost its fortune when Ward
was a young man. He had gone south to Raleigh and
methodically built himself a career in public service.
He was North Carolina's senior senator and
worshipped by the entire state. Under Buchanan's
classification system, Rusty Ward would be
absolutely labeled a "Believer." He was familiar
with every political game ever played. Ward knew
all the inside stories on everyone in this town. He
knew people's strengths and, more important, their
weaknesses. Physically, the man was a wreck,
Buchanan knew, with problems ranging from
diabetes to the prostate. Yet mentally, Ward was
sharp as ever. Those who underestimated the man's
massive intellect because of the physical ailments
had all lived to regret it.

Ward looked up from his menu. "Anything
interesting on your plate these days, Danny?"

Ward's voice was deep and sonorous, and so
wonderfully southern, all traces of clipped Yankee
long gone. Buchanan could sit and listen to the man
for hours. And he had done so on many occasions.

Buchanan replied, "Same old, same old. You?"

"Had an interesting hearing this morning. Senate
Intelligence. CIA."

"Is that right?"

"You ever hear of a gentleman by the name of
Thornhill? Robert Thornhill?"

Buchanan's features were impassive. "Can't say
that I know the man at all. Tell me about him."

"He's one of the old powers there. Associate DDO.
Smart, cunning, lies his ass off with the best of them.
I don't trust him."

"Doesn't sound like you should."

"I have to give the man his due though. He's done
terrific work, outlasted numerous CIA directors.
Really served his country extraordinarily well. He's

217

actually a legend over there. They let him do more or less what he wants because of that. Such a policy, however, is dangerous."

"Really? He sounds like a real patriot."

"That's what worries me. People who believe themselves to be true patriots tend to be zealots. Zealots, in my opinion, are one short step from lunatics. History has given us enough examples of that." Ward grinned. "I remember this one time he came in to deliver the usual bullshit. He looked so smug I decided I had to tweak him a little."

Buchanan looked very interested. "How'd you do that?"

"I asked him about death squads." Ward paused and looked around for a moment. "We've had problems with the CIA over that in the past. They fund these little insurgency groups, outfit and train 'em, then turn 'em loose, like an old coon dog. Then, unlike a good coon dog, they go and do things they weren't supposed to be doing. At least according to the official agency rules."

"What'd he say to that?"

"Well, it wasn't part of his little script. He looked through his briefing book like he was attempting to shake out a small band of armed men." Ward laughed deeply. "Then he threw me some gobbledy-gook that really amounted to nothing. Said that the 'new' CIA was merely a collector and analyzer of information. When I asked him if he was conceding that there was something wrong with the 'old' CIA, I thought he might come over the table at me." Ward laughed again. "Same old, same old."

"So what's he up to now that's got you ticked off?"

Ward smiled. "Trying to get me to reveal confidences?"

"Of course."

Ward glanced around again and then leaned

218

forward and spoke quietly. "He was withholding information, what else? You know the spooks, Danny, they want more and more funding but when you start to ask questions about what they're doing with that money, Jesus, it's like you killed their mother. But what else am I going to do when I'm presented with reports from the CIA's inspector general that have so many damn redactions the paper looks black? So I brought that fact to Mr. Thornhill's attention."

"How did he react to that? Pissed off? Cool and collected?"

"Why are you so curious about him?"

"You started it, Rusty. Don't blame me if I find your work fascinating."

"Well, he said those reports had to be censored to protect the identities of intelligence sources. That it was a very fine line and that the CIA walked it the best it could. I told him that it was kind of like my granddaughter playing hopscotch. She can't hit all the squares just right, so she misses some of them on purpose. I told him it was damn cute. When *little kids* did it.

"Now, I have to give the man his due. He made some sense. He said that it's a delusion that we're going to knock out entrenched dictators with simple satellite photos and high-speed modems. We need old-fashioned assets on the ground. We need people inside their organizations, within their inner circles. That's the only way we win. I understand that well enough. But the arrogance of the man, well, it gets to me. And I'm convinced that even if Robert Thornhill had no reason to lie, the man still wouldn't tell the truth. Hell, he has this little system where he taps his pen against the table and one of his aides pretends to whisper in his ear so he'll have a couple extra breaths to think of some lie. He's been using that same code all these years. I guess he thinks I'm some kind of horse's ass and wouldn't ever catch on."

"I'd like to think this Thornhill fellow knows better than to underestimate you."

"Oh, he's good. I have to admit he got the better of today's jousting. I mean, the man can say absolutely nothing and make it sound as strong and noble as the Ten Commandments. And when he got backed into a corner, he pulled out his national security bullshit counting on the fact that it would scare everybody to death. Bottom line: He promised me all these answers. And I told him I looked forward to working with him." Ward sipped his water. "Yep, he won today. But there's always tomorrow."

The waiter returned with their drinks and they gave their orders. Buchanan worked on a glass of Scotch and water while Ward nuzzled a bourbon, neat.

"So how's your better half? Faith burning the midnight oil for another client looking to ravage us poor, defenseless elected officials?"

"Actually, right now I believe she's out of town. Personal reasons."

"Nothing serious, I hope."

Buchanan shrugged. "Jury's still out on that. I'm sure she'll pull through."

"I guess we're all survivors. I don't know how much longer this tired old carcass of mine will hold out, though."

Buchanan raised his drink. "Outlive us all, word of Danny Buchanan."

"God, I hope not." Ward looked at him keenly. "It's hard to believe that it's been forty years since we left Bryn Mawr. You know, sometimes I envy you having grown up in that apartment over our garage."

Buchanan smiled. "Funny, I was jealous of you for

growing up in the mansion with all that money while my family waited on yours. Now which of us sounds drunk?"

"You're the best friend I ever had."

"And you know that sentiment is reciprocated, Senator."

"It's even more remarkable that you've never asked me for a damn thing. You damn well know I sit on a couple committees that could help your causes."

"I like to avoid the appearance of impropriety."

"You must be the only one in this town." Ward chuckled.

"Let's just say our friendship is more important to me than even that."

Ward spoke softly. "I never told you, but what you said at my mother's funeral touched me deeply. I swear, I think you knew the woman better than I did."

"She was a class act. Taught me all I ever needed to know about everything. She deserved a grand sendoff. What I said didn't come close by half."

Ward stared into his glass. "If my stepfather could have only lived off my family's inheritance and not tried to play businessman we might have kept the estate, and he wouldn't have taken his head off with a shotgun. But then maybe I wouldn't have gotten to play senator all these years if I'd had a trust fund to blow."

"If more people played the game the way you do, Rusty, the country would be far better off."

"I wasn't fishing for a compliment, but I appreciate you saying it."

Buchanan drummed his fingers against the table. "I drove out to the old place the other day."

Ward looked up, surprised. "Why?"

Buchanan shrugged. "Not really sure. I was close

221

by, I had some time. It hasn't changed much. Still beautiful."

"I haven't been there since I left for college. Don't even know who owns it now."

"A young couple. I saw the wife and kids through the gate, playing on the front lawn. Investment banker or Internet mogul, probably. An idea and ten bucks in his pocket yesterday, a red-hot company and a hundred million in stock today."

Ward lifted his glass. "God bless America."

"If I had had the money back then, your mother wouldn't have lost that house."

"I know that, Danny."

"But everything happens for a reason, Rusty. Like you said, you might not have gone into politics. You've had a grand career. You're a Believer."

Ward smiled. "Your little classification system has always intrigued me. You have it all written down somewhere? I'd like to compare it with my own conclusions about my distinguished colleagues."

Buchanan tapped his forehead. "It's all up here."

"All that gold, stored in one man's brain. What a pity."

"You know everything about everybody in this town too." Buchanan paused and then added quietly, "So what do you know about me?"

Ward seemed surprised by the question.

"Don't tell me the world's greatest lobbyist is having self-doubt? I thought the book on Daniel J. Buchanan was unshakable confidence, encyclopedic mind and a keen insight into the psychology of windbag politicians and their innate weaknesses, which could fill the Pacific, by the way."

"Everybody has doubts, Rusty, even people like you and me. That's why we last so long. One inch from the edge. Death at any minute if you let down your guard."

The way he said this made Ward drop his amused look. "You got something you'd like to talk about?"

"Not in a million years," Buchanan said with a sudden smile. "If I start telling the sorry likes of you all my secrets, then I'll have to take my lemonade stand somewhere else and start over. And I'm way too old for that."

Ward leaned back against the soft cushion and looked his friend over. "What makes you do it, Danny? Not money, surely."

Buchanan slowly nodded in agreement. "If I did it solely for the dollars, I would've been gone ten years ago." He swallowed the rest of his drink and looked over at the doorway, where the ambassador from Italy and his substantial entourage stood, along with several senior Hill staffers, a couple of senators and three women in short black dresses who looked like they had been rented for the evening, and very well might have been. The Monocle was filling up with so many VIPs now you could hardly spit without nailing some leader of something. And they all wanted the world. And they all wanted you to get it for them. Eat you up and leave nothing and then call you a friend. Buchanan knew all the lyrics to that song.

He looked up at an old photograph on the wall. A bald-headed man with a beak nose, dour look and ferocious eyes peered down at him. Long dead now, he had once been one of the most powerful men in Washington for decades. And most feared. Power and fear seemed to go hand in hand here. Now Buchanan couldn't even remember the man's name. Didn't that speak volumes.

Ward put down his glass. "I think I know. Your causes have become much more benevolent over the years. You're out to save a world few even care

223

about. You're really the only lobbyist I know who does it."

Buchanan shook his head. "A poor Irish lad who brought himself up by the bootstraps and made a fortune sees the light and then uses his golden years helping the less fortunate? Hell, Rusty, I'm driven more by fear than altruism."

Ward looked at him curiously. "How's that?"

Buchanan sat up very straight, put his palms together and cleared his throat. He had never told anyone this. Not even Faith. Maybe it was time. He would look insane, of course, but at least Rusty would keep it to himself.

"I have this recurring dream, you see. In my dream America keeps getting richer and richer, fatter and fatter. Where an athlete gets a hundred million dollars to bounce a ball, a movie star earns twenty million to act in trash and a model gets ten million to walk around in her underwear. Where a nineteen-year-old can make a billion dollars in stock options by using the Internet to sell us more things we don't need faster than ever." Buchanan stopped and smiled grimly at his bread plate. "And where a lobbyist can earn enough to buy his own plane. We keep hoarding the wealth of the world. Anybody gets in the way, we crush them, in a hundred different ways, while selling them the message of America the Beautiful. The world's remaining superpower, right?

"Then, little by little, the rest of the world wakes up and sees us for what we are: a fraud. And they start coming for us. In log boats and propeller planes and God knows how else. First by the thousands, then by the millions and then by the billions. And they wipe us out. Stuff us all down some pipe and flush us for good. You, me, the ballplayers, the movie stars, the supermodels, Wall Street,

Hollywood and Washington. The true land of make believe."

Ward stared at him wide eyed. "My God, a dream or a nightmare?"

Buchanan shot him a stern glance. "You tell me."

"Your country, love it or leave it, Danny. There's an element of truth in that slogan. We're not so bad."

"We also suck up a disproportionate share of the wealth and energy in the world. We pollute more than any other country. We trash foreign economies and never look back. But still, for a lot of big and small reasons that I really can't explain, I do love my country. That's why this nightmare disturbs me so much. *I don't want it to happen*. But it's getting harder and harder to feel any hope."

"If that's the case, why *do* you do it?"

Buchanan stared at the old photograph again and said, "Do you want something pithy or philosophical?"

"How about the truth?"

Buchanan looked at his old friend. "I deeply regret never having children," he began slowly, then paused. "A good friend of mine has a dozen grandchildren. He was telling me about a PTA meeting he had attended at his granddaughter's elementary school. I asked him why he was bothering with doing that. Wasn't that the parents' job? I said. You know what he told me? He said that with the way the world is now, we all have to think about things beyond our lifetime. Beyond our children's lifetime, in fact. It's our right. It's our duty, my good friend told me."

Buchanan smoothed out his napkin. "So maybe I do what I do because the sum of the world's tragedies outweighs its happiness.

"Other than that, I haven't the faintest idea."

TWENTY-EIGHT

Brooke Reynolds was just finished saying grace, and they all started on their meals. She had burst through the door ten minutes earlier, determined to eat dinner with her family. Her regular hours at the Bureau were eight-fifteen A.M. to five P.M. That was the funniest joke at the Bureau: regular hours. She had changed into jeans and a sweatshirt and exchanged her suede flats for Reeboks. Reynolds took much pleasure in scooping out spoonfuls of peas and mashed potatoes for all their plates. Rosemary poured out milk for the kids while her teenage daughter Theresa helped three-year-old David cut up his meat. It was a nice, quiet family gathering, which Reynolds had come to cherish and which she did everything possible to make each evening, even if it meant going back to work later.

Reynolds rose from the table and poured herself a glass of white wine. While half her brain focused on finding Faith Lockhart and her new confederate, Lee Adams, the other part was looking ahead with much anticipation to Halloween, less than a week away. Sydney, her six-year-old daughter, was dead set on being Eeyore, for the second year in a row. David would be the bouncy Tigger, a character that fit the perpetual-motion child perfectly. After that, Thanksgiving, perhaps a trip to her parents' in Florida, if she could find the time. Then Christmas. This year Reynolds was taking the kids to see Santa

226

Claus. She had missed last year because of – what else? – Bureau business. This year she would pull her 9mm on anyone who tried to stop her appointment with Kris Kringle. All in all, a good plan, if she could just make it work. Conception was easy; execution was the key that so often fell out of the lock.

As she put the cork back in the bottle, she looked sadly around a home that would not be hers much longer. Her son and daughter sensed that the change was coming. David hadn't slept through the night in over a week. Reynolds, home after working fifteen-hour days, would hold the quivering, wailing little boy, trying to calm him, rock him back to sleep. She tried to tell him that things would be just fine, when she was as uncertain as anyone whether they would be. It was sometimes terrifying being a parent, particularly in the midst of a divorce and all the pain it caused, which you saw every day etched into the faces of your children. More than once Reynolds had thought about calling off the divorce for that reason alone. But hanging on for the sake of the children wasn't the answer, she felt. At least not for her. They would have a better life without the man than they'd had with him. And her ex, she thought, might be a better father after the divorce than he had been before. Well, at least she could hope. Reynolds simply did not want to let her children down.

When Reynolds caught her daughter Sydney looking apprehensively at her, she smiled as naturally as she could. Sydney was six going on sixteen, so mature beyond her years that it scared Reynolds to death. She picked up on everything, missed nothing of significance. Reynolds had never in her career interrogated a suspect as thoroughly as Sydney did her mother nearly every day. The child dug deep, trying to understand what was going on, what their future would hold, and Reynolds had no ready answers for any of it.

More than once, she had found Sydney holding her crying brother in his bed late at night, attempting to soothe him, relieve his fears. Reynolds had recently told her daughter that she didn't need to assume the responsibility too, that her mother would always be there. Her statement had a hollow ring, and Sydney's face plainly showed a lack of belief. The fact that her daughter had not accepted this statement as dead, solid truth had aged Reynolds several years in several seconds. The memory of the palm reader and her predictions of premature death had come back to roost with a vengeance.

"Rosemary's chicken is awesome, isn't it, honey?" Reynolds said to Sydney.

The little girl nodded.

"Thank you, ma'am," Rosemary said, pleased.

"Are you okay, Mom?" Sydney asked. At the same time, she moved her little brother's milk away from the edge of the table. David had a propensity for spilling any liquid within his reach.

That subtle act of motherhood and her daughter's earnest question moved Reynolds almost to tears. She had been on such an emotional roller coaster of late that it didn't take much to set her off. She took a sip of wine, hoping it would prevent her from actually collapsing into a crying fit. It was like being pregnant again. The littlest thing affected her as if it were life or death. But then her common sense kicked in. She was a mom, things would work out. She had the luxury of a devoted live-in nanny. Sitting around whining, feeling sorry for yourself, wasn't the answer. So their life wasn't perfect. Whose was? She thought of what Anne Newman was going through right now. Suddenly Reynolds's problems didn't seem so bad.

"Everything's really good, Syd. Really good. Congratulations on your spelling test. Ms. Betack said you were the star of the day."

"I like school a lot."

"And it shows, young lady."

Reynolds was about to sit back down when the phone rang. She had caller ID and checked the readout screen. The ID screen came up blank. The caller must have ID block or his number was unlisted. She debated whether to answer it or not. The problem was that every FBI agent she knew had unlisted numbers. Ordinarily, though, anyone from the Bureau would call her on her pager or cell phone, both of which numbers she closely guarded; and calls to those two she would always answer. It was probably a random computer dialer and she would be told to wait until a real person came on and tried to sell her a time-share in Disney World. Still, something made her reach out and pick up the phone.

"Hello?"

"Brooke?"

Anne Newman sounded distressed. And as she listened to the woman, Reynolds sensed that there was something in addition to her husband's violent death – poor Anne, what worse could there be?

"I'll be there in thirty minutes," Reynolds said.

She grabbed her coat and car keys, took a bite out of a slice of the bread on her plate and kissed her children.

"Will you be back in time to read us a story, Mom?" Sydney asked.

"Three bears, three pigs, three goats." David promptly recited his favorite nighttime storytelling ritual to Brooke, his favorite story reader. His sister Sydney favored reading the stories herself, every night, sounding out each word along the way. Little David now took a big gulp of milk, loudly burped and then excused himself in a fit of laughter.

Reynolds smiled. Sometimes when she was tired she would tell the stories so fast they almost blurred together. The pigs built their houses, the bears went for their walk while Goldilocks burglarized the joint and the three billy goats gruff trounced the evil troll and lived happily ever after in their new pasture of grass. Sounded nice. Where could she buy some? And then, undressing for bed, Reynolds would endure spasms of crushing guilt. The reality was that her kids would be grown and gone before she blinked her eyes twice, and she routinely short-changed them on three short fairy tales because she wanted to do something so unimportant as sleep. Sometimes it was better not to think too much. Reynolds was a classic over-achiever and a perfectionist, to boot, while a "perfect parent" was the world's greatest oxymoron.

"I'll try my best. I promise."

The disappointed look on her daughter's face made Reynolds turn and flee the room. She stopped at the small room on the first floor that served as her study. From the top of a cabinet she removed a squat, heavy metal box, which she unlocked. Removing her SIG 9mm, she loaded in a fresh mag, pulled the slide back to chamber a round, clicked the safety on, slid the weapon in her clip holster and was out the door before she could think any more about another interrupted meal in a long string of disappointments for her children. Superwoman: career, kids, she had it all. Now, if she could only clone herself. Twice.

TWENTY-NINE

Lee and Faith had made two stops on the way to North Carolina, once for a late lunch at a Cracker Barrel and another at a large strip mall in southern Virginia. Lee had seen a billboard off the highway advertising a week-long gun show. The parking lot was packed with pickup trucks, RVs and cars with fat tires and engines erupting through their hoods. Some of the men were dressed in Polo and Chaps, and others in Grateful Dead T-shirts and ragged jeans. Americans of all backgrounds apparently loved their guns.

"Why here?" Faith asked as Lee got off the bike.

"Virginia law requires that licensed gun dealers conduct on-the-spot background checks on people trying to buy weapons," he explained. "You have to fill out a form, have your gun permit and two forms of identification. But the law doesn't apply to gun shows. All they want is your money. Which, by the way, I need."

"Do you *really* have to have a gun?"

He stared at her as though she had just hatched from an egg. "Everybody coming after *us* has them."

Unable to dispute this devastating logic, she said nothing more, gave him the cash and huddled on the bike as he went inside. Leave it to the man to say something that would paralyze her very soul.

Inside, Lee purchased a Smith & Wesson double-action autopistol with a fifteen-round mag, chambering 9mm Parabellums. The autopistol tag

231

was misleading. You had to pull the trigger each time to fire. The "auto" term referred to the fact that the pistol automatically loaded a new round with each pull of the trigger. He also bought a box of ammo and a cleaning kit and then returned to the parking lot.

Faith watched closely as he packed the gun and ammo away in the motorcycle's storage compartment.

"Feel safer now?" she asked dryly.

"Right now I wouldn't feel safe sitting in the Hoover Building with a hundred FBI agents staring at me. Gee, I wonder why."

They made Duck, North Carolina, by nightfall, and Faith gave Lee directions to the house in the Pine Island community.

When they pulled up in front, Lee stared at the immense structure, tugged off his helmet and turned to her. "I thought you said it was small."

"Actually, I think you referred to it as small. I said it was comfortable."

She climbed off the Honda and stretched out her body. Every bit of her, especially her butt, was one solid knot.

"It must be at least six thousand square feet." Lee continued to stare at the three-story, wooden-shingle-siding house that had dual stone chimneys and a cedar shake roof. Two broad veranda-style porches ran across the second and third floors, which gave it a plantation feel. There were gabled turrets and walls of lattice and glass; and immense displays of fountain grass erupted from the ground. Lee watched as the automatic sprinklers came on, along with the exterior landscape lighting. Behind the house he could hear the pounding surf. The house was situated at the end of a quiet cul-de-sac, although there were similar monster homes painted yellow, blue, green and gray lined up on the beach side in both directions as far as the eye could see. Although the air was warm and slightly humid, they were approaching November, and virtually all the other homes were dark.

Faith said, "I've never really bothered to add up the square footage. I rent it out April through September. It covers the mortgage and nets me about thirty thousand a year – just in case you're interested." Taking off her helmet and running her hands through her sweaty hair, she said, "I need a shower and some food. The kitchen should be stocked. You can put the bike in the carport."

Faith unlocked the front door and went inside while Lee parked the Honda in one of two bays of the carport and then carried in the bags. The inside of the house was even more beautiful than the outside. Lee was also grateful to see that the place had a security system. As he looked around, he took in the soaring ceilings, pickled wood beams and paneling, an enormous kitchen, Italian tile floors in some places, high-dollar Berber carpeting elsewhere. He counted six bedrooms, seven bathrooms and discovered an outdoor Jacuzzi on the back porch big enough for at least six drunken adults to flop around in. There were also three fireplaces, including a gas one in the master suite. The furniture was overstuffed rattan and wicker, all seemingly designed to beckon one to catnap.

Lee opened a set of French doors off the kitchen, stepped on to the deck and looked down into the enclosed courtyard. A kidney-shaped pool was situated down there. The chlorinated water sparkled under the glow of the pool lights. A Creepy Crawly made its way through the water, sucking up bugs and debris.

Faith joined him on the deck. "I had the people

come out this morning and get everything going. They maintain the pool all year 'round anyway. I've skinny-dipped down here in December. It's gloriously peaceful."

"There doesn't seem to be anybody else in the other houses."

"Certain parts of the Outer Banks are pretty full about nine or even ten months out of the year now, what with the nice weather. But you always have the chance of hurricanes this time of year, and this area is pretty expensive. The houses rent out for a small fortune, even in the off season. Unless you can get a big group together to rent them, your average family isn't going to be staying here. Mostly, you see the owners come down this time of year. But with kids in school, it's tough to do that during the week. So empty we have."

"Empty I like."

"The pool's heated, if you want to take a dip."

"I didn't bring my trunks."

"Not into skinny-dipping, huh?" She smiled and was very relieved that it was too dark for her to really see his eyes. If his baby blues had hit her just right, she might have pushed him in the pool, dived after him and everything else be damned.

"There are plenty of places in town to get some swimming stuff. I keep clothes down here, so I'm okay. We'll buy you some things tomorrow."

"I think I'm fine with what I brought."

"You don't want to stick out here, do you?"

"I'm not sure we'll be here long enough for that."

Faith looked out toward the wooden walkways leading past the sand dunes to where the Atlantic Ocean pitched and bellowed. "You never know. I don't think there's a better place to sleep than at the beach. There's nothing like the sound of waves crashing in your ears to drive you into unconsciousness. Back in D.C. I never sleep well. Too many things to worry about."

"Funny, I sleep just fine there."

She glared at him. "To each his own."

"What's for dinner?"

"First, a shower. You can have the master suite."

"It's your place. I'm fine on a couch."

"With six bedrooms, I don't think that would make much sense. Take the one at the end of the hall upstairs. It opens out on to the back porch. The Jacuzzi's out there. Feel free. Even without trunks. Don't worry, I won't peek."

They went inside. Lee grabbed his bag and followed her upstairs. He showered and put on a clean pair of khakis, a sweatshirt and sneakers without socks, since he had forgotten to bring the latter. He didn't bother to dry his new buzz cut. He caught himself looking in the mirror. The haircut didn't look so bad on him. In fact, it had taken a few years off. He slapped his hard gut, even did an exaggerated flex in the mirror.

"Yeah, right," he said to his reflection. "Even if she were your type, which she sure as hell ain't." He left his room and was about to head downstairs when he stopped in the hallway.

Faith's bedroom was at the other end of the corridor. He could still hear her shower running. She was probably taking her time under the hot water after the long ride. She had held up well, he had to admit, hadn't complained too much. He was edging down the hallway the whole time he was thinking this, because it just occurred to him that Faith might at this very minute be escaping out the back door while using the running shower as a ruse. For all he knew, she had arranged for a rental car that was parked down the street, and she was about to drive

235

off, leaving him with not much of a life. Was she just like her old man? Running away into the night when things got tough?

He knocked on her door. "Faith?" There was no answer, so he knocked louder. "Faith? Faith!" The water was still running. "Faith!" he yelled. He tried the door. It was locked. He pounded on the door again and yelled her name.

Lee was about to hustle down the stairs when he heard footsteps and the door was flung open. Faith stood there, her hair soaked and hanging in her face, water dripping down her legs, a towel covering, barely, the front of her.

"What?" she demanded. "What's wrong?"

Lee found himself staring at the elegant bone development of her shoulders, the now fully revealed Audrey Hepburn neck, the tightness of her arms. Then his gaze slid down to her upper thighs and he quickly concluded that her arms had nothing on her legs.

"What the hell is it, Lee?" she said loudly.

He snapped back. "Oh. I was just wondering, um, how about I make dinner?" He smiled weakly.

She stared incredulously at him as a puddle of water collected on the carpet at her feet. As she wrapped the mostly wet towel around her, Faith's small, firm breasts were now fully outlined against the thin wet fabric. That's when Lee began thinking seriously about taking another shower, only this time with water cold enough to turn certain parts of his anatomy the same color as his eyes.

"Fine." She slammed the door in his face.

"Very fine," Lee said quietly to the door.

He went downstairs and examined the contents of the refrigerator. He decided on a menu and started pulling food and pans. He had been living alone for so long that he had finally decided, after years of

Golden Arches food, that he had better learn how to cook properly. He actually found it therapeutic, and he fully expected to live an extra twenty years now that he had cleaned his arteries of all the grease. At least until he met Faith Lockhart. Now all bets on a long life were off.

Lee laid out talapia on a baking sheet, brushed the fish with butter he had melted in a pan and let it soak in. Then he added garlic, lemon juice and some other secret spices handed down to him through generations of Adamses and put the fish in the wall oven to broil. He sliced up tomatoes and a slab of mozzarella, arranged them nicely on a serving plate and doused them with olive oil and seasoning. Next he prepared a salad and then slit a length of French bread, buttered it, added garlic and placed it in the lower oven. He got out two plates, silverware and cloth napkins he found in a drawer and set the table. There were candles on the table, but lighting them seemed like a cheesy idea. This wasn't a honeymoon, and they still had that nationwide manhunt thing to consider.

He opened a small, built-in wine cooler next to the fridge and selected a chilled bottle of white. As he was pouring out two glasses of wine, Faith came down the stairs. She wore an unbuttoned blue denim shirt with a white T-shirt underneath, a pair of loose-fitting white slacks and red sandals. He noted she still wore no makeup, at least that he could detect. A silver bangle bracelet dangled at her wrist. She also wore turquoise earrings done in a loopy southwestern design.

She looked surprised at the kitchen activity. "A man who can shoot a gun, lose the Feds and cook too. You just never cease to amaze me."

He handed her a wine glass. "A good meal, a quiet evening and then we get down to serious business."

237

She glanced coolly at him as he clinked his glass against hers. "You clean up well," she said.

"Another one of my talents." He went to check the fish while Faith went over to the wall of windows and stared out.

They ate quietly, both of them apparently feeling a little awkward now that they had arrived at their destination. Getting here, ironically enough, seemed to be the easy part.

Faith insisted on cleaning up the kitchen while Lee turned on the TV.

"Did we make the news?" Faith asked.

"Not that I can see. But there must have been reports of the FBI agent being found. A murdered Fed is still pretty damn rare even in this day and age, thank God. I'll get a newspaper tomorrow."

Faith finished cleaning up, poured herself another glass of wine and joined him.

"Okay, our bellies are full, the booze has us about as mellow as we're ever going to get, so now's the time to talk," Lee said. "I need to hear the whole story, Faith. As sweet and simple as that."

"So you feed a girl a nice meal, fill her with wine and you think she's yours for the asking?" She smiled coyly.

He frowned. "I'm serious, Faith."

Her smile disappeared, along with her coyness. "Let's go for a walk on the beach."

Lee started to protest but then stopped. "Okay. It's your turf, home rules apply." He headed up the stairs.

"Where are you going?"

"Be right back."

When Lee came back down, he had on a wind-breaker.

"You didn't need a jacket, it's still pretty warm."

He spread open the front of the jacket, revealing

the clip holster and the Smith & Wesson in it. "Didn't want to spook any sand crabs we come across."

"Guns frighten me to death."

"Guns also prevent death, when *properly* used. Usually sudden, violent death."

"No one could have followed us. No one knows we're here."

His reply chilled her to the bone.

"I hope to God you're right."

THIRTY

Reynolds didn't use her bubble light but would have if a patrol car had tried to pull her over, as she was exceeding the speed limit by more than twenty miles per hour on the few open stretches of the Beltway before having to slow down in a sea of red brake lights. She checked her watch: seven-thirty. When wasn't there a rush hour in this damn area? People got up earlier and earlier to go to work, or stayed later and later before going home to avoid the traffic. Pretty soon the two groups would smack right into each other and the twenty-four-hour-a-day highway parking lot would officially begin. Luckily Anne Newman's house was only a few exits down from hers.

As she drove, Reynolds thought about her visit to Adams's apartment building. Reynolds had thought she had seen and heard everything by now, but Angie Carter's statement about the FBI had stunned her, and the shock of it had moved her and Connie into hyperspeed. They'd notified their superiors at the Bureau and quickly determined that no FBI operations had been conducted at Adams's address. Then the shit had really hit the fan. The impersonation of FBI agents got the attention of the director himself, and he had personally issued orders on the case. Even though the back door to Adams's apartment had been knocked off its hinges and they could have walked right in, a search warrant was fast-tracked and executed, again with the director's personal blessing. Reynolds was actually relieved about that because she didn't want to have any slip-ups on this one. Any mistakes would come home to roost right on her head.

The apartment was thoroughly searched by one of the Bureau's crack forensics teams, pulled off another high-profile case. In the end they didn't find much. There was no tape in the answering machine. That had really ticked Reynolds off. If the phony FBI people had taken the tape, there must have been something important on it. Her search team had continued to strike out. There were no travel documents, maps consulted, nothing that would hint as to where Adams and Lockhart were going. They had found fingerprints matching Faith Lockhart's, so that was something. They were checking into Adams's background. He had family in the area; maybe they knew something.

They had discovered the roof hatch in the empty apartment next door to Adams's. Clever. Reynolds had also noted the extra locks, video surveillance, steel door and frame and the copper shield over the alarm panel. Lee Adams knew what he was doing.

They had retrieved the bag of hair and hair coloring from one of the trash cans behind the apartment. That, together with the snips they had seen of the airport surveillance tapes, showed that Adams was now a blond, Lockhart a brunette. Not that this helped much. They were checking into whether either of them had other residences listed in their names elsewhere in the country. That was a needle in a haystack, she knew, even if they had used their real names. She doubted they would be that stupid. And even if they had used their aliases, the names Suzanne Blake and Charles Wright were too common to aid Reynolds very much.

The police officers who responded to the call at

Adams's apartment were pulled in and questioned. The men posing as FBI agents had fed them a story that Lee Adams was wanted in connection with a kidnapping ring across state lines. The FBI posers' credentials looked real, both police officers were quick to point out. And they carried the firepower and the professional swagger one normally associated with federal law enforcement. They were searching the place expertly and had made no move to run when the cruiser had shown up. The imposters talked the talk and walked the walk in all respects, said the two police officers, who were both veterans on the street. They had been given the name of the supposed special agent in charge. It was run through the FBI personnel database and came up negative. No surprise there. The police officers had given descriptions of the men they had seen, and a Bureau technician was creating computer images of them. Still, all in all, it was a dead end, with frightening implications. Implications that struck very close to home for Reynolds.

She had received another visit from Paul Fisher. He came with orders right from Massey, as he was quick to point out. Reynolds was to proceed with all due speed, but with the utmost caution, to find Faith Lockhart, and she could be assured of all the support she needed.

"Just don't make any more mistakes," he had said.

"I wasn't aware I had made any mistakes, Paul."

"An agent killed. Faith Lockhart falls into your lap and you let her get away. What would you call those?"

"Leaked information caused Ken to die," she had fired back. "I fail to see how that was my fault."

"Brooke," Fisher had said, "if you really believe that, then you might want to request reassignment right now. The buck stops with you. As far as the

Bureau is concerned, if there is a leak, every member of your squad, including you, is at the top of the list. And that's how the Bureau's following that up."

As soon as he left her office, Reynolds had thrown her shoe against the closed door. Then she had thrown the other one, just to be sure he was aware of her extreme displeasure. Paul Fisher was officially off her sexual fantasy list.

Reynolds raced down the exit ramp, hung a left on Braddock Road and fought through some late traffic backup until she turned off and entered the quiet residential neighborhood of the slain FBI agent. She slowed when she reached the Newmans' street. The house was dark, a single car in the driveway. Reynolds parked her government-issue sedan at the curb, got out and hustled up to the door.

Anne Newman must have been watching for her, because the door opened before Reynolds could ring the bell.

Anne Newman didn't attempt to make small talk or ask Reynolds if she wanted anything to drink. She led the FBI agent directly to a small back room that had been set up as an office with a desk, metal file cabinet, computer and fax machine. On the wall were framed baseball cards and other sports memorabilia. On the desk were stacks of silver dollars encased in hard plastic and neatly labeled.

"I was looking through Ken's office. I don't know why. It just seemed . . ."

"You don't have to explain, Anne. There are no set rules for what you're going through."

Anne Newman wiped away a tear as Reynolds studied her. Clearly the woman was near the breaking point, on all fronts. She was dressed in an old robe, her hair unwashed, eyes red and puffy. Yesterday afternoon, the most pressing decision she probably had to make was what to have for dinner,

Reynolds assumed. God, it could all turn on a dime. Ken Newman wasn't the only one being buried. Anne was right there beside him. The only catch was she still had to go on living.

"I found these photo albums. I didn't even know they were back here. They were in a box with some other things. I know this might look bad, but . . . but if it helps in finding out what happened to Ken . . ." She faded out for a moment as more tears plunked down on to the photo album with its tattered, seventies-style psychedelic cover.

"Calling you was the right thing to do," Anne finally said with a bluntness that was both painful and gratifying for Reynolds to hear.

"I know this is terribly difficult for you." Reynolds eyed the album, not wanting to prolong this any more than absolutely necessary. "Can I see what you found?"

Anne Newman sat down on a small sofa and opened the album and pulled up the clear plastic sheet that kept the photos securely inside. On the page she had opened to was an eight-by-ten photo of a group of men in hunting garb holding rifles. Ken Newman was one of the men. She pulled out the photo, revealing a piece of paper and a small key pressed into the album page. She handed Reynolds both and watched her closely as the FBI agent examined them.

The piece of paper was an account statement for a safe-deposit box at a local bank. The key, presumably, fit that box.

Reynolds looked at her. "You didn't know about this?"

Anne Newman shook her head. "We have a safe-deposit box. But not at that bank. And of course that's not all."

Reynolds looked back at the bank statement and

244

she jerked involuntarily. The name of the boxholder was not Ken Newman. Nor was the billing address for the house she was in. "Who's Frank Andrews?"

Anne Newman looked like she would burst into tears again. "God, I have no idea."

"Did Ken ever mention that name to you?" Newman shook her head.

Reynolds took a deep breath. If Newman had a safe-deposit box under a false name, he would have needed one thing to set up the account.

She sat on the sofa next to Anne and took her hand. "Have you found any identification around here that might match the name Frank Andrews?"

The tears welled in the stricken woman's eyes and Reynolds truly felt for her.

"You mean with Ken's picture on it? Showing that he was this Frank Andrews person?"

"Yes, that's what I mean," Reynolds said softly.

Anne Newman put her hand in her robe and pulled out a Virginia driver's license. The name on it was Frank Andrews. The license number, which in Virginia was the person's Social Security number, was on there. And in the small accompanying photo Ken Newman was staring back at her.

"I thought about going to open the safe-deposit box myself, but then I realized they wouldn't let me. I'm not on the account. And I wouldn't be able to explain that it was my husband, but just under a false name."

"I know, Anne. I know. You were right to bring me in. Now, where exactly did you find the fake ID?"

"In another one of the photo albums. They weren't family albums, of course. I keep those, been through them a zillion times. These albums were pictures of Ken and his hunting and fishing buddies. They took trips every year. Ken was good about taking

245

pictures. I never knew he kept them in albums. I wasn't all that interested in looking at those pictures, you see." She stared wistfully at the far wall. "Sometimes it seemed Ken was happier with his buddies shooting at ducks or at his coin and card shows than he was at home." She caught a quick breath, put a hand over her mouth and looked down.

Reynolds could sense Anne had never meant to share that personal bit of information with her, a semi-stranger. She said nothing. Experience told her to allow Anne Newman to work her way through this. A minute later the woman started speaking again.

"I never would have found it, I suppose, unless . . . what happened to Ken . . . you know. I guess life is funny sometimes."

Or terribly cruel. "Anne, I need to check this out. I'm going to take these items, and I don't want you to mention it to anyone. Not friends, family . . ." She paused, choosing her words as carefully as she could. "Or anyone else at the Bureau. Not until I dig a little bit."

Anne Newman looked up at her with frightened eyes. "What do you think Ken was involved in, Brooke?"

"I don't know yet. Let's not jump to conclusions on this. The safe-deposit box might be empty. Ken might have leased it a long time ago and then forgotten about it."

"And the fake ID?"

Reynolds licked her dry lips. "Ken worked some undercover over the years. This might be a souvenir of those days." Reynolds knew this was a lie, and Anne Newman probably did too, she thought. The license had a recent issue date on it. And those working undercover in the FBI didn't usually take

246

home the props with their secret identities on them once their tasks were completed. The fake license, she was fairly certain, was unrelated to his FBI duties. It was her job to discover what it *was* connected to.

"Anne, not a word to anyone. It's for your own safety as much as anything."

Anne Newman clutched her arm as Reynolds stood. "Brooke, I've got three kids. If Ken was mixed up in something . . ."

"I'll put the house under twenty-four-hour surveillance. Anything remotely suspicious catches your eye, you call me." She handed her a card with her direct-dial numbers on it. "Day or night."

"I didn't know where else to turn. Ken thought a lot of you, he really did."

"He was a damn good agent and he had a terrific career." If she discovered that Ken Newman had been a sell-out, however, the Bureau would crush his memory, his reputation, everything about his professional life. That would, of course, destroy his private side as well, including the woman Reynolds was looking at, and her children. But that was life. Reynolds didn't make the rules, didn't always agree with the rules, but she lived by them. However, she would check out the safe-deposit box by herself. If there was nothing suspicious in there, she would tell no one. She would continue to investigate why Newman was using an alias, but that would be done on her own time. She wasn't going to destroy his memory without a very compelling reason. She owed the man that.

She left Anne Newman sitting on the sofa, the photo album open in her lap. The ironic thing was, if Newman was the leak on the Lockhart case, he had probably helped himself to an early death. Now that Reynolds thought about it, whoever might have hired him had probably hoped to eliminate the mole and the main target in one efficient thrust. Only a slug deflecting off a pistol barrel had saved Faith Lockhart from joining Ken Newman on a slab. And perhaps the assistance of Lee Adams as well?

Whoever had orchestrated it clearly knew what he was doing. Which was bad for Reynolds. Contrary to popular fiction and film, most criminals weren't that accomplished and couldn't so easily out-maneuver the police at every turn. The majority of murderers, rapists, burglars, robbers, drug dealers and other felons were usually uneducated or scared; or drugged-out punks or drunks terrified of their own shadows when off the needle or bottle, yet demons when high. They left many clues behind and were usually caught, or turned themselves in, or were ratted on by their "friends." They were prosecuted and did jail time or, in rare cases, were executed. They were in no sense of the word professionals.

Reynolds knew that this was not the case here. Amateurs didn't find ways to pay off veteran FBI agents. They didn't hire hit men who lurked in the woods waiting for their prey. They didn't impersonate FBI agents with credentials so authentic they had scared off the cops. Sinister theories of conspiracy swirled in her head, sending a shiver of fear down her back. No matter how long you did this, the fear was always there. To be alive was to be afraid. To not be afraid was to be dead.

As she walked out, Reynolds passed under a blinking fire detector that was in the hallway. There were three other such devices in the house, including one in Ken Newman's office. While they were plugged into the home's electrical wiring and did function as designed, they all also housed sophisticated surveillance cameras with pinhole lenses. Two of the wall outlets on each level were similarly "modified." The modifications had taken place two weeks ago when the Newmans had taken a rare three-day vacation. This type of surveillance mode was based upon PLCs, power line carrier technology favored by the FBI. And the Central Intelligence Agency.

Robert Thornhill was on the prowl. And his attention would now turn to Brooke Reynolds.

As she climbed in her car, Reynolds understood very clearly that she was perhaps at the crossroads of her career. She would probably need every bit of ingenuity and inner strength she could muster to survive this. And yet the only thing she really wanted to do right now was drive home and tell her two beautiful children the story of the three pigs, just as slowly, accurately and colorfully as she possibly could.

THIRTY-ONE

T he wind, it turned out, was blowing hard along the beach, and the temperature had dropped drastically. Faith buttoned her overshirt; then, despite the cold, she took off her sandals and held them in one hand.

"I like to feel the sand," she explained to Lee. The tide was low, so they had a broad beach on which to meander. The sky held scattered clouds, the moon almost full, the stars winks of light staring down upon them. Far out on the water they saw the blink of what was probably a ship's light or stationary buoy. Except for the wind, it was completely quiet. No cars, no blaring TVs, no planes, no other people.

"It's really nice out here," Lee finally said as he watched a sand crab do its funny sideways scuttle into its tiny home. Stuck in the sand was a piece of PVC pipe. Lee knew that fishermen would stick their poles in the hollow tube when they were fishing from the beach.

"I've thought of moving here permanently," said Faith. She broke ranks with him and ventured into the water up to her ankles. Lee slipped off his shoes, rolled up his pants legs and joined her.

"Colder than I thought it would be," he said. "No swimming out here."

"You wouldn't believe how invigorating a swim in cold water can be."

"You're right, I wouldn't."

"I'm sure you've been asked this a million times,

but how did you become a private investigator?"

He shrugged and looked out toward the ocean. "Sort of fell into it. My dad was an engineer and I was a gadget guy, like him. But I never had the book smarts he did. I was sort of a rebel too, like you. But I didn't go to college. I joined the Navy."

"Please tell me you were a Navy SEAL. I'd sleep better."

Lee smiled. "I can barely shoot straight. I can't build a nuclear device out of toothpicks and gum wrappers, and the last time I checked, I couldn't disable a man simply by pressing my thumb against his head."

"I guess I'll keep you anyway. Sorry to interrupt."

"Not much more to it. I studied telephony, communications, that sort of thing in the Navy. Got married, had a kid. Worked at the phone company as a repairman. Then I lost my daughter in a messy divorce. I quit my job, answered an ad at a private security firm for someone experienced in electronic surveillance. I figured with my technical background I could learn what I needed to know. The job really got into my blood. I started my own private investigation firm, got some decent clients, made mistakes along the way but then got a firm footing. Now you see me today as the head of a mighty empire."

"How long have you been divorced?"

"A long time." He looked at her. "Why?"

"Just curious. Ever gotten close to the altar since then?"

"No. I guess I'm terrified of making the same mistakes." He stuffed his hands into his pockets. "Quite honestly, the problems came from both ends. I'm not easy to live with." He smiled. "I think God makes two kinds of people: those who should marry and procreate and those who should remain alone

251

and have sex only for fun. I think I'm in the latter group."

Faith looked down. "Save some room for me."

"Not to worry. There's plenty of space left."

He touched her elbow. "Let's talk. We're running out of time."

Faith led him back up on to the beach and plopped down cross-legged on a patch of dry sand. He sat next to her.

"Where would you like to begin?" she asked.

"How about the beginnings?"

"No, I mean do you want me to tell you all first, or do you want to spill *your* secrets first?"

He looked startled. "*My* secrets? Sorry, I'm fresh out."

She picked up a stick, drew the letters *d* and *b* in the sand and then glanced at him. "Danny Buchanan. What do you really know about him?"

"Just what I told you. He's your partner."

"He's also the man who hired you."

Lee couldn't find his voice for a few seconds. "I told you I didn't know who had hired me."

"That's right. That's what you *told* me."

"How do you know he hired me?"

"While I was in your office, I listened to a message from Danny, and he sounded quite anxious to know where I was and what you had found out. He left his phone number for you to call him back. He was more distressed than I've ever heard him. I guess I would be too if someone I had arranged to have killed was still alive and kicking."

"You're sure it was him on the phone?"

"After fifteen years of working with him I think I know his voice. So you didn't know?"

"No, I didn't."

"You know that's really hard to believe."

"I guess it is," he agreed. "But it happens to be the

252

truth." He scooped up some sand and let it run through his fingers. "So I take it that phone call is why you tried to give me the slip at the airport? You don't trust me."

She licked her dry lips and glanced at the holstered gun, which was visible as the wind whipped Lee's jacket around. "I *do* trust you, Lee. Otherwise I wouldn't be sitting on a lonely beach in the dark with an armed man who's still pretty much a stranger to me."

Lee let his shoulders slump. "I was hired to follow you, Faith. That's all."

"Don't you first find out if the client or his intentions are legitimate?"

Lee started to say something and then stopped. That was a reasonable question. The fact was business had been slow recently and the assignment and cash had been timely. And the file he had been given had a photo of Faith. And then he had seen her in person. Well, what the hell could he say? Most of his targets weren't as attractive as Faith Lockhart. In the photo her face had suggested vulnerability. After meeting her, he knew that impression wasn't necessarily true. But it was a very potent combination for him. For any man.

"Normally, I like to meet with a client, get to know him and his agenda before I agree to accept a job."

"But not here?"

"It was a little difficult, since I didn't know who had hired me."

"So instead of returning the cash, you accepted the offer and started following me – blindly, as it were."

"I didn't see any harm in just following you."

"But they could have been using you to get to me."

"It's not exactly like you were in hiding. Like I said, I thought you might be having some sort of affair. When I went inside the cottage, I knew that

253

wasn't the case. The rest of the night's events damn sure reinforced that conclusion. That's all I really know."

Faith stared out toward the ocean, to the horizon, where water met sky. It was a visual collision of sorts that happened every day and was comforting for some reason. It gave her hope when she probably had no other reason to feel it. Other than the man sitting beside her, perhaps.

"Let's go back to the house," she said.

THIRTY-TWO

They sat in the spacious family room. Faith picked up a remote control, hit a button and the flames in the gas fireplace crept to life. She poured another glass of wine, offered one to Lee, but he declined. They sat on the overstuffed couch.

Faith took a sip of wine and stared out the window, her eyes focusing on nothing. "Washington represents the richest, most enormous pie in the history of mankind. And everyone in the whole world wants a slice of it. There are certain people who hold the knife that portions out that pie. If you want a slice, you have to go through them."

"That's where you and Buchanan come in?"

"I lived, breathed and ate my career. Sometimes I worked more than twenty-four hours in a day because I'd cross the International Date Line. I can't tell you the hundreds of details, nuances, mind-reading, gut checks and sheer nerve and perseverance that lobbying on the scale we did requires." She put down her wine glass and focused on him. "I had a great teacher in Danny Buchanan. He almost never lost. That's remarkable, don't you think?"

"I guess never losing at anything is pretty remarkable. We can't all be Michael Jordan."

"In your line of work can you guarantee to your client that a certain result will occur?"

Lee smiled. "If I could foresee the future, I'd start playing the lottery."

"Danny Buchanan could guarantee the future."

Lee stopped smiling. "How?"

"He who controls the gatekeepers controls the future."

Lee slowly nodded in understanding. "So he was paying off people in government?"

"On a more sophisticated scale than anyone's done before."

"Congressmen on the payroll? That sort of thing?"

"Actually, they did it for free."

"What—"

"Until they left office. Then Danny had a whole world of goodies lined up for them. Lucrative do-nothing jobs in companies he had set up. Income from private portfolios of stocks and bonds, and cash funneled through legitimate businesses under the cover of services rendered. They could play golf all day, make a couple of sham phone calls to the Hill, take a few meetings and live like Kings. Hell, it's like a super 401(k). You know how Americans are so into their stocks. Danny worked them hard while they were on the Hill, but he would give them the best golden years money could buy."

"How many of them have 'retired'?"

"None, as yet. But everything is set up for when they do. Danny's been doing this only about ten years."

"He's been in D.C. a lot longer than ten years."

"I mean he's been bribing people for only ten years. Before then, he was a much more successful lobbyist. Since the start of his private company, he's made a lot less money."

"I thought guaranteeing results would bring him a lot *more* money."

"The last ten years have been pretty much a charitable decade for him."

"The man must have deep pockets."

"Danny has pretty much gone through his money. We started representing paying clients again so we could continue what we were doing. And the longer his people do what they are told, the more they will receive later. And by waiting until they're out of office to be paid, the chances any of them will be caught go down considerably."

"They must really trust Buchanan's word."

"I'm sure he's had to show them proof of what's waiting for them. But he's also an honorable man."

"All crooks are, aren't they? Who are some of the people on his retirement plan?"

She looked at him suspiciously. "Why?"

"Just humor me."

Faith named two of the men.

"Correct me if I'm mistaken, but aren't they the current vice president of the United States and the Speaker of the House?"

"Danny doesn't work with middle management. He actually started working with the vice president before he rose to that office, back when he was a House whip. But when Danny needs the man to pick up the phone and put the screws to someone, the man does."

"Holy shit, Faith. What the hell did you need that kind of firepower for? Are we talking military secrets?"

"Actually, something much more valuable." She picked up her wine glass. "We represent the poorest of the world's poor. African nations, in issues of humanitarian aid, food, medicine, clothing, farm equipment, crop seed, desalinization systems. In Latin America, money for vaccines and other medical supplies. The export of legal birth control devices, sterile needles and health information in the poorest countries."

Lee looked skeptical. "You're saying you were

bribing government officials to help third world countries?"

She set down her wine glass and looked directly at him. "Actually, the official lexicon has changed. The rich nations have developed very politically correct terminology for their destitute neighbors. The CIA publishes a manual on them, in fact. So instead of 'third world,' you have new categories: LDCs are 'less-developed countries,' meaning they're in the bottom group of the hierarchy of developed countries. There are officially one hundred and seventy-two LDCs, or the vast majority of countries in the world. Then there are the LLDCs. They're the 'least developed countries.' They're the bottom of the barrel, dead in the water. There are *only* forty-two of them. This may surprise you, but about half of the people on this planet live in abject poverty."

"And that makes it right?" Lee said. "That makes bribery and cheating right?"

"I'm not asking you to condone any of it. I don't really care if you agree with it or not. You wanted the facts, I'm giving them to you."

"America gives lots of foreign aid. And we don't *have* to give a dime."

She gave him a fierce look, one he had never seen from her before. "If you talk facts with me, you lose," she said sharply.

"Come again?"

"I've been researching this – hell, living this – for more than ten years! We pay farmers in this country more *not* to grow crops than we do on humanitarian relief overseas. Of the total federal budget, foreign aid represents about one percent, with the majority of that going to two countries, Egypt and Israel. Americans spend a hundred times as much money on makeup or fast food or video rentals in a year's time than we do on feeding starving children in third world countries in a decade. We could wipe out a dozen serious childhood diseases in undeveloped countries around the world with less money than we spend on Beanie Babies."

"You're naïve, Faith. You and Buchanan are probably just filling the lining of some dictator's pockets."

"No! That's an easy excuse, and one that I'm sick of. The money we do manage to get goes directly to legitimate humanitarian relief organizations, and never to the government directly. I've personally seen enough health ministers in African countries wearing Armani and driving a Mercedes while babies starve at their feet."

"And there aren't starving children in this country?"

"They get a lot of aid, and rightfully so. All I'm saying is that Danny and I had our agenda, and ours involved the *foreign* poor. Human beings are dying, Lee, by the millions. Children all over the world are perishing for no reason other than neglect. Every day, every hour, every minute."

"And do you really expect me to believe you two did this out of the goodness of your hearts?" He looked around the house. "This isn't exactly a soup kitchen, Faith."

"The first five years I worked with Danny I did my job, represented the big clients and I made a lot of money. A *lot* of money. I'll be the first to admit I'm one materialistic hardass. I like the money, and I loved what the money could buy."

"And then what happened? You found God?"

"No, he found me." Lee looked bewildered, and Faith quickly continued. "Danny had begun lobbying on behalf of the foreign poor. He was getting nowhere. No one cared, he kept telling me. The other partners at our firm were getting tired of

259

Danny's charitable endeavors. They wanted to represent IBM and Philip Morris, not Sudan's starving masses. Danny came to my office one day, said he was forming his own firm and wanted me to go with him. We weren't taking any clients, but Danny told me not to worry, that he'd take care of me."

Lee appeared mollified. "That much I can believe: You didn't know he was bribing people, or at least planning to."

"Of course I knew about it! He told me everything. He wanted me to go into this with eyes wide open. That's how he is. He's not some crook."

"Faith, do you know what you're saying? You *went along*, even though you knew you'd be breaking the law?"

She fixed a cold gaze upon him. "If I could fix it so that cigarette companies could keep selling cancer on a stick to anybody with a fresh set of lungs and gun manufacturers could roll out machine guns to anyone with a heartbeat, I guess I felt nothing was beneath me. And the goal here was something I could actually be proud of."

"Materialistic hardass goes soft?" Lee said with contempt.

"It's been known to happen," she shot back.

"How did you two work it?" Lee said in a baiting tone.

"I was Mister Outside, working all the people we didn't have in our back pockets. I was also good at getting celebrities to appear at some events, even travel to some of the countries. Photo ops, meet-and-greets with members." She sipped her wine. "Danny was Mister Inside. He worked all the people on the take while I pushed from the outside."

"And you kept this up for ten years?"

Faith nodded. "About a year ago Danny started

running out of money. A lot of our lobbying expenses he paid out of his own pocket. It wasn't like our clients could afford to pay us anything. And he had to invest a lot of his own money into these 'trust' funds, as he called them, for the members we were bribing. Danny took that part very seriously. He was their trustee. Every cent he promised would be there."

"Honor among thieves."

Faith ignored the barb. "That's when he told me to concentrate on paying clients while he carried the torch on the other matters. I offered to sell my house, and this house, to help raise money. He refused. He said I'd done enough." She shook her head. "Maybe I should still sell it – believe me, no one could ever do enough."

She fell silent for a bit and Lee chose not to break it. She stared across at him. "We really were accomplishing a lot of good."

"What do you want, Faith? You want me to break out in applause?"

Her eyes flashed at him. "Why don't you get on that stupid motorcycle and get the hell out of my life?"

"All right," Lee said calmly, "if you thought so highly of what you were doing, how did you turn out to be a witness for the FBI?"

Faith covered her face with her hands, as though she were about to start bawling. When Faith finally looked at him she seemed so distressed, Lee felt his anger slip away.

"For some time Danny had been acting strangely. I suspected that maybe someone was on to him. That scared the hell out of me. I didn't want to go to prison. I kept asking him what was wrong, but he wouldn't talk to me about it. He kept withdrawing, became more and more paranoid, finally even

261

asking me to leave the firm. I felt so alone, for the first time in a long time. It was like I had lost my father again."

"So you went to the FBI, tried to cut a deal. You for Buchanan."

"No!" she exclaimed. "Never!"

"What, then?"

"About three months ago there was a lot of news coverage about the FBI breaking a major public corruption case, involving a defense contractor bribing several congressmen to help it win a large federal contract. A couple of employees at the defense contractor contacted the FBI and revealed what was going on. They were actually part of the conspiracy early on, but were granted immunity in exchange for their testimony and assistance. That sounded like a good deal to me. Maybe I could get a deal too. Since Danny wouldn't confide in me, I decided to go for it. The lead agent was named in the article: Brooke Reynolds. I called her.

"I didn't know what to expect from the FBI but I knew one thing: I wouldn't tell them much right away, no names or anything, not until I saw what the lay of the land was. And I had leverage. They needed a live witness with a head full of dates, times, names, meetings, records of votes and agendas to make this work."

"And Buchanan was ignorant of all this?"

"I guess not, considering he hired someone to kill me."

"We don't know that he did."

"Oh, come on, Lee, who else could it be?"

Lee thought back to the other men he had seen at the airport. The device in the man's hand was a high-tech blowgun of sorts. Lee had seen a demonstration of one at a seminar on counterterrorism. The gun and ammo were constructed solely from plastic to allow passage through metal detectors. You hit the palm trigger and the air compression fired a tiny needle either tipped or filled with a deadly toxin, like thallium or ricin, or the all-time favorite of assassins, curare, because it reacted so damn fast in the body that there was no known antidote. In a crowd, the act could be carried out and the assassin gone before the victim fell dead.

"Go on," he said.

"I offered to bring Danny into the fold."

"And how did they react to that?"

"They made it very clear that Danny was going down."

"I'm not following your logic. If you *and* Buchanan were going to turn witness, who were the Feds going to prosecute: the foreign countries?"

"No. Their representatives didn't know what we were doing. As I said, the money didn't go directly to the governments. And it's not like CARE or the Catholic Relief Services or UNICEF would ever condone bribery. Danny was their unofficial and unpaid lobbyist-in-residence but they had no idea what he was doing. He represented about fifteen such organizations. It was tough going. They all had their agendas, took a scattergun approach. They typically proposed hundreds of single-issue bills, instead of a few comprehensive ones. Danny got them organized, working together, sponsoring a small number of bills containing more comprehensive legislation. He taught them what they had to do to be more effective."

"So tell me exactly who were you going to testify against, then?"

"The politicians we paid off," she said simply. "They did it just for the money. It's not like they gave a damn about children with dead eyes living in Hepatitis Heaven. I saw it every day in their greedy faces. They just expected a rich reward – thought it was their due."

"Don't you think you're coming down a little heavy on these guys?"

"Why don't *you* stop being so naïve? How do you think people get elected in this country? They get elected by the groups who *organize* the voters, who shape citizens' decisions on who and what to vote for. And do you know who those groups are? They're big business and special interests, and the wealthy who fill the coffers of political candidates every year. Do you really think ordinary people attend five-thousand-dollar-a-plate dinners? And then do you really think these groups give all that money out of the goodness of *their* collective hearts? When the politicians get into office, you better believe they're expected to deliver."

"So you're saying all politicians in this country are corrupt. That still doesn't make what you did right."

"No? What congressman from the state of Michigan would vote to do anything to seriously hurt the automobile industry? How long do you think she'd be in office? Or high-tech in California? Or farmers in the Midwest? Or tobacco in the South? It's like a self-fulfilling prophecy in a way. Business and labor and other special interests have a lot at stake. They're focused, they have big dollars, they have PACs and lobbyists blasting their messages to Washington nonstop. Big and small business employ just about everybody. Those same people vote in elections. They vote their pocketbooks. Voilà, there's your big, dark conspiracy of American politics. I see Danny as the first visionary ever to outsmart greed and selfishness."

"But what about the foreign aid? If this story came out, wouldn't that kill the pipeline?"

"That's the thing! Can you imagine all the positive

attention it would get? The poorest countries on earth forced to bribe greedy American politicians to get the help they so desperately needed because it was unavailable any other way. You get stories like that in the media, then maybe some real, substantive changes would be made."

"That all sounds pretty far-fetched. I mean, come on."

"Maybe so, but my options weren't exactly flowing over. It's real damn easy to second-guess, Lee."

Lee sat back as he muddled this over. "Okay, okay. Do you *really* think Buchanan would try to kill you?"

"We were partners, friends. Actually, more than that. In many ways he was like a father to me. I . . . I just don't know. Maybe he found out I went to the FBI. He would think I betrayed him. That could have driven him over the edge."

"There's a major problem with the theory that Buchanan is behind all this."

She looked over at him curiously.

"I *hadn't reported back* to Buchanan, remember? So unless he has someone else working for him, he doesn't know you're dealing with the FBI. And it takes time to set up a professional-caliber hit. You can't just call your local shooter and ask him to pop somebody for you and charge it to your Visa."

"But he might have known a hired killer already, and then he planned to somehow set you up for the murder."

Lee was shaking his head before she finished. "He would have had no idea I would be there that night. And if you had been killed, he'd have the problem of me finding out about it and maybe going to the police with the result that everything gets traced back to him. Why bring all that misery on himself?

Think about it, Faith, if Buchanan was planning to kill you, he would not have hired me."

She slumped in a chair. "My God, what you're saying makes perfect sense." Terror seeped into Faith's eyes as she thought about what all this meant. "Then you're saying . . .?"

"I'm saying that somebody else wants you dead."

"Who? Who?" She almost shouted this at him.

"I don't know," he said.

Faith abruptly stood and stared into the fire. The shadows of the flames lapped against her face. When she spoke her voice was calm, almost resigned. "Do you see your daughter much?"

"Not much. Why?"

"I thought marriage and kids could wait. And then months turned to years and years to decades. And now this."

"You're not in your golden years yet."

She looked at him. "Can you tell me I'll be alive tomorrow, a week from tomorrow?"

"Nobody has that guarantee. We can always go to the FBI, and now maybe we should."

"I can't do that. Not after what you've just told me."

He stood and gripped her shoulder. "What are you talking about?"

She moved away from him. "The FBI won't let me bring Danny in. Either he goes to jail or I do. When I thought he was behind trying to have me killed, I probably would have gone back and testified. But I can't do that now. I can't be part of him going to prison."

"If there hadn't been an attempt on your life, what were you going to do?"

"I was going to give them an ultimatum. If they wanted my cooperation, then Danny would have to be given immunity."

"And if they turned you down, like they did?"

"Then Danny and I would have been long gone. Somehow." She stared directly at him. "I'm not going back. For a lot of reasons. Not wanting to die being right at the top."

"And exactly where the hell does that leave me?"

"This isn't such a bad place, is it?" Faith said weakly.

"Are you crazy? We can't stay here forever."

"Then we better think of another place to run to."

"And what about my home? My life? I *do* have a family. Do you expect me to just kiss it all good-bye?"

"Whoever wants me dead will assume you know everything I do. You won't be safe."

"That's *my* decision, not yours."

"I'm sorry, Lee. I never thought anyone else would be dragged into this. Especially not someone like you."

"There has to be another way."

She headed for the stairs. "I'm very, very tired. And what else is there to talk about?"

"Dammit, I can't just walk away and start over."

Faith was halfway up the stairs. She stopped, turned and looked down at him.

"Do you think things will look better in the morning?" she asked.

"No," said Lee frankly.

"Which is why there's nothing left for us to talk about. Good night."

"Why do I think you made your decision not to go back a long time ago? Like the minute you met me."

"Lee—"

"You sucker me into going with you, pull that stupid stunt at the airport and now I'm trapped too. Thanks a helluva lot, lady."

"I didn't plan it like this! You're wrong."

267

"And you really expect me to believe you?"

"What do you want me to say?"

Lee stared up at her. "Granted it's not much, but I like my life, Faith."

"I'm sorry." She fled upstairs.

THIRTY-THREE

Lee grabbed a six-pack of Red Dog from the refrigerator and slammed the side door on his way out. He stopped at the Honda, wondering whether he should just climb on the big machine and run until his gas, money or sanity were gone. Then another possibility occurred to him. He could go to the Feds alone. Turn Faith in and claim ignorance about all of this. And he *was* ignorant. He hadn't done anything wrong. And he owed the woman nothing. In fact, she had been a source of misery, terror and near-death experiences. Turning her in should be an easy decision. So why the hell wasn't it?

He went out the rear gate and on to the walkway leading past the dunes. Lee intended to go down to the sand, watch the ocean and drink beer until either his mind ceased to function or he came up with a brilliant plan that would save them both. Or at least him. For some reason, he turned to look back at the house for a moment. The light was on in Faith's bedroom. The mini-blinds were down but not closed.

As Faith came into view, Lee stiffened. She didn't close the blinds. She moved through the room, disappeared into the bathroom for a minute and then reappeared. As she started to undress, Lee looked around to see if anyone was watching him watching her. The police responding to a Peeping-Tom call would put the finishing touches on a

269

spectacular day in the charmed life of Lee Adams. The other homes were dark, however; he could safely continue his voyeurism. Her shirt came off first, then her pants. She kept shedding clothes until all the window was filled with skin. And she didn't slip into any pajamas or even a T-shirt. Apparently this highly paid lobbyist-turned-Joan-of-Arc slept in the raw. Lee had a fairly clear view of things the towel had only hinted at. Maybe she knew he was out here and was putting on a peep show for him. What, as compensation for destroying his life? The bedroom light went out and Lee popped a beer, turned and headed for the beach. The show was over.

He had finished the first beer by the time he hit the sand. The tide was starting to roll in, and he didn't have to venture far to be in water past his ankles. He cracked another beer and went in farther, up to his knees. The water was freezing, but he went in farther still, almost to his crotch, and then stopped, for a practical reason: A wet pistol wasn't particularly useful.

He sloughed back to the sand, dropped the beer, slipped off his waterlogged sneakers and started to run. He was tired, but his legs moved seemingly of their own accord, his limbs scissoring, his breath coming in great chunks of foggy air. He did a quick mile, one of his fastest ever, it seemed to him. Then he dropped to the sand, sucking oxygen from the damp air. He felt hot and then chilled. He thought about his mother and father, his siblings. He envisioned his daughter Renee when she was young, falling off her great horse and calling for Daddy, her cries finally dying away to nothing when he did not come. It was as though his flow of blood had been reversed; it was all backing up, not knowing where to go. He felt the walls of his body giving way, unable to hold everything inside.

He stood on shaky legs, jogged unsteadily back to the beer and his shoes. He sat on the sand for a while, listened to the ocean scream at him and downed another two cans of Red Dog. He squinted into the darkness. It was funny. A few beers and he could see clearly the end of his life at the edge of the horizon. Always wondered when it was going to happen. Now he knew. Forty-one years, three months and fourteen days and the Man upstairs had pulled his ticket. He looked to the sky, waved. *Thanks a lot, God.*

He rose and moved on to the house but didn't go inside. Instead he went to the enclosed courtyard, put his pistol on the table, stripped off all his clothes and dived into the pool. The water temperature, he figured, hovered around eighty-five degrees. His chills quickly disappeared and he went under, touched bottom, did an awkward handstand, blowing freshly chlorinated water out his nostrils, and then floated on the surface, staring at a sky smeared with clouds. He swam some more, practiced his crawl and breast strokes and then drifted over to the side and downed another beer.

He crawled up on the pool deck and thought of his ruined life and of the woman who had done it to him. He dove back in, did another few laps and then climbed out of the pool for good. He looked down, surprised. That was a real kicker. He looked up at the dark window. Was she asleep? How could she be? How in hell could she be, after all this?

Lee decided he would find out for certain. No one could screw up his life and then fall into peaceful sleep. He looked down at himself again. Shit! He glanced at his soggy, sandy clothes and then up at the window. He finished another can of beer in quick gulps, his pulse seemingly spiking with each swallow. He wouldn't need the threads. He'd leave his pistol down here too. If things got out of hand, he didn't want lead to start flying. He pitched the last can of Red Dog over the fence, unopened. Let the birds pry it open and get a buzz. Why should he have all the fun?

He opened the side door quietly and took the stairs two at a time. He thought about kicking her bedroom door in but found it unlocked. He pushed the door open, peered in, letting his eyes adjust to the darkness here. He could make her out on the bed, one long hump. *One long hump.* To his alcohol-saturated mind, that phrase was immensely funny. He took three quick strides and was next to the bed.

Faith stared up at him. "Lee." It wasn't a question, how she said it. It was a simple statement that he didn't know the meaning of.

He knew she could see he was naked. Even in the darkness he trusted she could see he was fully aroused. With a sudden thrust of his arm he stripped the cover off her.

"Lee?" she said again, this time a question.

He looked down at the fine curves and softness of her naked body. His pulse rose, the blood rocketed through his veins, delivering a devilish potency to a man severely wronged. He roughly bulled between her legs, flopped down chest-to-chest. She made no move to resist, her body limp. He started to kiss her on the neck and then stopped. It was not that sort of thing. No tenderness. He clenched her wrists hard.

She just lay there, saying nothing, not telling him to stop. This angered him. He breathed heavily in her face. He wanted her to know it was the beer, not her. He wanted her to feel, to know this was not about her or how she looked or how he felt about her or anything else. He was a red-eyed drunken sonofabitch and she was easy meat. That was all. He loosened his grip. He wanted her to scream, to slug

272

him as hard as she could. Then he would stop. But not before.

Her voice broke through the sounds of what he was doing. "I'd appreciate if you'd get your elbows off my chest."

He wouldn't stop, however, kept going. Hard elbow against soft tissue. The king and the peasant. *Give it to me, Faith. Clean my clock.*

"You don't have to do it like this."

"Whad'cha have in mind?" he slurred back. Navy shore leave in New York City was the last time he had even come close to being this drunk. Intense pain clacked against his temples. Five beers and a few glasses of wine and he was pretty damn well blitzed. God, he was getting old.

"Me on top. You're obviously too intoxicated to know what you're even doing." Her tone was blunt, reproachful.

"On top? Always the boss, even between the sheets? The hell with you." He squeezed her wrists so tightly his thumbs and index fingers touched together. To her credit she didn't even make a whimper, though he could sense the pain coursing through her in how her body tensed under him. He pawed her breasts and buttocks, roughly pummeled her legs and torso. He made no move, though, to enter her. And it wasn't because he was too drunk to accomplish the mechanics; it was because not even alcohol could make him do that to a woman. He kept his eyes closed, didn't want to look at her. But he dipped his face to hers. Lee wanted Faith to smell the stink of his sweat, to soak in the barley and hops base of his lust.

"I just thought you might enjoy it more, that's all," she said.

"Dammit!" he roared. "Are you just gonna let me do this?"

"Would you have me call the police?"

Her voice was like a twirling drill bit against his already throbbing skull. He hovered over her, arms locked, the cords of his triceps bulging.

He felt a tear escape his eye, touch his cheeks, like a single wandering snowflake – homeless, just like him. "Why aren't you kicking the shit out of me, Faith?"

"Because it's not your fault."

Lee started to feel sick to his stomach, his arms weakening. She moved her arm, and he let it go, releasing her without Faith having to say a word. She touched his face, very gently, like a feather dropped from the sky. With a simple motion she rubbed the single tear away. When she spoke, her voice was hoarse. "Because I took your life."

He nodded in understanding. "So if I run with you, do I get this every night? My little dog biscuit?"

"If that's what you want." She suddenly took her hand away, let it drop to the bedding.

He made no move to take it again.

He finally opened his eyes and stared down at the numbing sadness in her gaze, the lingering pain in the tightness of her neck and face; pain he had inflicted and she had taken, silently; the outline of her own hopeless tears against pale cheeks. They all were like searing heat that somehow flashed right past his skin, collided with his heart, vaporizing it.

He pulled himself off her, staggered into the bathroom. He barely made it to the toilet, where the beer and dinner came out much faster than it had gone in. Then Lee passed out on the very expensive Italian tile floor.

The tingle of the cold washcloth against his forehead brought him around. Faith was behind him, cradling him. She seemed to be wearing some kind of long-

274

sleeved T-shirt. He could make out her long, muscular calves and her skinny, curved toes. Lee felt a thick towel across his middle. He was still nauseous, and cold, his teeth chattering. She helped him sit up and then stand, her arm around his waist. He was wearing a pair of Jockeys. She must have done it; he wouldn't have been capable. As it was, he felt like he'd been hog-tied to a whirlybird for about two days. Together they made it back to the bed and she helped him in, covering him with the sheet and comforter.

"I'll sleep in another room," she said softly.

He said nothing, refusing to open his eyes once more.

He could hear her move to the door. Right before she left, he said, "I'm sorry, Faith." He swallowed; his tongue felt big as a damn pineapple.

Before she closed the door, he heard her say so very quietly, "You won't believe this, Lee, but I'm more sorry than you."

THIRTY-FOUR

Brooke Reynolds looked calmly around the interior of the bank. It had just opened and there were no other customers in the branch. In another life she might have been casing the place for future robbery. The thought actually brought a rare smile to her face. She had several scenarios she could have played out, but the very young man sitting behind the desk, with the title of assistant branch manager on a name plate in front of him, had decided the matter.

He looked up as she approached. "Can I help you?"

His eyes grew appreciably larger when the FBI creds came out, and he sat up much straighter, as though attempting to show her that he indeed had a backbone beneath the boyish facade. "Is there a problem?"

"I need your assistance, Mr. Sobel," Reynolds said, eyeing the name on the brass plate. "It has to do with an ongoing Bureau investigation."

"Of course, certainly, whatever I can do," he said.

Reynolds sat down across from him and spoke in a quiet, direct manner. "I have a key here that fits a safe-deposit box at this branch. It was obtained during the investigation. We think whatever's in the box might lead to serious consequences. I need to get inside that box."

"I see. Well, um—"

"I have the account statement with me, if that'll help."

Bankers loved paper, she knew; and the more numbers and statistics, the better. She handed it across to him.

He looked down at the statement.

"Do you recognize the name Frank Andrews?" she asked.

"No," he said. "But I've only been at this branch for a week. Bank consolidation, it never ends."

"I'm sure; even the government is cutting way back."

"I hope not with you people. Lot of crime out there."

"I guess, being in bank management, you see a lot."

The young man looked smug and sipped his coffee. "Oh, the stories I could tell you."

"I bet. Is there any way to tell how often Mr. Andrews visited the box?"

"Absolutely. We transfer those logs to the computer now." He punched in the account number on his computer and waited while it crunched the data. "Would you like some coffee, Agent Reynolds?"

"Thanks, no. How large a box is it?"

He glanced at the statement. "From the monthly fee, it's our deluxe, double width."

"I guess it can hold a lot."

"They're very roomy." He leaned forward and spoke in a low voice. "I bet this has to do with drugs, doesn't it? Laundering, that sort of thing? I've taken a class on the subject."

"I'm sorry, Mr. Sobel, it's an ongoing investigation, and I really can't comment. You understand."

He quickly leaned back. "Absolutely. Sure. We all have rules – you wouldn't believe what we have to deal with at this place."

"I'm sure. Anything come up on the computer?"

"Oh, right." Sobel looked at the screen. "He's actually been in here quite a bit. I can print the log out for you, if you'd like."

"That would be a big help."

As they walked toward the vault a minute later, Sobel started looking nervous. "I'm just wondering if I should check upstairs first. I mean, I'm sure they'd have no problem and all, but still, they're incredibly strict with safe-deposit box access."

"I understand, but I thought the assistant branch manager would have the authority. I won't be taking anything out, just reviewing the contents. And depending on what I find, the box may have to be impounded. It's not the first time the Bureau's had to do this. I'll take full responsibility. Don't worry."

That seemed to relieve the young man and they proceeded into the vault. He took Reynolds's key and his own master and pulled out the large box.

"We have a private room where you can look at it."

He showed her into the small room and Reynolds closed the door. She took a deep breath and noticed that her palms were sweaty. In this box might be something that could shatter any number of lives and perhaps careers. She slowly raised the lid. What she saw made her swear under her breath.

The cash was neatly bundled with thick rubber bands, old, not new bills. She did a quick count. Tens of thousands. She put the lid back down.

Sobel was standing outside the booth when she opened the door. He returned the box to the vault.

"Can I see the sign-in register for this box?"

He showed her the signature log. It was Ken Newman's handwriting; she knew it well. A murdered FBI agent and a box full of cash under an alias. God help them.

278

"Did you find anything helpful?" Sobel asked.

"I need this box impounded. Anyone shows up wanting to get inside, you're to call me immediately at these numbers." She handed him her card.

"This is serious, isn't it?" Sobel suddenly looked very unhappy that he had been assigned to this branch.

"I appreciate your help, Mr. Sobel. I'll be in touch."

Reynolds returned to her car and drove as quickly as possible toward Anne Newman's house. She called from her car and confirmed the woman would be home. The funeral was scheduled to take place in three days. It would be a big affair, with top officials from the Bureau as well as law enforcement agencies from across the country attending. The funeral motorcade would be especially long and would pass between columns of somber, respectful federal agents and men and women in blue. The FBI buried its agents who died in the line of duty with the great honor and dignity they deserved.

"What did you find out, Brooke?" Anne Newman wore a black dress, her hair was nicely styled, and there was a touch of makeup on her face. Reynolds could hear talk coming from the kitchen. There were two cars parked out front when she had arrived. Probably family or friends offering condolences. She also noted platters of food on the dining room table. Cooking and condolences seemed, ironically, to go hand in hand; grief was better digested on a full stomach, apparently.

"I need to see records of your and Ken's bank accounts. Do you know where they are?"

"Well, Ken always handled the finances, but I'm sure they're in his office." She led Reynolds down the hallway and they went into Ken Newman's home office.

"Do you have more than one bank you deal with?"

"No. That much I do know. I always get the mail. It's just the one bank. And we only have a checking account, no savings. Ken said the interest they paid was a joke. He was really good about money. We own some good stocks, and the kids have their college accounts."

While Anne looked for the records, Reynolds idly glanced around the room. Stacked on one bookshelf were numerous hard plastic containers in various colors. While she had noted the coins encased in clear plastic on her previous visit, she hadn't really focused on these.

"What's in those containers?"

Anne looked at where she was pointing. "Oh, those are Ken's sports cards. Coins too. He was really good at it. He even took a course and became certified to grade both cards and coins. Just about every weekend he was at some show or another." She pointed up to the ceiling. "That's why there's a fire detector in here. Ken was really afraid of fire, in this room especially. All that paper and plastic. It could go up in a minute."

"I'm surprised he found the time for collecting."

"Well, he made the time. He really loved it."

"Did you or the kids ever go with him?"

"No. He never asked us to."

Her tone made Reynolds drop that line of inquiry. "I hate to ask this, but did Ken have life insurance?"

"Yes. A lot."

"At least you won't have to worry about that. I know it's little enough consolation, but so many people never think about those things. Ken obviously wanted you all to be taken care of if anything happened to him. Acts of love often speak louder than words." Reynolds was sincere, yet that last statement had sounded so incredibly lame that she decided to shut her mouth on the subject.

Anne pulled out a three-inch red notebook and handed it to Reynolds.

"I think this is what you're looking for. There are more in the drawer. This is the most current one."

Reynolds looked down at the binder. There was a laminated label affixed to the front flap of the notebook indicating that it contained checking account statements for the current year. She flipped it open. The statements were neatly labeled and organized chronologically by month, the most recent month on top.

"The canceled checks are in the other drawer. Ken kept them divided by year."

Damn! Reynolds kept her financial records stuffed in an assortment of drawers in her bedroom and even in the garage. Tax time at the Reynolds household was an accountant's worst nightmare.

"Anne, I know you have company. I can look through these by myself."

"You can take them with you if you want."

"If you don't mind, I'll look at them here."

"Okay. Would you like something to drink or eat? Lord knows we've got plenty of food. And I just put on a fresh pot of coffee."

"Actually, coffee would be great, thanks. Just a little cream and sugar."

Anne suddenly looked nervous. "You still haven't told me if you found out anything."

"I want to make absolutely sure before I say anything. I don't want to be wrong." As Reynolds looked into the poor woman's face, she felt tremendous guilt. Here she was letting the man's wife unknowingly assist her in possibly tarnishing her husband's memory.

"How are the kids holding up?" Reynolds asked, doing her best to shake this traitorous feeling.

281

"How any children would be, I suppose. They're sixteen and seventeen, so they understand things better than a five-year-old would. But it's still hard. For all of us. Only reason I'm not still bawling is that I ran out of tears this morning. I sent them to school. I decided it couldn't be any worse than sitting around here while a parade of people came through talking about their dad."

"You're probably right."

"You can only do the best you can. I knew there was always the possibility. God, Ken was an agent for twenty years. The only time he ever got hurt on duty was when his car got a flat and he wrenched his back changing the tire." Anne smiled briefly at this memory. "He was even talking about retirement. Maybe moving away when the kids were both at college. His mother lives in South Carolina. She's getting to the age where she needs some family close by."

Anne looked like she might start crying again. If she did, Reynolds wasn't sure she wouldn't join her, given her own mental state right now.

"You have children?"

"Boy and girl. Three and six."

Anne smiled. "Oh, still babies."

"I understand it gets tougher as they get older."

"Well, let's put it this way, it gets more complex. You go from spitting, biting, potty-training, to battles over clothes, boys, money. About age thirteen they suddenly can't stand being around Mom and Dad. That one was tough, but they finally came back. Then you worry yourself sick over alcohol and cars and sex and drugs."

Reynolds managed a weak smile. "Gee, I can't wait."

"How long have you been with the Bureau?"

"Thirteen years. Joined after one incredibly boring

year as a corporate lawyer."

"It can be a dangerous business."

Reynolds stared at her. "It certainly can be."

"You're married?"

"Technically, yes, but in a couple of months, no."

"Sorry to hear that."

"Believe me, it's best all around."

"You're keeping the children?"

"Absolutely."

"That's good. Children belong with their mothers, I don't care what the politically correct folk say."

"In my case, I wonder – I work long, unpredictable hours. All I know is that my children belong with me."

"You say you have a law degree?"

"From Georgetown."

"Lawyers make good money. And it's not nearly as dangerous as being an FBI agent."

"I suppose not." Reynolds finally realized where this was going.

"You might want to think about a career change. Too many nuts out there now. And too many guns. When Ken started at the Bureau, there weren't kids just out of diapers running around with machine guns shooting people down like they were in some damn cartoon."

Reynolds had no answer for that. She just stood there hugging the notebook to her chest, thinking of her kids.

"I'll bring your coffee."

Anne closed the door behind her and Reynolds sank into the nearest chair. She was having a sudden vision of her body being put inside a black pouch while the palm reader delivered the bad news to her bereaved children. *I told your mother so.* Shit! She shook off these thoughts and opened the notebook. Anne returned with her coffee, and then, left to herself, Reynolds made considerable progress. What she found out was very disturbing.

For at least the last three years, Ken Newman had made deposits, all in cash, to his checking account. The amounts were small – a hundred dollars here, fifty there – and they were made at random times. She pulled out the log Sobel had given her and ran her eye down the dates Newman had visited the safe-deposit box. Most of them corresponded with the dates he had also deposited cash into his checking account. Visit the box, put fresh cash in, take some old cash out and deposit it in the family bank account, she surmised.

It all added up to a significant amount of money, yet not a vast fortune. The thing was, the total balance of the checking account was never very large because there were always checks written on the account that depleted this balance. Newman's FBI payroll checks were on direct deposit, she noted. And there were numerous checks written to a stock brokerage firm. Reynolds found those records in another drawer and quickly determined that while Newman was far from wealthy, he'd had a nice stock portfolio going, and the records showed he religiously added to it. With the long bull market still steaming along, his investments had grown considerably.

Except for the cash deposits, what she was looking at wasn't really that unusual. He had saved money and invested it well. He wasn't wealthy, but he was comfortable. Dividends from the investment account were also deposited to the Newmans' checking account, further muddling the income picture. Simply put, it would be difficult to conclude that there was anything suspicious about the agent's finances unless one really took a very close look. And unless one knew about the safe-deposit box cash, the amount of money seemingly at issue just didn't warrant that level of scrutiny.

The confusing thing was the amount of cash she had seen in the safe-deposit box. Why keep that much in the box where it was earning no interest? What puzzled her almost as much as the cash was what she *wasn't* finding. When Anne came to check on her, she decided to ask her directly.

"I'm not finding any mortgage or credit card payments recorded here."

"We don't have a mortgage. That is, we did, a thirty-year one, but Ken made extra payments and finally paid it off early."

"Good for him. When was that?"

"About three or four years ago, I think."

"What about credit cards?"

"Ken didn't believe in them. What we bought, we bought with cash. Appliances, clothes, even cars. We never bought new, only used."

"Well, that's smart. Saves a ton in finance charges."

"Like I said, Ken was really good with the money."

"If I'd known how good, I would've had him help me."

"Do you need to look at anything else?"

"One more thing, I'm afraid. Your tax returns for the last couple of years, if you have them."

The large amount of cash in the box made sense now to Reynolds. If Newman paid cash for everything, then he would have no need to deposit it in his checking account. Of course, for things like the mortgage, the utilities and the phone bill, he needed to write a check, so he would have to deposit cash to cover those checks. And this also meant that for the money he didn't deposit into his checking account there was no record that he ever had the money in the box at all. Cash was cash, after all. And that meant that the IRS would have no way of knowing Newman ever had it either.

He wisely hadn't changed his lifestyle. Same house, no fancy cars, and he hadn't gone on insane shopping binges that had toppled so many thieves. And with no mortgage or credit card payments, he had a lot of free cash flow; on a cursory examination, this would seem to explain the ability to make the regular stock investments. Someone would have to really dig as Reynolds had to uncover the truth.

Anne found tax returns for the last six years in the metal filing cabinet standing against one wall. These were as well organized as the rest of the man's financial records. A quick look at the returns for the last three years confirmed Reynolds's suspicions. The only income listed was Newman's FBI salary and some miscellaneous investment interest and dividends and bank interest.

Reynolds put the files back and slipped on her coat. "Anne, I'm so sorry I had to come and do all this in the middle of everything you're having to deal with."

"I asked *you* for help, Brooke."

Reynolds felt another stab of guilt. "Well, I don't know how much help I've been."

Anne gripped her arm. "Now can you tell me what's going on? Has Ken done anything wrong?"

"All I can tell you right now is that I found some things I can't explain. I won't lie to you, they are very troubling."

Anne slowly took her hand away. "I guess you'll have to report what you've found."

Reynolds stared at the woman. Technically what she should do was go directly to OPR and tell them everything. The Office of Professional Responsibility was officially under the umbrella of the Bureau but was actually run by the Department of Justice. OPR investigated allegations of misconduct by Bureau personnel. They had a reputation for being very thorough. An OPR investigation could put a scare into even the toughest FBI agent.

Yes, from a simple technical point of view, it was a no-brainer. If life could only be so simple. The devastated woman standing before Reynolds made her decision much less simple. In the end she went with her human side and put aside the Bureau manual for now. Ken Newman would be buried a hero. The man had been an agent for two decades; he at least deserved that.

"At some point, yes, I'll have to report my findings. But not right now." She paused and gripped the woman's hand. "I know when the funeral is. I'll be there with everyone else, paying our respects to Ken."

Reynolds gave Anne a reassuring hug and then walked out, her mind whirling so fast she felt a little dizzy.

If Ken Newman was on the take, he had been doing it for a while. Was he the leak on Reynolds's investigation? Had he sold out other investigations as well? Was he just a freelancing mole selling to the highest bidder? Or was he a regular snitch working for the same party? If so, why was such a party interested in Faith Lockhart? There were foreign interests involved. Lockhart had told them that much. Was that the key? Was Newman working for a foreign government all this time, a foreign government that was also coincidentally caught up in Buchanan's scheme?

She sighed. The whole thing was snowballing into something so big, she halfway felt like running home and pulling the covers over her head. Instead she would get in her car, drive to the office and continue chipping away at this case, as she had hundreds of others over the years. She had won more than she had lost. And that was the best anyone in her line of work could ever hope for.

THIRTY-FIVE

Lee had awoken very late with the mother of all hangovers and decided to run it off. At first, each of his strides on the sand sent lethal darts through his brain. Then, as he loosened up, breathed the chilly air, felt the salty wind on his face, at about the one-mile point in his run, the effects of his crushed grape and Red Dog shooters disappeared. When he got back to the beach house, he went around to the pool and retrieved his clothes and his gun. He sat in a sling chair for a while, letting the sun warm him. When he went back inside, he smelled coffee and eggs.

Faith was in the kitchen, pouring a cup of coffee. She had on jeans and a short-sleeved shirt and was barefoot. When she saw him come in, she pulled out another mug and filled it. For a moment, this simple act of companionship pleased him. And then his actions of the night before washed that feeling away, like ocean waves brutally wiping out sand castles.

"I figured you'd sleep all day," she said. Her tone was excessively casual, he thought, and she didn't look at him when she spoke.

This qualified for the most awkward moment in Lee's entire life. What was he supposed to say? *Hey, sorry about that little sexual assault thing last night.*

He came into the kitchen area, fingered the mug, half hoping the large lump in his throat would end up strangling him to death. "Sometimes the best remedy for doing something incredibly stupid and inexcusable is to run until you drop." He glanced at the eggs. "Smells good."

"Doesn't compare to the meal you made last night. But then again, I'm no whiz in the kitchen. I guess I'm a room-service kind of girl. But I'm sure you already figured that out." As she moved over to the stove, he noted she walked with a slight limp. He also couldn't fail to notice the bruises on her uncovered wrists. He laid the pistol down on the counter before he could impulsively use it to blow his brains out.

"Faith?"

She didn't turn around, just kept scrambling the eggs around in the pan.

"If you want me to leave, I'll leave," said Lee.

While she seemed to consider this, he decided to say what he had been thinking during his run. "What happened last night, what I *did* to you last night, there's no excuse for. I've never, ever done anything like that in my life. That's not who I am. I can't blame you if you don't believe that. But it's the truth."

She suddenly turned to him, her eyes glistening. "Well, I can't say I hadn't imagined something happening between us, even in the nightmare we're in. I just didn't think it would be like that. . . ." Her voice broke off and she just as quickly turned away from him.

He looked down and nodded slightly, her words doubly devastating to him. "You see, I'm in a bit of a dilemma here. My gut and my conscience tell me to get out of your life so you won't have to be reminded of what happened last night every time you see me. But I don't want to leave you alone with all this. Not when someone's out to kill you."

She turned the burner off and set out two plates, shoveled the eggs on them, buttered two pieces of toast and put everything on the table. Lee didn't move. He just watched her, moving slowly, her cheeks wet from her tears. The bruises on her wrists were like permanent shackles around his soul.

He sat down across from her and picked at his eggs.

"I could have stopped you last night," she said bluntly. The tears slid down her cheeks and she made no attempt to wipe them away.

Lee felt his own eyes begin to burn with the beginnings of tears. "I wish to God you had."

"You were drunk. I'm not saying that's an excuse for what you did, but I also know you wouldn't have done it if you had been sober. And you also didn't go all the way. I choose to believe you would never sink so low as that. In fact, if I weren't absolutely sure of that, I would've shot you with your gun when you passed out." She paused, seemed to be searching for the right combination of words. "But maybe what I've done to you is much more awful than what you could have done to me last night." She pushed her plate away and looked out the window at what was shaping up to be a beautiful day.

When she next spoke, it was in a wistful, faraway tone that was curiously both hopeful and tragic. "When I was a little girl, I had my whole life planned out. I was going to be a nurse. And then a doctor. And I was going to get married and have ten kids. Dr. Faith Lockhart was going to save lives during the day and then come home to a wonderful man who loved her and be the perfect mother to her perfect children. After moving around all those years with my father, I just wanted *one* home. I'd live there the rest of my life. My children would always, always know where to find me. It seemed so simple, so . . . achievable, when I was only eight years old." She finally used her paper napkin to dab at her eyes, only then seeming to feel the wetness on her face.

She looked back at Lee. "But I have this life instead." Her gaze roamed the lovely room. "I actually had a pretty good run. Made a lot of money. What do I have to complain about? That's the American dream, isn't it? Money? Power? Owning beautiful things? Hell, I even ended up doing a little good, even if I did it illegally. But then I went and ruined everything. The best of intentions, but I struck out in the end. Just like my father. You're right, the nut didn't fall far from the tree." She paused again, played with her silverware, precisely placing the fork and butter knife perpendicular to one another.

"I don't want you to leave." On this she rose, quickly crossed the room and then raced up the stairs.

Lee heard her bedroom door slam shut.

Lee took a deep breath, stood and was surprised to find his legs so rubbery. It wasn't from the run, he knew. He showered, changed and came back downstairs. Faith's door was still closed and he had no intention of interrupting whatever she was doing in there. With his nerves unraveling, he decided to spend an hour with the mundane task of thoroughly cleaning his gun. The downside to salt and water was that they were tough on weapons, and automatic pistols were notoriously finicky anyway. If the ammo wasn't of a very high quality, you could count on the thing misfiring and then jamming – or a little sand and grit could cause the same malfunction. And you couldn't clear a pistol by simply pulling the trigger and bringing up a clean cylinder, as you would a revolver. By the time you got your pistol all straightened out, you'd be dead. And with Lee's luck to date, it would happen right when he absolutely needed the thing to fire true and straight. However, on the plus side, the 9mm Parabellums fired by the compact Smith & Wesson had excellent stopping power. Whatever they hit would drop. He prayed he wouldn't have to use the gun, however. Because that would probably mean someone was shooting at him.

He reloaded the fifteen-shot magazine, inserted it in the grip and chambered a round. He clicked the safety on and holstered the gun. He thought about taking the Honda down to the store for a newspaper but decided he didn't quite have the energy or desire to undertake even such a simple task. He also didn't want to leave Faith alone. When she came downstairs, he wanted to be here.

When Lee went to get a drink of water at the kitchen sink, he glanced out the window and almost had a heart attack. Across the road, above a tall hedge that ran about as far as the eye could see, suddenly exploding into his line of vision was a small plane! That's when Lee remembered the runway Faith had told him about. It was across from the house and shielded by the tall hedge.

Lee hurried to the front door to watch the landing. By the time he got outside, the plane had already disappeared. Then whizzing above the top of the hedge was the tail of the plane. It flashed in front of him and then continued past at a fast clip.

He went up on the second-story front porch and watched as the plane taxied to a stop and the passengers deplaned. A car was waiting to pick them up. Bags were off-loaded and stored in the car, which left with the passengers. The pilot got out of the twin-prop plane, checked a few things and then climbed back in. A few minutes later the plane taxied to the other end of the runway and turned around. The pilot opened the throttle and came roaring down the runway in the same direction he had landed, and then lifted gracefully into the air.

The plane headed out toward the water, made a turn and quickly disappeared into the horizon.

Lee went back inside and tried to watch some TV, while at the same time listening for Faith. After roaming through about a thousand channels, he concluded there was absolutely nothing worth watching, and he played a game of solitaire. He enjoyed losing so much, he played another dozen games, with the same result. He wandered downstairs and shot some pool in the game room. When lunchtime came around, he fixed a tuna sandwich and some beef barley soup and ate out on the deck overlooking the pool. He watched the same plane land once more around one o'clock. It shed its passengers and soared once more. He thought about knocking on Faith's door to see if she was hungry and then decided against it. He went for a swim in the pool and then lay on the cool concrete and caught some rays from the intense sun. He felt guilty every minute for enjoying it.

The hours passed and when it started to grow dark, he began contemplating cooking dinner. He would go and get Faith this time, and make her eat. He was just about to head up the stairs when her door opened and she came out.

The first thing that caught his eye was what she was wearing: a white cotton dress, knee-length and clingy, paired with a light blue cotton sweater. Her legs were bare, and she wore simple sandals that managed to look very classy. Her hair was nicely styled; a touch of makeup highlighted her features and pale red lipstick completed the look. She held a small clutch purse. The sweater covered the bruises on her wrists. Probably why she had picked it, he thought. He was thankful that her limp seemed to be gone.

"Going out?" Lee asked.

"Dinner. I'm starving."

"I was going to make something."

"I'd rather eat out. I'm getting cabin fever."

"So where are you going?"

"Well, actually I thought *we* might go."

Lee looked down at his faded khakis, deck shoes and short-sleeved Polo shirt. "I look sort of ragged next to you."

"You look fine." She glanced at the holstered gun. "I'd leave the six-shooter behind, though."

He looked at her dress. "Faith, I'm not sure how comfortable you'll be on the Honda in that."

"The country club's only a half mile up the road. It has a public restaurant. I thought we could walk. Looks to be a beautiful evening."

Lee finally nodded, understanding that getting out made perfect sense, for a lot of reasons. "Sounds good. Give me a sec." He ran upstairs, slipped off his gun and put it in a drawer in his room. He splashed water on his face, wet down his hair a little, grabbed his jacket and joined Faith at the front door, where she was activating the alarm. They left the house and crossed the service road. Reaching the sidewalk, which ran parallel to the main road, they strolled along under a sky that had changed to pink from blue as the sun sank. Landscape lighting had come on in the common areas and so had the underground sprinklers. The sound of the pressurized water was soothing to Lee. The lighting lent a nice mood to the walk, he thought. The whole place seemed to possess almost an ethereal glow, as though they were in a perfectly lit scene from a movie.

Lee looked up in time to see the same twin-prop airplane coming in for a landing. He shook his head.

"Scared the hell out of me the first time I saw that thing this morning."

"It would have scared me too, except the first time

295

I came here I was flying on it. That's the last flight for the evening. It's getting too dark now."

They reached the restaurant, which was decorated with a distinctly nautical theme: a big ship's wheel at the front entrance, diving helmets hung on the wall, fish netting suspended from the ceiling, knotty pine walls, rope banisters and hand rails and an enormous aquarium filled with castles, plant life and an odd assortment of fish peeking out here and there. The servers were young, energetic and attired in cruise line uniforms. The one attending Faith and Lee's table was particularly bubbly. She took their drink orders. Lee opted for iced tea. Faith ordered a wine spritzer. That done, the waitress proceeded to sing the specials of the day in a pleasant if wavering alto. After she left, Faith and Lee looked at each other and had to laugh.

While they waited for their drinks, Faith looked around the room.

Lee shot her a glance. "See anybody you recognize?"

"No. I never really went out when I came down here. I was afraid I'd run into someone I knew."

"Stay cool. You look very different from Faith Lockhart." He looked her over. "And I should have said this before, but you look really . . . well, you really look pretty tonight. I mean really fine." He suddenly looked embarrassed. "Not that you don't look good all the time. I meant . . ." Thoroughly tongue-tied, Lee lapsed into silence, sat back and perused his menu.

Faith looked over at him, feeling just as awkward as he did, she was sure, but a smile still eased across her lips. "Thank you."

They were there for two pleasant stolen hours, discussing innocuous subjects, telling stories of times past and learning more about each other. Since it was the off-season and a weekday, there were few other patrons. They finished their meal, then had coffee and shared a thick slice of coconut cream pie. They paid in cash and left a very generous tip, which would probably make their waitress sing all the way home.

Faith and Lee walked slowly back, enjoying the crisp night air and digesting their meals. Instead of going to the house, though, Faith led Lee down to the beach after dropping her purse off by the back door of the beach house. She slipped off her sandals and they continued their stroll on the sand. It was completely dark now, the wind light and refreshing, and they had the beach entirely to themselves.

Lee looked over at her. "Going out was a good idea. I really enjoyed myself."

"You can be very charming when you want to be."

He looked annoyed for a moment until he realized she was kidding him. "I guess going out together made for a fresh start of sorts too."

"That did cross my mind." She stopped and sat down on the beach, sinking her feet into the sand. Lee remained standing, looking out to the ocean.

"So what do we do now, Lee?"

He sat next to her, slipped off his shoes and curled his toes under the sand. "It would be great if we could stay here, but I don't think we can."

"Then where? I'm fresh out of houses."

"I've been thinking about that. I've got some good buddies in San Diego. Private investigators like me. They know everybody. If I ask, I'm sure they'll help us slip across the border into Mexico."

Faith didn't look very enthusiastic about that idea. "Mexico? And from there?"

Lee shrugged. "I don't know. We can maybe get some fake documents and use them to get to South America."

"South America? And you work the cocaine fields while I labor in a brothel?"

"Look, I've been there. It's not just drugs and prostitutes. We'll have lots of options."

"Two fugitives from justice with God knows who else after them?" Faith looked down at the sand and shook her head doubtfully.

"If you have a better idea, I'm listening," said Lee.

"I've got money. A lot of it in a numbered account in Switzerland."

He looked skeptical. "They really have those things?"

"Oh, yes. And all those global conspiracies you've probably heard about? Secret organizations ruling the planet? Well, they're all true." She smiled and tossed sand on him.

"Well, if the Feds search your home or office, will they find records for it? If they know the account numbers, they can put a tag on it. Trace the money."

"The whole purpose of a Swiss numbered account is to ensure absolute confidentiality. If Swiss bankers ran around giving out that information to anyone who asked for it, their whole system sort of topples."

"The FBI isn't just anyone."

"Not to worry, I didn't keep any records. I have the access information with me."

Lee looked unconvinced. "So do you have to go to Switzerland to get the money? Because that would be, you know, sort of impossible."

"I went there to open the account. The bank appointed a fiduciary, a bank employee, with a power of attorney to handle the transaction in person. It's pretty elaborate. You have to show your access numbers, give positive ID, then provide your signature, which they compare with the one they have on file."

"So from then on you call the fiduciary and he

does all that for you?"

"Right. I've done small transactions in the past, just to make sure it works. It's the same guy. He knows me and my voice. I give him the numbers and where I want the money to go. And it happens."

"You know you can't deposit it in Faith Lockhart's checking account."

"No, but I have a bank account down here under the name of SLC Corporation."

"And you're a signatory as an officer?"

"Yes, as Suzanne Blake."

"The problem is, the Feds know that name. Remember, from the airport."

"Do you know how many Suzanne Blakes there are in this country?"

Lee shrugged. "That's true."

"So at least we'll have money to live off. It won't last us forever, but it's something."

"Something is good."

They fell silent for a bit. Faith alternated between nervously looking at him and then out toward the ocean.

He glanced at her, having noticed her scrutiny. "What is it? Do I have coconut pie on my chin?"

"Lee, when the money comes, you can take half and leave. You don't have to come with me."

"Faith, we've already been through this."

"No, we haven't. I practically ordered you to come with me. I know it would be difficult to go back without me, but at least you'll have the money to go somewhere. Look, I can even call the FBI. I'll tell them you had no involvement. You were just blindly helping me. And that I gave you the slip. Then you can go back home."

"Thanks, Faith, but let's take it one step at a time. And I can't leave until I know you're safe."

"Are you sure?"

299

"Yes, I'm really sure. I won't go unless you tell me to. And then even if you do, I'll still stalk you, to make sure you're okay."

She reached out and took his arm. "Lee, I can never thank you enough for all you've done for me."

"Just consider me the big brother you never had."

The look they shared, though, held more than sibling affection. He looked down at the sand, trying to get his head straight. Faith looked back out at the water. When Lee looked over at her a minute later, Faith was moving her head from side to side and smiling.

"What are you thinking?" he asked.

She stood and looked down at him. "I'm thinking that I'd like to dance."

He stared up at her in amazement. "Dancing? How much *did* you have to drink?"

"How many nights do we have left here? Two? Three? Then it's off to play fugitive for the rest of our lives? Come on, Lee, last chance to party." She slipped off her sweater and let it fall to the sand. The white dress had spaghetti straps. She slipped them off her shoulders, gave him a heart-stopping wink and held out her hands for Lee to take. "Let's go, big boy."

"You're crazy, you truly are." However, Lee gripped her hands and stood. "Fair warning, I haven't danced in a long time."

"You're a boxer, right? Your footwork is probably better than mine. I'll lead first, and then you take over."

Lee took a few halting steps and dropped his hands. "This is silly, Faith. What if somebody's watching? They'll think we're nuts."

She looked at him stubbornly. "I've spent the last fifteen years of my life worrying about what everybody thought about everything. So right now, I don't give a damn about what anybody thinks about anything."

"But we don't even have any music."

"Hum a tune. Listen to the wind, it'll come."

And surprisingly it did. They started slowly at first, Lee feeling clumsy and Faith unused to leading. Then, as they started to get more familiar with each other's movements, they began making wider circles in the sand. After about ten minutes, Lee's right hand was perched comfortably on Faith's hip, hers was around his waist, their other pair of hands were interlocked and held chest high.

Then they grew noticeably braver and started doing some spins and twirls and other moves reminiscent of Big Band swing and Lindy hop. It was difficult, even in the hard-packed sand, but they gave it an inspired effort. Anyone watching would have thought them either intoxicated or reliving their youth and having the time of their lives. And, in a way, both observations would have been true.

"I haven't done this since high school," Lee said, smiling. "Although Three Dog Night was the big thing back then, not Benny Goodman."

Faith said nothing as she twirled and dipped around him, her moves growing more and more daring, more and more seductive; a flamenco dancer in white flaming heat.

She hiked her skirt up to give herself more freedom of movement, and Lee felt his heart race at the sight of her pale thighs.

They even ventured out into the water, splashing mightily as they went about their increasingly intricate dance steps. They had some tumbles into the sand and even into the salty, chilly water, but they got back up and kept going. Occasionally a truly spectacular combination, perfectly executed, left them both breathless and grinning like school-kids at a prom.

They finally reached the point where they both grew silent, their smiles faded and they drew closer to each other. The spins and twirls stopped, their heavy breaths eased and they found their bodies touching as their dance circles grew smaller. Finally they stopped altogether and simply stood there rocking slightly side to side, the last dance of the evening, arms around each other, faces close, eyes directly on one another as the wind whistled around them, the waves pitched and crashed hard, the stars and the moon watched from above.

Faith finally stepped away from him, her eyelids heavy, her limbs starting to once again erotically move to a silent tune.

Lee reached out to take her back. "I don't feel like dancing anymore, Faith." His meaning was crystal clear.

She reached out to him too, and then, quick as the snap of a whip, she shoved him hard in the chest and he flopped backward into the sand. She turned and ran, her peals of laughter descending over him as he looked after her, stunned. He grinned, jumped up and raced after her, catching her at the stairs going up to the beach house. He slung her over his shoulder and carried her the rest of the way, her legs and arms flailing in mock protest. They had forgotten the house alarm was set and went in the back door. Faith had to race like mad to the front door to disarm it in time.

"God, that was close. Like we really want the police coming by," she said.

"I don't want anybody coming by."

Gripping his hand tightly, Faith led Lee up to her bedroom. They sat on the bed in the darkness for a few minutes holding one another, gently rocking back and forth as though extending their movements on the beach to this more intimate place.

Finally she eased back from him, cupped his chin with her hand. "It's been a while, Lee. It's been a long time, in fact." Her tone was almost one of embarrassment, and Faith did feel embarrassed at this admission. She didn't want to disappoint him.

He stroked her fingers gently, held her gaze with his as the sounds of the waves reached them through the open window. It was comforting, she thought, the water, the wind, the touches of skin; a moment she may not experience again for a very long time, if ever.

"It'll never be easier for you, Faith."

This surprised her. "Why do you say that?"

Even in the darkness the glow of his eyes surrounded her, held her – protectively, she felt. The fifth-grade romance finally consummated? And yet she was with a man, not a boy. A very unique man, in his own right. She looked him over. No, definitely not a boy.

"Because I can't believe you've ever been with a man who feels the way I do about you."

"Easy to say," she murmured, though in fact his words had touched her deeply.

"Not for me," Lee said.

These few words were spoken with such depth of sincerity, with not a trace of the glibness, the self-servedness of the world she had thrived in for the last fifteen years, that Faith honestly didn't know how to react. But the time for talk had passed. She found herself sliding Lee's clothes off, and then he disrobed her. He massaged her shoulders and neck as he did so. Lee's big fingers were surprisingly gentle. She would've expected them to be rough.

All of their movements were unhurried, natural, as though they had done this thousands of times

303

over the course of a long, happy marriage, seeking just the right spots to work, to please the other.

They slid under the covers. Ten minutes later Lee slumped down, breathing heavy. Faith was under him, gasping for air as well. She kissed his face, his chest, his arms. Their sweat mingled, their limbs intertwined, they lay there talking and slowly kissing for another two hours, falling in and out of sleep as they did so. About three in the morning they made love again. And then both collapsed into deep, exhausted sleep.

THIRTY-SIX

Reynolds was sitting at her desk when the phone call came. It was Joyce Bennett, the lawyer representing Reynolds in her divorce.

"We have a problem, Brooke. Your husband's attorney just called, ranting and raving about you hiding assets."

Brooke's face collapsed in disbelief. "Are you serious? Well, tell him to let me in on it. I could use the extra money."

"This isn't a joke. He faxed me some account statements he says he just discovered. Under the children's names."

"For God's sake, Joyce, those are the kids' college accounts. Steve knew about those. That's why I didn't list them with my assets. Besides, they only have a few hundred dollars in them."

"Actually, the statements I'm looking at show a balance of fifty thousand dollars in each."

Reynolds's mouth went dry. "That's not possible. There must be some mistake."

"The other troubling thing is that the accounts are set up as Uniform Transfer to Minor's Act accounts. That means they're revocable at the discretion of the donor and trustee. You're the listed trustee, and I'm assuming you would be the donor of the funds as well. In essence, it's your money. You should have told me about these, Brooke."

"Joyce, there was nothing to tell. I have no idea

where that money came from. What do the statements show as the origin of funds?"

"Several wire transfers of roughly equal amounts. It doesn't show where they came from. Steve's attorney is threatening to go to court and claim fraud. Brooke, he also says he's called the Bureau."

Reynolds squeezed the phone and sat rigidly. "The Bureau?"

"You're sure you don't know where the money came from? How about your parents?"

"They don't have that kind of money. Can we trace the funds?"

"It's *your* account. I think you better do something. Keep me posted."

Reynolds hung up the phone and stared blankly at the papers on her desk, her mind reeling from this latest development. When the phone rang again a few minutes later, she almost didn't answer it. She knew who it was.

Paul Fisher spoke more coldly than ever to her. She was to come to the Hoover Building immediately. That was all he would tell her. As she walked down the stairs to the parking garage, her legs threatened to collapse under her several times. Every instinct she had told her she had just been summoned to her own professional execution.

The conference room at the Hoover Building was small and windowless. Paul Fisher was there, along with the ADIC, Fred Massey. Massey sat at the head of the table, twirling a pen between his fingers, his gaze locked on her. She recognized the two other people in the room: a Bureau lawyer and a senior investigator from OPR.

"Sit down, Agent Reynolds," Massey said firmly.

Reynolds sat. She wasn't guilty of anything, so why did she feel like Charlie Manson with a bloody knife in his sock?

"We have some things to discuss with you." He glanced at the Bureau lawyer. "I have to advise you, however, that you have the right to have counsel present, if you so wish."

She tried to act surprised, but couldn't really, not after the phone call from Joyce Bennett. Her forced reaction certainly increased her guilt in their eyes, she felt sure. She wondered about the timing of that phone call from Bennett. Not a big believer in conspiracies, Reynolds suddenly began to reconsider that stance.

"And why would I need counsel?"

Massey eyed Fisher, who turned to Reynolds. "We received a phone call from the attorney representing your husband in the divorce."

"I see. Well, I just received a call from my attorney, and I can assure you I'm as much in the dark as anyone else about how that money got into those accounts."

"Really?" Massey looked at her skeptically. "So you're saying it's a mistake that someone very recently dumped a hundred thousand dollars into accounts under your children's names, monies which are solely controlled by you?"

"I'm saying I don't know what to think. But I will find out, I can assure you."

"The timing, as you can understand, has us deeply troubled," Massey said.

"Not as troubled as me. It's my reputation at stake."

"Actually, it's the reputation of the Bureau we're concerned about," Fisher bluntly pointed out.

Reynolds gave him a cold stare and then looked back at Massey. "I don't know what's going on. Feel free to investigate; I've got nothing to hide."

Massey glanced down at a file in front of him. "Are you quite certain of that?"

307

Reynolds looked at the file. This was a classic interrogation technique. She had used it herself. Bluff the subject by suggesting you had incriminating evidence that would catch him in a lie and hope he'd cave. The only thing was, she didn't know if Massey was really bluffing or not. She suddenly knew what it was like to be on the other side of the interrogation. It wasn't fun.

"Am I quite certain of what?" she said, buying time.

"That you have nothing to hide?"

"I really resent that question, sir."

He tapped the file with his index finger. "You know what has deeply distressed me about Ken Newman's death? The fact that on the night he was murdered, he had taken your place. At your instruction. But for that order, he would be alive today. Would you?"

Reynolds's face turned red and she stood, towering over Massey. "Are you accusing me of being involved in Ken's murder?"

"Please sit down, Agent Reynolds."

"Are you?"

"I'm saying the coincidence, if it is one, has me concerned."

"It *was* a coincidence, since I didn't happen to know there was someone waiting there to kill him. If you recall, I showed up almost in time to stop it."

"Almost in time. That was convenient. Almost like a built-in alibi. A coincidence, or perfect timing? Perhaps too perfect timing?" Massey's gaze burned into her.

"I was working another case and finished sooner than I thought I would. Howard Constantinople can corroborate that."

"Oh, we plan to talk to Connie. You and he are friends, aren't you?"

"We're professional colleagues."

308

"I'm sure he wouldn't want to say anything that would implicate you in any way."

"I'm *sure* he'll tell you the truth if you just ask him."

"So you're saying there is no connection between Ken Newman's murder and the money showing up in your account?"

"Let me put it a little more strongly than that. I'm saying it's all bullshit! If I were guilty, why would I have anyone put a hundred grand into one of my accounts so close to the time Ken was killed? Don't you think that's a little obvious?"

"But it wasn't really your account, was it? It was in your children's names. And according to your personnel records, you're not due for a Bureau five-year check for another two years. I rather doubt the money would be in the account at that time, and by then I'm sure you'd have a good answer in case anyone did discover that money had once been there. The point is, if your husband's attorney hadn't dug it up, no one would know. That hardly qualifies as obvious."

"Okay, if it's not a mistake, then someone is setting me up."

"And who exactly would be doing that?"

"The person who killed Ken, and who tried to kill Faith Lockhart. Maybe he's afraid I'm getting too close."

"So Danny Buchanan is trying to set you up, is that what you're saying?"

Reynolds glanced at the Bureau lawyer and the representative from OPR. "Do they have clearance to hear this?"

"Your investigation has taken a backseat to these more recent charges," Fisher said.

Reynolds glared at him with rising anger. "Charges! They're unsubstantiated garbage."

Massey opened the file. "So are you saying that your *private* investigation into Ken Newman's finances is garbage?"

On this Reynolds froze and then abruptly sat down. She pressed sweaty palms against the table and tried to get her emotions under control. Her temper was not doing her any good. She was playing right into their hands. Indeed, Fisher and Massey exchanged what she saw as pleased glances at her obvious distress.

"We talked to Anne Newman. She told us everything you've done," Fisher said. "I can't even begin to tell you how many Bureau rules you've broken."

"I was trying to protect Ken and his family."

"Oh, please!" Fisher exclaimed.

"It's true! I was going to go to OPR, but not until after the funeral."

"That was so very considerate of you," Fisher said sarcastically.

"Why don't you go to hell, Paul."

"Agent Reynolds, keep a civil tongue in your head," Massey commanded.

Reynolds sat back and rubbed her forehead. "May I ask how you found out about what I was doing? Did Anne Newman come to you?"

"If you don't mind, we'll ask the questions." Massey leaned forward and made a pyramid with his fingers. "What exactly did you find in the safe-deposit box?"

"Cash. A lot. Thousands."

"And Newman's financial records?"

"A lot of unexplained income."

"We've also talked to the bank branch you visited. You told them not to allow access to the box to anyone except yourself. And you told Anne Newman not to tell anyone about it, not even anyone

310

at the Bureau."

"I didn't want anybody getting to that money. It was material evidence. And I told Anne to keep quiet until I had a chance to dig further. It was for her own protection, until I found out who was behind it."

"Or did you want the time to get the money for yourself? With Ken dead and Anne Newman apparently not even aware her husband had the safe-deposit box, you would be the only one who knew the money was there." Massey stared directly at her; his tiny eyes resembled twin bullets coming for her.

Fisher piped in: "It's curious that when Newman dies you access a box with thousands of dollars in it that he had under a fake name, and about the same time, accounts controlled by you fill up with a hundred thousand dollars."

"If you're somehow trying to say I had Ken killed because of the money in the box, you're way off base. Anne called and asked for my help. I never knew Ken had a safe-deposit box until she told me about it. I had no idea what was in the box until after Ken was already dead."

"So you say," Fisher said.

"So I know," Reynolds replied hotly. She looked at Massey. "Am I being formally charged with anything?"

Massey sat back and put his hands behind his head. "You must realize how very, very bad this all looks. If you were sitting in my chair, what would your conclusions be?"

"I can see how you might have your suspicions. But if you just give me the chance—"

Massey closed his file and stood. "You're suspended, Agent Reynolds, effective immediately."

Reynolds was stunned. "Suspended? I haven't

311

even been formally charged. You don't even have any specific evidence that I've done anything wrong. And you're suspending me?"

"You should be grateful it's not worse," Fisher said.

"Fred," Reynolds said, half rising from her chair, "I can understand your taking me off this assignment. You can transfer me somewhere else while you investigate, but don't suspend me. Everybody in the Bureau will assume I'm guilty. It's not right."

Massey's face did not soften at all. "Please turn in your credentials and sidearm to Agent Fisher. You are not to return to your office. And you are not to leave the area for any reason."

The blood drained from Reynolds's face and she fell back into her chair.

Massey went to the door. "Your highly suspicious actions, coupled with the murder of an agent and reports of unknown people impersonating FBI agents, does not allow me the option of merely reassigning you, Reynolds. If you're innocent as you claim, then you'll be reinstated with no loss in pay, seniority or responsibility. And I'll make absolutely certain there's no permanent damage to your reputation. If you're guilty, well, you know better than most what awaits you." Massey closed the door behind him.

Reynolds stood to leave, but Fisher blocked her way.

"Creds and gun. Now."

Reynolds slipped them out and handed them over. It was as though she were giving up one of her children. She looked at Fisher's triumphant features. "Gee, Paul, try not to enjoy it so much. You'll look like less of a fool when I'm exonerated."

"Exonerated? You'll be lucky if you're not under arrest by day's end. But we want this case to be airtight. And if you're thinking of running, we'll be watching. So don't even try."

"I wouldn't dream of it. I want to be here to see your face when I come and get my gun and badge back. Don't worry, I won't ask you to kiss my ass."

Reynolds walked down the hallway and out of the building, feeling as though every pair of eyes in the entire Bureau were fully upon her.

313

THIRTY-SEVEN

Lee got up before Faith, showered, changed his clothes and then stood next to the bed, watching her as she slept. For a few seconds he allowed himself to forget about everything except the wonderful night the two had spent together. He knew it had changed his life forever, and that thought scared him to death.

He went downstairs, moving a little slowly. Parts of him were aching that hadn't in a long time. And it wasn't just from the dancing. He went into the kitchen and made coffee. While it was brewing, he thought about last night. In his mind, Lee had made a very strong commitment to Faith Lockhart. Perhaps an old-fashioned sentiment to some, but sleeping with a woman meant you had deep feelings for her, at least as far as Lee was concerned.

He poured a cup of coffee and went out to sit on the deck off the kitchen. It was a warm day, sunny, but off in the distance, Lee could see darkening clouds approaching. Ahead of the storm was the twin-prop plane as it floated in for a landing with another load of passengers. Faith had told him that during the summer months, the planes might make ten or so trips a day. Now it was down to three; morning, noon and early evening. And so far none of the plane passengers had remained on this street. They had driven off to other places, which suited Lee just fine.

As he sipped his coffee, Lee concluded that he did

have such feelings for Faith, even though he had only known her a few days. Stranger things had happened. Did he love Faith Lockhart? He knew that right now he didn't want to be away from her. He wanted to protect her from harm. He wanted to hold her, spend every minute with her and, yes, have incredibly energetic sex with her as often as his body could manage. Did that constitute love?

On the other hand, she had participated in a bribery scheme involving government officials and was wanted by the FBI, among others. Yes, he thought with a sigh, things had gotten very complicated indeed. Right before they were taking off to God knew where. It wasn't like they could go to a church or even a justice of the peace and get married. *That's right, Father, we're the fugitive couple. Could you please hurry it up?*

Lee rolled his eyes and slapped his forehead hard. Marriage! Good God, was he nuts? Maybe that was how he felt, but what about Faith? Maybe she was into one-night stands, although everything he had observed about the woman argued against such a conclusion. Did she love him? Maybe she was infatuated, caught up in his role as her protector. Last night could be explained away by alcohol, the intoxication of the danger swirling around them or perhaps just simple lust. And he wasn't going to ask her how she felt. She had enough going on.

He focused on the immediate future. Was traveling cross-country on the Honda to San Diego the best plan? Mexico and then South America? He felt a pang of guilt when he thought of the family he would be leaving behind. Then he thought about something else: what everybody would think. His reputation. If he ran, he would be admitting guilt of sorts. And if they did get caught while running, who would believe them?

315

He slumped back in his chair and suddenly pondered a very different strategy. A few minutes before, flight seemed the wisest choice. Faith, understandably, didn't want to go back and help send Buchanan to prison. Lee really didn't have much interest in doing that either, not after hearing why the man had been bribing the politicians. Danny Buchanan probably should be sainted instead. That's when an idea started to form in his head.

Lee went back inside and picked up his cell phone from the coffee table. He had one of those mega-minute deals with no long distance or roaming charges, so that he rarely even used his hard-line phone anymore. It had voice mail, text mail, caller ID. It even had a news banner where you could check out late-breaking stories, or how your stocks were doing, not that he had any.

When he had first started out as a private investigator, Lee had used an IBM typewriter; touch-tone phones were cutting edge; and fax machines spit out curly thermal paper and were the domain of only the largest companies. That was less than fifteen years ago. Now he was holding a global communications command center in the palm of his hand. Change that fast just couldn't be healthy. But still, who could live without these damn things now?

He plopped down on the couch and stared at the slowly revolving ceiling fan's rattan blades, contemplating the pros and cons of what he was thinking about doing. Then he made up his mind, and slipped his wallet out of his back pocket. The piece of paper was in there with the number his client, Danny Buchanan, had originally given him. The one he had been unable to trace. Then doubt seized him. What if he was wrong about Buchanan's not being involved in the attempt on Faith's life? He stood and paced. When he looked out the window at the blue sky, he saw only possible disaster looming in the approaching storm clouds. Still, Buchanan had hired him. He was technically working for the man. Maybe it was time to report in. He said a silent prayer, picked up his cell phone and punched in the numbers from the piece of paper.

THIRTY-EIGHT

Connie did not look happy as Paul Fisher leaned toward him and addressed him in a conspiratorial tone.

"We have every reason to believe that she's in on it, Connie. Despite what you've told us."

Connie glared at the man. He hated everything about Fisher, from his perfect hair and rocky-ledge chin down to his ramrod-straight posture and wrinkle-free shirts. He had been sitting in here for half an hour. He had told Fisher and Massey his side of the story, and they had told him theirs. They were not going to find any middle ground.

"That's bullshit with a capital *B*, Paul."

Fisher sat back and looked at Massey. "You heard the facts. How can you sit there and defend her?"

"Because I know she's innocent, how about that?"

"Do you have any facts to back that up, Connie?" Massey wanted to know.

"I've been sitting here telling you the facts, Fred. We had a hot lead at Agriculture on another case. Brooke didn't even want Ken to go with Lockhart that night. She wanted to go."

"Or so she told you," Massey replied.

"Look, I've got twenty-five years' worth of experience that says Brooke Reynolds is as clean as they come."

"She investigated Ken Newman's finances without telling anyone."

"Come on, it's not the first time an agent's gone off

318

the manual. She gets a hot one and wants to follow it up. But she doesn't want to bury Ken's reputation along with the body. Not until she's sure."

"And the hundred thousand dollars in her kids' accounts?"

"Planted."

"By whom?"

"That's what we have to figure out."

Fisher shook his head in frustration. "We're going to have her followed. Every minute until we break this."

Connie leaned forward and did his best to keep his big hands from flying to Fisher's neck. "What you should be doing, Paul, is following up the leads from Ken's murder. And trying to track down Faith Lockhart."

"If you don't mind, Connie, we'll run the investigation."

Connie looked over at Fred Massey. "You want a tail on Reynolds, I'm your guy."

"You! No way!" Fisher protested.

"Hear me out, Fred," Connie said, his gaze locked on Massey. "I admit, things look bad for Brooke. But I also know there's not a finer agent in the Bureau. And I don't want to see a good agent's career go down the toilet because somebody made the wrong call. I've been down that road myself. Right, Fred?"

Massey looked intensely troubled at this last statement. He seemed to shrink in his chair under Connie's withering gaze.

"Fred," Fisher said, "we need an independent source—"

Connie interrupted, "*I* can be independent. If I'm wrong, then Brooke goes down, and I'll be the first one to break the news to her. But I'm betting she's going to come back and pick up her badge and gun.

In fact, in ten years I see her running this whole damn place."

"I don't know, Connie," Massey began.

"I think *somebody* owes me that opportunity, Fred," Connie said very quietly. "What do you think?"

There was a long moment of silence while Fisher looked back and forth between the two men.

"All right, Connie, you follow her," Massey said. "And you report back to me at regular intervals. Exactly what you see. No more. No less. I'm counting on you. For old times' sake."

Connie rose from the table and flicked a victorious glance at Fisher. "Thanks for the vote of confidence, gentlemen. I won't disappoint."

Fisher followed Connie out into the hallway.

"I don't know what you just pulled in there, but remember this: Your career already has one black mark against it, Connie. It can't afford another. And anything you report to Massey, I want to know about."

Connie crowded the much taller Fisher back against the wall.

"Listen up, Paul." He paused, ostensibly to pick a piece of lint off Fisher's shirt. "I understand that, technically, you're my superior here. Don't confuse that, though, with reality."

"You're treading a dangerous line, Connie."

"I like danger, Paul, that's why I joined the Bureau. That's why I carry a gun. I've killed somebody with mine. How about you?"

"You're not making sense. You're throwing your career away." Fisher felt the wall behind him; his face was growing red as Connie continued to lean into him like a listing oak against a picket fence.

"Is that right? Well, let me make some sense of this for you. Somebody is setting Brooke up. Now, who

320

could that be? It's got to be the leak here at the Bureau. Somebody wants to discredit her, bring her down. And if you ask me, Paul, you're trying awfully hard to do just that."

"Me? You're accusing me of being the leak?"

"I'm not accusing anybody of anything. I'm just reminding you that until we do find that leak, nobody, and I mean nobody, from the director down to the guys who clean the johns here, is above suspicion in my book."

Connie moved away from Fisher. "Have a nice day, Paul. I'm off to catch some bad guys."

Fisher stared after him, slowly shaking his head, something close to fear in his eyes.

THIRTY-NINE

The phone number Lee called was linked to a pager, so that Buchanan would know the instant the number was called. When the pager went off, Buchanan was at home packing his briefcase for a meeting at a downtown law firm that was doing pro bono work for one of Buchanan's clients. He had given up hope of the damn beeper ever sounding. When it did, he thought he would suffer a stroke.

Now Buchanan's dilemma was apparent. How to check the message and call back without Thornhill knowing about it. Then he thought of a plan. He called his driver. It was Thornhill's man, of course. It always was. They drove downtown to the law firm.

"I'll be a couple of hours. I'll phone when I'm done," he told the driver.

Buchanan went into the building. He had been here before, knew the layout well. He didn't go to the elevator bank, but instead went through the main lobby and passed through a door in the back that also served as a rear entrance to the parking garage. He took the elevator down two levels and stepped off. He went through the underground lobby area and out into the parking level. Right next to the door leading out from the lobby was a pay phone. He put in his coins and dialed the number that would allow him to check the message. His reasoning was clear: If Thornhill could intercept a random hard-line call under a

322

thousand tons of concrete, he was the devil himself and Buchanan had no chance of beating him anyway.

On the message Lee's voice was tight, his words few. And the impact on Buchanan was enormous. He had left a number. Buchanan dialed it. A man answered the phone immediately.

"Mr. Buchanan?" Lee asked.

"Is Faith all right?"

Lee gave a sigh of relief. He was hoping that would be the man's first question. That told him a lot. But still, he had to be cautious. "Just to verify it's really you: You sent me a package of information. How did you send it, and what was in it? And let me have the answers fast."

"Personal courier. I use Dash Services. The packet had a photo of Faith, five pages of background information on her and my firm, the contact phone number, a summary of my concerns and what I wanted you to do. It also had five thousand dollars in cash in denominations of fifties and twenties. I also called you three days ago at your office and left a message on your machine. Now please tell me that Faith is all right."

"She's fine, for now. But we have some problems."

"Yes, we do. For starters, how do I know you're Adams?"

Lee thought quickly. "I have a great Yellow Pages ad with a corny magnifying glass and everything. I have three brothers. The youngest works at a motorcycle shop in south Alexandria. He goes by Scotty, but his nickname in college was Scooter because he played football and could run so damn fast. If you want you can call him, check it out and call me back."

"Not necessary. I'm convinced. What happened? Why did you run?"

"Well, you would have too if someone tried to kill you."

"Tell me everything, Mr. Adams. Leave nothing out."

"Well, I know *who* you are, but I'm not sure I trust *you*. What can you do about that?"

"You tell me *why* Faith went to the FBI. That much I do know. And then I'll tell you who you're really up against. And it's not me. When I tell you who it is, you'll wish it were me."

Lee debated this for a moment. He could hear Faith getting up and heading probably to the shower. *Well, here goes.* "She was scared. She said you had been acting strangely, jumpy for a while. She had tried to talk to you about it, but you blew her off, even asked her to leave the firm. That made her even more fearful. She was afraid the authorities were on to you. She went to the FBI with the idea of bringing you in to testify too. Against the people you were bribing. You both cut a deal and walk."

"That would never have worked."

"Well, as she's fond of telling me, it's easy to second-guess."

"So she's told you everything?"

"Pretty much. She thought maybe you were the one who tried to kill her. But I put that notion to rest." *I hope I was right.*

"I had no idea Faith had even gone to the FBI until after she disappeared."

"It's not just the FBI after her. There are some other people too. They were at the airport. And they were carrying something I've only seen at a seminar on counterterrorism."

"Who sponsored the seminar?"

This question puzzled Lee. "The counterterrorism stuff was put on by the official spooks. You know, I guess the guys at CIA."

Buchanan said, "Well, at least you have encountered the enemy and you're still alive. That's good."

"What are you talking . . ." The blood suddenly seemed to pool over Lee's temples. "Are you saying what I think you're saying?"

"Let's just put it this way, Mr. Adams: Faith is not the only one working for a prominent federal agency. At least her involvement was voluntarily. Mine wasn't."

"Oh, shit."

"To put it mildly, yes. Where are you?"

"Why?"

"Because I need to get to you."

"And how can you do that without bringing the ACME assassin squad down on us? I assume you're under surveillance."

"Unbelievably, astonishingly tight surveillance."

"Okay, so you're not coming anywhere near us."

"Mr. Adams, the only chance we have is to work together. That can't be done from a distance. I have to come to you, because I don't think it wise for you to come here."

"You're not convincing me."

"I won't come if I can't lose them."

"Lose them? Look, who do you think you are, Houdini reincarnated? Well, let me tell you, not even Houdini could lose *both* the FBI *and* the CIA."

"I'm neither a spy nor a magician. I'm a humble lobbyist, but I have one advantage: I know this city better than anyone alive. And I have friends in both high and low places. And right now, they are equally valuable to me. Rest assured, I will get to you alone. And then we might be able to survive this. Now I want to speak to Faith."

"I'm not sure that's a good idea, Mr. Buchanan."

"Yes, it is."

Lee whirled around and saw Faith standing on the stairs in a T-shirt. "It's time, Lee. In fact, it's way past time."

He took a deep breath and held out the phone.

"Hello, Danny," she said into the phone.

"God, Faith, I'm sorry. For all of this." Buchanan's voice cracked in midsentence.

"I should be apologizing. I started this whole nightmare by going to the FBI."

"Well, we have to finish it. We may as well do it together. How is Adams? Is he capable? We're going to need some support."

Faith glanced over at Lee, who was anxiously watching her. "In my informed opinion, we have no problems there. In fact, that's probably our one ace in the hole."

"Tell me where you are, and I'll be down as quickly as possible."

She did. She also told Buchanan everything she and Lee knew. When she hung up, she looked over at Lee.

He shrugged. "I figured it was our only shot. Either that or we spend the rest of our lives running."

She sat on his lap, curled her legs up and laid her head against his chest. "You did the right thing. Whoever's involved in this, they'll find a tough opponent in Danny."

Lee's hopes, however, had plummeted. The CIA. Hired assassins, legions of people expert in all sorts of nasty things: computers, satellites, covert operations, air guns with poisoned bullets, all coming for him. If he was smart, he'd throw Faith on the Honda and run like hell.

"I'm going to grab a shower," Faith said. "Danny said he'd be down as soon as he could."

"Right," Lee said, a faraway look in his eyes.

As Faith headed up the stairs, Lee picked up his phone, glanced at it and froze. Lee Adams had never been more stunned in his life. And with the events of the last few days, the bar on what surprised him had risen to about the level of the sun. The text message on the cell phone's screen was concise. And it came close to stopping even Lee's very strong heart.

Faith Lockhart for Renee Adams, it said. There was a phone number to call. They wanted Faith in exchange for his daughter.

FORTY

Reynolds sat in her living room cradling a cup of tea and staring into a fire that was slowly dying. The last time she could remember being home at this time of the day was when she had been on maternity leave with David. Her son had been as surprised to see her come through the door as Rosemary. David was now napping, and Rosemary was busy doing laundry. Just another normal day for them. Reynolds simply stared into the embers of the fire, wishing that something, anything about her life could be normal.

It had started to rain hard, which fit in perfectly with her deep depression. Suspended. She felt naked without her gun and credentials. All those years at the Bureau, never a blemish, and now she was a step away from a ruined career. Then what would she do? Where could she go? Without her job, would her husband try to take the kids? Could she stop him if he did?

She put her cup down, kicked off her shoes and sank back on the couch. The tears started to come fast and heavy, and she put an arm across her face both to soak them up and muffle her sobs. The ringing doorbell made her sit up, wipe at her face and head to the door. She looked through the peephole and found herself staring at Howard Constantinople.

Connie stood in front of the fire he had just stoked,

328

warming his hands. An embarrassed Reynolds quickly dabbed at her eyes with a tissue. He could not have missed her red eyes and splotchy cheeks, she knew, but he had tactfully said nothing.

"Did they talk to you?" she asked.

Connie turned and dropped into a chair, nodding as he did so. "And I came damn close to being suspended myself. I was about two seconds from punching out Fisher, that shit-faced excuse for an agent."

"Don't go and crater your career for me, Connie."

"If I had sugged the guy, believe me, it would've been for me, not you." He popped a big knuckle, as though emphasizing the point, and then looked across at her. "The thing that kills me is, they actually believe you're somehow involved in this. I told them the truth. Something came up, we were working another case. You wanted to go with Lockhart because you had the relationship with her, but we had this potential whistleblower over at Agriculture we were committed to. I told them you were fretting like all get-out because you didn't know if Ken going with Lockhart out there was the right thing to do."

"And?"

"And they weren't listening. They've already made up their minds."

"Because of the money? Did they tell you about that?"

Connie nodded slowly and suddenly hunched forward. For a big man his movements could be quick, agile. "I don't like kicking you while you're down, but why in hell did you go sniffing around Newman's accounts without telling somebody? Like me, for instance? You know detectives go in pairs for lots of reasons, not the least of which is to cover the other's ass. Now you've got nobody to corroborate shit for you, except Anne Newman. And as far as they're concerned, she doesn't count."

Reynolds threw up her hands. "I never in a million years thought this would happen. I was trying to do right by Ken and his family."

"Well, if he was being paid off, maybe Ken doesn't deserve that sort of consideration. And that's coming from a good friend of his."

"We don't know that he was bad yet."

"Cash in a safe-deposit box under a fake name? Yeah, I guess everybody does that, don't they?"

"Connie, how did they know I was investigating Ken's finances? I can't believe Anne would have called the Bureau. She asked me for help."

"I asked Massey, but he's a clam. Figures I'm the enemy too. I nosed around a bit, though, and I think they got a phone tip. Anonymous, of course. Massey told me you were screaming frame-up. And you know what, I think you're right, even if they don't."

The sight of Connie at the door had been welcome. The fact that he was still loyal meant a lot to her. And she wanted to do right by him too. Especially him. "Look, this isn't going to help your career, being seen with me, Connie. I'm sure Fisher has a tail on me."

"Actually, I'm your tail."

"You're kidding."

"No, the hell I am not. I talked the ADIC into it. Called in a few markers. For old times' sake, Massey said. In case you didn't know, Fred Massey was the guy who asked me to take the dive on the Brownsville case all those years ago. If he thinks this evens us up, he's brain-dead. But don't get all excited. They know I have every incentive to cover *my* ass on this. And that means if you fall, they don't have to go putting blame anywhere else.

330

Including on yours truly." Connie paused and made a mock show of surprise. "ADIC? Come to think of it, that acronym really fits. Massey's a little shit too."

"You don't have much respect for your chain of command." Reynolds smiled. "What do you think of me, Agent Constantinople?"

"I think you screwed up big-time, and you just gave the Bureau a face-saving scapegoat," he said bluntly.

Reynolds's face grew serious. "You don't sugar-coat."

"Do you want me to waste time doing that?" Connie stood. "Or do you want to clear your name?"

"I *have* to clear my name. If I don't, I could lose it all, Connie. My kids, my career. All of it." Reynolds could feel herself trembling again and she took several deep breaths to counteract the panic she was feeling. She felt like a high schooler who had just learned she was pregnant. "But I'm suspended. No creds, no gun. No authority."

In answer Connie pulled on his overcoat. "Well, you've got me. I've got creds, a gun and, while I'm only a humble field agent after two and a half decades of doing this crap, I can do authority with the best of them. So get your coat and let's try to track down Lockhart."

"Lockhart?"

"I figure we deliver her, the pieces start to fall into place. The more they do, the more the blame gets shifted off you. I've talked to the VCU boys. They're spinning their wheels waiting on lab results and crap like that. And now Massey has them going hot and heavy on your angle and to hell with Lockhart for now. You know nobody's even gone to her house looking for clues?"

Reynolds looked miserable. "We were so reactive

on the whole thing. Ken killed. Lockhart gone. The fiasco at the airport. Then people calling themselves the FBI at Adams's apartment. We never really had a chance to take the proper investigative steps."

"So I figure we follow up some leads while they're still hot. Like checking out Adams's family in the area. I've got the list of names and addresses. If he went on the run, he might have gotten one of them to help."

"You could get into deep trouble for this, Connie."

He shrugged. "Not for the first time. Besides, we don't have a squad supervisor anymore. I don't know if you heard, but she was suspended for being stupid."

They exchanged smiles.

Connie continued. "So, as second-in-command, I'm entitled to investigate an active case I happened to be assigned to. My instructions are to find Faith Lockhart, so that's what I'm going to do. They just don't know I'm doing it with you. And I talked to the VCU guys. They know what I'm up to, so we won't run into another team going through Adams's relatives."

"I need to tell Rosemary I might be gone overnight."

"Then go." He looked at his watch. "I guess Sydney's still in school. Where's your boy?"

"Sleeping."

"Whisper in his ear that Mommy's gonna kick some butt."

When Reynolds returned, she went straight to the closet and got her coat. She hustled toward her study and then stopped.

"What's wrong?" Connie asked.

She looked at him, slightly embarrassed. "I was going to get my gun. Old habits die hard."

"Not to worry. You'll get yours back soon enough.

But you have to make me a promise. When you go to get your gun and creds, take me with you. I want to see their faces."

She opened the door for him. "Deal."

FORTY-ONE

Buchanan made a number of other phone calls from the parking garage as he worked out his arrangements. He then went up to the law firm and spent time on an important matter he suddenly cared nothing about. He was driven home, his mind working the whole time as he devised his plan against Robert Thornhill. That was one area of his being that the CIA man could never penetrate or control: Buchanan's mind. That fact was enormously comforting. Buchanan was slowly regaining his confidence. Maybe he could give the man a run for his money.

Buchanan unlocked the front door to his home and went inside. He lay his briefcase down on a chair and passed the darkened library. He turned on the light to gaze at his beloved painting, to give him strength for what lay ahead. As the light came on, Buchanan stared in disbelief at the empty frame. He staggered over to it, put his hands through the frame and touched the wall. He had been robbed. Yet he had a very good security system, and it had not been tripped.

He raced across to the phone to call the police. As his hand touched the receiver, it rang. He picked it up.

"Your car will be around in a couple of minutes, sir. Going to the office?"

At first Buchanan's mind didn't register.

"To the office, sir?"

"Yes," Buchanan was finally able to say.

He put the phone down and stared over at where his painting had hung. First Faith, and now his painting. All Thornhill's doing. *All right, Bob, first point to you. Now it's my turn.*

He went upstairs, washed his face and changed his clothes, carefully selecting what he needed to wear. He had a custom-built entertainment system in his bedroom housing a TV, stereo, VCR and DVD player. It was relatively safe from burglars since one couldn't take the components out without un-screwing numerous wooden pieces, a very time-consuming process. Buchanan did not watch TV or movies. And when he wanted music, he put a 33 platter on his old phonograph.

Sticking his hand in the slot of the VCR, Buchanan pulled out his passport, credit card and ID, all under an alias, and a slim bundle of hundred-dollar bills and put it all in a zippered inner pocket of his coat. Coming back downstairs, he looked outside and saw his car waiting. He would let him wait for a few more minutes, just for the hell of it.

When that time had passed, Buchanan picked up his briefcase and walked out to the car. He climbed in and the car drove off.

"Hello, Bob," Buchanan said as calmly as he could.

Thornhill glanced down at the briefcase.

Buchanan nodded his head toward the tinted window.

"I'm going to the office. The FBI will expect me to take my briefcase. Unless you assume they haven't tapped my phone line by now."

Thornhill nodded. "You have the makings of a good field operative in you, Danny."

"Where is the painting?"

"In a very safe place, which is far more than you deserve under the circumstances."

"What exactly does that mean?"

"That exactly means Lee Adams, private investigator. Hired by you to follow Faith Lockhart."

Buchanan feigned being taken aback for a minute. As a young man he'd had notions of being an actor. Not in the movies, but on the stage. For him, lobbying was the next best thing. "I didn't know she had gone to the FBI when I did that. I was only concerned for her safety."

"And why was that?"

"I think you know the answer."

Thornhill looked offended. "Why in the world would I want to harm Faith Lockhart? I don't even know the woman."

"Do you have to know someone before you destroy her?"

Thornhill's tone was mocking. "You were wrong to have done it, Danny. The painting will probably be returned to you. But for now, learn to live without it."

"How did you get into my house, Thornhill? I have a security system."

Thornhill looked as though he might burst out laughing. "A *home* security system? Oh, dear."

It was all Buchanan could do not to fling himself on the man.

"You amuse me, Danny, you really do. Running around trying to save the have-nots. Don't you understand? That's what makes the world go 'round. The rich and the poor. The powerful and the powerless. We'll always have them, until the world ends. And nothing you do will change that. Just as people will always hate each other, will betray each other. If it weren't for the evil qualities in humanity, I wouldn't have a job."

"I was just thinking that you missed your calling as a psychiatrist," said Buchanan. "For the criminally insane. You'd have so much in common with your patients."

Thornhill smiled. "That's how I got on to you, you know. Someone you tried to help ended up betraying you. Jealous of your success, your wanting to do good, I suppose. He didn't know about your little scheme, but he aroused my curiosity. And when I focus on someone's life, well, kept secrets are not an option. I tapped your home, your office, even your clothing, and found myself a treasure trove. We so enjoyed listening to you."

"Fascinating. Now tell me where Faith is."

"I was hoping you could tell me that."

"What do you want with her?"

"I want her to come and work for me. There is a friendly competition between the two agencies, but between the FBI and my agency, I would have to say that we play much fairer with our people. I've been working on this project longer than the Bureau. I don't want all my efforts to be in vain."

Buchanan chose his words carefully. He knew he was in great personal danger here. "What can Faith possibly give you that I haven't already?"

"In my line of work, two is always better than one."

"Would your math include the FBI agent you had killed, Bob?"

Thornhill took out his pipe and fiddled with it.

"You know, Danny, you would be well advised to keep yourself focused on your part of this puzzle only."

"I consider *every* part my part. I read the newspapers. You told me Faith had gone to the FBI. An FBI agent is killed working on an undisclosed case. Faith disappears at the same time. You're right, I hired Lee Adams to find out what was going on. I haven't heard from him. Did you have him killed too?"

"I'm a public servant. I don't have people killed."

"The FBI got on to Faith somehow, and you couldn't allow that, because your whole plan goes down the tubes if they find out the truth. And did you really think I believed you'd let me walk away with a slap on the back for a job well done? I didn't survive this long in the business by being a damned idiot."

Thornhill put his pipe away. "Survival, interesting concept. You consider yourself a survivor, and yet you come to me and make all these sorts of unfounded accusations—"

Buchanan leaned forward and placed his face right next to Thornhill's. "I've forgotten more about the subject of survival than you ever knew. I don't have armies of people with guns running around doing my bidding while I sit safely behind the walls of Langley analyzing the field of battle like it was a chess game. The minute you came into my life, I made contingency plans that will absolutely *destroy* you if anything happens to me. Didn't you ever consider the possibility that someone might be half as agile as yourself? Or have all your successes really gone to your head?"

Thornhill simply stared at him, so Buchanan kept going. "Now, I consider myself a partner of sorts with you, no matter how loathsome that thought is. And I want to know if you killed the FBI agent, because I want to know exactly what I have to do to get out of this nightmare. And I want to know if you killed Faith and Adams as well. And if you don't tell me, the minute I leave this car, my next stop will be the FBI. And if you think yourself so invincible as to try and kill me while the Feds are back there, then go ahead. However, if I die, you go down too."

Buchanan leaned back and allowed himself a

smile. "You know the old story of the frog and the scorpion, don't you? The scorpion needs a ride across the water and tells the frog he won't sting it if the frog will provide that ride. And the frog knows that if the scorpion does sting it, that the scorpion will drown, so he gives it the ride. Halfway across the water, the scorpion, against all reason, does sting the frog. As it's dying, the frog cries out, 'Why did you do it? Now you'll die too.' And the scorpion simply tells him, 'It's my nature.'" Buchanan made a mock show of waving. "Hello, Mr. Frog."

The two men sat staring at each other for the next mile until Thornhill broke the silence.

"Lockhart needed to be eliminated. The FBI agent was with her. So he had to die too."

"But you missed Faith?"

"With your private investigator's help. But for your blunder, this crisis would never have happened."

"It never *occurred* to me that you would be planning to kill anyone. So you have no idea where she is?"

"It's only a matter of time. I have a number of irons in the fire. And where there's bait, there's always hope."

"Meaning what?"

"Meaning I'm done talking with you."

The next fifteen minutes passed in complete silence. The car drove into the underground parking garage of Buchanan's building. A gray sedan waited on the lower level, its engine running. Before Thornhill got out, he gripped Buchanan's arm.

"You claim to have the ability to destroy me if anything happens to you. Well, here's my side. If your colleague and her new 'friend' bring all that I've worked for crashing down, you will all be eliminated. Immediately." He removed his hand.

"Just so we understand one another, Mr. Scorpion," Thornhill added scornfully.

A minute later, the gray sedan pulled out of the parking garage. Thornhill was already on the phone.

"Buchanan is not to be out of sight for even one second." He clicked off and began to think of how to attack this new development.

340

FORTY-TWO

"This is the last place," Connie said as they pulled up to the motorcycle shop in his sedan.

They got out and Reynolds looked around. "His younger brother?"

Connie nodded as he checked his list. "Scott Adams. Manages the place."

"Well, let's hope he's a little more helpful than the others."

They had covered all of Lee's relatives in the area. None had seen or heard from him in the last week. Or at least that's what they said. Scott Adams might be their last chance. However, when they got inside they were told he was out of town for a friend's wedding and wouldn't be back for a couple of days.

Connie handed the young man behind the counter his card. "Tell him to call me when he gets in."

Rick, the salesman who had obnoxiously flirted with Faith, looked down at the card. "Does this have anything to do with his brother?"

Connie and Reynolds eyed him. "Do you know Lee Adams?" Reynolds asked.

"Can't say I know him. He don't know my name or nothing. But he's come by a few times. Just a couple of days ago, in fact."

The two agents looked Rick up and down, gauging his credibility.

"Was he alone?" Reynolds asked.

"No. He had some chick with him."

Reynolds took out a photo of Lockhart and handed it over to him. "Think short hair, not long, black, not auburn."

Rick nodded as he stared at the photograph. "Yep, that's her. And Lee's hair was different too. Short and blond. And he had a beard and mustache too, but I'm real good at noticing things."

Reynolds and Connie looked at each other, trying hard to hide their excitement.

"Any idea where they might have gone?" Connie asked.

"Maybe. But I sure know why they came here."

"Really? Why's that?"

"They needed wheels. Took a bike. One of the big Gold Wings."

"Gold Wing?" Reynolds repeated.

"Yeah." Rick rifled through a stack of color brochures on the counter and flipped one around so Reynolds could see. "This one here. The Honda Gold Wing SE. If you're going long distance, nothing beats this baby. Trust me."

"And you say Adams took one. Got a color, license plate number?"

"I can look the plate up. The color's the same as on the brochure. That was a demo. Scotty let him take it."

"You said you might have an idea where they went," Reynolds prompted.

"What do you want with Lee?"

"We want to talk with him. And the lady he's with," she said amiably.

"They do something wrong?"

"Won't know until we talk to them," Connie replied. He stepped forward a little. "It's an ongoing FBI investigation. You a friend of theirs or something?"

Rick paled at the suggestion. "Hell, no, that chick

342

is bad news. A real attitude. While Lee was inside, I went out to the sales lot and tried to help her. Real professional-like, and she jumped all over me. And Lee's no better. When he came out, he gave me some lip. I came close to kicking his ass, in fact."

As Connie looked at the beanpole Rick, he recalled the surveillance tape of the physically imposing Lee Adams. "Kick his ass? Is that right?"

Rick looked defensive. "He's got some weight on me, but he's an old guy. And I'm into tae kwon do."

Reynolds studied Rick closely. "So you're saying that Lee Adams was inside for a while, and the woman was out in the lot by herself?"

"That's right."

Reynolds and Connie traded a quick glance. "If you have information as to where they went, the Bureau would greatly appreciate it," Reynolds said, growing impatient. "That and the plate number on the bike. Like right now, if you don't mind. We're sort of in a hurry."

"Sure. Lee also got a map for North Carolina. We sell 'em here, but Scotty just gave it to him. That's what Shirley, the girl who usually works the desk, said."

"Is she in today?"

"Nope. Sick. I'm it."

"Can I get one of those Carolina maps?"

Rick pulled one out and handed it to her. "How much?"

He smiled. "Hey, it's on the house. Just being a good citizen. You know, I'm thinking about joining the FBI."

"Well, we could always use a good man," Connie said with a blank expression, his gaze averted.

Rick looked up the plate number on the demo and gave it to Connie. "You guys let me know what happens," Rick said as they started to leave.

343

"You'll be the first," Connie called back over his shoulder.

The two agents settled back in the car.

Reynolds looked at her partner. "Well, Lockhart isn't being held by Adams against her will. He left her outside by herself. She could've taken off."

"They sure look to be a team of sorts. At least right now."

"North Carolina," Reynolds said almost to herself.

"Big state," Connie said back.

Reynolds looked at him with a wry expression. "Well, let's see if we can cut it down some. At the airport, Lockhart bought two tickets for a flight to Norfolk International."

"So why the map for North Carolina?"

"They couldn't take the plane. We'd have been waiting for them in Norfolk. At least Adams seemed to know that. He was probably aware we have an arrangement with the airlines, and that's how we scored Lockhart at the airport."

"Lockhart screwed up by using her real name for the second ticket. But that was probably all she could do, unless she had a third fake ID," Connie added.

"So no plane. Can't use a credit card, so no rental car. Adams figures we have the bus and railroad terminals covered. So they get the Honda from his brother and a map for their true destination: North Carolina."

"Meaning that when they got to Norfolk by plane they were either going to drive or hop another plane to someplace in Carolina."

Reynolds shook her head. "But that doesn't make sense. If they were going to North Carolina, why not just take a plane directly there? There are tons of flights to Raleigh and Charlotte out of National. Why go through Norfolk?"

"Well, maybe you'd go through Norfolk if you

weren't going to Charlotte or Raleigh or anyplace near them," Connie ventured, "but still wanted to go to someplace in North Carolina."

"But why not still go through one of those two major airports?"

"Well, what if Norfolk is a lot closer to where they wanted to go than Charlotte or Raleigh are?"

Reynolds thought a moment. "Raleigh's roughly in the middle of the state. Charlotte is west."

Connie snapped his fingers. "East! The coast. The Outer Banks?"

Reynolds found herself nodding in agreement. "Maybe. The Outer Banks has thousands of beach houses where one could hide."

Connie suddenly looked less hopeful. "Thousands of beach houses," he muttered.

"Well, the first thing you can do is call the Bureau's airline liaison and find out what flights run out of Norfolk for the Outer Banks. And we have some times to work with. Their flight was scheduled to get into Norfolk at noon. I don't see them cooling their heels any longer than necessary at a public place, so the flight out had to be relatively close to noon or so. Maybe one of the commuters has regular service. We already checked with the major airlines. They didn't reserve with any of them out of Norfolk."

Connie picked up the car phone and placed the call. It didn't take long before they got an answer.

Connie's features looked hopeful again. "You're not going to believe this, but there's only one commuter service to the Outer Banks from Norfolk International."

Reynolds smiled broadly and shook her head. "Finally, some luck in this damn case. Talk to me."

"Tarheel Airways. They fly out of Norfolk to five places in Carolina: Kill Devil Hills, Manteo,

Ocracoke, Hatteras and a place called Pine Island, near Duck. There're no regular departures. You call ahead and the plane is waiting for you."

Reynolds spread open the map and scanned it. "Okay, there are Hatteras and Ocracoke. They're the farthest south." She put a finger on the map. "Kill Devil Hills is here. Manteo south of that. And Duck is here, to the north."

Connie looked at where she was pointing. "I've been down there on vacation. You cross the bridge over the sound and head north for Duck. South for Kill Devil. They're fairly equidistant from each other at that point."

"So what do you think? North or south?"

"Well, if they were going to North Carolina, it was probably at Lockhart's prompting." Reynolds looked at him curiously. "Because Adams took the map," Connie explained. "If he knew the area, he wouldn't have done that."

"Nice, Sherlock, what else?"

"Well, Lockhart has some serious money. One look at her house in McLean will tell you that. If I were her, I'd have a safe house under my phony name in case the roof caved in."

"But we're still at square one: north or south?"

They sat there stewing over this until Reynolds suddenly slapped her forehead. "God, how stupid. Connie, if you have to call Tarheel to arrange for a flight, our answer's right there."

Connie's eyes grew wide. "Damn, talk about blind." He picked up the phone, got the number for Tarheel and placed the call, relaying the date and approximate time and the name Suzanne Blake.

He hung up and looked at her. "A reservation for two people with Tarheel was made by our Ms. Blake two days ago to fly out of Norfolk around two P.M. They were pissed because she never showed. They

346

normally take a credit card, but she'd flown with them before, and so they just took her on her word."

"And their destination?"

"Pine Island."

Reynolds couldn't help but smile. "God, Connie, we might actually pull this off."

Connie put the car in gear. "Only bad thing is, I don't rate one of the Bureau's planes. We're stuck with the old Crown Vic here. I figure six hours or so, not counting stops." He checked his watch. "With stops, that'll put us there about one in the morning."

"I'm not supposed to leave the area."

"Bureau Rule Number One: You can go anywhere so long as you have your guardian angel along."

Reynolds looked troubled. "What do you think about calling in reinforcements?"

He eyed her quizzically. "Well, I guess we could call Massey and Fisher and let them take all the credit."

Reynolds suddenly smiled. "Like you said, screw international relations. Give me a minute to call home and then let's roll."

FORTY-THREE

It had taken Lee several agonizing hours, but he had finally tracked down Renee. Her mother had flatly refused to give him her phone number at college, but in a series of calls to the admissions office, among others, Lee had lied, begged and threatened until the number had been given up. It figured. He hadn't called his daughter for a long time, and when he did, it had to be for something like this. Boy, she was really going to cherish her old man now.

Renee's roommate at UVA swore on her grave that Renee had left for class accompanied by two members of the football team, one of whom she was dating. After telling the young woman who he was and leaving a number for Renee to call, Lee had hung up the phone and then gotten the telephone number for the Albermarle County Sheriff's office. He talked his way to a deputy sheriff and told the woman that someone had made threats against Renee Adams, a student at UVA. Would they please send someone to check on her? The woman asked questions that Lee could not answer, including wanting to know who the hell he was. *Just check the latest most-wanted list,* he wanted to tell her. Sick with worry, he tried his best to impress upon her the sincerity of what he was saying. Then he hung up and stared down at the digital missive once more: "Renee for Faith," he slowly said to himself.

"What?"

He jerked around and stared at Faith, there on the stairs, her eyes wide, her mouth open.

"Lee, what is it?"

Lee was out of ideas at the moment. He simply held up the phone for Faith, his face an anguished mess.

She looked at the message and then stared at him. "We have to call the police."

"She's okay, I just talked to her roommate. And I called the police. Somebody's blowing smoke at us. Trying to spook us."

"You don't know that."

"You're right, I don't," he said miserably.

"Are you going to call the number back?"

"That's probably what they want me to do."

"You mean so they can trace the call? Can you trace a cellular call?"

"It's possible, if you have the right equipment. Phone carriers have to be able to trace a cell call to determine the location of a 911 caller. It uses a time difference of arrival method by measuring signal distances between cell towers and kicks out a string of possible locations. . . . Shit, my daughter's head might be in the guillotine and I sound like a damn walking science magazine."

"But not an exact location."

"No, at least I don't think so. It's not as precise as satellite positioning, that's for certain. But who the hell really knows? Some geeky asshole invents some new piece of shit every second that rips away a little bit more of your privacy. I know, my ex-wife married one."

"You should call, Lee."

"And what the hell am I supposed to say? They want to trade you for her."

She put one hand on his shoulder, rubbed his neck and then leaned against him. "Call them. And then we'll see what we can do. Nothing is going to happen to your daughter."

He looked at her. "You can't guarantee that."

"I *can* guarantee that I will do everything I can to make sure she's not harmed."

"Including walking into their hands?"

"If it comes to that, yes. I'm not going to let an innocent person get hurt because of me."

Lee slumped back against the couch. "I'm supposed to be so good under pressure too and I can't even think straight."

"Call them," Faith said very firmly.

Lee took a long breath and punched in the numbers. With Faith sitting beside him and listening in, they waited as the phone rang once and then was answered.

"Mr. Adams?" Neither of them recognized the voice. It had a mechanical quality to it, making them both think it was being altered somehow. It sounded inhuman enough to make their skin tingle with absolute dread.

"This is Lee Adams."

"Nice of you to leave your cell phone number at your apartment. It made contacting you much more convenient."

"I just checked on my daughter. She's fine. And the cops are on the scene. So your little kidnapping plan—"

"I have no need to kidnap your daughter, Mr. Adams."

"Then I'm not sure why I'm talking to you."

"You needn't abduct someone to kill her. Your daughter can be eliminated today, tomorrow, next month, next year. While going to class, lacrosse practice, driving on holiday, even while she's sleeping. Her bed is right next to a window, first floor. She often stays late at the library. It couldn't be easier, really."

"You sick bastard! You sonofabitch!" Lee looked like he wanted to break the phone in two.

Faith gripped his shoulders, trying to calm him down.

The voice continued with irritating calm. "Histrionics won't help your daughter. Where is Faith Lockhart, Mr. Adams? That's all we want. Give her up and all your problems go away."

"And I'm supposed to just accept that as gospel?"

"You really don't have a choice."

"How do you know I've even got the woman?"

"Do you want your daughter to die?"

"I'm telling the truth, Lockhart got away."

"Fine, next week you can bury Renee."

Faith jerked at Lee's arm and pointed at the phone.

"Wait, wait!" Lee said. "Okay, okay, if I have Faith, what do you propose?"

"A meeting."

"She's not going to come voluntarily."

"I don't really care how you get her there. That's your responsibility. We'll be waiting."

"And you'll just let me walk away?"

"Drop her off and drive away. We'll take care of the rest. You don't interest us."

"Where?"

Lee was given an address outside of Washington D.C., on the Maryland side. He knew it well: very isolated.

"I have to drive it. And the cops are everywhere. I need a few days."

"Tomorrow night. Twelve sharp."

"Dammit, that's not a lot of time."

"Then I suggest you start right now."

"Listen, if you lay a hand on my daughter, I'll find you, somehow I will. I swear it. First I'll break every bone in your body, and then I'll really hurt you."

351

"Mr. Adams, consider yourself the luckiest human being on the face of the earth that we don't see you as a threat. And do yourself a favor. When you walk away don't ever, ever look back. You won't turn to salt, but it still won't be pretty." The line went dead.

Lee put the phone down. For a few minutes he and Faith just sat there without speaking. "Now what do we do?" Lee finally managed to say.

"Danny said he'd be here as soon as he could."

"Great. I've got a deadline: tomorrow, midnight."

"If Danny's not here in time we'll drive to the place they gave you. But first we'll call in some reinforcements."

"Like who, the FBI?" Faith nodded. "Faith, I'm not sure we could explain all this to the Feds in one year, much less one day."

"It's all we have, Lee. If Danny gets here in time and has a better plan, so be it. Otherwise I'll call Agent Reynolds. She'll help us. I'll make it work." She squeezed his arm. "Nothing is going to happen to your daughter. I promise."

Lee gripped her hand, hoping with all his heart that the woman was right.

FORTY-FOUR

Buchanan had a number of meetings on Capitol Hill scheduled for the early evening, pitching to an audience that didn't want to hear him. It was like throwing a ball at a wave. It would either be kicked back in your face or lost at sea. Well, today was the end. No more.

His car dropped him off near the Capitol. He went up the front steps and over to the Senate side of the building, where he climbed the broad staircase to the second floor, which was mostly restricted space, and continued to the third floor, where people could freely wander.

Buchanan knew he was being followed by more people now. While there were lots of dark suits around, he had trekked these halls long enough to sense who should be here as opposed to those who looked out of place. He assumed they were the FBI and Thornhill's men. After the encounter in the car, the Frog would have deployed more resources. Good. Buchanan smiled. He would, from now on, refer to the CIA man as the Frog. Spies liked code names. And he couldn't think of a more appropriate one for Thornhill. Buchanan just hoped that his stinger was ready, filled to the hilt with poison, and that the Frog's shiny, inviting back wouldn't prove too slippery.

The door was the first one a person would come to upon reaching the third floor and turning left. A middle-aged man in a suit stood next to it. There was no brass plate to identify whose office this was. Right next door was the office of Franklin Graham, the Senate sergeant-at-arms. The sergeant-at-arms was the Senate's principal law enforcement, administrative support and protocol officer. Graham was a good friend of Buchanan's.

"Good to see you, Danny," the man in the suit said.

"Hello, Phil, how's that back of yours?"

"Doc says I should have the surgery."

"Listen to me, don't let them cut you. When you're feeling the pain, have a nice, pleasing shot of Scotch, sing a song at the top of your lungs and then make love to your wife."

"Drinking, dancing and loving – sounds like good advice to me," Phil said.

"What'd you expect from an Irishman?"

Phil laughed. "You're a good man, Danny Buchanan."

"You know why I'm here?"

Phil nodded. "Mr. Graham told me. You can go right in."

He unlocked the door and Buchanan passed through, and then Phil closed the door and stood guard. He didn't notice the two pairs of people who had idly watched this exchange.

The agents reasonably figured they could wait for Buchanan to come out and then take up their surveillance once more. They were on the third floor, after all. It wasn't like the man could fly away.

Inside the room, Buchanan grabbed a raincoat off the hook on the wall. Lucky for him it was drizzly outside. There was also a yellow hard hat on another wall hook. He slipped this on as well. Then he pulled Coke-bottle glasses and work gloves from his briefcase. At least from a distance, with his briefcase under the raincoat, he would change from lobbyist to laborer.

Going to another door at the end of the room, Buchanan removed the chain locking this door and opened it. He went up the stairs and then opened a hatchlike door, which revealed a ladder leading up. Buchanan put his feet on the rungs and started climbing. At the top, he popped another hatch and found himself on the roof of the Capitol.

The attic room was how the pages accessed the roof to change the flags that flew over the Capitol. The inside joke was that the flags were constantly changed, some flying only for seconds, so that members could send generous constituents back home a continuous supply of Stars and Stripes that had "flown" over the Capitol. Buchanan rubbed his brow. God, what a town.

Buchanan looked down at the front grounds of the Capitol. People were scurrying here and there, running for meetings with people they desperately needed help from. And with all the egos, factions, agendas, crisis upon crisis and stakes greater than anything that had come before in the world's history, everything somehow seemed to work out. A large anthill came to mind as Buchanan looked down upon this well-oiled machine of democracy. At least the ants did it for survival. But maybe in a way, we did too, he thought.

He looked up at Lady Liberty on her century-and-a-half perch atop the Capitol's dome. She had recently been removed via helicopter and stout cable, and the grime of a hundred fifty years had been thoroughly cleaned away. Too bad the sins of people weren't as easy to scrape off.

For one insane moment, Buchanan contemplated jumping. He might have, too, except the desire to beat Thornhill was simply too strong. And that would be the coward's way out anyway. Buchanan was many things, but a coward was not one of them.

There was a catwalk that ran across the roof of the Capitol, and it would take Buchanan to the second part of his journey. Or, more accurately, his escape. The House wing of the Capitol building had a similar attic room, which its pages used to raise and lower its flags. Buchanan quickly went across the catwalk and through the hatch on the House side. He climbed down the ladder and into the attic room, where he removed the hard hat and gloves, but kept on the glasses. He pulled a snap-brim hat from his briefcase and put it on. Pulling up the collar on the raincoat, he took a deep breath, opened the door to the attic room and passed through. People milled here and there, but no one really gave him a second glance.

In another minute he had left the Capitol through a rear doorway known only to the few veterans of the place. A car was waiting for him there. A half hour later he was at National Airport, where a private plane, its twin engines revving, awaited its sole passenger. Here was where the friend in *high* places earned his money. The plane received clearance for takeoff a few minutes later. Soon thereafter Buchanan looked out the window of the plane as the capital city slowly disappeared from view. How many times had he seen that sight from the air?

"Good riddance," he said under his breath.

FORTY-FIVE

Thornhill was heading home early after a very productive day. With Adams now in the fold, they would soon have Faith Lockhart. The man might try to dupe them, but Thornhill didn't think so. He had heard the very real fear in Adams's voice. Thank God for families. Yes, all in all, a productive day. The ringing phone would soon change all that.

"Yes?" Thornhill's confident look vanished as the man reported to him that somehow, some way, Danny Buchanan had utterly vanished, from the very top floor of the Capitol, no less.

"Find him!" Thornhill roared into the phone before slamming it down. What could the man's game be? Had he decided to begin his escape a little early? Or was it for another reason? Had he contacted Lockhart somehow? That was intensely troubling. Shared information between the two was not good for Thornhill. He thought back to their meeting in the car. Buchanan had displayed his usual temper, his little word games – empty bluster, really – but had otherwise been fairly subdued. What could have precipitated this latest development?

In his agitation, Thornhill drummed his fingers on the briefcase, he had in his lap. As he looked down at the hard leather, his mouth dropped open. The briefcase! The damn briefcase! He had provided one for Buchanan. It had a backup recorder in it. The conversation in the car. Thornhill admitting he had

had the FBI agent killed. Buchanan had tricked him into betraying himself and then taped him. Taped him with CIA-issue equipment. That two-faced sonofabitch!

Thornhill grabbed the phone; his fingers were shaking so badly he misdialed twice. "His briefcase, the tape in it. Find it. And him. You must get it. You *have* to get it."

He dropped the phone and slumped back in the seat. The master strategist of over a thousand clandestine operations spanning nearly four decades was absolutely stunned by this development. Buchanan could take him down with this. He was running loose with the evidence to crush him. But Buchanan would go down too, had to, there was no way around it.

Wait. The scorpion! The frog! Now it all made sense. Buchanan was going to go down and take Thornhill with him. The CIA man loosened his tie, wedged himself into the seat and fought the panic he felt flooding his body.

This is not how it will end, Robert, he told himself. *After thirty-five years this is not damn well how it's going to end. Calm down. Now is when you need to think. Now is where you earn your place in history. This man will not beat you.* Slowly, steadily, Thornhill's breathing returned to normal.

It could be that Buchanan would simply use the tape as insurance. Why spend the rest of his life in prison when he could quietly disappear? No, it made no sense that he would take the tape to the authorities. He had as much to lose as Thornhill, and he couldn't possibly be that vindictive. Thornhill had a sudden thought: Perhaps it was the painting, the idiotic painting. Maybe that was what had started this whole thing. Thornhill should never have taken the damned thing. He would leave a message on Buchanan's machine at once, telling him his precious object had been returned. Thornhill left the message and arranged for the painting to be returned.

As Thornhill sat back and looked out the window, his confidence returned. He had one ace in the hole. A good commander always held something in reserve. Thornhill made another phone call and received some positive news, a piece of intelligence that had just come in. His face brightened, the visions of doom receding. It would be all right after all. His mouth eased into a smile. The snatch of victory from the jaws of defeat; it could either age a man several decades overnight or give him bronze balls. Or sometimes both.

In another few minutes Thornhill was getting out of his car and walking up the sidewalk to his lovely house. His impeccably dressed wife met him at the door and gave him a perfunctory peck on the cheek. She had just come back from a country club function. In fact, she was always coming back from a country club function, he thought, muttering to himself. While he agonized over terrorists sneaking into the country with nuclear-bomb-making materials, she lounged at fashion shows where young, vacuous women with legs stretching to their inflated bosoms pranced about in outfits that didn't even bother to cover their derrieres. He was out every day saving the world, and his spouse ate finger sandwiches and drank champagne in the afternoon with other ladies of considerable means. The idle rich were as stupid as the uneducated poor – more brainless than cows, in fact, was Thornhill's opinion. At least cows had a reasonable understanding that they were the slaves. *I'm an underpaid civil servant*, Thornhill mused, *and if I ever let my defenses down, the only thing left of the wealthy and powerful in this country would be the echoes of their screams.* It was a powerful, mesmerizing thought.

He barely heard his wife's inconsequential ramblings on "her day" as he put down his briefcase, mixed a drink and escaped to his study and closed the door. He never told the woman about *his* day. She'd chat about it to her one-name, oh-so-chic glorified barber, who would tell another client, who would let it slip to someone else and the world would stop tomorrow. No, he never talked shop with the wife. But he did indulge her in just about everything else. But finger sandwiches indeed!

Ironically, Thornhill's home office was much like Buchanan's. There were no plaques, testimonials or souvenirs of his long career on display. He was a spy, after all. Was he supposed to act like the idiotic FBI and wear T-shirts and hats emblazoned with CIA? He almost choked on his whiskey at the thought. No, his career had been invisible to the public, but highly visible to those who mattered. The country was far better off because of him, though the ordinary folk would never know it. That was all right. To seek accolades from the great and ignorant public was the vice of a fool. He did what he did because of pride. Pride in himself, in his devotion to his country.

Thornhill thought back to his beloved father, a patriot who carried his secrets, his distinguished triumphs to the grave. Service and honor. That was what it was all about.

Soon, with a little luck, the son would notch another triumph in his own career. When Faith showed up, she would be dead within an hour. And Adams? Well, he would have to die too. Certainly Thornhill had lied to the man on the phone. Thornhill understood quite clearly that deceit was nothing more nor less than a highly effective tool of the trade. One just had to make sure that lies at work didn't interfere with one's personal life. But Thornhill had always been good with compartmentalization. Just ask his country club wife. He could initiate a covert action in Central America in the morning and play, and win, at bridge at the Congressional Country Club in the evening. Now, dammit, *that* was compartmentalization!

And whatever anyone said about him within the confines of the Agency, he had always been good with his people. He pulled them out of situations when they needed to be pulled. He had never left an agent or case officer spinning in the wind, helpless. But he also kept them in the field when he knew they could carry it home. He had developed an instinct for such things, and it had hardly ever proved wrong. He also didn't play political games with intelligence collection. He had never told the politicians simply what they wanted to hear, as others at the Agency had – sometimes with disastrous consequences. Well, he could only do what he could. In two years it would be someone else's problem. He would leave the organization in as strong a state as he could. His parting gift. There was no need to thank him. Service and honor. He lifted his drink in memory of his late father.

FORTY-SIX

"**S**tay low, Faith," Lee said as he edged close to a window overlooking the street. He had his gun out and was watching a car drop a man off out front. "Is that Buchanan?" he asked.

Faith anxiously peered over the windowsill and then immediately relaxed.

"Yes."

"Okay, answer the front door. I'll cover you."

"I told you it was Danny."

"Great, then go let *Danny* in. I'm not taking any unnecessary chances."

Frowning at this remark, Faith went to the front door and opened it. Buchanan slipped through and she closed and locked the door behind him. They exchanged a prolonged hug as Lee watched from the stairs, his gun in plain sight in his belt clip. He felt a pang of jealousy at this embrace. It quickly passed, though, as he sensed the exchange of affection was clearly that of a father and his daughter.

"You must be Lee Adams," Buchanan said, extending his hand. "I'm sure you regret the day you ever took on this assignment."

Lee came down and shook his hand. "Nah. This one's been a piece of cake. I'm actually thinking about specializing in this area, especially considering no one else would be stupid enough to do it."

"I thank God you were there to protect Faith."

"Actually, I've gotten pretty good at saving Faith." Lee and Faith exchanged smiles, then Lee looked back at Buchanan. "But the fact is we have one additional complication. A very important one," Lee added. "Let's go to the kitchen. You might want to hear it over a drink."

As they sat at the kitchen table, Lee filled Buchanan in on the situation with his daughter.

Buchanan looked furious. "That bastard."

Lee eyed him keenly. "This bastard have a name? I'd love to know it, for future reference."

Buchanan eyed him keenly and then shook his head. "Trust me, you don't want to go down that route."

"Who is behind all this, Danny?" Faith touched his arm. "I think I have a right to know."

Buchanan looked at Lee.

"Sorry," Lee said, putting up his hands, "that's your call."

Buchanan gripped Faith's arm. "They're very powerful people and they happen to work for this country. That's all I can really say without endangering you even more."

Faith sat back astonished. "*Our* own government is trying to kill us?"

"The gentleman I've been dealing with tends to go his own way. But he does have resources, lots of them."

"So Lee's daughter is in real danger?"

"Yes. This man will usually say rather less than what he actually intends."

"Why'd you come here, Buchanan?" Lee wanted to know. "You got away from the guy. At least for our sakes I hope you did. You could've lost yourself in a million different places. Why come here?"

"I got you both into this. I intend to get you out."

"Well, whatever plan you have better include

363

saving my daughter or else you can count me out. I'll park myself inside her skin for the next twenty years if I have to."

Faith said, "I thought I could call the FBI agent I was working with, Brooke Reynolds. We can tell her what's going on. She could place Lee's daughter in protective custody."

"For the rest of her life?" Buchanan shook his head. "No, that won't work. We have to cut the hydra's head off and then burn the stub. Otherwise we're just wasting time."

"And exactly how do we do that?" Lee asked.

Buchanan opened his briefcase and pulled out the tiny cassette tape from a hidden crevice. "With this. I was able to record the gentleman I've been talking about. On this tape he admits that he had the FBI agent killed, among other incriminating things."

For the first time Lee looked hopeful. "Are you serious?"

"Trust me, I would never joke about this man."

"So we use this tape to keep the hound at bay. He hurts us, we destroy him? He knows that. Then we've pulled his fangs."

Buchanan slowly nodded. "Exactly."

"And you know how to contact him?" asked Lee.

Buchanan nodded. "I'm sure that he's figured out what I did and is right now trying to deduce what my intention is."

"Well, *my* intention is that you call up this asshole right this second and tell him to stay the hell away from my daughter. I want it in blood. And I don't trust the sonofabitch, so I still want something like a company of SEALs outside her dorm room for good measure. And I still plan on heading up there myself. Just in case. They want Renee? They go through me."

"I'm not sure that's a good idea," Buchanan said.

"I don't remember asking for your permission," Lee fired back.

"Lee, please," Faith said. "Danny's just trying to help."

"I wouldn't be in this nightmare if this guy had been straight with me up front. So excuse the hell out of me if I don't treat him like he's my best buddy."

"I don't blame you for feeling that way," Buchanan said. "But you called me for help, and I'll do whatever I can to help you. And your daughter. That I swear."

Lee's guarded manner relaxed somewhat in the face of this seemingly frank declaration.

"Okay," he said grudgingly. "I admit you get points for coming here. You'll get more points when you call off the assassins. And then after that we should get the hell out of here. I've already called this psycho once on my cell phone. I'm assuming that at some point he'll be able to narrow our location down from that. When you call him, it'll give them even more info to work with."

"Understood. I have a plane at my disposal at a private airstrip not too far from here."

"Your friends in high places?"

"*Friend*. Senior senator from this state, Russell Ward."

"Good old Rusty," Faith said, smiling.

"You're sure you weren't followed?" Lee glanced at the front door.

"No one could have followed me. I'm not sure of much anymore, but I am certain of that."

"If this guy is as good as you seem to think he is, I wouldn't feel too certain of anything." Lee held out his cell phone. "Now please make the call."

FORTY-SEVEN

Thornhill was in his study at home when Buchanan's phone call came in. His communication link was such that the call was not traceable to Thornhill, if Buchanan was perhaps sitting at FBI headquarters. And Thornhill's phone also had a voice scrambler that would make voice ID impossible. On the other hand, Thornhill's people were working on tracing Buchanan's location, but as yet they hadn't been successful. Even the CIA had its limits, what with the explosion in the field of communications technology. There were so many electronic signals flying through the air, it made it damn near impossible to trace a wireless call to a precise location.

The National Security Agency would be able to trace the call with its stadium-size circular antennas. The super-secret NSA possessed technological might that made anything the CIA had pale by comparison, Thornhill well knew. It was said that the intelligence the NSA perpetually swept out of the air could fill the Library of Congress every *three* hours, gobbling up information in avalanche-byte mouthfuls. Thornhill had availed himself of the NSA's services before. However, the NSA (the inside joke was that the acronym stood for "no such agency") was often difficult for anyone to control. Thus Thornhill didn't want to involve them in this highly sensitive matter. He would handle it himself.

"You know why I'm calling?" Buchanan said.

"A tape. A highly personal one."

"It's good doing business with someone who considers himself omniscient."

"I would appreciate some small bit of evidence, if it's not too much trouble," Thornhill said placidly.

Buchanan played a snatch of the earlier conversation between the two men.

"Thank you, Danny. Now, your terms?"

"Point one, you don't go near Lee Adams's daughter. That is called off. Now and forever."

"Do you happen to be with Mr. Adams and Ms. Lockhart right now?"

"Second, all three of us are off limits as well. If anything remotely suspicious happens, then the tape goes directly to the FBI."

"During our last conversation you said you already had the means to destroy me."

"I lied."

"Do Adams and Lockhart know of my involvement?"

"No."

"How can I trust you?"

"It would only have put them in more danger to tell them. All they want to do is survive. It seems a common enough goal these days. And I'm afraid you'll just have to take my word for it."

"Even though you just admitted lying to me?"

"Exactly. Tell me, how does it feel?"

"And my long-term plan?"

"I really don't give a damn at this point."

"Why did you run?"

"Put yourself in my place; what would you have done?"

"I would never have allowed myself to be put in your place," said Thornhill.

367

"Thank God we can't all be like you. Do we have an agreement?"

"I don't have much choice, do I?"

"Join the club," said Buchanan. "However, you can be absolutely certain that if anything happens to any of us, it's over for you. But if you play fair, you accomplish your goal. Everyone lives to celebrate."

"Good doing business with you too, Danny."

Thornhill clicked off and sat there seething for a few moments. Then he made another call but came away disappointed. The trace had not been made. Well, that was all right. He hardly expected it to be so easy. He still had his ace in the hole. He made one more phone call and this time the information brought a broad smile to his lips. As Danny had said, Thornhill did know all there was to know, and he thanked God for his omniscience. When you planned for every possible contingency you were difficult to beat.

Buchanan was with Lockhart, of that he was almost certain. His two golden birds were occupying the same nest. That made his task infinitely simpler. Buchanan had outsmarted himself.

He was just about to refill his scotch when his wife popped her head in. Would he like to go to the club with her? There was a bridge tournament going on. She had just gotten a call. A couple had canceled and wanted to know if the Thornhills could take their place.

"Actually," he said, "I'm very much engaged in a game of chess." His wife looked around the empty room. "Oh, it's long-distance, dear," Thornhill explained, nodding at his desktop computer. "You know the things one can do with technology these days. You can do battle and never even see your opponent."

"Well, don't stay up too late," she said. "You've

been working very hard and you're not a young man anymore."

"I see light at the end of the tunnel," Thornhill replied. And this time he was telling the absolute truth.

FORTY-EIGHT

Reynolds and Connie reached Duck, North Carolina, around one in the morning after only a single stop for fuel and food and reached Pine Island a short while later. The streets were dark, the businesses closed. They were fortunate in finding an all-night gas station, however. While Reynolds got two coffees and some pastries, Connie found out from the clerk on duty where the airplane runway was located. They sat in the gas station lot, ate, and mulled things over.

"I checked in at WFO," Connie told Reynolds as he stirred sugar into his coffee. "Interesting twist. Buchanan's disappeared."

She swallowed a bite of her pastry and stared at him. "How the hell did that happen?"

"Nobody knows. That's why so many people are catching grief over it."

"Well, at least they can't blame that one on us."

"Don't be too sure of that. Laying blame is a fine art in D.C., and the Bureau ain't no exception."

Reynolds had a sudden thought. "Connie, do you think Buchanan could be trying to rendezvous with Lockhart? That may be why he disappeared."

"If we could nail them both at the same time, you might get appointed director."

Reynolds smiled. "I'll settle for having my suspension lifted. But Buchanan might be on his way here. What time did they say they lost the tail?"

"Late this afternoon."

"Then he could already be here, if he took a plane."

Connie sipped his coffee, while he thought this over. "Why would Buchanan and Lockhart be doing anything together?" he asked slowly.

"Don't forget, if we're right about Buchanan hiring Adams, then maybe Adams called Buchanan and they hooked up that way."

"*If* Adams is innocent in all this. But he sure as hell wouldn't call Buchanan if he thought the guy had anything to do with trying to knock off Lockhart. After all we've found out, I'm gauging the guy as her protector, of sorts."

"I think you're right about that. But maybe Adams found out something that made him believe Buchanan didn't order the hit. If that was the case, he might try to team with Buchanan to figure out together what the hell was going on and who else was out there trying to kill Lockhart."

"Somebody else behind this? One of the foreign governments Buchanan was working with, maybe? If the truth came out, they'd be sitting out there with world-class egg on their face. That's plenty of incentive to kill somebody," Connie said.

"I wonder," Reynolds began, as Connie watched her closely. "There's just been something about this case that's never added up," she said. "We've got somebody impersonating FBI agents. Somebody who seems to know our every move."

"Ken Newman?"

"Maybe. But that doesn't seem to make sense either. Ken's had cash coming in for a long time. Has he been somebody's mole for that long a period of time? Or is it somebody else?"

"And don't forget about whoever's trying to frame you. Moving money around accounts like that takes some expertise."

"Exactly. But I just don't see operatives of a

foreign government being able to do all that, and no one the wiser."

"Brooke, countries conduct industrial espionage against us every day. Shit, our staunchest allies even do it, ripping off our technology because they're not smart enough to do it on their own. And our borders are so open it doesn't take much to get in. You know that."

Reynolds let out a deep sigh as she stared into the darkness lying right outside the gas station's harsh ring of lights. "I suppose you're right. I guess instead of trying to figure out who's behind this, we should try to find Lockhart and company and just ask them."

"Now, that's a plan I can relate to." Connie put the car in gear and they sped off into the darkness.

After locating the runway, Reynolds and Connie cruised the dark streets looking for the Honda Gold Wing. Virtually all of the beach houses appeared vacant now, which made their search both easier and more difficult. It cut down the number of places they had to focus on, but it also made the agents stand out more.

Connie finally spotted the Honda in the carport of one of the beach houses. Reynolds eased out of the car and got a close enough look to confirm that the license tag matched the bike Lee Adams had borrowed from his brother's shop. Then they drove to the other end of the street, hit the lights and talked it over.

"Maybe it's as simple as me going in the front and you going in the back," Reynolds said as she studied the dark house. Her skin was tingling with the thought that a bare fifty feet away were two or possibly the three key people in this whole investigation.

Connie shook his head. "I don't like that. The Honda being there means Adams is in there too."

"We've got his gun."

"A guy like that, first thing he would've done is get another one. And we go in, even if we surprise him, he knows the lay of the land better than we do. He might get one of us." He added, "And you don't even have a gun, so we're not splitting up."

"You're the one who said you thought Adams wasn't a bad guy."

"Thinking something and being absolutely certain of it are two different things. And that difference is not something I'm willing to risk anybody's life over. And rushing in on anybody, good or bad, in the middle of the night, mistakes can happen. I intend on getting you back to your kids in one piece. And I wouldn't mind doing the same."

"So how do we play it? Wait for daylight and call in reinforcements?"

"Calling in the locals will probably mean every TV station down here will be on the block an hour after we do. That won't earn us many points at HQ."

"Well, I guess we can wait for them to ride off on the Honda and then pull them."

"Other things being equal, I'm inclined to watch the place and see what happens. If they come out, we move in. If we get real lucky, Lockhart will surface without Adams and we can take her. After that, I'm figuring we can bait Adams out pretty easy."

"And if they don't come out, together or singly?"

"Then we'll cross that bridge when we come to it."

"I don't want to lose them again, Connie."

"It's not like they can just take off down the beach or swim to England. Adams went to a lot of trouble to get those wheels. He's not going to abandon the bike because he doesn't have another way to replace it. Where he goes, that Honda goes. And that Honda ain't going anywhere without us seeing it."

They settled down and waited.

FORTY-NINE

His pistol resting on his belly, Lee had spent a few fitful hours on the couch downstairs. Every few minutes he thought he heard someone breaking in, and each time it proved to be nothing more than his very tired imagination doing its best to drive him crazy. Since he couldn't sleep, he had finally decided to get ready to leave for Charlottesville. He grabbed a quick shower and changed his clothes. He was packing his bag when a soft knock came on his door.

Faith was dressed in a long white robe; her puffy cheeks and tired-looking eyes were stark testaments to her inability to sleep.

"Where's Buchanan?" he asked.

"Actually dozing, I think. I never came close."

"Tell me about it." He finished packing and closed his bag.

"Are you sure you don't want me to come with you?" she asked.

He shook his head. "I don't want you anywhere near this guy and his goons if they show up. I got through to Renee last night. First time I've talked to her in I don't know how long and I have to tell her she might be the target of some psycho because of something her stupid dad did."

"How did she take it?"

On this Lee brightened. "Actually, she seemed happy to hear from me. I didn't tell her everything that was going on. I didn't want to panic her, but I think she's looking forward to seeing me."

"I'm glad to hear that. I'm really happy for you, Lee."

"The cops at least took my call seriously. Renee said a patrolman came by and a marked car's been cruising the area."

He put his bag down, took her hand. "I don't feel good about leaving you."

"It's your daughter. We'll be fine. You heard Danny. He's got this person over a barrel."

Lee looked unconvinced. "The last thing you should do right now is let down your guard. The car will be here at eight to take you and Buchanan to the plane. You head back to D.C."

"And then what?"

"Go to a motel in the suburbs. Register under a false name and then call me on my cell phone. As soon as things are okay with Renee I'll head back. I already talked it over with Buchanan. He's in agreement."

"And then?" Faith persisted.

"Let's just take it a step at a time. I told you there are no guarantees in this."

"I was actually talking about *us*."

Lee played with the strap on his bag. "Oh," was all that came out, and it sounded idiotic.

"I see."

"You see what?" Lee demanded.

"Wham, bam, thank you, ma'am."

"Where do you get off thinking like that? Don't you know what kind of a man I am by now?"

"Actually, I thought I did. But I guess I forgot. You're in the loner group: sex only for fun. Right?"

"Why are we doing this? Like we don't have enough going on. We can talk about it later. It's not like I'm not coming back."

Lee didn't mean to put her off, but – hell, why

375

couldn't she see there was no time for this right now?

Faith sat down on the bed.

"Like you said, no guarantees," she said.

He put a hand on her shoulder. "I am coming back, Faith. I didn't come this far to desert you now."

"Okay," was all she said. She stood, wiped her face and gave him a quick hug. "Please, please, be careful."

Faith let him out the rear door. As she turned to go back in, Lee's gaze was riveted on her. He took in everything, from the bare feet to the short dark hair and all points in between. For one troubling moment, he wondered if this was the last time he would ever see her.

Lee climbed on the Honda and quickly started up the bike.

As Lee roared out the driveway and hit the street, Brooke Reynolds raced back to the Crown Vic and threw open the door. Breathless, she looked inside.

"Shit, I knew the minute I left the car to get a closer look at the house this would happen. He must have come out a rear door. He didn't even turn on the carport light. I never saw him until the bike cranked up. So what do we do? House or the bike?"

Connie looked down the road. "Adams is already out of sight. And that bike is a lot more agile than this tank."

"I guess that leaves the house and Lockhart."

Connie suddenly looked worried. "We're presuming she's still inside. In fact, we don't even know if she was ever inside."

"Shit, I knew you were going to say that. She damn well better be. If we just let Adams go and Lockhart isn't in that house, *I* will swim to England. And you're going to have to be right beside me.

376

Come on, Connie, we have to go in the house."

Connie climbed out of the car, pulled his gun and looked around nervously. "Shit, I don't like this. It could be a setup. We could be walking right into an ambush. And we've got no backup."

"We don't have much choice, do we?"

"All right, but dammit, stay behind me."

They headed for the house.

FIFTY

Dressed in black sweats and tennis shoes, the three men raced along the beach, keeping low to the sand. Although the dawn was fast approaching, they were virtually invisible in their dark clothing against the backdrop of the ocean, and the pounding surf covered all sounds of their movements.

They had arrived in the area barely an hour ago and had just received some very disturbing news. Lee Adams had left the house. Lockhart wasn't with him. She must still be in the house. Or at least they hoped she was. Buchanan, they had been told, might be there as well. They would take those two over Adams. He could wait. They would eventually get him. In fact, they would not stop until they got him.

Each team member was equipped with an automatic pistol and a knife specially designed to take out the carotid in one efficient stroke. Each man was well skilled in exactly how to execute just such a lethal blow. Their orders were clear. Everyone in the house had to die. Perfectly executed, it could be a clean operation. They could be back in Washington by late morning.

They were proud men, professionals in their own right and long in the service of Robert Thornhill. As a team they had survived some dangerous times in the last twenty years with their wit, skill, physical strength and stamina. They had saved lives, made certain parts of the world safer, helped to ensure that the United States would become the world's sole remaining superpower. This would mean a fairer, more just world for many. Like Robert Thornhill, they had joined the Agency to perform a service, to engage in a public trust. To them, there was no higher calling.

All three men were also part of the group Lee and Faith had eluded at Adams's apartment. The episode had embarrassed them, tarnishing their reputation for near perfection. They had been hoping for a shot at redemption, and now they did not intend to waste it.

One man stayed near the top of the stairs to keep watch, while the other two hurried down the boardwalk to the rear of the house. The plan was simple, direct, unencumbered by layers of detail. They would hit the house hard and fast, starting on the ground floor and moving up. When they ran into anyone, they wouldn't ask questions or seek identification. Their suppressor-equipped pistols would fire one time for each victim, and then they would move on until every living thing in the house no longer was. Yes, it was definitely conceivable they could be back in Washington before lunch.

FIFTY-ONE

Lee slowed down the Honda and then stopped in the middle of the road, his feet coming down lightly on the asphalt. He looked back over his shoulder. The street was long, black and empty. The dawn would be coming soon, though. He could see it in the softening edges of the sky, like the streaked edges of a Polaroid slowly lapping to vibrancy.

So why couldn't he have waited? He could have waited until the car came to take Faith and Buchanan to the airstrip. It would only delay his trip to Charlottesville by a couple of hours at most. And it would certainly increase his peace of mind. Why the hell was he running away so fast? Renee was protected. What about Faith?

His gloved hand tapped against the Honda's throttle. It would also give him a chance to talk to the woman, to let Faith know that he cared very much for her.

He turned the Honda around and headed back. When he reached the street, he slowed the bike. The car was parked at the far end of the street. It was a big sedan that just screamed federal government. True, it was at the opposite end of the street and he wouldn't have passed it heading to the main road, but how the hell had his "expert" eyes missed that? God, was he really getting that old?

He drove directly at the car, figuring that if it was the Feds, he could cut off easily enough and lose them. As he drew closer, however, it was clear the

380

car was empty. Starting to panic, he swung the Honda around, drove up into the driveway of the beach house two lots down from Faith's and jumped off. Throwing down his helmet and pulling his pistol, Lee raced around to the rear courtyard of the house and then on to the boardwalk that criss-crossed the rear common areas connecting all the houses to the main steps going to the beach, like human veins leading to the heart's arteries. His own heart was pumping at a feverishly high pace.

He jumped off the boardwalk, squatted low behind some sawgrass and peered at the back of Faith's beach house. What he saw chilled him to the bone. The two men were dressed all in black and were sliding over the rear wall of Faith's courtyard. Were they the Feds? Or were they the men who had been prepared to assassinate Faith at the airport? *Please, God, don't let it be them.* The two men had already disappeared over the wall. In seconds they would be in the house. Had Faith reset the alarm system after she let him out? No, he thought, she probably hadn't.

Lee jumped up and dashed toward the house. As he crossed the boardwalk, he sensed something coming at him from the left as the darkness began to lift even more. That sensation was probably the only thing that saved his life.

The knife plunged into his arm instead of his neck as he ducked and rolled. He came up bleeding, but the rigid material of the bike suit had absorbed a good deal of the blow. His attacker didn't hesitate but leaped straight at him.

However, Lee timed it just right, managed to raise his good arm, pushed hard, levered the man over him, throwing him into the sawgrass, which was about as unpleasant as having a sharp knife driven into your flesh. Lee lunged for his gun, which he had lost when the guy had slammed into him. Lee had no qualms about shooting the guy down and raising a ruckus. Right now he would welcome any assistance the local police cared to provide.

His opponent made a stunning recovery, however, bursting out of the sawgrass with startling velocity and colliding with Lee before he could retrieve his pistol. The two men landed at the edge of the steps. Lee saw the knife thrust coming again but was able to grip the man's wrist before the blade hit him. The guy was strong; Lee could feel the steely tendons in the man's forearm and in the rocklike triceps as he grabbed the man's upper arm in an attempt to force the knife out of his hand. But Lee wasn't exactly a weakling either. He hadn't shoved tons of barbells around for years for nothing.

The guy he was battling was an experienced fighter as well because he had managed to get in two or three efficient gut punches with his free hand. After the first one, though, Lee tightened his abdominals and obliques and felt little pain from the other jabs. He had spent over two decades doing stomach crunches and having medicine balls slammed into his belly. After that punishment, the human fist offered very little difficulty for him, no matter how hard it was thrown.

Thinking that two could play at that game, Lee let go of the man's upper arm and landed a body uppercut to the diaphragm. He felt the wind go out of the guy, but the grip on the knife remained unbroken. Then Lee landed three successful kidney punches, about the most painful ones you could throw and still leave your opponent conscious. The knife fell from the man's hand, clattering down the steps.

Then both men rose to their feet, breathing hard, still clinging one to the other. Like a burst of wind,

382

the man executed a nifty loopkick that knocked Lee's legs from under him. He went down with a grunt but popped right back up when he saw the guy go for his pistol. Being seconds from death gave Lee's body resiliency he could never summon in less dangerous times. He hit the guy low and hard, linebacker to running back in a textbook impact, and they both went over the edge of the steps, bouncing painfully down each pressure-treated plank and landing in a pile of twisted arms, legs and torsos in the sand and then eating mouthfuls of salty water as they rolled into the water, the rising tide being almost up to the steps.

Lee had seen the pistol tumble away during the fall, so he kicked himself free and stood in ankle-deep water. The guy rose too, but not as swiftly. Lee, however, was tightly on guard. The guy knew karate; Lee had felt it in the kick at the top of the stairs; he was seeing it in the defensive posture the man now assumed, making himself into a little ball, leaving no angles, nothing of much width to hit. His brain working faster than conscious thought, Lee figured he had about four inches and fifty pounds on the guy, but if the man nailed him with a lethal foot to the head, Lee would go down. And then he and Faith and Buchanan were all dead. But if he didn't finish the guy within the next minute, Faith and Buchanan would be dead anyway.

The man aimed a crushing side kick to Lee's torso; however, his having to slosh through water to deliver the kick gave Lee the little extra time he needed. Lee had to get in close, grab what he could and not give Chuck Norris Jr. enough space to do his martial arts magic. Lee was a boxer; in-close fighting, where whipping legs couldn't do much damage, was where he could be absolutely devastating. Lee braced himself and absorbed the rib-rattling leg shot

to the body but then held on to the limb with his
bloodied arm, clinching it to his side in a viselike
grip. With his free hand, he landed a cartilage-
shattering blow to the guy's knee, driving it
backward to a degree knees were not designed to go.
The man screamed. Then Lee delivered a crunching
straight jab to the guy's face, feeling the nose flatten
under the impact. Finally, in a flash of almost
choreographed movement, Lee dropped the leg,
curled low and then erupted out of that position
with a cannonball left hook that carried all two
hundred and twenty pounds of his bulk plus
whatever multiplying factor pure fury brought to
the table. When his fist hit facial bone, which
promptly yielded under the terrible impact, Lee
knew he had won. Nobody short of a professional
heavyweight had a jaw that hard.

The man went down as though shot through the
head. Lee instantly flipped him on his stomach and
pushed his head under the water. He didn't have
time to actually drown the guy, so he brought his
elbow down with all his might dead center on the
back of the man's neck. The resulting sound was
unmistakable, even with the water lapping all over
them, as though God wanted Lee to damn well
know what he'd done, and didn't want him to ever
forget it.

The body went limp and Lee rose over the dead
man. Lee had been in more than his share of fights
both in and out of the boxing ring, but he had never
killed anyone before. As he looked down at the
body, he knew it was nothing to be proud of. Lee
was just grateful it wasn't him lying dead.

Sick to his stomach, suddenly feeling the full force
of the pain in his wounded arm, Lee looked up the
steps leading to the beach houses. He had only two
other beasts to conquer and then he could call it a

day. And it was clear they weren't the FBI. FBI agents didn't run around trying to kill people with fancy knives and karate kicks; they pulled their shield and guns and told you to stop right in your tracks. And if you were smart, you did.

No, they were the other guys. The CIA robokillers. He raced up the steps, found his pistol and hustled as fast as he could to the beach house, hoping with every labored breath that he was not too late.

FIFTY-TWO

Faith had changed into jeans and a sweatshirt and now sat on her bed staring at her bare feet. The sounds of the motorcycle had disappeared as though into an enormous vacuum. As she looked around the room, it was as though Lee Adams had never even been here, had never been real. She had spent so much time and energy trying to lose the man, and now that he was gone, all of her spirit seemed to have been swept into the void Lee had left behind.

At first she thought the sound she heard in the stillness of the house was Buchanan stirring. Then she thought it might actually be Lee returning. It had sounded like the back door. As she rose from the bed, it suddenly occurred to her that it couldn't be Lee because she hadn't heard the motorcycle pull into the carport; as this thought hit her, her heartbeat went through the roof.

Had she locked the door? She couldn't remember. She knew she hadn't set the alarm. Could it be just Danny stumbling around? For some reason Faith knew it wasn't.

She eased over to the doorway and peered out, her ears straining to hear any sound. She knew she hadn't imagined the noise. Someone had come in the house, she was sure of it. Someone was in the house right now. She looked down the hallway. There was another alarm control panel in the bedroom Lee had used. Could she reach it, activate the system, the

386

motion detector? She dropped to her knees and crawled out into the hallway.

Connie and Reynolds had gone in the side door and made their way down the lower-floor hallway. Connie had his gun pointed ahead. Reynolds was behind him, feeling naked and useless without her own pistol. They eased open each door on the lower level and found each room empty.

"They must be upstairs," Reynolds whispered into Connie's ear.

"I hope there's somebody here," he whispered back, his voice carrying an ominous tone.

They both froze when a sound came from somewhere within the house. Connie motioned upstairs with his finger and Reynolds nodded in agreement. They approached the stairs and headed up. Fortunately, the stairs were carpeted and absorbed the sounds of their footsteps. They reached the first landing and paused, listening intently. Silence. They moved forward again.

The family area was empty, as far as they could see. They moved along one wall, their heads swiveling in near-synchronized motion.

Right above them, in the upstairs hallway, Faith was flat on her stomach on the floor. She peered over the edge and relaxed slightly as she saw that it was Agents Reynolds and Constantinople. When she saw the two other men moving up the stairs from the lower level, her fear instantly returned.

"Look out," Faith yelled.

Connie and Reynolds turned back to look at her and saw where she was pointing. Connie swung his gun in the direction of the two men, who also had their guns out, pointed directly at the two agents.

"FBI," Reynolds barked out to the men in black.

"Drop your weapons." Usually when she said that, she felt fairly confident of the response. Now, with two guns against one, she was not nearly as confident.

The two men didn't drop their weapons. They moved forward as Connie swung his gun back and forth between the two.

One of the men looked up at Faith. "Come down here, Ms. Lockhart."

"Stay up there, Faith," Reynolds called out, her gaze finding Faith's and holding on it. "Go to your room and lock the door."

"Faith?" Buchanan appeared in the hallway, his hair disheveled, his eyes blinking.

"You too, Buchanan. Now," the same man commanded. "Down here."

"No!" Reynolds said, moving forward. "Listen up, an HRT unit is on its way here right now. We're looking at an ETA of about two minutes. If you won't put your weapons down, then I suggest you run like hell if you want to go up against those guys."

The man looked at her and smiled. "There's no HRT unit coming, Agent Reynolds."

Reynolds could not hide her astonishment. That astonishment immeasurably increased with the man's next words.

"Agent Constantinople," the man said, looking over at Connie, "you can leave now. We have it under control, but we appreciate your assistance."

Slowly, Reynolds turned and looked at her partner, her mouth open in absolute shock.

Connie stared back at her, both extreme discomfort and a profound sense of resignation on his features.

"Connie?" Reynolds took a quick breath. "It can't be, Connie. Please tell me it's not."

Connie fingered his pistol and he shrugged. Gradually his taut posture relaxed. "My plan was to get you out of this alive *and* get your suspension lifted." He looked over at the two men. One of them shook his head decisively.

"You're the leak?" Reynolds said. "Not Ken?"

"Ken was no leak," Connie said.

"But the money in the safe-deposit box?"

"That came from his card and coin trading. He operated all in cash. I actually did some shows with him. I knew. He was cheating the tax guys. So who the hell cared? More power to him. Most of it was going to college funds for his kids anyway."

"You let me think he was the leak."

"Well, I didn't want you to think it was me. Obviously, that would not have been good."

One of the men ran upstairs and disappeared into one of the bedrooms. A minute later he emerged carrying Buchanan's briefcase. He escorted Faith and Buchanan down the stairs. The man popped open the briefcase and took out the cassette. He played a little of the tape to confirm what was on it. Then he cracked open the cassette, pulled out the tape and threw the long strands into the gas fireplace and hit the remote switch. They all watched in silence as the tape was quickly reduced to a gooey mess.

As Reynolds watched the tape disappear, she couldn't help but think she was being shown the next few minutes of her life. The *last* few minutes of her life.

Reynolds looked at the two men and then at Connie. "So they just tailed us all the way down? I didn't see anybody," she said bitterly.

Connie shook his head. "There was a transmitter in my car. They've been listening in. They let us find the right house and then followed."

"Why, Connie? Why turn traitor?"

Connie's tone was reflective. "I put in twenty-five years at the Bureau. Twenty-five damn good years, and I'm still at square one, still a grunt in the field. I got a dozen years on you and you're my boss. Because I wouldn't play the political game south of the border. Because I wouldn't lie and just go along, they tanked my career." He shook his head and looked down. When he stared back up at her, he looked apologetic. "Understand, I got nothing against you, Brooke. Nothing. You're a damn fine agent. I didn't want it to end like this. The plan was for us to stay outside and let these guys do their thing. When I got the all-clear, we'd go in and find the bodies. Your name would be cleared, everything would work out fine. Adams taking off like that blew our plan apart." Connie stared with unfriendly eyes at the man in black who had identified him by name. "But if this guy hadn't said anything, maybe I still could have figured out a way for you to walk away with me."

The man shrugged. "Sorry, I didn't know that was important to you. But you'd better get going. It's getting light outside. Give us half an hour. Then you can call the cops. Make up any cover story you want."

Reynolds never took her eyes off Connie. "Let me make up a cover story for you, Connie. It goes like this: We found the house. I go in the front while you cover the rear. I don't come out. You hear shots, you go in. Find us all dead." Reynolds's voice broke as she thought of her children, of never seeing them again. "You see someone leaving, empty your pistol at him. But you miss, give chase, are almost killed, but luckily barely survive. You call the cops. They get here. You call HQ, fill them in. They send people down. You get bitched at a little for coming down here with me, but you were just standing by your boss. Loyalty. Who could really blame you? They investigate and never reach a satisfactory answer. Probably think I'm the leak for sure, came down for a payoff. You can tell them it was my idea to come here, that I knew exactly where to go. I go in the house, get popped. And you, a poor innocent dupe, almost lost your life too. Case closed. How's that sound, Agent Constantinople?" She almost spat this last part out.

One of Thornhill's men looked over at Connie and smiled. "Sounds good to me."

Connie never took his eyes off Reynolds. "I'm sorry, Brooke, I really am."

Reynolds's eyes filled with tears and her voice cracked again when she spoke. "Tell Anne Newman that. Tell *my* kids that, you bastard!"

His eyes downcast, Connie moved past them and started to head down the stairs.

"We'll do them here, one by one," the first man said.

He looked at Buchanan. "You first."

"I take it that was a special request from your boss," Buchanan said.

"Who? I want a name," Reynolds demanded.

"What does it matter?" the second man said. "It's not like you're going to be around to testify—"

The instant he said this, the bullet hit him in the back of the head and he went down instantly.

The other man whirled, trying to aim his gun, but was too late and took a blast right in the face. He dropped, dead, next to his partner.

Connie came back up the stairs, a wisp of smoke still trailing from his pistol's muzzle. He looked down at the two dead men. "That was for Ken Newman, you assholes." He looked up at Reynolds. "I didn't know they were going to kill Ken, Brooke. I swear that on a stack of Bibles. But after it happened, there was nothing I could do but bide my time and see what happened."

"And let me chase a wild goose? Watch me get suspended. My career ruined."

"There wasn't much I could do about that. Like I said, my intent was to get you out of this, get you reinstated. Let you be the hero. Let Ken take the charge as snitch. He was dead, what did it matter?"

"It would matter to his family, Connie."

Connie's features turned angry. "Look, I don't have to stand here and explain shit to you or anybody else. I'm not proud of what I did, but I had my reasons. You don't have to agree with them, and I'm not asking you to, but don't stand there and lecture me about something you know nothing about, lady. You want'a talk pain and bitterness? I got about fifteen years of it on you."

Reynolds blinked and stepped back, eyeing the pistol.

"Okay, Connie, you just saved our lives. That'll count for a lot."

"You think so, do you?"

She pulled out her cell phone. "I'm going to call Massey and get a team down here."

"Put the phone away, Brooke."

"Connie—"

"Put the damn phone down. Now!"

Reynolds let the phone drop to the floor. "Connie, it's over."

"It's never over, Brooke, you know that. Stuff that happened years ago will always come back to bite you in the ass. People find out stuff and look you up and suddenly your life is over."

"Is that why you're involved in this? Somebody was blackmailing you?"

He slowly gazed about. "What the hell does it matter?"

"It matters to me!" said Reynolds.

Connie let out a deep sigh. "When my wife got cancer, our insurance wouldn't cover all the specialized treatments. The doctors thought the treatments might give her a chance, a few more months. I mortgaged the house to the hilt. I cleaned out our bank accounts. It still wasn't enough. What was I supposed to do? Just let her die?" Connie angrily shook his head. "So some coke and other stuff turned up missing from the Bureau evidence room. Some people found out about it later. And suddenly I had a new employer." He paused and looked down for a moment. "And the most damnable thing is June died anyway."

"I can help you, Connie. You can end this right now."

Connie smiled grimly. "Nobody can help me, Brooke. I made my deal with the devil."

"Connie, let them go. It's over."

He shook his head. "I came here to do a job. And you know me well enough to know that I always finish what I start."

"Then what? How will you talk yourself out of these?" She looked at the two dead men. "And now you're going to kill three *more* people? That's crazy. Please."

"Not as crazy as giving up and spending the rest of my life in prison. Or maybe getting the chair." He shrugged his big shoulders. "I'll think of something."

"Please, Connie. Don't do this. You can't do this. I know you. You can't."

Connie looked at his pistol and then knelt down and picked up one of the dead men's guns that had a suppressor attached. "I've got to. And I am sorry, Brooke."

They all heard the click. Connie and Reynolds

instantly recognized it as the cock of a semi-automatic pistol.

Lee barked, "Drop the pistol. Now! Or I put a tunnel in your head."

Connie froze and let the gun fall to the floor.

Lee came up the stairs and put the muzzle of his pistol against the agent's head. "I'm real tempted to shoot you anyway, but you did save me the trouble of tangling with two more gorillas." Lee looked at Reynolds. "Agent Reynolds, I'd appreciate if you'd pick up the pistol and keep it trained on your boy here."

Reynolds did so, her eyes burning into her partner's. "Sit down, Connie. Now!" she ordered.

Lee went over and put his arms around Faith.

"Lee," was all she said, leaning into him.

"Thank God I decided to come back."

"Can someone tell me what the hell this is all about?" Reynolds said.

Buchanan stepped forward. "I can, but it may not do any good. The proof I had was on that tape. I was planning on making copies, but I didn't have the chance to before I left Washington."

Reynolds looked down at Connie. "You obviously know what's going on. If you cooperate, it'll help your sentencing."

"I might as well strap myself in the chair," Connie said.

"Who? Dammit, who is behind this that everybody's so scared to death of?"

"Agent Reynolds," Buchanan said, "I'm sure that particular gentleman is waiting to hear the outcome of all this. If he doesn't get it soon, he'll send out more men. I suggest we stop that from happening."

Reynolds looked at him. "Why should I trust you? What I should do is call the cops."

Faith said, "The night Agent Newman was killed,

I told him I wanted Danny to come in and testify with me. Newman told me that would never happen."

"Well, he told you right."

"But I think if you know all the facts, you won't think that way. What we did was wrong, but there was *no other way*. . . ."

"Well, that makes it all perfectly clear," Reynolds replied.

"That can wait," Buchanan said with urgency. "Right now we have to take care of the man behind these people." He looked down at the dead men.

"You can add one more to that count," Lee said. "He's outside taking a dip in the ocean."

Reynolds looked exasperated. "Everybody except for me seems to know everything." She turned to Buchanan with a scowl. "Okay, I'm listening. What's your suggestion?"

Buchanan started to answer when they all heard the sound of a plane coming in. Their eyes went to the window, where the dawn had broken.

"It's just the commuter service. It's daylight. First flight in. The runway's across the street," Faith explained.

"That I *do* know," Reynolds said.

"I suggest we use your friend there," Buchanan said, nodding at Connie, "to communicate with this person."

"And tell him what?"

"That his operation was a total success, except that his men were killed in the ensuing battle. He'll understand that, of course. Losses happen. But that Faith and I were killed and the tape was destroyed. That way he'll feel safe."

"And me?" Lee said.

Buchanan glanced at him. "We'll let you be our wild card."

"And why exactly should I do that?" Reynolds wanted to know. "When I could take you and Faith, and him" – she flicked her pistol at Connie – "to the WFO, get my job back and walk away a hero."

"Because if you do that, the man who has caused all of this will go free. Free to do something like this again."

Reynolds looked confused and troubled.

Buchanan watched her closely. "It's up to you."

Reynolds looked at each of them and then her gaze came to rest on Lee. She noted the blood on his sleeve, the cuts and bruises on his face.

"You saved all of our lives. You're probably the most innocent person in this room. What do you think?"

Lee looked at Faith and then at Buchanan before coming back to Reynolds. "I don't think I can give you a great reason to do it, but if you want my gut, I'd say to go along with them."

Reynolds sighed and looked over at Connie. "You have a way of contacting this monster?" Connie said nothing. "Connie, you work with us on this, it'll help you. I know you were just prepared to kill all of us, and I shouldn't give a damn about what happens to you." She paused and looked down for a moment. "But I do. Last chance, Connie, what do you say?"

Connie's big hands clenched and unclenched nervously. He looked at Buchanan. "What exactly do you want me to say?"

Buchanan told him precisely, and Connie sat down on the couch, picked up the phone and dialed. When the line was answered, he said, "This is . . ." – Connie looked embarrassed for a moment – "this is Ace-in-the-Hole." Ten minutes later Connie put down the phone and looked at each of them. "Okay, it's done."

"Did he seem to buy it?" Lee asked.

"Yes, but you can never be sure with these guys."

"Good, enough; that gives us some time," Buchanan said.

"Well, right now we have some things to tend to," Reynolds said. "Like a number of dead bodies. And I've got to report in. And get you" – she looked at Connie – "into a cell."

Connie glared at her. "So much for loyalty," he said.

She glared back. "You made your choices. What you did for us *will* help you. But you're going to be in prison a long time, Connie. At least you get to live. That's more of a choice than Ken had."

She looked at Buchanan. "Now what?"

"I suggest we leave here immediately. Once we're out of the area, you can call the police. When we get back to Washington, Faith and I will meet with the FBI, tell them what we know. We must keep everything completely secret. If he knows we're working with the FBI, we'll never get the proof we need."

"This guy had Ken killed?"

"Yes."

"Is he with a foreign interest?"

"Actually, you both have the same employer."

Reynolds looked at him, stunned. "Uncle Sam?" she said slowly.

Buchanan nodded. "If you trust me, I will do my best to bring him to you. I have my own personal score to settle with him."

"And what exactly do you expect in return?"

"For me? Nothing. If I go to prison, I go to prison. But Faith goes free. Unless you can guarantee me that, you can just call the police right now."

Faith grabbed his arm. "Danny, you're not taking the fall for this."

"Why not? It was my doing."

397

"But your reasons—"

"Reasons are no defense. I knew I was taking a chance when I broke the law."

"Well, so did I, dammit!"

Buchanan turned back to Reynolds. "Do we have a deal? Faith does not go to prison."

"I'm really not in a position to offer you anything." She pondered the issue for a moment. "But I can promise you this: If you are shooting straight with me, I'll do everything in my power to see that Faith goes free."

Connie stood up, suddenly looking pale. "Brooke, I need to hit the john, like quick." He was wobbly on his feet; one hand slid to his chest.

She glanced at him suspiciously. "What's the matter?" She scrutinized his pallid features. "Are you all right?"

"To tell the truth, I've been better," he mumbled, his head rolling to one side, his left side drooping.

"I'll go with him," Lee said.

As the pair started to the stairs, Connie seemed to lose his balance and he pressed his hand hard against the center of his chest, his face contorted in pain. "Shit. Oh, God!" He dropped to one knee, moaning, saliva dripping out of his mouth; he started gurgling.

"Connie!" Reynolds started toward him.

"He's having a heart attack," Faith cried out.

"Connie!" Reynolds said again as she stared at her stricken partner, who was fast sinking to the floor, his body twitching uncontrollably.

The movement was fast. It seemed too fast for a man in his fifties, but then again, desperation could mix with adrenaline in a flash.

Connie's hand dipped to his ankle. A compact pistol was in a holster there. The gun was out and aimed before anyone could react. Connie had

398

multiple targets, but he chose Danny Buchanan and fired.

The only one who reacted as fast as Connie did was Faith Lockhart.

From where she was standing next to Buchanan, she saw the pistol come out before anyone else. She saw the barrel pointed at her friend. In her mind she could hear the explosion that would launch the bullet that would kill Buchanan. How she moved that fast was inexplicable.

The bullet hit Faith in the chest; she gasped once and then dropped at Buchanan's feet.

"Faith!" Lee screamed. Instead of tackling Connie, he lunged for her.

Reynolds's gun was trained on Connie. As he swung the pistol around in her direction, the image of the palm reader flashed through her mind. That all-too-short life line. MOTHER OF TWO, FEDERAL AGENT DEAD. She saw the headline fully and boldly in her mind. The whole thing was almost paralyzing. Almost.

She and Connie locked gazes. He was bringing up his pistol, lining it up with her. He would pull the trigger, she had no doubt. He clearly had the nerve, the balls to kill. Did she? Her finger tightened on her own trigger as the entire world seemed to slow to the pace of an underwater world, where gravity was either suspended or magnified. Her partner. An FBI agent. A traitor. Her children. Her own life. Now or never.

Reynolds pulled the trigger once and then a second time. The recoil was short, her aim perfect. As the bullets entered Connie's body, his bulk quivered, his mind perhaps still sending messages, not yet realizing that it was dead.

Reynolds thought she saw Connie stare searchingly at her as he started to go down, the gun falling from his hand. That image would haunt her forever. Only when Agent Howard Constantinople hit the floor and didn't move again did Brooke Reynolds take a breath.

"Faith, Faith!" Lee was tearing at her shirt, exposing the horribly bloody wound in her chest. "Omigod. Faith." She was unconscious, her breathing barely detectable.

Buchanan stared down in blank horror.

Reynolds knelt beside Lee. "How bad?"

Lee looked up in anguish. He couldn't speak.

Reynolds assessed the wound. "Bad," she said. "Slug's still in her. The hole's right near her heart."

Lee looked at Faith. Her skin was already beginning to pale. He could feel the warmth of life spilling out from her with each shallow breath she took. "Oh, God. No. Please!" he cried out.

"We've got to get her to a hospital. Fast," Reynolds said. She had no idea where the closest hospital was, let alone a trauma center, which was what Faith really needed. And searching the local area by car would be akin to signing the woman's death warrant. She could call the paramedics, but who knew how long it would take for them to get here? The roar of the plane engine outside made Reynolds glance at the window. The plan formed in her head within seconds. She raced back to Connie and lifted his FBI credentials from his body. For one brief moment she gazed at her former colleague. She shouldn't feel bad for what she had done. He had been well prepared to kill her. So why did she feel crushed by remorse? But Connie was dead. Faith Lockhart wasn't. At least not yet. Reynolds hustled back over to where Faith lay. "Lee, we're taking the plane. Hurry!"

The group raced outside, Reynolds in the lead. They could hear the plane's engines revving up as it prepared to take off. Reynolds sprinted ahead, tore her way through the hedge and found herself on the runway. She looked down at the opposite end. The plane was turning, getting ready to roar down the tarmac, lift into the air; their only hope would be gone in seconds. She ran down the asphalt, directly at the aircraft, waving the pistol, the badge, screaming, "FBI!" at the top of her lungs. The plane came racing at her, as Buchanan, holding clear an opening in the hedge, helped Lee carry Faith through. They burst on to the runway.

The pilot finally focused on the woman waving a pistol and coming at him. He pulled back on the throttle and the aircraft stopped its roll, the engines whined down.

Reynolds reached the plane, held up the badge and the pilot slid open his window.

"FBI," she said hoarsely. "I have a badly wounded person. I need your aircraft. You're going to fly us to the nearest hospital. Now."

The pilot looked at the badge, the gun and nodded dumbly. "Okay."

They all climbed on the plane, Lee cradling Faith against his chest. The pilot turned the aircraft around again, went back to the end of the runway and started his takeoff roll once more. A minute later the plane lifted into the air and rushed toward the embrace of the quickly lightening sky.

FIFTY-THREE

The pilot radioed ahead and a life-support ambulance was waiting on the tarmac at the airstrip in Manteo, which was thankfully only a few minutes of flight time away. Reynolds and Lee had used some bandages from the first-aid kit on the plane to try to stop the bleeding, and Lee had given Faith oxygen from the small canister on board, but none of it seemed to have any effect. She had not yet regained consciousness; they could barely get a pulse now. Her limbs were beginning to grow cold, even as Lee clung to her, tried to give her heat from his own body, as though that would do any good.

Lee rode in the ambulance with Faith over to Beach Medical Center, which had an emergency and trauma center. Reynolds and Buchanan were driven there in a car. On the way to the hospital, Reynolds called Fred Massey in Washington. She told him just enough that he was already running to catch a Bureau plane. Just him, Reynolds had insisted; no one else could come. Massey had accepted this condition without comment. Perhaps it had been the tone of her voice, or simply the stunning content of her very few words.

Faith was immediately taken to the emergency room, where doctors labored over her for almost two hours, trying to get her vitals up, her heart regulated, the internal bleeding stopped. None of it looked good. Once, the crash cart even had to be called.

Through the doors Lee had watched in the

numbest horror as Faith repeatedly jerked under the impact of the electrical current surging through the paddles. Only when he saw the heart monitor go from flat line to its regular peaks and valleys did he find he could even move.

Barely two hours later they had to cut her chest open, spread her ribs wide and massage her heart to get it going. Every hour seemed to bring a new crisis as she barely clung to life.

Lee paced the floor incessantly, hands shoved in his pockets, head down, talking to no one. He had said every prayer he could remember. He had made up some new ones. He was helpless to do anything for the woman, and that's what tore at him. How could he have let this happen? How could Connie, that old, bulky sonofabitch, have gotten that shot off? And him right beside the guy? And Faith, why had she taken the round? Why? Buchanan should be the guy lying on that gurney with people swarming over him, trying desperately to push life back into his wrecked body.

Lee slumped against the wall and slid down to the floor, covering his face with both hands as his big body shook.

In a private room, Reynolds waited with Buchanan, who had barely spoken a word since Faith had been shot. He just sat there and stared at the wall. To look at Buchanan, no one would have guessed that anger was building in him: the absolute hatred he was holding for Robert Thornhill, a man who had destroyed everything he had cared about.

About the time Fred Massey arrived, Faith was taken to the ICU. She was stabilized for the time being, the doctor told them. The bullet was one of those vicious dum-dums, he said. It had tumbled through her body like a runaway bowling ball, doing considerable damage to organs, and the internal hemorrhaging had been severe. She was strong and for now she was alive. She had a chance, that was all, he cautioned. They would know more soon.

As the doctor walked away, Reynolds put a hand on Lee's shoulder and handed him a fresh cup of coffee.

"Lee, if she survived until now, I have to believe she's going to make it."

"No guarantees," he mumbled to himself, unable to look at the woman.

They went to the private room, where Reynolds introduced Buchanan and Lee to Fred Massey.

"I think Mr. Buchanan should start telling you his story," Reynolds said to Massey.

"And he's willing to do that?" Massey asked skeptically.

At this Buchanan perked up. "Something more than willing. But before I do, tell me one thing. What's more important to you? What I did, or arresting the person who killed your agent?"

Massey leaned forward. "I'm not sure I'm prepared to discuss any sort of deal with you."

Buchanan put his elbows on the table. "When I tell you my story, you will be. But I'll do so on only one condition. You let me deal with this man. In my own way."

"Agent Reynolds informed me this person works for the federal government."

"That's right."

"Well, that's pretty damn unbelievable. Do you have proof?"

"You let me do this my way, and you'll have your proof."

Massey looked over at Reynolds. "The bodies at

404

the house. Do we know who they are yet?"

She shook her head. "I just checked in. The police and agents from D.C., Raleigh and Norfolk are on the scene. But it's too early yet to have that info. But everything's on the QT. The locals have been told nothing. We're controlling all flows of information. You won't see anything on the news about the bodies or about Faith being alive and in this hospital."

Massey nodded. "Good work." As though suddenly remembering something, he opened his briefcase, pulled out two objects and handed them to her.

Reynolds looked down at her pistol and creds.

"I'm sorry any of this happened, Brooke," Massey said. "I should have trusted you and I didn't. Maybe I've been out of the field too damn long. Pushing too many papers and not listening to my instincts anymore."

Reynolds holstered her gun and put the creds in her purse. She once more felt complete. "Maybe I wouldn't have either, in your position. But it's in the past, Fred, let's move on. We don't have much time."

"Rest assured, Mr. Massey," Buchanan said, "you'll never identify those men. Or if you do, they'll have no ties to the person I'm talking about."

"How can you be so sure of that?" Massey demanded.

"Trust me, I know how this man operates."

"Look, why don't you just tell me who it is and I'll handle it from there?"

"No," Buchanan said firmly.

"What do you mean no? We're the FBI, mister, we do this for a living. If you want any sort of deal—"

"You will listen to me." Buchanan hardly raised his voice, but his eyes bored into Massey with such overwhelming force that the ADIC lost his train of thought and fell silent. "We have one chance to bring him in. One! He's already infiltrated the FBI. Constantinople may not be the only mole. There may be others."

"I highly doubt that—" Massey began.

Now Buchanan raised his voice. "Can you guarantee me that there aren't? Can you?"

Massey sat back, looking uncomfortable. He glanced at Reynolds, who shrugged.

"If they could turn Connie, they could turn anybody," she said.

Massey looked miserable, shaking his head slowly. "Connie . . . I still can't believe it."

Buchanan tapped the tabletop. "And if there is another spy in your ranks and you try to trap this man on your own, you will absolutely fail. And your chance will be gone. Forever. Do you really want to risk that?"

Massey rubbed his smooth chin, thinking it over. When he looked up at Buchanan, his expression was wary but interested.

"Do you really think you can nail this guy?"

"I'm prepared to die trying. And I need to work the phones. Call in some very special help." Buchanan smiled to himself. A lobbyist to the very end. He turned to Lee. "And I need your help, Lee. If you're willing."

Lee looked surprised. "Me? What can I do to help anybody?"

"I spoke with Faith about you last night. She told me about your 'special' abilities. She said you were a good man to have in a bad situation."

"I guess she was wrong about that. Otherwise she wouldn't be lying up there with a hole in her chest."

Buchanan put a hand on Lee's arm. "I can barely function with the guilt I have, for her having stepped in front of that bullet. But I can't change that now.

406

What I can do is try to make sure she didn't risk her life for nothing. There's great danger for you. Even if we get this man, he has many at his back. There'll always be some out there."

Buchanan settled back in his chair and watched Lee closely. Massey and Reynolds stared at the PI too. Lee's muscular arms and broad shoulders were in stark contrast to the fragility of the look deep within his eyes.

Lee Adams took a deep breath. What he really wanted to do was stand next to Faith's bed and never leave until she woke up, saw him, smiled, said she'd be okay. And then, so would he. But, Lee knew, one rarely got what one wished for in this life. So instead, he looked at Buchanan and said, "I guess I'm your man."

FIFTY-FOUR

The black sedan pulled up to the front of the house. Robert Thornhill and his wife, dressed in formal evening clothes, came out the front door. Thornhill locked the house, then the two got in the car and were driven away. The Thornhills were attending an official dinner at the White House.

The sedan passed the phone-line control pedestal belonging to the community where the Thornhills lived. The metal box was large, bulky and painted light green. It had been placed there about two years ago when the phone company had upgraded the communications lines for this old neighborhood. The metal box had been a sudden eyesore in an area that prided itself on splendid homes and high-dollar landscaping. Thus, the residents had paid for a number of large bushes to be planted around the aboveground pedestal. These bushes now hid the box completely from the road, which meant that the telephone servicemen had to approach it from the rear side, which faced the woods. Aesthetically pleasing, the bushes were also very welcome to the man who had watched the sedan pass by and then had opened the box and begun delicately picking his way through its electronic guts.

Lee Adams identified the line going to the Thornhills' residence with a special piece of his own customized equipment. His background in communications hardware was serving him well. The Thornhills' home had a good security system.

However, every security system had an Achilles' heel: the phone line. Always the phone line. Thank you, Mr Bell.

Lee went through the steps in his head. When an intruder broke into someone's home, the alarm went off and the computer dialed the central monitoring station to inform them of the break-in. Then the security person at the monitoring station called the home to see if everything was okay. If the owner answered, he had to give his special code or else the police would be sent. If no one answered the phone, the police would be sent automatically.

Simply put, Lee was making sure that the home's computer would never reach the monitoring station, yet would let it think that it had. He was accomplishing this by building an in-line component or phone simulator. He had dropped the Thornhill home from the landline feed, effectively severing outside phone communication. Now he had to trick the alarm computer into thinking it had phone service. To do this, he installed the in-line component and threw the switch, effectively giving the Thornhills' home a dial tone and phone line that went absolutely nowhere.

He had also found out that the Thornhills' alarm system had no cellular backup, just the regular landline. That was a big hole. A cellular backup was incapable of being fooled, since it was a wireless system with no way for Lee to access its feed line. Virtually all alarm systems in the country had the very same backbone land- and data-lines. And, thus, they all had back doors in. Lee had just completed his.

He packed up his tools and made his way through the woods to the rear of the Thornhills' home. He located a window that was not visible from the street. He had a copy of the Thornhills' floor plan

409

and alarm layout. It had been provided to him by Fred Massey. By accessing this window, he could reach the upstairs alarm panel without passing any motion detector points.

He pulled a stun gun from his backpack and held it flush against the window. The windows were all wired, even the second-floor ones, he knew. And both top and bottom window components had contacts. Most homes only had contacts at the bottom window casement; if that had been the case here, Lee would have simply picked the window lock and slid down the top window, without breaking any contacts.

He pulled the trigger on the stun gun and then moved it to another position on the window where he thought the contact elements were probably located. In all, he fired eight shots into the window frame from the stun gun. The electrical charge from the gun would melt the contacts, fusing them together and rendering them inoperable.

He picked the sash lock, held his breath and slid the window up. No alarm sounded. He quickly climbed through the window and closed it. Pulling a small flashlight from his pocket, he found the stairs and headed up. The Thornhills, he quickly observed, lived in extremely comfortable luxury. The furnishings were mostly antique; real oil paintings hung on the walls; and his feet melted into the thick and, he assumed, expensive carpet.

The alarm panel was where all such alarm panels were located; on the upper floor in the master bedroom. He unscrewed the plate and found the wire for the sound cannon. Two snips and the alarm system had suddenly developed laryngitis. Now he was free to roam. He went downstairs and passed in front of the motion detector, waving his arms in defiance, even giving it the finger, pretending it was

Thornhill there scowling at him, helpless to do anything about the intrusion. The red light came on and the alarm system was activated, although the system no longer could scream its warning. The computer would soon be dialing the central station, only its call would never get there. It would dial the number eight times, get no answer and then it would stop trying and go back to sleep. At the central station, everything would seem perfectly normal: a burglar's dream.

Lee watched as the red light on the motion detector disappeared. Each time he passed in front of it, though, it would go through the same routine, with the same result. Call eight times and then stop. Lee smiled. So far, so good. Before the Thornhills came home he would reattach the wires for the sound cannons: Thornhill would be suspicious if the normal beeping sound didn't occur when he opened the door. But for now, Lee had work to do.

411

FIFTY-FIVE

The White House dinner was very memorable for Mrs. Thornhill. Her husband, on the other hand, was working. He sat at the long table and made inconsequential conversation when called upon, but spent most of his time listening intently to the guests. There were a number of foreign visitors tonight, and Thornhill knew that good intelligence might come from unusual sources, even a White House dinner. Whether the foreign guests knew he was with the CIA, he wasn't sure. That was certainly not public knowledge. The guest list that would be printed in the *Washington Post* the next morning would identify them only as Mr. and Mrs. Robert Thornhill.

Ironically, the invitation to the dinner had not come because of Thornhill's position at the Agency. Who was invited to White House functions such as this, and why, were the greatest of mysteries in the capital city. However, the Thornhills' invitation had been extended because of his wife's well-known philanthropic work for the District of Columbia poor – a charitable endeavor in which the first lady herself was much involved as well. And Thornhill had to admit, his wife was dedicated to this cause. When she wasn't at the country club, of course.

The ride home was uneventful; the couple talked of mundane things while most of Thornhill's mind was focused on the phone call from Howard Constantinople. Losing his men had been a blow to

Thornhill, both personally and professionally. He had worked with them for years. How all three had been killed was beyond his comprehension. He had people down in North Carolina right now finding out as much as possible.

He had not heard anything further from Constantinople. Whether the man had run was unknown. But Faith and Buchanan were dead. And so was the other FBI agent, Reynolds. At least he was almost certain they were dead. The fact that no newspaper reports had come out regarding at least six dead bodies at a beach house in an affluent area in the Outer Banks was particularly troubling. It had been over a week, and nothing. It might be the Bureau's doing, covering up what was quickly building to a PR nightmare for them. Yes, he could see them doing that. Unfortunately, without Constantinople he had lost his eyes and ears at the Bureau. He would have to do something about that soon. It would take time to cultivate a new mole, yet nothing was impossible.

Well, the trail could never lead back to him. His three operatives had cover buried so deeply that the authorities would be incredibly fortunate if they managed to dig through even the surface layer. They would find nothing after that. Well, the three had died heroes. He and his colleagues had toasted their memory in the underground chamber upon learning of their deaths.

There was one more troubling loose end: Lee Adams. He had gone off on his motorcycle, presumably to Charlottesville to make sure his daughter was safe. He had never arrived in Charlottesville, that Thornhill knew for a fact. So where was he? Had he come back and managed to kill Thornhill's men? And yet one man taking out all three of them was incomprehensible. But

Constantinople had not mentioned Adams in the call.

As the car drove along, Thornhill felt much less confident than he had at the beginning of the evening. He would have to watch the situation very carefully. Perhaps there would be some message waiting for him at home.

As the car pulled into their driveway, Thornhill glanced at his watch. It was late, and he had an early morning. He had to testify tomorrow before Rusty Ward's committee. He had finally tracked down the answers the senator wanted, meaning he was prepared to throw out so much bullshit that the room would have to be fumigated after he had finished.

Thornhill disarmed the security system, kissed his wife good night and watched as she went up the stairs to her bedroom. She was still a very attractive woman, slender, fine-boned. Retirement would be coming soon. Perhaps it wouldn't be so bad. He'd had nightmares about it; his sitting in agony at interminable bridge games, country club dinners, fund-raisers; or hacking his way through infinite rounds of golf, his insufferably perky wife at his side for all of it.

However, as he watched the woman's nicely shaped backside gliding up the stairs, Thornhill suddenly saw more enticing possibilities for his golden years. They were relatively young, wealthy; they could travel the world. He even thought he might turn in early tonight, and take advantage of the physical urges he was suddenly feeling as he watched Mrs. Thornhill gracefully ascend the stairs to their bedroom. He liked the way she slid her high heels off, exposing black-hosed feet; moved a hand along her curvy hip; let her hair down her back, her shoulder muscles tensing with each movement.

Those hours at the country club certainly hadn't all been wasted. He would just pop in his study to check his messages and then head upstairs.

He clicked on the light in his study and went over to his desk. He was about to check for any messages on his secure phone when he heard a noise. He turned to the French doors that opened out on to the garden. The doors were opening and a man was stepping through.

Lee put a finger to his lips and smiled, his gun pointed directly at Thornhill. The CIA man stiffened, his eyes darting left and right, looking for escape, but there was none to be had. If he ran or screamed, he would be dead; he could see that in the man's eyes. Lee crossed the room and closed, then locked the door to the study. Thornhill watched him silently.

Thornhill received a second shock when another man stepped through the French doors, closing and locking them too.

Danny Buchanan looked so calm as to be almost asleep, yet a high level of energy danced behind his eyes.

"Who are you? What are you doing in my house?" Thornhill demanded.

"I expected something a little more original, Bob," said Buchanan. "How often is it that you see a ghost from the very recent past?"

"Sit," Lee ordered Thornhill.

Thornhill eyed the gun one more time, then went over and sat on the leather couch facing the two men. He undid his bow tie and dropped it on the couch, trying, with some difficulty, to assess the situation and decide on a course of action.

"I thought we had a deal, Bob," Buchanan said. "Why did you send your team of killers down? A lot of people lost their lives unnecessarily. Why?"

Thornhill looked at him suspiciously and then at Lee.

"I don't know what you're talking about. I don't even know who the hell you are."

It was clear what Thornhill was thinking: Lee and Buchanan were wired. Perhaps they were working with the FBI. And they were in his house. His wife was upstairs undressing, and these two men were in his house asking him these sorts of questions. Well, they would get nothing for their troubles.

"I" – Buchanan stopped and glanced at Lee – "we came here, as the sole survivors, to see what sort of arrangement we can work out. I don't want to keep looking over my shoulder for the rest of my life."

"Arrangement? How about I yell up to my wife to call the police? You like that arrangement?" Thornhill eyed Buchanan closely and then pretended recognition. "I know I've seen you somewhere before. In the newspapers?"

Buchanan smiled. "That certain tape Agent Constantinople told you was destroyed?" He slid his hand in his coat pocket and pulled out a cassette. "Well, he didn't get it exactly right."

Thornhill stared at the cassette as if it were plutonium about to be shoved down his throat. He reached into his own jacket.

Lee raised the pistol.

Thornhill gave him a disappointed look and slowly edged out his pipe and lighter, taking a moment to light it. Several soothing puffs later, he eyed Buchanan.

"Since I don't even know what you're talking about, why don't you play the tape? I'd be interested to know what's on it. It might explain why two complete strangers have broken into my house." *And if that tape had me talking about killing an FBI agent, neither of you would be here, and I'd already be under*

416

arrest. Bluff, bluff, bluff, Danny.

Buchanan slowly tapped the cassette against his palm, while Lee looked nervous.

"Come now, don't tease me with something and then pull it away," said Thornhill.

Buchanan dropped the cassette on the desk. "Maybe later. Right now I want to know what you're going to do for us. Something that will make us not go to the FBI and tell them what we know."

"And what might that be? You talked about people getting killed. Are you insinuating that I might have killed somebody? I'm assuming that you know I'm employed by the CIA. Are you foreign agents attempting some sort of bizarre blackmail scheme? The problem with that is, you need to have something to blackmail me with."

Lee said, "We know enough to bury you."

"Well, then I suggest you go get your shovel and start digging, Mr. . . . ?"

"Adams, Lee Adams," Lee said with a fierce scowl.

"Faith is dead, you know, Bob," Buchanan said. As he said this, Lee looked down. "She almost made it. Constantinople killed her. He also killed two of your men. Payback for your killing the FBI agent."

Thornhill looked suitably bewildered. "Faith? Constantinople? What the hell are you talking about?"

Lee came and stood directly in front of Thornhill. "You bastard! You kill people like stepping on ants. A game. That's all it is to you."

"Please put the gun away and leave my house. Now!"

"Damn you!" Lee aimed his pistol directly at Thornhill's head.

Buchanan was next to him in an instant. "Lee, please don't. That won't do any good."

417

"I would listen to your friend if I were you," Thornhill said as calmly as he could. He had had a gun pulled on him once before, when his cover had been blown in Istanbul many years ago. He had been lucky to get out alive. He wondered if his luck would hold tonight.

"Why should I listen to anybody?" Lee growled.

"Lee, please," Buchanan said.

Lee's finger hovered on the trigger for an instant, his gaze locked with Thornhill's. Finally, he lowered the gun, slowly.

"Well, I guess we'll have to go to the Feds with what we have," Lee said.

"I just want you out of my house."

"And all I want," Buchanan said, "is your personal assurances that no one else will be killed. You've got what you want. You don't have to harm anyone else."

"Right. Right, whatever you say. I won't kill anybody else," Thornhill said sarcastically. "Now if you'll please leave my house. I don't want to upset my wife. She has no idea she's married to a mass murderer."

"This is no joke," Buchanan said angrily.

"No, it really isn't, and I hope you get the help you so obviously need," said Thornhill. "And please take care that your gun-toting friend doesn't hurt anyone." *That should sound very nice on the tape. I am actually caring about others.*

Buchanan picked up the cassette.

"Not leaving the evidence of my crimes?"

Buchanan swiveled around and eyed him severely. "Under the circumstances, I don't think it will be necessary."

He looks like he wants to kill me, Thornhill thought. *Good, very good.*

Thornhill watched as the two men hurried down

his driveway and disappeared on to the darkened street. A minute later he heard a car start up. He raced to the phone and then stopped. Was it tapped? Was this whole thing a charade to trick him into a mistake? He stared at the window. Yes, they could be out there right now. He hit a button under his desk. All the drapes in the room descended and then a small whooshing sound commenced at each of the windows: white noise. He slid open his drawer and pulled out his secure phone. It had so many security and scrambling features that not even the NSA jocks could lift it from the air. Like the technology used on military aircraft, the phone threw out electronic chaff that jammed attempts to intercept its signal. *So much for electronic eavesdropping, you amateurs.*

"Buchanan and Lee Adams were in my study," he said into the phone. "Yes. In my home, dammit! They just left. I want all the men we can spare. We're only minutes from Langley. You should be able to find them." He paused to relight his pipe. "They sang some bullshit song about the cassette tape where I admitted to having the FBI agent killed. But Buchanan was just bluffing. The tape is gone. I figured they were wired, and I played dumb with everything. It almost cost me my life. That idiot Adams was two seconds away from blowing my head off. Buchanan said Lockhart was dead, which is good for us, if it's true. But I don't know if they're somehow working with the FBI. But without that tape they've got no evidence of what we've done. What? No, Buchanan was begging for us to leave him alone. We could go ahead with the blackmail plan, just let him live. It was pitiful, actually. When I first saw them, I thought they had come to kill me. That Adams is dangerous. And they told me Constantinople killed two of our men. Constantinople must be dead, so we need to get another spy at the FBI. But whatever you do, you find them. And this time no mistakes. They are dead. And after that, it's time to execute the plan. I can't wait to see those pitiful faces on Capitol Hill when I hit them with this."

Thornhill clicked off and sat at his desk. It was funny, their coming here that way. A desperate act. From desperate men. Did they really think they could bluff a man such as himself? It was rather insulting. But he had won in the end. The reality was that tomorrow or soon thereafter they would be dead and he wouldn't be.

He rose from behind the desk. Having survived that little scare had actually made him feel quite invigorated. He had been brave, cool under pressure. It was rather intoxicating, primal. He bounded up the stairs. To see Mrs. Thornhill. To demonstrate for her quite clearly who the man of the house was.

FIFTY-SIX

The Dirksen Senate Office Building was bustling as usual on this crisp morning. Robert Thornhill walked with special purpose down the long hallway, swinging his briefcase cavalierly at his side. Last night had been quite something, a success in many ways. The only downside was that they had failed to find Buchanan and Adams.

The rest of the night had been simply marvelous. Mrs. Thornhill had been impressed with his animalistic zeal. The woman had even gotten up early and made him breakfast, dressed in a sheer, clingy black outfit. That hadn't happened in years: making his breakfast or the clingy number.

The hearing room was at the far end of the hallway. Rusty Ward's little fiefdom, Thornhill thought with a snort. He ruled with a Southern fist, meaning velvet-gloved, yet with granite knuckles underneath. Ward would lull you to sleep with his ridiculously syrupy drawl and when you least expected it, he would pounce and shred you, his intense gaze and oh-so-precise words melting the unsuspecting foe right in his uncomfortable, government-issue hot seat.

Everything about Rusty Ward painfully assaulted Thornhill's old-school, Ivy-League sensibilities. But this morning he was ready. He would talk death squads and redactions until the cows came home, to borrow one of Ward's favorite lines; and the senator would be left with no more information at the end of the day than when he had started.

Before entering the hearing room, Thornhill took one energizing deep breath. He envisioned the setting that he was about to confront: Ward and company behind their little bench, the chairman pulling at his suspenders, his fat face looking here and there as he rustled through his briefing papers, missing nothing in the confines of his pathetic kingdom. When Thornhill entered, Ward would look at him, smile, nod, give him some little innocent greeting intended to disarm Thornhill's defenses, as if that were even a possibility. *But I guess he has to go through the motions. Teaching an old dog new tricks indeed.* That was another of Ward's stupid little sayings. How dreary.

Thornhill pulled open the door and strode confidently down the aisle of the hearing room. About halfway down, he realized that the room held many more people than usual. The small space was literally bursting with bodies. And as he looked around, he noted numerous faces he did not recognize. As he approached the witness table, he received another shock. There were already people sitting there, their backs to him.

He looked up at the committee. Ward stared back at him. There was no smile, no inane greeting from the portly chairman.

"Mr. Thornhill, take a seat in the front row, will you? We have one person testifying before you."

Thornhill looked dazed. "Excuse me?"

"Just sit down, Mr. Thornhill," Ward said again.

Thornhill looked at his watch. "I'm afraid I have limited time today, Mr. Chairman. And I wasn't told about anyone else testifying." Thornhill glanced at the witness table. He didn't recognize the men sitting there. "Perhaps we should just reschedule."

422

Ward looked past Thornhill. The latter turned and followed his gaze. The uniformed Capitol Hill police officer ceremoniously closed the door to the hearing room and then stood with his broad back against it, as though daring anyone to try to get past him.

Thornhill looked back around at Ward. "Am I missing something here?"

"If you are, it will be made crystal clear in a minute," Ward replied ominously. Then he looked over at one of his aides and nodded.

The aide disappeared through a small doorway behind the committee. He was back in a few seconds. And then Thornhill received what amounted to the greatest shock of his life, as Danny Buchanan walked through the doorway and made his way to the witness table. He never even looked at Thornhill, who just stood there in the middle of the aisle, his briefcase now resting motionless against his leg. The men rose from the witness table and took seats in the audience.

Buchanan stood in front of the witness table, raised his right hand, was sworn in and then sat down.

Ward glanced over at Thornhill, who still hadn't moved.

"Mr. Thornhill, will you please sit down so we can get started here?"

Thornhill couldn't take his eyes off Buchanan. He shuffled sideways toward the one remaining empty seat in the front row. The large man sitting at the end of the row moved aside so Thornhill could pass by. As Thornhill sat, he glanced over at the man and found himself staring at Lee Adams.

"Good to see you again," Lee said with a smile before settling back in his chair and turning his attention toward the front of the room.

"Mr. Buchanan," Ward began. "Can you tell us why you're here today, sir?"

"To provide testimony regarding a shocking conspiracy at the Central Intelligence Agency," Buchanan replied in a calm, assured tone. Over the years he had testified before more committees than all the Watergate folk combined. He was on familiar ground, his best friend in the world doing the questioning. This was his time. Finally.

"Then I guess you should start at the beginning, sir."

Buchanan placed his hands neatly in front of him, leaned forward and spoke into the microphone.

"Approximately fifteen months ago I was approached by a high-level official at the CIA. The gentleman was quite familiar with my lobbying practice. He was aware that I knew many of the members on the Hill intimately. He wanted me to help him with a very special project."

"What sort of project?" Ward prompted.

"He wanted me to help him gather evidence against congressmen that could be used to blackmail them."

"Blackmail? How?"

"He knew of my efforts to lobby on behalf of impoverished countries and world humanitarian organizations."

"We all are aware of your efforts in that regard," Ward said magnanimously.

"As you can imagine, it's a tough sell up here. I've used most of my own money in that crusade. The man knew that too. He felt I was desperate. An easy mark, I believe is what he said."

"Precisely how would this blackmail scheme work?"

"I would approach certain congressmen and bureaucrats who could help influence foreign-aid dollars and other overseas relief. I would only approach those who needed money. I would tell them that in return for their help, they would be compensated after they left office. They didn't know it, of course, but the CIA would finance these 'retirement' packages. If they agreed to help, then I would wear a wire provided by the CIA and record incriminating conversations with these men and women. They would also be placed under surveillance by the CIA. All this 'illegal' activity would be captured and subsequently used against them by the man at the CIA."

"How so?"

"Many of the people I was supposed to bribe for foreign aid also serve on committees overseeing the CIA. For example, two of the members of this very committee, Senators Johnson and McNamara, also sit on the appropriations committee for foreign operations. The gentleman from CIA gave me a list of names of all the people he wanted to target. Senators Johnson and McNamara were on that list. The plan was to blackmail them and others into using their committee positions to help the CIA. Increased budgets for the CIA, greater responsibilities, less congressional oversight. That sort of thing. In return, I would be paid a large sum of money."

Buchanan looked at Johnson and McNamara, men he had recruited so easily ten years ago. They stared back at him with exactly the proper look of shock and anger. Over the last week Buchanan had met with every single one of his bribees and had explained what was happening. If they wanted to survive, they would back up every word of the lie he was now telling. What choice did they have? They would also continue to support Buchanan's causes, and they wouldn't be getting a dime from him for doing so. Their efforts would really turn out to be "charitable." Praise God.

And he had confided in Ward as well. His friend had taken it better than Buchanan had thought possible. He had not condemned Buchanan's actions, but he had decided to stand by his old friend. There were greater crimes to punish.

"This is all the truth, Mr. Buchanan?"

"Yes sir," Buchanan said, with the look of a saint.

Thornhill sat impassively in his seat. The man's expression was akin to the condemned walking alone to the gas chamber – a mixture of bitterness, terror and disbelief. Buchanan had obviously cut a deal. The politicians were backing his story. He could see it in Johnson's and McNamara's faces. How could Thornhill attack their claims without revealing his own participation? He could hardly jump up and say, "That's not how it happened. Buchanan was already bribing them, I just caught him and used him for my own blackmail purposes." His Achilles' heel. It had never occurred to him. The frog and the scorpion, only the scorpion was going to survive.

"What did you do?" Ward asked Buchanan.

"I immediately went to the people on the list and told them what had happened, including Senators Johnson and McNamara. I'm sorry we were unable to bring you into the loop at the time, Mr. Chairman, but absolute confidentiality was the key. We collectively decided to set up a sting of sorts. I would pretend to go along with the CIA's plan, and the targets would pretend to be part of the plan. Then, while the CIA was gathering its blackmail material, I would secretly gather evidence against the CIA. When we felt the case was strong enough, we planned to go to the FBI with what we had."

Ward took off his glasses and dangled them in

426

front of his face. "Damn risky business, Mr. Buchanan. Was this blackmail operation officially sanctioned by the CIA, do you know?"

Buchanan shook his head. "It was clearly the work of one official there, and not the CIA."

"What happened then?"

"I gathered my evidence, but then my associate, Faith Lockhart, who was unaware of any of this, became suspicious of me. She thought, I suppose, that I was actually involved in a blackmail scheme. I, of course, couldn't confide in her. She went to the FBI with her story. They commenced an investigation. The man from the CIA found out about this development and arranged to have Ms. Lockhart killed. Thankfully, she escaped, but an FBI agent was killed."

The entire room began buzzing at this.

Ward looked pointedly at Buchanan. "Are you telling me that an official from the CIA was responsible for the murder of an FBI agent?"

Buchanan nodded. "Several other deaths have also occurred, including" – Buchanan looked down for a moment, his lips trembling – "Faith Lockhart. That is what has prompted my appearance here today. To stop the killing."

"Who is this man, Mr. Buchanan?" Ward said with as much indignity and curiosity as he could feign.

Buchanan turned and pointed directly at Robert Thornhill.

"Associate Deputy Director of Operations Robert Thornhill."

Thornhill erupted from his chair, waving an angry fist in the air, and roared, "This is a damnable lie! This entire event is a circus, an abomination the likes of which I have never witnessed in all my years in government. You bring me here under false

427

pretenses and then subject me to the preposterous, outrageous accusations of this person. They – they were in my home last night. This Buchanan person, and this man!" Thornhill pointed an angry finger at Lee. "This man held a gun to my head. They threatened me with this same insane story. They claimed to have evidence of this nonsense, but when I called their bluff, they ran off. I demand that you place them under immediate arrest. I intend to press full charges. And now, if you'll excuse me, I have legitimate business elsewhere."

Thornhill tried to get past Lee, but the PI stood up and blocked his way.

Thornhill looked at Ward. "Unless you do something right this instant, Mr. Chairman, I will be forced to call the police on my portable phone. I doubt if it would look very good on the evening news."

"I have proof of all that I've said," Buchanan said.

"What," Thornhill cried out, "the silly tape you threatened me with last night? If you have it, produce it. But whatever's on it is obviously forged."

Buchanan opened a briefcase, which rested on the table in front of him. Instead of an audiocassette, he took out a videocassette and handed it to an aide of Ward's.

Everyone in the room watched as another aide wheeled a television, with a VCR attached, out into a corner of the room where everyone could see the screen. The aide took the tape and inserted it in the VCR, hit the remote, stepped back. Everyone in the room watched breathlessly as the screen came to life.

On the TV Lee and Buchanan were just leaving Thornhill's study. Then Thornhill was at his desk, picking up his phone. He spoke into it anxiously. His conversation of the night before was played out before the entire room. His blackmail scheme, the

428

killing of the FBI agent, his ordering the murders of Buchanan and Lee Adams. The look of triumph on his face as he put down the phone was in monumental contrast to the look the man wore now.

As the screen went to black, Thornhill continued to stare at the TV, his mouth slightly open, his lips moving but no words coming out. His briefcase, with all its important papers, fell to the floor, forgotten.

Ward tapped his pen against the microphone, his eyes squarely on Thornhill. There was some satisfaction in the Senator's features, but it could not overcome the horror there as well. Ward was sickened by what he had just seen; he was ready to pitch his political career and go sit on his back porch and watch his grandchildren play games of complete innocence. He didn't want to do this anymore.

"I suppose that since you've admitted that these men were in your home last night, then you won't claim this piece of evidence is a forgery, Mr. Thornhill?" Ward said.

Danny Buchanan sat quietly at the table, his eyes downcast. On his features were relief, sadness, hope; and uneasiness for what lay ahead. He too had clearly had enough.

Lee watched Thornhill intently. The other task he had performed at the Thornhill residence last night had been a relatively simple one. The underlying technology was known as PLC, or power line carrier technology. It was a wireless system with a 2.4-gigahertz transmitter, covert camera and antenna installed in a device that looked just like the smoke alarm in Thornhill's study and actually performed the functions of a smoke detector while it simultaneously conducted surveillance. It was powered by the home's regular electrical current and produced clear, crisp video and audio of everything in its range. Thornhill had stopped his incriminating conversation from leaving his house, but it had never occurred to him that there was a miniature Trojan horse *inside* his house.

"I will be available to testify at the trial," said Danny Buchanan. He rose, turned and started to walk up the aisle.

Lee put a hand on Thornhill's shoulder. "Excuse me," he said politely. He made his way past the frozen Thornhill and joined Buchanan. The two men quietly walked out together.

FIFTY-SEVEN

One month to the day after Buchanan's testimony to Ward's committee, Robert Thornhill bounded down the steps of the federal courthouse in Washington, leaving his lawyers in his liberated, if anxious, wake. The car was waiting for him. He slid inside. He had been granted bail, after four weeks of sitting behind bars. Now it was time to get to work. Now it was damn well time for revenge.

"Have they all been contacted?" Thornhill asked the driver.

The man nodded. "They're already there. Waiting for you."

"Buchanan and Adams? Status?"

"Buchanan is in Witness Protection, but we have some leads. Adams is right out in the open. Available anytime to take out."

"Lockhart?"

"Dead."

"You're certain?"

"We haven't actually dug up her body, but everything else points to her having died from her wounds at the hospital in North Carolina."

Thornhill leaned back against his seat with a sigh. "Lucky her."

The car entered a public garage, where Thornhill left the vehicle. He stepped directly into a van waiting there for him, which then pulled out from the garage and headed in the opposite direction. So much for any tail the FBI had.

Within forty-five minutes he was at the small abandoned strip mall. He stepped into the elevator and was zipping several hundred feet down into the earth. The lower he was carried, the better Thornhill felt. This thought deeply amused him.

The doors parted and he literally burst out of the confines of the elevator. The men, his colleagues, were all there. His chair at the head of the table was empty. His trusty comrade Phil Winslow was in the seat to the immediate right. Thornhill allowed himself a grateful smile. Back in business, ready to go.

He sat down, looked around.

"Congratulations on getting bail, Bob," Winslow said.

"Four weeks later," Thornhill said bitterly. "I think the Agency needs to upgrade its legal counsel."

"Well, that video was very damaging," said Aaron Royce, the younger man who had butted heads with Thornhill at the previous meeting here. "I'm actually surprised you were able to get bail at all. And, quite frankly, I'm a little stunned that the Agency even saw fit to provide counsel."

"Of course it was damaging," Thornhill said scornfully. "And the Agency provided counsel because of loyalty. It doesn't forget its people. Unfortunately, however, it means I have to disappear. The lawyers think we have a shot at suppressing the video, but I think all would agree that, despite having technical legal deficiencies, the subject matter of the tape was a little too detailed to allow me to continue in my present capacity." Thornhill looked saddened for a moment. His career over, and not in the way he had planned. But then his features reassumed their usual steeliness; his resolve flooded back into him like an oil gusher. He looked around the room in triumph. "But I will lead the battle from a distance. And we will win the war. Now, I understand Buchanan went underground. But Adams didn't. We'll go the path of least resistance. Adams first. Then Buchanan. I want someone at the U.S. marshal's service. We have people there. We locate good old Danny and make his life disappear. Next, I want to make damn *sure* Faith Lockhart is no more." He looked at Winslow. "Are my travel documents ready, Phil?"

"Actually, no, Bob," Winslow said slowly.

Royce stared at Thornhill. "This operation has cost us too much," he said. "Three operatives dead. You indicted. The Agency's turned upside down. The FBI is all over us. It's a total and complete disaster. This makes Aldrich Ames seem like a bounced check."

Thornhill noticed that every man in the room, Winslow included, was looking at him with a very unfriendly face. "We will survive this, make no mistake about that," Thornhill said in an encouraging tone.

"I'm quite sure *we* will survive it," Royce said forcefully.

Royce was definitely beginning to bother Thornhill. He was showing backbone in a way that had to be quickly quashed. But for now Thornhill decided to ignore him. "The damn FBI," complained Thornhill. "Bugging my house. Is the Constitution not applicable to them?"

"Thank God you didn't mention my name during the phone call that night," Winslow said.

Thornhill looked at him again, struck by the curious tone in his friend's voice. "About my documents . . . I should prepare to leave the country as soon as possible."

"That won't be necessary, Bob," Royce said. "And

433

frankly, despite your constant outbursts to the contrary, until you screwed everything up, we had quite a good working relationship with the FBI. Cooperation is the key these days. Turf battles make losers of everyone. You made us into dinosaurs and you're dragging us down into the mud with you."

Thornhill gave him an exasperated look and then glanced at Winslow. "Phil, I don't have time for this. You deal with him."

Winslow coughed nervously. "I'm afraid he's right, Bob."

Thornhill froze for a moment and then looked around the table before settling back on Winslow. "Phil, I want my documents and my cover, and I want them right now."

Winslow looked at Royce and gave a slight nod of the head.

Aaron Royce rose from his chair. He didn't smile; he showed no signs of triumph. Just as he had been trained.

"Bob," he said, "there's been a change in plan. We won't be needing your assistance in this matter any further."

Thornhill's face flushed with anger. "What the hell are you talking about? I'm running this operation. And I want Buchanan and Adams dead. Now!"

"There will be no more killing," Winslow said fiercely. "No more killing of innocent people," he added quietly.

He stood. "I'm sorry, Bob. I truly am."

Thornhill stared at him, the first tremors of the truth hitting him. Phil Winslow had been his classmate at Yale, his fraternity brother. The two men were members of Skull & Bones. Winslow had been his best man. They'd been lifelong friends. Lifelong.

"Phil?" Thornhill said cautiously.

Winslow motioned to the other men, who rose too. They all headed for the elevator.

"Phil?" Thornhill said again, his mouth going dry.

When the group reached the elevator, Winslow looked back. "We can't let this matter go any further. We can't let it go to trial. And we can't let you steal away. They'll never stop looking for you. We need closure, Bob."

Thornhill half rose from his chair. "Then we can fake my death. My suicide."

"I'm sorry, Bob. We need complete and *honest* closure."

"Phil!" Thornhill screamed out. "Please!"

When all the men were inside the elevator, Winslow looked at his friend one last time. "Sacrifices are sometimes necessary, Bob. You know that better than anyone. For the good of the country."

The elevator doors closed.

FIFTY-EIGHT

Lee carefully held the basket of flowers in both hands as he walked down the hospital corridor. Once she'd regained enough strength, Faith had been transferred to a hospital outside of Richmond, Virginia. There she was listed under an alias, though, and an armed guard was stationed outside her room at all times. The hospital was considered far enough away from Washington to maintain absolute secrecy on her whereabouts, yet close enough for Brooke Reynolds to keep a close watch on her.

This was the first time Lee had been allowed in to see her, despite his frantic pleas to Reynolds. At least she was alive. And getting better every day, he had been told.

Thus he was very surprised when he approached her room and there was no guard outside. He knocked on the door, waited, then pushed it open. The room was empty, the bed stripped. He walked around the room in a daze for a few seconds and then ran back out into the hallway where he nearly collided with a nurse. He grabbed the woman's arm.

"The patient in 212? Where is she?" he asked.

The nurse glanced at the empty room and then back at him, her expression a sad one. "Are you family?"

"Yes," he lied.

She looked at the flowers and her expression grew even more distressed. "Didn't anyone call you?"

"Call me? About what?"

"She passed away last night."

Lee's face paled. "Passed away," he said numbly. "But she was out of danger. She was going to make it. What the hell are you talking about – passing away?"

"Please, sir, there are other patients here." She took his arm and steered him away from the room. "I don't know the exact details. I wasn't on duty. I can refer you to someone here who can answer your questions."

Lee pulled his arm free. "Look, she can't be dead, okay? That was just a story. To keep her safe."

"What?" The woman looked puzzled.

"I'll take it from here," a voice said.

They both turned and looked at Brooke Reynolds standing there. She held out her badge for the nurse to see. "I'll take it from here," she said again. The nurse nodded and walked quickly away.

"What the hell is going on?" Lee demanded.

"Let's go to a quiet place and talk this over."

"Where is Faith?"

"Lee, not here! Dammit, do you want to ruin everything?" She pulled on his arm, but he wasn't budging, and she knew she couldn't physically make him.

"Why should I go with you?"

"Because I'm going to tell you the truth."

They got in Reynolds's car and she pulled out of the parking lot.

"I knew you were coming today, and I was planning on being at the hospital ahead of you, waiting. I didn't quite make it. I'm sorry you had to hear about it from a nurse: that's not what I intended." Reynolds looked down at the flowers he still held tightly, and her heart went out to him. She

437

wasn't an FBI agent for this moment – she was simply a fellow human being sitting next to someone whose heart, she knew, was being torn apart. And what she had to tell him would only make it worse.

"Faith has been placed in Witness Protection. Buchanan too."

"*What?* Buchanan I can understand! But Faith isn't a witness to anything!" Lee's relief was matched only by his outrage. This was all wrong.

"But she is in need of protection. If certain people knew she was still alive – well, you know what could happen."

"When's the damn trial?"

"Actually, there isn't going to be a trial."

He stared over at her. "Don't tell me that sonofabitch Thornhill copped some sort of sweetheart deal. Don't tell me that."

"He didn't."

"So why no trial?"

"A trial needs a defendant." Reynolds tapped her fingers against the steering wheel and then slid on a pair of sunglasses. She proceeded to fiddle with the heating control.

"I'm waiting," Lee said. "Or don't I qualify for an explanation?"

Reynolds sighed and straightened up. "Thornhill is dead. He was found in his car on a back-country road with a single gunshot wound to the head. Suicide."

Lee was stunned into silence. After a minute he was able to mutter, "The coward's way out."

"I think everyone's relieved, actually. I know the people at CIA are. To say this whole thing rocked them to their super-secretive bones is an understatement. I guess for the good of the country, it's better to be spared a lengthy, embarrassing trial."

"Right, dirty laundry and all," Lee said acidly.

"Hooray for the country." Lee gave a mock salute to a flag flying in front of a post office they passed. "So if Thornhill's out of the way, why does Faith need Witness Protection?"

"You know the answer to that. When Thornhill died, he took the identity of everyone else involved in this with him to the grave. But they're out there, we know they are. Remember the videotape you orchestrated? Thornhill was talking to somebody on that phone, and that somebody is still out there. The CIA is doing an internal investigation to try to ferret them out, but I'm not holding my breath. And you know these people will do their best to get to Faith and Buchanan. For pure revenge, if nothing else." She touched his arm. "And you too, Lee."

He glanced over at her, read her mind. "No. There is no way I'm going into Witness Protection. I can't deal with a new name. I have a hard enough time remembering my real one. Might as well wait for Thornhill's sidekicks. Least I'll have some fun before I die."

"Lee, this is no joke. If you don't go underground, you'll be in great danger. And we can't follow you around twenty-four hours a day."

"No? After all I did for the Bureau? Does this also mean I don't get the FBI decoder ring and free T-shirt?"

"Why are you being such a smartass about this?"

"Maybe I don't give a shit anymore, Brooke. You're a smart lady, didn't that one ever occur to you?"

Neither said a word for the next couple of miles.

"If it were up to me, you'd get anything you wanted, including your own island somewhere with servants, but it's not up to me," Reynolds finally said.

He shrugged. "I'll take my chances. If they want to

439

come after me, so be it. They'll find me a little tougher bite than they think."

"Isn't there anything I can say to change your mind?"

He held up the flowers. "You can tell me where Faith is."

"I can't do that. You know I can't do that."

"Oh, come on, sure you can. You just have to *say* it."

"Lee, please—"

He smashed his big fist against the dashboard, cracking it. "Dammit, Brooke, you don't understand. I have to see Faith. I have to!"

"You're wrong, Lee, I do understand. And that's why this is so hard for me. But if I tell you and you go to her, that puts her in danger. And you too. You know that. That breaks all the rules. And I'm not going to do that. I'm sorry. You don't know how terrible I feel about all this."

Lee laid his head against the back of the seat and the two remained silent for another several minutes as Reynolds drove aimlessly.

"How is she?" he finally asked quietly.

"I won't lie to you. That bullet did a lot of damage. She's recovering, but slowly. They almost lost her a couple more times along the way."

Lee put his hand over his face, slowly shook his head.

"If it's any consolation, she was as upset as you are about this arrangement."

"Boy," Lee said, "that just makes everything wonderful. I'm the friggin' king of the world."

"That's not how I meant it."

"You're really not going to let me see her, are you?"

"No, I'm really not."

"Then you can drop me at the corner."

440

"But your car's back at the hospital."

He opened the car door before she came to a stop. "I'll walk."

"It's miles," Reynolds said, her voice strained. "And it's freezing outside. Lee, let me drive you. Let's go get some coffee. Talk about this some more."

"I need the fresh air. And what's there to talk about? I'm all talked out. I may never talk again." He climbed out and then leaned back in. "You *can* do something for me."

"Just name it."

He handed her the flowers. "Could you see that Faith gets these? I'd appreciate it." Lee shut the door and walked off.

Reynolds gripped the flowers and looked at Lee as he trudged away, head down, hands stuffed in his pockets. She saw his shoulders quiver. And then Brooke Reynolds lay back against the seat as the tears trickled down her face.

FIFTY-NINE

Nine months later Lee was staking out the hideaway townhouse of a man soon to be involved in an acrimonious divorce proceeding with his many-times-cheated-on wife. Lee had been hired by the very suspicious spouse to collect dirt on her hubby, and it hadn't taken him long to fill up bag after bag, as Lee watched a parade of pretty young things flounce through the premises. The wife wanted a nice-size financial settlement from the guy, who had about five hundred million bucks worth of stock options at some high-tech Internet outfit he had cofounded. And Lee was very happy to help her get it. The adulterous husband reminded him of Eddie Stipowicz, his ex-wife's billion-dollar man. Collecting evidence on this guy was a little bit like hurling rocks at little Eddie's bloated head.

Lee took out his camera and shot some pictures of a tall, blond, miniskirted number sauntering up to the townhouse. The photo of the bare-chested guy standing at the door awaiting her, beer can in hand, a goofy, lascivious smile on his fat face, would be exhibit numero uno for the wife's lawyers. No-fault divorce laws had seriously depressed the business of PIs running around digging up dirt, but when it came time to split the marriage loot, the slimy ooze still carried weight. Nobody liked being embarrassed with that stuff. Especially when there were kids involved, as there were here.

The long-legged blond couldn't have been more than twenty, about his daughter Renee's age, while the hubby was pushing fifty. God, those stock options. Must be nice. Or maybe it was the man's bald head, diminutive stature and soft pooch. You couldn't figure some women. *Nah, must be the dough,* Lee told himself. He put the camera away.

It was August in Washington, which meant just about everybody, other than cheating husbands and their bimbos, and PIs who spied on them, was out of town. It was hot, muggy, miserable. Lee had his window rolled down, praying for even the slightest movement of air, as he munched on trail mix and bottled water. The hardest thing with this type of surveillance was the lack of pee-pee breaks. That's why he preferred bottled water. The empty plastic containers had come in handy more than once for him.

He checked his watch; it was close on midnight. Most lights in the apartments and townhouses in the area had long since gone out. He was thinking about heading on, himself. He had gotten enough stuff in the last few days, including some embarrassing shots of a late-night romp in the townhouse's outdoor hot tub, to make the guy easily fork up half his net worth. Two naked girls who looked young enough to be thinking about the senior prom, frolicking in the bubbly water with a guy old enough to know better – this probably wouldn't sit too well with the upstanding stockholders of the husband's nice little high-tech concern, Lee imagined.

His own life had taken on a routine bordering on obsessive monotony, or so he had dubbed it. He got up early, worked out hard, pounding the bag, crunching the stomach and hoisting the weights until he thought his body would raise the white flag and then present him with an aneurysm. Then he went to work and kept at it nonstop until he barely made it to dinner at the McDonald's late-night drive-through near his apartment. Then he went home, alone, and tried to sleep, but found that he was never able to actually accomplish total unconsciousness. So he would prowl the apartment, look out the window, wonder about a whole bunch of things he couldn't do a damn thing about. His life's "what if" book was filled up. He'd have to go buy another one.

There had been some positives. Brooke Reynolds had made it her mission to send as much business his way as possible, and it had been quality, good-paying stuff. She had also had a number of ex-FBI agent buddies now in corporate security offer him full-time employment with, of course, stock options. He had turned them all down. The gesture was appreciated, he had told Reynolds, but he worked alone. He was not a suit type. He didn't like eating the kinds of lunches that required silverware. Traditional elements of success would undoubtedly be hazardous to his health.

He had seen Renee a great deal, and each time, things had gotten better between them. For about a month after everything had shaken out, he had barely left her side, making sure that nothing would happen to her because of Robert Thornhill and company. After Thornhill had killed himself his concerns had faded, although he was always on her to stay alert. She was going to come and visit him before school started up again. Maybe he'd drop Trish and Eddie a postcard, telling them what a fabulous job they'd done raising her. Or maybe he wouldn't.

Life was good, he kept telling himself. Business was good, he was in good health, his daughter was back in his life. He wasn't six feet under helping to fertilize grass. And he had served his country. All good shit. Which made him wonder why he was so unhappy, so out-and-out miserable. Actually, he knew, but there was absolutely nothing he could do about it. Wasn't that a kicker? Story of his life. Know the blues, but just can't change them.

A car's headlights flicked across his side mirror. His gaze immediately went to the car that had just pulled up behind him. It wasn't a cop wondering why he had parked here for several hours. He frowned and looked over at the townhouse. He wondered if his naughty tech mogul had noticed him and called in some reinforcements to help teach the curious PI a little lesson. Lee hoped that was the case. He had his crowbar in the seat next to him. This might actually be fun. Kicking the crap out of somebody might be the depression antidote he needed; get those endorphins going. At least it might get him through the night.

He was surprised when only one person emerged from the passenger side and headed his way. The person was small, slender, hidden inside an ankle-length coat with a hood, not exactly your recommended attire for a ninety-degree thermometer and one hundred percent humidity. His hand tightened on the crowbar. As the figure came up to his passenger door, he hit the door lock. The next moment, his lungs had locked up and he was gasping for air.

The face looking in at him was very pale and very thin. And very Faith Lockhart. He unlocked the door and she slid in.

He looked at her, finally found his voice down near his knees. "God, is it really you?"

She smiled, and suddenly she didn't seem so pale, so drawn, so frail. She slid off her long, hooded coat. Underneath she had on a short-sleeved shirt and khaki shorts. Her feet were in sandals. Her legs were

445

very pale and thinner than he remembered; all of her was. Months in a hospital had decimated her, he realized. Her hair had grown out and was longer, though far from its original length. She looked better with her real hair color, he thought. Actually, he would have taken the woman bald.

"It's me," she said quietly. "At least, what's left."

"Is that Reynolds back there?"

"Nervous and upset that I talked her into it."

"You look beautiful, Faith."

She smiled in a resigned fashion. "Liar. I look like hell. I can't even bear to look at my chest. God!" She said the words in a joking manner, but Lee could sense the anguish behind the light tone.

He very gently touched her face with his hand. "I'm not lying, and you know it."

She put her hand around his and gripped it with amazing strength. "Thank you."

"How are you really doing? I want facts, nothing but."

She stretched her arm slowly, the pain in her face so evident from such a simple movement. "I'm officially retired from the aerobics circuit, but I'm hanging in there. Actually, each day it gets better. The doctors expect a full recovery. Well, in the ninety percentile anyway."

"I never thought I'd see you again."

"I couldn't let that happen."

He slid over to her, put his arm around her. She winced a little as he did this, and he quickly backed off.

"I'm sorry, Faith, I'm sorry."

She smiled and put his arm back around her, patting his hand as she did so. "I'm not that fragile. And the day you can't put your arm around me is the day I call it a life."

"I'd ask you where you're living, but I don't want

446

to do anything that could put you in danger."

"Helluva way to have to live, don't you think?" Faith asked.

"Yes."

She leaned against him, resting her head against his chest. "I saw Danny right after I got out of the hospital. When they told us Thornhill had killed himself, I didn't think he was ever going to stop smiling."

"Can't say I felt any different."

She looked at him. "How are *you*, Lee?"

"Me! Nothing happened to me. Nobody shot me. Nobody tells me where I have to live. I'm doing fine. I got the best deal of all."

"Lie or the truth?"

"Lie," he said softly.

They exchanged a quick kiss and then a longer one. The movements were so easy, Lee thought, their heads turning at just the right angle, their arms going around each other with no wasted motion, like pieces in a puzzle someone was sliding together. They could be waking up at the beach house, the morning after. The nightmare never having occurred. How was it possible that one could know another person for such a short period of time and have it feel like several lifetimes? God would only let that happen once, if ever. And in Lee's case, he had taken it away. It wasn't fair, it wasn't right. He pressed his face into her hair, soaking up every particle of her scent.

"How long are you here?" he asked.

"What did you have in mind?"

"Nothing fancy. Dinner at my place, a quiet talk. Letting me hold you all night."

"As wonderful as that sounds, I'm not sure I'm up to that last part just yet."

He looked at her. "I'm being literal, Faith. I just

447

want to hold you. That's all. That's all I've been thinking about all these months. Just holding you."

Faith looked as though she might start crying. Instead she brushed away the lone tear that had tumbled down Lee's face.

Lee glanced in the rearview mirror. "But I guess that's not in Reynolds's agenda, is it?"

"I doubt it."

He looked back at her. "Faith," he said softly, "why did you step in front of that bullet? I know you care for Buchanan and all, but why?"

She took a shallow breath. "Like I said, he's unique, I'm ordinary. I couldn't let him die."

"I wouldn't have done it."

"Would you have done it for me?" she asked.

"Yes."

"You sacrifice for people you care about. And I care a great deal about Danny."

"I guess the fact that you had all the means to disappear – fake ID, Swiss bank account, safe house – and instead went to the FBI to try and save Buchanan should have clued me in on that."

She clutched his arm. "But I survived. I made it. Maybe that makes me just a little extraordinary, in a way?"

He cupped her face with his hand. "Now that you're here, I really don't want you to go, Faith. Like I would give everything I have, do anything I can, if you wouldn't leave me."

She traced his mouth with her fingers, kissed his lips, stared at his eyes, which even in the darkness seemed to have the blinding heat of the sun behind them. She never thought she would ever see those eyes again; maybe the fact that she might, if she were to survive, had been the only thing that had saved her, had not let her die. Right now she wasn't sure what else she had to live for. Other than the apparently depthless love of this man.

"Start the car," she said.

Puzzled, he looked at her but said nothing. He turned the key in the ignition, put the car in gear.

"Go ahead," Faith said.

He pulled the car away from the curb and the vehicle behind them immediately did the same.

They drove along, the car following them.

"Reynolds must be pulling her hair out," Lee said.

"She'll get over it."

"Where to?" he said.

"How much gas do you have in the car?" Faith asked.

He looked surprised. "I was on a stakeout. Full tank."

She was settled against him, her arm curling around his middle, her hair tickling his nose; she smelled so wonderful he felt dizzy.

"Let's go get some takeout Chinese. We can drive to the lookout spot off the GW Parkway." She looked at the star-filled sky. "I can show you the constellations."

He looked at her. "Been chasing stars lately?"

She smiled at him. "Always."

"And after that?"

"They can't keep me in Witness Protection against my will, can they?"

"No. But you'd be in danger."

"How about *we'd* be in danger?"

"In a second, Faith. In a second. But what happens when we run out of gas?"

"For now, just drive."

And that's exactly what he did.

449

ACKNOWLEDGMENTS

To my dear friend Jennifer Steinberg, for tracking down so much information for me. You'd make a great PI!

To my wife, Michelle, for always telling me the truth about the books.

To Neal Schiff at the FBI for his continued help and cooperation with my novels.

A very special thanks to FBI Special Agent Shawn Henry, who was very generous with his time, expertise, and enthusiasm, and who helped me avoid some serious gaffes in the story. Shawn, your comments made the book much better.

To Martha Pope for her valuable, insightful knowledge on Capitol Hill matters, and her patience with a political neophyte. Martha, you'd make a great teacher!

To Bobby Rosen, Diane Dewhirst, and Marty Paone for sharing their experiences and institutional memories with me.

To Tom DePont, Dawn Bailey, and Charles Nelson of NationsBank for assistance on financial and tax matters.

To Joe Duffy for enlightening me on foreign aid policy and procedures. And to his wife, Anne Wexler, for sharing her valuable time and insight with me.

A very, very special thanks to my friend Bob Schule for going above and beyond the call of duty in helping me on this book, by not only providing fascinating details about his long and distinguished career in Washington, but also for casting a wide net among his friends and colleagues in order to help me better understand politics, lobbying, and how Washington really works. Bob, you're a wonderful friend and a true professional.

To Congressman Rod Blagojevich (D. Ill) for allowing me a glimpse into the life of a member of Congress.

To Congressman Tony Hall (D. Ohio) for helping me better understand the plight of the world's poor, and how that issue plays out (or doesn't) in Washington.

To my good friend and family member Congressman John Baldacci (D. Maine) for his support and assistance with this project. If everyone in Washington were like John, the plot of this book would seem totally implausible.

To Larry Benoit and Bob Beene for their help on everything from lobbying to the nuts and bolts of governing, to all the little nooks and crannies in the U.S. Capitol building. To them I owe one of the best scenes in the book.

To John Deutch for his generous assistance in helping me to better understand the Central Intelligence Agency.

To Mark Jordan of Baldino's Lock and Key for educating me on the ways of security and phone systems and how to crack them. Mark, you're the best.

To Steve Jennings for reading every word as usual and helping to make them better.

To my dear friends David and Catherine Broome for exposing me to the North Carolina settings and for their continued encouragement and support.

To all those other people who contributed to this novel but for various reasons wish to remain anonymous. I couldn't have done it without all of you.

To my editor and my friend Frances Jalet-Miller. Her skill, encouragement, and gentle persuasion are all that any writer could ever want in an editor. To many more books together, Francie.

Last, but absolutely not least, to Larry, Maureen, Jamie, Tina, Emi, Jonathan, Karen Torres, Martha Otis, Jackie Joiner, and Jackie Meyer, Bruce Paonessa and Peter Mauceri, and all the rest of the Warner Books family. It takes *all* of us to make this happen. Friends for life.

All the people listed above gave me the knowledge and help I needed to write this novel. How I used all of that assistance to conjure up all sorts of shenanigans, misdeeds, outright crimes, and depictions of felonious and conspiratorial souls in *Saving Faith*, however, is my responsibility alone.

Praise for Victoria Aveyard

'A sizzling, imaginative thriller, where romance and revolution collide, where power and justice duel. It's exhilarating. Compelling. Action-packed. Unputdownable' *USA Today*

'Aveyard weaves a compelling new world of action-packed surprises . . . inventive, character-driven' *Kirkus*

'With world building to rival the likes of George R. R. Martin, a cast of fiery and powerful characters and betrayals which left many gaping, *Red Queen* is a victory worthy of its debut Crown' *Guardian*

'A whirlwind of betrayal and plot twists' *Sci-Fi Now*

'A clever blend of *The Hunger Games*, *The Selection*, *Graceling* and *Divergent*' *Starbust*

'The dystopian novel will please fans of *The Hunger Games* but uses a supernatural twist to explore the theme of social injustice'
We Love This Book

'If you're having hangovers over the *Divergent* series, or having withdrawal symptoms from *The Hunger Games*, then this is the book that will get you out of that funk' Dark Readers

'A wonderful mash up of Ancient Rome and Marie Antoinette with a dash of Catherine Fisher's *Incarceron* and Ridley Scott's *Gladiator*, not to mention some of Marvel Comic's box of tricks . . . Exciting and original' Sam Hawksmoor, author of *The Repossession* Trilogy

DISCARDED

014198053 X

Victoria Aveyard was born and raised in East Longmeadow, Massachusetts, a small town known only for the worst traffic rotary in the continental United States. She moved to Los Angeles to earn a BFA in screenwriting at the University of Southern California. She currently splits her time between the East and West coasts. As an author and screenwriter, she uses her career as an excuse to read too many books and watch too many movies.

Find out more at www.victoriaaveyard.com or follow her on Twitter and Instagram @VictoriaAveyard

Also by Victoria Aveyard

Novels
Red Queen
Glass Sword

Short Story Collection
Cruel Crown

DISCARDED